CRIME AND PUNISHMENT

Crime and Punishment

A NOVEL IN SIX PARTS WITH EPILOGUE BY

Fyodor Dostoevsky

TRANSLATED AND ANNOTATED
BY RICHARD PEVEAR AND
LARISSA VOLOKHONSKY

ALFRED A. KNOPF   NEW YORK
1992

This Is a Borzoi Book
· *Published by Alfred A. Knopf, Inc.*

Translation copyright © 1992
by Richard Pevear and Larissa Volokhonsky

All rights reserved under International and Pan-American Copyright Conventions. Published in the United States by Alfred A. Knopf, Inc., New York, and simultaneously in Canada by Random House of Canada Limited, Toronto. Distributed by Random House, Inc., New York.

This translation has been made from the Russian text of the Soviet Academy of Sciences edition, volumes six and seven (Leningrad, 1973). Quotations from Dostoevsky's letters and notebooks in the foreword are from Konstantin Mochulsky, *Dostoevsky: His Life and Work,* translated by Michael A. Minihan (Princeton, N.J.: Princeton University Press, 1967).

Library of Congress Cataloging-in-Publication Data

Dostoyevsky, Fyodor, 1821-1881
   [Prestuplenie i nakazanie.   English]
   Crime and punishment / Fyodor Dostoevsky.—1st ed.
     p.   cm.
   Translation of: Prestuplenie i nakazanie.
   Includes bibliographical references.
   ISBN 0-679-40557-7
   I. Title.
PG3326.P713   1992
891.73'3—dc20   91-53120
                                                 CIP

Manufactured in the United States of America
First Edition

Contents

Foreword

"I want to do an unprecedented and eccentric thing, to write thirty printed sheets [480 printed pages] within the space of four months, forming two separate novels, of which I will write one in the morning and the other in the evening, and to finish them by a fixed deadline. Do you know, my dear Anna Vasilievna, that even now such eccentric and extraordinary things utterly delight me. I simply don't fit into the category of staid and conventional people . . ." In this typically ebullient fashion, Dostoevsky described to a friend the predicament he found himself in during the summer of 1866. He was then forty-five, and had behind him ten years of imprisonment and exile for "antigovernment activities," the death of his first wife and of his closest brother Mikhail, and debts amounting to some 43,000 roubles. A year earlier he had gone abroad to escape his creditors with 175 roubles in his pocket and an agreement with an unscrupulous bookseller, F. T. Stellovsky, to produce a new novel for him by November 1, 1866, failing which (and Stellovsky hoped he would fail) all his existing and future works would become the bookseller's property.

Fortunately, Dostoevsky managed to bring off this "unprecedented . . . thing," though not quite in the way he envisaged. Work on one novel, which had been appearing serially in the *Russian Herald* since January 1866, continued to preoccupy him into the fall, and meanwhile not a word of the book for Stellovsky got written. Finally, on the advice of friends, he hired a stenographer, the young Anna Grigorievna Snitkin, who soon became his second wife. *The Gambler*, dictated to her in October, was handed to the bookseller on time, and in November he went on to finish the longer, serialized work—*Crime and Punishment*, the first of the five great novels that crowned Dostoevsky's artistic labors during the final fifteen years of his life.

The attempts of critics and literary scholars to define, or simply account for, what they have found in these novels may remind one of the Hindu parable of the blind men describing an elephant, each by feeling a different part—"a snake," "a hog weed," "a tree," "a broom," "a wall." Dostoevsky's own summaries in his letters and notebooks tend to be dry, schematic, and therefore misleading, because no novels are less dry or schematic than these. Furthermore, he was always ready to revise his plans when new material, discovered in the process of writing, demanded it. Thus he wrote to his friend Baron Vrangel, in December 1865, that the story he had been working on for several months (the first version of *Crime and Punishment*) had grown into "a big novel, in six parts. I had much of it written and ready by the end of November. *I burned it all.* Now I can confess it. I wasn't pleased with it myself. A *new form*, a *new plan* captivated me and so I began over again. I'm working day and night, and for all that I'm not working very much. A novel is a work of poetry. In order to write it, one must have tranquility of spirit and of impression . . ." A novel, at least a Dostoevsky novel, is a "work of poetry"—that is, a simultaneous composition on multiple planes—and the critics can therefore be forgiven their perplexity about where to take hold of it, since the first perplexity of criticism is that it must speak monosemantically of the polysemous.

But besides that, these were novels of a new kind, their multiple planes so divergent and even contradictory as to all but baffle definition. So much so that one line of criticism, rightly noting the dramatic technique and high seriousness of Dostoevsky's writing, has called his late works "novel-tragedies," while another, with equal rightness, finds their roots in Ménippean satire and a carnival sense of the world. Dostoevsky's uniqueness as an artist lies in his invention of a form capable of combining such opposites, of sounding such depths (carnival laughter has as much depth as tragedy), while never ceasing to portray the contemporary world, the everyday in all the detail of its everydayness. What's more, Dostoevsky's novels refuse to stay put in their own period, where the novels of Tolstoy, Turgenev, Goncharov have settled; they leap out of their historical situation and confront us as if they had not yet spoken their final word.

The question is what inspired this form-making impulse in Dostoevsky, what reality do his novels imitate, or can we still speak here of an "imitation of reality"? To suggest an answer, we must turn to *Notes from Underground,* published in 1864, just a year before he began work on *Crime and Punishment.* This paradoxical little novel marked a break, a new beginning in his art, and in a sense all his later works grew out of it. It seems to have come almost as a surprise to Dostoevsky himself. He had been attempting to write a critical response to the utopian communist N. G. Chernyshevsky, whose programmatic novel, *What Is to Be Done?,* appeared in 1863. Instead of an article, he produced the tale—at once apologia and confession—of the nameless man from underground.

Dostoevsky's polemics with the radicals of the 1860s appear to represent a change in his convictions, though such questions are never simple. He had started out in literary life as a liberal, critical of the imperial autocracy, sympathizing with the little man, drawn to the ideas of the French utopians Fourier and Saint-Simon. In the late 1840s he had attended meetings of the clandestine Petrashevsky circle, which owned a printing press and planned to publish Fourier's writings. This had led to his arrest in 1849, to penal servitude and exile. In *Notes from the Dead House,* a semi-fictional account of his prison experiences first published in 1860, a year after his return to Petersburg, he describes how he would sit looking at a corner of blue sky and think that there, beyond the prison walls, was another life, there was freedom, and one day he would leave his prison behind and find that free life waiting for him, and he would then live nobly, gratefully, and make no more mistakes.

Was Dostoevsky's opposition to the radical ideology of the 1860s the expression of a repentant sinner, ready to embrace monarchy and orthodoxy and the goodness of this world that he had not appreciated before? Not at all, if we judge by *Notes from Underground.* Something else rose up in him in the person of the underground man, this "man of heightened consciousness," with his mocking attacks on the laws of nature and arithmetic, on sensibleness, utility, profit, on development, civilization, and reason itself. He puts his tongue out at the "crystal palace" of Chernyshevsky's scientific-utopian future, but he goes beyond that when he declares: "Two times two is four is no longer life, gentlemen, but the beginning of death." It should be noted that the early 1860s saw the reforms brought about by the tsar-liberator Alexander II—the abolition of serfdom, the institution of public trial by jury, land reform, the relaxation of censorship—changes that the liberals of the 1840s had only dreamed of. It is by no means clear that the underground man, if he paid attention to such things, would find this reformed society any more to his liking than the "future reasonableness" of the radicals. To all such worlds he prefers his underground. And yet at one point he cries out, "But here, too, I'm lying! Lying, because I myself know, like two times two, that it is not at all the underground that is better, but something different, completely different, which I thirst for but cannot ever find!"

Clearly, the terms of this polemic, if polemic it is, go beyond the opposing of one set of ideas with another. Something strange seems to have happened to Dostoevsky after his return from exile. It is as if the world he had imagined in prison, the world of the blue sky and freedom, ceased to be recognizable to him, and another reality appeared in its place, one he was unprepared for and could only search out gropingly. In fact, he once described his experience of such an uncanny moment of vision, but he placed it in his past. The description, however, appeared in *Petersburg Visions in Verse and Prose*, a short work written in 1861. As a young man, he was returning home one evening and stopped to look along the Neva:

> It seemed, in the end, that all this world, with all its inhabitants, both the strong and the weak, with all their habitations, whether beggars' shelters or gilded palaces, at this hour of twilight resembled a fantastic, enchanted vision, a dream which in its turn would instantly vanish and waste away as vapor into the dark blue heaven. Suddenly a certain strange thought began to stir inside me. I started and my heart was as if flooded in that instant by a hot jet of blood which had suddenly boiled up from the influx of a mighty sensation which until now had been unknown to me. In that moment, as it were, I understood something which up to that time had only stirred in me, but had not as yet been fully comprehended. I saw clearly, as it were, into something new, a completely new world, unfamiliar to me and known only through some obscure hearsay, through a certain mysterious sign. I think that in those precise minutes, my real existence began . . .

Most important are the further details of this experience:

> I began to look about intently and suddenly I noticed some
> strange people. They were all strange, extraordinary figures, com-
> pletely prosaic, not Don Carloses or Posas to be sure, rather
> down-to-earth titular councilors and yet at the same time, as it
> were, sort of fantastic titular councilors. Someone was grimacing
> in front of me, having hidden himself behind all this fantastic
> crowd, and he was fidgeting some thread, some springs through,
> and these little dolls moved, and he laughed and laughed away.

The ambiguous laughter of this demiurge or demon can be heard in
all of Dostoevsky's later works. Here, in germ, was the reality that
challenged his powers of imitation, an indefinite "something new," a
completely new and unfamiliar world, prosaic and at the same time
fantastic, which could have no image until he gave it one, but was *more
real* than the vanishing spectacle he contemplated on the Neva. That
he recorded this moment of vision when he did suggests that in some
way he was reliving it.

Behind the ideas of radicals like Chernyshevsky, Dostoevsky could
hear the demiurge's laughter (not that he underestimated the serious
consequences of these ideas; he foresaw them only too clearly). His
response was the world as viewed by the man from underground,
whose ruminations are circumscribed by the same ideas, but who has
recognized that his life cannot be accounted for by them, that in fact
it cannot be accounted for by any laws or with any logical consistency.
Nor can it be narrated as a meaningful sequence of events, in harmonious and dignified prose. It is all discontinuous, full of the sudden and
the unexpected, disharmonious and undignified, terrible and at the
same time comical. From this basis he generalizes his attack on
the world view of enlightened Europe, particularly as adopted by the
Russian intelligentsia.

No one before Dostoevsky had ever written such a book. That it
failed in its immediate purpose, as a reply to the radical ideology of the
day, is not surprising: its dialectic was much too complex for the purpose, and artistically it was too strange, even offensive, for the common
reader. Indeed, to make such admissions about oneself as the underground man does, and to lash out with such sarcastic wit at the most

self-evident "truths" of society and human reason, is more a transgression than an argument, as the nameless hero is aware. *Notes from Underground* gives voice to the double-mindedness, at once guilty and defiant, of the conscious transgressor. But the man from underground transgresses only inwardly, philosophically, for the sake of a truth that he clings to although he cannot name it, knowing that the limits he is violating are false in any case, even if he can never find the "something different" that is better than his underground.

In *Crime and Punishment,* published two years later, the hero is an actual transgressor—the "theoretician-murderer" Raskolnikov. And the relations between the viewer, the spectacle of the world, and this "something new" or "something different" (betrayed by the demiurge's laughter), essentially the same in *Notes from Underground* and in the "vision on the Neva," appear once again. Indeed, there is a passage in part two of *Crime and Punishment* that almost exactly parallels the moment Dostoevsky had described in *Petersburg Visions.* The day after he commits the murder, Raskolnikov is crossing a bridge over the Neva and stops to gaze at the city:

> He stood and looked long and intently into the distance; this place was especially familiar to him. While he was attending the university, he often used to stop, mostly on his way home, at precisely this spot (he had done it perhaps a hundred times), and gaze intently at the indeed splendid panorama, and to be surprised almost every time by a certain unclear and unresolved impression. An inexplicable chill always breathed on him from this splendid panorama; for him the magnificent picture was filled with a mute and deaf spirit . . . He marveled each time at this gloomy and mysterious impression, and, mistrusting himself, put off the unriddling of it to some future time. Now suddenly he abruptly recalled these former questions and perplexities, and it seemed no accident to him that he should recall them now.

The loud laughter has here become a chill breath, the demiurge a "mute and deaf spirit"—the riddle remains, but the tonality has darkened considerably. Raskolnikov received this impression many times; it does not come as the result of his crime; on the contrary, he recalls it now as if his act were somehow the first step in its unriddling. *Crime and Punishment* is a highly unusual mystery novel: the most mystified character in it is the murderer himself.

We know a good deal about the genesis of the novel from Dostoevsky's letters and notebooks. When he went abroad in July 1865, he had plans in mind for two separate works—one, a long novel to be called *The Drunkards,* dealing with "the current problem of drunkenness," as he wrote when proposing it to the editor of *Fatherland Notes* (who turned it down); the other, "the psychological account of a crime," an idea that had first come to him in prison fifteen years earlier. He hoped to finish *The Drunkards* quickly, but instead got carried away by the other story. In September 1865 he was able to send a detailed outline of it to Mikhail Katkov, editor of the *Russian Herald.* Originally he conceived of it as a short work, written in the first person—the confession of the criminal himself. The murderer, as he wrote to Katkov, would be "an intellectually developed young man who even has good inclinations" and who kills "under the influence of some of those strange, 'incomplete' ideas which go floating about in the air . . ." In other words, the tale was to be a further exploration of the consequences of Russian radical ideology, particularly the ideology of the so-called Nihilists who emerged in the mid-1860s. In form it would have been similar to *Notes from Underground.* This was the version that Dostoevsky eventually burned.

In its new form, the novel retained the general features of the hero as he had outlined them for Katkov, but the material was greatly expanded, and it was no longer cast as a confession. By chance, close to the beginning of *Crime and Punishment,* Raskolnikov makes the acquaintance of a certain Semyon Zakharovich Marmeladov. The story of this unemployed official, his consumptive wife Katerina Ivanovna, and their family came to the novel from the abandoned pages of *The Drunkards;* the organic link between the two initially unrelated works would be Marmeladov's daughter Sonya. Just after this meeting, Raskolnikov receives a long letter from his mother, introducing yet another story involving his sister, Dunya, the man of affairs Luzhin, and the sinister but charming Svidrigailov. There were now three plots instead of one; and we begin to see something of Dostoevsky's method of composition in this juxtaposition—within an extremely foreshortened narrative time—of large scale, self-dramatizing *speakers.* Part one ends with the murder itself but is already rich in possibilities for future encounters, exchanges, conflicts.

Important questions remained unresolved in Dostoevsky's mind when the first part of the novel appeared in the January 1866 issue of the *Russian Herald.* His notebook for February shows him still working out Sonya's role and, more significantly, Raskolnikov's real motive for his crime. In some sketches, he was to be a much more articulate spokesman for the Nihilists, who combined "rational egoism" with a view of themselves as benefactors of mankind. This idea was supplanted by the Napoleonic figure of the "strong individual" who acts for the sake of his own power. In one version, Raskolnikov was to end with a vision of Christ and a heroic deed of self-sacrifice and reconciliation; in the other, his rebellion would become truly demonic, and he would finally shoot himself. Dostoevsky eventually decided against both outcomes, and Raskolnikov's motives were left unresolved, to the great advantage of the novel. And to Sonya, whom he had thought of making a more articulate opponent of Raskolnikov's idea, who would confront him sharply and even write him letters "possessing high artistic qualities," he finally gave only the almost mute witness of example. Instead of the vision of Christ, there is her reading of the Gospel account of the raising of Lazarus in part four. The rational egoism goes mostly to the miserly Luzhin, the bullet to Svidrigailov.

As the material of the novel grew into its new form, emphasis shifted away from Dostoevsky's original idea of "the psychological account of a crime" and from his ongoing polemics with the Nihilists. The pointedness of *Notes from Underground* had yielded to an inclusive, expanding image of the world caught in a moment of time—a world of rather down-to-earth and yet at the same time fantastic tradesmen, tavern keepers, house painters, money-lenders, the easily amused servant Nastasya, the open-palmed policeman Zamyotov, the fanatic little radical Lebezyatnikov, the explosive Lieutenant Gunpowder. Dostoevsky's art gives even the most minor characters a spectacular presence, and they are constantly upstaging each other.

Yet *Crime and Punishment* is still the most singly focused of Dostoevsky's later novels. Its characters and events all converge on the enigma of Raskolnikov. He appears in thirty-seven of the novel's forty scenes, and we are allowed entry only into his consciousness and, more briefly, Svidrigailov's. On the other hand, the plane of happening is considerably enlarged; or, rather, the limits of accountable reality, the limits of man-in-nature, fall away. Dreams, waking visions, even ghosts, are as much a part of this world as are the buildings, bridges, and canals of Petersburg; the line dividing the outer from the inner, the solid from the fantasmagorical, wavers. This is a fluid world, full of coincidences, chance but fatal meetings, crucial words accidentally overheard, embodied in the communicating streets and squares, the adjoining rooms and apartments of the city. Petersburg is not a backdrop for the events Dostoevsky narrates, but a constant participant in them, and a mirror of Raskolnikov's soul. The enigma of the city and the enigma of the hero are one.

This is not to say that Raskolnikov is a neurotic who cannot keep from projecting his inner states upon the world. The truth is that we all see as we feel, or, better, that our vision is always complex, always moral, always spiritual: we "see" beauty and ugliness, we "see" good and evil. The struggle to empty himself of such complexities leads to the terrible splits and estrangements in Raskolnikov. His name comes from the word *raskolnik*, meaning "schismatic," one who has split away from the body of the Church; but he is also divided against himself. He is, as the critic Konstantin Mochulsky wrote, "a demon embodied in a humanist." Reason, in which he trusts, leads him to murder, yet reason cannot provide him with an axe when he needs one. Chance does that, and chance continues to abet him and to mock him. His transgression, his step over (the Russian word for "crime" means literally "over-stepping"), confronts him with dimensions of the world and of himself that he did not anticipate and cannot understand. He had been studying law at the university, but it is a representative of the law, that most unlikely and fascinating of investigators, Porfiry Petrovich, who says to him:

> It must be observed that the general case, the one to which all legal forms and rules are suited, and on the basis of which they are all worked out and written down in the books, simply does not exist, for the very reason that every case, let's say, for instance, every

crime, as soon as it actually occurs, turns at once into a completely particular case, sir; and sometimes, just think, really completely unlike all the previous ones, sir.

This may be taken to apply to the laws of reason and nature as well. The world Raskolnikov begins to discover when he leaves his "closet" and goes to commit his rational crime does not stand upon any laws, but, again, on "something different." It is the same Porfiry Petrovich who tells him, near the end of the novel, that he still has many years ahead of him, and that he should "embrace suffering" and live: "Don't be too clever about it, just give yourself directly to life, without reasoning." But there is perhaps no scene in all of Dostoevsky more perfectly ambiguous than this one.

Ambiguity is not incidental to Dostoevsky's vision. It is most obvious here in the comical, even farcical, scandals and absurdities surrounding the gruesome death of Marmeladov and the memorial meal following his funeral. But comical incidents abound throughout the novel. Even the central story of Raskolnikov and his struggle with "fate" keeps verging on comedy. Then, too, much of the action has an oddly theatrical quality, and Dostoevsky often uses stage terminology for setting scenes (he refers a number of times to "the public," so unexpectedly that earlier translators have paraphrased the term away). Are these real people, or actors in some sort of show? It is essential to Dostoevsky's art that the "view" is constantly shifting and may drop into horror or rise into laughter at any moment. Yet this ambiguity does not make light of suffering. On the contrary, what writer has ever revealed it so nakedly? And that precisely because he does not allow us our usual rational or sentimental evasions. Suffering is unmitigated in *Crime and Punishment;* there is no answer to it; there is no law of suffering. Ambiguity touches its essence but not its reality.

Evil is the final ambiguity. Reason cannot accept it; rationalizing ideologies deny its existence. No one calls it by name, and this silence weighs heavily on the novel, because the world of *Crime and Punishment* is saturated with evil, so much so that it becomes palpable. It is the dense element through which Raskolnikov moves without recognition. The vision of evil, which he lacks, seems to be granted in the end to Svidrigailov. The action in the second to last chapter of the novel is literally and metaphysically drenched—with a torrential downpour, with Svidrigailov's fear of water, with his dreams of the flooding of the Neva, the drowned girl, the wet child he tries to help. The "natural man," the man of instinct and appetite, thinks he can reach the point at which evil turns into innocence, but what is possible for a stone or a tiger is not possible for a human being. Svidrigailov is soaked through with what Simone Weil described as "the monotony of evil: never anything new, everything here is *equivalent*. Never anything real, everything here is imaginary. It is because of this monotony that quantity plays so great a part . . . Condemned to a false infinity. This is hell itself." Svidrigailov cannot get out of it. Raskolnikov, though he is full of lies and self-deceptions, may still "lie his way to the truth," as his friend Razumikhin puts it. There is movement in his soul. There is none in Svidrigailov's, for all his winning honesty.

Only one "event" answers to the overwhelming presence of evil in the novel. This is the raising of Lazarus. And, of course, it is only quoted, only read into the text by Sonya. Reason cannot accept this either. In what sort of world can Lazarus be raised from the dead? Such an event violates all the laws of reason and nature. It is the quintessential "particular case." Raskolnikov the schismatic, the man of reason, the would-be "strong individual," stands between Sonya and Svidrigailov and cannot make up his mind. Even at the end his pride rises up against this world that he thinks has defeated him by means of some blind mechanism. But the part of him which is not bound by reason, and from which he is so terribly separated, has begun to work against his will. He spends the night in the same drenching rainstorm as Svidrigailov, yet he cannot resolve to take the same way out. He turns to Sonya, and with painfully slow steps begins to move toward "a new, hitherto completely unknown reality." There Dostoevsky leaves him.

And here we shall leave the reader of this foreword, with everything still to be said—for the life of a novel is not in the conception but in the performance, which eludes summary. In every cadence, every tone, the realization of every character and scene of this densely composed "work of poetry," Dostoevsky shows his mastery. If our translation has managed to follow him attentively enough, it will be the best commentary.

—RICHARD PEVEAR

Translators' Note

The names of the novel's main characters are given here with diminutives and variants. Russian names are composed of first name, patronymic (from the father's first name), and family name. Formal address requires the use of first name and patronymic; diminutives are commonly used among family and intimate friends; a shortened form of the patronymic (e.g., Romanych instead of Romanovich), used only in speech, also suggests a certain familiarity. Accented syllables are given in italics.

Raskolnikov, Rodion Romanovich, or Romanych (*Rod*ya, *Rod*ka)
————, Pul*cher*ia Alex*an*drovna
————, Av*dot*ya Romanovna (*Dun*ya, *Dun*echka)
Marme*la*dov, Sem*yon* Za*khar*ovich, or Za*khar*ych
————, Kate*ri*na I*van*ovna
————, *Sof*ya Sem*yon*ovna (*Son*ya, *Son*echka)
————, Po*li*na Mi*khail*ovna (*Pol*ya, *Pol*enka, *Pol*echka)
————, *Kol*ya (*Kol*ka)
————, *Len*ya (first called *Lid*a, or *Lid*ochka)
Svidri*gail*ov, Ar*kad*y I*van*ovich
————, *Mar*fa Pe*trov*na
Razu*mikh*in (or Vrazu*mikh*in), *Dmi*tri Pro*kof*ych
Por*fir*y Pe*trov*ich (no family name)
*Luzh*in, *Pyo*tr Pe*trov*ich
Lebe*zyat*nikov, An*drei* Sem*yon*ovich, or Sem*yon*ych
Zam*yot*ov, Alex*an*der Grig*or*ievich
N*as*tasya Pe*trov*na (no family name; *Nas*tenka, Na*stas*yushka)
Al*yon*a I*van*ovna (no family name)
Liza*vet*a I*van*ovna (no family name)
Il*ya* Pe*trov*ich, nicknamed "Gunpowder" (no family name)

*Lip*pewechsel, Ama*l*ia I*v*anovna (also called Lud*w*igovna and *Fyodo-*
  rovna)
Zos*s*imov (no first name or patronymic)
Niko*lai* De*ment*iev (no patronymic; Miko*lai*, Miko*l*ka, Niko*lash*ka)

The name Raskolnikov comes from *raskolnik,* a schismatic, from *ras-*
kol, schism (the *Raskolniki* are members of the sect of Old Believers,
who broke away from the Russian Orthodox Church in the seven-
teenth century); the root verb is *raskolot,* to split. Razumikhin comes
from *razum,* reason, mind, intelligence. Lebezyatnikov comes from
the verb *lebezit,* to fawn or flatter in an eager, fidgety, tail-wagging
manner.

A note on the topography of Petersburg: the city, formally known as
Saint Petersburg but normally referred to as Petersburg, was built on
the orders of Tsar Peter the Great in the early eighteenth century. It
is situated on the marshy delta where the river Neva flows westward
into the Gulf of Finland, at a point where the Neva divides into three
streams: the Neva, the Little Neva, and the Nevka. The main part of
the city is on the south bank of the Neva, and is crisscrossed by canals
designed to control flooding. The two smaller streams form the areas
of the city known as Vasilievsky Island (between the Neva and the
Little Neva), and the Petersburg side (between the Little Neva and the
Nevka). Farther down the Neva is the well-to-do residential and
amusement area called the Islands.

  Often, though not consistently, Dostoevsky blanks out the names of
specific streets and other topographical points. Scholars armed with
maps have traced Raskolnikov's movements around the city and discovered the missing names, which some translators have then inserted
into their versions of the novel. We have consistently followed Dostoevsky's inconsistency here, assuming it had an artistic purpose.

Part One

I

A<small>T THE BEGINNING</small> of July, during an extremely hot spell, towards evening, a young man left the closet he rented from tenants in S——y Lane, walked out to the street, and slowly, as if indecisively, headed for the K——n Bridge.

He had safely avoided meeting his landlady on the stairs. His closet was located just under the roof of a tall, five-storied house, and was more like a cupboard than a room. As for the landlady, from whom he rented this closet with dinner and maid-service included, she lived one flight below, in separate rooms, and every time he went out he could not fail to pass by the landlady's kitchen, the door of which almost always stood wide open to the stairs. And each time he passed by, the young man felt some painful and cowardly sensation, which made him wince with shame. He was over his head in debt to the landlady and was afraid of meeting her.

It was not that he was so cowardly and downtrodden, even quite the contrary; but for some time he had been in an irritable and tense state, resembling hypochondria. He was so immersed in himself and had isolated himself so much from everyone that he was afraid not only of meeting his landlady but of meeting anyone at all. He was crushed by poverty; but even his strained circumstances had lately ceased to burden him. He had entirely given up attending to his daily affairs and did not want to attend to them. As a matter of fact, he was not afraid of any landlady, whatever she might be plotting against him. But to stop on the stairs, to listen to all sorts of nonsense about this commonplace rubbish, which he could not care less about, all this badgering for payment, these threats and complaints, and to have to dodge all the while, make excuses, lie—oh, no, better to steal catlike down the stairs somehow and slip away unseen by anyone.

This time, however, as he walked out to the street, even he was struck by his fear of meeting his creditor.

"I want to attempt such a thing, and at the same time I'm afraid of such trifles!" he thought with a strange smile. "Hm . . . yes . . . man has it all in his hands, and it all slips through his fingers from sheer cowardice . . . That is an axiom . . . I wonder, what are people most afraid of? A new step, their own new word, that's what they're most afraid of . . . I babble too much, however. That's why I don't do anything, because I babble. However, maybe it's like this: I babble because I don't do anything. I've learned to babble over this past month, lying in a corner day in and day out, thinking about . . . cuckooland. Why on earth am I going now? Am I really capable of *that*? Is *that* something serious? No, not serious at all. I'm just toying with it, for the sake of fantasy. A plaything! Yes, a plaything, if you like!"

It was terribly hot out, and moreover it was close, crowded; lime, scaffolding, bricks, dust everywhere, and that special summer stench known so well to every Petersburger who cannot afford to rent a summer house—all at once these things unpleasantly shook the young man's already overwrought nerves. The intolerable stench from the taverns, especially numerous in that part of the city, and the drunkards he kept running into even though it was a weekday, completed the loathsome and melancholy coloring of the picture. A feeling of the deepest revulsion flashed for a moment in the young man's fine features. Incidentally, he was remarkably good-looking, taller than average, slender and trim, with beautiful dark eyes and dark blond hair. But soon he lapsed as if into deep thought, or even, more precisely, into some sort of oblivion, and walked on no longer noticing what was around him, and not wishing to notice. He only muttered something to himself from time to time, out of that habit of monologues he had just confessed to himself. And at the same moment he was aware that his thoughts sometimes became muddled and that he was very weak: it was the second day that he had had almost nothing to eat.

He was so badly dressed that another man, even an accustomed one, would have been ashamed to go out in such rags during the daytime. However, the neighborhood was such that it was hard to cause any surprise with one's dress. The proximity of the Haymarket, the abundance of certain establishments, a population predominantly of craftsmen and artisans, who clustered in these central Petersburg streets and lanes, sometimes produced such a motley of types in the general panorama that to be surprised at meeting any sort of figure would even have been strange. But so much spiteful contempt was already stored up in the young man's soul that, for all his sometimes very youthful touchiness, he was least ashamed of his rags in the street. It was a different matter when he met some acquaintances or former friends, whom he generally disliked meeting . . . And yet, when a drunk man who was just then being taken through the street in an enormous cart harnessed to an enormous cart-horse, no one knew why or where, suddenly shouted to him as he passed by: "Hey, you, German hatter!"—pointing at him and yelling at the top of his lungs—the young man suddenly stopped and convulsively clutched his hat. It was a tall, cylindrical Zimmerman hat,[1] but all worn out, quite faded, all holes and stains, brimless, and dented so that it stuck out at an ugly angle. Yet it was not shame but quite a different feeling, even more like fear, that seized him.

"I just knew it!" he muttered in confusion. "It's just as I thought! That's the worst of all! Some stupid thing like that, some trivial detail, can ruin the whole scheme! Yes, the hat is too conspicuous . . . Ludicrous, and therefore conspicuous . . . My rags certainly call for a cap, even if it's some old pancake, not this monster. Nobody wears this kind, it can be noticed a mile away, and remembered . . . above all, it will be remembered later, so there's evidence for you. Here one must be as inconspicuous as possible . . . Details, details above all! . . . It's these details that ruin everything always . . ."

He did not have far to go; he even knew how many steps it was from the gate of his house: exactly seven hundred and thirty. Once, when he was far gone in his dreaming, he had counted them. At that time he did not yet believe in these dreams of his, and only chafed himself with their ugly but seductive audacity. Whereas now, a month later, he was beginning to look at them differently and, despite all those taunting monologues about his own powerlessness and indecision, had grown used, even somehow involuntarily, to regarding the "ugly" dream as a real undertaking, though he still did not believe himself. Now he was even going to make a *trial* of his undertaking, and at every step his excitement grew stronger and stronger.

With a sinking heart and nervous trembling he came up to a most enormous house that faced a canal on one side and ——y Street on the other. The house was all small apartments inside, and was inhabited by all sorts of working people—tailors, locksmiths, cooks, various Germans, girls living on their own, petty clerkdom, and so on. People kept coming and going, darting through both gateways and across both courtyards. Three or four caretakers worked there. The young man was very pleased not to have met any one of them, and slipped inconspicuously from the gate directly to the stairway on the right. The stairway was dark and narrow, a "back" stairway, but he had known and made a study of all that before, and he liked the whole situation: in that darkness even a curious glance was no danger. "If I'm so afraid now, what if it really should somehow get down to the business itself? . . ." he thought involuntarily, going up to the fourth floor. There his way was blocked by some porters, ex-soldiers who were moving furniture out of one apartment. He already knew from before that a German, an official, had been living in that apartment with his family: "It means the German is now moving out; which means that on the fourth floor of this stairway, on this landing, for a while only the old woman's apartment will be left occupied. That's good . . . just in case . . ." he thought again, and rang at the old woman's apartment. The bell jingled feebly, as though it were made not of brass but of tin. In the small apartments of such houses almost all the bells are like that. He had forgotten the ring of this bell, and now its peculiar ring seemed suddenly to remind him of something and bring it clearly before him . . . He jumped, so weak had his nerves become this time. In a short while the door was opened a tiny crack: the woman lodger was looking at the visitor through the crack with obvious mistrust, and only her little eyes could be seen glittering from the darkness. But seeing a number of people on the landing, she took courage and opened the door all the way. The young man stepped across the threshold into the dark entryway, divided by a partition, behind which was a tiny kitchen. The old woman stood silently before him, looking at him inquiringly. She was a tiny, dried-up old crone, about sixty, with sharp, spiteful little eyes and a small, sharp nose. She was bareheaded, and her colorless and only slightly graying hair was thickly greased. Her long, thin neck, which resembled a chicken's leg, was wrapped in some flannel rags, and, despite the heat, a fur-trimmed jacket, completely worn out and yellow with age, hung loosely from her shoulders. The little old woman coughed and groaned all the time. The young man must have glanced at her with some peculiar glance, because the earlier mistrust suddenly flashed in her eyes again.

"Raskolnikov, a student, I was here a month ago," the young man hastened to mutter with a half bow, recalling that he should be more courteous.

"I remember, dearie, I remember very well that you were," the old woman said distinctly, still without taking her inquiring eyes from his face.

"And so again, ma'am . . . on the same little business . . ." Raskolnikov continued, a bit disconcerted and surprised by the old crone's mistrust.

"Though maybe she's always like that, and I didn't notice it last time," he thought, with an unpleasant feeling.

The old crone was silent for a moment, as if hesitating; then she stepped aside and, pointing towards the door to the room, allowed the visitor to go ahead, saying:

"Come in, dearie."

The small room into which the young man walked, with yellow wallpaper, geraniums and muslin curtains in the windows, was at that moment brightly lit by the setting sun. "So the sun will be shining the same way *then!* . . ." flashed as if haphazardly through Raskolnikov's mind, and with a quick glance he took in everything in the room, in order to study and remember the layout as well as possible. But there was nothing special in the room. The furniture, all very old and of yellow wood, consisted of a sofa with a huge, curved wooden back, a round table of an oval shape in front of the sofa, a dressing table with a mirror between the windows, chairs against the walls, and two or three halfpenny prints in yellow frames portraying German damsels with birds in their hands—that was all the furniture there was. In the corner, an oil lamp was burning in front of a small icon. Everything was very clean: both furniture and floor were polished to a high lustre; everything shone. "Lizaveta's work," the young man thought. There was not a speck of dust to be found in the whole apartment. "It's wicked old widows who keep everything so clean," Raskolnikov continued to himself, and he cast a curious sidelong glance at the cotton curtain hanging in the doorway to the second tiny room, where the old woman's bed and chest of drawers stood, and where he had not yet peeked even once. The whole apartment consisted of these two rooms.

"What's your business?" the little old woman said sternly, coming into the room and, as before, standing directly in front of him, so as to look him directly in the face.

"I've brought something to pawn; here, ma'am!" And he took an old, flat silver watch from his pocket. A globe was engraved on its back. The chain was of steel.

"But the time is up for your last pledge. It was a month to the day before yesterday."

"I'll give you interest for another month; be patient."

"That's as I please, dearie, whether I'll be patient or sell your thing right now."

"How much will you give for the watch, Alyona Ivanovna?"

"You bring me trifles, dearie, in my opinion it's not worth anything. Last time I gave you two roubles for your ring, and you could buy one new from a jeweler for a rouble and a half."

"Give me four roubles anyway—I'll redeem it, it's my father's. I'll be getting money soon."

"A rouble and a half, sir, and interest paid in advance, if you like, sir."

"A rouble and a half!" the young man exclaimed.

"As you please." And the old crone held the watch out to him. The young man took it and became so angry that he wanted simply to leave; but he at once thought better of it, remembering that there was nowhere else to go and that he had also come for another reason.

"I'll take it!" he said rudely.

The old crone felt in her pocket for her keys and went into the other room behind the curtain. The young man, left alone in the middle of the room, was listening with curiosity and figuring things out. She could be heard opening the chest of drawers. "Must be the top drawer," he figured. "So she carries the keys in her right pocket . . . All in one bunch on a steel ring . . . And there's one key, the biggest of them, three times bigger, with a toothed bit, certainly not for a drawer . . . It means there's also some coffer, or a trunk . . . Now that's curious. Trunks always have keys like that . . . But how mean this all is . . ."

The old crone came back.

"Here you are, dearie: if it's ten kopecks to the rouble per month, you'll owe me fifteen kopecks on a rouble and a half for the month to come, sir. And you also owe me twenty kopecks by the same reckoning for the previous two roubles. That makes thirty-five altogether. I now owe you altogether one rouble and fifteen kopecks for your watch. Here, take it, sir."

"What! So now it's one rouble and fifteen kopecks!"

"Right you are, sir."

The young man did not argue and took the money. He looked at the old woman and made no move to leave, as if he still wanted to say or do something, but he himself did not seem to know precisely what . . .

"One of these days, Alyona Ivanovna, I may bring you yet another thing . . . silver . . . nice . . . a cigarette case . . . once I get it back from a friend of mine . . ." He became confused and fell silent.

"So, we'll talk then, dearie."

"Good-bye, ma'am . . . And you stay at home alone like this, your sister's not here?" he asked as casually as he could, walking out to the entryway.

"What business do you have with her, dearie?"

"Nothing special. I just asked. And right away you . . . Good-bye, Alyona Ivanovna!"

Raskolnikov went out decidedly troubled. This trouble kept increasing more and more. On his way down the stairs he even stopped several times, as if suddenly struck by something. And finally, already in the street, he exclaimed:

"Oh, God, how loathsome this all is! And can it be, can it be that I . . . no, it's nonsense, it's absurd!" he added resolutely. "Could such horror really come into my head? But then, what filth my heart is capable of! . . . Above all, filthy, nasty, vile, vile! . . . And for the whole month I . . ."

But neither words nor exclamations could express his agitation. The feeling of boundless loathing that had begun to oppress and sicken his heart while he was still only on his way to the old woman now reached such proportions and became so clearly manifest that he did not know where to flee from his anguish. He went down the sidewalk like a drunk man, not noticing the passers-by and running into them, and was in the next street before he came to his senses. Looking around, he noticed that he was standing by a tavern, the entrance to which was downstairs from the sidewalk, in the basement. At that same moment two drunks came walking out the door and, supporting and cursing each other, climbed up to the street. Without another thought, Raskolnikov immediately went down the stairs. He had never gone into taverns before, but his head was spinning now, and besides he was tormented by a burning thirst. He wanted to drink some cold beer, all the more so in that he attributed his sudden weakness to hunger. He sat down in a dark and dirty corner, at a sticky little table, asked for beer, and greedily drank the first glass. He immediately felt all relieved, and his thoughts became clear. "It's all nonsense," he said hopefully, "and there was nothing to be troubled about! Just some physical disorder! One glass of beer, a piece of dry bread, and see—in an instant the mind gets stronger, the thoughts clearer, the intentions firmer! Pah, how paltry it all is! . . ." But in spite of this scornful spitting, he already looked cheerful, as if he had freed himself all at once of some terrible burden, and cast an amiable glance around at the people there. Yet even at that moment he had a distant foreboding that all this receptiveness to the good was also morbid.

There were few people left in the tavern by then. Just after the two drunks he had run into on the stairs, a whole party left together, five men or so, with one wench and an accordion. After them the place became quiet and roomy. There remained one man who looked like a tradesman, drunk, but not very, sitting over a beer; his friend, fat, enormous, in a tight-waisted coat, and with a gray beard, who was quite drunk, had dozed off on a bench, and every once in a while, as if half awake, would suddenly start snapping his fingers, spreading his arms wide and jerking the upper part of his body without getting up from the bench, while he sang some gibberish, trying hard to recall the verses, something like:

"The whole year long he loved his wife,
The who-o-ole year lo-o-ong he lo-o-oved his wife . . ."

Or again, suddenly waking up:

> "Down Podyacheskaya he did go,
> He met a girl he used to know . . ."

But no one shared his happiness; his silent friend even looked upon all these outbursts with hostility and mistrust. There was yet another man there who in appearance resembled a retired official. He was sitting apart over his little crock, taking a sip every once in a while and looking around. He also seemed somewhat agitated.

II

RASKOLNIKOV was not used to crowds and, as has already been mentioned, fled all company, especially of late. But now something suddenly drew him to people. Something new was happening in him, as it were, and with that a certain thirst for people made itself felt. After a whole month of this concentrated anguish, this gloomy excitement of his, he was so tired out that he wished, if only for a moment, to draw a breath in another world, whatever it might be, and, despite all the filthiness of the situation, it was with pleasure that he now went on sitting in the tavern.

The proprietor of the establishment was in another room, but frequently came into the main room, descending a flight of stairs from somewhere, his foppish black boots with their wide red tops appearing first. He was wearing a long-skirted coat and a terribly greasy black satin waistcoat, with no necktie, and his whole face was as if oiled like an iron padlock. Behind the counter was a lad of about fourteen, and there was another younger lad who served when anything was asked for. There were chopped pickles, dry black bread, and fish cut into pieces, all quite evil-smelling. It was so stuffy that it was almost impossible to sit there, and everything was so saturated with wine-smell that it seemed one could get drunk in five minutes from the air alone.

We sometimes encounter people, even perfect strangers, who begin to interest us at first sight, somehow suddenly, all at once, before a word has been spoken. Such was precisely the impression made on Raskolnikov by the guest who sat apart and looked like a retired official. Later the young man recalled this first impression more than once and even ascribed it to a presentiment. He kept glancing at the official, also no doubt because the latter was looking persistently at him, and one could see that he very much wanted to start a conversation. But at the others in the tavern, not excluding the proprietor, the official looked somehow habitually and even with boredom, and at the same time also with a certain shade of haughty disdain, as at people of lower position and development with whom he saw no point in talking. He was a man already past fifty, of average height and solid build, with some gray in his hair and a large bald spot, with a yellow, even greenish, face, swollen from constant drinking, and with puffy eyelids behind which his reddish eyes shone, tiny as slits, but lively. Yet there was something very strange in him; his eyes seemed even to be lit with rapture—perhaps there were sense and reason as well, but at the same time there seemed also to be a flicker of madness in them. He was dressed in an old, completely ragged black frock coat, which had shed all its buttons. Only one still somehow hung on, and this one he kept buttoned, obviously not wishing to shirk convention. From under his nankeen waistcoat a shirtfront stuck out, all crumpled, soiled, and stained. His face had been shaved in official style, but a good while ago, so that thick, blue-gray bristles were beginning to show on it. And there was indeed something solidly official in his ways. Yet he was agitated, kept ruffling his hair, and every once in a while leaned his head on his hands in anguish, resting his torn elbows on the spilt-upon and sticky table. Finally he looked straight at Raskolnikov and said loudly and firmly:

"May I venture, my dear sir, to engage you in a conversation of decency? For though you are not of important aspect, my experience nevertheless distinguishes in you an educated man, and one unaccustomed to drink. I myself have always respected education, coupled with the feelings of the heart, and moreover I am a titular councillor.[2] Marmeladov—such is my name—titular councillor. May I venture to ask whether you have been in government service?"

"No, studying . . ." the young man replied, surprised partly at the peculiarly ornate turn of speech and partly at being addressed so directly, point-blank. In spite of his recent momentary wish for at least some communion with people, at the first word actually addressed to him he suddenly felt his usual unpleasant and irritable feeling of loathing towards any stranger who touched or merely wanted to touch his person.

"A student, then, or a former student!"[3] the official cried. "Just as I thought! Experience, my dear sir, oft-repeated experience!" And he put his finger to his forehead in a sign of self-praise. "You were a student, or were engaged in some scholarly pursuit! Allow me . . ." He rose slightly, swayed, picked up his little crock and glass, and sat himself down with the young man, somewhat catercorner to him. He was drunk, but spoke loquaciously and glibly, only now and then getting a bit confused in places and dragging out his speech. He even fell upon Raskolnikov with a sort of greediness, as though he, too, had not talked to anyone for a whole month.

"My dear sir," he began almost solemnly, "poverty is no vice, that is the truth. I know that drunkenness is also no virtue, and that is even more so. But destitution, my dear sir, destitution is a vice, sir. In poverty you may still preserve the nobility of your inborn feelings, but in destitution no one ever does. For destitution one does not even get driven out of human company with a stick; one is swept out with a broom, to make it more insulting; and justly so, for in destitution I am the first to insult myself. Hence the drinking! My dear sir, a month ago Mr. Lebezyatnikov gave my wife a beating, and my wife is a far cry from me! Do you understand, sir? Allow me to ask you something else, if only for the sake of curiosity: did you ever happen to spend your nights on the Neva, on the hay barges?"[4]

"No, never," Raskolnikov replied. "Why do you ask?"

"Well, sir, but that's where I've come from, and it's already the fifth night, sir . . ."

He poured himself a glass, drank it, and lapsed into thought. Indeed, one could see bits of hay stuck here and there on his clothes and even in his hair. It was quite possible that he had not undressed and washed for five days. His hands were especially dirty—greasy, red, with black under the nails.

His conversation seemed to arouse general, if lax, attention. The lads at the counter began to snigger. It seemed the proprietor came down from the upstairs room on purpose to listen to the "funnyman," and sat some distance away, occasionally yawning lazily but grandly. It was obvious that Marmeladov had long been a familiar there. And his penchant for ornate speech he had probably acquired as a result of his habit of frequent tavern conversation with various strangers. This habit turns into a necessity for certain drunkards, mostly those who are treated harshly and ordered about at home. Hence, in a company of drinkers, they always seem eager to solicit justification for themselves and, if possible, even respect as well.

"Funnyman," the proprietor said loudly. "And why don't you work, why don't you serve, since you're an official?"

"Why do I not serve, my dear sir?" Marmeladov picked up, addressing Raskolnikov exclusively, as if it were he who had asked the question. "Why do I not serve? And does my heart not ache over this vain groveling? When Mr. Lebezyatnikov gave my wife a beating a month ago, with his own hands, while I was lying there in my cups, did I not suffer? Excuse me, young man, has it ever happened to you . . . hm . . . let's say, to ask hopelessly for a loan of money?"

"It's happened . . . that is, what do you mean by hopelessly?"

"That is, completely hopelessly, sir, knowing beforehand that nothing will come of it. Say, for example, you know beforehand and thoroughly well that this man, this most well-intentioned and most useful citizen, will under no circumstances give you any money—for why should he, may I ask? He knows I won't repay it. Out of compassion? But Mr. Lebezyatnikov, who follows all the new ideas, explained the other day that in our time compassion is even forbidden by science, as is already happening in England, where they have political economy. Why, then, should he give, may I ask? And so, knowing beforehand that he will not give anything, you still set out on your way and . . ."

"But why go?" Raskolnikov put in.

"And what if there is no one else, if there is nowhere else to go! It is necessary that every man have at least somewhere to go. For there are times when one absolutely must go at least somewhere! When my only-begotten daughter went out for the first time with a yellow pass,[5] and I went, too, then . . . (for my daughter lives on a yellow pass, sir . . .)," he added parenthetically, glancing somewhat worriedly at the young man. "Never mind, my dear sir, never mind!" he hastened to declare at once and with apparent calm, when both lads at the counter snorted and the proprietor himself smiled.

"Never mind, sir. I am not troubled by this wagging of heads, for everything is already known to everyone, and everything hidden will be made manifest;[6] I regard it not with disdain, but with humility. Let it be! Let it be! 'Behold the man!'[7] Excuse me, young man, but can you . . . Or, no, to expound it more forcefully and more expressively: not *can* you, but would you *venture,* looking upon me at this hour, to say of me affirmatively that I am not a swine?"

The young man did not answer a word.

"Well, sir," the orator went on, having waited sedately and this time with greater dignity for the renewed sniggering in the room to die down. "Well, sir, so I am a swine, and she is a lady! I have the image of a beast, and Katerina Ivanovna, my spouse, is an educated person and by birth an officer's daughter. Granted, granted I am a scoundrel, while she has a lofty heart and is full of sentiments ennobled by good breeding. And yet . . . oh, if only she felt pity for me! My dear sir, my dear sir, but it is necessary that every man have at least one such place where he, too, is pitied! And Katerina Ivanovna, though she is a magnanimous lady, is unjust . . . And though I myself understand that when she pulls me by these tufts of mine, she does it for no other reason than her heart's pity—for, I repeat it without embarrassment, she does pull these tufts of mine, young man," he confirmed with increased dignity, having heard more sniggering, "but, God, if she would only just once . . . But no! no! it is all in vain, and there is no use talking, no use talking! . . . for my wish has already been granted more than once, and already more than once I have been pitied, but . . . such is my trait, and I am a born brute!"

"That you are!" the proprietor remarked, yawning.

Marmeladov banged his fist resolutely on the table.

"Such is my trait! Do you know, do you know, sir, that I even drank up her stockings? Not her shoes, sir, for that would at least somehow resemble the order of things, but her stockings, I drank up her stockings, sir! Her angora kerchief I also drank up—a gift, a former one, hers, not mine; and our corner is cold, and this winter she caught a chill and took to coughing, with blood now. And we have three small children, and Katerina Ivanovna works day and night, scrubbing and cleaning and washing the children, for she has been used to cleanliness since childhood, and she has a weak chest and is inclined to consumption, and I feel it. Do I not feel it? And the more I drink, the more I feel it. It is for this I drink, that in drinking I may seek compassion and feeling. It is not joy I seek, but sorrow only . . . I drink, for I wish doubly to suffer!" And he bent his head to the table as if in despair.

"Young man," he continued, unbending again, "in your face I read, as it were, a certain sorrow. I read it when you entered, and therefore I addressed you at once. For by telling you the story of my life, I do not wish to expose myself to disgrace before these lovers of idleness, who know everything anyway, but am seeking a sensitive and educated man. Know, then, that my spouse was educated in an aristocratic provincial institute for the nobility and at her graduation danced with a shawl before the governor and other notables,[8] for which she received a gold medal and a certificate of merit. The medal . . . well, we sold the medal . . . long ago . . . hm . . . the certificate of merit is still lying in her trunk, she showed it to our landlady just recently. And though she is in the most ceaseless strife with our landlady, still she wished to feel proud before someone at least and to tell of the happy days gone by. And I do not judge, I do not judge, for this is the last thing left to her in her memories, and the rest has all gone to ruin! Yes, yes, she is a hot, proud, and unbending lady. She washes the floors herself and eats black bread, but disrespect for herself she will not tolerate. That is why she would not let Mr. Lebezyatnikov get away with his rudeness, and when Mr. Lebezyatnikov gave her a beating for it, she took to her bed, not so much from the beating as from emotion. She came to me already a widow, with three children, each one smaller than the next. She had married her first husband, an infantry officer, out of love, and eloped with him from her parental home. She loved her husband exceedingly, but he got into card-playing, was taken to court, and thereupon died. He used to beat her towards the end; and though she would not let him get away with it, as I am informed of a certainty and with documents, yet to this day she remembers him with tears and holds him up to me in reproach—and I am glad, I am glad, for at least in her imaginings she beholds herself as having once been happy . . . And after him she was left with three young children in a remote and savage district, where I was living at the time, and she was left in such hopeless destitution as I, though my adventures have been many and varied, am scarcely able to describe. And her relations had all renounced her. Besides, she was proud, much too proud . . . And it was then, my dear sir, it was then that I, being a widower myself, and having a fourteen-year-old daughter from my first wife, offered her my hand, for I could not look on at such suffering. You may judge thereby what degree her calamities had reached, if she, well educated and well bred, and of a known family, consented to marry me! But she did! Weeping and sobbing and wringing her hands—she did! For she had nowhere to go. Do you understand, do you understand, my dear sir, what it means when there is no longer anywhere to go? No! That you do not understand yet . . . And for a whole year I fulfilled my duties piously and sacredly and did not touch this" (he jabbed a finger at his bottle), "for I do have feelings. But even so I could not please her; and then I lost my position, also through no fault of my own, but because of a change of staff, and then I did touch it! . . . It is now a year and a half since we finally ended up, after much wandering and numerous calamities, in this splendid capital adorned with numerous monuments. And here I found a position . . . Found it, and lost it again. Do you understand, sir? This time I lost it through my own fault, for this trait of mine appeared again . . . We now live in a corner at Amalia Fyodorovna Lippewechsel's, and what we live on and pay with I do not know.[9] There are many others living there besides ourselves . . . A Sodom, sir, a most outrageous one . . . hm . . . yes . . . And meanwhile my daughter from my first marriage also grew up, and what she had to suffer from her stepmother while she was growing up, that I shall pass over in silence. For though Katerina Ivanovna is filled with magnanimous feelings, she is a hot and irritable lady, and an abrupt one . . . Yes, sir! Well, no use going over that! Sonya, as you can imagine, received no education. I tried four years ago to teach her geography and world history; but since I myself was not firm in this knowledge, and there were besides no suitable textbooks, for whatever books we had left . . . hm! . . . well, there are no books anymore, so that was the end of all education. We stopped at Cyrus of Persia.[10] Later, having reached maturity, she read several books of a novelistic purport, and recently, thanks to Mr. Lebezyatnikov, one more book—Lewes's *Physiology*,[11] perhaps you know it, sir?—read it with great interest and even recited some extracts aloud for us: that is the whole of her enlightenment. And now, my dear sir, I will address you with a private question of my own: how much, in your opinion, can a poor but honest girl earn by honest labor? . . . Not even fifteen kopecks a day, sir, if she is honest and has no special talents, and even then only if her hands are never still for a moment. And even then the state councillor[12] Klopstock, Ivan Ivanovich—perhaps you've heard of him?—has not only still not paid for the half dozen holland shirts she made him, but even offended her and chased her away, stamping his feet and calling her bad names, on the pretext that the collars were the wrong size and too pointed. And here the children were hungry . . . And here Katerina Ivanovna was pacing the room, wringing her hands, and flushed spots came out on her cheeks—as always happens with this illness: 'You live with us,' she says, 'you good-for-nothing, you eat and drink and use up warmth'—and what is there to eat and drink, if even the children don't see a crust of bread for three days on end! I was lying there . . . well, what of it! . . . lying there in my cups, sir, and I heard Sonya say (she's uncomplaining, and has such a meek little voice . . . she's fair, her face is always so pale, thin), and so she said, 'What, Katerina Ivanovna, must I really go and do such a thing?' And Darya Frantsevna, an ill-meaning woman and one oft-known to the police, had already made inquiries three times through the landlady. 'And what,' Katerina Ivanovna answered mockingly, 'what's there to save? Some treasure!' But do not blame her, do not blame her, my dear sir, do not blame her! She said this not in her right mind but in emotional agitation, in sickness, and with the children crying from hunger, and said it, besides, more for the sake of the insult than in any strict sense . . . For such is Katerina Ivanovna's character, and when the children get to crying, even if it's from hunger, she starts beating them at once. So then, some time after five, I see Sonechka get up, put on her kerchief, put on her wrap, and go out, and she came back home after eight. She came in, went straight to Katerina Ivanovna, and silently laid thirty roubles on the table in front of her. Not a word with it, not even a glance; she just took our big green flannel shawl (we have this one flannel shawl for all of us), covered her head and face with it completely, and lay down on her bed, face to the wall; only her little shoulders and her whole body kept trembling . . . And I was lying there in the same aspect as previously, sir . . . And then I saw, young man, after that I saw Katerina Ivanovna go over to Sonechka's bed, also without saying a word, and for the whole evening she stayed kneeling at her feet, kissing her feet, and would not get up, and then they both fell asleep together, embracing each other . . . both . . . both . . . yes, sir . . . and I . . . was lying there in my cups, sir."

Marmeladov fell silent, as though his voice had failed him. Then suddenly he poured a quick glass, drank it, and grunted.

"Since then, my dear sir," he went on after some silence, "since then, owing to an unfortunate occurrence and reports made by ill-meaning persons—which Darya Frantsevna especially abetted, on the pretext that she had not been shown due respect—since then my daughter, Sofya Semyonovna, has been obliged to carry a yellow pass, and under such circumstances could no longer remain with us. For the landlady, Amalia Fyodorovna, would not allow it (though she herself had abetted Darya Frantsevna before), and Mr. Lebezyatnikov also . . . hm . . . It was because of Sonya that this story happened between him and Katerina Ivanovna. First he sought after Sonya himself, but then he suddenly got puffed up: 'What?' he said. 'Is such an enlightened man as myself to live in the same apartment with such a woman?' And Katerina Ivanovna would not let that pass, she interfered . . . well, so it happened . . . And now Sonechka comes to us mostly at dusk, and helps Katerina Ivanovna, and brings whatever means she can . . . But she lives at the tailor Kapernaumov's, she rents a room from him, and Kapernaumov is lame and tongue-tied, and the whole of his extremely numerous family is also tongue-tied. And his wife, too, is tongue-tied . . . They occupy one room, and Sonya has her own, separately, with a partition . . . Hm, yes . . . The poorest people, and all of them tongue-tied . . . yes . . . So I got up that next morning, sir, put my rags on, lifted up my hands to heaven, and went to see his excellency, Ivan Afanasyevich. Do you know his excellency, Ivan Afanasyevich? No? Then you have missed knowing a man of God! He is wax . . . wax before the face of the Lord; as the wax melteth![13] . . . He even shed a tear when he heard it all. 'Well, Marmeladov,' he said, 'you have deceived my expectations once already. . . . I am taking you one more time, on my personal responsibility'—that's just what he said. 'Remember that,' he said, 'and now go!' I kissed the dust at his feet—mentally, because in reality he would not have allowed it, being a dignitary, and a man of the new political and educated thinking; I went home again, and when I announced that I had been taken back into the service and would have a salary, Lord, what went on then! . . ."

Marmeladov again stopped in great agitation. At that moment a whole party of drinkers walked in from the street, already drunk to begin with, and from the entrance came the sounds of a hired barrel organ and a child's cracked seven-year-old voice singing "The Little Farm."[14] It became noisy. The proprietor and servants occupied themselves with the newcomers. Marmeladov, ignoring the newcomers, went on with his story. He seemed to have grown quite weak, but the drunker he got, the more loquacious he became. The recollection of his recent success in the service seemed to animate him and was even reflected in his face as a sort of radiance. Raskolnikov listened attentively.

"That was all five weeks ago, sir. Yes . . . As soon as the two of them, Katerina Ivanovna and Sonechka, found out, Lord, it was just as though I'd moved into the Kingdom of God. I used to lie there like a brute, all I heard was abuse! But now they were tiptoeing around, quieting the children: 'Semyon Zakharych is tired from his work, he's resting, shh!' They brought me coffee before work, with scalded cream! They started getting real cream, do you hear! How they managed to knock together eleven roubles and fifty kopecks to have me decently outfitted, I don't understand. Boots, cotton shirtfronts—most magnificent, a uniform, they cooked it all up for eleven fifty, in the most excellent aspect, sir. The first day I came home after a morning's work, I saw that Katerina Ivanovna had prepared two courses, soup and corned beef with horseradish, which we'd had no notion of before then. She doesn't have any dresses . . . I mean, not any, sir, and here it was as if she were going to a party, all dressed up, and not just in anything, no, she knows how to do it all out of nothing: she fixed her hair, put on some clean collar, some cuffs, and—quite a different person emerged, younger and prettier. Sonechka, my dove, contributed only money, and as for herself, she said, for the time being it's not proper for me to visit you too often, or only when it's dark, so no one can see me. Do you hear? Do you hear? I went to take a nap after dinner, and what do you suppose? Katerina Ivanovna simply couldn't help herself: just a week earlier she had quarreled to the ultimate degree with the landlady, Amalia Fyodorovna, and now she invited her for a cup of coffee. They sat whispering for two hours: 'So,' she said, 'Semyon Zakharych has work now and is getting a salary, and he went to his excellency himself, and his excellency came out in person, and told everyone to wait, and took Semyon Zakharych by the arm, and led him past everyone into the office.' Do you hear? Do you hear? ' "Of course I remember your merits, Semyon Zakharych, and though you were given to that frivolous weakness, since you have now promised, and, moreover, since without you things have gone badly for us" ' (hear that, hear that!), ' "I shall now place my hopes," he said, "in your gentleman's word" '—that is, I must tell you, she up and invented it all, and not really out of frivolousness, not merely to boast, sir! No, she believed it all, she delights in her own fancies, by God, sir! And I do not condemn that, no, I do not condemn it! . . . And six days ago, when I brought home my first salary—twenty-three roubles and forty kopecks—brought it in full, she called me a sweet little thing: 'You sweet little thing!' she said. We were by ourselves, sir, you understand. And what sort of beauty would you say is in me, and what sort of husband am I? But no, she pinched my cheek and said, 'You sweet little thing!' "

Marmeladov stopped, wanted to smile, but suddenly his chin began to tremble. He restrained himself, however. The pot-house, the depraved look of the man, the five nights on the hay barges, the half-litre bottle, and at the same time this morbid love for his wife and family, bewildered his listener. Raskolnikov listened tensely, but with a morbid sensation. He was annoyed that he had stopped at the place.

"My dear sir, my dear sir!" Marmeladov exclaimed, recovering himself. "Oh, sir, perhaps it's all just a laughing matter for you, as it is for everyone else, and I am merely bothering you with the foolishness of all these measly details of my domestic life, but for me it's no laughing matter! For I can feel it all . . . And in the course of that whole paradisal day of my life and of that whole evening I spent in fleeting dreams—that is, how I would arrange it all, and would dress the children, and would give her peace, and would bring back my only-begotten daughter from dishonor into the bosom of the family . . . And so much, so much . . . It's permissible, sir. And then, my dear sir" (Marmeladov suddenly gave a sort of start, raised his head, and looked straight at his listener), "and then, sir, the very next day after all those dreams (that is, exactly five days ago), towards evening, by means of cunning deceit, like a thief in the night, I stole the key to Katerina Ivanovna's trunk from her, took out all that remained of the salary I had brought home, I don't remember how much, and now, sir, look at me, all of you! Five days away from home, they're looking for me there, and it's the end of my service, and my uniform is lying in a tavern near the Egyptian Bridge, and these garments I received in exchange for it . . . and it is the end of everything!"

Marmeladov struck himself on the forehead with his fist, clenched his teeth, closed his eyes, and leaned heavily on the table with his elbow. But a moment later his face suddenly changed and, glancing at Raskolnikov with a certain affected coyness and forced insolence, he laughed and said:

"And today I went to see Sonya and asked her for the hair of the dog! . . . Heh, heh, heh!"

"Did she give it to you?" one of the newcomers shouted from the side, shouted and guffawed at the top of his lungs.

"This very bottle here was bought on her money, sir," Marmeladov said, addressing Raskolnikov exclusively. "She took out thirty kopecks for me, with her own hands, the last she had, I saw it myself . . . She didn't say anything, she just looked at me silently . . . That is not done on earth, but up there . . . people are grieved for, wept over, and not reproached, not reproached! And it hurts more, it hurts more, sir, when one is not reproached! . . . Thirty kopecks, yes, sir. And doesn't she also need them now, eh? What do you think, my dear gentlemen? For she has to observe her cleanliness now. This cleanliness—of a special sort, you understand—costs money. Understand? And to buy a bit of pomade as well, can't do without that, sir; starched petticoats, some shoes of a frippery sort to show off her foot when she steps over a puddle. Do you understand, do you understand, sir, what this cleanliness means? So, sir, and now I, her blood father, snatched these thirty kopecks for the hair of the dog! And I'm drinking, sir! And I've already drunk them up, sir! . . . So, who's going to pity the likes of me? Eh? Do you pity me now, sir, or do you not? Speak, sir, do you or do you not? Heh, heh, heh, heh!"

He wanted to pour some more, but there was nothing left. The bottle was empty.

"Why pity you?" shouted the proprietor, who turned up near them again.

There was laughter and even swearing. The laughter and swearing came both from those who were listening and from those who were not listening but merely looking at the figure of the retired official.

"Pity! Why pity me!" Marmeladov suddenly cried out, rising with his hand stretched forth, in decided inspiration, as if he had only been waiting for these words. "Why pity me, you say? Yes! There's nothing to pity me for! I ought to be crucified, crucified on a cross, and not pitied! But crucify, O judge, crucify, and having crucified, pity the man! And then I myself will come to you to be crucified, for I thirst not for joy, but for sorrow and tears! . . . Do you think, wine-merchant, that this bottle of yours brought me sweetness? Sorrow, sorrow I sought at its bottom, sorrow and tears, and I tasted it and found it; and He will pity us who pitied everyone, and who understood all men and all women, He alone, and He is the judge. On that day He will come and ask, 'Where is the daughter who gave herself for a wicked and consumptive stepmother, for a stranger's little children? Where is the daughter who pitied her earthly father, a foul drunkard, not shrinking from his beastliness?' And He will say, 'Come! I have already forgiven you once . . . I have forgiven you once . . . And now, too, your many sins are forgiven, for you have loved much[15] . . .' And He will forgive my Sonya, He will forgive her, I know He will . . . Today, when I was with her, I felt it in my heart! And He will judge and forgive all, the good and the wicked, the wise and the humble . . . And when He has finished with everyone, then He will say unto us, too, 'You, too, come forth!' He will say. 'Come forth, my drunk ones, my weak ones, my shameless ones!' And we will all come forth, without being ashamed, and stand there. And He will say, 'Swine you are! Of the image of the beast and of his seal;[16] but come, you, too!' And the wise and the reasonable will say unto Him, 'Lord, why do you receive such as these?' And He will say, 'I receive them, my wise and reasonable ones, forasmuch as not one of them considered himself worthy of this thing . . .' And He will stretch out His arms to us, and we will fall at His feet . . . and weep . . . and understand everything! Then we will understand everything! . . . and everyone will understand . . . and Katerina Ivanovna . . . she, too, will understand . . . Lord, Thy kingdom come!"[17]

And he sank down on the bench, exhausted and weak, not looking at anyone, apparently oblivious of his surroundings and deep in thought. His words produced a certain impression; for a moment silence reigned, but soon laughter and swearing were heard again:

"Nice reasoning!"

"Blather!"

"A real official!"

And so on and so forth.

"Let us go, sir," Marmeladov said suddenly, raising his head and turning to Raskolnikov. "Take me . . . Kozel's house, through the courtyard. It's time . . . to Katerina Ivanovna . . ."

Raskolnikov had long been wanting to leave, and had himself thought of helping him. Marmeladov, who turned out to be much weaker on his feet than in his speeches, leaned heavily on the young man. They had to go two or three hundred steps. Confusion and fear took more and more possession of the drunkard as he neared home.

"It's not Katerina Ivanovna I'm afraid of now," he muttered in agitation, "and not that she'll start pulling my hair. Forget the hair! . . . The hair's nonsense! I can tell you! It's even better if she starts pulling it; that's not what I'm afraid of . . . I . . . it's her eyes I'm afraid of . . . yes . . . her eyes . . . I'm also afraid of the flushed spots on her cheeks, and also—her breathing . . . Have you ever seen how people with that illness breathe . . . when their feelings are aroused? And I'm afraid of the children's crying, too . . . Because if Sonya hasn't been feeding them, then . . . I don't know what! I really don't! And I'm not afraid of a beating . . . Know, sir, that such beatings are not only not painful, but are even a delight to me . . . For I myself cannot do without them. It's better. Let her beat me, to ease her soul . . . it's better . . . Here's the house. Kozel's house. A locksmith, a German, a rich one . . . take me in!"

They entered through the courtyard and went up to the fourth floor. The higher up, the darker the stairway became. It was nearly eleven o'clock by then, and though at that time of year there is no real night in Petersburg,[18] it was very dark at the top of the stairs.

At the head of the stairs, at the very top, a small, soot-blackened door stood open. A candle-end lighted the poorest of rooms, about ten paces long; the whole of it could be seen from the entryway. Everything was scattered about and in disorder, all sorts of children's rags especially. A torn sheet hung across the back corner. Behind it was probably a bed. The only contents of the room itself were two chairs and an oilcloth sofa, very ragged, before which stood an old pine kitchen table, unpainted and uncovered. At the edge of the table stood an iron candlestick with the butt of a tallow candle burning down in it. It appeared that this room of Marmeladov's was a separate one, not just a corner, though other tenants had to pass through it. The door to the further rooms, or hutches, into which Amalia Lippewechsel's apartment had been divided, was ajar. Behind it there was noise and shouting. Guffawing. Card-playing and tea-drinking seemed to be going on. Occasionally the most unceremonious words would fly out.

Raskolnikov immediately recognized Katerina Ivanovna. She was a terribly wasted woman, slender, quite tall and trim, still with beautiful dark brown hair, and indeed with flushed spots on her cheeks. She was pacing the small room, her hands pressed to her chest, her lips parched, her breath uneven and gasping. Her eyes glittered as with fever, but her gaze was sharp and fixed, and with the last light of the burnt-down candle-end flickering on it, this consumptive and agitated face produced a painful impression. To Raskolnikov she appeared about thirty years old, and Marmeladov was indeed no match for her . . . She did not hear or notice them as they entered; she seemed to be in some sort of oblivion, not hearing or seeing anything. The room was stuffy, yet she had not opened the window; a stench came from the stairs, yet the door to the stairs was not shut; waves of tobacco smoke came through the open door from the inner rooms, she was coughing, yet she did not close the door. The smallest child, a girl of about six, was asleep on the floor, sitting somehow crouched with her head buried in the sofa. The boy, a year older, stood in the corner crying and trembling all over. He had probably just been beaten. The older girl, about nine, tall and thin as a matchstick, wearing only a poor shirt, all in tatters, with a threadbare flannel wrap thrown over her bare shoulders, probably made for her two years before, since it now did not even reach her knees, stood in the corner by her little brother, her long arm, dry as a matchstick, around his neck. She was whispering something to him, apparently trying to calm him, doing all she could to restrain him so that he would not somehow start whimpering again, and at the same time following her mother fearfully with her big, dark eyes, which seemed even bigger in her wasted and frightened little face. Marmeladov knelt just at the door, without entering the room, and pushed Raskolnikov forward. The woman, seeing the stranger, stopped distractedly in front of him, having come to her senses for a moment, and appeared to be asking herself why he was there. But she must have fancied at once that he was going to some other room and only passing through theirs. Having come to this conclusion, and taking no further notice of him, she went to the entryway to close the door and suddenly gave a cry, seeing her husband kneeling there in the doorway.

"Ah!" she cried in a frenzy, "he's come back! The jailbird! The monster! . . . Where's the money? What's in your pocket, show me! And those aren't the same clothes! Where are your clothes? Where is the money? Speak! . . ."

And she fell to searching him. Marmeladov at once spread his arms humbly and obediently, to make the search of his pockets easier. Not a kopeck was left of the money.

"But where is the money?" she shouted. "Oh, Lord, did he really drink up all of it? There were twelve roubles left in the trunk! . . ." And suddenly, in a rage, she seized him by the hair and dragged him into the room. Marmeladov made her efforts easier by meekly crawling after her on his knees.

"And it's a delight to me! It's not painful, it's a deli-i-ight, my de-e-ear sir," he kept crying out, being pulled by his hair all the while and once even bumping his forehead on the floor. The child who was asleep on the floor woke up and started to cry. The boy in the corner could not help himself, trembled, cried out, and rushed to his sister in a terrible fright, almost a fit. The older girl, half awake, was trembling like a leaf.

"Drank it up! Drank up all of it, all of it!" the poor woman kept shouting in despair. "And they're not the same clothes! Hungry! Hungry!" (she pointed at the children, wringing her hands). "Oh, curse this life! And you, aren't you ashamed," she suddenly fell upon Raskolnikov, "coming from the pot-house! Were you drinking with him? Were you drinking with him, too? Get out!"

The young man hastened to leave without saying a word. Besides, the inner door had been thrown wide open and several curious faces were peering through it. Insolent, laughing heads with cigarettes or pipes, in skullcaps, craning their necks. One glimpsed figures in dressing gowns that hung quite open, or in indecently summerish costumes, some with cards in their hands. They laughed with particular glee when Marmeladov, dragged about by his hair, shouted that it was a delight to him. They even started edging into the room. Finally an ominous shrieking was heard: this was Amalia Lippewechsel herself tearing her way through, to restore order in her own fashion and frighten the poor woman for the hundredth time with an abusive command to clear out of the apartment by the next day. As he was leaving, Raskolnikov managed to thrust his hand into his pocket, rake up whatever coppers he happened to find from the rouble he had changed in the tavern, and put them unobserved on the windowsill. Afterwards, on the stairs, he thought better of it and wanted to go back.

"What a stupid thing to have done," he thought. "They have their Sonya, and I need it myself." But realizing that it was now impossible to take it back, and that he would not take it back in any case, he waved his hand and went home to his own apartment. "Sonya needs a bit of pomade as well," he went on, and grinned caustically as he strode along the street. "This cleanliness costs money . . . Hm! And maybe Sonechka will also go bankrupt today, because there's the same risk in it . . . trapping . . . prospecting for gold . . . and so tomorrow, without my money, they'd all be on dry beans . . . Bravo, Sonya! What a well they've dug for themselves, however! And they use it! They really do use it! And they got accustomed to it. Wept a bit and got accustomed. Man gets accustomed to everything, the scoundrel!"

He fell to thinking.

"But if that's a lie," he suddenly exclaimed involuntarily, "if man in fact is not a *scoundrel*—in general, that is, the whole human race—then the rest is all mere prejudice, instilled fear, and there are no barriers, and that's just how it should be! . . ."

III

HE WOKE UP LATE the next day, after a troubled sleep, but sleep had not fortified him. He woke up bilious, irritable, and angry, and looked with hatred at his little room. It was a tiny closet, about six paces long, of a most pathetic appearance, with yellow, dusty wallpaper coming off the walls everywhere, and with such a low ceiling that a man of any height at all felt creepy in it and kept thinking he might bump his head every moment. The furniture was in keeping with the place. There were three old chairs, not quite in good repair; a painted table in the corner, on which lay several books and notebooks (from the mere fact that they were so covered with dust, one could see that no hand had touched them for a long time); and finally a big, clumsy sofa, which occupied almost the entire wall and half the width of the room, and had once been upholstered in chintz but was now all ragged and served as Raskolnikov's bed. He often slept on it just as he was, without undressing, without a sheet, covering himself with his old, decrepit student's coat,[19] and with one small pillow under his head, beneath which he put whatever linen he had, clean or soiled, to bolster it. In front of the sofa stood a small table.

To become more degraded and slovenly would have been difficult; but Raskolnikov even enjoyed it in his present state of mind. He had decidedly withdrawn from everyone, like a turtle into its shell, and even the face of the maid who had the task of serving him, and who peeked into his room occasionally, drove him to bile and convulsions. This happens with certain monomaniacs when they concentrate too long on some one thing. It was two weeks since his landlady had stopped sending food up to him, but it had not yet occurred to him to go and have a talk with her, though he was left without dinner. Nastasya, the landlady's cook and only servant, was glad in a way that the tenant was in such a mood, and stopped tidying and sweeping his room altogether; only once a week, just by accident, she would some-times take a besom to it. It was she who woke him now.

"Enough sleeping! Get up!" she shouted over him. "It's past nine. I've brought you tea; want some tea? You must be wasting away!"

The tenant opened his eyes, gave a start, and recognized Nastasya.

"Is it the landlady's tea, or what?" he asked, slowly and with a pained look raising himself a little on the sofa.

"The landlady's, hah!"

She placed in front of him her own cracked teapot, full of re-used tea, and two yellow lumps of sugar.

"Here, Nastasya, please take this," he said, feeling in his pocket (he had slept in his clothes) and pulling out a handful of copper coins, "and go and buy me a roll. And a bit of sausage, too, whatever's cheapest, at the pork butcher's."

"I'll bring you a roll this minute, but don't you want some cabbage soup instead of the sausage? It's good cabbage soup, made yesterday. I saved some for you yesterday, but you came back late. Good cabbage soup."

Once the soup was brought and he had begun on it, Nastasya sat down beside him on the sofa and started chattering. She was a village woman, and a very chattery one.

"And so Praskovya Pavlovna wants to make a complaint against you with the poliss," she said.

He winced deeply.

"With the police? What does she want?"

"You don't pay her the money and you won't vacate the room. What do you think she wants?"

"Ah, the devil, that's all I need," he muttered, grinding his teeth. "No, it's just the wrong time for that . . . now . . . She's a fool," he added aloud. "I'll stop and have a talk with her today."

"A fool she may be, the same as I am, and aren't you a smarty, lying around like a sack and no good to anybody! You say you used to go and teach children before, so why don't you do anything now?"

"I do something . . ." Raskolnikov said, reluctantly and sternly.

"What do you do?"

"Work . . ."

"Which work?"

"I think," he replied seriously, after a pause.

Nastasya simply dissolved in laughter. She was the sort much given to laughter, and when something made her laugh, she laughed inaudibly, heaving and shaking her whole body, until she made herself sick.

"And a fat lot of money you've thought up, eh?" she was finally able to say.

"One can't teach children without boots. Anyway, I spit on it."

"Don't go spitting in the well."[20]

"They pay small change for children. What can one do with kopecks?" he went on reluctantly, as if answering his own thoughts.

"And you'd like a whole fortune at once?"

He gave her a strange look.

"Yes, a whole fortune," he said firmly, after a pause.

"Hey, take it easy, don't scare a body; I'm scared as it is. Shall I get you a roll?"

"If you want."

"Ah, I forgot! A letter came for you yesterday while you were out."

"A letter! For me! From whom?"

"I don't know from whom; I gave the mailman my own three kopecks. Will you pay me back?"

"But bring it here, for God's sake, bring it here!" Raskolnikov cried, all excited. "Oh, Lord!"

The letter appeared in a moment. Sure enough, it was from his mother, from R—— province. He even turned pale as he took it. It was long since he had received any letters. But now something else, too, suddenly wrung his heart.

"Leave, Nastasya, for God's sake; here are your three kopecks, only for God's sake leave quickly."

The letter trembled in his hands; he did not want to open it in front of her: he wished to be left *alone* with this letter. When Nastasya had gone, he quickly brought it to his lips and kissed it; then for a long time he gazed at the handwriting of the address, familiar and dear to him, the small and slanted handwriting of his mother, who had once taught him to read and write. He lingered; he even seemed afraid of something. Finally, he opened it: it was a big, thick letter, almost an ounce in weight; two big sheets of stationery covered with very small script.

"My dear Rodya," his mother wrote, "it is over two months now since I've spoken with you in writing, and I myself have suffered from it, and even spent some sleepless nights thinking. But you surely will not blame me for this unwilling silence of mine. You know how I love you; you are all we have, Dunya and I, you are everything for us, all our hope and our trust. What I felt when I learned that you had left the university several months ago because you had no way of supporting yourself, and that your lessons and other means had come to an end! How could I help you, with my pension of a hundred and twenty roubles a year? The fifteen roubles I sent you

four months ago I borrowed, as you know yourself, on the security of
that same pension, from our local merchant, Afanasy Ivanovich Vakhrushin. He is a kind man and used to be your father's friend. But,
having given him the right to receive my pension for me, I had to wait
until the debt was repaid, which has happened only now, so that all
this while I could not send you anything. But now, thank God, I think
I can send you more, and generally now we can even boast of our good
fortune, of which I hasten to inform you. And, first of all, guess what,
dear Rodya, your sister has been living with me for a month and a half
already, and in the future we shall not part again. Thanks be to God,
her torments are over, but I will tell you everything in order, so that
you will know how it all was and what we have been concealing from
you until now. When you wrote me two months ago that you had
heard from someone that Dunya was suffering much from rudeness in
Mr. and Mrs. Svidrigailov's house, and asked me for precise explanations—what could I then write you in reply? If I had written you the
whole truth, you might have dropped everything and come to us, on
foot if you had to, because I know your character and your feelings
and that you would brook no offense to your sister. And I was in
despair myself, but what was one to do? I myself did not even know
the whole truth then. And the greatest difficulty was that when Dunechka entered their home last year as a governess, she took a whole
hundred roubles in advance, against monthly deductions from her
salary, and therefore could not even leave her position without paying
back the debt. And this sum (I can now explain everything to you, my
precious Rodya) she took mainly in order to send you sixty roubles,
which you needed so much then and which you received from us last
year. We deceived you then, we wrote that it was from previous
money Dunechka had saved, but that was not so, and now I am telling
you the whole truth, because now everything, by God's will, has
suddenly changed for the better, and so that you will know how
Dunya loves you and what a precious heart she has. Indeed, Mr.
Svidrigailov treated her very rudely at first and gave her all sorts of
discourtesy and mockery at table . . . But I do not want to go into all
these painful details, so as not to trouble you for nothing, now that it
is all over. In short, despite good and noble treatment from Marfa
Petrovna, Mr. Svidrigailov's wife, and all the rest of the household, it

was very hard for Dunechka, especially when Mr. Svidrigailov, from his old regimental habit, was under the influence of Bacchus. And how did it finally turn out? Imagine, this madcap had long since conceived a passion for Dunya, but kept hiding it behind the appearance of rudeness and contempt for her. Perhaps he was ashamed and horrified himself, seeing that he was not so young anymore and the father of a family, while having such frivolous hopes, and was therefore angry with Dunya involuntarily. Or perhaps by his mockery and the rudeness of his treatment he simply wanted to cover up the truth from everyone else. But in the end he could not restrain himself and dared to make Dunya a vile and explicit proposition, promising her various rewards, above all that he would abandon everything and go with her to another village, or perhaps abroad. You can imagine how she suffered! To leave her position at once was impossible, not only because of the money she owed, but also to spare Marfa Petrovna, who might suddenly have formed suspicions, and it would have meant sowing discord in the family. And for Dunechka, too, it would have been a great scandal; that was unavoidable. There were also many other reasons, so that Dunya could not hope to escape from that terrible house for another six weeks. Of course, you know Dunya, you know how intelligent she is and what a firm character she has. Dunechka can endure much, and even in the most extreme situations she can find enough magnanimity in herself so as not to lose her firmness. She did not write about everything even to me, so as not to upset me, though we exchanged news frequently. The denouement came unexpectedly. Marfa Petrovna chanced to overhear her husband pleading with Dunya in the garden and, misinterpreting everything, laid the whole blame on Dunya, thinking she was the cause of it all. There was a terrible scene between them, right there in the garden: Marfa Petrovna even struck Dunya, refused to listen to anything, and shouted for a whole hour, and in the end ordered Dunya to be sent back to me in town at once, in a simple peasant cart, with all her belongings, linen, clothing thrown into it haphazardly, not even bundled or packed. Just then it started to pour, and Dunya, insulted and disgraced, had to ride with a peasant in an open cart the whole ten miles. Now think, what could I have written you in reply to your letter, which I had received two months earlier, and what could I have said? I was in despair myself; I did not dare write you the truth, because you would have been very unhappy, upset, and indignant, and, besides, what could you have done? You might even have ruined yourself, and, besides, Dunechka kept forbidding me; and to fill a letter with trifles and whatnot, while there was such grief in my soul, was beyond me. For a whole month there was gossip going around town about this story, and it came to the point where Dunya and I could not even go to church because of the scornful looks and whispers and things even said aloud in our presence. And all our acquaintances avoided us, they all even stopped greeting us, and I learned for certain that the shopclerks and officeboys wanted to insult us basely by smearing the gates of our house with tar,[21] so that the landlord began demanding that we move out. The cause of it all was Marfa Petrovna, who succeeded in accusing and besmirching Dunya in all houses. She is acquainted with everyone here, and during that month was constantly coming to town, and being a bit chatty and fond of telling about her family affairs, and especially of complaining about her husband to all and sundry, which is very bad, she spread the whole story in no time, not only around town but all over the district. I became ill, but Dunechka was firmer than I, and if only you could have seen how she bore it all, comforting me and encouraging me! She is an angel! But by God's mercy our torments were shortened: Mr. Svidrigailov thought better of it and repented, and, probably feeling sorry for Dunya, presented Marfa Petrovna with full and obvious proof of Dunechka's complete innocence, in the form of a letter Dunya had been forced to write and send him, even before Marfa Petrovna found them in the garden, declining the personal explanations and secret meetings he was insisting on— which letter had remained in Mr. Svidrigailov's possession after Dunechka's departure. In this letter she reproached him, in the most ardent manner and with the fullest indignation, precisely for his ignoble behavior with respect to Marfa Petrovna, reminding him that he was a father and a family man, and, finally, that it was vile on his part to torment and make unhappy a girl who was already unhappy and defenseless as it was. In short, dear Rodya, this letter was written so nobly and touchingly that I wept as I read it, and to this day cannot read it without tears. Besides, there finally emerged the evidence of the servants to vindicate Dunya; they had seen and knew much more than

Mr. Svidrigailov himself supposed, as always happens. Marfa Petrovna was utterly astonished and 'devastated anew,' as she herself confessed to us, but at the same time she became fully convinced of Dunechka's innocence, and the very next day, a Sunday, she went straight to the cathedral, knelt down, and prayed in tears to our sovereign Lady for the strength to endure this new trial and fulfill her duty. Then she came straight from the cathedral to us, without stopping anywhere, told us everything, wept bitterly, and in full repentance embraced Dunya, imploring her forgiveness. That same morning, without the slightest delay, she went straight from us to every house in town, and restored Dunechka's innocence and the nobility of her feelings and behavior everywhere, in terms most flattering to Dunechka, shedding tears all the while. Moreover, she showed everyone the letter Dunechka had written with her own hand to Mr. Svidrigailov, read it aloud, and even let it be copied (which I think was really unnecessary). Thus she had to go around for several days in a row visiting everyone in town, because some were offended that others had been shown preference, and thus turns were arranged, so that she was expected at each house beforehand and everyone knew that on such-and-such a day Marfa Petrovna would read the letter in such-and-such a house, and for each reading people even gathered who had heard the letter several times already, in their own homes and in their friends' as well. It is my opinion that much, very much of this was unnecessary; but that is Marfa Petrovna's character. In any case she fully restored Dunechka's honor, and all the vileness of the affair lay as an indelible disgrace on her husband as the chief culprit, so that I am even sorry for him; the madcap was dealt with all too harshly. Dunya was immediately invited to give lessons in several houses, but she refused. Generally, everyone suddenly began treating her with particular respect. All of this contributed greatly towards that unexpected occasion by means of which our whole fate, one might say, is now changing. You should know, dear Rodya, that a suitor has asked to marry Dunya, and that she has already had time to give her consent, of which I hasten to inform you as quickly as possible. And although this matter got done without your advice, you will probably not bear any grudge against me or your sister, for you will see from the matter itself that it was impossible to wait and delay until we received your answer. And you

could not have discussed everything in detail without being here yourself. This is how it happened. He is already a court councillor,[22] Pyotr
Petrovich Luzhin, and a distant relation of Marfa Petrovna, who contributed much to all this. He began by expressing, through her, the
desire of making our acquaintance; he was received properly, had
coffee, and the very next day sent a letter in which he quite politely
expressed his proposal and asked for a speedy and decisive answer. He
is a man of affairs and busy, and he is now hastening to go to Petersburg, so that every minute is precious to him. Of course, we were quite
amazed at first, because it all happened too quickly and unexpectedly.
We spent that whole day reasoning and considering together. He is
a trustworthy and established man; he serves in two posts, and already
has his own capital. True, he is already forty-five years old, but he is
of rather pleasing appearance and can still be attractive to women, and
generally he is quite a solid and decent man, only a bit sullen and, as
it were, arrogant. But perhaps he only seems so at first sight. And let
me warn you, dear Rodya, when you meet him in Petersburg, which
will happen very soon, do not judge him too quickly and rashly, as you
tend to do, if something in him does not appeal at first sight. I am
saying this just in case, though I am sure he will make a pleasant
impression on you. And besides, if one wants to know any man well,
one must consider him gradually and carefully, so as not to fall into
error and prejudice, which are very difficult to correct and smooth out
later. And Pyotr Petrovich, at least from many indications, is a quite
respectable man. At his very first visit, he declared to us that he was
a positive man, but in many ways shares, as he himself put it, 'the
convictions of our newest generations,' and is an enemy of all prejudices. He said much more as well, because he seems to be somewhat
vain and likes very much to be listened to, but that is almost not a vice.
I, of course, understood little, but Dunya explained to me that, though
he is a man of small education, he is intelligent and seems to be kind.
You know your sister's character, Rodya. She is a firm, reasonable,
patient, and magnanimous girl, though she has an ardent heart, as I
have come to know very well. Of course, there is no special love either
on her side or on his, but Dunya, besides being an intelligent girl, is
at the same time a noble being, like an angel, and will regard it as her
duty to ensure the happiness of her husband, who in turn would be

looking out for her happiness, and this last point, so far, we have no great reason to doubt, though one must admit that the matter has been done a bit too quickly. Besides, he is a very calculating man and, of course, will see for himself that the happier Dunechka is with him, the more his own marital happiness will be assured. And as for some unevenness of character, some old habits, perhaps also some differences of thinking (which cannot be avoided even in the happiest marriages), Dunechka has told me that in this respect she trusts to herself; that there is nothing here to worry about, and that she can endure much, provided their further relations are honest and just. At first, for example, he seemed somewhat abrupt to me; but that could be precisely the result of his being a straightforward man, and so it must be. For example, at his second visit, when he had already received her consent, he expressed in the course of the conversation that even before knowing Dunya he had made up his mind to marry an honest girl without a dowry, one who must already have experienced hardship; because, as he explained, a husband ought to owe nothing to his wife, but it is much better if a wife looks upon her husband as a benefactor. I should add that he expressed it somewhat more softly and tenderly than I have written it, because I have forgotten his actual expression and remember only the thought, and, besides, it was by no means said deliberately, but apparently escaped him in the heat of the conversation, so that he even tried to amend and soften it afterwards; but all the same it seemed to me a bit abrupt, as it were, and I later said so to Dunya. But Dunya answered me, even with some vexation, that 'words are not yet deeds,' and, of course, that is true. The night before she made her decision, Dunechka did not sleep at all and, thinking that I was already asleep, got out of bed and paced up and down the room all night; finally she knelt and prayed ardently before the icon for a long time, and in the morning announced to me that she had made her decision.

"I have already mentioned that Pyotr Petrovich is now going to Petersburg. He has big doings there, and wants to open a private attorney's office in Petersburg. He has been occupied for a long time with various suits and litigations, and won an important case just the other day. It is necessary for him to go to Petersburg because he has an important matter before the Senate.[23] So, dear Rodya, he may also be quite useful to you, even in everything, and Dunya and I have already decided that from this very day you could definitely begin your future career and consider your lot already clearly determined. Oh, if only this could come true! It would be such a benefit that we should regard it as the direct mercy of the Almighty towards us. That is all Dunya dreams about. We have already risked saying a few words in this regard to Pyotr Petrovich. He expressed himself cautiously and said that, of course, since he would be unable to do without a secretary, it would naturally be better to pay a salary to a relative than to a stranger, on condition that he proves capable of doing the work (as if you could prove incapable!), but at the same time he expressed doubt that your university studies would leave you any time to work in his office. For the time being we left it at that, but Dunya now thinks of nothing else. For the past few days she has simply been in a sort of fever and has already made up a whole project for how you could go on to become an assistant and even a partner of Pyotr Petrovich in his lawsuit affairs, more especially as you are in the department of jurisprudence. I fully agree with her, Rodya, and share in all her plans and hopes, seeing them as fully possible; and despite Pyotr Petrovich's present, quite understandable evasiveness (since he does not know you yet), Dunya is firmly convinced that she will achieve everything by her good influence on her future husband, and she is convinced of it. Of course, we took care not to let Pyotr Petrovich in on these further dreams of ours, above all that you will become his partner. He is a positive man, and would perhaps take it very dryly, since it would all just seem nothing but dreams to him. Likewise, neither Dunya nor I have said even half a word to him about our firm hope that he will help us to assist you with money while you are at the university; we did not speak of it, first of all, because it will come about by itself later on, and he will most likely offer it without much talk (as if he could refuse that to Dunechka), especially as you may become his right hand in the office and receive his assistance not as a boon, but as a well-earned salary. That is how Dunya wants to arrange it, and I fully agree with her. And secondly, we did not speak of it because I would especially like to put you on an equal footing in our now forthcoming meeting. When Dunya spoke rapturously about you with him, he replied that in order to judge a man, one must first observe him more closely, and that he would leave it to himself to form an opinion of you after making your acquaintance. You know, my precious Rodya, it seems to me from certain considerations (by no means relating to Pyotr Petrovich, incidentally, but just so, from my own personal and perhaps even old-womanish caprice), it seems to me that I would perhaps do better, after their marriage, to live separately, as I do now, and not with them. I am fully convinced that he will be so noble and delicate as to invite me himself and will suggest that I no longer be parted from my daughter, and if he has not said anything yet, that is naturally because it goes without saying; but I shall refuse. I have noticed more than once in my life that husbands do not much warm up to their mothers-in-law, and I not only do not want to be even the slightest burden to anyone, but I also want to be fully free myself, as long as I have at least a crust of bread of my own, and such children as you and Dunechka. If possible, I will settle near you both, because the most pleasant thing, Rodya, I have saved for the end of my letter: you must know, my dear friend, that we shall all perhaps come together again very soon and embrace each other after an almost three-year separation! It has already been decided *for certain* that Dunya and I are to leave for Petersburg, precisely when I do not know, but in any case very, very soon, perhaps even in a week. It all depends on Pyotr Petrovich's instructions, and as soon as he has had a look around Petersburg, he will let us know at once. He would like, from certain considerations, to hasten the wedding ceremony, and even celebrate the wedding, if possible, before the next fast, or, if that does not work out, because time is short, then right after our Lady's feast.[24] Oh, how happy I will be to press you to my heart! Dunya is all excited at the joy of seeing you, and said once, as a joke, that she would marry Pyotr Petrovich for that alone. She is an angel! She will not add anything now to my letter, and has only told me to write that she has so much to tell you, so much that she cannot bring herself to take the pen now, because one cannot say anything in a few lines, and only gets upset; but she has told me to embrace you warmly and send you countless kisses. But despite the fact that we shall perhaps be together in person very soon, I shall still send you money one of these days, as much as I can. Now that everyone has learned that Dunechka is marrying Pyotr Petrovich, my credit has suddenly gone up, and I know for certain that Afanasy Ivanovich will now trust me, on the security of my pension, even for as much as seventy-five roubles, so that I will be able to send you twenty-five or even thirty. I would send more, but I am afraid of our travel expenses; and although Pyotr Petrovich has been so good as to take upon himself part of the cost of our trip to the capital—that is, he has volunteered to pay for the delivery of our luggage and the big trunk (somehow through his acquaintances)—even so, we must calculate for our arrival in Petersburg, where we cannot appear without a kopeck, at least for the first few days. However, Dunya and I have already calculated it all precisely, and it turns out that we will not need much for the road. It is only sixty miles from here to the railway, and we've already made arrangements ahead of time with a peasant driver we know; and there Dunechka and I will be quite satisfied to travel third class. So that perhaps I can contrive to send you not twenty-five but certainly thirty roubles. But enough; I've covered two sheets with writing, there is not even any space left—our whole story, but so many events had accumulated! And now, my precious Rodya, I embrace you until we meet soon, and I give you my maternal blessing. Love your sister Dunya, Rodya; love her as she loves you, and know that she loves you boundlessly, more than herself. She is an angel, and you, Rodya, you are everything for us—all our hope, and all our trust. If only you are happy, then we shall be happy. Do you pray to God, Rodya, as you used to, and do you believe in the goodness of our Creator and Redeemer? I fear in my heart that you have been visited by the fashionable new unbelief. If so, I pray for you. Remember, my dear, in your childhood, when your father was alive, how you prattled out your prayers sitting on my knee, and how happy we all were then! Goodbye, or, better, *till we meet again!* I embrace you very, very warmly, and send you countless kisses.

Yours till death,
Pulcheria Raskolnikov."

ALMOST ALL THE WHILE he was reading, from the very beginning of the letter, Raskolnikov's face was wet with tears; but when he finished, it was pale, twisted convulsively, and a heavy, bilious, spiteful smile wandered over his lips. He laid his head on his skinny, bedraggled pillow and thought, thought for a long time. His heart was beating violently, and the thoughts surged violently. Finally, he felt too stifled and cramped in that yellow closet, which more resembled a cupboard or a trunk. His eyes and mind craved space. He grabbed his hat and went out, this time with no fear of meeting anyone on the stairs—he forgot all about it. He made his way towards Vasilievsky Island, along V——y Prospect, as though hurrying there on business, but, as usual, he walked without noticing where he was going, whispering and even talking aloud to himself, to the surprise of passers-by. Many took him for drunk.

IV

HIS MOTHER'S LETTER had tormented him. But concerning the main, capital point he had not a moment's doubt, not even while he was reading the letter. The main essence of the matter was decided in his mind and decided finally: "This marriage will not take place as long as I live, and to the devil with Mr. Luzhin!

"Because the thing is obvious," he muttered to himself, grinning and maliciously triumphant beforehand over the success of his decision. "No, mama, no, Dunya, you won't deceive me! . . . And they still apologize for not asking my advice and deciding the matter without me! Well they might! They think it's impossible to break it off now; but we'll see whether it's impossible or not! And what a capital excuse: 'Pyotr Petrovich is just such a busy man, such a busy man that he can't even get married any other way than posthaste, almost right on the train.' No, Dunechka, I see it all and know what this *so much* is that you want to talk to me about; I also know what you were thinking about all night, pacing the room, and what you prayed about to the Kazan Mother of God[25] that stands in mama's bedroom. It's hard to ascend Golgotha.[26] Hm . . . So it's settled finally: you, Avdotya Romanovna, are so good as to be marrying a practical and rational man, who has his own capital (who *already* has his own capital; that's more solid, more impressive), who serves in two posts and shares the convictions of our newest generations (as mama writes), and who 'seems to be kind,' as Dunechka herself remarks. That *seems* is the most splendid of all! And that very same Dunechka is going to marry that very same *seems!* . . . Splendid! Splendid! . . .

". . . Curious, however; why did mother write to me about the 'newest generations'? Simply to characterize the man, or with the further aim of putting Mr. Luzhin in my good graces? Oh, you sly ones! It would also be curious to have one more circumstance clarified: to what extent were they sincere with each other that day and that night and in all the time since? Were all the *words* between them spoken directly, or did they understand that each of them had the same thing in her heart and mind, so that there was no point in saying it all aloud and no use letting on? Most likely it was partly that way; one can see it in the letter: to mother he seemed abrupt, just *a bit,* and naive mother thrust her observations on Dunya. And Dunya, naturally, got angry and 'answered with vexation.' Well she might! Who wouldn't get furious if the thing is clear without any naive questions, and it's been decided that there's nothing to talk about. And what's she doing writing to me: 'Love Dunya, Rodya, and she loves you more than herself'? Can it be that she's secretly tormented by remorse at having agreed to sacrifice her daughter for the sake of her son? 'You are our hope, you are our everything'! Oh, mother . . ." Anger boiled up in him more and more, and he thought that if he met Mr. Luzhin right then, he might kill him!

"Hm, it's true," he went on, following the whirlwind of thoughts spinning in his head, "it's true that one must 'approach a man gradually and carefully in order to find him out,' but Mr. Luzhin is clear. The main thing is that he's 'a practical man and *seems* kind': no joke, he took the luggage upon himself, delivers a big trunk at his own expense! Oh, yes, he's kind! And the two of them, the *bride* and her mother, hire a peasant and a cart, covered with straw matting (I've traveled like that)! Never mind! It's only sixty miles, and then 'we'll be quite satisfied to travel third class' for another six hundred miles. That's reasonable: cut your coat according to your cloth; but you, Mr. Luzhin, what about you? She's your bride . . . Can you possibly be unaware that her mother is borrowing money on her pension for the journey? Of course, you've set up a joint commercial venture here, a mutually profitable enterprise, and with equal shares, so the expenses should also be divided equally; bread and butter for all, but bring your own tobacco, as the saying goes. And even here the businessman has hoodwinked them a bit: the luggage costs less than the trip, and it may even go for nothing. Don't they both see it, or are they ignoring it on purpose? And they're pleased, pleased! And to think that this is just the blossom; the real fruit is still to come! What matters here is not the stinginess, the cheese-paring, but the *tone* of it all. Because that is the future tone after the marriage, a prophecy . . . And mother, why is she going on such a spree, incidentally? What will she have left when she gets to Petersburg? Three roubles, or two 'little bills,' as that . . . old crone . . . says. Hm! What is she hoping to live on afterwards in Petersburg? Because she already has reasons to believe that it will be *impossible* for her to live with Dunya after the marriage, even at the beginning. The dear man must have *let it slip* somehow, betrayed himself, though mother waves it away with both hands: 'I shall refuse it myself,' she says. What, then, what is she hoping for? A hundred and twenty roubles of pension, minus what's owed to Afanasy Ivanovich? She also knits winter kerchiefs and embroiders cuffs, ruining her old eyes. But these kerchiefs add only twenty roubles a year to her hundred and twenty, and I know it. So they're putting their hopes on the nobility of Mr. Luzhin's feelings after all: 'He'll suggest it himself, he'll beg us to accept.' Good luck to them! And that's how it always is with these beautiful, Schilleresque souls:[27] till the last moment they dress a man up in peacock's feathers, till the last moment they hope for the good and not the bad; and though they may have premonitions of the other side of the coin, for the life of them they will not utter a real word beforehand; the thought alone makes them cringe; they wave the truth away with both hands, till the very moment when the man they've decked out so finely sticks their noses in it with his own two hands. Curious, does Mr. Luzhin have any decorations? I'll bet he has the Anna on the breast[28] and wears her when he's invited to dinner with contractors and merchants! Maybe he'll even wear her for his wedding! Ah, anyway, devil take him! . . .

". . . Mother, well, let her be, God bless her, that's how she is; but what about Dunya? I know you, Dunechka, my dear! You were going on twenty when we saw each other last: I already understood your character then. Mother writes that 'Dunechka can endure much.' I know she can! I knew it two and a half years ago, and for two and a half years I've been thinking about that, precisely about that, that 'Dunechka can endure much.' If she was able to endure Mr. Svidrigailov, with all the consequences, then indeed she can endure much. And now they imagine, she and mother, that one can also endure Mr. Luzhin, expounding his theory about the advantages of wives rescued from destitution by their benefactor husbands, and expounding it almost the moment they first met. Well, suppose he just 'let it slip,' though he's a rational man (in which case maybe he didn't let it slip at all, but precisely meant to explain it then and there), but Dunya, what of Dunya? The man is clear to her, and she'll have to live with this man. She could eat only black bread and wash it down with water, but she would never sell her soul, she would never trade her moral freedom for comfort; she wouldn't trade it for all Schleswig-Holstein,[29] let alone Mr. Luzhin. No, Dunya was not like that as far as I knew her, and . . . well, of course, she's no different now! . . . What's there to talk about! Svidrigailovs are hard! It's hard to spend your life as a governess, dragging yourself around the provinces for two hundred roubles, but all the same I know that my sister would sooner go and be a black slave for a planter or a Latvian for a Baltic German[30] than demean her spirit and her moral sense by tying herself to a man she doesn't respect and with whom she can do nothing— forever, merely for her own personal profit! And even if Mr. Luzhin were made entirely of the purest gold, or a solid diamond, she still would not consent to become Mr. Luzhin's lawful concubine! Then why has she consented now? What's the catch? What's the answer? The thing is clear: for herself, for her own comfort, even to save herself from death, she wouldn't sell herself; no, she's selling herself for someone else! For a dear, beloved person she will sell herself! That's what our whole catch consists of: for her brother, for her mother, she will sell herself! She'll sell everything! Oh, in that case, given the chance, we'll even crush our moral feeling; our freedom, peace of mind, even conscience—all, all of it goes to the flea market. Perish our life! So long as these beloved beings of ours are happy. Moreover, we'll invent our own casuistry, we'll take a lesson from the Jesuits,[31] and we may even reassure ourselves for a while, convince ourselves that it's necessary, truly necessary, for a good purpose. That's exactly how we are, and it's all clear as day. It's clear that the one who gets first notice, the one who stands in the forefront, is none other than Rodion Romanovich Raskolnikov. Oh, yes, of course, his happiness can be arranged, he can be kept at the university, made a partner in the office, his whole fate can be secured; maybe later he'll be rich, honored, respected, and perhaps he'll even end his life a famous man! And mother? But we're talking about Rodya, precious Rodya, her firstborn! How can she not sacrifice even such a daughter for the sake of such a firstborn son! Oh, dear and unjust hearts! Worse still, for this we might not even refuse Sonechka's lot! Sonechka, Sonechka Marmeladov, eternal Sonechka, as long as the world stands! But the sacrifice, have the two of you taken full measure of the sacrifice? Is it right? Are you strong enough? Is it any use? Is it reasonable? Do you know, Dunechka, that Sonechka's lot is in no way worse than yours with Mr. Luzhin? 'There can be no love here,' mother writes. And what if, besides love, there can be no respect either, if on the contrary there is already loathing, contempt, revulsion—what then? So it turns out once again that it will be necessary *'to observe cleanliness.'* It's true, isn't it? Do you understand, do you understand what this cleanliness means? Do you understand that this Luzhinian cleanliness is just the same as Sonechka's cleanliness and maybe even worse, nastier, meaner, because in your case, Dunechka, some extra comfort can still be reckoned on, while there it's quite simply a matter of starving to death! 'It's costly, Dunechka, this cleanliness is costly!' And if it gets to be too much for you, and you repent later? Think of all the anguish, the grief, curses, tears, hidden from everyone—because you're not Marfa Petrovna, after all! And what will happen with mother then? She's uneasy, tormented even now; but then, when she sees it all clearly? And me? What, indeed, do you take me for? I don't want your sacrifice, Dunechka, I don't want it, mama! It won't happen as long as I live, it won't, it won't! I don't accept it!"

He suddenly came to his senses and stopped.

"It won't happen? And how are you going to keep it from happening? Forbid it? What right do you have? What can you promise them in return for such a right? To devote your whole fate, your whole future to them, *once you finish your studies and find a position?* We've heard that before, but it's still a *blind deal,* and what about now? It's necessary to do something now, do you understand? And what are you doing now? You're fleecing them. Because they get the money on the credit of a hundred-rouble pension, or as an advance from the Svidrigailovs! How are you going to protect them from the Svidrigailovs, from Afanasy Ivanovich Vakhrushin, you future millionaire, you Zeus disposing of their fates? In ten years? But in ten years your mother will go blind from those kerchiefs, and maybe from tears as well; she'll waste away with fasting; and your sister? Go on, think what may happen to your sister after those ten years, or during those ten years. Have you guessed?"

He kept tormenting and taunting himself with these questions, even taking a certain delight in it. None of the questions was new or sudden, however; they were all old, sore, long-standing. They had begun torturing him long ago and had worn out his heart. Long, long ago this present anguish had been born in him, had grown, accumulated, and ripened recently and become concentrated, taking the form of a horrible, wild, and fantastic question that tormented his heart and mind, irresistibly demanding resolution. And now his mother's letter suddenly struck him like a thunderbolt. Clearly, he now had not to be anguished, not to suffer passively, by mere reasoning about unresolvable questions, but to do something without fail, at once, quickly. Decide at all costs to do at least something, or . . .

"Or renounce life altogether!" he suddenly cried out in frenzy. "Accept fate obediently as it is, once and for all, and stifle everything in myself, renouncing any right to act, to live, to love!"

"Do you understand, do you understand, my dear sir, what it means when there is no longer anywhere to go?" he suddenly recalled Marmeladov's question yesterday. "For it is necessary that every man have at least somewhere to go . . ."

Suddenly he gave a start: a certain thought, also from yesterday, raced through his head again. But he started not because this thought raced through his head. Indeed, he knew, he had *anticipated* that it would certainly "race through his head," and was already expecting it; and it was not yesterday's thought at all. But the difference was that a month ago, and even yesterday, it was only a dream, whereas now . . . now it suddenly appeared not as a dream, but in some new, menacing, and quite unfamiliar form, and he suddenly became aware of it himself . . . It hit him in the head, and everything went dark before his eyes.

He glanced hastily around; he was looking for something. He wanted to sit down, and was looking for a bench; at the moment he was walking along the K——y Boùlevard. He could see a bench ahead, about a hundred steps away. He walked as quickly as he could; but on the way a small adventure befell him, which for a few minutes took all his attention.

As he was looking out for a bench, he had noticed a woman walking ahead of him, about twenty steps away, but at first he did not rest his attention on her any more than on all the other objects flashing in front of him. It had happened to him many times before that he would arrive at home, for example, having absolutely no recollection of which way he had come, and he had already grown used to going around that way. But there was something so strange about this walking woman, and so striking, even at first glance, that little by little his attention became riveted on her—reluctantly at first and as if with annoyance, but then more and more strongly. He suddenly wanted to understand what precisely was so strange about this woman. First of all, she had to be very young, a girl, and she was walking bareheaded in such heat, with no parasol or gloves, swinging her arms somehow ridiculously. She was wearing a dress of some light, silken material, which was also somehow oddly put on, barely buttoned, and torn behind at the waist, near the very top of the skirt; a whole strip had come away and was hanging loosely. A little kerchief was thrown over her bare neck, but it stuck out somehow crookedly and sideways. To top it off, the girl was walking unsteadily, stumbling and even reeling this way and that. The encounter finally aroused all of Raskolnikov's attention. He caught up with the girl just by the bench, but she, having reached the bench, simply collapsed on it at one end, threw her head against the back of the bench, and closed her eyes, apparently from extreme fatigue. Taking a close look at her, Raskolnikov realized at once that she was completely drunk. It was strange and wild to see such a phenomenon. He even thought he might be mistaken. Before him was an extremely young little face, about sixteen years old, perhaps only fifteen—small, fair, pretty, but all flushed and as if swollen. The girl seemed to understand very little; she crossed one leg over the other, exposing it much more than she ought, and by all appearances was scarcely aware that she was in the street.

Raskolnikov did not sit down and did not want to go away, but stood perplexed in front of her. That boulevard was generally deserted anyway, but just then, past one o'clock in the afternoon, and in such heat, there was almost no one about. And yet, a short distance away, about fifteen steps, at the edge of the boulevard, a gentleman had stopped, who by all evidence would also have liked very much to approach the girl with certain intentions. He, too, had probably noticed her from afar and was overtaking her, but Raskolnikov had hindered him. The man kept glancing at him angrily, trying at the same time to keep him from noticing it, and was waiting impatiently for his turn, when the vexatious ragamuffin would leave. The thing was clear: this gentleman was about thirty, thickset, fat, full-blooded, with pink cheeks and a little moustache, and very foppishly dressed. Raskolnikov became terribly angry; he suddenly wanted to insult the fat dandy in some way. He left the girl for a moment and went up to the gentleman.

"Hey, you—Svidrigailov![32] What do you want here?" he shouted, clenching his teeth and laughing, his lips foaming with spite.

"What is the meaning of this?" the gentleman asked sternly, scowling in haughty amazement.

"Get out of here, that's what!"

"How dare you, *canaille!* . . ."

And he brandished his whip. Raskolnikov fell on him with both fists, not stopping to think that the thickset gentleman could take on two men like him. But at that moment someone seized him firmly from behind; a policeman stepped between them.

"Enough, gentlemen; no fighting in public places, if you please. What do you want? Who are you?" he addressed Raskolnikov sternly, having noticed his rags.

Raskolnikov looked at him attentively. He had a good soldier's face, with gray moustache and side-whiskers, and sensible eyes.

"You're just what I want," he cried, gripping his arm. "I am a former student, Raskolnikov . . . You may as well know that, too," he turned to the gentleman, "and you, come with me, I want to show you something."

Gripping the policeman's arm, he pulled him towards the bench.

"Here, look, she's completely drunk, she just came walking down the boulevard: who knows who she is, but it doesn't look like it's her profession. Most likely they got her drunk somewhere and deceived her . . . for the first time . . . understand? . . . and then just put her out in the street. Look how her dress is torn, look how it's put on; she's been dressed, she didn't do it herself, and it was clumsy male hands that dressed her. That's obvious. And now look over there: that dandy I was going to fight with is a stranger to me, I've never seen him before; but he, too, noticed her on the way just now, drunk, out of her senses, and he's dying to come and intercept her—seeing what state she's in—and take her somewhere . . . And it's certainly so; believe me, I'm not mistaken. I saw myself how he was watching her and following her, only I hindered him, and now he's waiting until I go away. There, now he's moved off a little, pretending he's rolling a cigarette . . . How can we keep him from her? How can we get her home? Think, man!"

The policeman understood and figured it all out at once. The fat gentleman was no mystery, of course; what remained was the girl. The good soldier bent down to look at her more closely, and genuine commiseration showed in his features.

"Ah, what a pity!" he said, shaking his head. "Seems quite a child still. Deceived, that's what it is. Listen, miss," he began calling her, "tell me, where do you live?" The girl opened her tired and bleary eyes, looked dully at her questioners, and waved her hand.

"Listen," said Raskolnikov, "here" (he felt in his pocket and took out twenty kopecks that happened to be there), "here, hire a coachman and tell him to take her to her address. If only we could find out her address!"

"Miss, eh, miss?" the policeman began again, taking the money. "I'll call a coachman now and take you home myself. Where shall I take you, eh? Where is your home?"

"Shoo! . . . pests! . . ." the girl muttered, and again waved her hand.

"Oh, oh, that's not nice! Oh, what a shame, miss, what a shame!" And again he began shaking his head, chiding, pitying, indignant. "This is a real problem!" he turned to Raskolnikov, and at the same time gave him another quick glance up and down. He, too, must surely have seemed strange to him: in such rags, and handing out money!

"Did you find her far from here?" he asked him.

"I tell you she was walking ahead of me, staggering, right here on the boulevard. As soon as she came to the bench, she just collapsed."

"Ah, what shame we've got in the world now! Lord! Such an

ordinary young girl, and she got drunk! She's been deceived, that's just what it is! Look, her little dress is torn . . . Ah, what depravity we've got nowadays! And she might well be from gentlefolk, the poor sort . . . We've got many like that nowadays. She looks like one of the pampered ones, like a young lady," and he bent over her again.

Perhaps his own daughters were growing up in the same way—"like young ladies and pampered ones," with well-bred airs and all sorts of modish affectations . . .

"The main thing," Raskolnikov went on fussing, "is to prevent that scoundrel somehow! What if he, too, abuses her! You can see by heart what he wants: look at the scoundrel, he just won't go away!"

Raskolnikov spoke loudly and pointed straight at him. The man heard him and was about to get angry again, but thought better of it and limited himself to a scornful glance. Then he slowly moved off another ten steps or so and stopped again.

"Prevent him we can, sir," the policeman replied pensively. "If only she'd say where to deliver her; otherwise . . . Miss, hey, miss!" he bent down again.

She suddenly opened her eyes wide, gave an attentive look, as if she understood something or other, rose from the bench, and walked back in the direction she had come from.

"Pah! Shameless . . . pests!" she said, waving her hand once again. She walked off quickly, but staggering as badly as before. The dandy walked after her, but along the other side of the boulevard, not taking his eyes off her.

"Don't worry, I won't let him, sir!" the moustached policeman said resolutely, and started after them.

"Ah, what depravity we've got nowadays!" he repeated aloud, with a sigh.

At that moment it was as if something stung Raskolnikov, as if he had been turned about in an instant.

"Hey, wait!" he shouted after the moustached policeman.

The man looked back.

"Forget it! What do you care? Leave her alone! Let him have fun" (he pointed to the dandy). "What is it to you?"

The policeman stared uncomprehendingly. Raskolnikov laughed.

"A-ach!" the good soldier said, waving his hand, and he went after the dandy and the girl, probably taking Raskolnikov for a madman or something even worse.

"He kept my twenty kopecks," Raskolnikov said spitefully when he found himself alone. "Well, let him; he'll take something from that one, too, and let the girl go with him, and that will be the end of it . . . Why did I go meddling in all that! Who am I to help anyone? Do I have any right to help? Let them all gobble each other alive—what is it to me? And how did I dare give those twenty kopecks away? Were they mine?"

In spite of these strange words, it was very painful for him. He sat down on the abandoned bench. His thoughts were distracted . . . And generally it was painful for him at that moment to think about anything at all. He would have liked to become totally oblivious, oblivious of everything, and then wake up and start totally anew . . .

"Poor girl! . . ." he said, having looked at the now empty end of the bench. "She'll come to her senses, cry a little, and then her mother will find out . . . First she'll hit her, then she'll give her a whipping, badly and shamefully, and maybe even throw her out . . . And if she doesn't, the Darya Frantsevnas will get wind of it anyway, and my girl will start running around here and there . . . Then right away the hospital (it's always like that when they live with their honest mothers and carry on in secret), well, and then . . . then the hospital again . . . wine . . . pot-houses . . . back to the hospital . . . in two or three years she'll be a wreck, so altogether she'll have lived to be nineteen, or only eighteen years old . . . Haven't I seen the likes of her? And how did they come to it? Just the same way . . . that's how . . . Pah! And so what! They say that's just how it ought to be. Every year, they say, a certain percentage has to go . . . somewhere . . . to the devil, it must be, so as to freshen up the rest and not interfere with them.[33] A percentage! Nice little words they have, really: so reassuring, so scientific. A certain percentage, they say, meaning there's nothing to worry about. Now, if it was some other word . . . well, then maybe it would be more worrisome . . . And what if Dunechka somehow gets into the percentage! . . . If not that one, then some other? . . .

"And where am I going to?" he thought suddenly. "Strange. I was going for some reason. As soon as I read the letter, off I went . . . To Vasilievsky Island, to Razumikhin's, that's where I was going . . .

now I remember. What for, however? And how is it that the thought of going to see Razumikhin flew into my head precisely now? Remarkable!"

He marveled at himself. Razumikhin was one of his former university friends. It was remarkable that Raskolnikov had almost no friends while he was at the university, kept aloof from everyone, visited no one, and had difficulty receiving visitors. Soon, however, everyone also turned away from him. General gatherings, conversations, merrymaking—he somehow did not participate in any of it. He was a zealous student, unsparing of himself, and was respected for it, but no one loved him. He was very poor and somehow haughtily proud and unsociable, as though he were keeping something to himself. It seemed to some of his friends that he looked upon them all as children, from above, as though he were ahead of them all in development, in knowledge, and in convictions, and that he regarded their convictions and interests as something inferior.

Yet for some reason he became close with Razumikhin—that is, not really close, but he was more sociable, more frank with him. However, it was impossible to be on any other terms with Razumikhin. He was an exceptionally cheerful and sociable fellow, kind to the point of simplicity. However, this simplicity concealed both depth and dignity. The best of his friends understood that; everyone loved him. He was far from stupid, though indeed a bit simple at times. His appearance was expressive—tall, thin, black-haired, always badly shaved. He could be violent on occasion, and was reputed to be a very strong man. Once, at night, in company, he knocked down a six-and-a-half-foot keeper of the peace with one blow. He could drink ad infinitum, or he could not drink at all; he could be impossibly mischievous, or he could not be mischievous at all. Razumikhin was also remarkable in that no setbacks ever confounded him, and no bad circumstances seemed able to crush him. He could make his lodgings even on a rooftop, suffer hellish hunger and extreme cold. He was very poor, and supported himself decidedly on his own, alone, getting money by work of one sort or another. He knew an endless number of sources to draw from—by means of working, of course. Once he went a whole winter without heating his room, asserting that he even found it more pleasant, because one sleeps better in the cold. At present he, too, had been forced to leave the university, but not for long, and he was trying in all haste to straighten out his circumstances so that he could continue. Raskolnikov had not visited him for about four months now, and Razumikhin did not even know his address. Once, some two months ago, they had chanced to meet in the street, but Raskolnikov had turned away and even crossed to the other side so as not to be noticed. And Razumikhin, though he did notice, passed by, not wishing to trouble a *friend*.

V

"In fact, just recently I was meaning to go to Razumikhin and ask him for work, to get me some lessons or something . . ." Raskolnikov went on puzzling, "but how can he help me now? Suppose he does get me lessons, suppose he even shares his last kopeck with me, if he has a kopeck, so that I could even buy boots and fix up my outfit enough to go and give lessons . . . hm . . . Well, and what then? What good will five coppers do me? Is that what I need now? Really, it's ridiculous to be going to Razumikhin . . ."

The question of why he was now going to Razumikhin troubled him more than he was even aware; he anxiously tried to find some sinister meaning for himself in this seemingly quite ordinary act.

"So, then, did I really mean to straighten things out with Razumikhin alone? To find the solution for everything in Razumikhin?" he asked himself in surprise.

He went on thinking and rubbing his forehead, and, strangely, somehow by chance, suddenly and almost of itself, after very long reflection, there came into his head a certain most strange thought.

"Hm . . . to Razumikhin," he said suddenly, quite calmly, as if with a sense of final decision, "I will go to Razumikhin, of course I will . . . but—not now . . . I will go to him . . . the next day, after *that*, once *that* is already finished and everything has taken a new course . . ."

And suddenly he came to his senses.

"After *that*," he cried out, tearing himself from the bench, "but will *that* be? Will it really be?"

He abandoned the bench and started walking, almost running; he had been about to turn back home, but going home suddenly became terribly disgusting to him; it was there, in that corner, in that terrible cupboard, that for more than a month now all *that* had been ripening; and so he just followed his nose.

His nervous trembling turned into some sort of feverishness; he even began shivering; in such heat he was getting a chill. As if with effort, almost unconsciously, by some inner necessity, he began peering at every object he encountered, as though straining after some diversion, but he failed miserably, and every moment kept falling into revery. And when he would raise his head again, with a start, and look around, he would immediately forget what he had just been thinking about and even which way he had come. In this fashion he went right across Vasilievsky Island, came to the Little Neva, crossed the bridge, and turned towards the Islands.[34] At first the greenness and freshness pleased his tired eyes, accustomed to city dust, lime, and enormous, crowding and crushing buildings. Here there was no closeness, no stench, no taverns. But soon these pleasant new sensations turned painful and irritating. Occasionally he would stop in front of a summer house decked out in greenery, look through the fence, and see dressed-up women far away, on balconies and terraces, and children running in the garden. He took special interest in the flowers; he looked longer at them than at anything else. He also met with luxurious carriages, men and women on horseback; he would follow them with curious eyes and forget them before they disappeared from sight. Once he stopped and counted his money; it came to about thirty kopecks. "Twenty to the policeman, three to Nastasya for the letter—so I gave the Marmeladovs some forty-seven or fifty kopecks yesterday," he thought, going over his accounts for some reason, but soon he even forgot why he had taken the money from his pocket. He remembered about it as he was passing an eating-house, a sort of cook-shop, and felt that he wanted to eat. Going into the cook-shop, he drank a glass of vodka and ate a piece of pie with some sort of filling. He finished it on the road. He had not drunk vodka for a very long time and it affected him at once, though he had drunk only one glass. His feet suddenly became heavy, and he began feeling a strong inclination to sleep. He started for home; but having reached Petrovsky Island, he stopped in complete exhaustion, left the road, went into the bushes, collapsed on the grass, and in a moment was asleep.

In a morbid condition, dreams are often distinguished by their re-markably graphic, vivid, and extremely lifelike quality. The resulting picture is sometimes monstrous, but the setting and the whole process of the presentation sometimes happen to be so probable, and with details so subtle, unexpected, yet artistically consistent with the whole fullness of the picture, that even the dreamer himself would be unable to invent them in reality, though he were as much an artist as Pushkin or Turgenev.[35] Such dreams, morbid dreams, are always long remembered and produce a strong impression on the disturbed and already excited organism of the person.

Raskolnikov had a terrible dream.[36] He dreamed of his childhood, while still in their little town. He is about seven years old and is strolling with his father on a feast day, towards evening, outside of town. The weather is gray, the day is stifling, the countryside is exactly as it was preserved in his memory: it was even far more effaced in his memory than it appeared now in his dream. The town stands open to view; there is not a single willow tree around it; somewhere very far off, at the very edge of the sky, is the black line of a little forest. A few paces beyond the town's last kitchen garden stands a tavern, a big tavern, which had always made the most unpleasant impression on him, and even frightened him, when he passed it on a stroll with his father. There was always such a crowd there; they shouted, guffawed, swore so much; they sang with such ugly and hoarse voices, and fought so often; there were always such drunk and scary mugs loitering around the tavern . . . Meeting them, he would press close to his father and tremble all over. The road by the tavern, a country track, was always dusty, and the dust was always so black. It meandered on, and in another three hundred paces or so skirted the town cemetery on the right. In the middle of the cemetery there was a stone church with a green cupola, where he went for the liturgy with his father and mother twice a year, when memorial services were held for his grandmother, who had died a long time before and whom he had never seen. On those occasions they always made *kutya*[37] and brought it with them on a white platter, wrapped in a napkin, and *kutya* was sugary, made of rice, with raisins pressed into the rice in the form of a cross. He loved this church and the old icons in it, most of them without settings, and the old priest with his shaking head. Next to his grandmother's grave, covered with a flat gravestone, there was also the little grave of his younger brother, who had died at six months old, and whom he also did not know at all and could not remember; but he had been told that he had had a little brother, and each time he visited the cemetery, he crossed himself religiously and reverently over the grave, bowed to it, and kissed it. And so now, in his dream, he and his father are going down the road to the cemetery, past the tavern; he is holding his father's hand and keeps looking fearfully at the tavern over his shoulder. A special circumstance attracts his attention: this time there seems to be some sort of festivity, a crowd of dressed-up townspeople, peasant women, their husbands, and all kinds of rabble. Everyone is drunk, everyone is singing songs, and near the porch of the tavern stands a cart, but a strange cart. It is one of those big carts to which big cart-horses are harnessed for transporting goods and barrels of wine. He always liked watching those huge horses, long-maned and thick-legged, moving calmly, at a measured pace, pulling some whole mountain behind them without the least strain, as if the load made it even easier for them. But now, strangely, to such a big cart a small, skinny, grayish peasant nag had been harnessed, one of those—he had often seen it—that sometimes overstrain themselves pulling a huge load of firewood or hay, especially if the cart gets stuck in the mud or a rut, and in such cases the peasants always whip them so painfully, so painfully, sometimes even on the muzzle and eyes, and he would feel so sorry, so sorry as he watched it that he almost wept, and his mother would always take him away from the window. Then suddenly it gets very noisy: out of the tavern, with shouting, singing, and balalaikas, come some big peasants, drunk as can be, in red and blue shirts, with their coats thrown over their shoulders. "Get in, get in, everybody!" shouts one of them, still a young man, with a fat neck and a beefy face, red as a carrot. "I'll take everybody for a ride! Get in!" But all at once there is a burst of laughter and exclamations:

"Not with a nag like that!"

"Are you out of your mind, Mikolka—harnessing such a puny mare to such a cart!"

"That gray can't be less than twenty years old, brothers!"

"Get in, I'll take everybody!" Mikolka cries again, and he jumps into the cart first, takes the reins, and stands up tall in the front. "The bay just left with Matvei," he shouts from the cart, "and this little runt of a mare breaks my heart—I might as well kill her, she's not worth her feed. Get in, I say! I'll make her gallop! Oh, how she'll gallop!" And he takes a whip in his hand, already enjoying the idea of whipping the gray.

"Get in, why not!" guffaws come from the crowd. "She'll gallop, did you hear?"

"I bet she hasn't galloped in ten years!"

"She will now!"

"Don't spare her, brothers, take your whips, get ready!"

"Here we go! Whip her up!"

They all get into Mikolka's cart, joking and guffawing. About six men pile in, and there is still room for more. They take a peasant woman, fat and ruddy. She is dressed in red calico, with a bead-embroidered *kichka*[38] on her head and boots on her feet; she cracks nuts and giggles all the while. The crowd around them is laughing, too, and indeed how could they not laugh: such a wretched little mare is going to pull such a heavy load at a gallop! Two fellows in the cart take up their whips at once to help Mikolka. To shouts of "Giddap!" the little mare starts pulling with all her might, but she can scarcely manage a slow walk, much less a gallop; she just shuffles her feet, grunts, and cowers under the lashes of the three whips showering on her like hail. The laughter in the cart and in the crowd redoubles, but Mikolka is angry, and in his rage he lashes the mare with quicker blows, as if he really thinks she can go at a gallop.

"Let me in, too, brothers!" one fellow, his appetite whetted, shouts from the crowd.

"Get in! Everybody get in!" cries Mikolka. "She'll pull everybody! I'll whip her to death!" And he lashes and lashes, and in his frenzy he no longer even knows what to lash her with.

"Papa, papa," he cries to his father, "papa, what are they doing? Papa, they're beating the poor horse!"

"Come along, come along!" says his father. "They're drunk, they're playing pranks, the fools—come along, don't look!" and he wants to take him away, but he tears himself from his father's hands and, beside himself, runs to the horse. But the poor horse is in a bad way. She is panting, she stops, tugs again, nearly falls.

"Whip the daylights out of her!" shouts Mikolka. "That's what it's come to. I'll whip her to death!"

"Have you no fear of God, or what, you hairy devil!" an old man shouts from the crowd.

"Who ever saw such a puny little horse pull a load like that?" someone else adds.

"You'll do her in!" shouts a third.

"Hands off! It's my goods! I can do what I want. Get in, more of you. Everybody get in! She's damn well going to gallop! . . ."

Suddenly there is a burst of guffaws that drowns out everything: the mare cannot endure the quick lashing and, in her impotence, has begun to kick. Even the old man cannot help grinning. Really, such a wretched mare, and still kicking!

Two fellows from the crowd get two more whips and run to whip the horse from the side. Each takes a side.

"On the muzzle, on the eyes, lash her on the eyes!" shouts Mikolka.[39]

"Let's have a song, brothers!" someone shouts from the cart, and everyone in the cart joins in. A drunken song breaks out, a tambourine rattles, they whistle to the refrain. The peasant woman cracks nuts and giggles.

. . . He runs past the horse, runs ahead of her, sees how they are lashing her on the eyes, right on the eyes! He is crying. His heart is in his throat, the tears are flowing. One of the whips grazes his face, he does not feel it, he wrings his hands, he shouts, he rushes to the gray-bearded old man, who is shaking his head in disapproval of it all. A woman takes him by the hand and tries to lead him away; but he breaks free and runs back to the horse. She is already at her last gasp, but she starts kicking again.

"Ah, go to the hairy devil!" Mikolka cries out in a rage. He drops his whip, bends down, and pulls a long and stout shaft from the bottom of the cart, takes one end of it in both hands and, with an effort, swings it aloft over the gray horse.

"He'll strike her dead!" people cry.

"He'll kill her!"

"It's my goods!" shouts Mikolka, and with a full swing he brings the shaft down. There is a heavy thud.

"Whip her, whip her! Why did you stop!" voices cry from the crowd.

Mikolka takes another swing, and another blow lands full on the miserable nag's back. Her hind legs give way, but then she jumps up and pulls, pulls with all the strength she has left, pulls this way and that, trying to move the cart; but six whips come at her from all sides, and the shaft is raised again and falls for a third time, then a fourth, in heavy, rhythmic strokes. Mikolka is furious that he was unable to kill her with one blow.

"She's tough!" they shout.

"She'll drop this time, brothers; it's the end of her!" one enthusiast yells from the crowd.

"Take an axe to her! Finish her off fast," shouts a third.

"Eh, let the fleas eat you! Step aside!" Mikolka cries out frenziedly, and he drops the shaft, bends down again, and pulls an iron crowbar from the bottom of the cart. "Look out!" he yells, and he swings it with all his might at the poor horse. The blow lands; the wretched mare staggers, sinks down, tries to pull, but another full swing of the crowbar lands on her back, and she falls to the ground as if all four legs had been cut from under her.

"Give her the final one!" shouts Mikolka, and he leaps from the cart as if beside himself. Several fellows, also red and drunk, seize whatever they can find—whips, sticks, the shaft—and run to the dying mare. Mikolka plants himself at her side and starts beating her pointlessly on the back with the crowbar. The nag stretches out her muzzle, heaves a deep sigh, and dies.

"He's done her in!" they shout from the crowd.

"But why wouldn't she gallop!"

"It's my goods!" Mikolka cries, holding the crowbar in his hands, his eyes bloodshot. He stands there as if he regretted having nothing else to beat.

"Really, you've got no fear of God in you!" many voices now shout from the crowd.

But the poor boy is beside himself. With a shout he tears through the crowd to the gray horse, throws his arms around her dead, bleeding muzzle, and kisses it, kisses her eyes and mouth . . . Then he suddenly jumps up and in a frenzy flies at Mikolka with his little fists. At this moment his father, who has been chasing after him all the while, finally seizes him and carries him out of the crowd.

"Come along, come along now!" he says to him. "Let's go home!"

"Papa! What did they . . . kill . . . the poor horse for!" he sobs, but his breath fails, and the words burst like cries from his straining chest.

"They're drunk, they're playing pranks, it's none of our business, come along!" his father says. He throws his arms around his father, but there is such strain, such strain in his chest. He tries to take a breath, to cry out, and wakes up.

He awoke panting, all in a sweat, his hair damp with sweat, and started up in terror.

"Thank God it was only a dream!" he said, leaning back against a tree and drawing a deep breath. "But what's wrong? Am I coming down with a fever? Such a hideous dream!"

His whole body was as if broken; his soul was dark and troubled. He leaned his elbows on his knees and rested his head in both hands.

"God!" he exclaimed, "but can it be, can it be that I will really take an axe and hit her on the head and smash her skull . . . slip in the sticky, warm blood, break the lock, steal, and tremble, and hide, all covered with blood . . . with the axe . . . Lord, can it be?"

He was trembling like a leaf as he said it.

"But what's wrong with me?" he went on, straightening up again, and as if in deep amazement. "I knew very well I could never endure it, so why have I been tormenting myself all this while? Even yesterday, yesterday, when I went to make that . . . *trial*, even yesterday I fully realized I could not endure it . . . So what is this now? Why have I doubted all along? Just yesterday, going down the stairs, I myself said it was mean, nasty, vile, vile . . . the mere thought of it made me vomit *in reality* and threw me into horror . . .

"No, I couldn't endure it, I couldn't endure it! Suppose, suppose there are even no doubts in all those calculations, suppose all that's been decided in this past month is clear as day, true as arithmetic. Lord! Even so, I wouldn't dare! I couldn't endure it, I couldn't! . . . What, what has this been all along? . . ."

He got to his feet, looked around as if wondering how he had ended up there, and walked towards the T——v Bridge. He was pale, his eyes were burning, all his limbs felt exhausted, but he suddenly seemed to breathe more easily. He felt he had just thrown off the horrible burden that had been weighing him down for so long, and his soul suddenly became light and peaceful. "Lord!" he pleaded, "show me my way; I renounce this cursed . . . dream of mine!"

Walking across the bridge, he looked calmly and quietly at the Neva, at the bright setting of the bright, red sun. In spite of his weakness, he was not even aware of any fatigue in himself. It was as if an abscess in his heart, which had been forming all that month, had suddenly burst. Freedom, freedom! He was now free of that spell, magic, sorcery, obsession!

Later on, when he recalled this time and all that happened to him during these days, minute by minute, point by point, feature by feature, he was always struck to superstition by one circumstance which, though in fact not very unusual, afterwards constantly seemed to him as if it were a sort of predetermination of his fate.

Namely, he could in no way understand or explain to himself why he, for whom it would have been most profitable, tired and worn out as he was, to return home by the shortest and most direct way, instead returned home through the Haymarket, where he had no need at all to go. The detour was not a long one, but it was obvious and totally unnecessary. Of course, it had happened to him dozens of times that he would return home without remembering what streets he had taken. But why, he always asked, why had such an important, decisive, and at the same time highly accidental encounter in the Haymarket (where he did not even have any reason to go) come just then, at such an hour and such a moment in his life, to meet him precisely in such a state of mind and precisely in such circumstances as alone would enable it, this encounter, to produce the most decisive and final effect on his entire fate? As if it had been waiting for him there on purpose!

It was about nine o'clock when he walked through the Haymarket. All the merchants with tables or trays, in shops big and small, were locking up their establishments, removing or packing away their wares, and going home, as were their customers. Numbers of various traffickers and ragpickers of all sorts were crowding around the ground floor cook-shops, in the dirty and stinking courtyards of the houses on the Haymarket, and more especially near the taverns. Raskolnikov liked these places most, as well as all the neighboring side streets, in his aimless wanderings. Here his rags attracted no supercilious attention, and one could go about dressed in anything without scandalizing people. Just at K——ny Lane, on the corner, a tradesman and a woman, his wife, had been selling their wares from two tables: thread, trimmings, cotton handkerchiefs, and so on. They, too, were heading for home, but lingered, talking with a woman acquaintance who had come up to them. This woman was Lizaveta Ivanovna, or simply Lizaveta, as everyone called her, the younger sister of that same old woman, Alyona Ivanovna, widow of a collegiate registrar,[40] the money-lender whom Raskolnikov had visited the day before to pawn his watch and make his *trial* . . . He had long known all about this Lizaveta, and she even knew him slightly. She was a tall, awkward, timid, and humble wench of thirty-five, all but an idiot, and was a complete slave to her sister, worked for her day and night, trembled before her, and even suffered her beatings. She stood hesitantly before the tradesman and the woman, holding a bundle and listening to them attentively. They were explaining something to her with particular ardor. When Raskolnikov suddenly saw her, some strange sensation, akin to the deepest amazement, seized him, though there was nothing amazing in this encounter.

"Why don't you decide for yourself, Lizaveta Ivanovna," the tradesman was saying loudly. "Come tomorrow, between six and seven. Those people will also arrive."

"Tomorrow?" Lizaveta said slowly and pensively, as if she were still undecided.

"See how Alyona Ivanovna's got you scared!" the hawker's wife, a perky little woman, started pattering. "You're just like a little child to look at you. And she isn't even your real sister, just a half sister, but see, she does what she likes with you."

"This time just don't say anything to Alyona Ivanovna," the husband interrupted, "that's my advice—just come to us without asking. It's a profitable deal. Later on your sister will realize it herself."

"Should I, really?"

"Between six and seven tomorrow, and one of those people will arrive, so you can make the deal in person."

"Around the samovar," his wife added.

"All right, I'll come," Lizaveta said, still hesitant, and slowly started to leave.

At that point Raskolnikov had already passed by them and did not hear the rest. He was walking softly, inconspicuously, trying not to miss even a single word. His initial amazement gradually gave way to horror, like a chill running down his spine. He had learned, he had learned suddenly, all at once, and quite unexpectedly, that tomorrow, at exactly seven o'clock in the evening, Lizaveta, the old woman's sister and only companion, would not be home, and that therefore, at exactly seven o'clock in the evening, the old woman *would be left at home alone.*

It was only a few more steps to his place. He walked in like a man condemned to death. He was not reasoning about anything, and was totally unable to reason; but he suddenly felt with his whole being that he no longer had any freedom either of mind or of will, and that everything had been suddenly and finally decided.

Of course, even if he had waited years on end for a good opportunity, having his design in mind, he could not have counted with certainty on a more obvious step towards the success of this design than the one that had suddenly presented itself now. In any case, it would have been difficult to learn for certain, the day before, with greater precision, yet without the least risk, without any dangerous inquiries or investigations, that the next day at such-and-such an hour, such-and-such an old woman, on whose life an attempt was being prepared, would be at home as alone as could be.

VI

LATER, RASKOLNIKOV somehow happened to find out precisely why the tradesman and the woman had invited Lizaveta to come back. It was a most ordinary matter, and there was nothing very special about it. A family that had moved to the city and fallen into poverty was selling things off, dresses and so on, all women's things. Since it was not profitable to sell them in the market, they were looking for a middleman, and that was what Lizaveta did: she took a commission, handled the deals, and had a large clientele, because she was very honest and always named a final price: whatever she said, that the price would be. Generally she spoke little and, as has been mentioned, was humble and timid . . .

But Raskolnikov had lately become superstitious. Traces of superstition remained in him for a long time afterwards, almost indelibly. And later on he was always inclined to see a certain strangeness, a mysteriousness, as it were, in this whole affair, the presence as of some peculiar influences and coincidences. The previous winter a student acquaintance of his, Pokorev, before leaving for Kharkov, had told him once in conversation the address of the old woman, Alyona Ivanovna, in case he might want to pawn something. For a long time he did not go to her, because he was giving lessons and getting by somehow. About a month and a half ago he had remembered the address; he had two things suitable for pawning: his father's old silver watch, and a small gold ring with three little red stones of some kind, given him as a keepsake by his sister when they parted. He decided to pawn the ring. Having located the old woman, who, from the very first glance, before he knew anything particular about her, filled him with insurmountable loathing, he took two "little bills" from her, and on his way back stopped at some wretched tavern. He asked for tea, sat down, and fell into deep thought. A strange idea was hatching in his head, like a chicken from an egg, and occupied him very, very much.

Almost next to him, at another table, sat a student he did not know or remember at all and a young officer. They had been playing billiards and were now drinking tea. Suddenly he heard the student talking with the officer about a money-lender, Alyona Ivanovna, widow of a collegiate secretary, and telling him her address. That in itself seemed somehow strange to Raskolnikov: he had just left her, and here they were talking about her. By chance, of course; but just then, when he could not rid himself of a certain quite extraordinary impression, it was as if someone had come to his service: the student suddenly began telling his friend various details about this Alyona Ivanovna.

"She's nice," he was saying, "you can always get money from her. She's rich as a Jew, she could hand you over five thousand at once, but she's not above taking pledges for a rouble. A lot of us have gone to her. Only she's a terrible harpy . . ."

And he began telling how wicked she was, how capricious; how, if your payment was one day late, your pledge was lost. She gives four times less than the thing is worth, and takes five or even seven percent a month, and so on. The student went on chattering and said, among other things, that the old woman had a sister, Lizaveta, and that the disgusting little hag used to beat her all the time and kept her completely enslaved, like a little child, though Lizaveta was at least six feet tall . . .

"She's quite a phenomenon herself!" the student cried out, and guffawed.

They began talking about Lizaveta. The student spoke of her with some special pleasure and kept laughing, and the officer, who listened with great interest, asked the student to send this Lizaveta to him to mend his linen. Raskolnikov did not miss a word and at once learned everything: Lizaveta was the old woman's younger half sister (they had different mothers) and was thirty-five years old. She worked day and night for her sister, was cook and laundress in the house, and besides that sewed things for sale, and even hired herself out to wash floors, and gave everything to her sister. She did not dare take any orders or any work without the old woman's permission. Meanwhile, the old woman had already made her will, a fact known to Lizaveta, who, apart from moveable property, chairs and so forth, did not stand to get a penny from this will; all the money was to go to a monastery in N——y province, for the eternal remembrance of her soul. Lizaveta was a tradeswoman, not of official rank; she was unmarried and of terribly awkward build, remarkably tall, with long, somehow twisted legs, always wore down-at-heel goatskin shoes, but kept herself neat. Above all the student was surprised and laughed at the fact that Lizaveta was constantly pregnant . . .

"But you say she's ugly?" the officer remarked.

"Well, yes, she's dark-skinned, looks like a soldier in disguise, but, you know, she's not ugly at all. She has such a kind face and eyes. Very much so. A lot of men like her—there's the proof. She's so quiet, meek, uncomplaining, agreeable—she agrees to everything. And she does have a very nice smile."

"Ah, so you like her, too!" the officer laughed.

"For the strangeness of it. No, but I'll tell you one thing: I could kill and rob that cursed old woman, and that, I assure you, without any remorse," the student added hotly.

The officer guffawed again, and Raskolnikov gave a start. How strange it was!

"Excuse me, I want to ask you a serious question," the student began ardently. "I was joking just now, but look: on the one hand you have a stupid, meaningless, worthless, wicked, sick old crone, no good to anyone and, on the contrary, harmful to everyone, who doesn't know herself why she's alive, and who will die on her own tomorrow. Understand? Understand?"

"So, I understand," the officer replied, looking fixedly at his ardent friend.

"Listen, now. On the other hand, you have fresh, young forces that are being wasted for lack of support, and that by the thousands, and that everywhere! A hundred, a thousand good deeds and under-takings that could be arranged and set going by the money that old woman has doomed to the monastery! Hundreds, maybe thousands of lives put right; dozens of families saved from destitution, from decay, from ruin, from depravity, from the venereal hospitals—all on her money. Kill her and take her money, so that afterwards with its help you can devote yourself to the service of all mankind and the common cause: what do you think, wouldn't thousands of good deeds make up for one tiny little crime? For one life, thousands of lives saved from decay and corruption. One death for hundreds of lives—it's simple arithmetic! And what does the life of this stupid, consumptive, and wicked old crone mean in the general balance? No more than the life of a louse, a cockroach, and not even that much, because the old crone is harmful. She's eating up someone else's life: the other day she got so angry that she bit Lizaveta's finger; they almost had to cut it off!"

"Of course, she doesn't deserve to be alive," the officer remarked, "but that's nature."

"Eh, brother, but nature has to be corrected and guided, otherwise we'd all drown in prejudices. Without that there wouldn't be even a single great man. 'Duty, conscience,' they say—I'm not going to speak against duty and conscience, but how do we really understand them? Wait, I'll ask you one more question. Listen!"

"No, you wait. I'll ask you a question. Listen!"

"Well?"

"You're talking and making speeches now, but tell me: would you *yourself* kill the old woman, or not?"

"Of course not! It's for the sake of justice that I . . . I'm not the point here . . ."

"Well, in my opinion, if you yourself don't dare, then there's no justice in it at all! Let's shoot another round!"

Raskolnikov was greatly agitated. Of course, it was all the most common and ordinary youthful talk and thinking, he had heard it many times before, only in different forms and on different subjects. But why precisely now did he have to hear precisely such talk and thinking, when . . . *exactly the same thoughts* had just been conceived in his own head? And why precisely now, as he was coming from the old woman's bearing the germ of his thought, should he chance upon a conversation about the same old woman? . . . This coincidence always seemed strange to him. This negligible tavern conversation had an extreme influence on him in the further development of the affair; as though there were indeed some predestination, some indication in it . . .

. . . .

Having returned from the Haymarket, he threw himself on the sofa and sat there for a whole hour without moving. Meanwhile it grew dark; he had no candle, and besides it did not occur to him to make a light. He was never able to recall whether he thought about anything during that time. In the end he became aware that he was still feverish, chilled, and realized with delight that it was also possible to lie down on the sofa. Soon a deep, leaden sleep, like a heavy weight, came over him.

He slept unusually long and without dreaming. Nastasya, who came into his room at ten o'clock the next morning, had difficulty shaking him out of it. She brought him tea and bread. It was re-used tea again, and again in her own teapot.

"Look at him sleeping there!" she cried indignantly. "All he does is sleep!"

He raised himself with an effort. His head ached; he got to his feet, took a turn around his closet, and dropped back on the sofa.

"Falling asleep again!" Nastasya cried. "Are you sick, or what?"

He made no reply.

"Want some tea?"

"Later," he said with an effort, closing his eyes again and turning to the wall. Nastasya stood over him for a while.

"Maybe he really is sick," she said, turned, and went out.

She came in again at two o'clock with soup. He lay as before. The tea remained untouched. Nastasya even got offended and began shaking him angrily.

"You're still snoring away!" she cried, looking at him with disgust. He raised himself slightly and sat up, but said nothing and stared at the ground.

"Are you sick or aren't you?" Nastasya asked, and again got no reply.

"You'd better go out at least," she said, after a pause, "you'd at least have some wind blowing on you. Are you going to eat, or what?"

"Later," he uttered faintly. "Go!" And he waved his hand.

She stood there a while longer, looking at him with compassion, and went out.

After a few minutes he raised his eyes and stared for a long time at the tea and soup. Then he took the bread, took the spoon, and began to eat.

He ate a little, three or four spoonfuls, without appetite, as if mechanically. His head ached less. Having finished his dinner, he stretched out on the sofa again, but could not sleep now: he lay motionless, on his stomach, his face buried in the pillow. He kept daydreaming, and his dreams were all quite strange: most often he imagined he was somewhere in Africa, in Egypt, in some oasis. The caravan is resting, the camels are peacefully lying down; palm trees stand in a full circle around; everyone is having dinner. And he keeps drinking water right from the stream, which is there just beside him, flowing and bubbling. And the air is so fresh, and the wonderful, wonderful water is so blue, cold, running over the many-colored stones and over such clean sand sparkling with gold . . . All at once he clearly heard the clock strike. He gave a start, came to, raised his head, looked at the window, realized what time it was, and suddenly jumped up, pulling himself together, as if someone had torn him from the sofa. He tiptoed to the door, quietly opened it a little, and began listening down the stairs. His heart was pounding terribly. It was all quiet on the stairs, as if everyone were asleep . . . It seemed wild and strange to him that he could have slept so obliviously since the day before and still have done nothing, prepared nothing . . . And meanwhile it might just have struck six o'clock . . . In place of sleep and torpor, an extraordinary, feverish, and somehow confused bustle came over him. The preparations, incidentally, were not many. He strained all his energies to figure everything out and not forget anything, and his heart kept beating, pounding, so that it was even hard for him to breathe. First he had to make a loop and sew it into his coat—a moment's work. He felt beneath his pillow and found one of his shirts among the linen stuffed under it, old, unwashed, completely fallen to pieces. From its tatters he tore a strip about two inches wide and fifteen inches long. He folded the strip in two, took off his sturdy, loose-fitting summer coat, made from some heavy cotton material (the only outer garment he owned), and began sewing the two ends inside it, under the left armhole. His hands trembled as he sewed, but he managed it so that nothing could be seen when he put the coat on again. The needle and thread had been made ready long ago and lay in the table drawer wrapped in a piece of paper. As for the loop itself, this was a very clever invention of his own: the loop was to hold the axe. He could not go through the streets carrying an axe in his hands. And if he were to hide it under his coat, he would still have to keep it in place with his hand, which would be noticeable. But now, with the loop, he had only to slip the axe-head into it, and the axe would hang quietly under his arm all the way. And with his hand in the side pocket of his coat, he could also hold the end of the axe handle to keep it from swinging; and since the coat was very loose, a real bag, it could not be noticed from the outside that he was holding something through the pocket with his hand. This loop he had also thought up two weeks ago.

Having finished that, he thrust his fingers into the small space between his "Turkish" sofa and the floor, felt near the left corner, and pulled out the *pledge* he had prepared long before and hidden there. This pledge was, incidentally, not a pledge at all, but simply a smoothly planed little piece of wood, about the size and thickness of a silver cigarette case. He had found this piece of wood by chance during one of his walks, in a courtyard, where there was some sort of workshop in one of the wings. Later he added to the piece of wood a thin and smooth strip of iron—probably a fragment of something—which he had also found in the street at the same time. Having put the two pieces together, of which the iron one was smaller than the wooden one, he tied them tightly, crisscross, with a thread, after which he wrapped them neatly and elegantly in clean, white paper, tied round with a thin ribbon, also crosswise, and with a little knot that would be rather tricky to untie. This was to distract the old woman's attention for a while, as she began fumbling with the knot, and thereby catch the right moment. And the iron strip was added for weight, so that at least for the first moment the old woman would not guess that the "article" was made of wood. All this had been kept for the time being under the sofa. He had no sooner taken out the pledge than someone shouted somewhere in the courtyard:

"It's long past six!"

"Long past! My God!"

He rushed to the door, listened, snatched his hat, and started down his thirteen steps, cautiously, inaudibly, like a cat. He was now faced with the most important thing—stealing the axe from the kitchen. That the deed was to be done with an axe he had already decided long ago. He also had a folding pruning knife, but he could not rely on the knife and still less on his own strength, and therefore finally decided on the axe. We may note, incidentally, one peculiarity with regard to all the final decisions he came to in this affair. They had one strange property: the more final they became, the more hideous and absurd they at once appeared in his own eyes. In spite of all his tormenting inner struggle, never for a single moment during the whole time could he believe in the feasibility of his designs.

If he had ever once managed to analyze and finally decide everything down to the last detail, and there were no longer any doubts left—at that point he would most likely have renounced it all as absurd, monstrous, and impossible. But there remained a whole abyss of doubts and unresolved details. As for where to get the axe, this trifle did not worry him in the least, because nothing could have been simpler. It so happened that Nastasya was constantly in and out of the house, especially during the evening: she would run to see the neighbors or to do some shopping, and would always leave the door wide open. That was the landlady's only quarrel with her. All one had to do, then, was go quietly into the kitchen when the time came, take the axe, and an hour later (when it was all over) go and put it back. But doubts also presented themselves: suppose he comes in an hour to put it back and there is Nastasya. Of course, he would have to pass by and wait until she went out again. But what if meanwhile she misses the axe, looks for it, starts shouting—there is suspicion for you, or at least the grounds for suspicion.

But these were still trifles he had not even begun to think about, nor did he have time. He had thought about the main thing, and put the trifles off until he himself was *convinced of everything*. But this last seemed decidedly unrealizable. At least it seemed so to him. He could in no way imagine, for example, that one day he would finish thinking, get up, and—simply go there . . . Even his recent *trial* (that is, his visit with the intention of making a final survey of the place) was only a *trying out* and far from the real thing, as if he had said to himself: "Why not go and try it—enough of this dreaming!" and he was immediately unable to endure it, spat, and fled, furious with himself. And yet it would seem he had already concluded the whole analysis, in terms of a moral resolution of the question: his casuistry was sharp as a razor, and he no longer found any conscious objections. But in the final instance he simply did not believe himself, and stubbornly, slavishly, sought objections on all sides, gropingly, as if someone were forcing him and drawing him to it. This last day, which had come so much by chance and resolved everything at once, affected him almost wholly mechanically: as if someone had taken him by the hand and pulled him along irresistibly, blindly, with unnatural force, without objections. As if a piece of his clothing had been caught in the cogs of a machine and he were being dragged into it.

At first—even long before—he had been occupied with one question: why almost all crimes are so easily detected and solved, and why almost all criminals leave such an obviously marked trail. He came gradually to various and curious conclusions, the chief reason lying, in his opinion, not so much in the material impossibility of concealing the crime as in the criminal himself; the criminal himself, almost any criminal, experiences at the moment of the crime a sort of failure of will and reason, which, on the contrary, are replaced by a phenomenal, childish thoughtlessness, just at the moment when reason and prudence are most necessary. According to his conviction, it turned out that this darkening of reason and failure of will take hold of a man like a disease, develop gradually, and reach their height shortly before the crime is committed; they continue unabated during the moment of the crime itself and for some time after it, depending on the individual; then they pass in the same way as any disease passes. But the question whether the disease generates the crime, or the crime somehow by its peculiar nature is always accompanied by something akin to disease, he did not yet feel able to resolve.

Having come to such conclusions, he decided that in his own personal case there would be no such morbid revolutions, that reason and will would remain with him inalienably throughout the fulfillment of what he had plotted, for the sole reason that what he had plotted—was "not a crime" . . . We omit the whole process by means of which he arrived at this latter decision; we have run too far ahead of ourselves as it is . . . We will only add that the factual, purely material difficulties of the affair generally played a most secondary role in his mind. "Since I will have kept all my will and reason over them, they, too, will be defeated in due time, once I have acquainted myself to the minutest point with all the details of the affair . . ." But the affair would not get started. He went on believing least of all in his final decisions, and when the hour struck, everything came out not that way at all, but somehow accidentally, even almost unexpectedly.

One quite negligible circumstance already nonplussed him even before he got down the stairs. Having reached the landlady's kitchen, wide open as always, he cautiously took a sidelong glance to see if the landlady herself might be there in Nastasya's absence, and, if not, whether the door to her room was tightly shut, so that she could not somehow peek out as he went in to take the axe. How great was his amazement when he suddenly saw that Nastasya was not only at home this time, in her kitchen, but was even doing something: taking laundry from a basket and hanging it on a line! Seeing him, she stopped hanging, turned towards him, and looked at him all the while he was passing by. He turned away and walked past as if noticing nothing. But the affair was finished: no axe! He was terribly struck.

"And where did I get the idea," he was thinking, as he went down to the gateway, "where did I get the idea that she was sure to be away right now? Why, why, why was I so certain of it?" He was crushed, even somehow humiliated. He wanted to laugh at himself in his anger . . . Dull, brutal rage was seething in him.

He stopped in the gateway, reflecting. To go out, to walk around the streets just for the sake of appearances, was revolting to him; to return home—even more revolting. "To lose such an opportunity forever!" he muttered, standing aimlessly in the gateway, directly opposite the caretaker's dark closet, which was also open. Suddenly he gave a start. From the caretaker's closet, which was two steps away from him, from under the bench to the right, the gleam of something caught his eye . . . He looked around—nobody. On tiptoe he approached the caretaker's room, went down the two steps, and called the caretaker in a faint voice. "Sure enough, he's not home! Must be nearby, though, somewhere in the yard, since the door is wide open." He rushed headlong for the axe (it was an axe) and pulled it from under the bench, where it lay between two logs; he slipped it into the loop at once, before going out, put both hands into his pockets, and walked out of the caretaker's room; no one noticed! "If not reason, then the devil!" he thought, grinning strangely. The incident encouraged him enormously.

He went quietly and *sedately* on his way, without hurrying, so as not to arouse any suspicions. He barely looked at the passers-by, even tried not to look at their faces at all and to be as inconspicuous as possible. Then he suddenly remembered his hat. "My God! I had money two days ago, and couldn't even change it for a cap!" A curse rose up in his soul.

Glancing into a shop by chance, out of the corner of his eye he noticed that the clock on the wall already showed ten minutes past seven. He had to hurry, and at the same time he had to make a detour, to get to the house from the other side . . .

Earlier, when he had happened to picture it all in his imagination, he sometimes thought he would be very afraid. But he was not very afraid now, even not afraid at all. He was even occupied at that moment with certain unrelated thoughts, though not for long. Passing the

Yusupov Garden, he even became much absorbed in the notion of setting up tall fountains, and of how they would freshen the air in all the public squares. Gradually he arrived at the conviction that if the Summer Garden were expanded across the entire Field of Mars and even joined with the garden of the Mikhailovsky Palace, it would be a wonderful and most useful thing for the city. At which point he suddenly became interested in precisely why the people of all big cities are somehow especially inclined, not really out of necessity alone, to live and settle in precisely those parts of the city where there are neither gardens nor fountains, where there is filth and stench and all sorts of squalor. At which point he recalled his own walks through the Haymarket and came to himself for a moment. "What nonsense," he thought. "No, better not to think anything at all.

"It must be the same for men being led out to execution—their thoughts must cling to every object they meet on the way," flashed through his head, but only flashed, like lightning; he hastened to extinguish the thought . . . But he was already close, here was the house, here were the gates. Somewhere a clock suddenly struck once. "What, can it be half past seven? Impossible; it must be fast!"

Luckily for him, everything again went well at the gates. Moreover, as if by design, a huge hay-wagon drove through the gates at that very moment, just ahead of him, concealing him completely all the while he was passing under the archway, and as soon as the wagon entered the courtyard, he slipped quickly to the right. On the other side of the wagon, several voices could be heard shouting and arguing, but no one noticed him, and he met no one coming his way. Many of the windows looking out onto the huge, square yard were open at that moment, but he did not raise his head—he had no strength. The stairway to the old woman's was close by, immediately to the right of the gates. He was already on the stairs . . .

Having caught his breath and pressed his hand to his pounding heart, at the same time feeling for the axe and straightening it once again, he began cautiously and quietly climbing the stairs, pausing every moment to listen. But the stairway also happened to be quite empty at the time; all the doors were shut; he met no one. True, one empty apartment on the second floor stood wide open, and painters were working in it, but they did not even look. He paused, thought for a moment, and went on. "Of course, it would be better if they weren't there at all, but . . . there are two more flights above them."

But here was the fourth floor, here was the door, here was the apartment opposite—the empty one. On the third floor, by all tokens, the apartment just under the old woman's was also empty: the calling card nailed to the door with little nails was gone—they had moved out! . . . He was gasping for breath. A thought raced momentarily through his mind: "Shouldn't I go away?" But he gave himself no reply and began listening at the old woman's door: dead silence. Then he listened down the stairs again, listened long, attentively . . . Then he took a last look around, pulled himself together, straightened himself up, and once more felt the axe in its loop. "Am I not pale . . . too pale?" he thought. "Am I not too excited? She's mistrustful . . . Shouldn't I wait a little longer . . . until my heart stops this . . . ?"

But his heart would not stop. On the contrary, as though on purpose, it pounded harder, harder, harder . . . He could not stand it, slowly reached for the bell, and rang. In half a minute he rang again, louder.

No answer. To go on ringing in vain was pointless, and it did not suit him. The old woman was certainly at home, but she was alone and suspicious. He was somewhat familiar with her habits . . . and once again pressed his ear to the door. Either his senses were extremely sharp (which in fact is difficult to suppose), or it was indeed quite audible, but he suddenly discerned something like the cautious sound of a hand on the door-latch and something like the rustle of a dress against the door itself. Someone was standing silently just at the latch, hiding inside and listening, in the same way as he was outside, and also, it seemed, with an ear to the door . . .

He purposely stirred and muttered something aloud, so as not to make it seem he was hiding; then he rang for the third time, but quietly, seriously, and without any impatience. Recalling it later, vividly, distinctly—for this moment was etched in him forever—he could not understand where he got so much cunning, especially since his reason seemed clouded at moments, and as for his body, he almost did not feel it on him . . . A second later came the sound of the latch being lifted.

VII

THE DOOR, as before, was opened a tiny crack, and again two sharp, mistrustful eyes stared at him from the darkness. Here Raskolnikov became flustered and made a serious mistake.

Fearing the old woman would be frightened that they were alone, and with no hope that his looks would reassure her, he took hold of the door and pulled it towards him so that the old woman should not somehow decide to lock herself in. Seeing this, she did not pull the door back towards her, but did not let go of the handle either, so that he almost pulled her out onto the stairway together with the door. Then, seeing that she was blocking the doorway and not letting him in, he went straight at her. The woman jumped aside in fear, was about to say something, but seemed unable to and only stared at him.

"Good evening, Alyona Ivanovna," he began, as casually as he could, but his voice would not obey him, it faltered and started trembling. "I've brought you . . . an article . . . but we'd better go over there . . . near the light . . ." And leaving her, he walked straight into the room uninvited. The old woman ran after him; her tongue came untied.

"Lord! What is it? . . . Who are you? What's your business?"

"For pity's sake, Alyona Ivanovna . . . you know me . . . Raskolnikov . . . here, I've brought you that pledge . . . the one I promised you the other day . . ." He was holding the pledge out to her.

The old woman glanced at the pledge, then at once fixed her eyes directly on the eyes of her uninvited visitor. She looked at him intently, spitefully, mistrustfully. A minute or so passed; he even thought he saw something like mockery in her eyes, as if she had already guessed everything. He felt himself becoming flustered, almost frightened, so frightened that it seemed if she were to look at him like that, without saying a word, for another half minute, he would run away from her.

"But why are you looking at me like that, as if you didn't recognize me?" he suddenly asked, also with spite. "If you want it, take it—otherwise I'll go somewhere else. I have no time."

He had not even intended to say this, but it suddenly got said, just so, by itself.

The old woman came to her senses, and her visitor's resolute tone seemed to encourage her.

"But what's the matter, dearie, so suddenly . . . what is it?" she asked, looking at the pledge.

"A silver cigarette case—I told you last time."

She held out her hand.

"But why are you so pale? Look, your hands are trembling! Did you go for a swim, dearie, or what?"

"Fever," he answered abruptly. "You can't help getting pale . . . when you have nothing to eat," he added, barely able to articulate the words. His strength was abandoning him again. But the answer sounded plausible; the old woman took the pledge.

"What is it?" she asked, once again looking Raskolnikov over intently and weighing the pledge in her hand.

"An article . . . a cigarette case . . . silver . . . take a look."

"But it doesn't seem like silver . . . Ehh, it's all wrapped up."

Trying to untie the string and going to the window, to the light (all her windows were closed, despite the stuffiness), she left him completely for a few seconds and turned her back to him. He unbuttoned his coat and freed the axe from the loop but did not quite take it out yet; he just held it in his right hand under the coat. His hands were terribly weak; he felt them growing more and more numb and stiff every moment. He was afraid he would let go and drop the axe . . . suddenly his head seemed to spin.

"Look how he's wrapped it up!" the old woman exclaimed in vexation, and made a move towards him.

He could not waste even one more moment. He took the axe all the way out, swung it with both hands, scarcely aware of himself, and almost without effort, almost mechanically, brought the butt-end down on her head. His own strength seemed to have no part in it. But the moment he brought the axe down, strength was born in him.

The old woman was bareheaded as always. Her thin hair, pale and streaked with gray, was thickly greased as usual, plaited into a ratty braid and tucked under a piece of horn comb that stuck up at the back of her head. Because she was short, the blow happened to land right on the crown of her head. She cried out, but very faintly, and her whole body suddenly sank to the floor, though she still managed to raise both hands to her head. In one hand she was still holding the "pledge." Then he struck her again and yet again with all his strength, both times with the butt-end, both times on the crown of the head. Blood poured out as from an overturned glass, and the body fell backwards. He stepped aside, letting it fall, and immediately bent down to her face; she was already dead. Her eyes bulged as if they were about to pop out, and her forehead and her whole face were contracted and distorted in convulsion.

He set the axe down on the floor by the dead woman, and immediately put his hand into her pocket, trying not to smear himself with the flowing blood—that same right pocket from which she had taken her keys the last time. He was in full possession of his reason, the clouding and dizziness had ceased, but his hands were still trembling. He recalled afterwards that he was even very attentive, careful, tried to be sure not to stain himself . . . He immediately pulled out the keys; they were all in one bunch, as before, on a steel ring. He immediately ran to the bedroom with them. This was a very small room; there was a huge stand with icons and, against the opposite wall, a large bed, quite clean, covered with a silk patchwork quilt. Against the third wall stood a chest of drawers. Strangely, as soon as he began applying the keys to the drawers, as soon as he heard their jingling, it was as if a convulsion ran through him. He again wanted suddenly to drop everything and leave. But only for a moment; it was too late to leave. He even grinned to himself, but then another anxious thought struck his mind. He suddenly fancied that the old woman might still be alive, and might still recover her senses. Abandoning both the keys and the chest of drawers, he ran back to the body, seized the axe and raised it one more time over the old woman, but did not bring it down. There was no doubt that she was dead. Bending over and examining her again more closely, he saw clearly that the skull was shattered and even displaced a little to one side. He was about to feel it with his finger, but jerked his hand back; it was obvious enough without that. Meanwhile a whole pool of blood had already formed. Suddenly he noticed a string around her neck; he tugged at it, but the string was strong and refused to snap; besides, it was soaked with blood. He tried simply pulling it out from her bodice, but something was in the way and it got stuck. Impatiently, he raised the axe again to cut the string where it lay on the body, but he did not dare, and with difficulty, smearing both his hands and the axe, after two minutes of fussing over it, he cut the string without touching the body with the axe, and took it off; he was not mistaken—a purse. There were two crosses on the string, one of cypress and the other of brass, besides a little enamel icon; hanging right there with them was a small, greasy suede purse with a steel frame and ring. The purse was stuffed full; Raskolnikov shoved it into his pocket without looking, dropped the crosses on the old woman's chest, and, taking the axe with him this time, rushed back to the bedroom.

He was terribly hurried, snatched up the keys, and began fumbling with them again. But somehow he had no luck: they would not go into the keyholes. It was not so much that his hands were trembling as that he kept making mistakes: he could even see, for instance, that the key was the wrong one, that it would not fit, and he still kept putting it in. Suddenly he recalled and realized that the big key with the toothed bit, which was dangling right there with the other, smaller ones, must certainly not be for the chest of drawers at all (as had also occurred to him the last time) but for some other trunk, and that it was in this trunk that everything was probably hidden. He abandoned the chest of drawers and immediately looked under the bed, knowing that old women usually keep their trunks under their beds. Sure enough, there stood a sizeable trunk, about two and a half feet long, with a bowed lid, upholstered in red morocco, studded with little steel nails. The toothed key fitted perfectly and opened it. On top, under a white sheet, lay a red silk coat lined with rabbit fur; beneath it was a silk dress, then a shawl, and then, deeper down, there seemed to be nothing but old clothes. First of all he began wiping his blood-stained hands on the red silk. "It's red; blood won't be so noticeable on red," he began to reason, but suddenly came to his senses: "Lord! Am I losing my mind?" he thought fearfully.

But no sooner had he disturbed these old clothes than a gold watch suddenly slipped out from under the fur coat. He hastened to turn everything over. Indeed, various gold objects were stuffed in among the rags—all of them probably pledges, redeemed and unredeemed—bracelets, chains, earrings, pins, and so on. Some were in cases, others simply wrapped in newspaper, but neatly and carefully, in double sheets, and tied with cloth bands. Without the least delay, he began stuffing them into the pockets of his trousers and coat, not choosing or opening the packages and cases; but he did not have time to take much . . .

Suddenly there was the sound of footsteps in the room where the old woman lay. He stopped, still as death. But everything was quiet; he must have imagined it. Suddenly there came a slight but distinct cry, or more as if someone softly and abruptly moaned and then fell silent. Again there was a dead silence for a minute or two. He sat crouched by the trunk and waited, barely breathing, then suddenly jumped up, seized the axe, and ran out of the bedroom.

Lizaveta was standing in the middle of the room, with a big bundle in her hands, frozen, staring at her murdered sister, white as a sheet, and as if unable to utter a cry. Seeing him run in, she trembled like a leaf, with a faint quivering, and spasms ran across her whole face; she raised her hand, opened her mouth, yet still did not utter a cry, and began slowly backing away from him into the corner, staring at him fixedly, point-blank, but still not uttering a sound, as if she did not have breath enough to cry out. He rushed at her with the axe; she twisted her lips pitifully, as very small children do when they begin to be afraid of something, stare at the thing that frightens them, and are on the point of crying out. And this wretched Lizaveta was so simple, so downtrodden, and so permanently frightened that she did not even raise a hand to protect her face, though it would have been the most necessary and natural gesture at that moment, because the axe was raised directly over her face. She brought her free left hand up very slightly, nowhere near her face, and slowly stretched it out towards him as if to keep him away. The blow landed directly on the skull, with the sharp edge, and immediately split the whole upper part of the forehead, almost to the crown. She collapsed. Raskolnikov, utterly at a loss, snatched up her bundle, dropped it again, and ran to the entryway.

Fear was taking hold of him more and more, especially after this second, quite unexpected murder. He wanted to run away from there as quickly as possible. And if he had been able at that moment to see and reason more properly, if he had only been able to realize all the difficulties of his situation, all the despair, all the hideousness, all the absurdity of it, and to understand, besides, how many more difficulties and perhaps evildoings he still had to overcome or commit in order to get out of there and reach home, he might very well have dropped everything and gone at once to denounce himself, and not even out of fear for himself, but solely out of horror and loathing for what he had done. Loathing especially was rising and growing in him every moment. Not for anything in the world would he have gone back to the trunk now, or even into the rooms.

But a sort of absentmindedness, even something like revery, began gradually to take possession of him: as if he forgot himself at moments or, better, forgot the main thing and clung to trifles. Nevertheless, glancing into the kitchen and seeing a bucket half full of water on a bench, it did occur to him to wash his hands and the axe. His blood-smeared hands were sticky. He plunged the axe blade straight into the water, grabbed a little piece of soap that was lying in a cracked saucer on the windowsill, and began washing his hands right in the bucket. When he had washed them clean, he also took the axe, washed the iron, and spent a long time, about three minutes, washing the wood where blood had gotten on it, even using soap to try and wash the blood away. Then he wiped it all off with a piece of laundry that was drying there on a line stretched across the kitchen, and then examined the axe long and attentively at the window. There were no traces, only the wood was still damp. He carefully slipped the axe into the loop under his coat. Then, as well as the light in the dim kitchen allowed, he examined his coat, trousers, boots. Superficially, at first glance, there seemed to be nothing, apart from some spots on his boots. He wet the rag and wiped them off. He knew, however, that he was not examining himself well, that there might indeed be something eye-catching which he had failed to notice. He stood pensively in the middle of the room. A dark, tormenting thought was rising in him—the thought that he had fallen into madness and was unable at that moment either to reason or to protect himself, and that he was perhaps not doing at all what he should have been doing . . . "My God! I must run, run away!" he muttered, and rushed into the entryway. But there such horror awaited him as he had surely never experienced before.

He stood, looked, and could not believe his eyes: the door, the outside door, from the entryway to the stairs, the same door at which he had rung, and through which he had entered earlier, stood unlatched, even a good hand's-breadth ajar: no lock, no hook the whole time, during the whole time! The old woman had not locked it behind him, perhaps out of prudence. But, good God, had he not seen Lizaveta after that? How, how could he fail to realize that she must have come in from somewhere! And certainly not through the wall!

He rushed to the door and hooked it.

"But no, again that's not it! I must go, go . . ."

He unhooked the door, opened it, and began listening on the stairs. He listened for a long time. Somewhere far away, downstairs, probably in the gateway, two voices were shouting loudly and shrilly, arguing and swearing. "What's that about?" He waited patiently. At last everything became quiet all at once, as though cut off; they went away. He was on the point of going out when suddenly, one floor below, the door to the stairs was noisily opened and someone started to go down humming a tune. "How is it they all make so much noise?" flashed through his head. He again closed the door behind him and waited. At last everything fell silent; there was not a soul. He had already stepped out to the stairs when again, suddenly, some new footsteps were heard.

The sound of these steps came from very far away, from the very bottom of the stairs, but he remembered quite well and distinctly how, right then, at the first sound, he had begun for some reason to suspect that they must be coming *here*, to the fourth floor, to the old woman's. Why? Could the sound have been somehow peculiar, portentous? The steps were heavy, regular, unhurried. Now *he* was already past the first floor, now he was ascending further, his steps were getting louder and louder. The heavy, short-winded breathing of the approaching man became audible. Now he was starting up the third flight . . . Here! And it suddenly seemed to him as though he had turned to stone, as though he were in one of those dreams where the dreamer is being pursued, the pursuers are close, they are going to kill him, and he is as if rooted to the spot, unable even to move his arms.

At last, and then only when the visitor started climbing to the fourth floor, he roused himself suddenly and had just time enough to slip quickly and adroitly from the landing back into the apartment and close the door behind him. Then he grasped the hook and quietly, inaudibly placed it through the eye. Instinct was helping him. Having done all that, he cowered, without breathing, just at the door. By then the uninvited visitor was also at the door. They now stood opposite each other, as he and the old woman had done earlier, with the door between them, but it was he who was listening.

The visitor drew several heavy breaths. "He must be big and fat," Raskolnikov thought, clutching the axe in his hand. Indeed, it was as if he were dreaming. The visitor grasped the bell-pull and rang firmly.

As soon as the bell gave its tinny clink, he suddenly seemed to fancy there was a stirring in the room. For a few seconds he even listened seriously. The stranger gave another clink of the bell, waited a bit, and suddenly began tugging impatiently at the door handle with all his might. Horrified, Raskolnikov watched the hook jumping about in the eye, and waited in dull fear for it to pop right out any moment. Indeed, it seemed possible: the door was being pulled so hard. It occurred to him to hold the hook in place, but then *he* might suspect. His head seemed to start spinning again. "I'm passing out!" flashed through him, but the stranger spoke, and he immediately recovered himself.

"What's up in there, are they snoring, or has somebody wrung their necks? Cur-r-rse it!" he bellowed, as if from a barrel. "Hey, Alyona Ivanovna, you old witch! Lizaveta Ivanovna, you indescribable beauty! Open up! Ohh, curse it all! Are they asleep, or what?"

And again, enraged, he pulled the bell ten times in a row as hard as he could. He was certainly an imperious man, and a familiar of the house.

At that same moment there was a sound of rapid, hurrying footsteps close by, on the stairs. Someone else was coming up. Raskolnikov did not even hear him at first.

"What, nobody home?" the newcomer cried in a ringing and cheerful voice, directly addressing the first visitor, who was still pulling the bell. "How do you do, Koch!"

"He must be very young, judging by his voice," Raskolnikov suddenly thought.

"Devil knows, I almost broke the lock," answered Koch. "And how do you happen to know me?"

"Well, I like that! Didn't I just beat you three times straight at billiards, the day before yesterday, at Gambrinus's?"

"A-a-ah . . ."

"So they're not there? Strange. Terribly stupid, though. Where could the old woman have gone? I'm here on business."

"I'm also here on business, my friend."

"Well, what's there to do? Go home, I guess. Bah! And I was hoping to get some money!" the young man cried.

"Go home, of course—but then why make an appointment? The old witch told me when to come herself. It's far out of my way. And where the devil she can have taken herself is beyond me. The old witch sits rotting here all year round with her bad legs, and all of a sudden she goes for an outing!"

"Maybe we should ask the caretaker?"

"Ask him what?"

"Where she's gone and when she'll be back?"

"Hm . . . the devil . . . ask him . . . But she never goes anywhere . . ." and he tugged at the door handle again. "Ah, the devil, nothing to be done; let's go!"

"Wait!" the young man suddenly shouted. "Look: do you see how the door gives when you pull?"

"So?"

"That means it's not locked, it's just latched, I mean hooked! Hear the hook rattling?"

"So?"

"But don't you understand? That means one of them is home. If they'd all gone out, they would have locked it from outside with a key, and not hooked it from inside. There, can you hear the hook rattling? And in order to fasten the hook from inside, someone has to be home, understand? So they're sitting in there and not opening the door!"

"Hah! Why, of course!" the astonished Koch exclaimed. "But what are they up to in there!" And he began to tug violently at the door.

"Wait!" The young man shouted again. "Don't tug at it! Something's not right here . . . you rang, you pulled . . . they don't open the door; it means they've both fainted, or . . ."

"Or what?"

"Listen, let's go get the caretaker; let him wake them up."

"Good idea!" They both started down the stairs.

"Wait! You stay here, and I'll run down and get the caretaker."

"Why stay?"

"You never know . . ."

"Maybe . . ."

"I'm studying to be a public investigator! It's obvious, ob-vi-ous that something's not right here!" the young man cried hotly, and went running down the stairs.

Koch stayed. He gave one more little tug at the bell, and it clinked once; then quietly, as if examining and reflecting, he began to move the door handle, pulling it and letting it go, to make sure once more that it was only hooked. Then he bent down, puffing, and tried to look through the keyhole; but there was a key in it, on the inside, and therefore nothing could be seen.

Raskolnikov stood there clutching the axe. He was as if in delirium. He was even readying himself to fight with them when they came in. Several times, while they were knocking and discussing, the idea had suddenly occurred to him to end it all at once and shout to them from behind the door. At times he wanted to start abusing them, taunting them, until they opened the door. "Just get it over with!" flashed through his head.

"Ah, the devil, he . . ."

Time was passing—one minute, two—no one came. Koch began to stir.

"Ah, the devil! . . ." he suddenly cried, and impatiently, abandoning his post, he, too, set off down the stairs, hurrying and stomping his feet as he went. His steps died away.

"Lord, what shall I do!"

Raskolnikov unfastened the hook, opened the door a little—not a sound. And suddenly, now without thinking at all, he went out, closed the door behind him as tightly as he could, and started down the stairs.

He had already gone three flights when a loud noise suddenly came from below—where could he go? There was nowhere to hide. He was turning to run back to the apartment again.

"Hey, you hairy devil! Stop him!"

With a shout, someone burst from one of the apartments below, and did not so much run as tumble down the stairs, shouting at the top of his lungs:

"Mitka! Mitka! Mitka! Mitka! Damn your eyes!"

The cry ended in a shriek; the last sounds already came from outside; then it was quiet. But at the same moment, several men, talking loudly and quickly, began noisily climbing the stairs. There were three or four of them. He heard the ringing voice of the young one. "It's them!"

In utter despair he marched straight to meet them: come what may! If they stopped him, all was lost; if they let him pass, all was lost anyway—they would remember him. In a moment they would come face to face; there was only one flight between them—and suddenly, salvation! A few steps away from him, on the right, was an empty and wide open apartment, that same second-floor apartment where the painters had been working and which, as if by design, they had now left. Surely it was they who had just run out with so much shouting. The floors were freshly painted; in the middle of the room was a small bucket of paint and a potsherd with a brush on it. He slipped through the open door in an instant and cowered behind the wall, and not a moment too soon: they were already on that very landing. Then they passed by and headed upstairs to the fourth floor, talking loudly. He waited, tiptoed out, and ran downstairs.

No one on the stairs! Nor in the gateway. He quickly walked through the gateway and turned left onto the street.

He knew very well, he knew perfectly well, that at that moment they were already in the apartment, that they were very surprised at finding it open, since it had just been locked, that they were already looking at the bodies, and that it would take them no more than a minute to realize and fully grasp that the murderer had just been there and had managed to hide somewhere, slip past them, get away; they would also realize, perhaps, that he had been there in the empty apartment while they were going upstairs. And yet by no means did he dare to quicken his pace, though there were about a hundred steps to go before the first turning. "Shouldn't I slip through some gate and wait somewhere on an unfamiliar stairway? No, no good. Shouldn't I throw the axe away somewhere? Shouldn't I take a cab? No good! No good!"

Here at last was the side street; he turned down it more dead than alive; now he was halfway to safety, and he knew it—not so suspicious; besides, there were many people shuttling along there, and he effaced himself among them like a grain of sand. But all these torments had weakened him so much that he could barely move. Sweat rolled off of him in drops; his whole neck was wet. "There's a potted one!" someone shouted at him as he walked out to the canal.

He was hardly aware of himself now, and the farther he went the worse it became. He remembered, however, that on coming out to the canal he had felt afraid because there were too few people and it was more conspicuous there, and had almost wanted to turn back to the side street. Though he was nearing collapse, he nevertheless made a detour and arrived home from the completely opposite side.

He was not fully conscious when he entered the gates of his house; at least he did not remember about the axe until he was already on the stairs. And yet a very important task was facing him: to put it back, and as inconspicuously as possible. Of course, he was no longer capable of realizing that it might be much better for him not to put the axe in its former place at all, but to leave it, later even, somewhere in an unfamiliar courtyard.

Yet everything worked out well. The caretaker's door was closed but not locked, meaning that the caretaker was most likely there. But by then he had so utterly lost the ability to understand anything that he went straight up to the door and opened it. If the caretaker had asked him, "What do you want?" he might simply have handed him the axe. But once again the caretaker was not there, and he had time to put the axe in its former place under the bench; he even covered it with a log, as before. He met no one, not a single soul, from then on all the way to his room; the landlady's door was shut. He went into his room and threw himself down on the sofa just as he was. He did not sleep, but was as if oblivious. If anyone had come into his room then, he would have jumped up at once and shouted. Bits and scraps of various thoughts kept swarming in his head; but he could not grasp any one of them, could not rest on any one, hard as he tried . . .

Part Two

I

HE LAY LIKE THAT for a very long time. Occasionally he seemed to wake up, and in those moments noticed that night had come long ago, yet it did not occur to him to get up. Finally he noticed light, as if it were already daytime. He was lying on his back on the sofa, still stupefied from his recent oblivion. Terrible, desperate screams came to him sharply from the street—which, by the way, he heard under his window every night between two and three o'clock. They were what wakened him now. "Ah! So the drunks are coming out of the taverns," he thought, "it's past two." And suddenly he jumped up as if someone had torn him from the sofa. "What! Past two already!" He sat down on the sofa and—remembered everything! Suddenly, in an instant, he remembered everything!

At first he thought he would lose his mind. A terrible chill seized him; but the chill was also caused by a fever that had begun long ago in his sleep. Now, however, he was suddenly stricken with such shivering that his teeth almost flew out and everything in him came loose. He opened the door and began to listen: the whole house was fast asleep. He looked with amazement at himself and everything in the room around him, unable to understand how, when he came back yesterday, he could forget to put the door on the hook, and throw himself on the sofa not only without undressing but even still wearing his hat: it had rolled off and was lying right there on the floor near his pillow. "If anyone had come in, what would he have thought? That I'm drunk, but . . ." He dashed to the window. There was light enough, and he hurriedly began looking himself all over, from head to foot, all his clothes: were there any traces? But that was no way to do it. Chilled and shivering, he began taking everything off and examining it all again more thoroughly. He turned everything over and over, to the last thread and scrap, and, not trusting himself, repeated the examination three times. But there seemed to be nothing, no traces, except in one place, where the cuff of his trousers was frayed and hung down like a fringe; there were thick traces of caked blood on this fringe. He seized a big clasp knife and cut the fringe off. There seemed to be nothing else. Suddenly he remembered that the purse and the things he had taken from the old woman's trunk were still in his pockets! Until now he had not even thought of taking them out and hiding them! He had not even remembered about them while he was examining his clothes! What was wrong with him? He rushed at once, took them out, and threw them on the table. Having taken everything out, and even reversed the pockets to make sure nothing was left, he carried the whole pile into a corner. There, in the very corner, low down, the wallpaper was coming away and was torn in one place: he at once began stuffing everything into this hole behind the paper. "It all fits! Everything, out of sight, and the purse, too!" he thought joyfully, straightening up and staring dumbly at the hole in the corner, which bulged more than ever. Suddenly he shook all over with horror: "My God," he whispered in despair, "what's wrong with me? Do you call that hidden? Is that any way to hide things?"

True, he had not been counting on things; he thought there would only be money and therefore did not prepare a place ahead of time. "But now, why was I rejoicing now? Is that any way to hide things? Reason truly is abandoning me!" Exhausted, he sat down on the sofa and was seized at once by an unbearable shivering. Mechanically, he pulled at his former student's greatcoat, warm but now almost in rags, which was lying next to him on a chair, covered himself with it, and once more sleep and delirium took hold of him. He sank into oblivion.

Not more than five minutes later he jumped up again, and immediately, in a frenzy, rushed again to his clothes. "How could I have fallen asleep again, when nothing has been done! That's it, that's it—the loop under the armhole—I haven't removed it yet! I forgot! Such a thing, such evidence, and I forgot!" He pulled the loop off and quickly began tearing it into pieces, stuffing them under the pillow among his linen. "Pieces of torn cloth will never arouse suspicion; no, probably not, probably not!" he repeated, standing in the middle of the room, and with painfully strained attention he began looking around again, on the floor and everywhere, to see if he had forgotten anything else. The conviction that everything, even memory, even simple reasoning-power was abandoning him, began to torment him unbearably. "What, can it be starting already, can the reckoning come so soon? See, see—there it is!" Indeed, the shreds of fringe he had cut off his trousers were simply lying on the floor, in the middle of the room, for the first comer to see! "What can be wrong with me!" he cried out again, like a lost man.

Here a strange thought came into his head: perhaps all his clothes were covered with blood, perhaps there were stains all over them, and he simply did not see, did not notice them, because his reason was failing, going to pieces . . . his mind darkening . . . Suddenly he remembered that there was also blood on the purse. "Bah! So then there must be blood inside the pocket as well, because the purse was still wet when I put it in my pocket!" He instantly turned the pocket out and, sure enough, there were traces, stains on the lining. "So reason hasn't deserted me altogether, so there's still some understanding and memory left, since I suddenly remembered and figured it out myself!" he thought triumphantly, taking a deep and joyful breath. "It was just feverish weakness, a momentary delirium." And he tore the whole lining out of the left pocket of his trousers. At that moment a ray of sunlight fell on his left boot: there, where his sock peeped out of the boot, marks seemed to have appeared. He kicked the boot off: "Marks, indeed! The whole toe of the sock is soaked with blood." So he must have carelessly stepped into that pool . . . "But what to do with it now? Where am I to put the sock, the fringe, the pocket?"

He raked it all up with his hand and stood in the middle of the room. "Into the stove? But they'll start rummaging in the stove first of all. Burn them? But what with? I don't even have any matches. No, better go out somewhere and throw it all away. Yes, better throw it all away!" he kept repeating, sitting down again on the sofa, "and right now, this minute, without delay! . . ." But instead, his head lay back on the pillow again; the unbearable chill again turned him to ice; again he pulled the greatcoat over him. And for a long time, for several hours, he kept imagining in fits and starts that it was "time to go, now, somewhere, without delay, and throw it all away, out of sight, quickly, quickly!" He tried several times to rise from the sofa, he wanted to get up but no longer could. Finally he was awakened by a loud knocking at the door.

"Open up! Are you alive in there? He just goes on snoring!" Nastasya shouted, banging on the door with her fist. "He just lies there snoring, day in and day out, like a dog! A dog, that's what he is! Open up, will you? It's past ten!"

"Maybe he's not home!" a male voice said.

"Bah! That's the caretaker's voice . . . What does he want?" He jumped and sat up on the sofa. His heart was pounding so hard that it even hurt.

"And who put it on the hook, then?" Nastasya objected. "See, he's locking himself in now! Are you afraid you'll get stolen, or what? Open the door, noodle, wake up!"

"What do they want? Why the caretaker? It's all been found out. Do I resist, or open? Ah, who gives a . . ."

He bent forward, reached out, and lifted the hook.

His whole room was of a size that made it possible to lift the hook without getting out of bed.

True enough, the caretaker and Nastasya were standing there.

Nastasya looked him over somehow strangely. He gave the caretaker a defiant and desperate look. The latter handed him a gray paper, folded in two and sealed with bottle wax.

"A summons, from the station," he pronounced, giving him the paper.

"What station?"

"The police, I mean; they're calling you in to the station. What other station . . ."

"The police! . . . What for? . . ."

"How should I know? They want you, so go." He looked at him intently, glanced around, and turned to leave.

"So you really got sick?" observed Nastasya, who had not taken her eyes off him. The caretaker also turned back for a moment. "He's had a fever since yesterday," she added.

He made no reply and held the paper in his hands without unsealing it.

"Don't get up, then," Nastasya continued, moved to pity and seeing that he was lowering his feet from the sofa. "Don't go, if you're sick; there's no fire. What's that in your hand?"

He looked: in his right hand were the cut-off pieces of fringe, the sock, and the scraps of the torn-out pocket. He had slept with them like that. Thinking about it afterwards, he recalled that even half-awakening in his fever, he would clutch them tightly in his hand and fall asleep again that way.

"Look, he's collected some rags and he sleeps with them like a treasure . . ." And Nastasya dissolved in her morbidly nervous laughter. He instantly shoved it all under the greatcoat and fixed her with a piercing look. Though at the moment he could understand very little in any full sense, he still felt that a man would not be treated that way if he were about to be arrested. "But . . . the police?"

"Have some tea. Would you like some? I'll bring it; I've got some left . . ."

"No . . . I'll go, I'll go now," he muttered, getting to his feet.

"But you won't even make it down the stairs."

"I'll go . . ."

"Suit yourself."

She left after the caretaker. He immediately rushed to the light to examine the sock and the fringe. "There are stains, but not very noticeable; it's all dirty, rubbed off, discolored by now. No one would see anything unless they knew beforehand. So Nastasya couldn't have noticed anything from where she was, thank God!" Then he tremblingly unsealed the summons and began to read; he spent a long time reading it and finally understood. It was an ordinary summons from the local police to come to the chief's office that day at half past nine.

"But this is unheard of. I've never had any personal dealings with the police! And why precisely today?" he thought, in tormenting bewilderment. "Lord, get it over with!" He fell on his knees to pray, but burst out laughing instead—not at praying, but at himself. He began hurriedly to dress. "If I'm to perish, let me perish, I don't care! Must put that sock on!" he suddenly thought. "It will rub away even more in the dust and the marks will disappear." But as soon as he put it on, he immediately pulled it off again with loathing and horror. He pulled it off, but, realizing that he had no other, he picked it up and put it on again—and again burst out laughing. "It's all conventional, all relative, all just a matter of form," he thought fleetingly, with only a small part of his mind, while his whole body trembled. "There, I put it on! I did finally put it on!" But his laughter immediately gave way to despair. "No, I'm not strong enough . . ." the thought came to him.

His legs were trembling. "From fear," he muttered to himself. His head was spinning and throbbing from high fever. "It's a ruse! They want to lure me there by a ruse and suddenly throw me off with everything," he continued to himself, walking out to the stairs. "The worst of it is that I'm almost delirious . . . I might blurt out some foolishness . . ."

On the stairs he remembered that he was leaving the things as they were, in the hole behind the wallpaper. "And there may be a search right now, while I'm out," he remembered and stopped. But such despair and, if one may put it so, such cynicism of perdition suddenly possessed him that he waved his hand and went on.

"Only get it over with! . . ."

Again it was unbearably hot out; not a drop of rain had fallen for all those days. Again dust, brick, lime; again the stench from the shops and taverns; again drunks all the time, Finnish peddlers, half-dilapi-dated cabbies. The sun flashed brightly in his eyes, so that it hurt him to look, and he became quite dizzy—the usual sensation of a man in a fever who suddenly steps outside on a bright, sunny day.

Coming to the turn onto *yesterday's* street, he peered down it with tormenting anxiety, at *that* house . . . and immediately looked away.

"If they ask, maybe I'll tell them," he thought, approaching the station.

The station was less than a quarter of a mile from his house. It had just been moved into new quarters, on the fourth floor of a different building. He had been in the former quarters once, briefly, but very long ago. Passing under the gateway, he saw a stairway to the right, with a peasant coming down it carrying a book. "Must be a caretaker; so the station must be there," and on that surmise he started up the stairs. He did not want to ask anyone about anything.

"I'll walk in, fall on my knees, and tell them everything . . ." he thought, going up to the fourth floor.

The stairway was narrow, steep, and all covered with swill. The doors to the kitchens of all the apartments, on all four floors, opened onto the stairs and stood open most of the day. This made it terribly stifling. Up and down the stairs went caretakers with books under their arms, messengers, and various people of both sexes—visitors. The door of the office itself was also wide open. He went in and stopped in the anteroom. Here a number of peasants were standing and waiting. And here, too, it was extremely stifling; moreover, from the newly painted rooms a nauseating odor of fresh, not quite cured paint, made with rancid oil, assailed his nostrils. After waiting a little while, he made the decision to move on, into the next room. All the rooms were tiny and low. A terrible impatience drew him farther and farther. No one took any notice of him. In the second room some scriveners were sitting and writing; they were dressed only slightly better than he was—a strange assortment of people by the look of it. He turned to one of them.

"What do you want?"

He showed him the summons from the office.

"You're a student?" the man asked, glancing at the summons.

"A former student."

The scrivener looked him over, though without any curiosity. He was a somehow especially disheveled man, with a fixed idea in his eyes.

"I won't get anything out of this one," Raskolnikov thought, "it's all the same to him."

"Go in there, to the clerk," said the scrivener, jabbing his finger forward, pointing to the very last room.

He entered that room (the fourth one down); it was small and chock-full of the public—people whose clothes were somewhat cleaner than in the other rooms. Among the visitors were two ladies. One of them was in mourning, humbly dressed, and sat across the table from the clerk, writing something to his dictation. The other, an extremely plump and conspicuous woman, with reddish-purple blotches, all too magnificently dressed, and with a brooch the size of a saucer on her bosom, stood to one side waiting for something. Raskolnikov handed his summons to the clerk. He gave it a passing glance, said "Wait," and continued to occupy himself with the mourning lady.

He breathed more freely. "Must be for something else!" Gradually he began to take heart; with all his might he exhorted himself to take heart and pull himself together.

"Some foolishness, some most trifling indiscretion, and I can give myself away completely! Hm . . . too bad it's so airless here," he added, "stifling . . . My head is spinning even more . . . my mind, too . . ."

He felt a terrible disorder within himself. He was afraid of losing his control. He tried to hang on to something, to think at least of something, some completely unrelated thing, but could not manage to do it. The clerk, however, interested him greatly: he kept hoping to read something in his face, to pry into him. This was a very young man, about twenty-two years old, with a dark and mobile physiognomy which looked older than its years, fashionably and foppishly dressed, his hair parted behind, all combed and pomaded, with many rings and signet-rings on his white, brush-scrubbed fingers, and gold chains on his waistcoat. He even spoke a few words of French, and quite satisfactorily, with a foreigner who was there.

"Why don't you sit down, Louisa Ivanovna," he said in passing to the bedizened reddish-purple lady, who remained standing as if she did not dare to sit down, though there was a chair beside her.

"Ich danke,"[1] she said, and quietly, with a silken rustling, lowered herself onto the chair. Her light-blue dress with white lace trimming expanded around the chair like a balloon and filled almost half the office. There was a reek of perfume. But the lady was obviously abashed that she was taking up half the space and that she reeked so much of perfume, and her smile, though cowardly and insolent at once, was also obviously uneasy.

The mourning lady finally finished and started to get up. Suddenly there was some noise and an officer came in, quite dashingly and somehow with a special swing of the shoulders at each step, tossed his cockaded cap on the table, and sat himself down in an armchair. The magnificent lady simply leaped from her seat as soon as she saw him, and began curtsying to him with some special sort of rapture; but the officer did not pay the slightest attention to her, and she now did not dare to sit down again in his presence. He was a lieutenant, the police chief's assistant, with reddish moustaches sticking out horizontally on both sides, and with extremely small features, which, incidentally, expressed nothing in particular apart from a certain insolence. He gave a sidelong and somewhat indignant glance at Raskolnikov: his costume really was too wretched, and yet, despite such humiliation, his bearing was not in keeping with his costume; Raskolnikov, from lack of prudence, looked at him too directly and steadily, so that he even became offended.

"What do you want?" he shouted, probably surprised that such a ragamuffin did not even think of effacing himself before the lightning of his gaze.

"I was summoned . . . by a notice . . ." Raskolnikov managed to reply.

"It's that case to do with the recovery of money, from him, the *student*," the clerk spoke hurriedly, tearing himself away from his papers. "Here, sir!" and he flipped the register over for Raskolnikov, pointing to a place in it. "Read this!"

"Money? What money?" Raskolnikov thought. "But . . . then it surely can't be *that!*" And he gave a joyful start. He suddenly felt terribly, inexpressibly light. Everything fell from his shoulders.

"And what time does it say you should come, my very dear sir?" the lieutenant shouted, getting more and more insulted for some unknown reason. "It says you should come at nine, and it's already past eleven!"

"It was brought to me only a quarter of an hour ago," Raskolnikov replied loudly, over his shoulder, becoming suddenly and unexpectedly angry himself, and even finding a certain pleasure in it. "It's enough that I came at all, sick with fever as I am."

"Kindly do not shout!"

"I'm not shouting, I'm speaking quite evenly; it's you who are shouting at me; but I am a student and I will not allow anyone to shout at me."

The assistant flared up so violently that for the first moment he was even unable to say anything articulate, and only some sort of spluttering flew out of his mouth. He leaped from his seat.

"Kindly be still! You are in an official place. No r-r-rudeness, sir!"

"But you, too, are in an official place," Raskolnikov cried, "and you are not only shouting but also smoking a cigarette, and thereby being disrespectful towards all of us!" Having said this, Raskolnikov felt an inexpressible delight.

The clerk was looking at them with a smile. The fiery lieutenant was visibly taken aback.

"That is none of your business, sir!" he finally yelled, in a somehow unnaturally loud voice. "You will kindly give the response that is demanded of you. Show him, Alexander Grigorievich. There are complaints against you! You owe money! Just look at this bright young falcon!"

But Raskolnikov was no longer listening and greedily took hold of the paper, hastening to find the answer. He read it over once, then twice, and did not understand.

"What is this?" he asked the clerk.

"It is a request for the recovery of money owed by you on a promissory note. You must either pay it, including all expenses, fines, and so forth, or give a written response stating when you will be able to pay, and at the same time sign an obligation not to leave the capital before payment is made and not to sell or conceal your property. And the creditor is free to sell your property, and to take action against you in accordance with the law."

"But I . . . don't owe anyone anything!"

"That is not our business. Our office has received for recovery a promissory note in the amount of one hundred and fifteen roubles, overdue and legally protested, which you gave to the widow of the collegiate assessor Zarnitsyn nine months ago, and which was given by her in payment to the court councillor Chebarov, for which reason we have invited you here to respond."

"But she's my landlady!"

"So what if she is your landlady?"

The clerk looked at him with a condescending smile of regret and, at the same time, of a certain triumph, as at a novice who has just come under fire for the first time: "Well," he seemed to be saying, "how do you feel now?" But what did he care, what did he care now about a promissory note and its recovery! Was it worth the least anxiety now, even the least attention? He stood, read, listened, replied, even asked questions himself, but all mechanically. The triumph of self-preservation, the rescue from overwhelming danger—that was what filled his entire being at the moment, with no foresight, no analysis, no future riddling and unriddling, no doubts or questions. It was a moment of complete, spontaneous, purely animal joy. But at that same moment something like thunder and lightning broke out in the office. The lieutenant, still all shaken by disrespect, all aflame, and apparently wishing to shore up his wounded pride, fell with all his thunderbolts upon the unfortunate "magnificent lady," who, ever since he walked in, had been looking at him with the most stupid smile.

"And you, you so-and-so," he suddenly shouted at the top of his lungs (the mourning lady had already gone out), "what went on at your place last night? Eh? More of your disgrace and debauchery, for the whole street to hear? More fighting and drinking? Are you longing for the penitentiary? Didn't I tell you, didn't I warn you ten times that you wouldn't get away the eleventh? And you do it again and again, you so-and-so, you!"

The paper simply dropped from Raskolnikov's hands, and he gazed wildly at the magnificent lady who had just been given such an unceremonious trimming; however, he quickly realized what it was all about and even began to enjoy the whole story very much. He listened with pleasure, so much so that he even wanted to laugh, laugh, laugh . . . All his nerves were twitching.

"Ilya Petrovich!" the clerk began solicitously, but stopped and bided his time, because the boiling lieutenant could be held back only by main force—he knew it from his own experience.

As for the magnificent lady, at first the thunder and lightning set her all atremble; but, strangely, the stronger and more numerous the curses, the more amiable she looked, and the more charming was the smile she turned on the terrible lieutenant. She kept shifting her feet and curtsying all the time, waiting impatiently until she got the chance to put a word in, and she finally did get it.

"I did not haff any noise und fighting, Mr. Kapitän," she suddenly started to patter, like peas spilling in a pan, in brisk Russian, but with a strong German accent, "und it vas not, it vas not any shcandal, but he came trunken, und I vill tell it all, Mr. Kapitän, und it is not my fault . . . mine is a noble house, Mr. Kapitän, und a noble behavior, Mr. Kapitän, und I alvays, alvays didn't vant any shcandal. But he is coming completely trunken, und then again is asking for three more pottles, und then he raised one of his foots und begint to play the fortepian mit his foot, und this is not nice at all in a noble house, und he ganz broke the fortepian, und he had no maniers, no maniers at all, und I tell him so. Und he took the pottle und begint to push everyone from behind mit the pottle. Und here I run und call the caretaker, und

Karl comes, und he hitten Karl in the eye, und he hitten Henriette in the eye, too, und me he shlapped five times on the cheek. Und this is so indelicate in a noble house, Mr. Kapitän, und I am yelling. Und he opened the vindow on the canal und shtarted sqvealing out the vindow like a little pig; und it is a disgrace. Und mit all his might he is sqvealing out the vindow to the street like a little pig; und vat a disgrace it is! Fui, fui, fui! Und Karl pulled him avay from the vindow by his frock coat, und here, it's true, Mr. Kapitän, he tore sein Rock. Und then he shouted that Mann muss pay him fifteen roubles fine. Und I myself, Mr. Kapitän, paid him five roubles for sein Rock. Und this is not a noble guest, Mr. Kapitän, und he did all sorts of shcandal. I vill gedrückt a big satire on you, he says, because I can write anything about you in all the newspapers."

"So he's one of those writers?"

"Yes, Mr. Kapitän, und he is such an unnoble guest, Mr. Kapitän, ven in a noble house . . ."

"So, so, so! Enough! I've told you before, I've told you over and over . . ."

"Ilya Petrovich!" the clerk said again, significantly. The lieutenant quickly glanced at him; the clerk nodded slightly.

". . . So, my most esteemed *Laviza* Ivanovna, here is my final word for you, and, believe me, it is final," the lieutenant continued. "If there is one more scandal in your noble house, I will send you in person to zugunder,[2] to use a high-class expression. Do you hear me? So a writer, a littérateur, took five roubles for his coattail in a 'noble house'? That's writers for you!" He cast a contemptuous glance at Raskolnikov. "There was a similar story in a tavern two days ago: one of them had dinner and then didn't want to pay for it—'or else I'll put you into a satire,' he said. Another one, on a steamboat last week, denounced a respectable family, a state councillor, his wife and daughter, in the foulest language. And another got himself kicked out of a pastry shop the other day. That's how they are, these writers, littérateurs, students, town criers . . . pah! Off with you! I'll stop by your place myself . . . so watch out! Do you hear?"

Louisa Ivanovna, with hurried amiability, began curtsying in all directions, and backed towards the door still curtsying; but in the doorway she bumped backwards into a fine officer with a fresh, open face and magnificent, bushy blond side-whiskers. This was the chief of police, Nikodim Fomich himself. Louisa Ivanovna hastily curtsied almost to the floor and, skipping with quick, small steps, flew out of the office.

"More blasts, more thunder and lightning, tornadoes, hurricanes!" Nikodim Fomich pleasantly and amicably addressed Ilya Petrovich. "His heart has been stirred up again, he's boiling again! I heard it way downstairs."

" 'Twas nothing!" Ilya Petrovich uttered with gentlemanly nonchalance (not even "nothing" but somehow " 'Twa-as na-a-awthing"), going to another table with some papers, and jerking his shoulders spectacularly with each step—a step here, a shoulder there. "Look, sir, if you please: mister writer here, or student, rather—a former one, that is—owes money and doesn't pay it, has given out all sorts of promissory notes, won't vacate his apartment, there are constant complaints about him, and he is so good as to start an altercation with me for smoking a cigarette in his presence! He's s-s-scoundrelly enough himself, and look at him, if you please, sir: here he is in all his attractiveness!"

"Come, come, my friend, poverty is no vice! We know you're like gunpowder, unable to bear an offense. You must have gotten offended with him for some reason and couldn't help saying something," Nikodim Fomich went on, amiably addressing Raskolnikov, "but you mustn't do that: he is a mo-o-st no-o-oble man, I must tell you, but gunpowder, gunpowder! He flares up, he boils up, he burns up—and that's it! All gone! And what's left is his heart of gold! In our regiment he was known as 'Lieutenant Gunpowder' . . ."

"And what a r-r-regiment it was!" exclaimed Ilya Petrovich, quite content to be so pleasantly tickled, but still sulking.

Raskolnikov suddenly wanted to say something extraordinarily pleasant to them all.

"I beg your pardon, Captain," he began quite casually, suddenly addressing Nikodim Fomich, "but you must also understand my position . . . I am even ready to ask his forgiveness if for my part I was in any way disrespectful. I am a poor and sick student, weighed down" (that was how he said it: *weighed down*) "by poverty. I am a former student because I cannot support myself now, but I will be getting some money . . . I have a mother and a sister in ——y province . . . They will send it, and I . . . will pay. My landlady is a kind woman, but she is so angry because I lost my lessons and haven't paid her for four months that she won't even send up my dinner . . . And I absolutely do not understand what this promissory note is! She's now demanding that I pay, but how can I? Judge for yourself! . . ."

"But that is not our business . . ." the clerk observed again.

"Allow me, allow me, I completely agree with you, but allow me to explain," Raskolnikov picked up again, still addressing himself not to the clerk but to Nikodim Fomich, but trying as hard as he could to address Ilya Petrovich as well, though he stubbornly pretended to be burrowing in his papers and contemptuously ignored him, "allow me, too, for my part, to explain that I have been living with her for about three years now, ever since I came from the province, and earlier . . . earlier . . . but then, why shouldn't I confess it, at the very beginning I made a promise that I would marry her daughter, a verbal promise, a completely free one . . . This girl was . . . however, I even liked her . . . though I wasn't in love . . . youth, in a word—that is, I mean to say that the landlady gave me considerable credit then, and my way of life was somewhat . . . I was quite thoughtless . . ."

"Such intimacies are hardly required of you, my dear sir, and we have no time for them," Ilya Petrovich interrupted rudely and triumphantly, but Raskolnikov hotly cut him off, though it had suddenly become very difficult for him to speak.

"But allow me, do allow me to tell everything, more or less . . . how things went and . . . in my turn . . . though it's unnecessary, I agree— but a year ago this girl died of typhus, and I stayed on as a tenant like before, and when the landlady moved to her present apartment, she told me . . . and in a friendly way . . . that she had complete trust in me and all . . . but wouldn't I like to give her this promissory note for a hundred and fifteen roubles, which was the total amount I owed her. Allow me, sir: she precisely said that once I'd given her this paper, she would let me have as much more credit as I wanted, and that she, for her part, would never, ever—these were her own words—make use of this paper before I myself paid her . . . And now, when I've lost my lessons and have nothing to eat, she applies for recovery . . . What can I say?"

"All these touching details, my dear sir, are of no concern to us," Ilya Petrovich insolently cut in. "You must make a response and a commitment, and as for your happening to be in love, and all these other tragic points, we could not care less about them."

"Now that's . . . cruel of you . . . really . . ." Nikodim Fomich muttered, and he, too, sat down at the table and started signing things. He felt somehow ashamed.

"Write," the clerk said to Raskolnikov.

"Write what?" he asked, somehow with particular rudeness.

"I'll dictate to you."

Raskolnikov fancied that after his confession the clerk had become more casual and contemptuous with him, but—strangely—he suddenly felt decidedly indifferent to anyone's possible opinion, and this change occurred somehow in a moment, an instant. If he had only cared to reflect a little, he would of course have been surprised that he could have spoken with them as he had a minute before, and even thrust his feelings upon them. And where had these feelings come from? On the contrary, if the room were now suddenly filled not with policemen but with his foremost friends, even then, he thought, he would be unable to find a single human word for them, so empty had his heart suddenly become. A dark sensation of tormenting, infinite solitude and estrangement suddenly rose to consciousness in his soul. It was not the abjectness of his heart's outpourings before Ilya Petrovich, nor the abjectness of the lieutenant's triumph over him, that suddenly so overturned his heart. Oh, what did he care now about his own meanness, about all these vanities, lieutenants, German women, proceedings, offices, and so on and so forth! Even if he had been sentenced to be burned at that moment, he would not have stirred, and would probably not have listened very attentively to the sentence. What was taking place in him was totally unfamiliar, new, sudden, never before experienced. Not that he understood it, but he sensed clearly, with all the power of sensation, that it was no longer possible for him to address these people in the police station, not only with heartfelt effusions, as he had just done, but in any way at all, and had they been his own brothers and sisters, and not police lieutenants, there would still have been no point in his addressing them, in whatever circumstances of life. Never until that minute had he experienced such a strange and terrible sensation. And most tormenting of all was that it was more a sensation than an awareness, an idea; a spontaneous sensation, the most tormenting of any he had yet experienced in his life.

The clerk began dictating to him the customary formal response for such occasions—that is, I cannot pay, I promise to pay by such-and-such a date (some day), I will not leave town, I will neither sell nor give away my property, and so on.

"You can't even write, you're barely able to hold the pen," the clerk observed, studying Raskolnikov with curiosity. "Are you sick?"

"Yes . . . dizzy . . . go on!"

"That's all. Sign it."

The clerk took the paper from him and busied himself with others. Raskolnikov gave back the pen, but instead of getting up and leaving, he put both elbows on the table and pressed his head with his hands. It was as if a nail were being driven into his skull. A strange thought suddenly came to him: to get up now, go over to Nikodim Fomich, and tell him all about yesterday, down to the last detail, then go to his apartment with them and show them the things in the corner, in the hole. The urge was so strong that he had already risen from his seat to carry it out. "Shouldn't I at least think it over for a moment?" raced through his head. "No, better do it without thinking, just to get it off my back!" But suddenly he stopped, rooted to the spot: Nikodim Fomich was talking heatedly with Ilya Petrovich, and he caught some of the words.

"It's impossible; they'll both be released! First of all, everything's against it; just consider, why would they call the caretaker if it was their doing? To give themselves away, or what? Out of cunning? No, that would be much too cunning! And, finally, both caretakers and the tradeswoman saw the student Pestryakov just by the gate, the very moment he came in: he was walking with three friends and parted with them just by the gate, and he asked the caretakers about lodgings while his friends were still with him. Now, would such a man ask about lodgings if he had come there with such an intention? As for Koch, he spent half an hour with the silversmith downstairs before he went to the old woman's, and left him to go upstairs at exactly a quarter to eight. Think, now . . ."

"But, excuse me, how did they end up with this contradiction: they assure us that they knocked and the door was locked, but when they came back with the caretaker three minutes later, it turned out that the door was not locked."

"That's just it: the murderer must have been there inside and put the door on the hook; and he would certainly have been caught there if Koch hadn't been fool enough to go for the caretaker himself. And it was precisely during that interval that *he* managed to get down the stairs and somehow slip past them. Koch keeps crossing himself with both hands: 'If I'd stayed there,' he says, 'he would have jumped out and killed me with an axe.' He wants to have a Russian *molieben* served, heh, heh! . . ."[3]

"And no one even saw the murderer?"

"But how could they, really? That house is like Noah's ark," observed the clerk, who was listening in from where he sat.

"The case is clear, quite clear!" Nikodim Fomich repeated hotly.

"No, the case is very unclear," Ilya Petrovich clinched.

Raskolnikov picked up his hat and made for the door, but he did not reach it . . .

When he came to his senses he saw that he was sitting in a chair, that some man was supporting him from the right, that another man was standing on his left holding a yellow glass filled with yellow water, and that Nikodim Fomich was standing in front of him, looking at him intently. He got up from the chair.

"What, are you ill?" Nikodim Fomich asked rather curtly.

"He could hardly hold the pen to sign his name," the clerk observed, sitting down in his place and going back to his papers.

"And how long have you been ill?" Ilya Petrovich called out from where he sat, also sorting through his papers. He, too, had of course looked at the sick man when he fainted, but stepped away at once when he came to.

"Since yesterday . . ." Raskolnikov muttered in reply.

"And did you go out yesterday?"

"Yes."

"Though you were ill?"

"Though I was ill."

"At what time?"

"After seven in the evening."

"And where, may I ask?"

"Down the street."

"Plain and simple."

Raskolnikov answered curtly, abruptly; he was white as a sheet and refused to lower his dark, feverish eyes before the gaze of Ilya Petrovich.

"He can barely stand on his feet, and you . . ." Nikodim Fomich began.

"Not-at-all!" Ilya Petrovich pronounced somehow specially. Nikodim Fomich was about to add something, but, having glanced at the clerk, who was also looking very intently at him, he fell silent. Everyone suddenly fell silent. It was strange.

"Very well, sir," Ilya Petrovich concluded, "we are not keeping you."

Raskolnikov walked out. After his exit an animated conversation began, which he could still hear, the questioning voice of Nikodim Fomich rising above the others . . . In the street he recovered completely.

"A search, a search, an immediate search!" he repeated to himself, hurrying to get home. "The villains! They suspect me!" His former fear again came over him entirely, from head to foot.

II

"AND WHAT IF there has already been a search? What if I find them there now?"

But here was his room. Nothing and nobody; no one had been there. Even Nastasya had not touched anything. But, Lord! How could he have left all those things in that hole?

He rushed to the corner, thrust his hand under the wallpaper, and began pulling the things out and loading them into his pockets. There turned out to be eight articles altogether: two small boxes with earrings or something of the sort—he did not look closely; then four small morocco cases. One chain was simply wrapped in newspaper. There was something else in newspaper, apparently a medal.

He stowed them all in different pockets of his coat and in the remaining right pocket of his trousers, trying to make them less conspicuous. He took the purse as well, together with the things. Then he went out of the room, this time leaving the door wide open.

He walked quickly and firmly, and though he felt broken all over, his consciousness remained with him. He was afraid of being followed, afraid that within half an hour, within a quarter of an hour, instructions would be issued to keep a watch on him; so meanwhile he had at all costs to cover his traces. He had to manage it while he still had at least some strength and some judgment . . . But where to go?

He had long since decided: "Throw everything into the canal, and the water will wash away all traces, and that will be the end of it." He had decided so during the night, in delirium, in those moments when, as he remembered, he had made several attempts to rise up and go "quickly, quickly, and throw it all away." But throwing it away turned out to be very difficult.

He wandered along the embankment of the Ekaterininsky Canal for half an hour, perhaps longer, and several times cast an eye at the landing steps as he passed by them. But he could not even think of carrying out his intention: either rafts were standing there and washerwomen were doing laundry on them, or boats were moored there, and people were simply swarming all over the place; besides, he could be seen, he could be noticed from anywhere along the embankments, from all sides: a man coming down on purpose, stopping and throwing something into the water, would look suspicious. And what if the cases floated instead of sinking? Yes, of course they would float. Everyone would see them. Indeed, they all kept staring at him as it was, looking him over, as if he were their only concern. "Why is that? Or does it just seem so to me?" he thought.

Finally it occurred to him that it might be better to go somewhere along the Neva. There were fewer people, it would not be so conspicuous, in any case it was more convenient, and, above all—it was farther away from those parts. And suddenly he was amazed: how could he have wandered for a whole half hour in anguish and anxiety, and in dangerous places, and not thought of it before! And he had killed a whole half hour over such a foolhardy matter simply because he had decided on it in his sleep, in delirium! He was becoming extremely distracted and forgetful, and he knew it. He decidedly had to hurry!

He walked along the V——y Prospect in the direction of the Neva; but on the way another thought suddenly came to him: "Why the Neva? Why in the water? Wouldn't it be better to go somewhere very far away, even to the Islands again, and there somewhere, in some solitary place, in the woods, under a bush, to bury it all, and maybe also make note of the tree?" And though he felt he could not consider it all clearly and soberly at that moment, it seemed a flawless idea.

But he was not destined to get to the Islands either; something else happened: coming out from the V——y Prospect to the square, he saw on his left the entrance to a courtyard, surrounded by completely blank walls. To the right, immediately inside the gateway, the blank, un-whitewashed wall of the four-storied house next door stretched back deep into the yard. To the left, parallel to the blind wall, and also just beyond the gate, a wooden fence extended about twenty paces into the yard and only then broke to the left. This was a fenced-off, out-of-the-way spot where some materials were lying about. Deeper into the yard, from behind the fence, the angle of a low, sooty stone shed peeked out—evidently part of some workshop. It was probably a carriage-maker's or a metalworker's shop, or something of the sort; everything, starting almost from the gate, was covered with black coal dust. "Why not abandon it here and go away!" suddenly crossed his mind. Not noticing anyone in the yard, he stepped through the gate and saw, just inside, a trough set up next to the fence (such as one often finds in places where there are many factory workers, teamsters, coachmen, and so on), and written in chalk on the fence above the trough was the inevitable witticism in such circumstances: "NO LOIDERING HEAR."[4] That was already a good thing; it meant there would be nothing suspicious about his going in and loitering. "Just dump it all in a heap somewhere, and get out!"

Having looked around one more time, he had already put his hand into his pocket when he suddenly noticed, up next to the outside wall, between the gate and the trough, where the whole space was a little more than two feet wide, a big, unhewn stone weighing perhaps fifty pounds, leaning right against the stone street-wall. The street, the sidewalk, were just beyond this wall; one could hear passers-by, always numerous there, shuttling back and forth; yet he could not be seen from outside the gate, but only if someone were to come in from the street, which, however, might very well happen, and therefore he had to hurry.

He bent down, gripped the top of the stone firmly with both hands, gathered all his strength, and rolled it over. The stone had made a shallow depression; he at once began throwing all the contents of his pockets into it. The purse ended up on top, and there was still some room in the depression. Then he took hold of the stone again, and with one heave rolled it back onto its former side, so that it ended up exactly in its former place, only it seemed perhaps a little, just a tiny bit, higher. But he raked up some dirt and tamped it around the edges with his foot. Nothing could be noticed.

He went out and headed for the square. Again, as that morning in the office, a strong, almost unbearable joy possessed him for a moment. "The traces are covered! And who, who would think of looking under that stone? It may have been lying there since the house was built, and may go on lying there as long again. And even if they find it, who will think of me? It's finished! No evidence!" And he laughed. Yes, he remembered afterwards that he laughed a rapid, nervous, inaudible, drawn-out laugh, and went on laughing all the while he was crossing the square. But when he turned down K——y Boulevard, where he had met that girl two days before, his laughter suddenly went away. Other thoughts started creeping into his head. He also suddenly fancied that it was terribly loathsome now for him to pass that bench where he had sat and pondered then, after the girl left, and that it would also be terribly difficult for him to meet that moustached officer again, the one to whom he had given the twenty kopecks: "Devil take him!"

He walked on, looking distractedly and spitefully about him. All his thoughts were now circling around some one main point, and he himself felt that it was indeed the main point, and that now, precisely now, he was left face-to-face with this main point—even for the first time after those two months.

"Ah, devil take it all!" he thought suddenly, in a fit of inexhaustible spite. "So, if it's begun, it's begun—to hell with her, and with the new life! Lord, how stupid it is! . . . And all the lying and groveling I produced today! How repulsively I fawned and flirted today with that nasty Ilya Petrovich! Ah, but that's nonsense, too! I spit on them, and on everyone, and on my own fawning and flirting! That's not it! Not it at all! . . ."

Suddenly he stopped. A new, totally unexpected, and extremely simple question all at once bewildered and bitterly astonished him:

"If indeed this whole thing was done consciously and not foolheadedly, if you indeed had a definite and firm objective, then how is it that so far you have not even looked into the purse and do not know what you've actually gained, or for what you accepted all these torments and started out on such a mean, nasty, vile business? Weren't you going to throw it into the water just now, this purse, along with all the other things which you also haven't seen yet? . . . How is that?"

Yes, it was true; it was all true. However, he had even known it before, and it was by no means a new question for him; and when the decision had been made that night to throw it all into the water, it had been made without any hesitation or objection, but in such a way as if it had to be so, as if it even could not be otherwise . . . Yes, he knew all that, and he remembered it all; it had been just about decided yesterday, at the very moment when he was sitting over the trunk, pulling the cases out of it . . . Yes, it was true!

"It's because I'm very sick," he finally decided glumly. "I've tormented and tortured myself, without knowing myself what I'm doing . . . And yesterday, and the day before yesterday, and all this time I've been torturing myself . . . I'll get well and . . . stop torturing myself . . . And what if I never get well? Lord! I'm so tired of it all! . . ."

He walked on without stopping. He longed terribly for some distraction, but he did not know what to do or what to undertake. One new, insurmountable sensation was gaining possession of him almost minute by minute: it was a certain boundless, almost physical loathing for everything he met or saw around him, an obstinate, spiteful, hate-filled loathing. All the people he met were repulsive to him—their faces, their walk, their movements were repulsive. If anyone had spoken to him, he would probably just have spat at him, bitten him . . .

When he walked out to the embankment of the Little Neva, on Vasilievsky Island, near the bridge, he suddenly stopped. "Here's where he lives, in that house," he thought. "Well, well, I seem to have brought myself to Razumikhin! The same story all over again . . . It's very curious, however: did I mean to come, or did I simply walk and end up here? Makes no difference; I said . . . two days ago . . . that I'd go and see him the day after *that;* well, so I'll go! As if I couldn't go now . . ."

He went up to Razumikhin's on the fifth floor.

He was at home, in his closet, busy writing at the moment, and opened the door himself. They had not seen each other for about four months. Razumikhin stood there in a dressing gown worn to tatters, with shoes on his bare feet, disheveled, unshaved, and unwashed. His face showed surprise.

"What's with you?" he cried, looking his entering friend over from head to foot; then he paused and whistled.

"It's that bad, is it? You've even outdone me, brother," he added, looking at Raskolnikov's rags. "Sit down, you must be tired!" And when he collapsed onto the oilcloth Turkish sofa, which was even worse than his own, Razumikhin suddenly noticed that his guest was ill.

"But you're seriously ill, do you know that?" He began feeling his pulse; Raskolnikov pulled his hand back.

"Don't," he said. "I've come . . . the thing is, I have no lessons . . . I wanted . . . however, I don't need any lessons . . ."

"You know what? You're raving!" observed Razumikhin, who was watching him closely.

"No, I'm not raving." Raskolnikov got up from the sofa. It had not occurred to him as he was going upstairs to Razumikhin's that he would therefore have to come face-to-face with him. But now, in an instant, he realized from his earlier experience that he was least of all disposed at that moment to come face-to-face with anyone in the whole world, whoever it might be. All his bile rose up in him. He nearly choked with anger at himself as soon as he crossed Razumikhin's threshold.

"Good-bye!" he said suddenly, and went to the door.

"But wait, wait, you crank!"

"Don't! . . ." the latter repeated, pulling his hand back again.

"And why the devil did you come, then! Are you cracked or something? I'm . . . almost hurt. I won't let you go like that."

"Well, listen: I came to you because aside from you I don't know anyone who would help . . . to start . . . because you're kinder than the rest of them—smarter, that is—and you're able to talk about things . . . But now I see that I need nothing, do you hear, absolutely nothing . . . no favors, no concern from anyone . . . I myself . . . alone . . . And enough! Let me be, all of you!"

"But wait a minute, you chimney sweep! This is completely crazy! You can do as you like for all I care. You see, I don't have any lessons either, and to hell with it, but there's a bookseller in the flea market named Cherubimov, and he's a sort of lesson in himself. I wouldn't exchange him now for five merchants' lessons. He does a bit of publishing, brings out little books on natural science—and how they sell! The titles alone are priceless! Now, you've always maintained that I'm stupid: by God, brother, there are some that are stupider! And lately he's also hooked on to the trend; he doesn't know beans about it, but, well, naturally I encourage him. Now, here we have two sheets and a bit more of German text—the stupidest sort of charlatanism, in my opinion; in short, it examines whether woman is or is not a human being. Well, and naturally it solemnly establishes that she is a human being. Cherubimov is preparing it in line with the woman question; I'm doing the translating; he'll stretch these two and a half sheets to six, we'll concoct a nice, frilly title half a page long, and peddle it for fifty kopecks. It'll do! I'll get six roubles a sheet for the translation, making it fifteen roubles in all, and I took six roubles in advance. That done, we'll start translating something about whales; then we've marked out some of the dullest gossip from the second part of the *Confessions* for translation—somebody told Cherubimov that Rousseau is supposedly a Radishchev in his own way.[5] Naturally, I don't contradict—devil take him! So, do you want to translate the second sheet of *Is Woman a Human Being?*[6] If you do, take the text right now, take some pens and paper—it's all supplied—and take three roubles, because I took the advance for the whole translation, first and second sheets, so three roubles would be exactly your share. When you finish the sheet, you'll get another three roubles. And one more thing, please don't regard this as some sort of favor on my part. On the contrary, the moment you walked in, I already saw how you were going to be of use to me. First of all, my spelling is poor, and second, my German just goes kaput sometimes, so that I have to make things up on my own instead, my only consolation being that it comes out even better. But who knows, maybe it comes out worse instead of better . . . Are you going to take it or not?"

Raskolnikov silently took the German pages of the article, took the three roubles, and walked out without saying a word. Razumikhin gazed after him in astonishment. But, having gone as far as the First Line,[7] Raskolnikov suddenly turned back, went up to Razumikhin's again, placed both the German pages and the three roubles on the table, and again walked out without saying a word.

"Have you got brain fever or what?" Razumikhin bellowed, finally enraged. "What is this farce you're playing? You've even got me all screwed up . . . Ah, the devil, what did you come for, then?"

"I don't want . . . translations . . ." Raskolnikov muttered, already going down the stairs.

"What the devil do you want?" Razumikhin shouted from above. The other silently went on down.

"Hey! Where are you living?"

There was no answer.

"Ah, the devil! . . ."

But Raskolnikov was already outside. On the Nikolaevsky Bridge he was once more brought fully back to his senses, owing to an incident that was most unpleasant for him. He was stoutly lashed on the back with a whip by the driver of a carriage, for almost falling under the horses' hoofs even after the driver had shouted to him three or four times. The stroke of the whip made him so angry that, as he jumped to the railing (for some unknown reason he had been walking in the very middle of the bridge, which is for driving, not for walking), he snarled and bared his teeth spitefully. Of course, there was laughter around him.

"He had it coming!"

"Some kind of scofflaw!"

"You know, they pretend they're drunk and get under the wheels on purpose, and then you have to answer for it."

"They live from it, my good sir, they live from it . . ."

But at that moment, as he stood by the railing rubbing his back and still senselessly and spitefully watching the carriage drive away, he suddenly felt someone put money in his hand. He looked; it was an elderly merchant's wife in a kerchief and goatskin shoes, with a girl beside her in a little hat and holding a green parasol, probably her daughter. "Take it, my dear, in Christ's name." He took it, and they went on. It was a twenty-kopeck piece. From his clothes and appearance, they could well have taken him for a beggar, for a real collector of half kopecks in the street, and the offering of so much as twenty kopecks he doubtless owed to the stroke of the whip's having moved them to pity.

He clutched the twenty kopecks in his hand, walked about ten steps, and turned his face to the Neva, in the direction of the palace.[8] There was not the least cloud in the sky, and the water was almost blue, which rarely happens with the Neva. The dome of the cathedral, which is not outlined so well from any other spot as when looked at from here, on the bridge, about twenty paces from the chapel, was simply shining, and through the clear air one could even make out each of its ornaments distinctly.[9] The pain from the whip subsided, and Raskolnikov forgot about the blow; one troublesome and not entirely clear thought now occupied him exclusively. He stood and looked long and intently into the distance; this place was especially familiar to him. While he was attending the university, he often used to stop, mostly on his way home, at precisely this spot (he had done it perhaps a hundred times), and gaze intently at the indeed splendid panorama, and to be surprised almost every time by a certain unclear and unresolved impression. An inexplicable chill always breathed on him from this splendid panorama; for him the magnificent picture was filled with a mute and deaf spirit . . . He marveled each time at this gloomy and mysterious impression, and, mistrusting himself, put off the unriddling of it to some future time. Now suddenly he abruptly recalled these former questions and perplexities, and it seemed no accident to him that he should recall them now. The fact alone that he had stopped at the same spot as before already seemed wild and strange to him, as if indeed he could imagine thinking now about the same things as before, and being interested in the same themes and pictures he had been interested in . . . still so recently. He even felt almost like laughing, yet at the same time his chest was painfully constricted. It was as if he now saw all his former past, and former thoughts, and former tasks, and former themes, and former impressions, and this whole panorama, and himself, and everything, everything, somewhere far down below, barely visible under his feet . . . It seemed as if he were flying upwards somewhere, and everything was vanishing from his sight . . . Inadvertently moving his hand, he suddenly felt the twenty-kopeck piece clutched in his fist. He opened his hand, stared at the coin, swung, and threw it into the water; then he turned and went home. It seemed to him that at that moment he had cut himself off, as with scissors, from everyone and everything.

He reached home only towards evening, which meant he had been walking for about six hours. Of where and how he came back, he remembered nothing. He undressed and, shivering all over like a spent horse, lay down on the sofa, pulled the greatcoat over him, and immediately sank into oblivion . . .

In the dark of evening he was jolted back to consciousness by terrible shouting. God, what shouting it was! Never before had he seen or heard such unnatural noises, such howling, screaming, snarling, tears, blows, and curses. He could never even have imagined such beastliness, such frenzy. In horror, he raised himself and sat up on his bed, tormented, and with his heart sinking every moment. But the fighting, screaming, and swearing grew worse and worse. And then, to his great amazement, he suddenly made out his landlady's voice. She was howling, shrieking, and wailing, hurrying, rushing, skipping over words, so that it was even impossible to make anything out, pleading for something—not to be beaten anymore, of course, because she was being mercilessly beaten on the stairs. The voice of her assailant became so terrible in its spite and rage that it was no more than a rasp, yet her assailant was also saying something, also rapidly, indistinctly, hurrying and spluttering. Suddenly Raskolnikov began shaking like a leaf: he recognized the voice; it was the voice of Ilya Petrovich. Ilya Petrovich was here, beating the landlady! He was kicking her, pounding her head against the steps—that was clear, one could tell from the sounds, the screaming, the thuds! What was happening? Had the world turned upside down, or what? A crowd could be heard gathering on all the floors, all down the stairs; voices, exclamations could be heard, people coming up, knocking, slamming doors, running. "But what for, what for, and how can it be?" he kept repeating, seriously thinking he had gone completely mad. But no, he could hear it too plainly! . . . But in that case it meant they would also come to him, "because . . . it must be on account of that same . . . on account of yesterday . . . Lord!" He would have liked to fasten the hook on his door, but he was unable to raise his arm . . . besides, it was useless! Fear, like ice, encased his soul, tormented him, numbed him . . . Then at last all this uproar, which had gone on for a good ten minutes, gradually began to subside. The landlady moaned and groaned; Ilya Petrovich still threatened and swore . . . Then at last he, too, seemed to grow subdued; then no more was heard from him. "Has he really gone? Lord!" Yes, now the landlady was going, too, still moaning and weeping . . . that was her door slamming shut . . . Now the crowd on the stairs was breaking up, going back to their apartments—exclaiming, arguing, calling to each other, raising their voices to a shout, then lowering them to a whisper. There must have been many of them; almost the whole house had gathered. "But, God, how can it all be! And why, why did he come here!"

Exhausted, Raskolnikov fell back on the sofa, but could no longer close his eyes; he lay for about half an hour in such suffering, such an unbearable feeling of boundless horror, as he had never experienced before. Suddenly a bright light shone in his room: Nastasya came in with a candle and a plate of soup. Looking at him closely and seeing that he was not asleep, she put the candle on the table and began setting out what she had brought: bread, salt, plate, spoon.

"I bet you haven't eaten since yesterday. You spent the whole day loafing about, and you shaking all over with fever."

"Nastasya . . . why were they beating the landlady?"

She looked at him intently.

"Who was beating the landlady?"

"Just now . . . half an hour ago, Ilya Petrovich, the police chief's assistant, on the stairs . . . Why was he beating her so? And . . . why was he here?"

Nastasya studied him silently, frowning, and went on looking at him like that for a long time. He began feeling very unpleasant, even frightened, under this scrutiny.

"Nastasya, why are you silent?" he finally said timidly, in a weak voice.

"It's the blood," she finally answered softly, as if speaking to herself.

"Blood! . . . What blood? . . ." he murmured, turning pale and drawing back towards the wall. Nastasya went on looking at him silently.

"No one was beating the landlady," she said, again in a stern and resolute voice. He looked at her, scarcely breathing.

"I heard it myself . . . I wasn't asleep, I was sitting up," he said even more timidly. "I listened for a long time . . . The police chief's assistant was here . . . Everyone came running out to the stairs, from all the apartments . . ."

"No one was here. It's the blood clamoring in you. When it can't get out and starts clotting up into these little clots, that's when you start imagining things . . . Are you going to eat, or what?"

He did not reply. Nastasya went on standing over him, looking at him steadily, and would not go away.

"Give me water . . . Nastasyushka."

She went downstairs and came back about two minutes later with water in a white earthenware mug; but he no longer remembered what happened next. He only remembered taking one sip of cold water and spilling some from the mug onto his chest. Then came unconsciousness.

III

HOWEVER, it was not that he was totally unconscious during the whole time of his illness: it was a feverish condition, with moments of delirium and semi-awareness. Afterwards he remembered a good deal. Once it seemed to him that many people were gathered around him and wanted to take him and carry him away somewhere, and there was much arguing and quarreling about him. Then suddenly he was alone in the room, everyone was gone, they were afraid of him, and only opened the door a crack from time to time to look at him, threaten him, arrange something among themselves, laugh and tease him. He remembered Nastasya being often with him; he also made out another person, who seemed very familiar, but precisely who it was he simply could not figure out, and he grieved over it, and even wept. At times it seemed to him that he had been lying there for at least a month, at other times that it was still the same day. But about *that*—about *that* he forgot completely; instead, he remembered every minute having forgotten something that must not be forgotten—he agonized, suffered, trying to remember, moaned, fell into a rage, or into terrible, unbearable fear. Then he tried to tear himself away, wanted to run, but there was always someone who stopped him by force, and he would fall into weakness and unconsciousness again. At last he fully recovered his senses.

This occurred in the morning, at ten o'clock. At that hour of the morning, on clear days, sunlight always came in a long stripe across the right wall of his room and lit up the corner by the door. Nastasya was standing at his bedside with another person, a man completely unknown to him, who was studying him with great curiosity. He was a young fellow in a caftan, with a little beard, and had the look of a company agent. The landlady was peeking through the half-opened door. Raskolnikov raised himself slightly.

"Who is this, Nastasya?" he asked, pointing to the fellow.

"Look, he's come to!" she said.

"He's come to!" echoed the agent. Realizing that he had come to, the landlady, who was peeking through the door, immediately closed it and hid herself. She had always been shy, and it was burdensome for her to endure conversations and explanations; she was about forty, round and fat, dark-browed, dark-eyed, kind out of fatness and laziness, and even quite comely. But unnecessarily bashful.

"Who . . . are you?" he continued to ask, addressing the agent himself. But at that moment the door was flung open again and Razumikhin came in, stooping a little because of his height.

"What a ship's cabin," he shouted, coming in. "I always bump my head; and they call it an apartment! So you've come to, brother? Pashenka just told me."

"He just came to," said Nastasya.

"He just came to," the agent agreed again, with a little smile.

"And who are you, sir, if you please?" Razumikhin asked, suddenly turning to him. "I, you may be pleased to know, am Vrazumikhin;[10] not Razumikhin, as everyone calls me, but Vrazumikhin, a student and a gentleman's son, and this is my friend. Well, sir, and who are you?"

"And I am the merchant Shelopaev's office agent, sir, here on business, sir."

"Take this chair, if you please." Razumikhin himself took the other, on the opposite side of the table. "So you've come to, brother, and it's a good thing you have," he went on, addressing Raskolnikov. "You hardly ate or drank anything for four days. Really, we gave you tea from a spoon. I brought Zossimov to you twice. Remember Zossimov? He examined you carefully and immediately said it was all trifles—something went to your head, or whatever. Some nervous nonsense, he says, or poor rations—they didn't dish you up enough beer and horseradish, hence the illness—but it's nothing, it'll go away, it'll all get through the hopper. Good old Zossimov! He's become quite a doctor! Well, sir, I don't want to keep you," he again turned to the agent, "will you kindly explain your errand? Note, Rodya, it's the second time they've sent someone from that office; only it wasn't this one before, it was someone else, and I talked with him. Who was it that came before?"

"Presuming it was two days ago, sir, that's right, sir, it would have been Alexei Semyonovich; he's also employed by our office, sir."

"And he seems to have a bit more sense than you do, wouldn't you say?"

"Yes, sir, he surely is a solider man, sir."

"Admirable. Well, sir, go on."

"Now then, sir, there's an order come through our office, by your mother's request, through Afanasy Ivanovich Vakhrushin, of whom I judge you've heard more than once, if you please, sir," the agent began, addressing Raskolnikov directly, "in the case that you're now in your right understanding, sir, to hand you over thirty-five rubles, sir, since Semyon Semyonovich, by your mother's request, received a notice to that effect from Afanasy Ivanovich, in the same way as before. You do know him, if you please, sir?"

"Yes . . . I remember . . . Vakhrushin . . ." Raskolnikov said pensively.

"You hear? He knows the merchant Vakhrushin!" Razumikhin exclaimed. "Of course he's in his right understanding! As a matter of fact, I see now that you, too, are a man of sense. Well, sir! It's always pleasant to hear intelligent talk."

"That same man, sir, Vakhrushin, Afanasy Ivanovich, by the request of your mama, who already did it once in the same way, through him, and he did not refuse this time either, sir, so the other day he sent notice from his parts to Semyon Semyonovich to give you thirty-five rubles, sir, in expectation of better things to come, sir."

"That 'in expectation of better things to come' came off better than anything else, though the part about 'your mama' wasn't too bad either. Well, what do you think, is he of completely sound mind, or not so completely? Eh?"

"I don't care, as for me, sir. Just so long as there's a little signature, sir."

"That he'll scribble for you. Have you got a book with you or something?"

"A book, sir, right here."

"Hand it to me. Now, Rodya, sit up. I'll support you. Scrawl your Raskolnikov for him, take the pen, brother, because we want money now more than a bear wants molasses."

"No need," Raskolnikov said, pushing the pen away.

"No need for what?"

"I won't sign."

"Pah, the devil, but we can't do without the signature!"

"I don't need . . . money . . ."

"You don't need money! Well, brother, that is a lie, and I'll be your witness! Don't worry, please, he's just . . . wandering again. By the way, the same thing happens to him when he's awake . . . You're a reasonable man, and we can guide him, I mean, simply guide his hand and he'll sign. Here we go . . ."

"By the way, I can come back some other time, sir."

"No, no, why trouble yourself. You're a reasonable man . . . Come on, Rodya, don't keep your visitor . . . look, he's waiting," and he seriously prepared to guide Raskolnikov's hand.

"No, don't, I'll do it myself . . ." he said, and he took the pen and signed the book. The agent laid out the money and departed.

"Bravo! And now, brother, do you want something to eat?"

"Yes," Raskolnikov answered.

"Have you got soup?"

"From yesterday," answered Nastasya, who had been standing right there all the while.

"With potatoes and rice?"

"With potatoes and rice."

"I know it by heart. Fetch your soup, and some tea as well."

"So I will."

Raskolnikov looked at everything with deep astonishment and dull, senseless fear. He decided to say nothing and wait for what would happen next. "I don't seem delirious," he was thinking, "this all seems real enough . . ."

In two minutes Nastasya came back with the soup and announced that tea would follow shortly. The soup arrived with two spoons, two plates, and a whole setting: salt, pepper, mustard for the beef, and so forth, which had not happened in such proper order for a long time. The tablecloth was clean.

"It wouldn't be a bad idea, Nastasyushka, if Praskovya Pavlovna dispatched us a couple of bottles of beer. We could do with a drink."

"Well, isn't he a fast one!" Nastasya muttered, and went to carry out the order.

Raskolnikov kept looking wildly and tensely about him. Meanwhile Razumikhin sat down next to him on the sofa, clumsy as a bear, put his left hand behind his head, though he was able to sit up by himself, and with his right hand brought a spoonful of soup to his mouth, having blown on it first so that he would not scald his tongue. But the soup was just barely warm. Raskolnikov greedily swallowed one spoonful, then a second, a third. After giving him several spoonfuls, however, Razumikhin suddenly stopped and declared that concerning any more he would have to consult Zossimov.

Nastasya came in carrying two bottles of beer.

"And will you have tea?"

"Yes, I will."

"Fetch us up some tea, too, Nastasya, because as far as tea is concerned, I think we can do without the medical faculty. Meanwhile, here's our beer!" He went back to his chair, pulled the soup and beef towards him, and started eating with as much appetite as though he had not eaten for three days.

"I, brother Rodya, now have dinner here like this every day," he mumbled as well as his beef-stuffed mouth would allow, "and it's all due to Pashenka, your little landlady, who honors me from the bottom of her soul. Naturally, I don't insist, but I don't protest either. And here's Nastasya with the tea. What a quick one! Want some beer, Nastenka?"

"Eh, deuce take you!"

"Some tea, then?"

"I wouldn't refuse."

"Pour some. Wait, I'll pour you some myself; sit down at the table."

He set things out at once, poured her tea, poured another cup, abandoned his breakfast, and went and sat on the sofa again. He put his left hand behind the sick man's head as before, raised him up, and began giving him tea from a spoon, again blowing on each spoonful repeatedly and with a special zeal, as though it were this process of blowing that constituted the main and saving point for recovery. Raskolnikov was silent and did not resist, though he felt strong enough to raise himself and sit on the sofa without any external help, strong enough not only to hold the spoon or the cup, but perhaps even to walk. But from some strange, almost animal cunning, it suddenly occurred to him to conceal his strength for the time being, to lie low, to pretend, if necessary, that he had even not quite recovered his wits, and meanwhile to listen and learn what was going on there. However, he was unable to control his loathing: having swallowed about ten spoonfuls of tea, he suddenly freed his head, pushed the spoon away testily, and fell back on the pillow. Under his head there now indeed lay real pillows—down pillows, in clean pillowcases; this, too, he noticed and took into consideration.

"Pashenka must send us up some raspberry preserve today, to make a drink for him," Razumikhin said, taking his chair again and going back to his soup and beer.

"And where is she going to get raspberries for you?" Nastasya asked, holding the saucer on her five outspread fingertips and sucking tea from it "through the sugar."[11]

"In the shop, my friend, that's where she'll get raspberries. You see, Rodya, a whole story has gone on here in your absence. When you ran out on me in such a rascally fashion, without even telling me your address, I suddenly got so mad that I resolved to find you and punish you. I started out that same day. I walked and walked, asked and asked! This apartment, the present one, I forgot about; I'd never have remembered it anyway, because I never knew about it. Well, and the previous one—I only remembered that it was near the Five Corners,[12] in Kharlamov's house. I searched and searched for this Kharlamov's house—and it turned out finally that it wasn't Kharlamov's house at all, but Buch's—that's how sounds can confuse you! So I got angry. I got angry and went the next day to try my luck at the address bureau, and what do you think: in two minutes they found you for me. They've got you registered."

"Registered!"

"Sure enough; but General Kobelev just refused to be found while I was there! Well, sir, it's a long story. Anyway, when I landed here, I immediately got to know about all your affairs; all of them, brother, all of them, I know everything, the girl here saw it—Ilya Petrovich was pointed out to me, Nikodim Fomich is my acquaintance now, and so is the caretaker, and Mr. Zamyotov, Alexander Grigorievich, the clerk in the local office, and finally Pashenka—to crown it all. The girl here knows . . ."

"He sweet-talked her," Nastasya muttered, grinning mischievously.

"Put that into your tea, Nastasya Nikiforovna."

"Go on, you dog!" Nastasya suddenly cried, and burst out laughing. "And I'm Petrovna, not Nikiforovna," she added suddenly, once she stopped laughing.

"We shall cherish that fact, ma'am. And so, brother, to avoid being superfluous, I first wanted to blast this whole place with electricity and wipe out all the prejudice in the local neighborhood at once; but Pashenka prevailed. I'd never have suspected she could be such a . . . winsome little thing . . . Eh, brother? What do you think?"

Raskolnikov remained silent, though he never for a moment tore his anxious eyes from him, and now went on stubbornly staring at him.

"Very much so, in fact," Razumikhin continued, not in the least embarrassed by the silence, and as if agreeing with the answer he had received, "and even quite all right, in all respects."

"Ah, the beast!" Nastasya cried out again, the conversation apparently affording her some inexplicable delight.

"Too bad you didn't know how to go about it from the very beginning, brother. That wasn't the right way with her. She is, so to speak, a most unexpected character! Well, her character can wait . . . Only how did it come about, for instance, that she dared to stop sending you your dinner? Or that promissory note, for example? You must be crazy to go signing any promissory notes! Or that proposed marriage, for example, when the daughter, Natalia Yegorovna, was still alive . . . I know everything! However, I see I'm touching a sensitive chord, and I am an ass; forgive me. Speaking of stupidity, incidentally, Praskovya Pavlovna is not at all as stupid as one might take her to be at first sight—eh, brother? Wouldn't you agree?"

"Yes . . ." Raskolnikov said through his teeth, looking away, but realizing that it was to his advantage to keep up the conversation.

"Isn't it the truth?" Razumikhin cried out, obviously happy to have received an answer. "But not very intelligent either, eh? A totally, totally unexpected character! I'm somewhat at a loss, brother, I assure you . . . She's got to be at least forty. She says thirty-six—and she has every right to. By the way, I swear to you that I'm judging her only mentally, by metaphysics alone; she and I have got such an emblem started here, you can forget about your algebra! I don't understand a thing! Well, it's all nonsense; only seeing that you were no longer a student, that you'd lost your lessons, and your outfit, and that after the girl's death there was no point in keeping you on a family footing, she suddenly got scared; and since you, for your part, hid yourself in a corner and wouldn't maintain things as before, she got a notion to chase you out of the apartment. And she'd been nursing that intention for a long time, but then she would have been sorry to lose the promissory note. Besides, you yourself kept assuring her that your mother would pay . . ."

"It was my own baseness that made me say that . . . My mother is nearly a beggar herself . . . and I was lying, so as to be kept on in this apartment and . . . be fed," Raskolnikov uttered loudly and distinctly.

"Well, that was only reasonable. But the whole catch was that Mr. Chebarov, court councillor and a man of business, turned up just at that moment. Pashenka would never have thought of anything without him; she's too bashful; well, but a man of business is not bashful, and he naturally asked her straight off: Is there any hope that this little note can be realized? Answer: There is, because there's this mama, who will help Rodya out with her hundred and twenty-five rouble pension even if she must go without eating herself, and there's this dear sister, who would sell herself into slavery for her dear brother. And he started from there . . . Why are you fidgeting? I've found out all your inner-most secrets now, brother; it was not for nothing that you opened your heart to Pashenka while you were still on a family footing with her, and I'm saying it out of love now . . . That's just the point: an honest and sensitive man opens his heart, and the man of business listens and goes on eating—and then he eats you up. So she let Chebarov have this little note, supposedly as payment, and he, feeling no shame, went and made a formal claim on it. When I found all that out, I wanted to give him a blast, too, just for conscience's sake, but around that time Pa-shenka and I got our harmony going, so I called a halt to the whole business, I mean at its very source, by vouching that you would pay. I vouched for you, brother, do you hear? We sent for Chebarov, stuck ten bills in his teeth, got the paper back, and here, I have the honor of presenting it to you—your word is good now—so, here, take it, I've even torn it a little, the way it's officially done."

Razumikhin laid the promissory note out on the table; Raskolnikov glanced at it and, without saying a word, turned his face to the wall. Even Razumikhin winced.

"I see, brother," he said after a moment, "that I have made a fool of myself again. I hoped to distract you and amuse you with my babbling, but it seems I've just stirred your bile."

"Was it you I didn't recognize in my delirium?" Raskolnikov asked, also after a moment's pause and without turning back again.

"It was me, and you even got into a frenzy then, especially the time I brought Zamyotov."

"Zamyotov? . . . The clerk? . . . What for?" Raskolnikov quickly turned and fixed his eyes on Razumikhin.

"But what's wrong with . . . Why be so worried? He wanted to make your acquaintance; he wanted it himself, because I talked about you a lot with him . . . Otherwise, who would have told me so much about you? He's a nice fellow, brother, quite a wonderful one . . . in his own way, naturally. We're friends now; we see each other almost every day. Because I've moved into this neighborhood. You didn't know yet? I've just moved. We've called on Laviza twice. Remember Laviza, Laviza Ivanovna?"

"Was I raving about something?"

"Sure enough! You were out of your mind, sir."

"What did I rave about?"

"Come now! What did he rave about? You know what people rave about . . . Well, brother, let's not waste any more time. To business!"

He got up from his chair and grabbed his cap.

"What did I rave about?"

"You just won't let go! Afraid about some secret, are you? Don't worry, you didn't say anything about the countess. But about some bulldog, and about some earrings and chains, and about Krestovsky Island, and about some caretaker or other, and about Nikodim Fomich, and about Ilya Petrovich, the police chief's assistant—there was quite a bit of talk about them. And, what's more, you were extremely interested in your own sock, extremely! You kept begging: 'Please, just give it to me.' Zamyotov himself went looking in all the corners for your socks, and handed you that trash with his own perfumed and be-ringed little hands. Only then did you calm down, and you went on clutching that trash in your hands day and night; you wouldn't part with it. It's probably still lying somewhere under your blanket. And then you also begged for some fringe for your trousers, and so tearfully! We tried to get you to say what sort of fringe it was, but we couldn't make anything out . . . Well, sir, and so to business! Here we have thirty-five roubles. I'm taking ten of them, and in about two hours I'll present you with an accounting for them. Meanwhile, I'll let Zossimov know, though he should have been here long ago, because it's already past eleven. And you, Nastenka, stop and see him as often as you can while I'm gone, find out if he needs anything to drink, or whatever . . . And I'll tell Pashenka what's needed myself. Good-bye!"

"Calls her Pashenka! Ah, you slyboots!" Nastasya said to his back; then she opened the door and began eavesdropping, but she could not restrain herself and ran downstairs. She was too eager to know what he was saying to the landlady; and generally it was clear that she was completely charmed by Razumikhin.

No sooner had the door closed behind her than the sick man threw off his blanket and jumped from his bed as if half crazed. With burning, convulsive impatience he had been waiting for them to leave, so that he could immediately get down to business in their absence. But get down to what? What business? That, of all things, he now seemed to have forgotten. "Lord! only tell me one thing: do they know all about it, or do they not know yet? And what if they already know and are just pretending, taunting me while I'm lying here, and are suddenly going to come in and say that everything has long been known and that they were just . . . What must I do now, then? I've forgotten, of all things; I remembered a moment ago, and suddenly forgot! . . ."

He stood in the middle of the room, looking around in painful bewilderment; he went over to the door, opened it, listened; but that was not it. Suddenly, as if recollecting, he rushed to the corner where the hole in the wallpaper was, began examining everything, thrust his hand into the hole, felt around in it, but that was not it either. He went to the stove, opened it, and began feeling around in the ashes: the bits of frayed cuff from his trousers and the torn pieces of his pocket were still lying there as he had thrown them in, so no one had looked there! Then he remembered the sock that Razumikhin had just been telling him about. Sure enough, there it was lying on the sofa under the blanket, but it had gotten so rubbed and dirty in the meantime that Zamyotov certainly could not have noticed anything.

"Bah, Zamyotov! . . . the office! . . . And why are they calling me to the office? Where is the summons? Bah! . . . I've mixed it all up: they summoned me before! I examined the sock that time, too, and now . . . now I've been sick. And why did Zamyotov come here? Why did Razumikhin bring him?" he was muttering weakly, sitting down on the sofa again. "What is it? Am I still delirious, or is this real? It seems real . . . Ah, I remember: I must flee, flee quickly! I must, I must flee! Yes . . . but where? And where are my clothes? No boots! They took them away! Hid them! I understand! Ah, here's my coat—they missed it! Here's the money on the table, thank God! Here's the promissory note . . . I'll take the money and leave, and rent another apartment, and they won't find me! But what about the address bureau? They will find me! Razumikhin will. Better to flee altogether . . . far away . . . to America, and spit on all of them! And take the promissory note with me . . . it will be useful there. What else shall I take? They think I'm sick! They don't know I can walk, heh, heh, heh! . . . I could tell by their eyes that they know everything! If only I can manage to get downstairs! But what if they have guards standing there—policemen! What's this, tea? Ah, there's some beer left, half a bottle, cold!"

He grabbed the bottle, which still held enough for a full glass, and delightedly emptied it at one gulp, as if extinguishing a fire in his chest. But in less than a minute the beer went to his head, and a light and even pleasant chill ran down his spine. He lay back and pulled the blanket over him. His thoughts, ill and incoherent to begin with, were becoming more and more confused, and sleep, light and pleasant, soon enveloped him. He settled his head delightedly on the pillow, wrapped himself tightly in the soft, quilted blanket that covered him now in place of the former tattered greatcoat, and fell into a deep, sound, healing sleep.

He woke up on hearing someone come into his room, opened his eyes, and saw Razumikhin, who had flung the door wide open and was standing on the threshold, uncertain whether he should enter or not. Raskolnikov quickly raised himself on the sofa and looked at him as if he were trying hard to recall something.

"Ah, since you're not asleep, here I am! Nastasya, drag that bundle up here!" Razumikhin called down to her. "You'll have the accounting presently . . ."

"What time is it?" Raskolnikov asked, looking around in alarm.

"You had yourself a good sleep, brother; it's evening outside, must be around six o'clock. You've slept more than six hours . . ."

"Lord! What's the matter with me! . . ."

"And why not? You're welcome to it! Are you in a hurry? Seeing a girl, or something? We've got all the time in the world. I've been waiting for you three hours already; I looked in twice, but you were asleep. I stopped twice at Zossimov's—no one home, and that's that! Never mind, he'll come! . . . I also did some little errands of my own. I got moved in today, completely moved in, with my uncle. I have an uncle now . . . So, well, devil take it, now to business! . . . Give me the bundle, Nastenka. Here we go . . . And how are you feeling, brother?"

"I'm well. I'm not sick . . . Listen, Razumikhin, were you here long?"

"Three hours, I told you."

"No, but before?"

"Before when?"

"How long have you been coming here?"

"But I told you all that earlier; don't you remember?"

Raskolnikov fell to thinking. The morning appeared to him as in a dream. He could not recall it by himself, and looked questioningly at Razumikhin.

"Hm!" said the latter, "he forgot! I rather fancied this morning that you still weren't in your right ... Now that you've slept, you're better ... Really, you look all better. Good boy! Well, to business! You'll remember now. Look here, my dear man."

He began untying the bundle, which appeared to interest him greatly.

"Believe me, brother, I've taken this especially to heart. Because we have to make a human being out of you, after all. Let's get started: we'll begin from the top. Take a look at this little chapeau," he began, pulling a rather nice but at the same time very ordinary and cheap cap from the bundle. "Allow me to try it on you."

"Later, after," Raskolnikov spoke, peevishly waving it away.

"No, no, brother Rodya, don't resist, later will be too late; besides, I won't be able to sleep all night, because I bought it without any measurements, at a guess. Just right!" he exclaimed triumphantly, having tried it on him. "Just the right size! Headgear, brother, is the foremost thing in an outfit, a recommendation in its way. Every time my friend Tolstyakov goes into some public place where everyone else is standing around in hats and caps, he's forced to remove his lid. Everyone thinks he does it out of slavish feelings, but it's simply because he's ashamed of that bird's nest of his—such a bashful man! Well, Nastenka, here's two examples of headgear for you: this Palmerston" (he took from the corner Raskolnikov's battered top hat, which for some unknown reason he called a Palmerston), "and this piece of jewelrywork. Give us an estimate, Rodya; how much do you think I paid for it? Nastasyushka?" he turned to her, seeing that the other said nothing.

"Offhand I'd say twenty kopecks," Nastasya replied.

"Twenty kopecks? Fool!" he cried, getting offended. "Even you would cost more than twenty kopecks these days—eighty kopecks! And that's only because it's second-hand. True, there's one condition: if you wear this one out, next year they'll give you another for nothing, by God! Well, sir, now let's start on the United Pants of America, as we used to call them in school. I warn you, I'm proud of them," and he displayed before Raskolnikov a pair of gray trousers, made of light-weight summer wool. "Not a hole, not a spot, and though they've seen some wear, they're quite acceptable—and there's a matching waistcoat, the same color, as fashion dictates. And the truth is they're even better second-hand: softer, tenderer . . . You see, Rodya, to make a career in the world, it's enough, in my opinion, if you always observe the season; don't ask for asparagus in January, and you'll have a few more bills in your purse; the same goes for this purchase. The season now is summer, so I made a summer purchase, because by fall the season will call for warmer material anyway, and you'll have to throw these out . . . more particularly because by then they'll have had time to fall apart anyway, if not from increased luxury, then from inner disarray. So, give me your estimate! How much do you think? Two roubles twenty-five kopecks! And, remember, again with the same condition: you wear these out, next year you get another pair free! At Fedyaev's shop they don't do business any other way: you pay once, and it's enough for your whole life, because in any case you'd never go back there again. Now, sir, let's look at the boots—how do you like them? You can see they've been worn, but they'll do for about two months, because they're foreign goods and foreign workmanship: a secretary from the British Embassy dumped them on the flea market last week; he'd worn them for only six days, but he was badly in need of money. Price—one rouble fifty kopecks. Lucky?"

"Maybe they won't fit!" Nastasya remarked.

"Won't fit? Look at this!" and he pulled Raskolnikov's old, stiff, torn, and mud-caked boot from his pocket. "I went equipped, and they reconstructed the right size from this monster. A lot of feeling went into this whole business. And with respect to linen, I made a deal with the landlady. Here are three shirts to begin with, hempen, but with fashionable fronts . . . So, sir, altogether that's eighty kopecks for the cap, two roubles twenty-five kopecks for the rest of the clothes, making it three roubles five kopecks in all; plus one rouble fifty kopecks for the boots—because they're so good. Four roubles fifty-five kopecks altogether, and five roubles for all the linen—I got it wholesale—so altogether it's exactly nine roubles fifty-five kopecks. Your change is forty-five kopecks in five-kopeck pieces—here, sir, be so good as to accept it—and thus, Rodya, you are now restored to your full costume, because in my opinion your coat will not only still serve, but even possesses a look of special nobility: that's what it means to buy from Charmeur![13] As for socks and the rest, I leave that up to you; we've got twenty-five nice little roubles left—and don't worry about Pashenka and the rent; I told you: the most unlimited credit. And now, brother, allow me to change your linen, because I think the only thing still sick about you is your shirt . . ."

"Let me be! I don't want to!" Raskolnikov waved his hands, having listened with loathing to Razumikhin's tensely playful account of purchasing the clothes . . .

"That, brother, is impossible; why else did I wear out all that good shoe-leather?" Razumikhin insisted. "Nastasyushka, don't be bashful, give me a hand, that's it!" and, in spite of Raskolnikov's resistance, he succeeded in changing his shirt. Raskolnikov fell back on the pillow and for about two minutes would not say a word.

"It'll be some time before they leave me alone!" he thought. "What money did you use to pay for all that?" he asked finally, staring at the wall.

"What money? I like that! It was your own money. An agent came this morning from Vakhrushin; your mother sent it; did you forget that, too?"

"I remember now . . ." Raskolnikov said, after long and sullen reflection. Frowning, Razumikhin kept glancing at him worriedly.

The door opened, and a tall, heavyset man came in, whose appearance also seemed already somewhat familiar to Raskolnikov.

"Zossimov! At last!" Razumikhin cried out with delight.

IV

ZOSSIMOV WAS a tall, fat man with a puffy, colorlessly pale, clean-shaven face and straight blond hair, wearing spectacles, and with a large gold ring on his fat-swollen finger. He was about twenty-seven years old. He had on a loose, foppish summer coat and light-colored summer trousers; generally everything on him was loose, foppish, and brand new; his linen was impeccable, his watch-chain massive. He was slow, almost languid, of manner, and at the same time studiously casual; a certain pretentiousness, though carefully concealed, kept showing itself every moment. All who knew him found him a difficult man, but said that he knew his business.

"I stopped twice at your place, brother . . . See, he's come to!" cried Razumikhin.

"I see, I see. So, how are we feeling now, eh?" Zossimov addressed Raskolnikov, looking at him attentively and sitting by his feet on the sofa, where he immediately sprawled as well as he could.

"Eh, he's still sulking," Razumikhin went on. "We just changed his shirt, and he almost started to cry."

"That's understandable; you might have waited with the shirt, if he didn't want . . . Pulse is fine. You still have a little headache, hm?"

"I'm well, I'm completely well!" Raskolnikov said insistently and irritably, raising himself suddenly on the sofa and flashing his eyes, but he immediately fell back on the pillow and turned his face to the wall. Zossimov was watching him attentively.

"Very good . . . everything's as it ought to be," he said languidly. "Has he eaten anything?"

They told him, and asked what he was allowed to have.

"Everything's allowed . . . soup, tea . . . no mushrooms, naturally, or cucumbers—well, and no need for any beef either, and . . . well, but what's there to talk about! . . ." He exchanged glances with Razumikhin. "No more medicine, no more anything; and tomorrow we'll see . . . Today wouldn't be . . . well, yes . . ."

"Tomorrow evening I'll take him for an outing!" Razumikhin decided. "To the Yusupov Garden, and then we'll go to the Palais de Cristal."[14]

"I wouldn't budge him tomorrow; though maybe . . . a little . . . well, we'll see."

"Too bad. I'm having a housewarming party tonight, just two steps away; he could come, too; at least he could lie on the sofa among us! And what about you?" Razumikhin suddenly addressed Zossimov. "Don't forget, you promised."

"Maybe a little later. What are you planning to have?"

"Nothing much—tea, vodka, pickled herring. There'll be a pie. For friends only."

"Who, precisely?"

"They're all from around here, and almost all of them new friends, actually—except maybe for the old uncle, and even he is new: came to Petersburg just yesterday on some little business of his; we see each other once in five years."

"What is he?"

"He's vegetated all his life as a provincial postmaster . . . gets some wretched pension, sixty-five years old, nothing to talk about . . . I love him, though. Porfiry Petrovich will be there, the local police inspector in the department of investigation . . . a lawyer. But I think you know . . ."

"He's also some sort of relative of yours?"

"A very distant one; but why are you frowning? So, you quarreled with him once, and now maybe you won't come?"

"I don't give a damn about him . . ."

"So much the better. And then some students, a teacher, one functionary, one musician, an army officer, Zamyotov . . ."

"Tell me, please, what you, or he, for instance" (Zossimov nodded towards Raskolnikov), "can possibly have in common with someone like Zamyotov?"

"Oh, these peevish ones! Principles! . . . You've all got principles in you like springs; you don't dare turn around by your own will; no, in my opinion, if he's a good man, there's a principle for you, and I don't want to know any more. Zamyotov is a most wonderful man."

"And he has an open palm."

"So what if he has an open palm! To hell with it! Who cares if he has an open palm!" Razumikhin suddenly cried, getting somehow unnaturally irritated. "Did I praise his open palm? I said he was a good man, only in his own way! And if we look straight, in all ways—will there be many good people left? No, in that case I'm sure that I, with all my innards, would be worth about as much as one baked onion, and then only with you thrown in! . . ."

"That's not enough; I'll give two for you . . ."

"And I'll give only one for you! Look at this wit! Zamyotov is still a boy, I can rough him up, because he ought to be drawn in and not pushed away. You won't set a person right by pushing him away, especially if he's a boy. You have to be twice as careful with a boy. Eh, you progressive dimwits, you really don't understand anything! You disparage man and damage yourselves . . . And if you'd like to know, we've even got something started together."

"I wonder what."

"It all has to do with the case of that painter—that house-painter, I mean . . . We're going to get him off! However, it won't be any trouble now. The case is perfectly clear now! We'll just put on some more heat."

"What about this house-painter?"

"You mean I didn't tell you? Really? Ah, that's right, I only told you the beginning . . . it's about the murder of the old woman, the pawn-broker, the official's widow . . . so now this house-painter is mixed up in it . . ."

"I heard about that murder before you, and am even interested in the case . . . somewhat . . . for a certain reason . . . and I've read about it in the papers! So, now . . ."

"They killed Lizaveta, too!" Nastasya suddenly blurted out, ad-dressing Raskolnikov. She had been standing in the room all the while, pressed up next to the door, listening.

"Lizaveta?" Raskolnikov muttered in a barely audible voice.

"Lizaveta, who sold things. She used to visit downstairs. She mended your shirts once."

Raskolnikov turned to the wall where, from among the little flowers on the dirty yellow wallpaper, he picked out one clumsy white flower with little brown lines and began studying it: how many leaves it had, what sort of serrations the leaves had, and how many little lines. There was no feeling in his arms and legs, as if they were paralyzed, but he did not even try to move and went on stubbornly staring at the flower.

"So what about the house-painter?" Zossimov interrupted Nas-tasya's babbling with some particular displeasure. She sighed and fell silent.

"They've also put him down as the murderer!" Razumikhin went on with fervor.

"They must have evidence or something?"

"The devil they have! Or, no, they precisely do have evidence, only this evidence is no evidence, that's what has to be proved! It's just the same as when they first picked up and suspected those, what's their names . . . Koch and Pestryakov. Pah! What a stupid way to do things; it's disgusting even for an outsider! Pestryakov may stop by my place today . . . Incidentally, Rodya, you know about this story, it happened just before your illness, exactly the day before you fainted in the office while they were talking about it . . ."

Zossimov glanced curiously at Raskolnikov; he did not move.

"And you know what, Razumikhin? You're a real busybody after all. Just look at you!" Zossimov remarked.

"Maybe so, but we'll still get him off!" Razumikhin shouted, banging his fist on the table. "Because you know what irks me the most about it? Not that they're lying; lying can always be forgiven; lying is a fine thing, because it leads to the truth. No, what irks me is that they lie and then worship their own lies. I respect Porfiry, but . . . What, for instance, was the first thing that threw them off? The door was locked, and when they came back with the caretaker it was unlocked. Well, so Koch and Pestryakov did the murder! That's their logic."

"Don't get so excited; they were simply detained; they couldn't just . . . Incidentally, I used to run into this Koch; so it turns out he bought unredeemed articles from the old woman, eh?"

"Yes, some sort of swindler! He also buys up promissory notes. A trafficker. Devil take him anyway! But this is what makes me so angry, do you understand? It's their routine that makes me angry, their decrepit, trite, inflexible routine . . . And here, just in this one case, it would be possible to open up a whole new way. From psychological facts alone one could show how to get on the right track. 'We have facts,' they say. But facts are not everything; at least half the game is knowing how to handle the facts!"

"And you know how to handle the facts?"

"But it's impossible to keep silent when you feel, palpably feel, that you could help with the case, if only . . . Ahh! . . . Do you know the case in detail?"

"I'm still waiting to hear about the house-painter."

"Yes, where was I! So, listen to the story: exactly three days after the murder, in the morning, while they were still nursing Koch and Pestryakov along—though they had both accounted for their every step; it was cryingly obvious—suddenly a most unexpected fact emerged. A certain peasant, Dushkin, the owner of a tavern across the street from that same house, came to the police with a jewelry case containing a pair of gold earrings, and with a whole tale to go with it: 'The day before yesterday, in the evening, some time after eight or thereabouts'—the very day and hour, you see?—'a workman, this painter, Mikolai, who had also stopped in earlier in the day, came running to me and brought me this box with gold earrings and little stones, and asked if he could pawn them for two roubles, and when I asked where he got them, he declared that he'd picked them up from the sidewalk. I didn't question him any more about it'—this is Dushkin speaking—'but I got him out one little note'—a rouble, that is—'because I thought if it wasn't me, he'd pawn them to someone else, and it makes no difference, because he'll drink it up anyway, and it's better if the thing stays with me—the deeper hidden, the closer to hand—and if something comes up, or there are any rumors, I can represent it at once.' Well, of course, that's all his old granny's dream, he's lying like a rug, because I know this Dushkin, he's a pawnbroker himself, and he receives stolen goods, and he filched a thirty-rouble article from Mikolai with no intention of 'representing' it. He simply got scared. But, devil take it, listen; Dushkin goes on: 'And that peasant there, Mikolai Dementiev, I know him since childhood, he's from our province, the Zaraisk district, because I'm from Riazan myself. And Mikolai's not a drunkard, but he does drink, and it was known to me that he was working in that house there, painting, him and Mitrei, the two of them being from the same parts. And when he got the rouble, he broke it straight off, drank two cups in a row, took the change, and left, and I didn't see Mitrei with him that time. And the next day I heard that Alyona Ivanovna and her sister Lizaveta was killed with an axe, and I used to know them, sir, and I got to wondering about the earrings—because we knew the deceased used to lend money on things like that. I went to their house and started making inquiries, cautiously, for myself, tiptoeing around, and first of all I asked if Mikolai was there. And Mitrei said Mikolai went on a spree, came home drunk at daybreak, stayed for about ten minutes, and left again, and Mitrei didn't see him after that and was finishing the job by himself. And their job is up the same stairway as the murder was, on the second floor. So I heard all that, but I didn't say nothing to nobody'—this is Dushkin speaking—'I just found out everything I could about the murder and went home again, still in the same doubts. And then this morning, at eight o'clock'—three days later, you see?—'Mikolai comes in, not sober, but not so drunk either, able to understand what's said to him. He sits down on the bench without a word. And besides him, right then there was just one stranger in the tavern, and another man, an acquaintance, asleep on a bench, and our two lads, sir. "Have you seen Mitrei?" I ask. "No, I haven't," he says. "You've been gone?" "Yes," he says, "since two days ago." "And where did you sleep last night?" "In Peski, with the boys from Kolomna."¹⁵ "So," I say, "where did you get those earrings?" "Found them on the sidewalk." But the way he says it don't ring true, and he's not looking at me straight. "And did you hear," I say, "thus and so happened that same night, and that same hour, up that same stairway?" "No, I didn't," and he listens with his eyes popping out, and suddenly he goes white as chalk. I'm telling him, and he's reaching for his hat and starting to get up. Right then I wanted to keep him there, so I said, "Wait, Mikolai, why don't you have a drink?" And I winked to the lad to hold the door, and I was getting out from behind the counter when he up and bolted on me, out into the street, and ran off down a back alley, and that's the last I saw of him. But I stopped doubting then, because the sin on him was clear . . .' "

"Sure enough! . . ." said Zossimov.

"Wait! Listen to the rest! Naturally, they set out hotfoot after Mikolai; Dushkin was detained, a search was carried out, and the same for Mitrei; they also ransacked the boys from Kolomna—then all at once, two days ago, Mikolai himself was brought in: he'd been detained near the ——sky Gate, at an inn. He'd gone in, taken off his cross, a silver one, and asked for a drink in exchange. They gave him one. A few minutes later a woman went out to the cow-shed and saw him through a crack in the wall of the adjoining shed: he'd tied his belt to a beam, made a noose, and was standing on a stump trying to put the noose around his neck. The woman screamed to high heaven; people came running: 'So that's what you're up to!' 'Take me to such-and-such police station, I'll confess everything.' So he was presented with all due honors at such-and-such police station—here, that is. And then this and that, who and what, how old are you—'Twenty-two'—and so on and so forth. Question: 'When you and Mitrei were working, did you see anyone on the stairs at such-and-such an hour?' Answer: 'Sure, some people maybe passed by, not so's we noticed.' 'And did you hear anything, any noise, or whatever?' 'Nothing special.' 'And was it known to you, Mikolai, that on such-and-such a day and hour, the widow so-and-so was murdered and robbed, and her sister as well?' 'No, sir, I never knew nothing about that, I first heard it from Afanasy Pavlovich three days after, in the tavern.' 'And where did you get the earrings?' 'Found them on the sidewalk.' 'Why didn't you come to work with Mitrei the next day?' 'Because I went on a spree.' 'Where?' 'In such-and-such.' 'Why did you run away from Dushkin?' 'Because then I got real scared.' 'Scared of what?' 'Having the law on me.' 'Why would you be scared if you felt you weren't guilty of anything? . . .' Now, you may believe it or not, Zossimov, but this question was asked, and literally in those words—I know positively, it was told to me accurately! How do you like that, eh? How do you like it?"

"Well, no, all the same there is evidence."

"But I'm not talking about evidence now, I'm talking about the question, about how they understand their essence! Ah, devil take it! . . . Well, so they pushed him and pushed him, pressed him and pressed him, and so he confessed: 'I didn't find them on the sidewalk, I found them in the apartment there where Mitrei and me was painting.' 'How was that?' 'It was just like this, that Mitrei and me was painting and painting all day till eight o'clock, and was just about to go, and Mitrei took the brush and slapped some paint on my mug; so he slapped some paint on my mug and ran away, and I ran after him. So I was running after him, shouting my head off; and when I turned from the stairs to the gateway, I ran smack into the caretaker and some gentlemen, and how many gentlemen it was I don't remember, and the caretaker swore at me for that, and the other caretaker also swore at me, and the caretaker's woman came out and swore at us, too, and there was a gentleman coming in the gate with a lady, and he also swore at us, because me and Mitka was lying there and blocking the way: I grabbed Mitka's hair and pulled him down and started punching him, and Mitka was under me and grabbed my hair and started punching me, and not because we was mad, it was all real friendly, for the fun of it. And then Mitka got free and ran out to the street, and I ran after him but I couldn't catch him, so I went back to the apartment by myself, because we had to tidy up. I started picking up and waiting for Mitrei, in case he came back. And by the door to the entryway, behind the wall, in the corner, I stepped on a box. I looked and it was lying there wrapped up in paper. I took the paper off, and saw these tiny little hooks, so I undid the hooks—and there was earrings inside the box . . ."

"Behind the door? It was behind the door? Behind the door?" Raskolnikov suddenly cried out, staring at Razumikhin with dull, frightened eyes, and slowly raising himself on the sofa with the support of his arm.

"Yes . . . but why? What's the matter? Why are you looking like that?" Razumikhin also rose from his seat.

"Nothing! . . ." Raskolnikov answered, barely audibly, sinking onto the pillow again and again turning to the wall. Everyone was silent for a short while.

"He must have been dozing and suddenly woke up," Razumikhin said at last, looking questioningly at Zossimov; the latter made a slight negative movement with his head.

"Well, go on," said Zossimov. "What then?"

"So, what then? As soon as he saw the earrings, he immediately forgot both the apartment and Mitka, grabbed his hat, and ran to Dushkin, and, as we know, got a rouble from him, lied to him that he had found them on the sidewalk, and at once went on a spree. And about the murder he keeps repeating the same thing: 'I never knew nothing about that, I first heard about it three days after.' 'And why did you not come before now?' 'From fear.' 'And why did you want to hang yourself?' 'From thinking.' 'Thinking what?' 'That I'd have the law on me.' Well, that's the whole story. Now, what do you suppose they drew from it?"

"What is there to suppose? There's a trace there, something at least. A fact. You don't think they should let your painter go free?"

"But they've put him right down as the murderer now! They don't even have any doubts . . ."

"Nonsense; you're too excited. And what about the earrings? You must agree that if on that same day and hour the earrings from the old woman's trunk got into Nikolai's hands—you must agree that they got there somehow? That's no trifle in such investigations."

"Got there somehow! But how did they get there?" Razumikhin cried out. "And can it be that you, a doctor, you, whose first duty it is to study man, and who have the opportunity before anyone else of studying human nature—can it be that you do not see, from all these facts, what sort of character this Nikolai is? Can you not see from the very first that everything he testified to during the interrogation is the most sacred truth? They got into his hands exactly as he testified. He stepped on the box and picked it up."

"The most sacred truth? Nevertheless, he himself admitted that he lied at first."

"Listen to me, listen carefully: the caretaker, and Koch, and Pestryakov, and the other caretaker, and the first caretaker's wife, and the market woman who was sitting with her in the caretaker's room at the time, and the court councillor Kriukov, who got out of a carriage that same moment and was coming through the gateway arm in arm with a lady—all, meaning eight or ten witnesses, testify with one voice that Nikolai was holding Dmitri down, was lying on him and punching him, and that the other grabbed his hair and was also punching him. They were lying across the entrance, blocking the way; people swear at them from all sides, and they, 'like little children' (as the witnesses literally said), are lying on each other, squealing, fighting, and laughing, each one louder than the other, with the most ridiculous faces, and then they run out to the street, like children, chasing each other. Hear that? Now, pay strict attention: the bodies upstairs are still warm, you hear, still warm; they were found that way! If they killed them, or just Nikolai alone, and broke into the trunk besides and robbed it, or merely took part in the robbery somehow, then allow me to ask you just one question: does such a state of mind—that is, squeals, laughter, a childish fight under the gateway—does it fit with axes, with blood, with criminal cunning, stealth, and robbery? They had only just killed them, only five or ten minutes earlier—that's how it comes out, since the bodies are still warm—and suddenly, abandoning the bodies and the open apartment, and knowing that people have just gone up there, and abandoning the loot, they go rolling around in the street like little children, laughing, attracting everybody's attention, and there are ten unanimous witnesses to it!"

"Strange, certainly! Impossible, in fact, but . . ."

"No *buts*, brother, because if the earrings, which on that day and hour turned up in Nikolai's hands, do constitute important factual evidence against him—directly explained, however, by his own testimony, and therefore still *disputable evidence*—we must also take into consideration certain exonerating facts, all the more so in that these facts are *irrefutable*. But do you think, seeing the nature of our jurisprudence, that they will or can accept such a fact—based solely on psychological impossibility alone, and on state of mind alone—as an irrefutable fact, demolishing all incriminating and material facts whatsoever? No, they won't, not for anything, because they've found the box, and the man wanted to hang himself, 'which could only be because he felt guilty'! That's the capital question, that's why I get so excited! You must understand!"

"Oh, I do see that you're excited. Wait, I forgot to ask: what proof is there that the box with the earrings indeed came from the old woman's trunk?"

"It's been proved," Razumikhin answered, frowning and as if with reluctance. "Koch recognized the article and led them to the owner, and he proved positively that the article indeed belongs to him."

"That's bad. Now another thing: did anyone see Nikolai during the time that Koch and Pestryakov were upstairs, and can it be proved somehow?"

"That's just it, nobody saw him," Razumikhin answered with vexation, "that's the worst of it: even Koch and Pestryakov didn't notice them as they were going upstairs, though their testimony wouldn't mean much now. 'We saw that the apartment was open,' they say, 'that someone must have been working in it, but we didn't pay attention as we passed by, and we don't remember exactly whether the workers were there at the moment or not.' "

"Hm. So the only defense they have is that they were punching each other and laughing. Granted it's strong evidence, but . . . Then how, may I ask, do you explain the whole fact yourself? How do you explain the finding of the earrings, if he indeed found them as he testifies?"

"How do I explain it? But what is there to explain; the thing is clear!

At least the path the case should take is clear and established, and it's precisely the box that establishes it. The real murderer dropped the earrings. The murderer was upstairs when Koch and Pestryakov were knocking, and had locked himself in. Like a fool, Koch went downstairs; then the murderer jumped out and ran downstairs himself, since he had no other choice. On the stairs he hid from Koch, Pestryakov, and the caretaker in the empty apartment at the precise moment when Dmitri and Nikolai had gone running out of it, stood behind the door while the caretaker and the others were going upstairs, waited until their steps died away, then went down as calmly as you please, precisely at the same moment that Dmitri and Nikolai ran out to the street and everyone left and there was no one in the gateway. Maybe someone saw him, but without paying any attention—there were enough people going by! And he dropped the box out of his pocket while he was standing behind the door, and didn't notice that he'd dropped it because he had other things on his mind. But the box clearly proves that he was standing precisely there. That's the whole trick!"

"Clever, brother! Really clever! Couldn't be cleverer!"

"But why, why?"

"Because of the timing . . . the way it all falls together so nicely . . . just like a stage play."

"A-a-ah!" Razumikhin began to shout, but at that moment the door opened and a new person, unknown to anyone present, walked in.

V

THIS WAS a gentleman already well past his youth, prim, stately, with a wary and peevish physiognomy, who began by stopping in the doorway and glancing about with offensively unconcealed astonishment, as if asking with his eyes: "Where on earth have I come to?" Mistrustfully, and even with a pretense of being somewhat alarmed, even almost affronted, he looked around Raskolnikov's cramped and low "ship's cabin." After which, with the same astonishment, he shifted his gaze and fixed it upon Raskolnikov himself, undressed, unkempt, unwashed, lying on his meagre and dirty sofa, who was also staring motionlessly at him. Then, with the same deliberateness, he began staring at the disheveled, uncombed, unshaven figure of Razumikhin, who with insolent inquisitiveness looked him straight in the eye, not moving from where he sat. The tense silence lasted for about a minute; then at last, as might be expected, a slight change of scene took place. The newly arrived gentleman must have realized from certain, albeit rather sharp, indications, that in this "ship's cabin" his exaggeratedly stern bearing would get him precisely nowhere, and, softening somewhat, he turned and addressed Zossimov, politely though not without sternness, rapping out each syllable of his question:

"Mr. Rodion Romanych Raskolnikov, a student, or a former student?"

Zossimov slowly stirred himself and would perhaps have answered if Razumikhin, who had not been addressed at all, had not immediately prevented him.

"He's here, lying on the sofa! What is it you want?"

This offhanded "What is it you want?" simply floored the prim gentleman; he even almost turned to Razumikhin, but managed to catch himself in time and quickly turned back to Zossimov.

"This is Raskolnikov," Zossimov drawled, nodding towards the sick man, and he yawned, opening his mouth extraordinarily widely as he did so, and keeping it that way for an extraordinarily long time. Then he slowly drew his hand up to his waistcoat pocket, took out an enormous, convex, gold-lidded watch, opened it, looked, and as slowly and sluggishly put it back into his pocket.

Raskolnikov himself lay silently on his back all the while, staring obstinately, though without any thought, at the man who had come in. His face, now turned away from the curious flower on the wallpaper, was extremely pale and had a look of extraordinary suffering, as though he had just undergone painful surgery or had just been released from torture. But the newly arrived gentleman gradually began to elicit more and more attention from him, then perplexity, then mistrust, then even something like fear. And when Zossimov, pointing to him, said: "This is Raskolnikov," he suddenly raised himself quickly, as if jumping up a little, sat up on his bed, and spoke in an almost defiant, but faltering and weak voice:

"Yes! I am Raskolnikov! What do you want?"

The visitor looked at him attentively and said imposingly:

"Pyotr Petrovich Luzhin. I have every hope that by now my name is not wholly unfamiliar to you."

But Raskolnikov, who had been expecting something quite different, looked at him dully and pensively and made no reply, as though he were decidedly hearing Pyotr Petrovich's name for the first time.

"What? Is it possible that you have received no news as yet?" Pyotr Petrovich asked, wincing slightly.

In response to which Raskolnikov slowly sank back on the pillow, flung his hands up behind his head, and began staring at the ceiling. Anguish flitted across Luzhin's face. Zossimov and Razumikhin began scrutinizing him with even greater curiosity, and he finally became visibly embarrassed.

"I had supposed and reckoned," he began to drawl, "that a letter sent more than ten days ago, almost two weeks, in fact . . ."

"Listen, why do you go on standing in the doorway?" Razumikhin suddenly interrupted. "If you've got something to explain, do sit down; there's not room enough there for both you and Nastasya. Step aside, Nastasyushka, let him pass! Come in, there's a chair for you right here! Squeeze by!"

He pushed his chair back from the table, made a small space between the table and his knees, and waited in that somewhat strained position for the visitor to "squeeze" through the crack. The moment was chosen in such a way that it was quite impossible to refuse, and the visitor started through the narrow space, hurrying and stumbling. Having reached the chair, he sat down and eyed Razumikhin suspiciously.

"Anyway, you oughtn't to be embarrassed," Razumikhin blurted out, "it's the fifth day that Rodya's been sick, for three days he was delirious, but now he's come to and even got his appetite back. Here sits his doctor, he's just finished examining him; and I am Rodka's friend, also a former student, and presently his nurse; so you oughtn't to count us or be confused, but just go ahead and say what it is you want."

"Thank you. But shall I not disturb the sick man with my presence and conversation?" Pyotr Petrovich turned to Zossimov.

"No-o-o," Zossimov drawled, "you may even divert him." And he yawned again.

"Oh, he's been conscious for a long time, since morning!" continued Razumikhin, whose familiarity had the appearance of such unfeigned ingenuousness that Pyotr Petrovich reconsidered and began to take heart, perhaps also partly because the insolent ragamuffin had had time to introduce himself as a student.

"Your mama . . ." Luzhin began.

A loud "Hm!" came from Razumikhin. Luzhin looked at him questioningly.

"Nothing; never mind; go on . . ."

Luzhin shrugged.

". . . Your mama began a letter to you, myself being among them at the time. Having arrived here, I waited purposely for a few days before coming to see you, so as to be completely certain that you had been informed of everything; but now, to my surprise . . ."

"I know, I know!" Raskolnikov suddenly said, with an expression of the most impatient annoyance. "That's you, is it? The fiancé? So, I know! . . . and enough!"

Pyotr Petrovich was decidedly hurt, but held his tongue. He hastened to try and understand what it all meant. The silence lasted for about a minute.

Meanwhile Raskolnikov, who had turned slightly towards him when he replied, suddenly began looking him over again, attentively and with some special curiosity, as if he had not managed to look him over well enough before, or as if he had been struck by something new in him; he even raised himself from his pillow on purpose to do so. Indeed, there was some striking peculiarity, as it were, in Pyotr Petrovich's general appearance—namely, something that seemed to justify the appellation of "fiancé" just given him so unceremoniously. First, it was evident, and even all too noticeable, that Pyotr Petrovich had hastened to try to use his few days in the capital to get himself fitted out and spruced up while waiting for his fiancée—which, incidentally, was quite innocent and pardonable. Even his own, perhaps all too smug awareness of his pleasant change for the better could be forgiven on such an occasion, for Pyotr Petrovich did indeed rank as a fiancé. All his clothes were fresh from the tailor and everything was fine, except perhaps that it was all too new and spoke overly much of a certain purpose. Even the smart, spanking-new top hat testified to this purpose: Pyotr Petrovich somehow treated it all too reverently and held it all too carefully in his hands. Even the exquisite pair of lilac-colored, real Jouvain gloves[16] testified to the same thing, by this alone, that they were not worn but were merely carried around for display. In Pyotr Petrovich's attire, light and youthful colors predominated. He was wearing a pretty summer jacket of a light brown shade, light-colored summer trousers, a matching waistcoat, a fine, newly purchased shirt, a little tie of the lightest cambric with pink stripes, and the best part was that it all even became Pyotr Petrovich. His face, very fresh and even handsome, looked younger than his forty-five years to begin with. Dark side-whiskers pleasantly overshadowed it from both sides, like a pair of mutton chops, setting off very handsomely his gleaming, clean-shaven chin. Even his hair, only slightly touched with gray, combed and curled by the hairdresser, did not thereby endow him with a ridiculous or somehow silly look, as curled hair most often does, inevitably making one resemble a German on his way to the altar. And if there was indeed something unpleasant and repulsive in this rather handsome and solid physiognomy, it proceeded from other causes. Having looked Mr. Luzhin over unceremoniously, Raskolnikov smiled venomously, sank onto the pillow again, and went back to staring at the ceiling.

But Mr. Luzhin checked himself, and apparently decided to ignore all this strangeness for the time being.

"I am quite, quite sorry to find you in such a state," he began again, breaking the silence with some effort. "If I had known you were unwell, I would have come sooner. But, you know, one gets caught up! . . . Moreover, in my line as a lawyer, I have a rather important case in the Senate. Not to mention those cares which you yourself may surmise. I am expecting your relations—that is, your mama and sister—any time now . . ."

Raskolnikov stirred and wanted to say something; a certain agitation showed on his face. Pyotr Petrovich stopped and waited, but since nothing followed, he went on.

". . . Any time now. I have found them an apartment for the immediate future . . ."

"Where?" Raskolnikov said weakly.

"Quite near here, in Bakaleev's house . . ."

"That's on Voznesensky," Razumikhin interrupted, "there are two floors of furnished rooms; the merchant Yushin runs the place; I've been there."

"Yes, furnished rooms, sir . . ."

"Utterly vile: filth, stench, and a suspicious place besides; things have happened there; and devil knows who the tenants are! . . . I went there on a scandalous occasion myself. But it's cheap."

"I, of course, was not able to gather so much information, being new here," Pyotr Petrovich objected touchily, "but in any case they are two quite, quite clean little rooms, and since it is for quite a short period of time . . . I have already found a real, that is, our future apartment," he turned to Raskolnikov, "and it is now being decorated; and I myself am squeezed into furnished rooms for the time being, two steps away, at Mrs. Lippewechsel's, in the apartment of a young friend of mine, Andrei Semyonych Lebezyatnikov; it was he who directed me to Bakaleev's house . . ."

"Lebezyatnikov?" Raskolnikov said slowly, as if recalling something.

"Yes, Andrei Semyonych Lebezyatnikov, a clerk in the ministry. Do you know him perchance?"

"Yes . . . no . . ." Raskolnikov replied.

"Excuse me, but your question made it seem that you did. I once used to be his guardian . . . a very nice young man . . . up-to-date . . . I am delighted to meet young people: one learns what is new from them." Pyotr Petrovich looked hopefully around at those present.

"In what sense do you mean?" Razumikhin asked.

"In the most serious, so to speak, in the very essence of things," Pyotr Petrovich picked up, as if delighted to be asked. "You see, it has been ten years since I last visited Petersburg. All these new things of ours, reforms, ideas—all this has touched us in the provinces as well; but to see better, and to see everything, one must be in Petersburg. Well, sir, it is precisely my notion that one sees and learns most of all by observing our younger generations. And I confess I am delighted . . ."

"With what, exactly?"

"A vast question. I may be mistaken, but it seems to me that I find a clearer vision, more criticism, so to speak, more practicality . . ."

"That's true," Zossimov said through his teeth.

"Nonsense, there's no practicality," Razumikhin seized upon him. "Practicality is acquired with effort, it doesn't fall from the sky for free. And we lost the habit of any activity about two hundred years ago . . . There may be some ideas wandering around," he turned to Pyotr Petrovich, "and there is a desire for the good, albeit a childish one; even honesty can be found, though there are crooks all over the place; but still there's no practicality! Practicality is a scant item these days."

"I cannot agree with you," Pyotr Petrovich objected with visible pleasure. "Of course, there are passions, mistakes, but one must also make allowances: passions testify to enthusiasm for the cause, and to the wrong external situation in which the cause finds itself. And if little has in fact been done, there also has not been much time. Not to mention means. But it is my personal view, if you like, that something has been done: useful new ideas have been spread, and some useful new books, instead of the former dreamy and romantic ones; literature is acquiring a shade of greater maturity; many harmful prejudices have been eradicated and derided . . . In short, we have cut ourselves off irrevocably from the past, and that in itself, I think, is already something, sir . . ."

"All by rote! Recommending himself!" Raskolnikov said suddenly.

"What, sir?" asked Pyotr Petrovich, who had not caught the remark, but he received no reply.

"That is all quite correct," Zossimov hastened to put in.

"Is it not, sir?" Pyotr Petrovich continued, glancing affably at Zossimov. "You yourself must agree," he went on addressing Razumikhin, but now with the shade of a certain triumph and superiority, and he almost added "young man," "that there is such a thing as prosperity or, as they now say, progress, if only in the name of science and economic truth . . ."

"A commonplace!"

"No, it is not a commonplace, sir! If up to now, for example, I have been told to 'love my neighbor,' and I did love him, what came of it?" Pyotr Petrovich continued, perhaps with unnecessary haste. "What came of it was that I tore my caftan in two, shared it with my neighbor, and we were both left half naked, in accordance with the Russian proverb which says: If you chase several hares at once, you won't overtake any one of them.[17] But science says: Love yourself before all, because everything in the world is based on self-interest. If you love only yourself, you will set your affairs up properly, and your caftan will also remain in one piece. And economic truth adds that the more properly arranged personal affairs and, so to speak, whole caftans there are in society, the firmer its foundations are and the better arranged its common cause. It follows that by acquiring solely and exclusively for myself, I am thereby precisely acquiring for everyone, as it were, and working so that my neighbor will have something more than a torn caftan, not from private, isolated generosities now, but as a result of universal prosperity. A simple thought, which unfortunately has been too long in coming, overshadowed by rapturousness and dreaminess, though it seems it would not take much wit to realize . . ."[18]

"Sorry, wit is what I happen to lack," Razumikhin interrupted sharply, "so let's stop. I did have some purpose when I started talking, but all this self-gratifying chatter, this endless stream of commonplaces, and all the same, always the same, has become so sickening after three years that, by God, I blush not only to say such things, but to hear them said in my presence. Naturally, you've hastened to recommend yourself with regard to your knowledge; that is quite pardonable, and I do not condemn it. For the time being I simply wanted to find out who you were, because, you know, there are all sorts of traffickers hanging on to this common cause who in their own interest have so distorted everything they've touched that they have decidedly befouled the whole cause. And so, enough, sir!"

"My dear sir," Mr. Luzhin began, wincing with extreme dignity, "do you mean to suggest so unceremoniously that I, too . . ."

"Oh, heavens, heavens . . . How could I! . . . And so, enough, sir!" Razumikhin cut him off and turned abruptly to Zossimov, to continue their previous conversation.

Pyotr Petrovich proved intelligent enough to believe the explanation at once. But he resolved to leave in two minutes anyway.

"I hope that our acquaintance, which has presently begun," he turned to Raskolnikov, "will, upon your recovery and in view of circumstances known to you, continue to grow . . . I wish especially that your health . . ."

Raskolnikov did not even turn his head. Pyotr Petrovich began to get up from his chair.

"The killer was certainly one of her clients!" Zossimov was saying assertively.

"Certainly one of her clients!" Razumikhin echoed. "Porfiry doesn't give away his thoughts, but all the same he's interrogating the clients . . ."

"Interrogating the clients?" Raskolnikov asked loudly.

"Yes. What of it?"

"Nothing."

"How does he get hold of them?" asked Zossimov.

"Koch has led him to some; the names of others were written on the paper the articles were wrapped in; and some came on their own when they heard . . ."

"Must be a cunning and experienced rogue! What boldness! What determination!"

"But he's not, that's precisely the point!" Razumikhin interrupted. "That's what throws you all off. I say he was not cunning, not experienced, and this was certainly his first attempt! Assume calculation and a cunning rogue, and it all looks improbable. Assume an inexperienced man, and it looks as if he escaped disaster only by chance, and chance can do all sorts of things! Good God, maybe he didn't even foresee any obstacles! And how does he go about the business? He takes things worth ten or twenty roubles, stuffs his pockets with them, rummages in a woman's trunk, among her rags—while in the chest, in the top drawer, in a strongbox, they found fifteen hundred roubles in hard cash, and notes besides! He couldn't even rob, all he could do was kill! A first attempt, I tell you, a first attempt; he lost his head! And he got away not by calculation, but by chance!"

"It seems you're referring to the recent murder of the official's old widow," Pyotr Petrovich put in, addressing Zossimov. He was already standing, hat and gloves in hand, but wished to drop a few more clever remarks before leaving. He was obviously anxious to make a favorable impression, and vanity overcame his good sense.

"True. Have you heard about it?"

"Of course. It was in the neighborhood."

"You know the details?"

"I cannot say that I do; but there is another circumstance in it that interests me—a whole question, so to speak. I am not even referring to the fact that crime has been increasing among the lower classes over the past five years; I am not referring to the constant robberies and fires everywhere; what is most strange to me is that crime has been increasing among the upper classes as well, and in a parallel way, so to speak. In one place they say a former student intercepted mail on the highway; in another, people of advanced social position have been counterfeiting banknotes; then, in Moscow, a whole band is caught making forged tickets for the latest lottery—and among the chief participants is a lecturer in world history; then one of our embassy secretaries is murdered abroad, for reasons mysterious and monetary . . .[19] And now, if this old pawnbroker was killed by one of her clients, it follows that he is a man of higher society—because peasants do not pawn gold objects—and what, then, explains this licentiousness, on the one hand, in the civilized part of our society?"

"There have been many economic changes . . ." Zossimov responded.

"What explains it?" Razumikhin took up. "It might be explained precisely by an all too inveterate impracticality."

"How do you mean that, sir?"

"It's what your Moscow lecturer answered when he was asked why he forged lottery tickets: 'Everybody else is getting rich one way or another, so I wanted to get rich quickly, too.' I don't remember his exact words, but the meaning was for nothing, quickly, without effort. We're used to having everything handed to us, to pulling ourselves up by other men's bootstraps, to having our food chewed for us. Well, and when the great hour struck, everyone showed what he was made of . . ."

"But morality, after all? The rules, so to speak . . ."

"What are you so worried about?" Raskolnikov broke in unexpectedly. "It all went according to your theory!"

"How according to my theory?"

"Get to the consequences of what you've just been preaching, and it will turn out that one can go around putting a knife in people."

"Good God!" cried Luzhin.

"No, that's not so," echoed Zossimov.

Raskolnikov was lying pale on the sofa, his upper lip trembling; he was breathing heavily.

"There is measure in all things," Luzhin continued haughtily. "An economic idea is not yet an invitation to murder, and if one simply supposes . . ."

"And is it true," Raskolnikov again suddenly interrupted, his voice, trembling with anger, betraying a certain joy of offense, "is it true that you told your fiancée . . . at the same time as you received her consent, that above all you were glad she was poor . . . because it's best to take a wife up from destitution, so that you can lord it over her afterwards . . . and reproach her with having been her benefactor? . . ."

"My dear sir!" Luzhin, all flushed and confused, cried out angrily and irritably, "my dear sir . . . to distort a thought in such a fashion! Excuse me, but I must tell you that the rumors which have reached you, or, better, which have been conveyed to you, do not have even the shadow of a reasonable foundation, and I . . . suspect I know . . . in short . . . this barb . . . your mama, in short . . . Even without this, she seemed to me, for all her excellent qualities, incidentally, to be of a somewhat rapturous and romantic cast of mind . . . But all the same I was a thousand miles from supposing that she could understand and present the situation in such a perversely fantastic form . . . And finally . . . finally . . ."

"And do you know what?" Raskolnikov cried out, raising himself on his pillow and looking point-blank at him with piercing, glittering eyes, "do you know what?"

"What, sir?" Luzhin stopped and waited, with an offended and defiant air. The silence lasted a few seconds.

"Just this, that if you dare . . . ever again . . . to mention my mother . . . even a single word . . . I'll send you flying down the stairs!"

"What's got into you!" cried Razumikhin.

"Ah, so that's how it is, sir!" Luzhin became pale and bit his lip. "Listen to me, sir," he began distinctly, restraining himself as much as he could, but still breathless, "even earlier, from the first moment, I guessed at your hostility, but I remained here on purpose to learn still more. I could forgive much in a sick man, and a relation, but now . . . you . . . never, sir . . ."

"I am not sick!" Raskolnikov cried out.

"So much the worse, sir . . ."

"Get the hell out of here!"

But Luzhin was already leaving on his own, without finishing his speech, again squeezing between the table and the chair; this time Razumikhin stood to let him pass. Without looking at anyone, without even nodding to Zossimov, who for a long time had been shaking his head at him to leave the sick man alone, Luzhin went out, cautiously raising his hat just to shoulder height and ducking a little as he stepped through the doorway. And even the curve of his back at that moment seemed expressive of the terrible insult he was bearing away with him.

"Impossible, simply impossible!" the bewildered Razumikhin said, shaking his head.

"Leave me, leave me, all of you!" Raskolnikov cried out frenziedly. "Will you tormentors never leave me! I'm not afraid of you! I'm not afraid of anyone now, not of anyone! Away from me! Alone, I want to be alone, alone, alone!"

"Come on!" said Zossimov, nodding to Razumikhin.

"Good God, can we leave him like this?"

"Come on!" Zossimov repeated insistently, and he walked out. Razumikhin thought a little and ran after him.

"It might get worse if we don't do as he says," Zossimov said, already on the stairs. "He shouldn't be irritated . . ."

"What is it with him?"

"He needs some sort of favorable push, that's all! He was strong enough today . . . You know, he's got something on his mind! Something fixed, heavy . . . That I'm very much afraid of; most assuredly!"

"But maybe it's this gentleman, this Pyotr Petrovich! You could see from what they said that he's marrying his sister, and that Rodya got a letter about it just before his illness . . ."

"Yes; why the devil did he have to come now; he may have spoiled the whole thing. And did you notice that he's indifferent to everything, doesn't respond to anything, except for one point that drives him wild: this murder . . ."

"Yes, yes!" Razumikhin picked up, "of course I noticed it! He gets interested, frightened. He got frightened the very day of his illness, in the police chief's office; he passed out."

"Tell me about it in more detail this evening, and then I'll tell you a thing or two. He interests me, very much so! I'll come and check on him in half an hour . . . There won't be any inflammation, though . . ."

"My thanks to you! And I'll wait at Pashenka's meanwhile, and keep an eye on him through Nastasya . . ."

Raskolnikov, after they left, looked at Nastasya with impatience and anguish; but she still lingered and would not go away.

"Will you have some tea now?" she asked.

"Later! I want to sleep! Leave me . . ."

He turned convulsively to the wall; Nastasya went out.

VI

BUT AS SOON AS she went out, he got up, hooked the door, untied the bundle of clothing that Razumikhin had brought earlier and had tied up again himself, and began to dress. Strangely, he seemed suddenly to become perfectly calm; there was none of the earlier half-crazed delirium, nor the panicky fear of that whole recent time. This was the first moment of some strange, sudden calm. His movements were precise and definite; a firm intention shone through them. "Today, today! . . ." he muttered to himself. He realized, however, that he was still weak, but emotional tension, so strong in him that it had reached the point of calm, of a fixed idea, gave him strength and self-confidence; he hoped, all the same, that he would not collapse in the street. Having fully dressed, in all new things, he looked at the money lying on the table, reflected, and put it in his pocket. There were twenty-five roubles. He also took all the five-kopeck pieces left as change from the ten roubles Razumikhin had spent on the clothes. Then he quietly unfastened the hook, stepped out of the room, went down the stairs, and peeked through the wide open door into the kitchen: Nastasya was standing with her back to him, bending over the landlady's samovar and blowing on the coals. She did not hear anything. Besides, who could imagine he would leave? In another moment he was in the street.

It was about eight o'clock; the sun was going down. It was as stifling as before, yet he greedily inhaled the stinking, dusty, city-infected air. He began to feel slightly giddy; a sort of wild energy suddenly shone in his inflamed eyes and in his pale and yellow, emaciated face. He did not know and did not think about where he was going; he knew only one thing—that "all *this* must be ended today, at once, right now; otherwise he would not go back home, because he *did not want to live like that.*" Ended how? Ended by what? Of that he had no idea, nor did he want to think about it. He kept driving the thought away; the thought tormented him. He simply felt and knew that everything had to change, one way or another, "no matter how," he repeated with desperate, fixed self-confidence and resolution.

By old habit, following the usual course of his former walks, he headed straight for the Haymarket. Just before the Haymarket, on the sidewalk in front of a grocery shop, stood a dark-haired young organ-grinder, turning out some quite heartfelt love song. He was accompanying a girl of about fifteen, who stood in front of him on the sidewalk, dressed like a young lady in a crinoline, a little cape, gloves, and a straw hat with a flame-colored feather—all of it old and shabby. She was singing a love song in a cracked but rather pleasant and strong street singer's voice, hoping to get two kopecks from the shop. Raskolnikov stopped alongside two or three listeners, listened for a while, took out a five-kopeck piece, and put it in the girl's hand. She suddenly cut off her song on the highest and most heartfelt note, as with a knife, shouted a curt "Enough!" to the organ-grinder, and they both trudged on to the next shop.

"Do you like street singing?" Raskolnikov suddenly addressed one not too young passer-by, who had been standing with him near the barrel-organ and looked like an idler. The man stared at him wildly and with amazement. "I do," Raskolnikov went on, looking as if he were not talking about street singing at all, "I like hearing songs to the barrel-organ on a cold, dark, and wet autumn evening—it must be a wet evening—when all the passers-by have pale green, sickly faces; or, even better, when wet snow is falling, straight down, with no wind— you know?—and the gaslights are shining through it . . ."

"I don't know, sir . . . Excuse me . . ." the gentleman muttered, frightened both by the question and by Raskolnikov's strange look, and he crossed to the other side of the street.

Raskolnikov went straight on and came to the corner of the Haymarket where the tradesman and the woman, the ones who had been talking with Lizaveta that day, had their stand; but they were not there now. Having recognized the spot, he stopped, looked around, and addressed a young fellow in a red shirt who was yawning in the doorway of a miller's shop.

"That tradesman and the woman, his wife, keep a stand here at the corner, eh?"

"All kinds of people keep stands here," the fellow replied, looking Raskolnikov up and down superciliously.

"What's his name?"

"Whatever he was baptized."

"Are you from Zaraisk, too? What's your province?"

The fellow gave Raskolnikov another look.

"Ours isn't a province, Your Excellency, it's a district, but the strict one is my brother, not me, so I couldn't say, sir . . . Therefore I hope you'll be so magnanimous as to forgive me, Your Excellency."

"Is this a cook-shop, the place upstairs?"

"It's a tavern; they've got billiards, and princesses on hand . . . oh-la-la!"

Raskolnikov crossed the square. There, on the corner, stood a thick crowd of people, all of them peasants. He made his way into the very thick of them, peering into their faces. For some reason he felt drawn to talk with everyone. But the peasants paid no attention to him; they were all cackling to each other, bunching together in little groups. He stood, thought a moment, then went to the right along the sidewalk, in the direction of V——y. Once past the square, he found himself in an alley.

He often used to take this short alley, which made an elbow and led from the square to Sadovaya. Recently, he had even been drawn to loafing around all these places, when he was feeling sick at heart, so as to make it "all the more sickening." But now he was not thinking anything as he entered it. A big building there was given over entirely to taverns and other eating and drinking establishments; women came running out of them every other minute, wearing whatever was worn "around the neighborhood"—bareheaded and only in dresses. They crowded in groups at two or three places along the sidewalk, mostly near the basement stairways, where a couple of steps led down to various rather pleasurable establishments. In one of these, at that moment, a clatter and racket were going on for the whole street to hear—the strumming of a guitar, singing, and great merrymaking. A large group of women crowded around the entrance; some were sitting on the steps, others on the sidewalk, the rest stood talking together. A drunken soldier with a cigarette was loafing in the street nearby, swearing loudly; he seemed to want to go in somewhere but had apparently forgotten where. A ragamuffin was swearing at another ragamuffin, and there was a man lying dead drunk in the middle of the street. Raskolnikov stopped near the large group of women. They were talking in husky voices; all of them were wearing cotton dresses, goatskin shoes, and nothing on their heads. Some were over forty, but there were some younger than seventeen; almost every one of them had a black eye.

For some reason he was interested in the singing and all the clatter and racket there, downstairs . . . Through the shrieks and guffaws, to the accompaniment of the guitar and the thin falsetto of a rollicking song, came the sound of someone desperately dancing, beating time with his heels. He listened intently, gloomily, pensively, bending down at the entrance and peering curiously from the sidewalk into the entryway.

> "My soldier-boy so fine and free,
>   What cause have you for beating me!"

the singer's thin voice poured out. Raskolnikov wanted terribly to catch the words, as if that were all that mattered to him.

"Why don't I go in?" he thought. "They're laughing loudly! Drunk. Well, suppose I get drunk?"

"Won't you go in, dear master?" one of the women asked in a ringing, not yet quite husky voice. She was young and not even repulsive—she alone of the whole group.

"Well, well, here's a pretty one!" he replied, straightening up and looking at her.

She smiled; the compliment pleased her very much.

"You're a real pretty one yourself," she said.

"But so skinny!" another observed in a bass voice. "Just checked out of the hospital, or what?"

"Look, they're all generals' daughters, and snub-nosed every nose of them!" a newly arrived peasant suddenly interrupted, tipsy, his coat unbuttoned, and with a slyly laughing mug. "Here's some fun, eh?"

"Go in if you're going!"

"That I will, my sweeties!"

And he tumbled down the steps.

Raskolnikov started to move on.

"Listen, dear master!" the girl called after him.

"What?"

She became embarrassed.

"I'd always be glad to spend some time with you, dear master, but right now I can't seem to settle my conscience on you. Give me six kopecks for a drink, my nice young gentleman!"

Raskolnikov took out what happened into his hand: three five-kopeck pieces.

"Ah, such a kind master!"

"What's your name?"

"Ask for Duklida."

"Just look at that, will you," one woman in the group suddenly remarked, shaking her head at Duklida. "I don't know how any-one could ask like that! I think I'd just drop down from conscience alone . . ."

Raskolnikov looked curiously at the one who had spoken. She was a pockmarked wench of about thirty, all covered with bruises, and with a swollen upper lip. She pronounced her judgment calmly and seriously.

"Where was it," Raskolnikov thought as he walked on, "where was it that I read about a man condemned to death saying or thinking, an hour before his death, that if he had to live somewhere high up on a cliffside, on a ledge so narrow that there was room only for his two feet—and with the abyss, the ocean, eternal darkness, eternal solitude, eternal storm all around him—and had to stay like that, on a square foot of space, an entire lifetime, a thousand years, an eternity—it would be better to live so than to die right now! Only to live, to live, to live! To live, no matter how—only to live![20] . . . How true! Lord, how true! Man is a scoundrel! And he's a scoundrel who calls him a scoundrel for that," he added in a moment.

He came out on another street. "Hah! The 'Crystal Palace'! Razumikhin was talking earlier about the 'Crystal Palace.' Only what was it I wanted to do? Ah, yes, to read! . . . Zossimov said he read about it in the newspapers . . ."

"Do you have the newspapers?" he asked, going into a quite spacious and even orderly tavern with several rooms, all of them rather empty, however. Two or three customers were having tea, and in a farther room a group of some four men sat drinking champagne. Raskolnikov fancied that one of them was Zamyotov, but it was hard to tell from a distance.

"So what if it is!" he thought.

"Will you be having vodka, sir?" the waiter asked.

"Bring me tea. And some newspapers, old ones—say, from the last five days—and I'll leave you a good tip."

"Right, sir. Here are today's, sir. And some vodka, sir?"

The old newspapers and the tea appeared. Raskolnikov sat down and began searching: "Izler . . . Izler . . . Aztecs . . . Aztecs . . . Izler . . . Bartola . . . Massimo . . . Aztecs . . . Izler . . . pah, the devil! Ah, the short notices: woman falls down stairs . . . tradesman burns up with drink . . . fire in Peski . . . fire on the Petersburg side . . . another fire on the Petersburg side . . . another fire on the Petersburg side . . . Izler . . . Izler . . . Izler . . . Izler . . . Massimo . . . Ah, here . . ."[21]

He finally found what he wanted and started reading; the lines danced in front of his eyes, but he nevertheless finished the whole "news item" and greedily began looking in other issues for later additions. His hands trembled with convulsive impatience as he leafed through the pages. Suddenly someone sat down next to him at his table. He looked up—it was Zamyotov, the same Zamyotov, with the same look, with the signet rings, the watch-chains, the part in his black, curly, and pomaded hair, wearing a foppish waistcoat, a somewhat worn jacket, and not very fresh linen. He was cheerful; at least he was smiling cheerfully and good-naturedly. His dark-skinned face was a little flushed from the champagne he had been drinking.

"What! You here?" he began in perplexity, and in a tone suggesting they had known each other for ages. "Razumikhin told me just yesterday that you were still unconscious. How strange! And I was there at your place . . ."

Raskolnikov had known he would come over. He laid the newspapers aside and turned to Zamyotov. There was a smirk on his lips, and in that smirk the trace of some new, irritable impatience.

"I know you were," he replied, "I heard about it, sir. You looked for my sock . . . And, you know, Razumikhin's lost his head over you; he says you went with him to Laviza Ivanovna, the one you took such trouble over that time, winking to Lieutenant Gunpowder, and he couldn't understand, remember? Yet one wonders how he could possibly not understand—it was clear enough . . . eh?"

"And what a rowdy he is!"

"Who, Gunpowder?"

"No, your friend Razumikhin . . ."

"Nice life you've got for yourself, Mr. Zamyotov; a toll-free entry into the most pleasant places! Who was that pouring champagne into you just now?"

"Yes, we were . . . having a drink . . . Pouring, really!"

"An honorarium! You profit in all ways!" Raskolnikov laughed. "Never mind, sweet boy, never mind!" he added, slapping Zamyotov on the shoulder. "I'm not saying it out of malice; it's all 'real friendly, for the fun of it,' as your workman said when he was punching Mitka, the one in the old woman's case."

"How do you know about that?"

"Maybe I know more than you do."

"You're a strange one, you are . . . You must still be very sick. You shouldn't have gone out . . ."

"So I seem strange to you?"

"Yes. What's this, you're reading newspapers?"

"Newspapers."

"There's a lot about fires . . ."

"I'm not reading about fires." Here he gave Zamyotov a mysterious look; a mocking smile again twisted his lips. "No, not about fires," he went on, winking at Zamyotov. "And confess it, my dear young man, aren't you terribly anxious to know what I was reading about?"

"Not at all; I just asked. Can't I ask? Why do you keep . . ."

"Listen, you're an educated man, a literary man, eh?"

"I finished the sixth class in gymnasium," Zamyotov answered with some dignity.

"The sixth class! Ah, my little sparrow! With a part in his hair and rings on his fingers—a rich man! Pah, what a dear little boy!" Here Raskolnikov dissolved into nervous laughter right in Zamyotov's face. The latter drew back, not really offended, but very much surprised.

"Pah, what a strange fellow!" Zamyotov repeated, very seriously. "I think you're still raving."

"Raving? Nonsense, my little sparrow! . . . So I'm strange, am I? Well, and are you curious about me? Are you curious?"

"I'm curious."

"Then shall I tell you what I was reading about, what I was looking for? See how many issues I had them drag out for me! Suspicious, eh?"

"So, tell me."

"Are your ears pricked up?"

"Why pricked up?"

"I'll tell you why later, and now, my dear, I declare to you . . . no, better: 'I confess' . . . No, that's not right either: 'I give testimony, and you take it'—that's best! So, I give testimony that I was reading . . . I was interested in . . . I was searching . . . I was looking for . . ." Raskolnikov narrowed his eyes and paused: "I was looking—and that is the reason I came here—for news about the murder of the official's old widow," he finally uttered, almost in a whisper, bringing his face extremely close to Zamyotov's face. Zamyotov looked straight at him, point-blank, without moving or drawing his face back from Raskolnikov's face. What seemed strangest afterwards to Zamyotov was that their silence lasted for exactly a full minute, and that for exactly a full minute they sat looking at each other that way.

"Well, so what if you were?" he suddenly cried out in perplexity and impatience. "Why should I care? What of it?"

"It's that same old woman," Raskolnikov went on, still in a whisper, not moving at Zamyotov's exclamation, "the same one, remember, that you started telling about in the office, and I fainted. So, do you understand now?"

"But what do you mean? 'Understand' . . . what?" said Zamyotov, almost alarmed.

Raskolnikov's frozen and serious expression transformed in an instant, and he suddenly dissolved into the same nervous laughter as shortly before, apparently quite unable to restrain himself. And in a flash he recalled, with the extreme clarity of a sensation, that recent moment when he was standing with the axe behind the door, the hook was jumping up and down, the people outside the door were cursing and trying to force it, and he suddenly wanted to shout to them, curse at them, stick his tongue out, taunt them, and laugh loudly—laugh, laugh, laugh!

"You're either crazy, or . . ." Zamyotov said, and stopped, as if suddenly struck by a thought that flashed unexpectedly through his mind.

"Or? Or what? Well, what? Go on, say it!"

"Nothing!" replied Zamyotov, exasperated. "It's all nonsense!"

Both fell silent. After his unexpected burst into a fit of laughter, Raskolnikov all at once became pensive and sad. He leaned his elbow on the table and propped his head in his hand. He seemed to forget Zamyotov entirely. The silence lasted for quite some time.

"Why don't you drink your tea? It'll get cold," said Zamyotov.

"Eh? What? Tea? . . . Maybe so . . ." Raskolnikov took a sip from the cup, put a piece of bread in his mouth, and, looking at Zamyotov, seemed suddenly to recall everything and rouse himself: at the same moment his face resumed its original mocking expression. He went on drinking tea.

"There's a lot of this crookedness around nowadays," said Zamyotov. "Just recently I read in the Moscow *Gazette* that they caught a whole gang of counterfeiters in Moscow. A whole organization. They were making bank notes."

"Oh, that was way back! I read about it a month ago," Raskolnikov replied calmly. "So they're crooks in your opinion?" he added, grinning.

"What else would you call them?"

"Them? They're children, greenhorns, not crooks! A full fifty of them went into such a thing together! How is it possible? Even three would be too many, and even then they'd have to be surer of each other than of themselves! Otherwise, if just one of them gets drunk and spills it out, the whole thing falls through. Greenhorns! They hire unreliable people to change the money in banks: trusting such a job to the first comer! Well, suppose the greenhorns even brought it off, suppose each one got a million changed—well, what then? For the rest of their lives? They have to depend on each other all the rest of their lives! No, better to hang oneself! But they couldn't even get it changed: one of them went to the bank, got five thousand changed, and his hands betrayed him. He counted through four thousand and then took the fifth without counting it, on faith, just to pocket it and run away quickly. So he aroused suspicion. And everything blew up because of one fool! How is it possible?"[22]

"That his hands betrayed him?" Zamyotov picked up. "No, that is possible, sir. No, I'm absolutely sure it's possible. Sometimes one just can't stand it."

"A thing like that?"

"And you think you could stand it? No, I couldn't. To risk such horror for a hundred-rouble reward! To take a false bank note, and where?—to a banking house, where they do know a hawk from a handsaw—no, I'd get flustered. Wouldn't you?"

Again Raskolnikov suddenly felt a terrible urge to "stick his tongue out." Shivers momentarily ran down his spine.

"I wouldn't do it that way," he began, remotely. "This is how I would get it changed: I'd count the first thousand four times or so, backwards and forwards, examining every note, and then go on to the next thousand; I'd start counting, count half way through, pull out a fifty-rouble note and hold it up to the light, turn it over, and hold it up to the light again—is it false or not? 'I'm afraid,' I'd say, 'I have a relative, and the other day she lost twenty-five roubles that way,' and I'd tell them the story. Then, when I started counting the third thousand—'No, sorry, I think, back there in the second thousand, I counted the seventh hundred incorrectly; I'm not sure'—and I'd leave the third thousand and start over again on the second; and so on for the whole five thousand. And when I was done, I'd pull out a note from the fifth thousand and one from the second, hold them up to the light again, and say in a doubtful voice: 'Change them, please.' And I'd have the clerk in such a lather by then that he'd do anything to be rid of me! When I was finally done with it all, I'd go and open the door—'No, sorry,' and I'd come back again to ask about something, to get some explanation—that's how I would do it!"

"Pah, what awful things you say!" Zamyotov laughed. "Only it's all just talk; in reality you'd be sure to make a slip. Here, let me tell you, not only you and I, but in my opinion even a seasoned, desperate man cannot vouch for himself. But why go far? Take, for example, this old woman who was murdered in our precinct. It looks like the work of a real daredevil; he risked it all in broad daylight, got away only by a miracle—and even so his hands betrayed him: he wasn't able to steal, he couldn't stand it; that's clear from the evidence . . ."

Raskolnikov looked offended.

"Clear! Go and catch him then!" he cried, gloatingly egging Zamyotov on.

"Oh, they'll catch him all right!"

"Who? You? You're going to catch him? You'll run yourselves into the ground! What's the main thing for you—whether the man spends the money or not? First he has no money, then he suddenly starts spending—who else could it be? A child so high could hoodwink you with that if he wanted to!"

"That's precisely it; they all do it that way," Zamyotov replied. "He kills cunningly, risks his life, and then immediately gets caught in some pot-house. They get caught spending. Not everyone is as cunning as you are. You wouldn't go to a pot-house, naturally?"

Raskolnikov frowned and looked fixedly at Zamyotov.

"It seems I've whetted your appetite. So, you want to know how I'd act in this case, too?" he asked with displeasure.

"Yes, I do," the other answered firmly and seriously. He had begun to look and sound all too serious.

"Very much?"

"Very much."

"All right. This is how I would act," Raskolnikov began, again suddenly bringing his face close to Zamyotov's, again looking point-blank at him, again speaking in a whisper, so that this time Zamyotov even gave a start. "Here's what I would do: I would take the money and the things, and as soon as I left there, immediately, without stopping anywhere, I'd go to some out-of-the-way place where there were only fences and almost no people around—some kitchen garden or the like. There would be a stone in this yard, which I would have picked out beforehand, weighing thirty or forty pounds, somewhere in a corner near the fence, that might have been sitting there since the house was built; I'd lift this stone—of course there would be a shallow hole under it—and put all the money and things into the hole. I'd put them there and replace the stone just the way it had been before, tamp it down with my foot, and go away. And I wouldn't touch it for a year, or two, or three—so, look all you like. Now you see me, and now you don't!"

"You are a madman," Zamyotov spoke for some reason also almost in a whisper, and for some reason suddenly drew back from Raskolnikov. Raskolnikov's eyes were flashing; he became terribly pale; his upper lip twitched and began to tremble. He leaned as close to Zamyotov as he could and began moving his lips without uttering anything; this went on for half a minute or so; he was aware of what he was doing, but could not stop himself. A terrible word was trembling on his lips, like the hook on that door: another moment and it would jump out; another moment and it would let go; another moment and it would be spoken!

"And what if it was I who killed the old woman and Lizaveta?" he said suddenly—and came to his senses.

Zamyotov looked wildly at him and went white as a sheet. His face twisted into a smile.

"But can it be?" he said, barely audibly.

Raskolnikov looked at him spitefully.

"Admit that you believed it! Right? Am I right?"

"Not at all! Now more than ever I don't!" Zamyotov said hastily.

"Got you at last! The little sparrow's caught! So you did believe it at first, if 'now more than ever you don't'?"

"No, not at all, really!" Zamyotov exclaimed, visibly confused. "Is that why you've been frightening me, so as to lead up to that?"

"You don't believe it, then? And what did you start talking about in my absence, when I left the office that time? And why did Lieutenant Gunpowder interrogate me after I fainted? Hey, you," he called to the waiter, getting up and taking his cap, "how much?"

"Thirty kopecks in all, sir," the waiter answered, running over.

"And here's twenty more for a tip. Look at all this money!" He held the notes out to Zamyotov with a trembling hand. "Red ones, blue ones, twenty-five roubles. Where from? And where did the new clothes come from? You know I didn't have a kopeck! I bet you've already questioned the landlady, eh? . . . Well, enough! *Assez causé!*[23] See you later . . . with the greatest pleasure! . . ."

He went out all atremble with some wild, hysterical feeling, in which there was at the same time a portion of unbearable delight—yet he was gloomy and terribly tired. His face was distorted, as if after some fit. His fatigue was increasing rapidly. His energy would now be aroused and surge up suddenly, with the first push, the first irritating sensation, and then rapidly grow weaker as the sensation weakened.

Zamyotov, left alone, went on sitting where he was for a long time, pondering. Raskolnikov had unwittingly overturned all his ideas on a certain point, and had finally settled his opinion.

"Ilya Petrovich is a blockhead!" he decided finally.

Raskolnikov had just opened the door to go out when he suddenly bumped into Razumikhin, right on the porch, coming in. Neither one saw the other even a step before, so that they almost bumped heads. They stood for some time looking each other up and down. Razumikhin was greatly amazed, but suddenly wrath, real wrath, flashed menacingly in his eyes.

"So here's where you are!" he shouted at the top of his lungs. "Ran away from your sick-bed! And I even looked for you under the sofa! We went to the attic! I almost gave Nastasya a beating because of you . . . And here's where he is! Rodka! What is the meaning of this! Tell the whole truth! Confess! Do you hear?"

"It means that I'm sick to death of all of you, and I want to be alone," Raskolnikov replied calmly.

"Alone? When you still can't walk, when your mug is white as a sheet, and you can barely breathe! Fool! . . . What were you doing in the 'Crystal Palace'? Confess immediately!"

"Let me be!" said Raskolnikov, and he tried to pass by. This now drove Razumikhin into a rage: he seized him firmly by the shoulder.

"Let you be? You dare tell me to let you be? And do you know what I'm going to do with you now? I'm going to pick you up, tie you in a knot, carry you home under my arm, and lock you in!"

"Listen, Razumikhin," Raskolnikov began softly and apparently quite calmly, "can't you see that I don't want your good deeds? And who wants to do good deeds for someone who . . . spits on them? For someone, finally, who only feels seriously burdened by them? Why did you seek me out at the start of my illness? Maybe I would have been quite happy to die! Didn't I make it sufficiently plain to you today that you are tormenting me, that I am . . . sick of you! Really, why do you want to torment people! I assure you that it all seriously interferes with my recovery, because it keeps me constantly irritated. Didn't Zossimov leave today so as not to irritate me? You leave me, too, for God's sake! And what right do you have, finally, to restrain me by force? Can't you see as I'm speaking now that I'm entirely in my right mind? How, teach me how to implore you, finally, not to pester me with your good deeds! Say I'm ungrateful, say I'm mean, only leave me alone, all of you, for God's sake, leave me alone! Leave me! Leave me!"

He had begun calmly, savoring beforehand all the venom he was going to pour out, but he finished frenzied and breathless, as earlier with Luzhin.

Razumikhin stood, thought, and let his hand fall.

"Go to the devil, then!" he said softly and almost pensively. "Wait!" he suddenly bellowed, as Raskolnikov tried to set off. "Listen to me. I announce to you that you're all, to a man, babblers and braggarts! Some little suffering comes along, and you brood over it like a hen over an egg! Even there you steal from other authors! There isn't a sign of independent life in you! You're made of spermaceti ointment, with whey instead of blood in your veins! I don't believe a one of you! The first thing you do in any circumstances is try not to resemble a human being! Wa-a-ait!" he cried with redoubled fury, seeing that Raskolnikov was making another attempt to leave. "Hear me out! You know I have people coming today for a housewarming party, maybe they've come already, but I left my uncle there—I ran over just now—to receive my guests. So, if you weren't a fool, a banal fool, an utter fool, a foreign translation . . . you see, Rodya, I admit you're a smart fellow, but you're a fool!—so, if you weren't a fool, you'd be better off spending the evening at my place than going around wearing out your boots for nothing. Since you've already gone out, what's the difference! I'll roll in a soft armchair for you, my landlord has one . . . A bit of tea, good company . . . Or else I can put you on the couch—anyway, you'll be lying there with us . . . Zossimov will be there, too. Will you come?"

"No."

"R-r-rot!" Razumikhin cried out impatiently. "How can you tell? You can't answer for yourself! Besides, you have no understanding of these things . . . I've fallen out with people like this a thousand times and gone running back . . . One gets ashamed—and goes back to the man! So remember, Pochinkov's house, third floor . . ."

"And in the same way, Mr. Razumikhin, you would probably let someone beat you for the pleasure of doing them good."

"Who, me? I'll twist your nose off just for thinking it! Pochinkov's house, number forty-seven, the official Babushkin's apartment . . ."

"I won't come, Razumikhin!" Raskolnikov turned and started to walk away.

"I bet you will!" Razumikhin called after him. "Otherwise you . . . otherwise I don't want to know you! Hey, wait! Is Zamyotov in there?"

"He is."

"You saw him?"

"I did."

"You spoke?"

"We spoke."

"What about? Ah, devil take you, don't tell me, then! Pochinkov's, forty-seven, Babushkin's, remember!"

Raskolnikov reached Sadovaya and turned the corner. Razumikhin followed him with his eyes, pondering. Finally he threw up his hands, went into the tavern, but stopped halfway up the stairs.

"Devil take it!" he continued, almost aloud. "He talks sense, but it's as if . . . still, I'm a fool, too! Don't madmen talk sense? I think that's what Zossimov is afraid of!" He tapped himself on the forehead with his finger. "And what if . . . no, he shouldn't be allowed to go by himself now! He might drown himself . . . Ech, I messed that one up! Impossible!" And he ran back outside after Raskolnikov, but the trail was already cold. He spat and with quick steps went back to the "Crystal Palace," hastening to question Zamyotov.

Raskolnikov walked straight to the ——sky Bridge, stopped in the middle of it, leaned both elbows on the railing, and began to look along. After parting with Razumikhin he became so weak that he had barely been able to get there. He longed to sit or lie down somewhere in the street. Leaning over the water, he gazed mechanically at the last pink gleams of the sunset, at the row of houses, dark in the thickening dusk, at one distant window, somewhere in a garret on the left bank, blazing as if aflame when the last ray of sunlight struck it for a moment, at the dark water of the canal—he stood as if peering intently into the water. Finally, red circles began spinning in his eyes, the houses began to sway, the passers-by, the embankments, the carriages—all began spinning and dancing around him. Suddenly he gave a start, perhaps saved from fainting again by a wild and ugly sight. He sensed that someone was standing next to him, to his right, close by; he looked— and saw a woman, tall, wearing a kerchief, with a long, yellow, wasted face and reddish, sunken eyes. She was looking straight at him, but obviously saw nothing and recognized no one. Suddenly she leaned her right forearm on the parapet, raised her right leg, swung it over the railing, then her left leg, and threw herself into the canal. The dirty water parted, swallowing its victim for a moment, but a minute later the drowning woman floated up and was gently carried downstream, her head and legs in the water, her back up, her skirt to one side and ballooning over the water like a pillow.

"She's drowned herself! Drowned herself!" dozens of voices were crying; people came running, both embankments were strung with spectators, people crowded around Raskolnikov on the bridge, pushing and pressing him from behind.

"Merciful God, it's our Afrosinyushka!" a woman's tearful cry came from somewhere nearby. "Merciful God, save her! Pull her out, dear people!"

"A boat! A boat!" shouts came from the crowd.

But by then there was no need for a boat; a policeman ran down the stairs, threw off his greatcoat and boots, and plunged into the water. It was not much of a task; the stream carried the drowning woman within two yards of the stairs; he seized her clothes with his right hand, with his left managed to get hold of the pole a fellow policeman held out to him, and the drowning woman was pulled out at once. They laid her on the granite slabs of the embankment. She quickly came around, raised herself a little, sat up, and began sneezing and snorting, senselessly wiping off her wet dress with her hands. She said nothing.

"Drank herself cockeyed, my dears, she drank herself cockeyed," the same woman's voice went on howling, next to Afrosinyushka now. "The other day, too, she went and tried to hang herself; we took her out of the noose. And now I had to go to the store, and I left a girl to keep an eye on her, and it all came to grief! She's a tradeswoman, my dear, like us, we're neighbors, second house from the corner, right here . . ."

People began to disperse; the policemen were still fussing over the nearly drowned woman; someone shouted something about the police station . . . Raskolnikov looked upon it all with a strange feeling of indifference and detachment. It was disgusting to him. "No, it's vile . . . the water . . . better not," he was muttering to himself. "Nothing'll come of it," he added, "no point in waiting. What's that—the police station? . . . And why isn't Zamyotov there in his office? The office is open past nine . . ." He turned his back to the railing and looked around him.

"Well, after all, why not!" he said resolutely, left the bridge, and set off in the direction of the police station. His heart was empty and blank. He did not want to reflect. Even his anguish had gone; and not a trace remained of his former energy, when he had left the house determined to "end it all!" Total apathy had taken its place.

"After all, it's a way out!" he thought, walking slowly and listlessly along the embankment of the canal. "Anyway, I'll end it because I want to . . . Is it a way out, though? But what's the difference! There'll be a square foot of space—hah! What sort of an end, though? Can it really be the end? Shall I tell them or shall I not tell them? Ah . . . the devil! Besides, I'm tired; I wish I could lie or sit down somewhere soon! What's most shameful is that it's so stupid! But I spit on that, too. Pah, what stupid things come into one's head . . ."

To get to the police station he had to keep straight on and take the second turn to the left: it was there, two steps away. But having reached the first turn, he stopped, thought, went down the side street, and made a detour through two more streets—perhaps without any purpose, or perhaps to delay for at least another minute and gain time. He walked along looking down. Suddenly it was as if someone whispered something in his ear. He raised his head and saw that he was standing in front of *that* house, right by the gate. He had not gone there, or even passed by, since *that* evening.

An irresistible and inexplicable desire drew him on. He went in, passed all the way under the gateway, turned to the first door on the right, and began going up the familiar stairs to the fourth floor. The narrow and steep stairway was very dark. He stopped on each landing and looked around with curiosity. The entire window frame on the first-floor landing had been taken out: "It wasn't like that then," he thought. Here was the second-floor apartment where Nikolashka and Mitka had been working then: "Closed and the door has been painted; that must mean it's for rent." Now it was the third floor . . . the fourth . . . "Here!" He was overcome with perplexity: the door to the apartment was wide open, there were people in it, voices could be heard; he had not expected that at all. After a short hesitation, he mounted the last steps and went into the apartment.

It, too, was being redecorated; workmen were there; he seemed to be struck by the fact. He had been imagining for some reason that he would find everything just as he had left it then, perhaps even the corpses in the same places on the floor. Instead, bare walls, no furniture—it was somehow strange! He walked over to the window and sat down on the sill.

There were two workmen, both young fellows, one on the older side, the other much younger. They were hanging fresh wallpaper, white with little purple flowers, in place of the former tattered and torn yellow paper. For some reason Raskolnikov was terribly displeased by this; he looked at the new wallpaper with animosity, as though he were sorry to see everything so changed.

The workmen were obviously late, and were now hastily rolling up their paper in preparation for going home. Raskolnikov's appearance drew almost no notice from them. They were talking about something. Raskolnikov crossed his arms and began to listen.

"So she comes to me in the morning," the older one was saying to the younger one, "really early, and she's all gussied up. 'What are you doing,' I says, 'sugar-and-spicing in front of me like that?' 'From henceforth, Tit Vasilievich,' she says, 'I want to stay under your complete will.' So that's how it is! And all gussied up, like a magazine, just like a magazine!"

"What's a magazine, pops?" asked the young one. "Pops" was obviously giving him lessons.

"A magazine is pictures, brother, colored pictures, and they get sent here to local tailors, every Saturday, by mail, from abroad, to tell how everybody should dress, the male sex the same as the female. Drawings,

I mean. The male sex is shown more in fancy suits, and in the female department, brother, there's such pompadours—give me all you've got and it won't be enough!"

"What you can't find here in Petersburg!" the young one exclaimed enthusiastically. "Except for your old granny, they've got everything!"

"Except for that, brother, there's everything to be found," the older one concluded didactically.

Raskolnikov stood up and walked into the other room, where the trunk, the bed, and the chest used to be; the room seemed terribly small to him without the furniture. The wallpaper was still the same; the place where the icon-stand had been was sharply outlined on the wallpaper in the corner. He looked around and returned to his window. The older workman was watching him out of the corner of his eye.

"What do you want, sir?" he asked, suddenly addressing him.

Instead of answering, Raskolnikov stood up, walked out to the landing, took hold of the bell-pull, and rang. The same bell, the same tinny sound! He rang a second, a third time; he listened and remembered. The former painfully horrible, hideous sensation began to come back to him more clearly, more vividly; he shuddered with each ring, and enjoyed the feeling more and more.

"What do you want? Who are you?" cried the workman, coming out to him. Raskolnikov walked back in the door.

"I want to rent this apartment," he said. "I'm looking it over."

"Nobody rents places at night; and besides, you should have come with the caretaker."

"The floor has been washed; are they going to paint it?" Raskolnikov went on. "Is there any blood?"

"What blood?"

"That old woman and her sister were murdered here. There was a whole pool of blood."

"What sort of man are you?" the workman cried worriedly.

"Me?"

"Yes, you."

"You want to know? . . . Let's go to the police, I'll tell you there."

The workman looked at him in perplexity.

"It's time we left, sir, we're late. Let's go, Alyoshka. We'll have to lock up," the older workman said.

"Let's go, then!" Raskolnikov replied indifferently, and he walked out first and went slowly down the stairs. "Hey, caretaker!" he cried as he passed under the gateway.

Several people were standing just at the street entrance, gazing at the passers-by: the two caretakers, a woman, a tradesman in a smock, and some others. Raskolnikov went straight up to them.

"What do you want?" one of the caretakers responded.

"Have you been to the police?"

"Just came back. So, what do you want?"

"They're all there?"

"They are."

"The assistant's there?"

"He was for a while. What do you want?"

Raskolnikov did not answer, but stood beside them, pondering.

"He came to look at the place," the older workman said, coming up.

"What place?"

"Where we're working. 'Why have you washed the blood up?' he said. 'There was a murder here, and I've come to rent the place.' And he started ringing the bell, all but tore it out. 'Let's go to the police,' he says, 'I'll prove it all there.' Just wouldn't leave off."

The caretaker scrutinized Raskolnikov, perplexed and frowning.

"But who are you?" he cried, a bit more menacingly.

"I am Rodion Romanych Raskolnikov, a former student, and I live at Shil's house, here in the lane, not far away, apartment number fourteen. Ask the caretaker . . . he knows me." Raskolnikov said all this somehow lazily and pensively, not turning, but gazing fixedly at the darkened street.

"Why did you go up there?"

"To look."

"What's there to look at?"

"Why not just take him to the police?" the tradesman suddenly mixed in, and then fell silent.

Raskolnikov cast a sidelong glance at him over his shoulder, looked at him attentively, and said, as slowly and lazily as before:

"Let's go."

"Just take him, then!" the encouraged tradesman picked up. "Why did he come about *that?* What's on his mind, eh?"

"God knows, maybe he's drunk, maybe he's not," the workman muttered.

"But what do you want?" the caretaker shouted again, beginning to get seriously angry. "Quit pestering us!"

"Scared to go to the police?" Raskolnikov said to him mockingly.

"Why scared? Quit pestering us!"

"Scofflaw!" cried the woman.

"Why go on talking to him?" shouted the other caretaker, a huge man in an unbuttoned coat and with keys on his belt. "Clear out! . . . Yes, he's a scofflaw! . . . Clear out!"

And seizing Raskolnikov by the shoulder, he threw him into the street. Raskolnikov nearly went head over heels, but did not fall. He straightened himself up, looked silently at all the spectators, and walked away.

"A weird man," the workman let fall.

"People turned weird lately," the woman said.

"We still should've taken him to the police," the tradesman added.

"No point getting involved," the big caretaker decided. "He's a scofflaw for sure! You could see he was foisting himself on us, but once you get involved, there's no getting out . . . Don't we know it!"

"Well now, shall I go or not?" thought Raskolnikov, stopping in the middle of the street, at an intersection, and looking around as if he were waiting for the final word from someone. But no reply came from anywhere; everything was blank and dead, like the stones he was walking on, dead for him, for him alone . . . Suddenly, in the distance, about two hundred paces away, at the end of the street, in the thickening darkness, he made out a crowd, voices, shouts . . . In the midst of the crowd stood some carriage . . . A small light started flickering in the middle of the street. "What's going on?" Raskolnikov turned to the right and went towards the crowd. It was as if he were snatching at anything, and he grinned coldly as he thought of it, because he had firmly decided about the police and knew for certain that now it was all going to end.

VII

I N THE MIDDLE of the street stood a jaunty, high-class carriage, harnessed to a pair of fiery gray horses; there were no passengers, and the coachman, having climbed down from his box, was standing by; the horses were being held by their bridles. A great many people were crowding around, the police in front of them all. One of them was holding a lantern and bending down, directing the light at something on the pavement, just by the wheels. Everyone was talking, shouting, gasping; the coachman looked bewildered and kept repeating every so often:

"What a shame! Lord, what a shame!"

Raskolnikov pushed his way through as well as he could and finally glimpsed the object of all this bustle and curiosity. A man just run over by the horses was lying on the ground, apparently unconscious, very poorly dressed, but in "gentleman's" clothes, and all covered with blood. Blood was flowing from his face, from his head. His face was all battered, scraped, and mangled. One could see that he had been run over in earnest.

"Saints alive!" wailed the coachman, "how could I help it! If I'd been racing, or if I hadn't hollered to him . . . but I was driving at a slow, steady pace. Everybody saw it, as true as I'm standing here. A drunk can't see straight, who doesn't know that! . . . I saw him crossing the street, reeling, nearly falling over—I shouted once, then again, then a third time, and then I reined in the horses; but he fell right under their feet! Maybe on purpose, or else he was really so drunk . . . The horses are young, skittish; they reared up, he gave a shout, they took off again . . . and so we came to grief."

"That's exactly how it was!" some witness responded from the crowd.

"He did shout, it's true, he shouted three times to him," another voice responded.

"Three times exactly, everybody heard it!" cried a third.

The coachman, however, was not very distressed or frightened. One could see that the carriage belonged to a wealthy and important owner, who was awaiting its arrival somewhere; how to see to this last circumstance was no small part of the policemen's concern. The trampled man had to be removed to the police station and then to the hospital. No one knew his name.

Meanwhile Raskolnikov pushed ahead and bent down closer. Suddenly the lantern shone brightly on the unfortunate man's face. He recognized him.

"I know him! I know him!" he cried, pushing all the way to the front. "He's an official, a retired official, a titular councillor, Marmeladov! He lives near here, in Kozel's house . . . A doctor, quickly! Here, I'll pay!" He pulled the money from his pocket and showed it to the policeman. He was surprisingly excited.

The police were pleased to have found out who the trampled man was. Raskolnikov gave his own name and address as well, and began doing his utmost to persuade them, as if it were a matter of his own father, to transport the unconscious Marmeladov to his lodgings.

"It's here, three houses away," he urged, "the house belongs to Kozel, a German, a rich man . . . He must have been trying to get home just now, drunk . . . I know him; he's a drunkard . . . He has a family, a wife, children, there's a daughter. It'll take too long to bring him to the hospital, and I'm sure there's a doctor there in the house! I'll pay, I'll pay . . . Anyway they'll take care of him, they'll help him at once, otherwise he'll die before he gets to the hospital . . ."

He even managed to slip them something unobserved; it was, however, a clear and lawful case, and in any event help was closer here. The trampled man was picked up and carried; people lent a hand. Kozel's house was about thirty steps away. Raskolnikov walked behind, carefully supporting the head and showing the way.

"This way, this way! Carry him head first up the stairs; turn him around . . . there! I'll pay, I'll thank you well for it," he muttered.

Katerina Ivanovna, as soon as she had a free moment, would immediately begin pacing her small room, from window to stove and back, her arms crossed tightly on her chest, talking to herself and coughing. Lately she had begun talking more and more often to her older daughter, the ten-year-old Polenka, who, though she understood little as yet, still understood very well that her mother needed her, and therefore always followed her with her big, intelligent eyes, and used all her guile to pretend that she understood everything. This time Polenka was undressing her little brother, who had not been feeling very well all day, getting him ready for bed. The boy, waiting for her to change his shirt, which was to be washed that same night, was sitting silently on the chair, with a serious mien, straight-backed and motionless, his little legs stretched out in front of him, pressed together, heels to the public and toes apart. He was listening to what his mama was saying to his sister, with pouting lips and wide-open eyes, sitting perfectly still, as all smart little boys ought to do when they are being undressed for bed. The even smaller girl, in complete rags, stood by the screen waiting her turn. The door to the stairs was open, to afford at least some protection from the waves of tobacco smoke that issued from the other rooms and kept sending the poor consumptive woman into long and painful fits of coughing. Katerina Ivanovna seemed to have grown even thinner over the past week, and the flushed spots on her cheeks burned even brighter than before.

"You wouldn't believe, you can't even imagine, Polenka," she was saying, pacing the room, "how great was the gaiety and splendor of our life in papa's house, and how this drunkard has ruined me and will ruin you all! Father had the state rank of colonel[24] and was nearly a governor by then, he only had one more step to go, so that everyone that called on him used to say, 'Even now, Ivan Mikhailovich, we already regard you as our governor!' When I . . . hem! . . . when I . . . hem, hem, hem . . . oh, curse this life!" she exclaimed, coughing up phlegm and clutching her chest. "When I . . . ah, at the marshal's last ball[25] . . . when Princess Bezzemelny saw me—the one who blessed me afterwards when I was marrying your father, Polya—she asked at once: 'Isn't this that nice young lady who danced with a shawl at the graduation?' . . . That rip should be mended; why don't you take the needle and darn it now, the way I taught you, otherwise tomorrow . . . hem, hem, hem! . . . it'll tear wo-o-orse!" she cried, straining herself. "At that same time, a kammerjunker, Prince Shchegolskoy,[26] had just come from Petersburg . . . he danced a mazurka with me, and the very next day wanted to come with a proposal; but I thanked him personally in flattering terms and said that my heart had long belonged to another. That other was your father, Polya; papa was terribly cross with me . . . Is the water ready? Now, give me the shirt; and the stockings? . . . Lida," she turned to the little daughter, "you'll just have to sleep without your shirt tonight, somehow . . . and lay out your stockings, too . . . so they can be washed together . . . Why doesn't that ragtag come home, the drunkard! He's worn his shirt out like some old dustcloth, it's all torn . . . I could wash it with the rest and not have to suffer two nights in a row! Lord! Hem, hem, hem, hem! Again! What's this?" she cried out, looking at the crowd in the entryway and the people squeezing into her room with some burden. "What's this? What are they carrying? Lord!"

"Is there somewhere to put him?" the policeman asked, looking around, when the bloodstained and unconscious Marmeladov had already been lugged into the room.

"On the sofa! Lay him out on the sofa, head this way," Raskolnikov pointed.

"Run over in the street! Drunk!" someone shouted from the entryway.

Katerina Ivanovna stood all pale, breathing with difficulty. The children were completely frightened. Little Lidochka cried out, rushed to Polenka, threw her arms around her, and began shaking all over.

Having laid Marmeladov down, Raskolnikov rushed to Katerina Ivanovna.

"For God's sake, calm yourself, don't be afraid!" he spoke in a quick patter. "He was crossing the street and was run over by a carriage; don't worry, he'll come round; I told them to bring him here . . . I was here once, you remember . . . He'll come round, I'll pay!"

"He finally got it!" Katerina Ivanovna cried desperately, and rushed to her husband.

Raskolnikov quickly noted that she was not one of those women who immediately fall into a faint. Instantly there was a pillow under the unfortunate man's head, something no one had thought of yet; Katerina Ivanovna began undressing him, examining him, fussing over him, not losing her presence of mind, forgetting herself, biting her trembling lips, and suppressing the cries that were about to burst from her breast.

Raskolnikov meanwhile persuaded someone to run and get a doctor. As it turned out, there was a doctor living two houses away.

"I've sent for a doctor," he kept saying to Katerina Ivanovna, "don't worry, I'll pay. Is there any water? . . . And bring a napkin, a towel, something, quickly; we don't know yet what his injuries are . . . He's been injured, not killed . . . rest assured . . . The doctor will say!"

Katerina Ivanovna rushed to the window; there, on a broken-seated chair, in the corner, a big clay bowl full of water had been set up, ready for the nighttime washing of her children's and husband's linen. This nighttime washing was done by Katerina Ivanovna herself, with her own hands, at least twice a week and sometimes more often, for it had reached a point where they no longer had any changes of linen, each member of the family had only one, and Katerina Ivanovna, who could not bear uncleanliness, preferred to wear herself out at night and beyond her strength, while everyone was asleep, so that the laundry would have time to dry on the line by morning and she could give them all clean things, rather than to see dirt in the house. She tried to lift the bowl and bring it over, as Raskolnikov had requested, but almost fell with the burden. But he had already managed to find a towel, and he wet it and began washing Marmeladov's bloodstained face. Katerina Ivanovna stood right there, painfully catching her breath and clutching her chest with her hands. She herself was in need of help. Raskolnikov began to realize that he had perhaps not done well in persuading them to bring the trampled man there. The policeman also stood perplexed.

"Polya!" Katerina Ivanovna cried, "run to Sonya, quickly. If you don't find her there, never mind, tell them that her father has been run over by a carriage and that she should come here at once . . . as soon as she gets back. Quickly, Polya! Here, put on a kerchief!"

"Run fas' as you can!" the boy suddenly cried from his chair, and, having said it, relapsed into his former silent, straight-backed sitting, wide-eyed, heels together, toes apart.

Meanwhile the room had become so crowded that there was no space for an apple to fall. The police had left, except for one who stayed for a time and tried to chase the public thronging in from the stairs back out to the stairs again. In their stead, almost all of Mrs. Lippewechsel's tenants came pouring from the inner rooms, crowding in the doorway at first, but then flooding into the room itself. Katerina Ivanovna flew into a rage.

"You might at least let him die in peace!" she shouted at the whole crowd. "A fine show you've found for yourselves! With cigarettes!

Hem, hem, hem! Maybe with your hats on, too! . . . Really, there's one in a hat . . . Out! At least have respect for a dead body!"

Coughing stopped her breath, but the tongue-lashing had its effect. Obviously, Katerina Ivanovna even inspired some fear; the tenants, one by one, squeezed back through the door, with that strange feeling of inner satisfaction which can always be observed, even in those who are near and dear, when a sudden disaster befalls their neighbor, and which is to be found in all men, without exception, however sincere their feelings of sympathy and commiseration.

Outside the door, however, voices were raised about the hospital, and how one ought not to disturb people unnecessarily.

"So one ought not to die!" cried Katerina Ivanovna, and she rushed for the door, to loose a blast of thunder at them, but in the doorway she ran into Mrs. Lippewechsel herself, who had just managed to learn of the accident and came running to re-establish order. She was an extremely cantankerous and disorderly German woman.

"Ach, my God!" she clasped her hands. "Your trunken husband has a horse trampled! To the hospital mit him! I am the landlady!"

"Amalia Ludwigovna! I ask you to consider what you are saying," Katerina Ivanovna began haughtily. (She always spoke in a haughty tone with the landlady, so that she would "remember her place," and even now she could not deny herself the pleasure.) "Amalia Ludwigovna . . ."

"I have told you how-many-times before that you muss never dare say to me Amal Ludwigovna. I am Amal-Ivan!"

"You are not Amal-Ivan, you are Amalia Ludwigovna, and since I am not one of your base flatterers, like Mr. Lebezyatnikov, who is now laughing outside the door" (outside the door there was indeed laughter, and someone cried: "A cat-fight!"), "I shall always address you as Amalia Ludwigovna, though I decidedly fail to understand why you so dislike this appellation. You see for yourself what has happened to Semyon Zakharovich; he is dying. I ask you to close this door at once and not allow anyone in. Let him at least die in peace! Otherwise, I assure you, tomorrow your action will be made known to the governor-general himself. The prince knew me as a young girl, and very well remembers Semyon Zakharovich, to whom he has shown favor many times. Everyone knows that Semyon Zakharovich had many friends and protectors, whom he himself abandoned out of noble pride, aware of his unfortunate weakness, but now" (she pointed to Raskolnikov) "we are being helped by a magnanimous young man who has means and connections, and whom Semyon Zakharovich knew as a child, and rest assured, Amalia Ludwigovna . . ."

All this was spoken in a rapid patter, faster and faster, but coughing all at once interrupted Katerina Ivanovna's eloquence. At that moment the dying man came to and moaned, and she ran to him. He opened his eyes and, still without recognition or understanding, began peering at Raskolnikov, who was standing over him. He breathed heavily, deeply, rarely; blood oozed from the corners of his mouth; sweat stood out on his forehead. Not recognizing Raskolnikov, he began looking around anxiously. Katerina Ivanovna looked at him sadly but sternly, and tears flowed from her eyes.

"My God! His whole chest is crushed! And the blood, so much blood!" she said in despair. "We must take all his outer clothes off! Turn over a little, Semyon Zakharovich, if you can," she cried to him.

Marmeladov recognized her.

"A priest!" he said in a hoarse voice.

Katerina Ivanovna went over to the window, leaned her forehead against the window frame, and exclaimed in desperation:

"Oh, curse this life!"

"A priest!" the dying man said again, after a moment's silence.

"They've go-o-one!" Katerina Ivanovna cried at him; he obeyed the cry and fell silent. He was seeking for her with timid, anguished eyes; she went back to him and stood by his head. He calmed down somewhat, but not for long. Soon his eyes rested on little Lidochka (his favorite), who was shaking in the corner as if in a fit and stared at him with her astonished, childishly attentive eyes.

"A . . . a . . ." he pointed to her worriedly. He wanted to say something.

"What now?" cried Katerina Ivanovna.

"Barefoot! Barefoot!" he muttered, pointing with crazed eyes at the girl's bare little feet.

"Be quiet!" Katerina Ivanovna cried irritably. "You know very well why she's barefoot!"

"Thank God, the doctor!" Raskolnikov cried joyfully.

The doctor came in, a trim little old man, a German, looking about him with mistrustful eyes; he went over to the sick man, took his pulse, carefully felt his head, and with Katerina Ivanovna's help unbuttoned his shirt, all soaked with blood, and bared the sick man's chest. His whole chest was torn, mangled, mutilated; several ribs on the right side were broken. On the left side, just over the heart, there was a large, ominous yellowish-black spot, the cruel blow of a hoof. The doctor frowned. The policeman told him that the injured man had been caught in a wheel and dragged, turning, about thirty paces along the pavement.

"It's surprising that he recovered consciousness at all," the doctor whispered softly to Raskolnikov.

"What is your opinion?" the latter asked.

"He will die now."

"There's no hope at all?"

"Not the slightest! He is at his last gasp . . . Besides, his head is dangerously injured . . . Hm. I could perhaps let some blood . . . but . . . it would be no use. In five or ten minutes he will certainly die."

"Try letting some blood, then!"

"Perhaps . . . However, I warn you it will be perfectly useless."

At that point more steps were heard, the crowd in the entryway parted, and a priest, a gray-haired old man, appeared on the threshold with the Holy Gifts.[27] A policeman had gone to fetch him while they were still in the street. The doctor immediately gave way to him, and they exchanged meaningful glances. Raskolnikov persuaded the doctor to stay at least for a little while. The doctor shrugged and stayed.

Everyone stepped aside. The confession lasted a very short time. The dying man probably did not understand much of anything; and he could utter only abrupt, inarticulate sounds. Katerina Ivanovna took Lidochka, got the boy down from his chair, went to the corner near the stove, knelt, and made the children kneel in front of her. The little girl went on shaking; but the boy, upright on his bare little knees, raised his hand regularly, making a full sign of the cross, and bowed to the ground, bumping with his forehead, which seemed to give him special pleasure. Katerina Ivanovna was biting her lips and holding back her tears; she, too, was praying, straightening the boy's shirt from time to time, and she managed to throw a kerchief over the girl's bare shoulders, taking it from the top of the chest of drawers as she prayed and without getting up from her knees. Meanwhile, curious people began opening the door from the inner rooms again. And more and more spectators, tenants from all down the stairs, crowded into the entryway, but without crossing the threshold. The whole scene was lighted by just one candle-end.

At that moment Polenka, who had run to fetch her sister, squeezed quickly through the crowd in the entryway. She came in, almost breathless from running hard, took off her kerchief, sought out her mother with her eyes, went to her, and said: "She's coming! I met her in the street!" Her mother pulled her down and made her kneel beside her. Timidly and inaudibly, a girl came in, squeezing through the crowd, and her sudden appearance was strange in that room, in the midst of poverty, rags, death, and despair. She, too, was in rags, a two-penny costume, but adorned in street fashion, to suit the taste and rules established in that special world, with a clearly and shamefully explicit purpose. Sonya stood in the entryway, just at the threshold but not crossing it, with a lost look, unconscious, as it seemed, of everything, forgetting her gaudy silk dress with its long and absurd train, bought at fourth hand and so unseemly here, and her boundless crinoline that blocked the entire doorway, and her light-colored shoes, and the little parasol, useless at night, which she still carried with her, and her absurd round straw hat with its flame-colored feather. From under this hat, cocked at a boyish angle, peered a thin, pale, and frightened little face, mouth open and eyes fixed in terror. Sonya was of small stature, about eighteen years old, thin but quite pretty, blond, and with remarkable blue eyes. She stared at the bed, at the priest; she, too, was breathless from walking quickly. Finally, certain whispered words from the crowd probably reached her. She looked down, took a step over the threshold, and stood in the room, though still just by the door.

Confession and communion were over. Katerina Ivanovna again went up to her husband's bed. The priest withdrew and, as he was leaving, tried to address a few words of admonition and comfort to Katerina Ivanovna.

"And what am I to do with these?" she interrupted sharply and irritably, pointing to the little ones.

"God is merciful; hope for help from the Almighty," the priest began.

"Ehh! Merciful, but not to us!"

"That is sinful, madam, sinful," the priest observed, shaking his head.

"And is this not sinful?" cried Katerina Ivanovna, pointing to the dying man.

"Perhaps those who were the inadvertent cause will agree to compensate you, at least for the loss of income . . ."

"You don't understand!" Katerina Ivanovna cried irritably, waving her hand. "What is there to compensate? He was drunk; he went and got under the horses himself! And what income? There wasn't any income from him, there was only torment. The drunkard drank up everything. He stole from us, and took it to the pot-house; he wasted their lives and mine in the pot-house! Thank God he's dying! We'll have fewer losses!"

"You would do better to forgive him in the hour of death. Such feelings are a sin, madam, a great sin!"

Katerina Ivanovna was bustling around the sick man, giving him water, wiping the sweat and blood from his head, straightening his pillow, as she talked with the priest, and only turned to him from time to time while doing other things. But now she suddenly fell upon him almost in a frenzy.

"Eh, father! Words, nothing but words! Forgive him! And what if he didn't get run over? He'd come home drunk, wearing his only shirt, all dirty and ragged, and flop down and snore, and I'd be sloshing in the water till dawn, washing his and the children's rags, and then I'd hang them out the window to dry, and as soon as it was dawn, I'd sit down right away to mend them—that's my night! . . . So what's all this talk about forgiveness! As if I hadn't forgiven him!"

Deep, terrible coughing interrupted her words. She spat into her handkerchief and thrust it out for the priest to see, holding her other hand to her chest in pain. The handkerchief was all bloody . . .

The priest hung his head and said nothing.

Marmeladov was in his final agony; he would not take his eyes from the face of Katerina Ivanovna, who again bent over him. He kept wanting to say something to her; he tried to begin, moving his tongue with effort and uttering unintelligible words, but Katerina Ivanovna, understanding that he wanted to ask her forgiveness, at once shouted at him peremptorily:

"Be quiet! Don't! . . . I know what you want to say! . . ." And the sick man fell silent; but at that same moment his wandering eyes rested on the doorway, and he saw Sonya . . .

He had not noticed her until then: she was standing in the corner, in the shadows.

"Who's there? Who's there?" he said suddenly, in a hoarse, breathless voice, all alarmed, in horror motioning with his eyes towards the doorway where his daughter stood, and making an effort to raise himself.

"Lie down! Lie do-o-own!" cried Katerina Ivanovna.

But with an unnatural effort he managed to prop himself on one arm. He gazed wildly and fixedly at his daughter for some time, as though he did not recognize her. And indeed he had never seen her in such attire. All at once he recognized her—humiliated, crushed, bedizened, and ashamed, humbly waiting her turn to take leave of her dying father. Infinite suffering showed in his face.

"Sonya! Daughter! Forgive me!" he cried, and tried to hold out his hand to her, but without its support he slipped from the sofa and went crashing face down on the floor; they rushed to pick him up, laid him out again, but by then he was almost gone. Sonya cried out weakly, ran and embraced him, and remained so in that embrace. He died in her arms.

"So he got it!" Katerina Ivanovna cried, looking at her husband's corpse. "Well, what now? How am I going to bury him! And how am I going to feed them tomorrow, all of them?"

Raskolnikov went up to Katerina Ivanovna.

"Katerina Ivanovna," he began, "last week your deceased husband told me all about his life and his circumstances . . . You may be sure that he spoke of you with rapturous respect. Since that evening, when I learned how devoted he was to all of you, and how he respected and loved you especially, Katerina Ivanovna, in spite of his unfortunate weakness, since that evening we became friends . . . Permit me now . . . to assist . . . to pay what is due to my deceased friend. Here are . . . twenty roubles, I think—and if this can serve to

help you, then . . . I . . . in short, I'll come again—I'll be sure to come
. . . maybe even tomorrow . . . Good-bye!"

And he quickly left the room, hastening to squeeze through the
crowd and reach the stairs; but in the crowd he suddenly ran into
Nikodim Fomich, who had learned of the accident and wished to take
a personal hand in the arrangements. They had not seen each other since
that scene in the office, but Nikodim Fomich recognized him instantly.

"Ah, it's you?" he asked.

"He's dead," Raskolnikov answered. "The doctor was here, a priest
was here, everything's in order. Don't trouble the poor woman too
much, she's consumptive as it is. Cheer her up with something, if you
can . . . You're a kind man, I know . . ." he added with a smirk, looking
him straight in the eye.

"But, really, you're all soaked with blood," Nikodim Fomich remarked, making out by the light of the lantern several fresh spots of
blood on Raskolnikov's waistcoat.

"Soaked, yes . . . I've got blood all over me!" Raskolnikov said, with
some peculiar look; then he smiled, nodded his head, and went down
the stairs.

He went down slowly, unhurriedly, all in a fever, and filled, though
he was not aware of it, with the new, boundless sensation of a sudden
influx of full and powerful life. This sensation might be likened to the
sensation of a man condemned to death who is suddenly and unexpectedly granted a pardon.[28] Halfway down he was overtaken by the priest
on his way home. Raskolnikov silently let him pass, exchanging wordless bows with him. But as he was going down the last few steps, he
suddenly heard hurried footsteps behind him. Someone was running
after him. It was Polenka; she was running after him and calling:
"Listen! Listen!"

He turned to her. She ran down the last flight and stopped very close
to him, just one step higher. A dim light came from the courtyard.
Raskolnikov made out the girl's thin but dear little face, smiling and
looking at him with childish cheerfulness. She had come running with
an errand, which apparently pleased her very much.

"Listen, what is your name? . . . and also, where do you live?" she
asked hurriedly, in a breathless little voice.

He put his two hands on her shoulders and looked at her with something like happiness. It gave him such pleasure to look at her—he did not know why himself.

"Who sent you?"

"My sister Sonya sent me," the girl replied, smiling even more cheerfully.

"I just knew it was your sister Sonya."

"Mama sent me, too. When my sister Sonya was sending me, mama also came over and said: 'Run quickly, Polenka!' "

"Do you love your sister Sonya?"

"I love her most of all!" Polenka said with some special firmness, and her smile suddenly became more serious.

"And will you love me?"

Instead of an answer, he saw the girl's little face coming towards him, her full little lips naively puckered to kiss him. Suddenly her arms, thin as matchsticks, held him hard, her head bent to his shoulder, and the girl began crying softly, pressing her face harder and harder against him.

"I'm sorry for papa!" she said after a minute, raising her tear-stained face and wiping away the tears with her hands. "We've had so many misfortunes lately," she added unexpectedly, with that especially solemn look children try so hard to assume when they suddenly want to talk like "big people."

"And did papa love you?"

"He loved Lidochka most of all," she went on, very seriously and no longer smiling, just the way big people speak, "he loved her because she's little, and because she's sick, and he always brought her treats, and us he taught to read, and me he taught grammar and catechism," she added with dignity, "and mama didn't say anything, but we still knew she liked that, and papa knew it, and mama wants to teach me French, because it's time I got my education."

"And do you know how to pray?"

"Oh, of course we do, since long ago! I pray to myself, because I'm big now, and Kolya and Lidochka pray out loud with mother; first they recite the 'Hail, Mary' and then another prayer: 'God forgive and bless our sister Sonya,' and then 'God forgive and bless our other papa,' because our old papa died already and this one is the other one, but we pray for that one, too."

"Polechka, my name is Rodion; pray for me, too, sometimes: 'and for the servant of God, Rodion'—that's all."

"I'll pray for you all the rest of my life," the girl said ardently, and suddenly laughed again, rushed to him, and again held him hard.

Raskolnikov told her his name, gave her the address, and promised to come the next day without fail. The girl went away completely delighted with him. It was past ten when he walked out to the street. Five minutes later he was standing on the bridge, in exactly the same spot from which the woman had thrown herself not long before.

"Enough!" he said resolutely and solemnly. "Away with mirages, away with false fears, away with spectres! . . . There is life! Was I not alive just now? My life hasn't died with the old crone! May the Lord remember her in His kingdom, and—enough, my dear, it's time to go! Now is the kingdom of reason and light and . . . and will and strength . . . and now we shall see! Now we shall cross swords!" he added presumptuously, as if addressing some dark force and challenging it. "And I had already consented to live on a square foot of space!

" . . . I'm very weak at the moment, but . . . all my illness seems to have gone. And I knew it would when I went out today. By the way, Pochinkov's house is just two steps away. To Razumikhin's now, certainly, even if it weren't two steps away . . . let him win the bet! . . . Let him have his laugh—it's nothing, let him! . . . Strength, what's needed is strength; without strength you get nowhere; and strength is acquired by strength—that's something they don't know," he added proudly and self-confidently, and he left the bridge barely able to move his legs. Pride and self-confidence were growing in him every moment; with each succeeding moment he was no longer the man he had been the moment before. What special thing was it, however, that had so turned him around? He himself did not know; like a man clutching at a straw, he suddenly fancied that he, too, "could live, that there still was life, that his life had not died with the old crone." It was perhaps a rather hasty conclusion, but he was not thinking of that.

"I did ask her to remember the servant of God, Rodion, however," suddenly flashed in his head. "Well, but that was . . . just in case!" he added, and laughed at once at his own schoolboy joke. He was in excellent spirits.

He had no trouble finding Razumikhin; the new tenant of Pochinkov's house was already known, and the caretaker immediately showed him the way. From halfway up the stairs one could already hear the noise and animated conversation of a large gathering. The door to the stairs was wide open; shouts and arguing could be heard. Razumikhin's room was quite big, and about fifteen people were gathered in it. Raskolnikov stopped in the anteroom. There, behind a partition, two of the landlady's serving-girls busied themselves with two big samovars, bottles, plates and platters with pies and hors d'oeuvres brought from the landlady's kitchen. Raskolnikov asked for Razumikhin. He came running out, delighted. One could tell at a glance that he had drunk an unusual amount, and though Razumikhin was almost incapable of getting really drunk, this time the effect was somewhat noticeable.

"Listen," Raskolnikov hurried, "I only came to tell you that you've won the bet, and that indeed nobody knows what may happen to him. But I can't come in; I'm so weak I'm about to fall over. So, hello and good-bye! Come and see me tomorrow . . ."

"You know what, I'm going to take you home! If you yourself say you're so weak, then . . ."

"What about your guests? Who's that curly one who just peeked out here?"

"Him? Devil knows! Must be some acquaintance of my uncle's, or maybe he came on his own . . . I'll leave my uncle with them, a most invaluable man, too bad you can't meet him right now. But devil take them all anyway! They've forgotten about me now, and besides, I need some cooling off, because you came just in time, brother: another two minutes and I'd have started a fight in there, by God! They pour out such drivel . . . You can't imagine to what extent a man can finally get himself wrapped up in lies! But why can't you imagine it? Don't we lie ourselves? Let them lie, then; and afterwards they won't lie . . . Sit down for a minute, I'll get Zossimov."

Zossimov fell upon Raskolnikov even with a sort of greediness; some special curiosity could be seen in him; soon his face brightened.

"To bed without delay," he decided, having examined the patient as well as he could, "and take a bit of something for the night. Will you? I've already prepared it . . . a little powder."

"Or two, even," Raskolnikov replied.

The powder was taken at once.

"It will be very good if you go with him," Zossimov remarked to Razumikhin. "We'll see what may happen tomorrow, but today it's not bad at all: quite a change from this morning. Live and learn . . ."

"You know what Zossimov whispered to me just now, as we were leaving?" Razumikhin blurted out as soon as they stepped into the street. "I'll tell you everything straight out, brother, because they're fools. Zossimov told me to chat you up on the way and get you to chat back, and then tell him, because he's got this idea . . . that you're . . . mad, or close to it. Imagine that! First, you're three times smarter than he is; second, if you're not crazy, you'll spit on him having such drivel in his head; and third, this hunk of meat—a surgeon by profession—has now gone crazy over mental illnesses, and what finally turned him around about you was your conversation today with Zamyotov."

"Zamyotov told you everything?"

"Everything, and it's an excellent thing he did. I now understand it all inside and out; Zamyotov understands it, too . . . Well, in short, Rodya . . . the point is . . . I'm a bit drunk now . . . but that doesn't matter . . . the point is that this notion . . . you understand? . . . was really hatching in them . . . you understand? That is, none of them dared to say it aloud, because it's the most absurd drivel, and especially once they'd picked up that house-painter, it all popped and went out forever. But how can they be such fools? I gave Zamyotov a bit of a beating then—that's between us, brother, don't let out even a hint that you know; I've noticed he's touchy; it was at Laviza's—but today, today it all became clear. This Ilya Petrovich, mainly! He took advantage of your fainting in the office that time, but afterwards he felt ashamed himself, that I know . . ."

Raskolnikov listened greedily. Razumikhin was drunk and telling all.

"I fainted that time because it was stuffy and smelled of oil paint," Raskolnikov said.

"He keeps explaining! And it wasn't only the paint: that inflammation had been coming on for a whole month; Zossimov is here to testify! But how mortified the boy is now, you can't even imagine! 'I'm not worth his little finger!' he says—meaning yours. He occasionally has decent feelings, brother. But the lesson, the lesson today in the 'Crystal Palace,' that tops them all! You really scared him at first, nearly drove him to convulsions! You really almost convinced him again about all that hideous nonsense, and then suddenly—stuck your tongue out at him: 'Take that!' Perfect! Now he's crushed, destroyed! By God, you're an expert; it serves them right! Too bad I wasn't there! He's been waiting terribly for you now. Porfiry also wants to make your acquaintance . . ."

"Ah . . . him, too . . . And why have I been put down as mad?"

"Well, not mad, exactly. It seems I've been spouting off too much, brother . . . You see, it struck him today that you were interested only in just that one point; now it's clear why you were interested; knowing all the circumstances . . . and how it irritated you then, and got tangled up with your illness . . . I'm a little drunk, brother, only devil knows about him, he's got some idea in his head . . . I tell you, he's gone crazy over mental illnesses. But you can spit . . ."

They were silent for half a minute or so.

"Listen, Razumikhin," Raskolnikov started to say, "I want to tell you straight out: I'm just coming from a dead man's house, some official who died . . . I gave them all my money . . . and besides, I was just kissed by a being who, even if I had killed someone, would still . . . in short, I saw another being there, too . . . with a flame-colored feather . . . but I'm getting confused; I'm very weak, hold me up . . . here's the stairs . . ."

"What is it? What is it?" asked the alarmed Razumikhin.

"I'm a little dizzy, only that's not the point, but I feel so sad, so sad!—like a woman . . . really! Look, what's that? Look! Look!"

"What?"

"Don't you see? A light in my room, see? Through the crack . . ."

They were standing before the last flight, next to the landlady's door, and looking up one could indeed see that there was a light in Raskolnikov's closet.

"Strange! Nastasya, maybe," observed Razumikhin.

"She never comes to my room at this hour; besides, she's long been asleep, but . . . I don't care! Farewell!"

"But what is it? I'll take you up, we'll go in together!"

"I know we'll go in together, but I want to shake your hand here and say farewell to you here. So, give me your hand, and farewell!"

"What's got into you, Rodya?"

"Nothing; let's go; you'll be a witness . . ."

They began climbing the stairs, and the thought flashed through Razumikhin's mind that Zossimov might be right after all. "Eh, I upset him with all my babbling!" he muttered to himself. Suddenly, coming up to the door, they heard voices in the room.

"What's going on here?" Razumikhin cried out.

Raskolnikov took the door first and flung it wide open, flung it open and stood rooted to the threshold.

His mother and sister were sitting on the sofa, and had already been waiting there for an hour and a half. Why was it that he had expected them least of all, and had thought of them least of all, even in spite of the earlier repeated news that they had left, were on their way, would arrive any moment? For the entire hour and a half they had been vying with each other in questioning Nastasya, who was standing before them even now and had managed to tell them the whole story backwards and forwards. They were beside themselves with fear when they heard that "he ran away today," sick, and, as appeared from the story, certainly delirious. "God, what's become of him!" They both wept, they both endured the agony of the cross during that hour and a half of waiting.

A cry of rapturous joy greeted Raskolnikov's appearance. Both women rushed to him. But he stood like a dead man; a sudden, unbearable awareness struck him like a thunderbolt. And his arms would not rise to embrace them; they could not. His mother and sister hugged him tightly, kissed him, laughed, wept . . . He took a step, swayed, and collapsed on the floor in a faint.

Alarm, cries of terror, moans . . . Razumikhin, who was standing on the threshold, flew into the room, took the sick man up in his powerful arms, and in an instant had him lying on the sofa.

"It's nothing, nothing!" he cried to the mother and sister, "he's just fainted, it's all rubbish! The doctor just said he was much better, completely well! Water! See, he's already recovering; see, he's come to! . . ."

And grabbing Dunechka's arm so hard that he almost twisted it, he bent her down to see how "he's already come to." The mother and sister both looked upon Razumikhin with tenderness and gratitude, as on Providence itself; they had already heard from Nastasya what he had been for their Rodya throughout his illness—this "efficient young man," as he was referred to that same evening, in an intimate conversation with Dunya, by Pulcheria Alexandrovna Raskolnikov herself.

Part Three

I

Raskolnikov raised himself and sat up on the sofa.

He waved weakly at Razumikhin to stop the whole stream of incoherent and ardent consolations he was addressing to his mother and sister, took both of them by the hand, and for about two minutes peered silently now at the one, now at the other. His mother was frightened by his look. A strong feeling, to the point of suffering, shone in his eyes, but at the same time there was in them something fixed, even as if mad. Pulcheria Alexandrovna began to cry.

Avdotya Romanovna was pale; her hand trembled in her brother's hand.

"Go home . . . with him," he said in a broken voice, pointing at Razumikhin, "till tomorrow; tomorrow everything . . . Did you arrive long ago?"

"In the evening, Rodya," Pulcheria Alexandrovna answered. "The train was terribly late. But, Rodya, I won't leave you now for anything! I'll spend the night here, beside . . ."

"Don't torment me!" he said, waving his hand irritably.

"I'll stay with him!" cried Razumikhin. "I won't leave him for a moment; devil take all the people at my place, let them climb the walls! They've got my uncle for a president."

"How can I ever thank you!" Pulcheria Alexandrovna tried to begin, again pressing Razumikhin's hands, but Raskolnikov interrupted her once more.

"I can't, I can't," he kept repeating irritably, "don't torment me! Enough, go away . . . I can't! . . ."

"Come, mama, let's at least leave the room for a moment," Dunya whispered, frightened. "You can see we're distressing him."

"But can I really not even look at him after three years!" Pulcheria Alexandrovna began to cry.

"Wait!" he stopped them again. "You keep interrupting me, and my thoughts get confused . . . Have you seen Luzhin?"

"No, Rodya, but he already knows of our arrival. We have heard, Rodya, that Pyotr Petrovich was so good as to visit you today," Pulcheria Alexandrovna added, somewhat timidly.

"Yes . . . was so good . . . Dunya, I told Luzhin I'd kick him down the stairs today, and threw him the hell out of here . . ."

"Rodya, what are you saying! Surely you . . . you don't mean . . ." Pulcheria Alexandrovna began fearfully, but stopped, looking at Dunya.

Avdotya Romanovna peered intently at her brother and waited to hear more. They had both been forewarned of the quarrel by Nastasya, as far as she had been able to understand and convey it, and had suffered in perplexity and anticipation.

"Dunya," Raskolnikov continued with effort, "I do not want this marriage, and therefore you must refuse him tomorrow, first thing, so that he won't drag his face here again."

"My God!" cried Pulcheria Alexandrovna.

"Brother, think what you are saying!" Avdotya Romanovna began hot-temperedly, but at once restrained herself. "Perhaps you're in no condition now, you're tired," she said meekly.

"Raving? No . . . You're marrying Luzhin for my sake. And I do not accept the sacrifice. And therefore, by tomorrow, write a letter . . . of refusal . . . Give it to me to read in the morning, and there's an end to it!"

"I cannot do that!" the offended girl cried out. "What right have you . . ."

"Dunechka, you're too hot-tempered yourself; stop now; tomorrow . . . Don't you see . . ." the frightened mother rushed to Dunya. "Ah, we'd better go!"

"He's raving!" the drunk Razumikhin shouted. "Otherwise how would he dare! Tomorrow all this foolishness will leave him . . . But he really did throw him out today. Just like he said. Well, and the other one got angry . . . He was playing the orator here, showing off his knowledge, and then he left with his tail between his legs . . ."

"So it's true?" Pulcheria Alexandrovna cried out.

"Until tomorrow, brother," Dunya said with compassion. "Come, mama . . . Good-bye, Rodya!"

"Listen, sister," he repeated to her back, summoning a last effort,

"I'm not raving; this marriage is a vile thing. Maybe I'm vile myself, but you mustn't . . . one is enough . . . and though I may be vile, I will not regard such a sister as a sister. It's either me or Luzhin! Go, both of you . . ."

"You're out of your mind! Despot!" Razumikhin roared, but Raskolnikov no longer answered, and was perhaps unable to answer. He lay back on the sofa and turned to the wall, completely exhausted. Avdotya Romanovna gave Razumikhin a curious look; her dark eyes flashed; Razumikhin even jumped under her glance. Pulcheria Alexandrovna stood as if stunned.

"I cannot possibly leave!" she whispered to Razumikhin, almost in despair. "I'll stay here, somewhere . . . Take Dunya home."

"You'll spoil the whole thing!" Razumikhin also whispered, losing his temper. "Let's at least go out to the stairs. Nastasya, a light! I swear to you," he continued in a half whisper, once they were on the stairs, "he almost gave us a beating earlier, the doctor and me! Do you understand? The doctor himself! And he gave in and left so as not to irritate him, and I stayed to keep watch downstairs, but he got dressed and slipped out. And he'll slip out now if you irritate him, in the dark, and do something to himself . . ."

"Ah, what are you saying!"

"Besides, it's impossible for Avdotya Romanovna to be in that place without you! Just think where you're staying! As if that scoundrel Pyotr Petrovich couldn't have found you better . . . You know, I'm a bit drunk, though; that's why I'm . . . calling names; don't pay any . . ."

"But I shall go to the landlady here," Pulcheria Alexandrovna insisted. "I shall plead with her to give me and Dunya a corner for tonight. I cannot leave him like this, I cannot!"

They were standing on the stairway as they spoke, on the landing just outside the landlady's door. Nastasya held the light for them from the bottom step. Razumikhin was extremely agitated. Half an hour earlier, as he was taking Raskolnikov home, though he had been unnecessarily talkative and he knew it, he had felt completely alert and almost fresh, despite the terrible quantity of wine he had drunk that evening. But now his condition even bordered on a sort of ecstasy, and at the same time it was as if all the wine he had drunk came rushing to his head again, all at once, and with twice the force. He stood with the two ladies, grasping them both by the hand, persuading them and presenting his arguments with amazing frankness, and at almost every word, probably for added conviction, he painfully squeezed their hands, very tightly, as in a vise, and he seemed to devour Avdotya Romanovna with his eyes, without being the least embarrassed by it. Once or twice the pain made them try to free their hands from his huge and bony grip, but he not only did not notice the reason for it, but drew them to him even more tightly. If at that moment they had ordered him to throw himself headlong down the stairs, as a service to them, he would have carried out the order at once, without argument or hesitation. Pulcheria Alexandrovna, alarmed as she was by the thought of her Rodya, though she felt that the young man was being much too eccentric and was pressing her hand too painfully, at the same time, since he was like her Providence, did not wish to notice all these eccentric details. But Avdotya Romanovna, who shared her alarm, though far from fearful by nature, was amazed and almost frightened to meet the eyes of her brother's friend, flashing with wild fire, and only the boundless trust inspired by Nastasya's stories about this strange man held her back from the temptation of running away from him and dragging her mother with her. She also understood that now, perhaps, they even could not run away from him. However, after about ten minutes she felt considerably reassured: Razumikhin had the property of speaking the whole of himself out at once, whatever mood he was in, so that everyone soon knew with whom they were dealing.

"It's impossible to go to the landlady, and it's terrible nonsense!" he cried out, reasoning with Pulcheria Alexandrovna. "You may be his mother, but if you stay, you'll drive him into a fury, and then devil knows what will happen! Listen, here's what I'll do: Nastasya will sit with him now, and I'll take you both to your place, because you can't go through the streets by yourselves; our Petersburg, in that respect . . . Well, spit on it! . . . Then I'll run back here at once, and in a quarter of an hour, on my greatest word of honor, I'll bring you a report: how he is, whether he's sleeping, and all the rest of it. Then—listen!—then from you I'll go straight to my place—I have guests there, all drunk— I'll pick up Zossimov—that's the doctor who's treating him, he's at my place now, not drunk; no, he's not drunk, he never gets drunk! I'll drag him to Rodka, and then straight to you, so within an hour you'll get two reports on him—one from the doctor, you understand, from the doctor himself; that's a whole lot better than from me! If he's bad, I swear I'll bring you here myself; if he's well, you can go to sleep. And I'll spend the whole night here, in the entryway, he won't hear me, and I'll tell Zossimov to sleep at the landlady's, so as to be on hand. So, what's better for him now, you or the doctor? The doctor is much more useful, much more. So go home, then! And staying with the landlady's impossible; possible for me, but impossible for you—she won't let you, because . . . because she's a fool. She'll get jealous of Avdotya Romanovna on account of me, if you want to know, and of you as well . . . And of Avdotya Romanovna certainly. She's a totally, totally unexpected character! However, I'm a fool myself . . . Spit on it! Let's go! Do you believe me? Well, do you believe me or not?"

"Come, mama," said Avdotya Romanovna, "he will surely do as he's promised. He already resurrected my brother, and if it's true that the doctor is willing to spend the night here, what could be better?"

"So you . . . you . . . you understand me, because you're an angel!" Razumikhin cried out rapturously. "Let's go! Nastasya! Upstairs this minute, and sit there by him, with a light; I'll be back in a quarter of an hour . . ."

Pulcheria Alexandrovna, though not fully convinced, no longer resisted. Razumikhin took both women by the arm and dragged them down the stairs. Nevertheless, she worried about him: "He may be efficient and kind, but is he capable of carrying out his promise? He's in such a state! . . ."

"Ah, I see you're thinking what a state I'm in!" Razumikhin interrupted her thoughts, having guessed them, and went striding along the sidewalk with his enormously long steps, so that the two ladies could barely keep up with him—which fact, however, he did not notice. "Nonsense! That is . . . I'm drunk as a dolt, but that's not the point; I'm drunk, but not with wine. The moment I saw you, it went to my head . . . But spit on me! Don't pay any attention: I'm talking nonsense; I'm unworthy of you . . . I'm unworthy of you in the highest degree! . . . But as soon as I've taken you home, I'll come straight here to the canal, and pour two tubs of water over my head, and be ready to go . . . If only you knew how I love you both! . . . Don't laugh, and don't be angry! . . . Be angry with everyone else, but don't be angry with me! I'm his friend, so I'm your friend, too. I want it that way . . . I had a presentiment . . . last year, there was a certain moment . . . Not a presentiment at all, however, because it's as if you fell from the sky. And maybe I won't even sleep all night . . . This Zossimov was afraid today that he might lose his mind . . . That's why he shouldn't be irritated."

"What are you saying!" the mother cried out.

"Did the doctor really say so himself?" Avdotya Romanovna asked, frightened.

"He did, but it's not that, not that at all. And he gave him some sort of medication, a powder, I saw it, and then you arrived . . . Eh! . . . If only you could have come a day later! It's a good thing we left. And in an hour Zossimov himself will give you a full report. He's certainly not drunk! And I won't be drunk either . . . Why did I get so cockeyed? Because they dragged me into an argument, curse them! I swore I wouldn't argue! . . . They pour out such hogwash! I almost got into a fight! I left my uncle there as chairman . . . Well, so they insist on total impersonality, can you believe it? And that's just where they find the most relish! Not to be oneself, to be least of all like oneself! And that they consider the highest progress. If only they had their own way of lying, but no, they . . ."

"Listen," Pulcheria Alexandrovna interrupted timidly, but she only added fuel to the fire.

"What do you think?" Razumikhin shouted, raising his voice even more. "You think it's because they're lying? Nonsense! I like it when people lie! Lying is man's only privilege over all other organisms. If you lie—you get to the truth! Lying is what makes me a man. Not one truth has ever been reached without first lying fourteen times or so, maybe a hundred and fourteen, and that's honorable in its way; well, but we can't even lie with our own minds! Lie to me, but in your own way, and I'll kiss you for it. Lying in one's own way is almost better than telling the truth in someone else's way; in the first case you're a man, and in the second—no better than a bird! The truth won't go away, but life can be nailed shut; there are examples. Well, so where are we all now? With regard to science, development, thought, invention, ideals, aspirations, liberalism, reason, experience, and everything,

everything, everything, we're all, without exception, still sitting in the first grade! We like getting by on other people's reason—we've acquired a taste for it! Right? Am I right?" Razumikhin shouted, shaking and squeezing both ladies' hands. "Am I right?"

"Oh, my God, I don't know," said poor Pulcheria Alexandrovna.

"Yes, you're right . . . though I don't agree with you in everything," Avdotya Romanovna added seriously, and immediately cried out, so painfully did he squeeze her hand this time.

"Right? You say I'm right? Well, then you . . . you . . ." he cried rapturously, "you are a wellspring of kindness, purity, reason, and . . . perfection! Give me your hand, give it to me . . . you give me yours, too; I want to kiss your hands, here and now, on my knees!"

And he knelt in the middle of the sidewalk, which at that hour was fortunately deserted.

"Stop, I beg you! What are you doing?" Pulcheria Alexandrovna cried out, extremely alarmed.

"Get up, get up!" Dunya was alarmed, too, but laughing.

"Never! Not until you give me your hands! There, and enough now! I get up, and we go! I'm a miserable dolt, I'm unworthy of you, and drunk, and ashamed . . . I'm not worthy to love you, but to worship you is every man's duty, unless he's a perfect brute! So, I have worshipped . . . Here's your rooming house—and for this alone Rodion was right to throw your Pyotr Petrovich out today! How dared he place you in such rooms? It's a scandal! Do you know who they let in here? And you're his fiancée! You are his fiancée, aren't you? Well, let me tell you in that case that your fiancé is a scoundrel!"

"Listen, Mr. Razumikhin, you are forgetting yourself . . ." Pulcheria Alexandrovna tried to begin.

"Yes, yes, you're right, I'm forgetting myself, shame on me!" Razumikhin suddenly checked himself. "But . . . but . . . you cannot be angry with me for speaking this way! For I'm speaking sincerely, and not because . . . hm! that would be base; in short, not because I'm . . . hm . . . with you . . . well, never mind, let's drop it, I won't tell you why, I don't dare! . . . And we all realized as soon as he came in today that he was not a man of our kind. Not because he came with his hair curled by a hairdresser, not because he was in a hurry to show off his intelligence, but because he's a stool pigeon and a speculator; because he's a Jew and a mountebank, and it shows. You think he's intelligent? No, he's a fool, a fool! So, is he a match for you? Oh, my God! You see, ladies," he suddenly stopped, already on the way up to their rooms, "they may all be drunk at my place, but they're all honest, and though we do lie—because I lie, too—in the end we'll lie our way to the truth, because we're on a noble path, while Pyotr Petrovich . . . is not on a noble path. And though I just roundly denounced them, I do respect them all—even Zamyotov; maybe I don't respect him, but I still love him, because he's a puppy! Even that brute Zossimov, because he's honest and knows his business . . . but enough, all's said and forgiven. Forgiven? Is it? So, let's go. I know this corridor, I was here once; here, in number three, there was a scandal . . . Well, which is yours? What number? Eight? So, lock your door for the night and don't let anyone in. I'll be back in a quarter of an hour with news, and in another half an hour with Zossimov—you'll see! Good-bye, I'm running!"

"My God, Dunechka, what will come of this?" said Pulcheria Alexandrovna, turning anxiously and fearfully to her daughter.

"Calm yourself, mama," Dunya answered, taking off her hat and cape, "God Himself has sent us this gentleman, though he may have come straight from some binge. We can rely on him, I assure you. And with all he's already done for my brother . . ."

"Ah, Dunechka, God knows if he'll come back! How could I bring myself to leave Rodya! And this is not at all, not at all how I imagined finding him! He was so stern, as if he weren't glad to see us . . ."

Tears came to her eyes.

"No, mama, it's not so. You didn't look closely, you kept crying. He's very upset from this great illness—that's the reason for it all."

"Ah, this illness! What will come of it, what will come of it! And how he spoke with you, Dunya!" her mother said, peeking timidly into her daughter's eyes in order to read the whole of her thought, and already half comforted by the fact that Dunya herself was defending Rodya and had therefore forgiven him. "I'm sure he'll think better of it tomorrow," she added, trying to worm it all out of her.

"And I am sure he'll say the same thing tomorrow . . . about that," Avdotya Romanovna cut her off, and here, of course, was the snag, because this was the point which Pulcheria Alexandrovna was simply too afraid to bring up now. Dunya went over and kissed her mother.

Her mother hugged her tightly and said nothing. Then she sat down, anxiously awaiting Razumikhin's return, and began timidly to watch her daughter who, also in expectation, crossed her arms and began to pace the room back and forth, thinking to herself. Such thoughtful pacing from corner to corner was a usual habit with Avdotya Romanovna, and her mother was somehow always afraid to interrupt her thinking at such times.

Razumikhin was of course ridiculous, with the sudden, drunken flaring up of his passion for Avdotya Romanovna; but one look at Avdotya Romanovna, especially now, as she paced the room with her arms crossed, sad and thoughtful, and many would perhaps have excused him, quite apart from his eccentric state. Avdotya Romanovna was remarkably good-looking—tall, wonderfully trim, strong, self-confident, as showed in her every gesture, but without in the least detracting from the softness and grace of her movements. She resembled her brother in looks, and could even be called a beauty. Her hair was dark blond, a little lighter than her brother's; her eyes were almost black, flashing, proud, and at the same time, occasionally, for moments, remarkably kind. She was pale, but not sickly pale; her face shone with freshness and health. Her mouth was somewhat small, and her lower lip, fresh and red, protruded slightly, as did her chin—the only irregularity in this beautiful face, but which lent it a specially characteristic quality and, incidentally, a trace of arrogance. The expression of her face was always serious and thoughtful rather than gay; but how becoming was her smile, how becoming her laughter—gay, young, wholehearted! It was understandable that Razumikhin, ardent, sincere, simple, honest, strong as a folk hero, and drunk, who had never seen anything like that, lost his head at first sight. Moreover, as if by design, chance showed him Dunya for the first time in a beautiful moment of love and joy at seeing her brother. Then he noticed how her lower lip trembled indignantly in response to her brother's impertinent and ungratefully cruel orders—and lost all resistance.

He was telling the truth, however, when he let out that drunken nonsense earlier, on the stairs, about Raskolnikov's eccentric landlady, Praskovya Pavlovna, becoming jealous on his account not only of Avdotya Romanovna, but perhaps of Pulcheria Alexandrovna as well. Although Pulcheria Alexandrovna was already forty-three years old, her face still kept the remnants of its former beauty, and besides, she looked much younger than her age, as almost always happens with women who keep their clarity of spirit, the freshness of their impressions, and the honest, pure ardor of their hearts into old age. Let us say parenthetically that keeping all this is the only means of preserving one's beauty even in old age. Her hair was already thinning and starting to turn gray, little radiating wrinkles had long since appeared around her eyes, her cheeks were sunken and dry from worry and grief, and still her face was beautiful. It was a portrait of Dunechka's face, only twenty years later, and lacking the expression of the protruding lower lip. Pulcheria Alexandrovna was sentimental, though not to the point of being saccharine; she was timid and yielding, but only up to a limit: she would yield much, would agree to much, even to something that went against her convictions, but there was always a limit of honesty, principle, and ultimate conviction beyond which no circumstances could make her step.

Exactly twenty minutes after Razumikhin left, there came two soft but hurried knocks on the door; he was back.

"No time to come in!" he began hastily, when they opened the door. "He's snoring away excellently, peacefully, and God grant he sleeps for ten hours. Nastasya's with him; I told her not to leave before I get back. Now I'll go and drag Zossimov there, he'll give you a report, and then you, too, should turn in; I see you're impossibly worn out."

And he set off again down the corridor.

"What an efficient and . . . devoted young man!" Pulcheria Alexandrovna exclaimed, exceedingly glad.

"He seems to be a nice person!" Avdotya Romanovna answered with some warmth, again beginning to pace the room back and forth.

Almost an hour later steps were heard in the corridor and there was another knock at the door. Both women were waiting, this time, with complete faith in Razumikhin's promise; and indeed he had managed to drag Zossimov along. Zossimov had agreed at once to leave the feast and go to have a look at Raskolnikov, but he came to the ladies reluctantly and with great mistrust, not trusting the drunken Razumikhin. Yet his vanity was immediately set at ease, and even flattered: he realized that he was indeed being awaited like an oracle. He stayed for exactly ten minutes and managed to convince Pulcheria Alexandrovna and set her at ease completely. He spoke with extraordinary sympathy, but with restraint and with a somehow eager seriousness, precisely like a twenty-seven-year-old doctor in an important consultation, not deviating from the subject by a single word or revealing the least desire to enter into more private and personal relations with the two ladies. Having noted upon entering how dazzlingly beautiful Avdotya Romanovna was, he immediately tried not to pay her any notice during the whole time of his visit, and addressed himself to Pulcheria Alexandrovna alone. All this gave him great inner satisfaction. About the patient himself he was able to say that at the present moment he found his condition quite satisfactory. Also, from his observations, the patient's illness had, apart from the poor material circumstances of the recent months of his life, some moral causes as well, "being, so to speak, a product of many complex moral and material influences, anxieties, apprehensions, worries, certain ideas . . . and other things." Having noted in passing that Avdotya Romanovna had begun to listen with special attentiveness, Zossimov expanded somewhat further on this subject. To Pulcheria Alexandrovna's anxious and timid question concerning "some supposed suspicions of madness," he replied, with a calm and frank smile, that his words had been overly exaggerated; that, of course, some fixed idea could be observed in the patient, something suggesting monomania—since he, Zossimov, was now especially following this extremely interesting branch of medicine—but it was also to be remembered that the patient had been delirious almost up to that day, and . . . and, of course, the arrival of his family would strengthen, divert, and have a salutary effect upon him, "if only it is possible to avoid any special new shocks," he added significantly. Then he got up, bowed his way out sedately and cordially, to the accompaniment of blessings, warm gratitude, entreaties, and even, without his having sought it, the offer of Avdotya Romanovna's little hand to shake, and left extremely pleased with his visit and still more with himself.

"And we'll talk tomorrow; go to bed, right now, you must!" Razumikhin clinched, following Zossimov out. "Tomorrow, as early as possible, I'll come with a report."

"But what a ravishing girl that Avdotya Romanovna is!" Zossimov observed, all but licking his chops, as they came out to the street.

"Ravishing? Did you say ravishing!" Razumikhin bellowed, and he suddenly flew at Zossimov and seized him by the throat. "If you ever dare . . . Understand? Understand?" he shouted, shaking him by the collar and pushing him against the wall. "Do you hear?"

"Let go, you drunken devil!" Zossimov fought him off and, when Razumikhin finally let go, looked at him closely and suddenly burst out laughing. Razumikhin stood before him, his arms hanging down, in dark and serious thought.

"I'm an ass, of course," he said, dark as a storm cloud, "but then . . . so are you."

"No, brother, not me. I don't have such foolish dreams."

They walked on silently, and only as they were nearing Raskolnikov's house did Razumikhin, who was greatly preoccupied, break the silence.

"Listen," he said to Zossimov, "you're a nice fellow, but, on top of all your other bad qualities, you're also a philanderer, I know that, and a dirty one. You're a piece of nervous, weak-willed trash, you're whimsical, you've grown fat and can't deny yourself anything—and I call that dirty, because it leads straight to dirt. You've pampered yourself so much that, I confess, the thing I'm least able to understand is how with all that you can still be a good and even selfless physician. You sleep on a feather bed (you, a doctor!), yet you get up in the night for a sick man! In three years or so you won't be getting up for any sick man . . . But, the devil, that's not the point; the point is that you'll be spending the night in the landlady's apartment (it took a lot to convince her!), and I in the kitchen—so here's a chance for you to get more closely acquainted! It's not what you're thinking! Not a shadow of it, brother . . ."

"But I'm not thinking anything."

"What you have here, brother, is modesty, reticence, shyness, fierce chastity, and for all that—a few sighs and she melts like wax, just melts away! Deliver me from her, in the name of all the devils in the world! She's such a winsome little thing! . . . I'll earn it, I'll earn it with my head!"

Zossimov guffawed more than ever.

"Well, you've really got it bad! But what do I need her for?"

"I guarantee it won't be much trouble; just talk whatever slop you like, just sit next to her and talk. Besides, you're a doctor, you can start treating her for something. I swear you won't regret it. She has a piano there; I can strum a little, you know; there's one song I sing, a Russian song, a real one: 'I'll bathe myself in bitter tears . . .' She likes the real ones—well, so it started with a little song; but you are a piano virtuoso, a maestro, a Rubinstein[1] . . . I guarantee you won't regret it."

"Why, did you give her some sort of promise? A formal receipt or something? Maybe you promised to marry . . ."

"Nothing, nothing, absolutely nothing of the sort! And she's not like that at all; Chebarov tried to . . ."

"Just drop her, then!"

"But I can't just drop her like that!"

"But why can't you?"

"Well, somehow I can't, that's all! There's a sucking-in principle here, brother."

"Then why have you been leading her on?"

"But I haven't been leading her on at all; maybe I got led on my-self, in my stupidity; and for her it makes absolutely no difference whether it's you or me, as long as somebody sits next to her and sighs. Look, brother . . . I don't know how to phrase it for you, but look—you know a lot about mathematics, for instance, and you're still studying it, I know . . . so, start teaching her integral calculus—by God, I'm not joking, I'm serious, it'll be decidedly all the same to her; she'll look at you and sigh, and so on for a whole year. I, inci-dentally, spent a very long time, two days in a row, telling her about the Prussian House of Lords[2] (because otherwise what can you talk to her about?)—and she just sighed and stewed! Only don't start talking about love—she's shy to the point of convulsions—but still make it look as if you can't leave her side—and that's enough. It's terribly comfortable, just like home—read, sit, lie down, write . . . You can even kiss her, if you do it carefully . . ."

"But what do I need her for?"

"Eh, really, I can't seem to explain it to you! You see, the two of you suit each other perfectly! I even thought about you before . . . You'll end up with it anyway! Do you care whether it's sooner or later? Here, brother, there's this feather-bed principle—eh, and not only a feather-bed principle! It sucks you in, it's the end of the world, an anchor, a quiet haven, the navel of the earth, the three-fish foundation of the world, the essence of pancakes, rich meat pies, evening samovars, soft sighs and warm vests, heated beds on the stove—well, just as if you died and were alive at the same time, both benefits at once! Well, the devil, brother, I've talked enough rot, it's time for bed! Listen, I sometimes wake up at night, so I'll go and look in on him. Only it's nothing, nonsense, everything's fine. You needn't worry especially, but if you want, you can look in once. But if you notice anything, delirium, for instance, or a fever, or whatever, wake me up immediately. It's not possible, though . . ."

II

PREOCCUPIED and serious, Razumikhin woke up the next day between seven and eight. In the morning he suddenly turned out to have many new and unforeseen perplexities. He had never before imagined that he would wake up like that one day. He recalled every last detail of the previous day, realizing that something uncommon had befallen him, and that he had received into himself a certain impression heretofore unknown to him and unlike any other. At the same time he clearly understood that the dream that had begun burning in his head was in the highest degree unrealizable—so unrealizable that he was even ashamed of it, and he hurried on to other, more urgent cares and perplexities bequeathed him by that "thrice-cursed yesterday."

His most terrible recollection was of how "base and vile" he had turned out to be, not only because he was drunk, but because, taking advantage of the girl's situation, he had abused her fiancé before her, out of stupidly hasty jealousy, not only knowing nothing of their mutual relations and commitments but not even knowing the man himself properly. And what right did he have to judge him so hastily and rashly? And who had invited him to be a judge! Was such a being as Avdotya Romanovna indeed capable of giving herself to an unworthy man for money? So there must be some worth in him. The rooms? But how, in fact, could he have known they were that sort of rooms? He was having an apartment made ready, after all . . . pah, how base it all was! He was drunk, but what sort of justification was that? A silly excuse, which humiliated him even more! The truth is in wine, and so this whole truth told itself—"that is, all the filth of his envious, boorish heart!" And was such a dream in any degree permissible for him, Razumikhin? Who was he compared with such a girl—he, a drunken brawler and yesterday's braggart? "Is such a cynical and ridiculous juxtaposition possible?" Razumikhin blushed desperately at the thought of it, and suddenly, as if by design, at the same moment he clearly recalled standing on the stairs yesterday, telling them that the landlady would be jealous of Avdotya Romanovna on account of him . . . that was really unbearable. He swung with all his might and hit the kitchen stove with his fist, hurting his hand and knocking out a brick.

"Of course," he muttered to himself after a moment, with some feeling of self-abasement, "of course, now I can never paint or smooth over all those nasty things . . . so there's no point in thinking about it, I must simply go silently and . . . do my duty . . . also silently . . . and not apologize or say anything, and . . . and, of course, all is lost now!"

Nevertheless, as he was getting dressed, he looked over his outfit more carefully than usual. He had no other clothes, and even if he had, he would perhaps not have put them on—"just so, I wouldn't, on purpose." But all the same he could not go on being a cynic and a dirty sloven: he had no right to offend other people's feelings, all the more so in that those others needed him and were calling him to them. He gave his clothes a careful brushing. And the linen he wore was always passable; in that sense he was particularly clean.

He washed zealously that morning—Nastasya found him some soap—washed his hair, his neck, and especially his hands. But when it came to the question of whether or not to shave his stubble (Praskovya Pavlovna had excellent razors, still preserved from the late Mr. Zarnitsyn), the question was resolved, even with a vengeance, in the negative: "Let it stay as it is! What if they should think I shaved in order to . . . and that's certainly what they would think! No, not for anything in the world!"

And . . . and, above all, he was so coarse, so dirty, with his tavern manners; and . . . and suppose he knew that he was still, let us say, a decent man at least . . . well, what was there to be proud of in being a decent man? Everyone ought to be a decent man, and even better than that, and . . . and still (now he remembered) there were some little turns laid to his account . . . not really dishonest, but all the same! . . . And what thoughts he sometimes had! Hm . . . and to set all that next to Avdotya Romanovna! "Well, so, the devil! Who cares! I'll be dirty, salacious, tavern-mannered on purpose, and to hell with it! I'll be even more so! . . ."

In these monologues he was found by Zossimov, who had spent the night in Praskovya Pavlovna's drawing room.

He was about to go home, and was hurrying to have a look at the sick man before he left. Razumikhin reported to him that he was sleeping like a log. Zossimov gave orders not to rouse him before he woke up on his own. And he promised to stop by some time after ten.

"I only hope he'll be here," he added. "Pah, the devil! No control over my own patient; just try treating him! Do you know if *he* will go to them or *they* will come here?"

"They'll come, I think," Razumikhin replied, understanding the intent of the question, "and, of course, they'll talk over their family affairs. I'll leave. As a doctor, naturally, you have more rights than I do."

"But I'm also not their father confessor. I'll come and go. I have enough to do without them."

"One thing troubles me," Razumikhin interrupted, frowning. "Yesterday, being drunk, I blurted out various foolish things to him as we walked along . . . various things . . . among them that you're afraid he . . . is inclined to madness."

"You blurted out the same thing to the ladies as well."

"I know it was stupid! Beat me if you like! And did you really have some firm idea?"

"But it's nonsense, I tell you; what firm idea! You yourself described him as a monomaniac when you brought me to him . . . Well, and then yesterday we added more fuel—that is, you did—with those stories . . . about the house-painter; a nice conversation that was, when it may have been just what made him lose his mind! If only I'd known exactly what happened in the office that time, and that some boor had . . . offended him with that suspicion! Hm . . . I wouldn't have allowed such a conversation yesterday. Because these monomaniacs turn a drop into an ocean, they think any sort of claptrap is a reality . . . As far as I remember, I understood half of this business from Zamyotov's story yesterday. But that's nothing! I know a case of a hypochondriac, a forty-year-old man, who couldn't stand an eight-year-old boy's daily mockery at the table, and put a knife in him! And there he was, all in rags, an insolent policeman, the start of an illness, and such a suspicion! For a wild hypochondriac! With such rabid, exceptional vanity! The whole starting point of the illness may well have been sitting right there! Well, so, the devil! . . . Incidentally, this Zamyotov really is a nice boy, only . . . hm . . . he shouldn't have told all that yesterday. An awful babbler!"

"But who did he tell? Me and you?"

"And Porfiry."

"So, why not Porfiry?"

"Incidentally, do you have any influence over those two, the mother and the sister? They should be more careful with him today . . ."

"They'll manage!" Razumikhin answered reluctantly.

"And why is he so much against this Luzhin? The man has money, she doesn't seem averse to him . . . and they don't have a bean, do they?"

"What are you trying to worm out of me?" Razumikhin cried irritably. "Bean or no bean, how do I know? Ask them yourself, maybe you'll find out . . ."

"Pah, how stupid you are sometimes! Yesterday's drunkenness is still sitting in you . . . Good-bye; thank your Praskovya Pavlovna for the night's lodging. She locked herself in, wouldn't answer my *bonjour* through the door, but she got up at seven o'clock, a samovar was brought to her through the corridor from the kitchen . . . I wasn't deemed worthy of beholding . . ."

At nine o'clock sharp Razumikhin arrived at Bakaleev's rooming house. The two ladies had been awaiting him for a long, long time, with hysterical impatience. They had risen at about seven, or even earlier. He came in looking dark as night, and bowed awkwardly, for which he immediately became angry—at himself, of course. He had reckoned without his host: Pulcheria Alexandrovna simply rushed to him, seized both his hands, and almost kissed them. He glanced timidly at Avdotya Romanovna, but that arrogant face had at the moment an expression of such gratitude and friendliness, such complete and, for him, unexpected esteem (instead of mocking looks and involuntary, poorly disguised contempt!) that it would truly have been easier for him if he had been met with abuse; otherwise it was too embarrassing. Fortunately, there was a ready topic of conversation, and he hastened to seize upon it.

Having heard that "he was not awake yet" but that "everything was excellent," Pulcheria Alexandrovna declared that it was all for the better, "because she needed very, very, very much to discuss things first." The question of tea followed, with an invitation to have it together; they had not had anything yet, since they were expecting Razumikhin. Avdotya Romanovna rang the bell, a dirty ragamuffin answered the summons, tea was ordered and eventually served, but in so dirty and improper a fashion that the ladies were ashamed. Razumikhin vehemently denounced the rooming house but, remembering about Luzhin, fell silent, became embarrassed, and was terribly glad when Pulcheria Alexandrovna's questions finally came pouring out one after another, without a break.

He spent three-quarters of an hour answering them, constantly interrupted and questioned again, and managed to convey the most important and necessary facts as he knew them from the last year of Rodion Romanovich's life, concluding with a detailed account of his illness. However, he omitted much of what was better omitted, including the scene in the office with all its consequences. His account was greedily listened to; but when he thought he had already finished and satisfied his listeners, it turned out that for them it was as if he had not yet begun.

"Tell me, tell me, what do you think . . . ah, forgive me, I still do not know your name!" Pulcheria Alexandrovna hurried.

"Dmitri Prokofych."

"Now then, Dmitri Prokofych, I should like very, very much to know . . . generally . . . how he looks at things now—that is, please understand me, how shall I put it—that is, better to say: what are his likes and dislikes? Is he always so irritable? What are his wishes and, so to speak, his dreams, if you can say? What precisely has a special influence on him now? In short, I should like . . ."

"Ah, mama, how can anyone answer so much all at once?" Dunya remarked.

"Ah, my God, but this is not at all, not at all how I expected to see him, Dmitri Prokofych."

"That's only natural," Dmitri Prokofych replied. "I have no mother, but my uncle comes here every year, and almost every time fails to recognize me, even externally, and he is an intelligent man; well, and in the three years of your separation a lot of water has flowed under the bridge. What can I tell you? I've known Rodion for a year and a half: sullen, gloomy, arrogant, proud; recently (and maybe much earlier) insecure and hypochondriac. Magnanimous and kind. Doesn't like voicing his feelings, and would rather do something cruel than speak his heart out in words. At times, however, he's not hypochondriac at all, but just inhumanly cold and callous, as if there really were two opposite characters in him, changing places with each other. At times he's terribly taciturn! He's always in a hurry, always too busy, yet he lies there doing nothing. Not given to mockery, and not because he lacks sharpness but as if he had no time for such trifles. Never hears people out to the end. Is never interested in what interests everyone else at a given moment. Sets a terribly high value on himself and, it seems, not without a certain justification. Well, what else? . . . It seems to me that your arrival will have a salutary effect on him."

"Ah, God grant us that!" Pulcheria Alexandrovna cried out, tormented by Razumikhin's assessment of her Rodya.

And Razumikhin at last looked more courageously at Avdotya Romanovna. He had glanced at her frequently during the conversation, but cursorily, for a moment only, looking away at once. Avdotya Romanovna now sat at the table and listened attentively, now got up again and began pacing from corner to corner, as was her habit, arms crossed, lips pressed together, occasionally asking a question without interrupting her pacing, and again falling into thought. She, too, had the habit of not hearing people out to the end. She was wearing a dark dress of some thin fabric, with a sheer white scarf tied around her neck. Razumikhin noted at once by many tokens that both women were in extremely poor circumstances. Had Avdotya Romanovna been dressed like a queen, he most likely would not have been afraid of her at all; but now, perhaps just because she was so poorly dressed and because he noticed this whole niggardly situation, fear crept into his heart, and he became apprehensive of every word, every gesture—which, of course, was inconvenient for a man who did not trust himself to begin with.

"You have said many curious things about my brother's character, and . . . have spoken impartially. That's good; I thought you were in awe of him," Avdotya Romanovna observed with a smile. "It also seems true that he ought to have a woman around him," she added pensively.

"I didn't say so, but perhaps you're right about that, too, only . . ."

"What?"

"He doesn't love anyone, and maybe he never will," Razumikhin said bluntly.

"You mean he's unable to love?"

"And you know, Avdotya Romanovna, you resemble your brother terribly much, in everything even!" he suddenly blurted out, unexpectedly for himself, but, recalling what he had just told her about her brother, he immediately blushed like a lobster and became terribly embarrassed. Looking at him, Avdotya Romanovna could not help laughing.

"You both may be mistaken about Rodya," Pulcheria Alexandrovna interrupted, somewhat piqued. "I'm not talking about now, Dunechka. What Pyotr Petrovich writes in this letter . . . and what you and I were supposing, may not be true, but you cannot even imagine, Dmitri Prokofych, how fantastical and, how shall I put it, capricious he is. I could never trust his character, even when he was only fifteen years old. I'm certain that even now he might suddenly do something with himself that no other man would ever think of doing . . . There's no need to look far: do you know how he astounded me, shocked me, and all but completely did me in a year ago, when he took it into his head to marry that—what's her name?—Zarnitsyn, his landlady's daughter?"

"Do you know any details of that story?" asked Avdotya Romanovna.

"Do you think," Pulcheria Alexandrovna continued hotly, "that my tears, my pleas, my illness, my possible death from grief, our poverty, would have stopped him? He would have stepped quite calmly over every obstacle. Yet can it be, can it be that he doesn't love us?"

"He never told me anything about that story himself," Razumikhin answered cautiously, "but I have heard a thing or two from Mrs. Zarnitsyn herself, who for her own part is also not a great talker, and what I heard is perhaps even a bit strange . . ."

"But what, what did you hear?" both women asked at once.

"Nothing so very special, really. I only learned that this marriage, which was already quite settled and failed to take place only because of the bride's death, was not at all to Mrs. Zarnitsyn's liking . . . Besides, they say the bride was not even good-looking—that is, they say she was even homely . . . and quite sickly and . . . and strange . . . though it seems she had some merits. There absolutely must have been some merits; otherwise none of it makes any sense . . . There was no dowry either, but he wouldn't have counted on a dowry . . . Generally, it's hard to judge in such matters."

"I'm sure she was a worthy girl," Avdotya Romanovna observed tersely.

"God forgive me, but I was glad of her death all the same, though I don't know which of them would have ruined the other, he her or she him," Pulcheria Alexandrovna concluded; then carefully, with pauses and constant glances at Dunya, who obviously did not like it, she again began to ask questions about the previous day's scene between Rodya and Luzhin. One could see that this event troubled her most of all, to the point of fear and trembling. Razumikhin went over everything again in detail, but this time also added his own conclusion: he accused Raskolnikov straight out of deliberately insulting Pyotr Petrovich, this time excusing him very little on account of his illness.

"He thought it all up before his illness," he added.

"I think so, too," Pulcheria Alexandrovna said, looking crushed. But she was greatly struck that Razumikhin this time spoke so carefully, even as if respectfully, about Pyotr Petrovich. Avdotya Romanovna was also struck by this.

"So this is your opinion of Pyotr Petrovich?" Pulcheria Alexandrovna could not help asking.

"I cannot be of any other opinion regarding your daughter's future husband," Razumikhin replied, firmly and ardently, "and I say it not only out of common politeness, but because . . . because . . . well, if only because Avdotya Romanovna herself, of her own free will, has deigned to choose this man. And if I abused him so much yesterday, it's because I was filthy drunk and . . . mad as well; yes, mad, off my head, out of my mind, completely . . . and today I'm ashamed of it! . . ." He got red in the face and fell silent. Avdotya Romanovna also blushed, but did not break her silence. She had not said a single word from the moment they began talking about Luzhin.

And meanwhile, without her support, Pulcheria Alexandrovna obviously felt hesitant. At last, faltering and glancing continually at her daughter, she declared that one circumstance troubled her greatly at present.

"You see, Dmitri Prokofych . . ." she began. "Shall I be completely frank with Dmitri Prokofych, Dunechka?"

"Of course, mama," Avdotya Romanovna remarked imposingly.

"This is what it is," her mother hurried on, as if a mountain had been lifted from her by this permission to voice her grief. "This morning, very early, we received a note from Pyotr Petrovich in reply to yesterday's message concerning our arrival. You see, he was to have met us yesterday, as he had promised, right at the station. Instead, some lackey was sent to meet us at the station, to give us the address of this rooming house and show us the way, and Pyotr Petrovich told him to tell us he would come to us today, in the morning. Instead of which, today, in the morning, this note came from him . . . It would be best if you read it yourself; there is a point in it that troubles me very much . . . You'll see now what this point is and . . . tell me your frank opinion, Dmitri Prokofych! You know Rodya's character best of all and can advise us better than anyone else. I warn you that Dunechka already resolved everything from the first moment, but I, I still do not know how to act and . . . and have been waiting for you."

Razumikhin unfolded the note, dated the previous day, and read the following:

DEAR MADAM, Pulcheria Alexandrovna,
I have the honor of informing you that owing to suddenly arisen delays I was unable to meet you on the platform, having sent a rather efficient man for that purpose. I must equally deprive myself of the honor of seeing you tomorrow morning, owing to urgent matters in the Senate,

and so as not to intrude upon your family reunion with your son, and Avdotya Romanovna's with her brother. I shall have the honor of calling upon you and paying my respects to you in your apartment not earlier than tomorrow evening at eight o'clock sharp, and with that I venture to add an earnest and, may I say, insistent request that Rodion Romanovich not be present at this general meeting of ours, inasmuch as he offended me in an unparalleled and discourteous way when I visited him yesterday in his illness, and wishing, moreover, to have a necessary and thorough discussion with you of a certain point, concerning which I should like to know your own interpretation. With that I have the honor of forewarning you beforehand that if, contrary to my request, I do encounter Rodion Romanovich, I shall be obliged to withdraw at once, and in that case you will have only yourself to blame. I write this with the understanding that Rodion Romanovich, who appeared so ill at the time of my visit, suddenly recovered two hours later, and may therefore be able to leave his room and come to you. This was confirmed for me by my own eyes, in the apartment of a certain drunkard, who was crushed by horses and died as a result, and to whose daughter, a girl of notorious behavior, he handed over as much as twenty-five roubles yesterday, on the pretext of a funeral, which surprised me greatly, knowing what trouble you had in gathering this sum. With that, and expressing my particular respect to the esteemed Avdotya Romanovna, I beg you to accept the respectfully devoted feelings of

> Your humble servant,
> P. Luzhin

"WHAT AM I to do now, Dmitri Prokofych?" Pulcheria Alexandrovna began to say, almost in tears. "How am I to suggest that Rodya not come? Yesterday he demanded so insistently that we refuse Pyotr Petrovich, and now we're told not to receive him! But if he finds out, he will come on purpose . . . and what will happen then?"

"Do as Avdotya Romanovna has decided," Razumikhin replied calmly and at once.

"Ah, my God! She says . . . she says God knows what, and she won't explain her purpose! She says it would be better—not really better, that is, but it's somehow supposedly necessary—that Rodya also come to-night, on purpose, at eight o'clock, and it's necessary that they meet . . . As for me, I didn't even want to show him the letter; I wanted to arrange it somehow slyly, through you, so that he wouldn't come . . . because he's so irritable . . . Besides, I don't understand a thing—who is this drunkard who died, and who is this daughter, and how could he give this daughter all the money he has left . . . that . . ."

"That cost you so dearly, mama," Avdotya Romanovna added.

"He was not himself yesterday," Razumikhin said thoughtfully. "If you knew what sort of things he poured out yesterday in the tavern, though it was all intelligent . . . hm! He was indeed saying something yesterday, as we were going home, about some dead man and some girl, but I didn't understand a word of it . . . However, yesterday I myself . . ."

"Best of all, mama, let's go to him ourselves, and there, I assure you, we'll see at once what to do. And besides, it's time—Lord, it's past ten!" she exclaimed, glancing at her magnificent gold and enamel watch, which hung round her neck on a fine Venetian chain and was terribly out of harmony with the rest of her attire. "A present from the fiancé," thought Razumikhin.

"Ah, it's time! . . . It's time, Dunechka, it's time!" Pulcheria Alexandrovna began bustling about in alarm. "He may think we're angry because of yesterday, since we're so long in coming. Ah, my God!"

She was busily throwing on her cape and putting on her hat as she spoke; Dunechka also readied herself. Her gloves were not only worn out but even torn, as Razumikhin noticed, and yet the obvious poverty of their dress even lent both ladies an air of some special dignity, as always happens with those who know how to wear poor clothing. Razumikhin looked at Dunechka with awe and was proud to be escorting her. "That queen," he thought to himself, "who mended her own stockings in prison—of course, she looked like a real queen at that moment, even more so than during the most splendid solemnities and appearances."[3]

"My God!" exclaimed Pulcheria Alexandrovna, "would I ever have thought I'd be afraid to meet my own son, my dear, dear Rodya, as I am now! . . . I am afraid, Dmitri Prokofych!" she added, glancing at him timidly.

"Don't be afraid, mama," Dunya said, kissing her. "Better to believe in him. I do."

"Ah, my God! So do I, but I didn't sleep all night!" the poor woman exclaimed.

They walked out to the street.

"You know, Dunechka, I no sooner fell asleep a little, towards morning, than I suddenly dreamed of the late Marfa Petrovna . . . all in white . . . she came up to me and took me by the hand, and she shook her head at me so sternly, so sternly, as if in disapproval . . . Does that bode well? Ah, my God, Dmitri Prokofych, you don't know yet: Marfa Petrovna died!"

"No, I didn't know. What Marfa Petrovna?"

"Quite suddenly! And imagine . . ."

"Later, mama!" Dunya interrupted. "He doesn't know yet who Marfa Petrovna is!"

"Ah, you don't know? And I thought you already knew everything. You must forgive me, Dmitri Prokofych, I'm quite addled these days. I really regard you as our Providence, and so I was convinced that you already knew everything. I regard you as one of our family . . . You won't be angry with me for saying so. Ah, my God, what's the matter with your right hand? Did you hurt it?"

"Yes, I hurt it," murmured the overjoyed Razumikhin.

"I sometimes speak too much from the heart, so that Dunya corrects me . . . But, my God, what a closet he lives in! Is he awake yet, I wonder? And that woman, his landlady, considers it a room? Listen, you say he doesn't like to show his heart; do you think perhaps I'll tire him out with my . . . weaknesses? . . . Won't you teach me, Dmitri Prokofych? How should I be with him? You know, I go about quite like a lost person."

"Don't question him too much about anything, if you see him making a wry face; especially avoid asking him too much about his health—he doesn't like it."

"Ah, Dmitri Prokofych, how difficult it is to be a mother! But here is the stairway . . . What an awful stairway!"

"Mama, you're even pale; calm yourself, my dear," Dunya said, caressing her. "He must be happy just to see you, and you torment yourself so," she added, flashing her eyes.

"Wait, I'll go ahead and find out if he's awake."

The ladies slowly followed after Razumikhin, who started up the stairs ahead of them. When they came to the fourth-floor landing, outside the landlady's door, they noticed that the door was open a tiny crack and that two quick black eyes were examining them both from the darkness. When their eyes met, the door was suddenly slammed shut with such a bang that Pulcheria Alexandrovna almost cried out in fright.

III

"HE'S WELL, he's well!" Zossimov cried cheerily to greet the people entering. He had been there for about ten minutes already, and was sitting on the same end of the sofa as yesterday. Raskolnikov was sitting on the opposite end, fully dressed and even carefully washed and combed—something that had not happened with him for a long time. The room filled up immediately, but Nastasya still managed to slip in with the visitors and began to listen.

Indeed, Raskolnikov was almost well, especially as compared with yesterday, only he was very pale, distracted, and sullen. Externally, he seemed to resemble a wounded man or a man suffering from some acute physical pain: his brows were knitted, his lips compressed, his eyes inflamed. He spoke little and reluctantly, as if forcing himself or fulfilling a duty, and a certain anxiety showed every now and then in his movements.

All that was lacking was some bandage or gauze wrapping to complete his resemblance to a man with, for example, a painful abscess on his finger, or an injured hand, or something of the sort.

However, even this pale and sullen face brightened momentarily, as if with light, when his mother and sister entered; but this seemed to lend only a more concentrated torment to his expression, in place of the former anguished distraction. The light quickly faded but the torment remained, and Zossimov, observing and studying his patient with all the youthful ardor of a doctor just beginning to get a taste of practice, was surprised to note in him, instead of joy at his family's arrival, something like a heavy, concealed determination to endure an hour or two of torture that could no longer be avoided. He saw later how almost every word of the ensuing conversation seemed to touch and reopen some wound in his patient; but at the same time he marveled somewhat that yesterday's monomaniac, who all but flew into a rage at the slightest word, today was able to control himself and keep his feelings hidden.

"Yes, I myself can now see that I am almost well," Raskolnikov said, kissing his mother and sister affably, at which Pulcheria Alexandrovna immediately beamed, "and I say it not *as I did yesterday,*" he added, addressing Razumikhin and giving him a friendly handshake.

"And I even marveled at him today," began Zossimov, who was glad to see the visitors, because in ten minutes he had already managed to lose the thread of his conversation with his patient. "If it goes on like this, in three or four days things will be just as they were—that is, as they were a month ago, or two . . . or maybe even three? Because this started and was coming on from way back . . . eh? Do you admit, now, that you yourself may be to blame?" he added with a cautious smile, as though still fearing to irritate him with something.

"Very likely," Raskolnikov answered coldly.

"What I'm driving at," Zossimov went on, with increasing relish, "is that your complete recovery now depends chiefly on you yourself. Since it's become possible to talk with you, I should like to impress upon you that it is necessary to eliminate the original, so to speak, radical causes that influenced the onset of your ill condition; only then will you be cured; otherwise it will get even worse. I do not know these original causes, but they must be known to you. You are an intelligent man and, of course, have observed yourself. It seems to me that the beginning of your disorder to some extent coincides with your leaving the university. You cannot remain without occupation, and it seems to me, therefore, that hard work and a firmly set goal could be of great help to you."

"Yes, yes, you're entirely right . . . I'll quickly get myself back into the university, and then everything will go . . . like clockwork."

Zossimov, who had begun his sage advice partly for effect in front of the ladies, was naturally somewhat taken aback when, glancing at his listener as he finished his speech, he noticed a look of unmistakable derision on his face. However, this lasted only a moment. Pulcheria Alexandrovna began at once thanking Zossimov, especially for last night's visit to their hotel.

"What? He went to see you during the night, too?" Raskolnikov asked, as if alarmed. "So then you didn't get any sleep after your journey."

"Ah, Rodya, it was all only until two o'clock. Dunya and I never go to bed before two, even at home."

"I, too, don't know how to thank him," Raskolnikov continued, frowning suddenly and looking down. "Setting aside the question of money—you will excuse me for mentioning it" (he turned to Zossimov), "I really don't know how I have deserved such special attention from you. I simply don't understand . . . and . . . and it's even burdensome to me, because I don't understand it—I'm speaking frankly with you."

"Now, don't get yourself irritated," Zossimov forced himself to laugh. "Suppose you're my first patient; well, and our kind, when we're just starting out in practice, love our first patients like our own children, and some almost fall in love with them. After all, I don't have such a wealth of patients."

"Not to mention him," Raskolnikov added, pointing to Razumikhin, "he, too, has had nothing but insults and trouble from me."

"Listen to this nonsense! Are you in a sentimental mood today, or what?" Razumikhin exclaimed.

Had he been more perceptive, he would have seen that there was no question here of a sentimental mood, but something even quite the opposite. Avdotya Romanovna noticed it. She was watching her brother closely and anxiously.

"And of you, mama, I don't even dare to speak," he went on, as if reciting a lesson learned by heart that morning. "Only today have I been able to realize something of the torment you must have suffered yesterday, waiting here for me to return." Having said this, he suddenly held out his hand to his sister, silently and with a smile. But this time there was a flash of genuine, unfeigned emotion in his smile. Dunya at once seized the hand he held out to her and pressed it ardently, with joy and gratitude. It was the first time he had addressed her since yesterday's falling-out. Their mother's face lit up with rapture and happiness at the sight of this final and wordless reconciliation of brother and sister.

"That's what I love him for!" whispered Razumikhin, who exaggerated everything, turning energetically on his chair. "These sudden gestures of his! . . ."

"And how well he does it all," his mother thought to herself. "He has such noble impulses, and how simply, how delicately he has ended yesterday's misunderstanding with his sister—just by offering her his hand at the right moment and giving her a nice look . . . And what beautiful eyes he has, what a beautiful face! . . . He's even better looking than Dunechka . . . But, my God, what clothes! How terribly he's dressed! The errand-boy Vasya, in Afanasy Ivanovich's shop, is dressed better! . . . I think I could just rush to him and embrace him, and . . . weep—but I'm afraid, afraid . . . he's so . . . Lord! He speaks so tenderly now, yet I'm afraid! What am I afraid of? . . ."

"Ah, Rodya," she suddenly picked up, hurrying to answer his remark, "you wouldn't believe how unhappy Dunechka and I were . . . yesterday! Now that everything's over and done with, and we're all happy again, I can tell you. Imagine, we came running here to embrace you, almost straight from the train, and that woman—ah, here she is! How do you do, Nastasya! . . . She suddenly told us you had been in a fever and had just run away from the doctor, out of the house, delirious, and that people had gone running to look for you. You wouldn't believe how we felt! I could only picture to myself the tragic death of Lieutenant Potanchikov, our acquaintance, your father's friend—you won't remember him, Rodya—who ran out in just the same way, also in delirium, and fell into the well in the yard, and they only managed to get him out the next day. And, of course, we exaggerated it even more. We were about to rush and look for Pyotr Petrovich, so that with his help at least . . . because we were alone, completely alone," she trailed off in a pitiful voice, and suddenly stopped altogether, remembering that it was still rather dangerous to start talking about Pyotr Petrovich, even though "everyone was now completely happy again."

"Yes, yes . . . it's all a pity, of course . . ." Raskolnikov muttered in reply, but with so distracted and almost inattentive an air that Dunya looked at him in amazement.

"What else was I going to say . . ." he continued, making an effort to recall. "Ah, yes: mama, and you, too, Dunechka, please do not think that I did not want to come to you first this morning and was waiting for you to come to me."

"But what is it, Rodya!" Pulcheria Alexandrovna cried out, also surprised.

"Is he just answering us out of duty, or what?" thought Dunechka. "He's making peace and asking forgiveness as if he were performing a service or had memorized a lesson."

"I was about to come as soon as I woke up, but I was delayed by my clothes; last night I forgot to tell her . . . Nastasya . . . to wash off that blood . . . I've only just managed to get dressed."

"Blood! What blood!" Pulcheria Alexandrovna became alarmed.

"Never mind . . . don't worry. It was blood from yesterday, when I was wandering around somewhat delirious and came upon a man who had been run over . . . some official . . ."

"Delirious? But you remember everything," Razumikhin interrupted.

"That's true," Raskolnikov replied, somehow especially carefully, "I remember everything, down to the smallest detail, but try asking me why I did this, or went there, or said that—I'd have a hard time explaining."

"A phenomenon known only too well," Zossimov mixed in. "The performance is sometimes masterful, extremely clever, but the control of the actions, their source, is deranged and depends on various morbid impressions. As in a dream."

"Perhaps it's even good that he considers me almost crazy," Raskolnikov thought.

"But healthy people are perhaps no different," Dunechka observed, looking anxiously at Zossimov.

"Quite a true observation," the latter replied. "Indeed, in that sense we're all rather often almost like mad people, only with the slight difference that the 'sick' are somewhat madder than we are, so that it's necessary to draw a line here. And the harmonious man, it's true, almost doesn't exist; out of tens, maybe hundreds of thousands, one will be found, and quite a weak specimen at that . . ."

The word "mad," imprudently dropped by Zossimov, whose favorite subject was running away with him, made everyone wince.

Raskolnikov sat as though he were not paying attention, deep in thought, and with a strange smile on his pale lips. He went on puzzling over something.

"Well, what about this man who was run over? I interrupted you!" Razumikhin hastened to exclaim.

"What?" the other asked, as if waking up. "Ah, yes . . . so I got stained with blood when I helped carry him into his apartment . . . Incidentally, mama, I did an unpardonable thing yesterday; I was truly out of my mind. Yesterday I gave all the money you sent me . . . to his wife . . . for the funeral. She's a widow now, consumptive, a pitiful woman . . . three little orphans, hungry . . . they have nothing in the house . . . and there's yet another daughter . . . Perhaps you'd have given her the money yourself, if you'd seen . . . However, I had no right, I admit, especially knowing how hard it was for you to get it. Before helping people, one must first have the right; otherwise—'*Crevez, chiens, si vous n'êtes pas contents!*' "[4] He laughed. "Right, Dunya?"

"No, not right," Dunya answered firmly.

"Bah! So you, too . . . have your notions! . . ." he muttered, looking at her almost with hatred and smiling derisively. "I should have realized it . . . Well, that's praiseworthy; it's better for you . . . and you'll come to a certain line, and if you don't cross it, you'll be unhappy, and if you do, maybe you'll be even more unhappy . . . However, it's all nonsense!" he added irritably, annoyed at getting involuntarily carried away. "I only wanted to say that I ask your forgiveness, mama," he concluded sharply and abruptly.

"Ah, Rodya, there's no need; I'm sure everything you do is wonderful!" his gladdened mother said.

"Don't be sure," he said, twisting his mouth into a smile. Silence ensued. There was something tense in this whole conversation, and in the silence, and in the reconciliation, and in the forgiveness, and everyone felt it.

"So they really are afraid of me," Raskolnikov thought to himself, glancing sullenly at his mother and sister. Indeed, the longer Pulcheria Alexandrovna remained silent, the more timid she became.

"I seemed to love them so much when they weren't here," flashed through his head.

"You know, Rodya, Marfa Petrovna died!" Pulcheria Alexandrovna suddenly popped up.

"What Marfa Petrovna?"

"Ah, my God—Marfa Petrovna—Svidrigailov! I wrote you so much about her."

"A-a-ah, yes, I remember . . . So she died? Ah, did she?" he suddenly roused himself, as if waking up. "She really died? Of what?"

"Just imagine, it was a sudden death!" Pulcheria Alexandrovna hurried on, encouraged by his curiosity. "And just at the same time as I sent you that letter, even the same day! Imagine, that terrible man seems to have been the cause of her death. They say he gave her a terrible beating!"

"Is that how they were?" he asked, turning to his sister.

"No, quite the opposite. He was always very patient with her, even polite. In many cases he was even too indulgent of her nature, for all those seven years . . . Somehow he suddenly lost patience."

"So he's not so terrible, if he managed to restrain himself for seven years? You seem to be vindicating him, Dunechka?"

"No, no, he's a terrible man! I can't even imagine anything more terrible," Dunya answered, almost with a shudder, and she frowned and lapsed into thought.

"That was in the morning," Pulcheria Alexandrovna hurriedly continued. "Afterwards she immediately ordered the horses to be harnessed, to go to town right after dinner, because she always used to go to town in such cases; they say she ate dinner with great appetite . . ."

"In spite of the beating, eh?"

". . . But then, that was always her . . . habit; and as soon as she finished dinner, so as not to be late to town, she went straight to the bathhouse . . . You see, she was taking some sort of bathing cure; they have a cold spring there, and she bathed in it regularly, every day, and as soon as she got into the water, she suddenly had a stroke!"

"Sure enough!" said Zossimov.

"And was it a bad beating?"

"That hardly matters," Dunya responded.

"Hm! Anyway, mama, why do you bother telling me about such

nonsense?" Raskolnikov suddenly said, irritably and as if inadvertently.

"Ah, my friend, I just didn't know what to talk about," escaped from Pulcheria Alexandrovna.

"What is it, are you all afraid of me or something?" he said with a twisted smile.

"In fact, it's true," said Dunya, looking directly and sternly at her brother. "Mama was so afraid coming up the stairs that she even crossed herself."

His face became all contorted as if in a spasm.

"Ah, Dunya, stop it! Rodya, please don't be angry . . . How could you, Dunya!" Pulcheria Alexandrovna started to say in confusion. "The truth is that as we were coming here, I was dreaming all the way, on the train, of how we would see each other, how we would tell each other everything . . . and I was so happy that I didn't even notice the journey! But what am I saying! I'm happy now, too . . . Dunya, you really shouldn't! It makes me happy just to see you, Rodya . . ."

"Enough, mama," he muttered in confusion, pressing her hand without looking at her. "We'll have time to talk all we want!"

Having said this, he suddenly became confused and turned pale: again that terrible, recent feeling passed like a deathly chill over his soul; again it suddenly became perfectly plain and clear to him that he had just uttered a terrible lie, that not only would he never have the chance to talk all he wanted, but that it was no longer possible for him to *talk* at all, with anyone, about anything, ever. The impression of this tormenting thought was so strong that for a moment he almost forgot himself entirely; he rose from his place and, without looking at anyone, started out the door.

"What are you doing?" Razumikhin exclaimed, seizing his arm.

He sat down again and began silently looking around him; everyone was looking at him in perplexity.

"But why are you all so dull!" he suddenly cried out, quite unexpectedly. "Say something! What's the point of sitting here like this! Well, speak! Let's talk . . . We got together and don't open our mouths . . . So, say something!"

"Thank God! I thought it was going to be the same as yesterday," Pulcheria Alexandrovna said, crossing herself.

"What is it, Rodya?" Avdotya Romanovna asked mistrustfully.

"Nothing. I just remembered something," he answered, and suddenly laughed.

"Well, that's good. At least it was something! Otherwise I'd have thought . . ." Zossimov muttered, rising from the sofa. "However, it's time I was going; maybe I'll stop by later . . . if you're here . . ."

He made his bows and left.

"What a wonderful man!" Pulcheria Alexandrovna observed.

"Yes, wonderful, excellent, educated, intelligent . . ." Raskolnikov suddenly started saying in a sort of unexpected patter, and with hitherto unusual animation. "I can't recall where I met him before my illness . . . I think I did meet him somewhere . . . And here is another good man!" He motioned towards Razumikhin. "Do you like him, Dunya?" he asked, and for no apparent reason suddenly burst out laughing.

"Very much," Dunya replied.

"Pah, you're a real . . . little swine!" said Razumikhin, frightfully abashed and blushing, and he rose from his chair. Pulcheria Alexandrovna smiled slightly, and Raskolnikov roared with laughter.

"But where are you off to?"

"I also . . . have to . . ."

"You don't have to at all; stay here! Zossimov left, so you also have to. Don't go . . . What time is it? Twelve already? What a pretty watch you have, Dunya! But why are you all silent again? I'm the only one who keeps talking! . . ."

"It was a present from Marfa Petrovna," Dunya replied.

"And a very expensive one," Pulcheria Alexandrovna added.

"Ahh! Look at the size of it—almost too big for a lady."

"I like it like that," said Dunya.

Razumikhin thought to himself: "So it's not from her fiancé," and for some reason he rejoiced.

"And I thought it was Luzhin's present," Raskolnikov remarked.

"No, he hasn't given Dunya anything yet."

"Ahh! And do you remember how I was in love, mama, and wanted to get married?" he said suddenly, looking at his mother, who was struck by this unexpected turn and the tone in which he began talking about it.

"Ah, my friend, of course!" Pulcheria Alexandrovna exchanged glances with Dunechka and Razumikhin.

"Hm! Yes! Well, what can I tell you. I don't even remember much. She was such a sickly girl," he went on, as if suddenly lapsing into thought again, and looking down, "quite ill; she liked giving alms and kept dreaming of a convent, and once she broke down in tears when she began talking about it; yes, yes . . . I remember . . . I remember very well. She was so . . . homely. Really, I don't know why I got so attached to her then; I think it was because she was always sick . . . If she'd been lame or hunchbacked, I think I would have loved her even more . . ." (He smiled pensively.) "It was just . . . some spring delirium . . ."

"No, it was not just a spring delirium," Dunechka said animatedly.

He looked with strained attention at his sister, but either did not hear or did not understand her words. Then he rose, deep in thought, went over to his mother, kissed her, returned to his place, and sat down.

"You love her even now!" Pulcheria Alexandrovna said, touched.

"Her? Now? Ah . . . you mean her! No. It's all as if in another world now . . . and so long ago. And everything around seems not to be happening here . . ."

He looked at them attentively.

"And you, too . . . it's as if I were looking at you from a thousand miles away . . . Besides, devil knows why we're talking about it! What's the point of asking questions?" he added in vexation, and fell silent, biting his nails and lapsing into thought again.

"What an awful apartment you have, Rodya; like a coffin," Pulcheria Alexandrovna said suddenly, breaking the heavy silence. "I'm sure it's half on account of this apartment that you've become so melancholic."

"Apartment? . . ." he replied distractedly. "Yes, the apartment contributed a lot . . . I've thought about that myself . . . But if you knew what a strange thought you just said, mama," he added suddenly, with a strange smirk.

A little longer and this company, this family, after their three-year separation, this familial tone of conversation, together with the complete impossibility of talking about anything at all, would finally become decidedly unbearable to him. There was, however, one pressing matter that absolutely had to be resolved that day, one way or the other—so he had resolved when he woke up in the morning. He was glad, now, to have this *matter* as a way out.

"Listen, Dunya," he began seriously and dryly, "I must, of course, ask your forgiveness for yesterday, but I consider it my duty to remind you again that I will not renounce my main point. It's either me or Luzhin. I may be vile, but you must not be. One of us is enough. And if you marry Luzhin, I will immediately cease to regard you as my sister."

"Rodya, Rodya! But this is all the same as yesterday," Pulcheria Alexandrovna exclaimed ruefully. "And why do you keep calling yourself vile—I can't bear it! It was the same yesterday . . ."

"Brother," Dunya replied firmly and also dryly, "there is a mistake on your part in all this. I thought it over during the night and found the mistake. The point is that you seem to think I'm sacrificing myself to someone and for someone. That is not so at all. I am marrying simply for myself, because things are hard for me; of course, I shall be glad if I also manage to be of use to my family, but that is not the main motive for my determination . . ."

"She's lying!" he thought to himself, biting his nails in anger. "The proud thing! She doesn't want to admit that she'd like playing the benefactress! Oh, base characters! They love, and it comes out like hate . . . Oh, how I . . . hate them all!"

"In short, I am marrying Pyotr Petrovich," Dunechka went on, "because I prefer the lesser of two evils. I intend honestly to fulfill all that he expects of me, and therefore I am not deceiving him . . . Why did you just smile like that?"

She, too, became flushed, and wrath shone in her eyes.

"You'll fulfill everything?" he asked, grinning venomously.

"Up to a point. Both the manner and the form of Pyotr Petrovich's proposal showed me at once what he requires. He may, of course, value himself too highly, but I hope that he also values me . . . Why are you laughing again?"

"And why are you blushing again? You're lying, sister, you're lying on purpose, solely out of your woman's stubbornness, just to insist on your point before me . . . You cannot respect Luzhin—I've seen him and talked with him. Which means you're selling yourself for money, and that means that in any case you're acting basely, and I'm glad you're at least able to blush!"

"It's not true, I'm not lying! . . ." Dunechka cried out, losing all her composure. "I won't marry him unless I'm convinced that he values and appreciates me; I won't marry him unless I'm convinced that I can respect him. Fortunately, I can be convinced of that quite certainly, and even today. And such a marriage is not vile, as you say! And if you were right, and I had really made up my mind to do something vile, isn't it merciless on your part to talk to me that way? Why do you demand a heroism of me that you may not even have in yourself? That is despotism; that is coercion! If I ruin anyone, it will only be myself . . . I haven't gone and put a knife into anyone yet! . . . Why are you looking at me like that? Why did you get so pale? Rodya, what's wrong? Rodya, dear!"

"Lord! She's made him faint!" Pulcheria Alexandrovna cried out.

"No, no . . . nonsense . . . it's nothing! . . . I just felt a little dizzy. Not faint at all . . . You and your faints! . . . Hm! yes . . . what was I going to say? Ah, yes: how could you be convinced today that you can respect him, and that he . . . values you, or however you put it? I think you said something about today? Or did I not hear right?"

"Mama, show my brother Pyotr Petrovich's letter," said Dunechka.

Pulcheria Alexandrovna handed over the letter with trembling hands. He took it with great curiosity. But before unfolding it, he suddenly looked at Dunya somehow with surprise.

"Strange," he said slowly, as if suddenly struck by a new thought, "why am I making such a fuss? Why all this outcry? Go and marry whomever you like!"

He spoke as if to himself, though he said it aloud, and looked at his sister for some time as if in bewilderment.

Finally he unfolded the letter, still with an expression of some strange surprise; then he began reading slowly and attentively, and read it twice. Pulcheria Alexandrovna was especially uneasy, and everyone also expected something special.

"It surprises me," he began, after some reflection, handing the letter back to his mother, but without addressing anyone in particular, "he handles cases, he's a lawyer, and his conversation is so . . . pretentious—yet his writing is quite illiterate."

Everyone stirred; this was not what they were expecting.

"But they all write like that," Razumikhin observed abruptly.

"So you've read it?"

"Yes."

"We showed him, Rodya, we . . . asked his advice," Pulcheria Alexandrovna began, embarrassed.

"It's legal style, as a matter of fact," Razumikhin interrupted, "legal documents are still written that way."

"Legal? Yes, precisely legal, businesslike . . . Not so very illiterate, and not too literary either—a business style!"

"Pyotr Petrovich makes it no secret that he had to scrape up pennies for his education, and even boasts of having made his own way in life," Avdotya Romanovna remarked, somewhat offended by her brother's new tone.

"Let him boast, he has some reason—I don't deny that. You seem to be offended, sister, that out of the entire letter I drew such a frivolous observation, and you think I began speaking of such trifles on purpose, in my vexation, just to put on an act in front of you. On the contrary, a certain observation to do with style occurred to me, which is not at all irrelevant in the present case. There is this one phrase: 'you will have only yourself to blame'—very significantly and clearly put; and then there is the threat that he will leave at once if I come. This threat to leave is the same as a threat to abandon you both if you disobey, and to abandon you now, when he has already brought you to Petersburg. Now, tell me: can such a phrase from Luzhin be as offensive as it would be if he had written it" (he pointed to Razumikhin), "or Zossimov, or any one of us?"

"N-no," Dunechka answered, perking up, "I understood very well that it was too naively expressed, and that he was perhaps simply not a very skillful writer . . . That's good reasoning, brother. I didn't even expect . . ."

"It's put in a legal manner, there's no other way to put it legally, and it came out coarser than he may have wanted. However, I must disappoint you somewhat: there is one other expression in this letter that is a bit of a slander against me, and rather a low one. Yesterday I gave money to a consumptive and broken-hearted widow, not 'on the pretext of a funeral,' but simply for the funeral, and I handed it not to the daughter—a girl, as he writes, 'of notorious behavior' (whom I saw yesterday for the first time in my life)—but precisely to the widow. In all this I see an overly hasty desire to sully me and make me quarrel with you. Again, he expresses himself legalistically—that is, revealing his purpose too plainly, and with rather naive haste. He's an intelligent man, but it takes something more than intelligence to act intelligently. All this portrays the man, and . . . I don't think he values you very much. I say this in admonition, because I sincerely wish you well . . ."

Dunechka did not reply; her decision had already been made, and she was only waiting for that evening.

"Well, what have you decided, Rodya?" asked Pulcheria Alexandrovna, troubled even more than before by his sudden, new *businesslike* tone of voice.

"What do you mean—'decided'?"

"But Pyotr Petrovich writes here that you mustn't be with us in the evening, and that he will leave . . . if you come. So, will you . . . come?"

"That is, of course, not up to me to decide, but up to you, first, if such a demand from Pyotr Petrovich does not offend you, and, second, up to Dunya, if she also is not offended. I will do as you think best," he added dryly.

"Dunechka has already decided, and I agree with her completely," Pulcheria Alexandrovna hastened to put in.

"I decided to ask you, Rodya, to ask you earnestly to join us at this meeting without fail," said Dunya. "Will you come?"

"I will."

"I ask you, too, to join us at eight o'clock," she turned to Razumikhin. "Mama, I'm inviting him, too."

"That's fine, Dunechka. Whatever you all decide," Pulcheria Alexandrovna added, "so let it be. And it's easier for me; I don't like lying and pretending; better to tell the whole truth . . . and let Pyotr Petrovich be angry if he chooses!"

IV

A T THAT MOMENT the door opened quietly, and a girl came into the
room, looking timidly around. Everyone turned to her with surprise and curiosity. Raskolnikov did not recognize her at first. It was
Sofya Semyonovna Marmeladov. He had seen her for the first time the
day before, but at such a moment, under such circumstances, and in
such attire that his memory retained the image of quite a different
person. Here, now, was a modestly and even poorly dressed girl, still
very young, looking almost like a little girl, with a modest and decent
manner and a bright but as if somewhat intimidated face. She was
wearing a very simple, everyday dress and an old hat no longer in
fashion, though she still carried yesterday's parasol. Suddenly seeing
a room full of people, she became not so much confused as quite lost,
timid as a little child, and even made a move to go out again.

"Ah . . . it's you?" Raskolnikov said, greatly surprised, and he
suddenly became embarrassed himself.

It occurred to him at once that his mother and sister had already
heard fleetingly, in Luzhin's letter, of a certain girl of "notorious"
behavior. He had just been protesting against Luzhin's slander and
stated that it was the first time he had seen the girl, and suddenly she
herself walked in. He also recalled that he had not protested in the least
against the expression "of notorious behavior." All this flitted vaguely
and instantly through his head. But, looking more attentively, he
suddenly saw that this humiliated being was already so humiliated that
he suddenly felt pity for her. And when she made a move to run away
in fear—it was as if something turned over inside him.

"I was not at all expecting you," he hurried, stopping her with his
eyes. "Be so good as to sit down. You must have come from Katerina
Ivanovna. Excuse me, not here; sit over there . . ."

When Sonya entered, Razumikhin, who had been sitting just by the
door on one of Raskolnikov's three chairs, rose to let her in. At first
Raskolnikov had shown her to the end of the sofa where Zossimov had
been sitting, but recalling that this sofa was too *familiar* a place, that
it served him as a bed, he hastily directed her to Razumikhin's chair.

"And you sit here," he said to Razumikhin, putting him on the end where Zossimov had been sitting.

Sonya sat down, all but trembling with fear, and glanced timidly at the two ladies. One could see that she herself did not know how she could possibly have sat down next to them. She became so frightened when she realized it that she suddenly stood up again and in complete embarrassment addressed Raskolnikov.

"I . . . I . . . have come just for a moment, excuse me for disturbing you," she began, faltering. "Katerina Ivanovna sent me, she had no one else . . . And Katerina Ivanovna told me to beg you please to come to the funeral service tomorrow, in the morning . . . to the liturgy . . . at the Mitrofanievsky Cemetery, and to stay afterwards for a meal . . . with us . . . with her . . . To do her the honor . . . She told me to ask you."[5]

Sonya faltered and fell silent.

"I will certainly try . . . certainly," Raskolnikov answered, also standing up, and also faltering and not finishing . . . "Be so good as to sit down," he said suddenly, "I must speak with you. Please— but perhaps you're in a hurry—be so good as to give me two minutes . . ."

And he moved the chair for her. Sonya sat down again and again quickly gave the two ladies a timid, lost glance, and suddenly looked down.

Raskolnikov's pale face became flushed; he cringed all over, as it were; his eyes lit up.

"Mama," he said, firmly and insistently, "this is Sofya Semyonovna Marmeladov, the daughter of that most unfortunate Mr. Marmeladov who was run over before my eyes yesterday, and about whom I have already spoken with you . . ."

Pulcheria Alexandrovna looked at Sonya and slightly narrowed her eyes. In spite of her confusion before Rodya's insistent and challenging look, she simply could not deny herself that pleasure. Dunechka stared seriously and fixedly straight in the poor girl's face and gazed at her in perplexity. Hearing the introduction, Sonya tried to raise her eyes, but became even more embarrassed than before.

"I wanted to ask you," Raskolnikov hastened to address her, "how things worked out with you today. Did you have any trouble? . . . With the police, for instance?"

"No, sir, everything went all right . . . It's only too clear what caused his death; we weren't troubled; except that the neighbors are angry."

"Why?"

"That the body's been there so long . . . it's hot now; there's a smell . . . so today, around vespers, they'll carry it over to the cemetery, to the chapel, till tomorrow. Katerina Ivanovna was against it at first, but now she sees herself that it's impossible . . ."

"Today, then?"

"She begs you to do us the honor of attending the funeral service in church tomorrow, and of coming to her afterwards for a memorial meal."

"She's preparing a meal?"

"Yes, sir, a light one; she told me to thank you very much for your help yesterday . . . without you we'd have nothing for the funeral." And her lips and chin suddenly quivered, but she collected herself and overcame her emotion by quickly looking down again.

As they spoke, Raskolnikov studied her closely. She had a thin little face, quite thin and pale, and rather irregular, somehow sharp, with a sharp little nose and chin. She could not even have been called pretty, but her blue eyes were so clear, and when they were animated, the expression of her face became so kind and simple-hearted, that one involuntarily felt drawn to her. There was, besides, a special, characteristic feature of her face and of her whole figure: despite her eighteen years, she looked almost like a little girl, much younger than her age, almost quite a child, and this sometimes even appeared comically in some of her movements.

"But can Katerina Ivanovna manage on such small means, and even plan to have a meal? . . ." Raskolnikov asked, determined to continue the conversation.

"But the coffin will be a simple one, sir . . . it will all be simple, so it won't cost much . . . Katerina Ivanovna and I calculated everything so as to have something left for the meal . . . and Katerina Ivanovna wants very much to have it. One can't really . . . it's a consolation to her . . . that's how she is, you know . . ."

"I understand, I understand . . . certainly . . . Why are you staring at my room? Mama here also says it's like a coffin."

"You gave us all you had yesterday!" Sonechka suddenly said in reply, in a sort of intense and quick whisper, again looking down. Her lips and chin quivered again. She had been struck much earlier by the poverty of Raskolnikov's furnishings, and now these words somehow escaped her of themselves. Silence ensued. Dunechka's eyes somehow brightened, and Pulcheria Alexandrovna even looked affably at Sonya.

"Rodya," she said, getting up, "we shall be dining together, of course. Dunechka, come . . . And you, Rodya, ought to go for a little walk, and then rest, lie down a bit, and afterwards come soon . . . I'm afraid we may have tired you . . ."

"Yes, yes, I'll come," he said, getting up and beginning to hurry . . . "I have some business, however . . ."

"You don't mean you'll dine separately!" Razumikhin exclaimed, looking at Raskolnikov in surprise. "What's got into you?"

"Yes, yes, I'll come, of course, of course . . . And you stay for a minute. You don't need him now, mama? Or am I perhaps taking him from you?"

"Oh, no, no! And you, Dmitri Prokofych, will you be so kind as to join us for dinner?"

"Please do," Dunya asked.

Razumikhin bowed, beaming all over. For a moment everyone suddenly became somehow strangely abashed.

"Good-bye, Rodya—I mean, for now; I don't like saying 'good-bye.' Good-bye, Nastasya . . . ah, I've said it again! . . ."

Pulcheria Alexandrovna was going to bow to Sonechka, but it somehow did not come off, and she hastened from the room.

But Avdotya Romanovna was waiting her turn, as it were, and, following her mother past Sonya, gave her an attentive, polite, and full bow. Sonechka became embarrassed and bowed somehow hastily and fearfully; a sort of pained feeling even showed in her face, as if Avdotya Romanovna's politeness and attention were burdensome and tormenting to her.

"Dunya, good-bye!" Raskolnikov called out from the doorway, "give me your hand!"

"But I did; don't you remember?" Dunya answered, turning to him tenderly and awkwardly.

"Well, then give it to me again!"

And he squeezed her fingers tightly. Dunechka smiled at him, blushed, quickly pulled her hand back, and went after her mother, all happy herself for some reason.

"Well, that's nice!" he said to Sonya, coming back into the room and looking at her brightly. "May the Lord grant rest to the dead, but the living have still got to live! Right? Right? Isn't that right?"

Sonya looked at his suddenly brightened face even with surprise; for a few moments he gazed at her silently and fixedly: the whole story her deceased father had told him about her swept suddenly through his memory . . .

"LORD, DUNECHKA!" Pulcheria Alexandrovna began to say, as soon as they came out to the street, "I really almost feel glad we've left; it's somehow easier. Now, would I have thought yesterday on the train that I could ever be glad of that!"

"I tell you again, mama, he's still very ill. Don't you see? Maybe it was suffering over us that upset him. One must be tolerant; then so much, so much can be forgiven."

"But you were not very tolerant!" Pulcheria Alexandrovna interrupted at once, hotly and jealously. "You know, Dunya, I was looking at the two of you, and you're the perfect picture of him, not so much in looks as in soul: you're both melancholic, both sullen and hot-tempered, both arrogant, and both magnanimous . . . Is it possible that he's an egoist, Dunechka? Eh? . . . When I think what may happen tonight at our place, my heart just sinks!"

"Don't worry, mama, what must be, will be."

"But, Dunechka, only think of the position we're in now! What if Pyotr Petrovich retracts?" poor Pulcheria Alexandrovna suddenly let out incautiously.

"What would he be worth after that!" Dunechka answered curtly and contemptuously.

"We did well to leave now," Pulcheria Alexandrovna hastened to interrupt. "He was hurrying somewhere on business; let him go out for a walk, get some air . . . his room is awfully stuffy . . . but where can one get any air here? It's the same outside as in a closed room. Lord, what a city! . . . Wait, look out, you'll be crushed, they're carrying something! Goodness, it's a piano . . . how they all push! . . . I'm also very afraid of this girl . . ."

"What girl, mama?"

"Why, this Sofya Semyonovna who was there just now . . ."

"What about her?"

"I just have a certain presentiment, Dunya. Well, believe it or not, as soon as she walked in, at that very moment I thought to myself: here is where the main thing lies . . ."

"Nothing's lying there at all!" Dunya exclaimed in vexation. "You and your presentiments, mother! He's only known her since yesterday, and he didn't recognize her today when she came in."

"Well, you'll see! . . . She disturbs me; but you'll see, you will! And I got so scared: she looked at me, just looked, with such eyes, I could hardly sit still—remember, when he began introducing her? And it's strange: Pyotr Petrovich writes such things about her, and then he introduces her to us, to you of all people! It means he cares for her!"

"What does it matter what he writes! People talked and wrote about us, too, don't forget! And I'm sure she's . . . wonderful, and that this is all nonsense!"

"God be with her!"

"And Pyotr Petrovich is a worthless gossip," Dunechka suddenly snapped.

Pulcheria Alexandrovna simply wilted. The conversation ceased.

"LISTEN, here's this business I have with you . . ." Raskolnikov said, drawing Razumikhin over to the window . . .

"I'll tell Katerina Ivanovna that you'll come, then . . ." Sonya hurried, bowing as she prepared to leave.

"One moment, Sofya Semyonovna; we have no secrets; you are not in our way . . . I'd like to say a couple of more words to you . . . Listen," he suddenly turned to Razumikhin, as if breaking off without finishing the sentence, "you do know this . . . what's his name! . . . Porfiry Petrovich?"

"Of course I do! My relative. What about it?" Razumikhin added with a sort of burst of curiosity.

"He's now in charge of . . . this case . . . well, this murder . . . the one you were talking about yesterday?"

"Yes . . . so?" Razumikhin suddenly goggled his eyes.

"He's been questioning the pawners, and I also pawned some things there—junk, really—but it's my sister's ring, which she gave me as a keepsake when I was coming here, and also my father's silver watch. Worth five or six roubles in all, but I care about them, as mementos. So what shall I do now? I don't want the things to be lost, especially the watch. I was trembling just now for fear mother would ask to see it when we started talking about Dunechka's watch. It's the only thing left of my father's. She'll be sick if it's lost! Women! So what shall I do, tell me! I know I should report it to the police! But wouldn't it be better to go to Porfiry himself, eh? What do you think? To be done with it sooner? Mama will still ask before dinner, you'll see!"

"Certainly not to the police, but to Porfiry—by all means!" Razumikhin cried in some unusual excitement. "I can't tell you how glad I am! But why wait? Let's go now, it's two steps away, we're sure to find him there."

"Why not . . . let's go . . ."

"And he'll be very, very, very, very glad to meet you! I've told him a lot about you at various times . . . And yesterday, too. Let's go! . . . So you knew the old woman! Well, there! . . . It's all turned out quite mag-ni-fi-cently! . . . Ah, yes . . . Sofya Ivanovna . . ."

"Sofya Semyonovna," Raskolnikov corrected him. "Sofya Semyonovna, this is my friend Razumikhin, and a good man he is . . ."

"If you have to go now . . ." Sonya tried to begin, without so much as looking at Razumikhin, and becoming even more abashed as a result.

"Let's go, then!" Raskolnikov decided. "I'll call on you today, Sofya Semyonovna, only tell me, where do you live?"

It was not that he was confused, but as if he were hurrying and avoiding her eyes. Sonya gave him her address and blushed. They went out together.

"Don't you lock the door?" Razumikhin asked, coming down the stairs behind them.

"Never! . . . Though I've been meaning to buy a lock for two years now," he added casually. "Happy are those who have nothing to lock up?" he turned to Sonya, laughing.

Outside, they stopped in the gateway.

"Are you going to the right, Sofya Semyonovna? By the way, how did you find me?" he asked, as if wishing to tell her something quite different. He kept wanting to look into her quiet, clear eyes, but somehow kept being unable to . . .

"But you gave Polechka your address yesterday."

"Polya? Ah, yes . . . Polechka! That . . . little one . . . is she your sister? So I gave her my address?"

"You mean you've forgotten?"

"No . . . I remember . . ."

"And I also heard about you before, from my late father . . . Only I didn't know your last name then, and he didn't know it himself . . . And I came just now . . . and since I learned your last name yesterday . . . I asked today, 'Where does Mr. Raskolnikov live?' . . . I didn't know you were also subletting a room . . . Good-bye, sir . . . I'll tell Katerina Ivanovna . . ."

She was terribly glad to get away at last; she walked looking down, hurrying, the sooner to be out of their sight, the sooner somehow to get through those twenty steps until she could turn the corner to the right and be alone at last, and then walk along, hurrying, not looking at anyone, not noticing anything, but thinking, remembering, pondering every word said, every circumstance. Never, never had she felt anything like this. A whole new world had descended vaguely and mysteriously into her soul. She suddenly remembered that Raskolnikov himself wanted to call on her that day, perhaps that same morning, perhaps at once!

"Only not today, please, not today!" she murmured with a sinking heart, as if pleading with someone, like a frightened child. "Lord! To me . . . in that room . . . he'll see . . . oh, Lord!"

And, of course, at that moment she could not have noticed the gentleman, unknown to her, who was keeping a close eye on her and following on her heels. He had been following her ever since she walked out the gate. When the three of them—she, Razumikhin, and Raskolnikov—stopped for a couple of words on the sidewalk, this passer-by, stepping around them, seemed suddenly to give a start, accidentally catching Sonya's words: "and I asked, where does Mr. Raskolnikov live?" He had looked quickly but attentively at all three of them, especially at Raskolnikov, whom Sonya was addressing; then he looked at the house and made a note of it. All this was done in a moment, as he walked, and the passer-by, trying not to let it show, went farther on, slowing his pace as if he were waiting. He was waiting for Sonya; he had seen that they were saying good-bye and that Sonya was about to go home.

"But where does she live? I've seen that face somewhere," he thought, remembering Sonya's face . . . "I must find out."

Coming to the corner, he crossed to the other side of the street, looked back, and saw that Sonya was already following after him, in the same direction, noticing nothing. Coming to the corner, she also turned down the same street. He followed her on the opposite sidewalk, without taking his eyes off her; after going some fifty steps, he crossed back to Sonya's side of the street, caught up with her, and kept on walking five steps behind her.

He was a man of about fifty, of above average height, portly, with broad and steep shoulders that gave him a stooping look. He was stylishly and comfortably dressed, and had the air of an imposing gentleman. He was carrying a beautiful cane with which he tapped the sidewalk at every step, and on his hands he wore a fresh pair of gloves. His broad face with its high cheekbones was quite pleasant, and he had a fresh, non-Petersburg complexion. His hair, still very thick, was quite blond, with perhaps only a touch of gray, and his broad, thick spade beard was even lighter than the hair on his head. His eyes were blue and had a cold, intent, and thoughtful look; his lips were scarlet. In general, he was an exceedingly well-preserved man, who seemed much younger than his years.

When Sonya came out to the canal, the two of them were alone on the sidewalk. Observing her, he had been able to notice how pensive and distracted she was. When she reached her house, Sonya turned in at the gate; he followed her, seeming somewhat surprised. Going into the courtyard, she turned to the right, towards the corner, where the stairway to her apartment was. "Hah!" the unknown gentleman muttered, and he started up the stairs behind her. Only then did Sonya notice him. She went up to the third floor, turned down the hallway, and rang at number nine, where the words KAPERNAUMOV, TAILOR were written on the door in chalk. "Hah!" the stranger repeated again, surprised at the strange coincidence, and rang at number eight next door. The two doors were about six paces apart.

"You live at Kapernaumov's!" he said, looking at Sonya and laughing. "He altered my waistcoat for me yesterday. And I'm staying here, next door to you, with Madame Resslich, Gertrude Karlovna. The way things do happen!"

Sonya looked at him attentively.

"We're neighbors," he went on, somehow especially cheerfully. "It's only my third day in the city. Well, good-bye for now."

Sonya did not answer; the door was opened and she slipped into her room. She felt ashamed for some reason, and seemed to have grown timid . . .

ON THE WAY to see Porfiry, Razumikhin was in an especially excited state.

"This is nice, brother," he repeated several times. "I'm glad, I'm so glad!"

"What are you so glad about?" Raskolnikov thought to himself.

"I didn't even know you also pawned things with the old woman. And . . . and . . . was it long ago? I mean, did you go to her long ago?"

("What a naive fool!")

"When was it? . . ." Raskolnikov paused, recollecting. "I went there, I think, about three days before her death. However, I'm not going to redeem the things now," he picked up, with a sort of hasty and special concern about the things, "I'm down to my last silver rouble again . . . thanks to that cursed delirium yesterday! . . ."

He mentioned the delirium with special significance.

"Ah, yes, yes, yes," Razumikhin hastily yessed him, who knows about what. "That's why you were struck . . . partly . . . that time . . . and, you know, you also kept saying something about rings and chains in your delirium! . . . Ah, yes, yes . . . It's clear, it's all clear now."

("So! The idea really spread around among them! Here's a man who would go to the cross for me, yet he's so glad it's *become clear* why I talked about rings in my delirium! It really got settled in them all! . . .")

"And will we find him in?" he asked aloud.

"We will, we will," Razumikhin hurried. "He's a nice fellow, brother, you'll see! He's a bit awkward—not to say he's not a man of the world, but I mean he's awkward in another sense. He's an intelligent type, intelligent, not stupid at all, only he has some peculiar way of thinking . . . Mistrustful, a skeptic, a cynic . . . he likes hoodwinking people, or not hoodwinking them but pulling their leg . . . Well, and then it's the old material method . . . But he knows his job, he really does . . . Last year he ran down a case involving a murder where almost all the traces were lost! He wants very, very, very much to make your acquaintance!"

"But why so much?"

"I mean, not that . . . you see, recently, when you were sick, I happened to talk about you a lot and quite often . . . So, he listened . . . and when he learned that you were studying law and couldn't finish your studies because of your circumstances, he said, 'What a pity!' So, I concluded . . . I mean, not just that, but all of it together; yesterday Zamyotov . . . You see, Rodya, I blabbed something to you yesterday while I was drunk, as we were walking home . . . so you see, brother, I'm afraid you may exaggerate . . ."

"What is it? That I'm supposed to be mad? But maybe it's true."

He grinned tensely.

"Yes . . . yes . . . I mean, no! Pah! Anyway, everything I was saying (and about other things, too) was all nonsense, on account of drink."

"But why are you apologizing! I'm so sick of all this!" Raskolnikov cried with exaggerated irritation. He was partly pretending, however.

"I know, I know, I understand. Believe me, I understand. It's shameful even to speak of . . ."

"If it's shameful, don't speak!"

They both fell silent. Razumikhin was more than delighted, and Raskolnikov realized this with loathing. He was also troubled by what Razumikhin had just said about Porfiry.

"I'll have to sing Lazarus for him, too," he thought,[6] turning pale, and with his heart pounding, "and sing it naturally. Most natural would be to sing nothing. Eagerly to sing nothing. No, *eagerly* would be unnatural again . . . Well, how things turn out there . . . we shall see . . . presently . . . Is it good that I'm going, or not good? A moth flying into the candle-flame. My heart is pounding—that's not good! . . ."

"In this gray house," said Razumikhin.

("Most important is whether or not Porfiry knows I was in that witch's apartment yesterday . . . and asked about the blood. I must find that out at once, from the very first step, the moment I walk in, by the look on his face; o-ther-wise . . . I'll find out, if it's the end of me!")

"You know what?" he suddenly turned to Razumikhin with an impish smile. "I've noticed that you've been in a state of some unusual excitement today, brother, ever since this morning. True?"

"Excitement? None whatsoever." Razumikhin cringed.

"No, really, brother, it's quite noticeable. You sat on the chair today as you never do, somehow on the edge of it, and kept jerking spasmodically. Kept jumping up for no apparent reason. You'd be angry, and then suddenly for some reason your mug would turn as sweet as a lollipop. You even blushed; especially when you were invited to dinner, you blushed terribly."

"Nothing of the kind! Lies! . . . What are you talking about?"

"But why are you dodging like a schoolboy! Pah, the devil, he's blushing again!"

"What a swine you are, though!"

"But why are you embarrassed? Romeo! Wait, I'm going to tell on you today—ha, ha, ha! Mama will have a laugh . . . and so will someone else . . ."

"Listen, listen, listen, but this is serious, it's . . . ah, the devil, I don't know what it is!" Razumikhin became utterly muddled and went cold with terror. "What are you going to tell them? I, brother . . . pah, what a swine you are!"

"Just like a rose in springtime! And you have no idea how it becomes you; a six-and-a-half-foot Romeo! And so well scrubbed today; you even cleaned under your fingernails, eh? When did that ever happen before! And, by God, you've even pomaded yourself! Bend down!"

"Swine!!!"

Raskolnikov laughed so much that it seemed he could no longer control himself, and, thus laughing, they entered Porfiry Petrovich's apartment. This was just what Raskolnikov wanted: from inside one could hear how they came in laughing and went on guffawing in the entryway.

"Not a word here, or I'll . . . beat you to a pulp!" Razumikhin whispered furiously, seizing Raskolnikov by the shoulder.

V

THE LATTER was already going into the apartment. He entered looking as though he had to use all his strength to keep from somehow breaking into giggles. Behind him, his physiognomy completely overthrown and ferocious, red as a peony, lanky and awkward, entered the abashed Razumikhin. His face and his whole figure were indeed comical at that moment, and justified Raskolnikov's laughter. Raskolnikov, not introduced as yet, bowed to their host, who was standing in the middle of the room looking at them inquiringly, and held out his hand to him, still with an obviously great effort to suppress his hilarity and to utter at least two or three words to introduce himself. But he had barely managed to assume a serious expression and mutter something when suddenly, as if involuntarily, he glanced at Razumikhin again, and here he could no longer restrain himself: the suppressed laughter broke through all the more irresistibly the more forcefully he had been trying to contain it until then. The remarkable ferocity with which Razumikhin was taking this "heartfelt" laughter gave the whole scene a look of the most genuine hilarity and, above all, naturalness. Razumikhin, as if on purpose, was helping things along.

"Pah, the devil!" he bellowed, waving his arm, and happened to hit a small round table on which stood an empty tea glass. Everything went flying and jingling.

"But why go breaking chairs, gentlemen! It's a loss to the exchequer!" Porfiry Petrovich exclaimed merrily.

The scene presented itself as follows: Raskolnikov, his hand forgotten in his host's hand, was finishing laughing but, knowing there were limits, was waiting for the moment to end it as quickly and naturally as possible. Razumikhin, embarrassed to the utmost by the fall of the table and the broken glass, looked gloomily at the fragments, spat, and turned sharply to the window, where he stood with his back to the public, his face scowling terribly, looking out the window but seeing nothing. Porfiry Petrovich was laughing, and willingly so, but it was obvious that explanations were called for. On a chair in the corner sat Zamyotov, who had risen when the guests entered and stood expectantly, widening his mouth into a smile, but looked at the whole scene with perplexity and even something like mistrust, and at Raskolnikov even with a certain bewilderment. The unexpected presence of Zamyotov struck Raskolnikov unpleasantly.

"This still needs some figuring out!" he thought.

"Excuse me, please," he began, trying to look abashed, "Raskolnikov . . ."

"But, my goodness, sir, how nice, and how nicely you came in . . . What, doesn't he intend even to say hello?" Porfiry Petrovich nodded towards Razumikhin.

"By God, I don't know why he's so furious with me. I simply told him on the way here that he resembled Romeo, and . . . and proved it. I can't think of anything else."

"Swine!" Razumikhin responded, without turning around.

"He must have had very serious reasons, if he got so angry over one little word," Porfiry laughed.

"Ah, you—investigator! . . . Ah, devil take you all!" Razumikhin snapped, and suddenly laughed himself, and with a cheerful face, as though nothing had happened, went up to Porfiry Petrovich.

"Enough! Fools all! To business now: this is my friend, Rodion Romanych Raskolnikov; first of all, he's heard about you and has been wanting to make your acquaintance, and, second, he has a little business with you. Hah! Zamyotov! What brings you here? You mean you know each other? Since when?"

"What's this now!" Raskolnikov thought uneasily.

Zamyotov seemed abashed, but not very.

"We met yesterday, at your place," he said offhandedly.

"So God spared me the trouble: last week he was begging me terribly to get him introduced to you somehow, Porfiry, but here you've rubbed noses without me . . . Where do you keep your tobacco?"

Porfiry Petrovich was casually dressed, in a house-jacket, a rather clean shirt, and down-at-the-heel slippers. He was a man of about thirty-five, of less than average height, stout and even pot-bellied, clean-shaven, with no moustache or side-whiskers, and with closely cropped hair on a large, round head that bulged somehow especially roundly at the back. His puffy, round, slightly pug-nosed face was of a sickly, dark yellow color, but rather cheerful and even mocking. It would even have been good-natured were it not for the expression of his eyes, which had a sort of liquid, watery gleam and were covered by nearly white eyelashes that blinked as though winking at someone. The look of these eyes was strangely out of harmony with his whole figure, which had something womanish about it, and lent it something a good deal more serious than might have been expected at first sight.

As soon as he heard that his guest had "a little business" with him, he at once asked him to sit down on the sofa, sat down himself at the other end, and stared at his guest, expecting an immediate account of the business, with the sort of eager and all too serious attention that from the first becomes burdensome and embarrassing, especially for a stranger, and especially when what is being recounted seems, in one's own opinion, out of all proportion to the unusually weighty attention accorded it. But Raskolnikov explained his business clearly and precisely, in brief and coherent terms, and was left so pleased with himself that he even managed to give Porfiry a thorough looking-over. Porfiry Petrovich, for his part, never once took his eyes off him during the whole time. Razumikhin, settling himself across the table from them, hotly and impatiently followed the account of the business, shifting his glance every second from one to the other and back, which was even a bit too much.

"Fool!" Raskolnikov cursed to himself.

"You ought to make a statement to the police," Porfiry replied with a most businesslike look, "that, having been informed of such-and-such an event—of this murder, that is—you ask in your turn to inform the investigator in charge of the case that such-and-such things belong to you, and that you wish to redeem them . . . or perhaps . . . however, they'll write it out for you."

"That's just the point, that at the present moment," Raskolnikov did his best to look as abashed as possible, "I am not exactly solvent

. . . and even such a trifle is more than . . . You see, for now I'd like simply to declare that the things are mine, and that when I have the money . . ."

"That doesn't matter, sir," Porfiry Petrovich answered, taking the explanation of finances coldly, "and, as a matter of fact, if you wish you can write directly to me, to the same effect, that having been informed of this and that, and declaring such-and-such things mine, I ask . . ."

"On ordinary paper?" Raskolnikov hastened to interrupt, interested again in the financial aspect of the matter.

"Oh, the most ordinary, sir!" Porfiry Petrovich suddenly looked at him somehow with obvious mockery, narrowing his eyes and as if winking at him. However, perhaps it only seemed so to Raskolnikov, because it lasted no more than an instant. There was something of the sort, at least. Raskolnikov would have sworn to God that he winked at him, devil knew why.

"He knows!" flashed in him like lightning.

"Excuse me for bothering you with such trifles," he went on, some-what disconcerted, "my things are worth only five roubles, but they are especially dear to me as mementos of those from whom I received them, and, I confess, as soon as I found out, I was very afraid . . ."

"That's why you got so roused up yesterday when I let on to Zossimov that Porfiry was questioning the pawners!" Razumikhin put in with obvious intention.

Now, this was insufferable. Raskolnikov could not help himself and angrily flashed a glance at him, his black eyes burning with wrath. But he immediately recovered himself.

"You seem to be taunting me, brother?" he turned to him with artfully feigned irritation. "I agree that in your eyes I may care too much about such trash, but you cannot regard me as greedy or egoistic for that, and in my eyes these two worthless little trinkets may not be trash at all. I told you just now that this two-penny silver watch is the only thing left of my father's. You may laugh, but my mother has come to visit me," he suddenly turned to Porfiry again, "and if she were to find out," he quickly turned back to Razumikhin, trying especially hard to make his voice tremble, "that this watch is lost, I swear she would be in despair! Women!"

"But it's not that at all! I meant it in a different way! Quite the opposite!" exclaimed the distressed Razumikhin.

"Well done? Natural? Not exaggerated?" Raskolnikov trembled within himself. "Why did I say 'women'?"

"Your mother has come to visit you?" Porfiry Petrovich inquired for some reason.

"Yes."

"When was that, sir?"

"Yesterday evening."

Porfiry paused, as if considering something.

"Your things would not be lost in any event," he went on calmly and coldly, "because I've been sitting here a long time waiting for you."

And as though nothing were the matter, he solicitously began offering an ashtray to Razumikhin, who was mercilessly flicking cigarette ashes on the carpet. Raskolnikov gave a start, but Porfiry, still solicitous for Razumikhin's cigarette, seemed not to be looking.

"Wha-a-at? Waiting? So you knew he had pawned things *there?*" exclaimed Razumikhin.

Porfiry Petrovich addressed Raskolnikov directly.

"Your two things, the ring and the watch, *she* had wrapped up in one piece of paper, with your name clearly written on it in pencil, together with the day and month when she received them from you . . ."

"How is it you're so observant? . . ." Raskolnikov grinned awkwardly, making a special effort to look him straight in the eye; but he could not help himself and suddenly added: "I just made that observation because there were probably many pawners . . . so that it would be difficult for you to remember them all . . . But, on the contrary, you remember them all so distinctly, and . . . and . . ."

("Stupid! Weak! Why did I add that!")

"Yes, almost all the pawners are known now; in fact, you are the only one who has not been so good as to pay us a visit," Porfiry replied, with a barely noticeable shade of mockery.

"I was not feeling very well."

"So I have heard, sir. I've even heard that you were greatly upset by something. You also seem pale now."

"Not pale at all . . . on the contrary, I'm quite well!" Raskolnikov snapped rudely and angrily, suddenly changing his tone. Anger was boiling up in him and he could not suppress it. "And it's in anger that I'll make some slip!" flashed in him again. "But why are they torment-ing me! . . ."

"Not feeling very well!" Razumikhin picked up. "Listen to that drivel! He was in delirium and almost unconscious until yester-day . . . Would you believe it, Porfiry, he could hardly stand up, but as soon as we—Zossimov and I—turned our backs yesterday, he got dressed and made off on the sly, and carried on somewhere till almost midnight—and all that, I tell you, in complete delirium, can you imagine it! A remarkable case!"

"Really, in *complete delirium?* You don't say!" Porfiry shook his head with a sort of womanish gesture.

"Ah, nonsense! Don't believe it! But then, you don't believe it anyway!" escaped from Raskolnikov, who was now much too angry. However, Porfiry Petrovich seemed not to hear these strange words.

"But how could you have gone out if you weren't delirious?" Razu-mikhin suddenly lost his temper. "Why did you go out? What for? . . . And why precisely on the sly? Was there any common sense in you then? Now that all the danger is past, I can say it straight out!"

"I got awfully sick of them yesterday," Raskolnikov suddenly turned to Porfiry with an insolently defiant grin, "so I ran away from them to rent an apartment where they wouldn't find me, and I took a pile of money with me. Mr. Zamyotov here saw the money. What do you say, Mr. Zamyotov, was I intelligent yesterday or delirious? Settle the argument!"

He could really have strangled Zamyotov at that moment, so much did he dislike his silence and the look in his eyes.

"In my opinion you spoke quite intelligently, and even cunningly, sir, only you were rather irritable," Zamyotov declared dryly.

"And Nikodim Fomich told me today," Porfiry Petrovich put in, "that he met you yesterday, quite late, in the apartment of an official who had been run over by horses . . ."

"Now, take this official, for instance!" Razumikhin picked up. "Now, weren't you crazy at the official's place? You gave all your money to the widow for the funeral! Now, if you wanted to help—

well, give her fifteen, give her twenty, leave three roubles for yourself at least—but no, you just forked over the whole twenty-five!"

"Maybe I found a treasure somewhere, and you don't know it. So I gave her money with both hands yesterday . . . Mr. Zamyotov here knows I found a treasure! . . . Excuse us, please," he turned to Porfiry with twitching lips, "for bothering you for half an hour with such a trivial exchange. You must be sick of it, eh?"

"My goodness, sir, on the contrary, on the co-o-ontrary! You have no idea how you interest me! It's curious both to look and to listen . . . and, I admit, I'm very glad that you have finally been so good as to come . . ."

"Well, give us some tea at least! Our throats are dry!" Razumikhin cried.

"A wonderful idea! Maybe everyone will join us. But wouldn't you like . . . something more substantial . . . before tea?"

"Ah, go on!"

Porfiry Petrovich went to send for tea.

Thoughts were spinning like a whirlwind in Raskolnikov's head. He was terribly annoyed.

"What's more, they don't even conceal it; they don't even care to stand on ceremony! What occasion did you have for talking about me with Nikodim Fomich, since you don't know me at all? It means they don't even care to conceal the fact that they're watching me like a pack of dogs! They spit in my mug quite openly!" He was trembling with fury. "Strike directly, then; don't play cat and mouse with me. It's not polite, Porfiry Petrovich, and I may still, perhaps, not allow it, sir! . . . I'll get up and blurt out the whole truth in your mugs; then you'll see how I despise you! . . ." He caught his breath with difficulty. "But what if it only seems so to me? What if it's a mirage, what if I'm completely mistaken, get angry on account of my inexperience, and fail to keep up my vile role? Maybe it's all unintentional? Their words are all ordinary, but there's something in them . . . All this can always be said, and yet there is something. Why did he come out with that 'she'? Why did Zamyotov add that I spoke *cunningly*? Why do they all speak in such a tone? Yes . . . that tone . . . Razumikhin has been sitting right here, why does he not imagine anything? The innocent dolt never imagines anything! I'm feverish again! . . . Did Porfiry wink at me just now, or not? Must be nonsense; why would he wink? Do they want to irritate my nerves, or are they taunting me? Either it's all a mirage, or they *know!* . . . Even Zamyotov is impertinent . . . Is Zamyotov impertinent? Zamyotov's changed his mind overnight. I had a feeling he'd change his mind! He seems quite at home here, yet it's the first time he's come. Porfiry doesn't treat him like a guest, turns his back to him. They've already rubbed noses. They must have rubbed noses *because of me!* They must have been talking about me before we came! . . . Do they know about the apartment? Just get it over with! . . . When I said I ran away yesterday to rent an apartment, he let it go, he didn't pick it up . . . It was clever to put that in about the apartment—I'll need it later! . . . In delirium, I said! . . . Ha, ha, ha! He knows all about yesterday evening! But he didn't know about mother's arrival! . . . And the witch wrote down the date with a pencil! . . . Lies! I won't let you get me! These aren't facts yet, they're only a mirage! No, just try giving me facts! The apartment is not a fact either, it's delirium; I know what to tell them . . . But do they know about the apartment? I won't go until I find out! Why did I come? But that I'm angry now—that, perhaps, is a fact! Pah, how irritable I am! But maybe that's good; the role of the sick man . . . He's feeling me out. He'll try to throw me off. Why did I come?"

All this swept like lightning through his head.

Porfiry Petrovich was back in an instant. He suddenly became somehow merry.

"Since your party yesterday, brother, my head . . . in fact, the whole of me is somehow unscrewed," he began in quite a different tone, laughing, to Razumikhin.

"Well, was it interesting? I left you yesterday at the most interesting point. Who won?"

"No one, naturally. We got on to the eternal questions, and it all stayed in the clouds."

"Just imagine what they got on to yesterday, Rodya: is there such a thing as crime, or not? He said they all lied themselves into the blue devils."

"What's so surprising? It's an ordinary social question," Raskolnikov replied distractedly.

"The question was not formulated that way," Porfiry observed.

"Not quite that way, it's true," Razumikhin agreed at once, hurrying and getting excited as usual. "You see, Rodion—listen and give your opinion, I want it. I was turning inside out yesterday waiting for you; I told them about you, too, that you were going to come . . . It started with the views of the socialists. Their views are well known: crime is a protest against the abnormality of the social set-up—that alone and nothing more, no other causes are admitted—but nothing! . . ."

"Now, that is a lie!" cried Porfiry Petrovich. He was growing visibly animated and laughing all the while, looking at Razumikhin, which fired him up all the more.

"N-nothing is admitted!" Razumikhin interrupted hotly. "I'm not lying! . . . I'll show you their books: with them one is always a 'victim of the environment'—and nothing else! Their favorite phrase! Hence directly that if society itself is normally set up, all crimes will at once disappear, because there will be no reason for protesting and everyone will instantly become righteous. Nature isn't taken into account, nature is driven out, nature is not supposed to be! With them it's not mankind developing all along in a historical, *living* way that will finally turn by itself into a normal society, but, on the contrary, a social system, coming out of some mathematical head, will at once organize the whole of mankind and instantly make it righteous and sinless, sooner than any living process, without any historical and living way! That's why they have such an instinctive dislike of history: 'there's nothing in it but outrage and stupidity'—and everything is explained by stupidity alone! That's why they so dislike the *living* process of life: there's no need for the *living soul!* The living soul will demand life, the living soul won't listen to mechanics, the living soul is suspicious, the living soul is retrograde! While here, though there may be a whiff of carrion, and it may all be made out of rubber—still it's not alive, still it has no will, still it's slavish, it won't rebel! And it turns out in the end that they've reduced everything to mere brickwork and the layout of corridors and rooms in a phalanstery![7] The phalanstery may be all ready, but your nature isn't ready for the phalanstery, it wants life, it hasn't completed the life process yet, it's too soon for the cemetery! You can't overleap nature with logic alone! Logic will presuppose three cases, when there are a million of them! Cut away the whole million, and reduce everything to the one question of comfort! The easiest solution to the problem! Enticingly clear, and there's no need to think! Above all, there's no need to think! The whole of life's mystery can fit on two printed pages!"

"He's broken loose again, drumming away! You've got to hold him by both arms," Porfiry laughed. "Imagine," he turned to Raskolnikov, "it was the same yesterday evening, with six voices, in one room, and with preliminary punch-drinking besides—can you picture that? No, brother, you're lying: 'environment' means a great deal in crime; I can confirm that."

"I know it means a great deal, but tell me this: a forty-year-old man dishonors a girl of ten—was it the environment that made him do it?"

"Well, strictly speaking, perhaps it is the environment," Porfiry observed with surprising solemnity. "The crime against the girl may very well be explained by the 'environment.' "

Razumikhin all but flew into a rage.

"And if you like I can *deduce* for you right now," he bellowed, "that you have white eyelashes solely because Ivan the Great[8] is two hundred and fifty feet high, and I can deduce it clearly, precisely, progressively, and even with a liberal tinge. I can! Want to bet?"

"I accept! Let's listen, please, to how he deduces it!"

"Ah, he just goes on pretending, devil take it!" Razumikhin cried out, jumped up, and waved his arm. "You're not worth talking to! He does it all on purpose, you don't know him yet, Rodion! And he took their side yesterday just so as to fool them all. And, Lord, the things he was saying! And didn't he make them happy! . . . He sometimes keeps it up like that for two weeks. Last year he assured us, who knows why, that he was going to become a monk: he stood by it for two months! Recently he decided to assure us he was getting married and that everything was set for the wedding. He even had a new suit made. We already started congratulating him. There was no bride, nothing—it was all a mirage!"

"Ah, that's a lie! I had the suit made before. It was because of the new suit that it occurred to me to pull your legs."

"Are you really such a dissembler?" Raskolnikov asked casually.

"And did you think I wasn't? Just wait, I'll take you in, too—ha, ha, ha! No, you see, I'll tell you the whole truth! Speaking of all these questions, crimes, the environment, little girls, I now recall, though it always interested me, a certain article of yours: 'On Crime' . . . or whatever it was, I don't remember the title, I've forgotten. I had the pleasure of reading it two months ago in *Periodical Discourse.*"

"My article? In *Periodical Discourse?*" Raskolnikov asked in surprise. "I did indeed write an article dealing with a certain book six months ago, when I left the university, but at the time I took it to *Weekly Discourse,* not *Periodical.*"

"Yet it got into *Periodical Discourse.*"

"But *Weekly Discourse* ceased to exist, which is why it wasn't printed then . . ."

"That's true, sir; and as it was ceasing to exist, *Weekly Discourse* merged with *Periodical Discourse,* and so your little article appeared two months ago in *Periodical Discourse.* And you didn't know?"

Raskolnikov indeed knew nothing.

"But, my goodness, you can demand payment from them for the article! What a character you have, though! Your life is so solitary that you don't even know things that concern you directly. It's a fact, sir."

"Bravo, Rodka! I didn't know either!" Razumikhin exclaimed. "I'll stop by the reading room today and look for that issue! Two months ago? What was the date? Anyway, I'll find it! What a thing! And he doesn't even say!"

"But how did you find out that the article was mine? I signed it with an initial."

"By chance, and only the other day. Through the editor, an acquaintance of mine . . . I was quite interested."

"As I recall, I was considering the psychological state of the criminal throughout the course of the crime."

"Yes, sir, and you maintain that the act of carrying out a crime is always accompanied by illness. Very, very original, but . . . as a matter of fact, what interested me was not that part of your article, but a certain thought tossed in at the end, which unfortunately you present only vaguely, by way of a hint . . . In short, if you recall, a certain hint is presented that there supposedly exist in the world certain persons who can . . . that is, who not only can but are fully entitled to commit all sorts of crimes and excesses and to whom the law supposedly does not apply."

Raskolnikov smiled at this forced and deliberate distortion of his idea.

"What? How's that? The right to commit crimes? But not because they're 'victims of the environment'?" Razumikhin inquired, even somewhat fearfully.

"No, no, not quite because of that," Porfiry replied. "The whole point is that in his article all people are somehow divided into the 'ordinary' and the 'extraordinary.' The ordinary must live in obedience and have no right to transgress the law, because they are, after all, ordinary. While the extraordinary have the right to commit all sorts of crimes and in various ways to transgress the law, because in point of fact they are extraordinary. That is how you had it, unless I'm mistaken?"

"But what is this? It can't possibly be so!" Razumikhin muttered in perplexity.

Raskolnikov smiled again. He realized all at once what the point was and where he was being led; he remembered his article. He decided to accept the challenge.

"That isn't quite how I had it," he began, simply and modestly. "I admit, however, that your summary is almost correct, even perfectly correct, if you like . . ." (It was as if he were pleased to agree that it was perfectly correct.) "The only difference is that I do not at all insist that extraordinary people absolutely must and are duty bound at all times to do all sorts of excesses, as you say. I even think that such an article would never be accepted for publication. I merely suggested that an 'extraordinary' man has the right . . . that is, not an official right, but his own right, to allow his conscience to . . . step over certain obstacles, and then only in the event that the fulfillment of his idea—sometimes perhaps salutary for the whole of mankind—calls for it. You have been pleased to say that my article is unclear; I am prepared to clarify it for you, as far as I can. I will perhaps not be mistaken in supposing that that seems to be just what you want. As you please, sir. In my opinion, if, as the result of certain combinations, Kepler's or Newton's discoveries could become known to people in no other way than by sacrificing the lives of one, or ten, or a hundred or more people who were hindering the discovery, or standing as an obstacle in its path, then Newton would have the right, and it would even be his duty

. . . to remove those ten or a hundred people, in order to make his discoveries known to all mankind. It by no means follows from this, incidentally, that Newton should have the right to kill anyone he pleases, whomever happens along, or to steal from the market every day. Further, I recall developing in my article the idea that all . . . well, let's say, the lawgivers and founders of mankind, starting from the most ancient and going on to the Lycurguses, the Solons, the Muhammads, the Napoleons, and so forth,⁹ that all of them to a man were criminals, from the fact alone that in giving a new law they thereby violated the old one, held sacred by society and passed down from their fathers, and they certainly did not stop at shedding blood either, if it happened that blood (sometimes quite innocent and shed valiantly for the ancient law) could help them. It is even remarkable that most of these benefactors and founders of mankind were especially terrible blood-shedders. In short, I deduce that all, not only great men, but even those who are a tiny bit off the beaten track—that is, who are a tiny bit capable of saying something new—by their very nature cannot fail to be criminals—more or less, to be sure. Otherwise it would be hard for them to get off the beaten track, and, of course, they cannot consent to stay on it, again by nature, and in my opinion it is even their duty not to consent. In short, you see that so far there is nothing especially new here. It has been printed and read a thousand times. As for my dividing people into ordinary and extraordinary, I agree that it is somewhat arbitrary, but I don't really insist on exact numbers. I only believe in my main idea. It consists precisely in people being divided generally, according to the law of nature, into two categories: a lower or, so to speak, material category (the ordinary), serving solely for the reproduction of their own kind; and people proper—that is, those who have the gift or talent of speaking a *new word* in their environment. The subdivisions here are naturally endless, but the distinctive features of both categories are quite marked: people of the first, or material, category are by nature conservative, staid, live in obedience, and like being obedient. In my opinion they even must be obedient, because that is their purpose, and for them there is decidedly nothing humiliating in it. Those of the second category all transgress the law, are destroyers or inclined to destroy, depending on their abilities. The crimes of these people, naturally, are relative and varie-

gated; for the most part they call, in quite diverse declarations, for the destruction of the present in the name of the better. But if such a one needs, for the sake of his idea, to step even over a dead body, over blood, then within himself, in his conscience, he can, in my opinion, allow himself to step over blood—depending, however, on the idea and its scale—make note of that. It is only in this sense that I speak in my article of their right to crime. (You recall we began with the legal question.) However, there's not much cause for alarm: the masses hardly ever acknowledge this right in them; they punish them and hang them (more or less), thereby quite rightly fulfilling their conservative purpose; yet, for all that, in subsequent generations these same masses place the punished ones on a pedestal and worship them (more or less). The first category is always master of the present; the second—master of the future. The first preserves the world and increases it numerically; the second moves the world and leads it towards a goal. Both the one and the other have a perfectly equal right to exist. In short, for me all men's rights are equivalent—and *vive la guerre éternelle*—until the New Jerusalem, of course!"[10]

"So you still believe in the New Jerusalem?"

"I believe," Raskolnikov answered firmly; saying this, as throughout his whole tirade, he looked at the ground, having picked out a certain spot on the carpet.

"And . . . and . . . and do you also believe in God? Excuse me for being so curious."

"I believe," Raskolnikov repeated, looking up at Porfiry.

"And . . . and do you believe in the raising of Lazarus?"[11]

"I be-believe. What do you need all this for?"

"You believe literally?"

"Literally."

"I see, sir . . . just curious. Excuse me, sir. But, if I may say so—returning to the previous point—they aren't always punished; some, on the contrary . . ."

"Triumph in their own lifetime? Oh, yes, some attain in their own lifetime, and then . . ."

"Start doing their own punishing?"

"If necessary, and, in fact, almost always. Your observation, generally speaking, is quite witty."

"Thank you, sir. But tell me this: how does one manage to distinguish these extraordinary ones from the ordinary? Are they somehow marked at birth, or what? What I'm getting at is that one could do with more accuracy here, more outward certainty, so to speak: excuse the natural uneasiness of a practical and law-abiding man, but wouldn't it be possible in this case, for example, to introduce some special clothing, the wearing of some insignia, or whatever? . . . Because, you must agree, if there is some sort of mix-up, and a person from one category imagines he belongs to the other category and starts 'removing all obstacles,' as you quite happily put it, well then . . ."

"Oh, it happens quite often! This observation is even wittier than your last one . . ."

"Thank you, sir . . ."

"Not at all, sir; but consider also that a mistake is possible only on the part of the first category, that is, the 'ordinary' people (as I have called them, perhaps rather unfortunately). In spite of their innate tendency to obedience, by some playfulness of nature that is not denied even to cows, quite a few of them like to imagine themselves progressive people, 'destroyers,' who are in on the 'new word,' and that in all sincerity, sir. And at the same time they quite often fail to notice the really *new* ones, and even despise them as backward, shabby-minded people. But in my opinion there cannot be any significant danger here, and there is really nothing for you to be alarmed about, because they never go far. Of course, they ought to receive an occasional whipping, to remind them of their place when they get carried away, but no more than that; there isn't even any need for someone to whip them: they'll whip themselves, because they're so well behaved; some perform this service for each other, and some do it with their own hands . . . all the while imposing various public penances on themselves—the result is beautiful and edifying; in short, there's nothing for you to be alarmed about . . . Such a law exists."

"Well, at least you've reassured me somewhat in that regard; but then there's this other worry: tell me, please, are there many of these people who have the right to put a knife into others—I mean, of these 'extraordinary' ones? I am ready to bow down, of course, but you'll agree, sir, it's a bit eerie if there are too many of them, eh?"

"Oh, don't worry about that either," Raskolnikov went on in the same tone. "Generally, there are remarkably few people born who have a new thought, who are capable, if only slightly, of saying anything *new*—strangely few, in fact. One thing is clear, that the ordering of people's conception, all these categories and subdivisions, must be quite correctly and precisely determined by some law of nature. This law is as yet unknown, of course, but I believe that it exists and may one day be known. An enormous mass of people, of material, exists in the world only so that finally, through some effort, some as yet mysterious process, through some interbreeding of stocks and races, with great strain it may finally bring into the world, let's say, at least one somewhat independent man in a thousand. Perhaps one in ten thousand is born with a broader independence (I'm speaking approximately, graphically). With a still broader independence—one in a hundred thousand. Men of genius—one in millions; and great geniuses, the fulfillers of mankind—perhaps after the elapsing of many thousands of millions of people on earth. In short, I have not looked into the retort where all this takes place. But there certainly is and must be a definite law; it can be no accident."

"What, are you two joking or something?" Razumikhin cried out at last. "Addling each other's brains, aren't you? Sitting there and poking fun at each other! Are you serious, Rodya?"

Raskolnikov silently raised his pale, almost sad face to him, and did not answer. And how strange this quiet and sad face seemed to Razumikhin next to the undisguised, intrusive, annoying, and *impolite* sarcasm of Porfiry.

"Well, brother, if it's really serious, then . . . You're right, of course, in saying that it's nothing new, and resembles everything we've read and heard a hundred times over; but what is indeed *original* in it all—and, to my horror, is really yours alone—is that you do finally permit bloodshed *in all conscience* and, if I may say so, even with such fanaticism . . . So this is the main point of your article. This permission to shed blood *in all conscience* is . . . is to my mind more horrible than if bloodshed were officially, legally permitted . . ."

"Quite right, it's more horrible," Porfiry echoed.

"No, you got carried away somehow! It's a mistake. I'll read it . . . You got carried away! You can't think like that . . . I'll read it."

"That's not all in the article; it's only hinted at," said Raskolnikov.

"Right, right, sir," Porfiry could not sit still. "It has now become almost clear to me how you choose to look at crime, sir, but . . . excuse my importunity (I'm bothering you so much; I'm quite ashamed!)— you see, sir, you have reassured me greatly concerning cases of a mistaken mixing of the two categories, but . . . I keep being bothered by various practical cases! Now, what if some man, or youth, imagines himself a Lycurgus or a Muhammad—a future one, to be sure—and goes and starts removing all obstacles to that end . . . We're faced with a long campaign, and for this campaign we need money . . . and so he starts providing himself for the campaign . . . you know what I mean?"

Zamyotov suddenly snorted from his corner. Raskolnikov did not even raise his eyes to him.

"I have to agree," he answered calmly, "that such cases must indeed occur. The vain and silly in particular fall for such bait; young men particularly."

"So you see, sir. Well, and what then, sir?"

"Then nothing," Raskolnikov smiled. "It's not my fault. That's how it is and always will be. Now, he just said" (he nodded towards Razumikhin) "that I permit the shedding of blood. What of it? Society is all too well provided with banishments, prisons, court investigators, hard labor camps—why worry? Go and catch your thief! . . ."

"And what if we do catch him?"

"Serves him right."

"You're logical, after all. Well, sir, and what about his conscience?"

"But what business is that of yours?"

"But just out of humaneness, sir."

"Whoever has one can suffer, if he acknowledges his error. It's a punishment for him—on top of hard labor."

"Well, and those who are the true geniuses—the ones who are granted the right to put a knife into others," Razumikhin asked, frowning, "they ought not to suffer at all, even for the blood they've shed?"

"Why this word *ought?* There's neither permission nor prohibition here. Let him suffer, if he pities his victim . . . Suffering and pain are always obligatory for a broad consciousness and a deep heart. Truly great men, I think, must feel great sorrow in this world," he suddenly added pensively, not even in the tone of the conversation.

He raised his eyes, gave them all a thoughtful look, smiled, and took his cap. He was too calm, compared with when he had first come, and he felt it. Everyone rose.

"Well, sir, curse me if you like, be angry if you like, but I cannot help myself," Porfiry Petrovich rounded off again. "Allow me one more little question (I really am bothering you, sir!); I would like to introduce just one little idea, simply so as not to forget, sir . . ."

"Very well, tell me your little idea," Raskolnikov stood expectantly before him, pale and serious.

"Now then, sir . . . I really don't know how best to express it . . . it's such a playful idea . . . a psychological idea . . . Now then, sir, it really cannot be—heh, heh, heh!—that when you were writing your little article you did not regard yourself—say, just the tiniest bit—as one of the 'extraordinary' people, as saying a *new word*—in your sense, I mean . . . Isn't that so, sir?"

"It's quite possible," Raskolnikov replied disdainfully.

Razumikhin stirred.

"And if so, sir, can it be that you yourself would venture—say, in view of certain worldly failures and constraints, or somehow for the furtherance of all mankind—to step over the obstacle? . . . well, for instance, to kill and rob? . . ."

And he somehow suddenly winked at him again with his left eye and laughed inaudibly—exactly as earlier.

"If I did, I would certainly not tell you," Raskolnikov answered with defiant, haughty disdain.

"No, sir, it's just that I'm interested, properly speaking, in under-standing your article, in a literary sense only, sir . . ."

"Pah, how obvious and insolent!" Raskolnikov thought in disgust.

"Allow me to observe," he answered dryly, "that I do not consider myself a Muhammad or a Napoleon . . . or any such person whatsoever, and am consequently unable, not being them, to give you a satisfactory explanation of how I would act."

"But, my goodness, who in our Russia nowadays doesn't consider himself a Napoleon?" Porfiry suddenly pronounced with horrible fa-miliarity. There was something particularly clear this time even in the tone of his voice.

"Might it not have been some future Napoleon who bumped off our Alyona Ivanovna with an axe last week?" Zamyotov suddenly blurted out from his corner.

Raskolnikov was silent, looking firmly and fixedly at Porfiry. Razumikhin frowned gloomily. He seemed to have begun noticing something even earlier. He looked wrathfully around him. A moment of gloomy silence passed. Raskolnikov turned to leave.

"Leaving already!" Porfiry said kindly, holding out his hand with extreme affability. "I'm very, very glad to have made your acquaintance. And concerning your request, do not be in any doubt. Simply write as I told you. Or, best of all, come to my office yourself . . . one of these days . . . tomorrow, even. I'll be there around eleven o'clock for certain. We can settle everything . . . and talk . . . Since you were one of the last to be *there*, you might be able to tell us something . . ." he added, with a most good-natured air.

"You want to question me officially, with all the trimmings?" Raskolnikov asked sharply.

"What for, sir? There's no need of that as yet. You misunderstand me. You see, I never let an opportunity go by, and . . . and I've already talked with all the other pawners . . . taken evidence from some . . . and since you're the last one . . . Oh, yes, by the way!" he exclaimed, suddenly happy about something, "by the way, I've just remembered—what's the matter with me! . . ." He turned to Razumikhin. "You were carping at me all the time about this Nikolashka . . . well, I know, I know myself that the lad is clear," he turned back to Raskolnikov, "but there was no help for it; we had to bother Mitka as well . . . The thing is, sir, the whole point is: going up the stairs that time . . . excuse me, you were there before eight, sir?"

"Before eight," Raskolnikov answered, at the same time with an unpleasant feeling that he need not have said it.

"So, passing by on the stairs before eight o'clock, did you at least notice two workers in the open apartment—remember?—on the second floor? Or at least one of them? They were painting, didn't you see? This is very, very important for them! . . ."

"Painters? No, I didn't see . . ." Raskolnikov answered slowly, as if rummaging through his memories, at the same time straining his whole being and frozen with anguish trying to guess where precisely the trap lay, and how not to overlook something. "No, I didn't see, and I didn't notice any open apartment either . . . but on the fourth floor" (he was now in full possession of the trap and was triumphant) "I do remember there was an official moving out of the apartment . . . opposite Alyona Ivanovna's . . . yes . . . that I remember clearly . . . soldiers carrying out some sofa and pressing me against the wall . . . but painters—no, I don't remember any painters being there . . . and I don't think there was any open apartment anywhere. No, there wasn't . . ."

"But what's the matter with you!" Razumikhin exclaimed suddenly, as if coming to his senses and figuring things out. "The painters were working on the day of the crime itself, and he was there two days earlier! Why ask him?"

"Pah! I got it all mixed up!" Porfiry slapped himself on the forehead. "Devil take it, my mind stumbles all over itself with this case!" he said to Raskolnikov, as if in apology. "It's so important for us to find out if anyone saw them in the apartment between seven and eight, that I fancied just now you also might be able to tell us . . . I got it totally mixed up!"

"Well, so you ought to be more careful," Razumikhin observed morosely.

These last words were spoken in the entryway. Porfiry Petrovich saw them right to the door, with extreme affability. They both came out to the street gloomy and sullen, and did not say a word for a few steps. Raskolnikov drew a deep breath . . .

VI

. . . I don't believe it! I can't believe it!" the puzzled Razumikhin repeated, trying his best to refute Raskolnikov's arguments. They were already approaching Bakaleev's rooming house, where Pulcheria Alexandrovna and Dunya had long been expecting them. In the heat of the conversation, Razumikhin kept stopping every moment, embarrassed and excited by the mere fact that they were talking openly about *that* for the first time.

"Don't, then!" Raskolnikov replied, with a cold and careless smile. "You noticed nothing, as is usual with you, but I weighed every word."

"You're insecure, that's why . . . Hm . . . I must admit Porfiry's tone was rather strange, and that scoundrel Zamyotov especially! . . . You're right, there was something in him—but why? Why?"

"Changed his mind overnight."

"But it's the opposite, the opposite! If they did have such a brainless idea, they'd try their best to conceal it and keep their cards hidden, so as to catch you later . . . But now—it was so insolent and reckless!"

"If they had any facts—real facts, that is—or somewhat well-founded suspicions at least, then they would indeed try to conceal their game, in hopes of bigger winnings (but then they would have made a search long ago!). They have no facts, however, not a one—it's all a mirage, all double-ended, just a fleeting idea—so they're using insolence to try to throw me off. Maybe he's angry himself that there are no facts, and his irritation broke through. Or maybe he has something in mind . . . It seems he's an intelligent man . . . Maybe he wanted to frighten me with his knowing . . . There's psychology for you, brother . . . But enough! It's disgusting to explain it all!"

"And insulting, insulting! I understand you! But . . . since we've started talking openly now (and it's excellent that we're talking openly; I'm glad!)—I will now confess to you straight out that I've noticed it in them for some time, this idea, all along; in the tiniest sense, naturally; a creeping suspicion—but why even a creeping one! How dare they! Where, where are its roots hidden? If you knew how furious I was! What, just because a poor student, crippled by poverty and hypochondria, on the verge of a cruel illness and delirium, which may already have begun in him (note that!), insecure, vain, conscious of his worth, who for six months has sat in his corner seeing no one, in rags, in boots without soles, is standing there in front of some local cops, suffering their abuse; and here there's an unexpected debt shoved in his nose, an overdue promissory note from the court councillor Chebarov, rancid paint, thirty degrees Réaumur,[12] a stifling atmosphere, a crowd of people, a story about the murder of a person he'd visited the day before—and all this on an empty stomach! How could anyone not faint! And to base everything on that, on that! Devil take it! I know it's annoying, but in your place, Rodka, I'd burst out laughing in their faces; or, better—I'd spit in their mugs, and lay it on thick, and deal out a couple of dozen whacks all around—wisely, as it should always be done—and that would be the end of it. Spit on them! Cheer up! For shame!"

"He explained it well, however," Raskolnikov thought.

"Spit on them? And tomorrow another interrogation!" he said bitterly. "Should I really get into explanations with them? I'm already annoyed that I stooped to Zamyotov yesterday in the tavern . . ."

"Devil take it! I'll go to Porfiry myself! And I'll pin him down *as a relative;* let him lay it all out to the roots! As for Zamyotov . . ."

"He's finally figured it out!" thought Raskolnikov.

"Wait!" cried Razumikhin, suddenly seizing him by the shoulder. "Wait! You're all wrong! I've just thought it over: you're all wrong! Look, what sort of ruse was it? You say the question about the workmen was a ruse? Get what I'm saying: if you had done *that,* would you let on that you'd seen the apartment being painted . . . and the workmen? On the contrary: you didn't see anything, even if you did! Who's going to come out against himself?"

"If I had done *that thing,* I would certainly say I had seen both the apartment and the workmen," Raskolnikov went on answering reluctantly and with obvious loathing.

"But why speak against oneself?"

"Because only peasants or the most inexperienced novices deny everything outright and all down the line. A man with even a bit of development and experience will certainly try to admit as far as possible all the external and unavoidable facts; only he'll seek other reasons for them, he'll work in some feature of his own, a special and unexpected one, that will give them an entirely different meaning and present them in a different light. Porfiry could precisely count on my being certain to answer that way, on my being certain to say I'd seen them, for the sake of plausibility, and working in something to explain it . . ."

"But he'd tell you immediately that there were no workmen there two days before, and that you had therefore been there precisely on the day of the murder, between seven and eight. He'd throw you off with nothing!"

"But that's what he was counting on, that I wouldn't have time to figure it out and would precisely hasten to answer more plausibly, forgetting that the workmen couldn't have been there two days before."

"But how could one forget that?"

"What could be easier! It's with such nothings that clever people are thrown off most easily. The cleverer the man, the less he suspects that he can be thrown off with the simplest thing. It's precisely the simplest thing that will throw off the cleverest man. Porfiry isn't as stupid as you think . . ."

"In that case he's a scoundrel!"

Raskolnikov could not help laughing. But at the same moment it struck him as strange that he had become so animated and had so willingly uttered this last explanation, when he had kept up the whole previous conversation with sullen loathing, obviously for some purpose, out of necessity.

"I'm beginning to relish certain points!" he thought to himself.

But at almost the same moment he began suddenly to be somehow uneasy, as if struck by an unexpected and alarming thought. His unease kept growing. They had already reached the entrance to Bakaleev's rooming house.

"Go alone," Raskolnikov said suddenly, "I'll be back right away."

"Where are you going? We're already here!"

"I must, I must . . . something to do . . . I'll be back in half an hour . . . Tell them."

"As you wish; I'll follow you!"

"So you want to torment me, too!" he cried out, with such bitter irritation, with such despair in his eyes, that Razumikhin dropped his hands. He stood for a while on the steps and watched glumly as Raskolnikov strode off quickly in the direction of his own lane. Finally, gritting his teeth and clenching his fists, and swearing on the spot that he would squeeze Porfiry out like a lemon that very day, he went upstairs to reassure Pulcheria Alexandrovna, alarmed by then at their long absence.

By the time Raskolnikov reached his house, his temples were damp with sweat and he was breathing heavily. He hastily climbed the stairs, walked into his unlocked apartment, and immediately put the door on the hook. Then he rushed fearfully and madly to the corner, to the same hole in the wallpaper where the things had lain, thrust his hand into it, and for several minutes felt around in it carefully, going over every cranny and every crease in the wallpaper. Finding nothing, he stood up and drew a deep breath. Just as he was coming to Bakaleev's steps, he had suddenly imagined that something, some chain, a cuff-link, or even a scrap of the paper they had been wrapped in, with a mark on it in the old woman's hand, might somehow have slipped down and lost itself in a crack, afterwards to confront him suddenly as unexpected and irrefutable evidence.

He stood as if pensively, and a strange, humiliated, half-senseless smile wandered over his lips. Finally he took his cap and walked quietly out of the room. His thoughts were confused. Pensively, he went down to the gateway.

"Why, here's the man himself!" a loud voice exclaimed. He raised his head.

The caretaker was standing by the door of his closet, pointing him out to some short man, a tradesman by the look of it, who was wearing something like a smock over his waistcoat, and from a distance very much resembled a woman. His head hung down in its greasy cap, and he was as if all hunched over. His flabby, wrinkled face told more than fifty years; his small, swollen eyes had a sullen, stern, and displeased look.

"What is it?" Raskolnikov asked, coming up to the caretaker.

The tradesman gave him a sidelong look, examining him closely, attentively, unhurriedly; then he turned slowly and, without saying a word, walked out the gate to the street.

"But what is it!" Raskolnikov cried.

"Just somebody asking if a student lived here—he gave your name— and who you rent from. You came down right then, I pointed you out, and he left. How about that!"

The caretaker, too, was somewhat perplexed, but not very, and after thinking a moment longer, he turned and slouched back to his closet.

Raskolnikov rushed after the tradesman and caught sight of him at once, going along the other side of the street at the same steady and unhurried pace, his eyes fixed on the ground, as if pondering something. He soon overtook him, but walked behind him for a while; finally he drew abreast of him and stole a glance at his face from the side. The man noticed him at once, quickly looked him over, then dropped his eyes again, and thus they walked on for about a minute, side by side, neither one saying a word.

"You were asking for me . . . at the caretaker's?" Raskolnikov said at last, but somehow very softly.

The tradesman made no reply and did not even look. Again there was silence.

"But why do you . . . come asking . . . and say nothing . . . what does it mean?" Raskolnikov's voice was faltering, and the words somehow did not want to come out clearly.

This time the tradesman raised his eyes and gave Raskolnikov an ominous, gloomy look.

"Murderer!" he said suddenly, in a soft but clear and distinct voice.

Raskolnikov was walking beside him. His legs suddenly became terribly weak, a chill ran down his spine, and it was as if his heart stood still for a moment; then all at once it began pounding as if it had jumped off the hook. They walked on thus for about a hundred steps, side by side, and again in complete silence.

The tradesman did not look at him.

"What do you . . . what . . . who is a murderer?" Raskolnikov muttered, barely audibly.

"*You* are a murderer," the man replied even more distinctly and imposingly, smiling as if with some hateful triumph, and again he looked straight into Raskolnikov's pale face and deadened eyes. Just then they came to an intersection. The tradesman turned down the street to the left and walked on without looking back. Raskolnikov remained on the spot and gazed after him for a long time. He saw him turn around, after he had gone fifty steps or so, and look at him standing there motionlessly on the same spot. It was impossible to see, but Raskolnikov fancied that the man once again smiled his coldly hateful and triumphant smile.

With slow, weakened steps, with trembling knees and as if terribly cold, Raskolnikov returned and went upstairs to his closet. He took off his cap, put it on the table, and stood motionlessly beside it for about ten minutes. Then, powerless, he lay down on the sofa and painfully, with a weak moan, stretched out on it; his eyes were closed. He lay that way for about half an hour.

He was not thinking of anything. There were just some thoughts, or scraps of thoughts, images without order or connection—the faces of people he had seen as a child, or had met only once somewhere, and whom he would never even have remembered; the belfry of the V——y Church; the billiard table in some tavern, an officer by the billiard table, the smell of cigars in a basement tobacco shop, a pothouse, a back stairway, completely dark, all slopped with swill and strewn with eggshells, and from somewhere the sound of Sunday bells ringing . . . One thing followed another, spinning like a whirlwind. Some he even liked, and he clung to them, but they would die out, and generally something weighed on him inside, but not very much. At times he even felt good . . . The slight chill would not go away, but that, too, felt almost good.

He heard Razumikhin's hurrying steps and his voice, closed his eyes, and pretended to be asleep. Razumikhin opened the door and for a while stood as if hesitating in the doorway. Then he stepped quietly into the room and cautiously approached the sofa. Nastasya could be heard whispering:

"Don't rile him; let him get some sleep; he can eat later."

"Right you are," answered Razumikhin.

They both went out cautiously and closed the door. Another half hour or so passed. Raskolnikov opened his eyes and heaved himself over on his back again, his arms flung behind his head . . .

"Who is he? Who is this man who came from under the ground? Where was he and what did he see? He saw everything, there's no doubt of it. But where was he standing then, where was he watching from? Why did he come from under the floor only now? And how could he have seen—how is it possible? . . . Hm . . ." Raskolnikov went on, turning cold and shuddering, "and the case that Nikolai found behind the door—how was that possible? Evidence? One little thing in a hundred thousand overlooked—and here's evidence as big as an Egyptian pyramid! A fly flew by and saw it! Is it possible this way?"

And he suddenly felt with loathing how weak he had become, physically weak.

"I should have known," he thought, with a bitter smile, "and how, knowing myself, *anticipating* myself, did I dare take an axe and bloody my hands! I had to have known beforehand . . . Eh! but I did know beforehand! . . ." he whispered in despair.

At times he stopped still at some thought.

"No, those people are made differently; the true *master*, to whom all is permitted, sacks Toulon, makes a slaughterhouse of Paris, *forgets* an army in Egypt, *expends* half a million men in a Moscow campaign, and gets off with a pun in Vilno; and when he dies they set up monuments to him—and thus *everything* is permitted.[13] No, obviously such men are made not of flesh but of bronze!"

All at once a sudden, extraneous thought almost made him laugh: "Napoleon, pyramids, Waterloo—and a scrawny, vile registrar's widow, a little old crone, a moneylender with a red trunk under her bed—well, how is Porfiry Petrovich, for instance, going to digest that! . . . It's not for them to digest! . . . Aesthetics will prevent them: would Napoleon, say, be found crawling under some 'little old crone's' bed! Eh, but what rot! . . ."

There were moments when he felt he was almost raving; he would fall into a feverishly ecstatic mood.

"The little old crone is nonsense!" he thought, ardently and impetuously. "The old woman was a mistake perhaps, but she's not the point! The old woman was merely a sickness . . . I was in a hurry to step over . . . it wasn't a human being I killed, it was a principle! So I killed the principle, but I didn't step over, I stayed on this side . . . All I managed to do was kill. And I didn't even manage that, as it turns out . . . A principle? Why was that little fool Razumikhin abusing the socialists today? They're hardworking, commercial people, concerned with 'universal happiness' . . . No, life is given to me only once, and never will be again—I don't want to sit waiting for universal happiness. I want to live myself; otherwise it's better not to live at all. And so? I just didn't want to pass by my hungry mother, clutching my rouble in my pocket, while waiting for 'universal happiness.' To say, 'I'm carrying a little brick for universal happiness, and so there's a feeling of peace in my heart.'[14] Ha, ha! But why did you leave me out? I have only one life; I, too, want . . . Eh, an aesthetic louse is what I am, and nothing more," he added, suddenly bursting into laughter like a madman. "Yes, I really am a louse," he went on, gloatingly seizing upon the thought, rummaging in it, playing and amusing himself with it, "if only because, first, I'm now reasoning about being a louse; second, because I've been troubling all-good Providence for a whole month, calling it to witness that I was undertaking it not to satisfy my own flesh and lust, but with a splendid and agreeable goal in mind—ha, ha! Third, because I resolved to observe all possible justice in carrying it out, weight, measure, arithmetic: I chose the most useless louse of all and, having killed her, decided to take from her exactly as much as I needed for the first step, no more and no less (and the rest would thus simply go to the monastery, according to her will—ha, ha!) . . . And ultimately, ultimately I am a louse," he added, grinding his teeth, "because I myself am perhaps even more vile and nasty than the louse I killed, and I had *anticipated* beforehand that I would tell myself so *after* I killed her. Can anything compare with such horror! Oh, triteness! Oh, meanness! . . . Oh, how well I understand the 'prophet' with his sabre, on his steed. Allah commands—obey, 'trembling' creature![15] He's right, the 'prophet' is right when he sets up a first-rate battery across a street somewhere and blasts away at the innocent and the guilty, without even stooping to explain himself! Obey, trembling creature and—*forget your wishes,* because—that's none of your business! . . . Oh, nothing, nothing will make me forgive the old crone!"

His hair was damp with sweat, his trembling lips were parched, his fixed eyes were turned up to the ceiling.

"My mother, my sister, how I loved them! Why do I hate them now? Yes, I hate them, hate them physically, I cannot bear having them near me . . . I went over and kissed mother this morning, I remember . . . To embrace her and think that if she found out, she . . . should I tell her, then? That would be just like me . . . Hm! *She* must be the same as I am," he added, making an effort to think, as though struggling against the delirium that was taking hold of him. "Oh, how I hate that little old crone now! If she recovered, I think I'd kill her again! Poor Lizaveta! Why did she have to turn up there! . . . Strange, though; why is it that I almost never think of her, as if I hadn't killed her? . . . Lizaveta! Sonya! Poor, meek ones, with meek eyes . . . Dear ones! . . . Why don't they weep? Why don't they moan? . . . They give everything . . . their eyes are meek and gentle . . . Sonya, Sonya! Gentle Sonya! . . ."

He became oblivious; it seemed strange to him that he did not remember how he could have ended up in the street. It was already late evening. The twilight was thickening, the full moon shone brighter and brighter, but the air was somehow especially stifling. People moved in crowds along the street; artisans and office workers were going home, others were out for a stroll; there was a smell of lime, dust, stagnant water. Raskolnikov walked along sad and preoccupied; he remembered very well that he had left the house with some purpose, that he had to do something, and quickly, but precisely what—he had forgotten. Suddenly he stopped and noticed that a man standing on the sidewalk across the street was waving to him with his hand. He started across the street towards him, but the man suddenly turned and went on as though nothing had happened, with his head down, not looking back or showing any sign that he had called him. "But did he call me, really?" Raskolnikov thought, and nevertheless started after him. When he was about ten steps away, he suddenly recognized the man— and was frightened: it was today's tradesman, in the same smock, hunched over as before. Raskolnikov stayed some distance behind him; his heart was pounding; they turned down a side street—he still re- fused to look back. "Does he know I'm following him?" thought Raskolnikov. The tradesman walked through the gates of a big house. Raskolnikov hastened up to the gates and looked in to see if he would turn and call him. Indeed, having passed under the gateway and on into the courtyard, he suddenly turned around and again seemed to wave to him. Raskolnikov immediately went through the gateway, but the tradesman was no longer in the courtyard. That meant he had gone straight up the first stairway. Raskolnikov rushed after him. He could indeed hear someone's steady, unhurried steps two flights above. Strangely, the stairway seemed familiar! Here was the first-floor win- dow; moonlight shone sadly and mysteriously through the glass; here was the second floor. Hah! It was the same apartment where the painters had been working . . . How had he not recognized it at once? The steps of the man ahead of him faded away: "that means he has stopped or is hiding somewhere." Here was the third floor; should he go any farther? How silent it was, even frightening . . . But he went on. The sound of his own steps scared and alarmed him. God, how dark! The tradesman was probably lurking somewhere here in a cor- ner. Ah! The apartment door was standing wide open; he thought a moment and went in. The entryway was very dark and empty, not a soul, as though everything had been taken out; quietly, on tiptoe, he moved on into the living room: the whole room was brightly flooded with moonlight; everything here was as it had been: the chairs, the mirror, the yellow sofa, the pictures in their frames. A huge, round, copper-red moon was looking straight in the window. "It's because of the moon that it's so silent," thought Raskolnikov, "asking some riddle, no doubt." He stood and waited, waited a long time, and the more silent the moon was, the harder his heart pounded—it was even becoming painful. And still the same silence. Suddenly there came a brief, dry crack like the snapping of a twig; then everything was still again. An awakened fly suddenly swooped and struck against the window, buzzing plaintively. At the same moment he made out what seemed to be a woman's wrap hanging in the corner between a small cupboard and the window. "Why is that wrap here?" he thought, "it wasn't here before . . ." He approached quietly and realized that someone seemed to be hiding there behind the wrap. He cautiously moved the wrap aside with his hand and saw a chair standing there, and on the chair, in the corner, sat the little old crone, all hunched up, with her head bent down so that there was no way he could see her face—but it was she. He stood over her. "Afraid!" he thought, and he quietly freed the axe from its loop and struck the old woman on the crown of the head, once and then again. But, strangely, she did not even stir under his blows, as though she were made of wood. He became frightened, bent closer, and began looking at her, but she also bent her head still lower. Then he bent down all the way to the floor and peeked into her face from below, peeked and went dead: the little old crone was sitting there laughing—simply dissolving in soft, inaudible laughter, trying her best not to let him hear her. He suddenly fancied that the door to the bedroom had opened a little, and there also seemed to be laughter and whispering there. Rage overcame him: he began hitting the old woman on the head with all his strength, but at every blow of the axe the laughing and whispering from the bedroom grew stronger and louder, and the little crone heaved all over with laughter. He wanted to run away, but now the whole entryway is full of people, all the doors to the stairs are wide open, and on the landings, on the stairway, farther down there are people, head to head, all looking—but all hushed and waiting, silent . . . His heart shrank, his feet became rooted and refused to move . . . He tried to cry out—and woke up.

He drew a deep breath—yet, strangely, it was as if the dream were still going on: his door was wide open, and a man completely unknown to him was standing on the threshold, studying him intently.

Raskolnikov had not yet managed to open his eyes fully, and he instantly closed them again. He lay on his back without stirring. "Is the dream still going on, or not?" he thought, and again imperceptibly parted his eyelashes a little: the stranger was standing in the same place and was still peering at him. All at once he cautiously stepped across the threshold, closed the door carefully behind him, went over to the table, waited for about a minute—not taking his eyes off him all the while—and softly, noiselessly, sat down on the chair by the sofa; he placed his hat beside him on the floor, leaned with both hands on his cane, and rested his chin on his hands. One could see that he was prepared to wait a long time. As far as could be made out through blinking eyelashes, this was a man no longer young, thickset, and with a bushy, fair, almost white beard . . .

About ten minutes went by. It was still light, but evening was approaching. There was total silence in the room. No sound came even from the stairs. Only a big fly buzzed and struggled, striking with a swoop against the window. Finally it became unbearable: Raskolnikov raised himself all at once and sat up on the sofa.

"Speak, then. What do you want?"

"Ah, I just knew you were not asleep, but only pretending," the unknown man answered strangely, with a quiet laugh. "Allow me to introduce myself: Arkady Ivanovich Svidrigailov . . ."

Part Four

"Can this be a continuation of my dream?" came once again to Raskolnikov's mind. Cautiously and mistrustfully he stared at his unexpected visitor.

"Svidrigailov? What nonsense! It can't be!" he finally said aloud, in perplexity.

The visitor seemed not in the least surprised at this exclamation.

"I have come here owing to two reasons: first, I wished to meet you personally, because I have long since heard much about you from a point that is curious and advantageous for you; and, second, I dream that you will perhaps not decline to help me in a certain undertaking directly concerned with the interests of your dear sister, Avdotya Romanovna. Owing to biased opinion, she will perhaps not allow me into the yard if I come on my own, without a recommendation; well, but with your help, on the other hand, I reckon . . ."

"Poor reckoning," Raskolnikov interrupted.

"They arrived only yesterday, if I may ask?"

Raskolnikov did not reply.

"It was yesterday, I know. I myself arrived only two days ago. Well, here is what I shall tell you in that regard, Rodion Romanovich; I consider it unnecessary to justify myself, but even so, allow me to say: what is there in all this, in the thing itself, that is so especially criminal on my part—I mean, judging soberly, and without prejudice?"

Raskolnikov went on studying him silently.

"That I pursued a defenseless girl in my own house and 'insulted her with my vile proposals'—is that it, sir? (I'm running ahead of myself!) But you need only suppose that I, too, am a man, *et nihil humanum*[1] . . . in short, that I, too, am capable of being tempted and of falling in love (which, of course, does not happen on command), and then everything is explained in the most natural way. The whole question here is: am I a monster, or a victim myself? Well, and what if I am a victim? For in offering to elope with my object to America or Switzerland, I may have been nurturing the most respectful feelings, and hoping, besides, to arrange for our mutual happiness! . . . For reason is the slave of passion; good heavens, perhaps I was ruining myself even more! . . ."

"But that is not the point at all," Raskolnikov interrupted with loathing. "You are quite simply disgusting, whether you are right or not, and so people don't want to have anything to do with you, they chase you away—so, go! . . ."

Svidrigailov suddenly burst out laughing.

"You, however . . . you simply will not be thrown off!" he said, laughing in the most genuine manner. "I tried to dodge round you, but no, you went straight to the most real point!"

"But you're continuing to dodge even now."

"What of it? What of it?" Svidrigailov repeated, laughing openheartedly. "It's *bonne guerre,* [2] as they call it, and the most admissible dodging! . . . Anyway, you interrupted me; one way or the other, I affirm again: there would have been no trouble, if it hadn't been for that incident in the garden. Marfa Petrovna . . ."

"And they say you also took care of Marfa Petrovna?" Raskolnikov interrupted rudely.

"So you've heard about that, too? But then, how could you not . . . Well, concerning the question you've raised, I really don't know what to say, though my own conscience is entirely at rest in that regard. I mean, do not think that I feared anything of the sort: it was all performed in perfect order and with complete precision; the medical experts diagnosed apoplexy, the result of bathing after a heavy meal and almost a full bottle of wine, and they could not have discovered anything else . . . No, sir, I was thinking about that myself for some time, especially on my way here, sitting in the train: didn't I contribute to this whole . . . misfortune, somehow morally, through irritation or something like that? But I concluded that this, too, was positively impossible."

Raskolnikov laughed.

"Not that you should worry!"

"And what is there to laugh at? Just think: I struck her only twice with a riding crop; there weren't even any marks . . . Please do not regard me as a cynic; I do know exactly how vile it was on my part, and so on; but I also know perfectly well that Marfa Petrovna may even have been glad of my, shall we say, enthusiasm. The story concerning your dear sister had been wrung out to the last drop. It was already the third day that Marfa Petrovna had been obliged to stay at home; she had nothing to take her to town, and besides they were all sick of her there, what with that letter of hers (you did hear about the reading of the letter?). And suddenly those two strokes fell as if from heaven! She ordered the carriage to be readied first thing! . . . I won't even mention the fact that there are occasions when women find it extremely agreeable to be insulted, for all their apparent indignation. Everyone has known them, these occasions; man in general finds it extremely pleasant to be insulted—have you noticed? But it's especially so with women. One might even say it's their only provender."

At one point Raskolnikov had wanted to get up and leave, thereby putting an end to the meeting. But a certain curiosity and even calculation, as it were, kept him for the moment.

"Do you enjoy fighting?" he asked distractedly.

"No, not really," Svidrigailov answered calmly. "And Marfa Petrovna and I hardly ever fought. Our life was quite harmonious, and she always remained pleased with me. In all those seven years I used the whip only twice (unless one counts a third rather ambiguous occasion): the first time was two months after our marriage, just after we came to the estate; and then in this last instance. And you were thinking I was such a monster, a retrograde, a serf-owner? Heh, heh . . . By the way, you must remember, Rodion Romanovich, how a few years ago, still in the days of beneficent freedom of expression, one of our noblemen was disgraced nationwide and presswide—I've forgotten his name!—he gave a whipping to a German woman on a train, remember? It was then, too, in that same year, I think, that the 'Outrageous Act of *The Age*' occurred (I mean the *Egyptian Nights*, the public reading, remember? Those dark eyes! Oh, where have you gone, golden days of our youth!).[3] So, sir, here is my opinion: I feel no deep sympathy for the gentleman who gave a whipping to the German woman, because it's really . . . well, what is there to sympathize with? But all the same I cannot help declaring that one sometimes runs across such provoking 'German women' that I don't think there's a single progressivist who could vouch for himself entirely. At the time no one looked at the subject from that point, and yet that point is the truly humane one, it really is, sir!"

Having said this, Svidrigailov suddenly laughed again. It was clear to Raskolnikov that this was a man who was firmly set on something, and who kept his own counsel.

"You must not have talked with anyone for several days?" he asked.

"Almost right. And so? You're no doubt surprised that I'm such a congenial man?"

"No, I'm surprised that you're a much too congenial man."

"Because I was not offended by the rudeness of your questions? Is that it? But . . . why be offended? As I was asked, so I answered," he added, with a surprisingly simple-hearted expression. "You see, there's not much that interests me especially, by God!" he went on, somehow pensively. "Especially now, nothing really occupies me . . . However, you may be permitted to think that I am ingratiating myself with you for some purpose, all the more so in that I have business with your dear sister, as I myself have declared. But I'll tell you frankly: I'm very bored! These last three days especially, so that I was even glad to see you . . . Don't be angry, Rodion Romanovich, but you yourself seem terribly strange to me for some reason. Like it or not, there's something in you; and precisely now—that is, not this very minute, but now generally . . . Well, well, I'll stop, I'll stop, don't scowl! I'm really not such a bear as you think."

Raskolnikov looked at him glumly.

"Perhaps you're not a bear at all," he said. "It even seems to me that you're of very good society, or can at least be a decent man on occasion."

"In fact, I'm not particularly interested in anyone's opinion," Svidrigailov answered dryly and even as if with a shade of haughtiness, "and therefore why not be a vulgar fellow for a while—the attire is so well suited to our climate, and . . . and especially if that is also one's natural inclination," he added, laughing again.

"I've heard, however, that you have many acquaintances here. You're what's known as 'not without connections.' In that case what do you need me for, if not for some purpose?"

"It's true, as you say, that I have acquaintances," Svidrigailov picked up, without responding to the main point. "I've met some already; this

is the third day I've been hanging about; I recognize people, and seem
to be recognized as well. I'm decently dressed, of course, and am not
reckoned a poor man; even the peasant reform didn't touch us: it's all
forests and water-meadows, so there was no loss of income,[4] but
. . . I won't go to them; I was sick of it even before: I've been walking
around for three days without telling anyone . . . And then there's this
city! I mean, tell me, how did we ever come up with it! A city of
functionaries and all sorts of seminarians! Really, there's much that I
never noticed before, when I was lolling about here some eight years
ago . . . I now place all my hopes in anatomy, by God!"

"Anatomy?"

"And as for these clubs, these Dussots, these *pointes* of yours,[5] this
progress, if you like—well, it can all do without us," he went on, again
ignoring the question. "Besides, who wants to be a sharper?"

"So you were a sharper, too?"

"What else? There was a whole group of us, a most respectable one,
about eight years ago; we whiled the time away; all well-mannered
people, you know, poets, capitalists. Generally, in our Russian society,
the best-mannered people are those who have been beaten—did you
ever notice that? It was on the estate that I started going to seed.
Anyway, they put me in prison then, for debt—a little Greek, from
Nezhin. And then Marfa Petrovna turned up, bargained a bit, and
bought me off for thirty thousand pieces of silver. (I owed seventy
thousand all told.) I entered into lawful marriage with her, and she
immediately took me home to her estate, like some treasure. She was
five years older than I, you see. She loved me very much. For seven
years I never left the estate. And, mark this, all her life she kept a
document against me, in somebody else's name, for the thirty thousand, so that if I ever decided to rebel at anything—there'd be a trap
right there! And she'd have done it! Women can keep all these things
together."

"And if it weren't for the document, you'd have skipped out?"

"I don't know what to say. The document was almost no hindrance
to me. I didn't want to go anywhere, though Marfa Petrovna herself
even suggested twice that I go abroad, seeing that I was bored. But
what for? I used to go abroad, and I always felt sick at heart. Nothing
special, really—here's the dawn coming up, here's the Bay of Naples,

the sea—you look, and it's somehow sad. The most disgusting thing is that you're always sad about something! No, the fatherland's better; here at least you can blame it all on everyone else and justify yourself. I might go on an expedition to the North Pole now, because *j'ai le vin mauvais*,[6] drinking disgusts me, and wine is the only thing I have left. I've tried. Listen, they say Berg is going to fly in a huge balloon from the Yusupov Garden on Sunday, and is inviting people to go with him for a certain fee—is it true?"[7]

"Why, would you go and fly?"

"Me? No . . . I just . . ." Svidrigailov muttered, as if he were indeed reflecting.

"What is he . . . really . . . or something?" Raskolnikov thought.

"No, the document was no hindrance to me," Svidrigailov went on reflectively. "I myself wouldn't leave the estate. And a year ago, on my name-day, Marfa Petrovna handed the document over to me, and gave me a significant sum on top of it. She had a fortune, you know. 'See how I trust you, Arkady Ivanovich'—really, that's what she said. You don't believe she said it? And you know, I got to be quite a manager on the estate; the whole neighborhood knows me. I ordered books. Marfa Petrovna approved at first, but then kept being afraid I'd overstudy."

"You seem to miss Marfa Petrovna very much?"

"Me? Perhaps. Perhaps, indeed. By the way, do you believe in ghosts?"

"What ghosts?"

"Ordinary ghosts. What do you mean, what ghosts?"

"Do you?"

"Well, perhaps not, *pour vous plaire*[8] . . . that is, not really not . . ."

"What, do they come to you?"

Svidrigailov gave him a somehow strange look.

"Marfa Petrovna has been so kind as to visit me," he said, twisting his mouth into a strange sort of smile.

"How do you mean, so kind as to visit you?"

"She's already come three times. I saw her first on the very day of the funeral, an hour after the cemetery. It was the day before I left to come here. The second time was two days ago, on the way, at dawn, in the Malaya Vishera station; and the third time was two hours ago, in the apartment where I'm staying, in my room; I was alone."

"And awake?"

"Wide awake. I was awake all three times. She comes, talks for a moment, and leaves by the door, always by the door. One even seems to hear it."

"Why did I think that something like that must be going on with you?" Raskolnikov said suddenly, and was at once surprised that he had said it. He was greatly excited.

"So-o-o? You thought that?" Svidrigailov asked in surprise. "Can it be? Now, didn't I tell you there was a common point between us, eh?"

"You never said that!" Raskolnikov replied sharply and with passion.

"Didn't I?"

"No!"

"I thought I did. Earlier, when I came in and saw that you were lying there with your eyes closed, pretending, I said to myself at once: 'This is the very man!' "

"What do you mean, the very man? What is this about?" Raskolnikov cried out.

"What is it about? I really don't know what . . ." Svidrigailov muttered frankly, becoming somehow confused.

For a moment they were silent. They were staring wide-eyed at each other.

"That's all nonsense!" Raskolnikov cried in vexation. "What does she say when she comes?"

"She? Imagine, she talks about the most worthless trifles, and—man is amazing!—that's just what makes me angry. The first time she came (I was tired, you know: the funeral service, 'Give rest with thy saints,' then the blessings, the food⁹—finally I was left alone in the study, lit myself a cigar, and began thinking), she came in the door: 'What with all this fuss, Arkady Ivanovich,' she said, 'you've forgotten to wind the clock in the dining room.' And indeed I had been winding that clock every week for seven years, and whenever I forgot, she would always remind me. The next day I was on my way here. I walked into the stationhouse at dawn—I'd been dozing during the night, all broken up, eyes still sleepy—had some coffee; I looked up—Marfa Petrovna suddenly sat down next to me, holding a deck of cards: 'Shall I tell your fortune, Arkady Ivanovich, for the road?' She used to be good at reading cards. Well, I'll never forgive myself for not asking her! I got scared and ran away; true, they were also ringing the bell. Then, today, I was sitting with a heavy stomach after a perfectly rotten meal in a cook-shop—sitting and smoking, when Marfa Petrovna suddenly came in again, all dressed up in a new green silk gown with a very long train: 'Good afternoon, Arkady Ivanovich! How do you like my gown? Aniska will never sew like this.' (Aniska is our village dressmaker, from a former serf family, went to Moscow for lessons—a pretty wench.) She was standing in front of me and turning around. I looked the gown over, then looked attentively in her face: 'Marfa Petrovna,' I said, 'why on earth do you trouble yourself coming to me with such trifles?' 'Good heavens, my dear, can't I bother you a little?' 'I'm going to get married, Marfa Petrovna,' I said, in order to tease her. 'That's just like you, Arkady Ivanovich; it does you little credit, after you've just buried your wife, to go and get married at once. And if only you'd choose well, but I know you—it won't be right for her or for you, you'll only make good people laugh.' Then she up and left, and I thought I could hear the rustling of her train. What nonsense, eh?"

"Or maybe it's all lies?" Raskolnikov responded.

"I rarely lie," Svidrigailov answered thoughtfully, as if he had not even noticed the rudeness of the question.

"And did you ever see ghosts before this?"

"Y-yes, I did, once before in my life, about six years ago. I had a household serf named Filka; we had just buried him, and I forgot and called out: 'Filka, my pipe!' He came in and went straight to the cabinet where I kept my pipes. I sat there thinking: 'It's his revenge on me,' because we had quarreled badly just before his death. 'How dare you come to me with a torn elbow,' I said. 'Get out, scoundrel!' He turned around, walked out, and never came back. I didn't tell Marfa Petrovna. I wanted to order a memorial service for him, but I was ashamed."

"You should see a doctor."

"I don't need you to tell me I'm not well, though I don't really know what's wrong with me; I think I'm five times healthier than you are.

I didn't ask whether you believe that people see ghosts. I asked if you believe that there are ghosts."

"No, I wouldn't believe it for anything!" Raskolnikov cried out, even somewhat spitefully.

"What is it they usually say?" Svidrigailov muttered as if to himself, turning aside and inclining his head slightly. "They say, 'You're sick, and therefore what you imagine is all just nonexistent raving.' But there's no strict logic here. I agree that ghosts come only to sick people; but that only proves that ghosts cannot appear to anyone but sick people, not that they themselves do not exist."

"Of course they don't!" Raskolnikov insisted irritably.

"No? You think not?" Svidrigailov went on, slowly raising his eyes to him. "And what if one reasons like this (come, help me now): 'Ghosts are, so to speak, bits and pieces of other worlds, their beginnings. The healthy man, naturally, has no call to see them, because the healthy man is the most earthly of men, and therefore he ought to live according to life here, for the sake of completeness and order. Well, but as soon as a man gets sick, as soon as the normal earthly order of his organism is disrupted, the possibility of another world at once begins to make itself known, and the sicker one is, the greater the contact with this other world, so that when a man dies altogether, he goes to the other world directly.' I've been reasoning it out for a long time. If one believes in a future life, one can believe in this reasoning."

"I do not believe in a future life," said Raskolnikov.

Svidrigailov sat thinking.

"And what if there are only spiders there, or something of the sort," he said suddenly.

"He's a madman," thought Raskolnikov.

"We keep imagining eternity as an idea that cannot be grasped, something vast, vast! But why must it be vast? Instead of all that, imagine suddenly that there will be one little room there, something like a village bathhouse, covered with soot, with spiders in all the corners, and that's the whole of eternity. I sometimes fancy something of the sort."

"But surely, surely you can imagine something more just and comforting than that!" Raskolnikov cried out with painful feeling.

"More just? Who knows, perhaps that is just—and, you know, if I had my way, it's certainly how I would do it!" Svidrigailov answered, smiling vaguely.

A sort of chill came over Raskolnikov at this hideous answer. Svidrigailov raised his head, looked at him intently, and suddenly burst out laughing.

"No, but realize," he cried, "that half an hour ago we had never even seen each other, we're supposed to be enemies, there's unfinished business between us; so we've dropped the business, and look what literature we've gone sailing into! Well, wasn't it true when I said we were apples from the same tree?"

"Do me a favor," Raskolnikov continued irritably, "allow me to ask you for a quick explanation of why you deem me worthy to be honored by your visit . . . and . . . and . . . I'm in a hurry, I have no time, I must go out . . ."

"By all means, by all means. Your dear sister, Avdotya Romanovna, is going to marry Mr. Luzhin, Pyotr Petrovich?"

"Could you not somehow avoid asking any questions about my sister or mentioning her name? I don't understand how you even dare to utter her name in my presence, if you are indeed Svidrigailov."

"But it's her that I came to speak about; how can I not mention her?"

"Very well; speak, but be quick!"

"I'm sure you've already formed an opinion of this Mr. Luzhin, to whom I am related through my wife, if you've spent as much as half an hour with him, or merely heard something true and accurate about him. He is no match for Avdotya Romanovna. In my opinion, Avdotya Romanovna is quite magnanimously and improvidently sacrificing herself in this affair for . . . for her family. It seemed to me, from all I had heard about you, that you, for your part, would be very pleased if this marriage could be broken off without harming anyone's interests. Now that I've met you in person, I'm even certain of it."

"This is all very naive on your part—excuse me, I was going to say insolent," Raskolnikov said.

"What you mean, I take it, is that I'm trying to grease my own skids. Don't worry, Rodion Romanovich, if I were going to bother about my own advantage, I would not speak so directly—I'm not a complete fool yet. In this regard, I shall reveal to you a psychological anomaly. Earlier, in justifying my love for Avdotya Romanovna, I said I was a victim myself. Well, let it be known to you that I no longer feel any love, none at all, which even seems strange to me now, because I did indeed feel something . . ."

"From idleness and depravity," Raskolnikov interrupted.

"I am indeed a depraved and idle person. Nevertheless, your dear sister possesses so many advantages that I could not help succumbing somewhat to the impression. But that is all nonsense, as I now see myself."

"How long ago did you see it?"

"I began to notice it even earlier, and finally became convinced two days ago, almost at the very moment of my arrival in Petersburg. In Moscow, however, I still imagined I was coming to seek Avdotya Romanovna's hand and to be Mr. Luzhin's rival."

"Excuse me for interrupting you, but kindly make it short, and go straight to the purpose of your visit. I'm in a hurry, I must go out . . ."

"With the greatest pleasure. Having arrived here, and having now decided to undertake a certain . . . voyage, I wished to make the necessary preliminary arrangements. My children have stayed behind with their aunt; they're rich, and do not need me personally. After all, what sort of father am I! For myself I took only what Marfa Petrovna gave me a year ago. It's enough for me. Sorry, I'm now coming to the business itself. Before this voyage, which may in fact take place, I also want to finish with Mr. Luzhin. Not that I find him so unbearable, but all the same it was through him that my quarrel with Marfa Petrovna came about, when I discovered she had cooked up this wedding. I now wish to see Avdotya Romanovna, with your mediation, and explain to her, perhaps even in your presence, first, that she will get not the slightest profit from Mr. Luzhin, but instead, and quite certainly, there will be a clear loss. Then, having asked her forgiveness for all those recent troubles, I would like to ask permission to offer her ten thousand roubles and thus facilitate her break with Mr. Luzhin, a break which I am sure she would not be averse to, if only the possibility should arise."

"But you are really and truly crazy!" Raskolnikov exclaimed, not even so much angry as surprised. "How dare you say that!"

"I knew you were going to make an outcry; but, first, though I'm not rich, I do have these ten thousand roubles at my disposal—that is, I absolutely, absolutely do not need them. If Avdotya Romanovna does not accept them, I may put them to some even more foolish use. That's one thing. Second, my conscience is entirely at rest; there is no calculation in my offer. You may not believe it, but later both you and Avdotya Romanovna will find it to be so. The whole thing is that I did indeed cause your dear, much esteemed sister some trouble and unpleasantness; therefore, feeling sincerely repentant, it is my heartfelt wish—not to buy myself off, not to pay for the unpleasantness, but purely and simply to do something profitable for her, on the grounds that I have not, after all, taken the privilege of doing only evil. If there were even a millionth part of calculation in my offer, I would not have made it so directly; and I would not be offering her only ten thousand, when I offered her much more just five weeks ago. Besides, it's possible that in a very, very short time I shall marry a certain girl, and consequently all suspicion of any attempts against Avdotya Romanovna should thereby be wiped out. In conclusion, I will say that in marrying Mr. Luzhin, Avdotya Romanovna will only be taking the same money from another hand . . . Don't be angry, Rodion Romanovich; consider it calmly and coolly."

Svidrigailov himself was extremely cool and calm as he said this.

"I beg you to finish," said Raskolnikov. "In any case, it's unforgivably impudent."

"Not in the least. Or else man can only do evil to men in this world, and, on the contrary, has no right to do even a drop of good, because of empty, conventional formalities. That is absurd. If I died, for example, and left this sum to your dear sister in my will, is it possible that even then she would refuse it?"

"Quite possible."

"Now, that can't be, sir. However, if so, so—let it be as you say. Only ten thousand is a wonderful thing on occasion. In any case, I ask that you tell Avdotya Romanovna what I've said."

"No, I won't."

"In that case, Rodion Romanovich, I shall be forced to try to obtain a personal meeting myself, and therefore to trouble her."

"And if I do tell her, you won't try to obtain a personal meeting?"

"I really don't know what to say. I would very much like to see her, just once."

"Hopeless."

"Too bad. However, you don't know me. Perhaps we'll become closer."

"You think we'll become closer?"

"And why not?" Svidrigailov said, smiling, and he stood up and took his hat. "It's not that I wished so much to trouble you, and I didn't even count on much in coming here, though, by the way, already this morning I was struck by your physiognomy . . ."

"Where did you see me this morning?" Raskolnikov asked uneasily.

"By chance, sir . . . I keep fancying there's something in you that suits my . . . But don't worry, I'm not a bore; I got along with sharpers, and I never bored Prince Svirbey, a distant relation of mine and a grand gentleman, and I was able to write about Raphael's Madonna in Madame Prilukov's album, and lived uninterruptedly for seven years with Marfa Petrovna, and spent a night or two in Vyazemsky's house on the Haymarket in days of old,[10] and will perhaps fly with Berg in his balloon."

"Well, very well, sir. May I ask if you will be going on your trip soon?"

"What trip?"

"That 'voyage' . . . You were just talking about it."

"Voyage? Ah, yes! . . . I did tell you about a voyage . . . Well, that is a vast question . . . You have no idea what you're asking, however!" he added, and suddenly burst into loud but short laughter. "Perhaps, instead of the voyage, I'll get married. They're matchmaking me with a fiancée."

"Here?"

"Yes."

"How have you had time?"

"But I rather wished to see Avdotya Romanovna once. A serious request. Well, good-bye . . . Ah, yes! See what I forgot! Tell your dear sister, Rodion Romanovich, that she is mentioned in Marfa Petrovna's will for three thousand roubles. That is positively so. Marfa Petrovna made the arrangements a week before her death, and it was done in my presence. In two or three weeks Avdotya Romanovna will be able to have the money."

"You're telling the truth?"

"The truth. Tell her. Well, sir, I am at your service. I'm staying quite nearby, you see."

As he was leaving, Svidrigailov ran into Razumikhin in the doorway.

I I

I T WAS NEARLY eight o'clock by then; they hurried off to Bakaleev's, in order to arrive before Luzhin.

"Well, who was that?" Razumikhin asked, as soon as they were in the street.

"That was Svidrigailov, the landowner in whose house my sister was offended when she was serving there as a governess. She left them on account of his amorous pursuits, having been turned out by his wife, Marfa Petrovna. Afterwards, this Marfa Petrovna begged Dunya's forgiveness, and now she has suddenly died. We were talking about her this morning. I don't know why, but I'm very afraid of the man. He came here right after his wife's funeral. He's very strange, and is set on something . . . He seems to know something . . . Dunya must be protected from him . . . that's what I wanted to tell you, do you hear?"

"Protected? But what can he do against Avdotya Romanovna? Well, thank you for telling me like this, Rodya . . . We'll protect her, that we will! . . . Where does he live?"

"I don't know."

"Why didn't you ask? Eh, too bad! But I'll find out!"

"Did you see him?" Raskolnikov asked, after some silence.

"Oh, yes, I noted him; I noted him well."

"You're sure you saw him? Saw him clearly?" Raskolnikov insisted.

"Oh, yes, I remember him clearly; I'd know him in a thousand; I have a good memory for faces."

Again there was a silence.

"Hm . . . well then . . ." Raskolnikov muttered. "Because, you know

. . . I was thinking . . . I keep imagining . . . it might have been a fantasy."

"What's this all about? I don't quite understand you."

"You've all been saying that I was mad," Raskolnikov went on, twisting his mouth into a smile, "and just now I imagined that perhaps I really am mad and was only seeing a ghost!"

"But what is this about?"

"And who knows! Maybe I really am mad, and everything that's happened during these days, maybe everything is just my imagination . . ."

"Eh, Rodya, you've been upset again! . . . But what did he say? Why did he come?"

Raskolnikov did not answer. Razumikhin reflected for a moment.

"Well, listen to my report," he began. "I stopped by your place; you were asleep. Then we had dinner, and then I went to Porfiry's. Zamyotov was still there. I tried to begin, but nothing came of it. I just couldn't begin talking in a real way. It's as if they don't understand, and cannot understand, and are not at all embarrassed. I took Porfiry over to the window and began talking, but again for some reason it didn't come out right; he looked away, and I looked away. Finally I brought my fist up to his mug and said I was going to smash him, in a familial way. He just stared at me. I spat and left, that's all. Very stupid. Not a word between me and Zamyotov. Only, you see, I thought I'd fouled things up, but as I was going down the stairs it occurred to me, it just dawned on me: what are we fussing about, the two of us? If there was anything to it, or any danger for you, then of course. But what is it to you? You've got nothing to do with it, so spit on them; we'll have the laugh on them afterwards, and in your place I'd even start mystifying them. Because they'll really be ashamed afterwards! Spit on it; you can give them a beating afterwards, but for now let's laugh!"

"You're right, of course!" Raskolnikov replied. "But what will you say tomorrow?" he thought to himself. Strangely, until then it had never once occurred to him: "What will Razumikhin think when he finds out?" Having thought of it, Raskolnikov looked at him intently. As for Razumikhin's present report of his visit to Porfiry, he was not very interested in it: so much had been lost and gained since then! . . .

In the corridor they ran into Luzhin: he had arrived at eight o'clock sharp and was searching for the room, so that all three entered together, but without greeting or looking at one another. The young men went in first, while Pyotr Petrovich, for propriety's sake, lingered a little in the entryway, taking off his coat. Pulcheria Alexandrovna went at once to meet him at the threshold. Dunya was greeting her brother.

Pyotr Petrovich walked in and quite affably, though with redoubled solemnity, bowed to the ladies. However, he looked as though he had been slightly thrown off and had not yet found himself. Pulcheria Alexandrovna, who also seemed embarrassed, hastened at once to seat everyone at the round table, on which a samovar was boiling. Dunya and Luzhin were placed opposite each other on two sides of the table. Razumikhin and Raskolnikov found themselves facing Pulcheria Alexandrovna—Razumikhin closer to Luzhin, Raskolnikov next to his sister.

A momentary silence ensued. Pyotr Petrovich unhurriedly pulled out a cambric handkerchief that gave off a whiff of scent, and blew his nose with the air of a man of virtue whose dignity has been somewhat offended and who, moreover, has firmly resolved to demand an explanation. While still in the entryway the thought had occurred to him of leaving without taking off his coat, thereby punishing the two ladies severely and impressively, so as to let them feel the whole weight of it. But he had not dared. Besides, the man did not like uncertainty, and here an explanation was called for: if his orders had been so openly defied, there must be something behind it, and therefore it was better to find it out now; as for punishment, there would always be time for that, and he had the upper hand.

"I trust the trip went well?" he addressed Pulcheria Alexandrovna in an official tone.

"Thank God, it did, Pyotr Petrovich."

"Pleased to hear it, madam. And Avdotya Romanovna did not find it too tiring either?"

"I'm young and strong, I don't get tired, but it was very hard on mother."

"There's no help for it; our nation's railways are quite long. Our so-called 'Mother Russia' is a vast country . . . And I, for all that I desired to do so, was simply unable to meet you. I trust, however, that everything went without any special trouble."

"Ah, no, Pyotr Petrovich, we were very disheartened," Pulcheria Alexandrovna hastened to declare, with a special intonation, "and would simply have perished if Dmitri Prokofych had not been sent to us, as I think, by God Himself. This is he, Dmitri Prokofych Razumikhin," she added, introducing him to Luzhin.

"Indeed, I had the pleasure . . . yesterday," Luzhin muttered, with an unfriendly sidelong glance at Razumikhin; then he frowned and fell silent. Generally speaking, Pyotr Petrovich belonged to that category of people who appear extremely affable in company, and with a special claim to affability, but who, as soon as something grates on them, instantly lose all their resources and begin to seem more like sacks of flour than offhand and convivial cavaliers. Everyone again fell silent; Raskolnikov was stubbornly silent, Avdotya Romanovna did not want to break the silence for the time being, Razumikhin had nothing to say—and so Pulcheria Alexandrovna started worrying again.

"Marfa Petrovna died, have you heard?" she began, falling back on her capital resource.

"Of course I have, madam. I was informed at the first rumor of it, and have even come now to tell you that Arkady Ivanovich Svidrigailov left in all haste for Petersburg immediately following his wife's funeral. That is so, at least, according to the most precise reports which I have received."

"To Petersburg? Here?" Dunechka asked worriedly, and she exchanged glances with her mother.

"Just so, madam, and surely not without purpose, considering the hastiness of his departure and the preceding circumstances in general."

"Lord! But can it be that he will not leave Dunechka alone even here?" Pulcheria Alexandrovna exclaimed.

"It seems to me that there is nothing to be particularly worried about, either for you or for Avdotya Romanovna, unless, of course, you yourselves wish to enter into some sort of relations with him. For my part, I am watching, and am now seeking to discover where he is staying . . ."

"Ah, Pyotr Petrovich, you wouldn't believe how you frightened me just now!" Pulcheria Alexandrovna went on. "I have seen him only twice, but I found him terrible, terrible! I'm sure he was the cause of the late Marfa Petrovna's death."

"Concerning that, no conclusion is possible. I have precise information. I will not dispute that he perhaps contributed to hastening the course of events, so to speak, by the moral influence of his offense; but concerning the behavior and the moral characteristics of the person in general, I agree with you. I do not know whether he is rich now or precisely what Marfa Petrovna left him; that will be known to me very shortly; but, of course, here in Petersburg, with at least some financial means, he will at once resume his old habits. He is the most depraved and vice-ridden of all men of his sort! I have significant grounds for supposing that Marfa Petrovna, who had the misfortune of falling so much in love with him and redeeming him from his debts eight years ago, served him in still another respect: solely as the result of her efforts and sacrifices, a criminal case was snuffed out at the very start, a case having a tinge of brutal and, so to speak, fantastic evildoing, for which he could quite, quite possibly have taken a trip to Siberia. That is what the man is like, if you wish to know."

"Ah, Lord!" cried Pulcheria Alexandrovna. Raskolnikov was listening attentively.

"And it's true that you have precise information about it?" Dunya asked sternly and imposingly.

"I say only what I myself heard in confidence from the late Marfa Petrovna. It should be noted that the case is rather obscure from a legal point of view. There was living here, and I believe she still lives here, a certain foreign woman named Resslich, a small-time money-lender, and engaged in other affairs as well. Mr. Svidrigailov had long been in some sort of rather close and mysterious relations with this Resslich. She had a distant relative living with her, a niece I think, a deaf and dumb girl of about fifteen, or even fourteen, whom this Resslich hated beyond measure and reproached for every morsel; she even used to beat her brutally. One day the girl was found hanging in the attic. The verdict was suicide. After the customary proceedings, the case was closed, but later there came a report that the child had been . . . cruelly abused by Svidrigailov. True, it was all obscure; the report came from another woman, also a German, a notorious woman and not to be trusted; in the end, essentially, there was no report, thanks to Marfa Petrovna's efforts and money; everything confined itself to rumor. Nevertheless, this rumor was highly portentous. While there, Avdotya Romanovna, you undoubtedly also heard about a story involving the servant Filipp, who died of brutal treatment about six years ago, still in the time of serfdom."

"I heard, on the contrary, that this Filipp hanged himself."

"Just so, madam; but he was driven or, better, inclined towards a violent death by Mr. Svidrigailov's system of constant punishments and persecutions."

"That I do not know," Dunya answered dryly. "I only heard some very strange story that this Filipp was a sort of hypochondriac, a sort of homemade philosopher; they said he 'read himself up,' and that he most likely hanged himself because of Mr. Svidrigailov's mockery, and not from any beatings. He treated the servants well while I was there, and they even liked him, though they, too, indeed accused him of Filipp's death."

"I see, Avdotya Romanovna, that you are somehow suddenly inclined to justify him," Luzhin remarked, twisting his mouth into an ambiguous smile. "He really is a cunning and seductive man when it comes to ladies, of which Marfa Petrovna, who died so strangely, serves as a lamentable example. I merely wanted to be of service to you and your mother with my advice, in view of his new and undoubtedly forthcoming attempts. As for me, I am firmly convinced that the man will undoubtedly disappear once again into debtors' prison. Marfa Petrovna by no means ever had the slightest intention of binding anything over to him, having her children to consider, and if she did leave him anything, it is only the most necessary, of little worth, ephemeral, not enough to last a man of his habits for even a year."

"Pyotr Petrovich, I beg you," said Dunya, "let us stop talking about Mr. Svidrigailov. It makes me weary."

"He just came to see me," Raskolnikov suddenly said, breaking his silence for the first time.

There were exclamations on all sides; everyone turned to him. Even Pyotr Petrovich became excited.

"About an hour and a half ago, while I was sleeping, he came in, woke me up, and introduced himself," Raskolnikov continued. "He was rather offhand and cheerful, and fully hopes I will become close with him. By the way, he very much begs and seeks to meet with you, Dunya, and has asked me to be an intermediary at this meeting. He has an offer for you; he told me what it was. Moreover, he informed me positively that Marfa Petrovna managed, a week before her death, to make a bequest of three thousand roubles to you, Dunya, and that now you will be able to have the money in the very nearest future."

"Thank God!" Pulcheria Alexandrovna cried out, and she crossed herself. "Pray for her, Dunya, pray for her!"

"That is actually true," escaped from Luzhin.

"Well, well, what else?" Dunya hurried.

"Then he said that he himself was not rich, that all the property would go to his children, who are now with their aunt. Then, that he was staying somewhere not far from me, but where, I don't know, I didn't ask . . ."

"But what, what does he want to offer Dunechka?" Pulcheria Alexandrovna asked, frightened. "Did he tell you?"

"Yes, he did."

"What is it?"

"I'll tell you later." Raskolnikov fell silent and turned to his tea.

Pyotr Petrovich took out his watch and looked at it.

"I must go and attend to some business, and thus will not be in your way," he added, looking somewhat piqued, and he began to rise from his chair.

"Do stay, Pyotr Petrovich," said Dunya. "You were planning to spend the evening. Besides, you yourself wrote that you wished to talk with mama about something."

"Just so, Avdotya Romanovna," Pyotr Petrovich said imposingly, taking his seat again, but still holding his hat in his hand. "Indeed, I wanted to talk both with you and with your most respected mother, and even about some quite important points. However, just as your brother is unable to speak in my presence concerning certain offers from Mr. Svidrigailov, so I am unwilling and unable to speak . . . in the presence of others . . . concerning certain quite, quite important points. Furthermore, my capital and most urgent request has not been fulfilled . . ."

Luzhin assumed a bitter expression and lapsed into dignified silence.

"Your request that my brother not be present at our meeting was not fulfilled solely at my insistence," said Dunya. "You wrote that my brother had insulted you; I think that this ought to be explained at once, and that you should make peace. And if Rodya did indeed insult you, he *must* and *will* ask your forgiveness."

Pyotr Petrovich immediately showed his mettle.

"There are certain insults, Avdotya Romanovna, which, for all one's good will, cannot be forgotten. There is a line in all things that it is dangerous to step over; for once one steps over, it is impossible to go back."

"As a matter of fact, Pyotr Petrovich, that is not what I was talking about," Dunya interrupted a little impatiently. "Do try to understand that our whole future depends on whether all this can or cannot be clarified and settled as soon as possible. I tell you outright, from the first word, that I cannot look upon it any other way, and if you value me at all, then, hard as it may be, this whole story must end today. I repeat that if my brother is at fault, he will ask your forgiveness."

"I am surprised that you put the question in such a way, Avdotya Romanovna." Luzhin was becoming more and more irritated. "While valuing and, so to speak, adoring you, I may at the same time quite, quite dislike someone of your household. Having claimed the happiness of your hand, I cannot at the same time take upon myself obligations incompatible with . . ."

"Ah, drop all this touchiness, Pyotr Petrovich," Dunya interrupted with feeling, "and be the noble and intelligent man I have always considered and want to consider you to be. I gave you a great promise, I am your fiancée; trust me in this matter, then, and believe me capable of judging impartially. That I am taking upon myself the role of judge is as much a surprise for my brother as it is for you. When I asked him today, after receiving your letter, to be sure to come to our meeting, I told him nothing of my intentions. Understand that if you do not make peace I shall have to choose between you: either you or him. That is how the question has been put both on his side and on yours. I do not want to make a wrong choice, and I must not. For your sake, I must break with my brother; for my brother's sake, I must break with you. I can and will find out now for certain whether he is a brother to me. And, about you, whether you appreciate me, whether you value me, whether you are a husband to me."

"Avdotya Romanovna," Luzhin pronounced, wincing, "your words are of all too great an import for me; I will say more, they are even offensive, in view of the position I have the honor of occupying in relation to you. To say nothing of the offensive and strange juxtaposition, on the same level, of myself and . . . a presumptuous youth, you allow, by your words, for the possibility of breaking the promise I was given. 'Either you or him,' you say, and thereby show me how little I mean to you . . . I cannot allow it, in view of the relations and . . . obligations existing between us."

"What!" Dunya flared up. "I place your interests alongside all that has so far been precious in my life, all that has so far constituted the *whole* of my life, and you are suddenly offended because I attach so *little* value to you!"

Raskolnikov smiled silently and caustically. Razumikhin cringed all over. But Pyotr Petrovich did not accept the objection; on the contrary, he grew more importunate and irritable with every word, as though he were acquiring a taste for it.

"Love for one's future life-companion, a future husband, ought to exceed the love for one's brother," he pronounced sententiously, "and in any case I am not to be placed on the same level . . . Although I insisted before that in your brother's presence I could not and did not wish to explain all that I came to say, I shall nevertheless ask your much respected mother here and now for the necessary explanation of one point I consider quite capital and offensive to myself. Yesterday," he turned to Pulcheria Alexandrovna, "in the presence of Mr. Rassudkin (or . . . is that right? Excuse me, I've forgotten your last name)"—he bowed politely to Razumikhin[11]—"your son offended me by distorting a thought I once expressed to you in private conversation, over coffee: namely, that marriage to a poor girl who has already experienced life's grief is, in my view, more profitable with regard to matrimony than marriage to one who has known prosperity, for it is better for morality. Your son deliberately exaggerated the meaning of my words to absurdity, accusing me of malicious intentions, and basing himself, as I think, on your own correspondence. I shall count myself happy, Pulcheria Alexandrovna, if you prove able to reassure me in the opposite sense and thereby set my mind considerably at rest. Tell me, then, in precisely what terms did you convey my words in your letter to Rodion Romanovich?"

"I don't remember," Pulcheria Alexandrovna was thrown off, "but I told it as I myself understood it. I don't know how Rodya told it to you. Perhaps he did exaggerate something."

"He could not have exaggerated without some suggestion from you."

"Pyotr Petrovich," Pulcheria Alexandrovna declared with dignity, "that we are *here* is proof that Dunya and I did not take your words in a very bad way."

"Well done, mama!" Dunya said approvingly.

"Then I am to blame in this as well!" Luzhin became offended.

"Now, Pyotr Petrovich, you keep blaming Rodion, but you yourself also wrote us something untrue about him in today's letter," Pulcheria Alexandrovna added, taking heart.

"I do not recall writing anything that was not true, madam."

"You wrote," Raskolnikov said sharply, without turning to Luzhin, "that I gave money yesterday not to the widow of the man who was run over, as it was in reality, but to his daughter (whom I had never seen until yesterday). You wrote it in order to make me quarrel with my family, and to that end added some vile expressions about the behavior of a girl whom you do not know. All that is gossip and meanness."

"Excuse me, sir," Luzhin replied, trembling with anger, "in my letter I enlarged upon your qualities and actions solely to fulfill thereby the request of your dear sister and your mama that I describe to them how I found you and what impression you made on me. With regard to what I mentioned in my letter, find even one line that is not right—that is, that you did not spend the money, and that in that family, unfortunate as they may be, there are no unworthy persons!"

"And I say that you, with all your virtues, are not worth the little finger of that unfortunate girl at whom you are casting a stone."

"Meaning that you might even decide to introduce her into the company of your mother and sister?"

"I have already done so, if you want to know. I sat her down beside mama and Dunya today."

"Rodya!" exclaimed Pulcheria Alexandrovna.

Dunechka blushed; Razumikhin knitted his brows. Luzhin smiled haughtily and sarcastically.

"You may see for yourself, Avdotya Romanovna," he said, "whether any agreement is possible here. I hope that the matter is now ended and explained once and for all. And I shall withdraw so as not to interfere with the further pleasantness of this family reunion and the imparting of secrets" (he rose from the chair and took his hat). "But in leaving I will venture to remark that henceforth I hope to be spared such meetings and, so to speak, compromises. On this subject I address myself particularly to you, most respected Pulcheria Alexandrovna, the more so as my letter was intended for you and you alone."

Pulcheria Alexandrovna became slightly offended.

"Why, you're really going about getting us into your power, Pyotr Petrovich. Dunya told you the reason why your wish was not fulfilled; her intentions were good. And, besides, you wrote to me as if it were an order. Should we really regard your every wish as an order? I will tell you, on the contrary, that you ought now to be especially delicate and forbearing towards us, because we have dropped everything and come here, entrusting ourselves to you, and therefore are almost in your power as it is."

"That is not quite correct, Pulcheria Alexandrovna, especially at the present moment, when Marfa Petrovna's legacy of three thousand roubles has just been announced—which seems to be very opportune, judging by the new tone in which I am being addressed," he added caustically.

"Judging by that remark, it may be supposed that you were indeed counting on our helplessness," Dunya observed irritably.

"But now, in any case, I cannot do so, and I especially have no wish to hinder the conveying of Arkady Ivanovich Svidrigailov's secret offers, with which he has empowered your dear brother, and which, as I perceive, have a capital, and perhaps also rather pleasant, significance for you."

"Ah, my God!" exclaimed Pulcheria Alexandrovna.

Razumikhin kept fidgeting in his chair.

"Well, sister, are you ashamed now?" asked Raskolnikov.

"Yes, I am ashamed, Rodya," said Dunya. "Pyotr Petrovich, get out!" she turned to him, pale with wrath.

Pyotr Petrovich was apparently not at all expecting such an outcome. He had relied too much on himself, on his power, on the helplessness of his victims. Even now he did not believe it. He became pale, and his lips trembled.

"Avdotya Romanovna, if I walk out that door now, with such parting words, then—consider—I shall never come back. Think it over well! My word is firm."

"What insolence!" cried Dunya, quickly rising from her place. "I don't want you to come back!"

"What? So tha-a-at's how it is!" cried Luzhin, who until the last moment absolutely did not believe in such a denouement, and therefore now lost the thread altogether. "It's that that it is, madam! And do you know, Avdotya Romanovna, that I could even protest?"

"What right have you to speak to her like that!" Pulcheria Alexandrovna broke in hotly. "How are you going to protest? And what are these rights of yours? Do you think I would give my Dunya to a man like you? Go, leave us altogether! It's our own fault for deciding to do a wrong thing, and mine most of all . . ."

"All the same, Pulcheria Alexandrovna," Luzhin was becoming frenzied in his rage, "you bound me by the word you gave, which you are now renouncing . . . and finally . . . finally, I have been drawn, so to speak, into expenses because of it . . ."

This last claim was so much in Pyotr Petrovich's character that Raskolnikov, who was growing pale from wrath and from his efforts to contain it, suddenly could not help himself and—burst out laughing. But Pulcheria Alexandrovna lost her temper:

"Expenses? What expenses? You're not talking about our trunk! But the conductor delivered it for nothing! Lord, and it's we who bound you! Come to your senses, Pyotr Petrovich; it is you who have bound us hand and foot, and not we you!"

"Enough, mama, please, enough!" Avdotya Romanovna pleaded. "Pyotr Petrovich, kindly leave!"

"I shall leave, madam, but just one last word!" he said, now losing almost all control of himself. "Your mother seems to have entirely forgotten that I decided to take you, so to speak, after a town rumor concerning your good name had spread throughout the neighborhood. Disregarding public opinion for your sake, and restoring your good name, I could quite, quite certainly hope for some retribution, and even demand your gratitude . . . And only now have my eyes been opened! I see myself that I perhaps acted quite, quite rashly in disregarding the public voice . . ."

"What, is he queer in the head or something?" cried Razumikhin, jumping up from his chair and preparing himself for reprisals.

"Mean and wicked man that you are!" said Dunya.

"Not a word! Not a gesture!" cried Raskolnikov, holding Razumikhin back; then, going up to Luzhin almost point-blank:

"Be so good as to get out!" he said, softly and distinctly. "And not a word more, or else . . ."

Pyotr Petrovich looked at him for a few seconds, his face pale and twisted with spite, then turned and went out; and rarely, of course, has anyone carried away so much spiteful hatred in his heart as this man felt for Raskolnikov. He blamed him, and him alone, for everything. Remarkably, as he was going down the stairs, he still imagined that the case was perhaps not lost at all, and, as far as the ladies alone were concerned, was even "quite, quite" remediable.

III

THE MAIN THING was that, until the very last moment, he had in no way expected such a denouement. He had stood on his mettle to the last limit, without supposing even the possibility that the two poor and defenseless women could get out from under his power. Vanity contributed much to this conviction, as did that degree of self-confidence which is best called self-admiration. Having risen from insignificance, Pyotr Petrovich had a morbid habit of admiring himself, highly valued his intelligence and abilities, and sometimes, alone with himself, even admired his own face in the mirror. But most of all in the world he loved and valued his money, acquired by labor and various means: it made him equal to all that was higher than himself.

In bitterly reminding Dunya just now that he had decided to take her in spite of the bad rumors about her, Pyotr Petrovich had spoken quite sincerely, and even felt deeply indignant at such "black ingratitude." And yet, when he was proposing to Dunya, he had already been fully convinced of the absurdity of all this gossip, universally refuted by Marfa Petrovna and long since dropped by the whole little town, which ardently vindicated Dunya. And he himself would not have denied now that he knew all that at the time. Nevertheless, he still valued highly his determination to elevate Dunya to himself, and regarded it as a great deed. In reprimanding Dunya about it just now, he had given voice to a secret, cherished thought of his, which he had already admired more than once, and was unable to understand how others could fail to admire his great deed. When he had gone to visit Raskolnikov the other day, he had entered with the feeling of a benefactor ready to reap his harvest and listen to the sweetest compliments. And now, going down the stairs, he most certainly considered himself offended and unacknowledged in the highest degree.

As for Dunya, she was simply necessary for him; it was unthinkable for him to renounce her. For a long time, for several years already, he had been having delectable dreams of marriage, but he kept hoarding up money and waited. In deepest secret, he entertained rapturous thoughts of a well-behaved and poor girl (she must be poor), very young, very pretty, well born and educated, very intimidated, who had experienced a great many misfortunes and was utterly cowed before him, a girl who would all her life regard him as her salvation, stand in awe of him, obey him, wonder at him and at him alone. How many scenes, how many delectable episodes he had created in imagination on this playful and seductive theme, as he rested quietly from his affairs! And now the dream of so many years was almost coming true: the beauty and education of Avdotya Romanovna struck him; her helpless position aroused him in the extreme. Here was something even a bit more than he had dreamed of: here was a proud, unusual, virtuous girl, superior to him in education and upbringing (that he could feel), and such a being would be slavishly grateful to him all her life for his great deed, and would reverently efface herself before him, and he—he would rule boundlessly and absolutely! . . . As if by design, shortly before then, after much anticipation and deliberation, he had at last decided finally to change his career and enter a wider sphere of activity, and, with that, to move little by little into higher society, the thought of which he had long been savoring. In short, he had decided to try Petersburg. He knew that here women could be "quite, quite" beneficial. The charm of a lovely, virtuous, and educated woman could do wonders to smooth his path, attract certain people, create an aura . . . and now it had all collapsed! This present, ugly breakup affected him like a bolt of lightning. It was some ugly joke, an absurdity! He had only shown his mettle a tiny bit; he had not even had time to speak himself out; he was merely joking, got carried away, and it ended so seriously! Finally, he had even come to love Dunya in his own way; he was already her master in his dreams—and suddenly! . . . No! Tomorrow, tomorrow at the latest, all this must be restored, healed, set right, and above all—this presumptuous brat, this youngster who was the cause of it all, must be destroyed. With a painful feeling he also somehow involuntarily remembered Razumikhin . . . however, he soon set himself at ease in that regard: "This is the last person who could be held up to him!" Indeed, if there was anyone he was seriously afraid of, it was—Svidrigailov . . . In short, many troubles lay ahead of him . . . .

"No, it's my fault most of all!" Dunechka was saying, embracing and kissing her mother. "I was tempted by his money, but I swear, brother—I never imagined he could be such an unworthy man. If I had seen through him sooner, I would never have been tempted! Don't blame me, brother!"

"God has delivered us! God has delivered us!" Pulcheria Alexandrovna muttered, but somehow unconsciously, as if she had not quite made sense of all that had happened.

They were all rejoicing; in five minutes they were even laughing. Only Dunechka occasionally became pale and knitted her brows, thinking back on what had happened. Pulcheria Alexandrovna would never have imagined that she, too, could be so glad; even that morning a breakup with Luzhin had seemed to her a terrible disaster. But Razumikhin was in ecstasy. He did not yet dare to express it fully, but was trembling all over as in a fever, as if a two-hundred-pound weight had fallen off his heart. Now he had the right to give his whole life to them, to serve them . . . And who knew what then! However, he drove all further thoughts away still more timorously, and was afraid of his own imagination. Only Raskolnikov went on sitting in the same place, almost sullen, even distracted. He who had insisted most on Luzhin's removal, now seemed to be the least interested in what had happened. Dunya thought unwillingly that he was still very angry with her, and Pulcheria Alexandrovna kept looking at him fearfully.

"So, what did Svidrigailov say?" Dunya went over to him.

"Ah, yes, yes!" exclaimed Pulcheria Alexandrovna.

Raskolnikov raised his head.

"He insists on making you a gift of ten thousand roubles, and at the same time says he wishes to see you once more, in my presence."

"To see her! Not for anything in the world!" Pulcheria Alexandrovna cried out. "And how dare he offer her money!"

Then Raskolnikov related (rather dryly) his conversation with Svidrigailov, omitting Marfa Petrovna's ghosts, so as not to go into superfluous matters, and feeling disgusted at starting any conversation at all beyond the most necessary.

"And what answer did you give him?" asked Dunya.

"First I said I wouldn't tell you anything. Then he said he would use every means possible to seek a meeting himself. He insisted that his passion for you was a whim, and that he now feels nothing for you . . . He does not want you to marry Luzhin . . . Generally, he was not very consistent."

"How do you explain him to yourself, Rodya? How did he seem to you?"

"I confess I don't understand any of it very well. He offers ten thousand, while saying he's not rich. He announces that he wants to go away somewhere, and ten minutes later forgets that he mentioned it. Suddenly he also says he wants to get married, and that a match has already been made for him . . . He has his purposes, of course—bad ones, most likely. Then again, it's somehow strange to suppose he'd approach this matter so stupidly, if he had bad intentions towards you . . . Of course, I refused this money on your behalf, once and for all. Generally, he seemed very strange to me, and . . . even . . . as if he showed signs of madness. But I could just as well be mistaken; there might simply be some sort of hoodwinking going on here. Marfa Petrovna's death seems to have made its impression on him . . ."

"Lord rest her soul!" exclaimed Pulcheria Alexandrovna. "I will pray to God for her eternally, eternally! Where would we be now, Dunya, without those three thousand roubles! Lord, just as though they fell from heaven! Ah, Rodya, this morning we had all of three roubles to our name, and were thinking, Dunya and I, of quickly pawning the watch somewhere, if only so as not to take anything from that man until he thought of it himself."

Dunya was somehow all too struck by Svidrigailov's offer. She was still standing deep in thought.

"He's contemplating something horrible!" she said to herself, almost in a whisper, all but shuddering.

Raskolnikov noticed this excessive fear.

"It seems I'll have to see him more than once," he said to Dunya.

"We'll keep an eye on him! I'll stay on his trail!" Razumikhin cried energetically. "I won't let him out of my sight! Rodya gave me his permission. He told me himself today: 'Protect my sister.' And do I have your permission, Avdotya Romanovna?"

Dunya smiled and gave him her hand, but the worry would not leave her face. Pulcheria Alexandrovna kept glancing at her timidly; however, the three thousand had obviously set her at ease.

A quarter of an hour later they were all in a most animated conversation. Even Raskolnikov, though he did not speak, listened attentively for some time. Razumikhin was holding forth.

"But why, why would you leave!" he overflowed rapturously in his ecstatic speech. "What are you going to do in a wretched little town? The main thing is that you're all together here, and you need one another—oh, you do need one another, believe me! Well, at least for the time being . . . Take me as a friend, a partner, and I assure you we can start an excellent enterprise. Listen, I'll explain it all to you in detail—the whole project! This morning, when nothing had happened yet, it was already flashing in my head . . . The point is this: I have an uncle (I'll introduce him to you; a most agreeable, most respectable old codger!), and this uncle has a capital of a thousand roubles; he himself lives on his pension and wants for nothing. For two years now he's been pestering me to take the thousand from him and pay him six percent on it. I see what he's up to: he simply wants to help me out. Last year I didn't need it, but this year I was just waiting for him to come and decided I'd take it. Then you can give another thousand out of your three; that way we'll have enough to start with, and so we'll join together. And what is it we're going to do?"

Here Razumikhin began developing his project, and spoke at length about how almost all our booksellers and publishers have little feeling for their wares, and are therefore also bad publishers, whereas decent publications generally pay for themselves and bring in a profit, sometimes a considerable one. And so Razumikhin's dream was to go into publishing, since he had already spent two years working for others, and knew three European languages quite well, though he had told Raskolnikov six days ago that his German was *"kaput,"* with the aim of convincing him to take half of his translation work and three roubles of the advance; not only was he lying then, but Raskolnikov had known that he was lying.

"Why, why should we let the chance slip, when we happen to have one of the main essentials—our own money?" Razumikhin was becoming excited. "Of course, it means a lot of work, but we will work—you, Avdotya Romanovna, and I, and Rodion . . . some books bring in a nice profit nowadays! And the main basis of the enterprise will be that we'll know precisely what to translate. We'll translate, and publish, and study, all at the same time. I can be useful here, because I've got experience. I've been poking around among publishers for nearly two years now; I know all the ins and outs—and there's no need for the divine spark, believe me! Why, why should we let the spoon miss our mouth? I myself know—I've been keeping it a secret—of two or three works that would bring a hundred roubles each just for the idea of translating and publishing them; as for one of them, I wouldn't sell the idea even for five hundred roubles. And you know, if I were to tell someone, he might just doubt it—blockheads that they are! As for the business end proper—typographers, paper, sales—you can leave that to me! I know all the ropes! We'll start little by little and wind up with something big; at least we'll have enough to eat, and in any case we'll get back what we put in."

Dunya's eyes were shining.

"I like what you're saying very much, Dmitri Prokofych," she said.

"I know nothing about it, of course," Pulcheria Alexandrovna responded, "it may be good, but then again, God knows. It's so new somehow, so unknown. Of course, it's necessary for us to stay here, at least for the time being."

She looked at Rodya.

"What do you think, brother?" Dunya said.

"I think his idea is a very good one," he answered. "Naturally, you shouldn't dream ahead of time of establishing a firm, but it is indeed possible to publish five or six books with unquestionable success. I myself know of one work that would be sure to do well. And as for his ability to handle the business, there's no doubt of it: he understands business . . . However, you have time enough to come to an agreement . . ."

"Hurrah!" cried Razumikhin. "Now wait, there's an apartment here, in this same building, with the same landlord. It's a private, separate one, not connected with the rooming house, and it's furnished—the price is moderate, three small rooms. So you take that to start with. I'll pawn your watch tomorrow and bring you the money, and later everything will be settled. And the main thing is that you can all three live together, and Rodya with you . . . Where are you off to, Rodya?"

"What, Rodya, you're leaving already?" Pulcheria Alexandrovna asked, even in alarm.

"At such a moment!" exclaimed Razumikhin.

Dunya looked at her brother with incredulous surprise. He had his cap in his hand; he was getting ready to go.

"It's not as if you were burying me or saying good-bye forever," he said, somehow strangely.

It was as if he smiled, but at the same time as if it were not a smile.

"Though, who knows, maybe this is the last time we'll see each other," he added inadvertently.

He was thinking it to himself, but somehow it got spoken aloud.

"What's the matter with you!" his mother cried out.

"Where are you going, Rodya?" Dunya asked, somehow strangely.

"No, I really must," he answered vaguely, as if hesitating over what he wanted to say. But there was a sort of sharp determination in his pale face.

"I wanted to tell you . . . as I was coming here . . . I wanted to tell you, mama . . . and you, Dunya, that it's better if we part ways for a while. I'm not feeling well, I'm not at ease . . . I'll come myself afterwards . . . when I can. I think of you and love you . . . Leave me! Leave me alone! I decided on it even before . . . I decided on it for certain . . . Whatever happens to me, whether I perish or not, I want to be alone. Forget me altogether. It's better . . . Don't make inquiries about me. When need be, I'll come myself, or . . . send for you. Perhaps everything will rise again! . . . But for now, if you love me, give in . . . Otherwise I'll start hating you, I feel it . . . Good-bye!"

"Lord!" cried Pulcheria Alexandrovna.

Mother and sister were both terribly frightened; so was Razumikhin.

"Rodya, Rodya! Make peace with us, let's be as we used to be!" his poor mother exclaimed.

He slowly turned towards the door, and slowly began walking out of the room. Dunya overtook him.

"Brother! What are you doing to mother!" she whispered, her eyes burning with indignation.

He gave her a heavy look.

"It's all right, I'll be back, I'll still come!" he muttered half aloud, as if not quite aware of what he wanted to say, and walked out of the room.

"Wicked, unfeeling egoist!" Dunya cried out.

"He's not unfeeling, he's cra-a-azy! He's mad! Don't you see that? If not, you're unfeeling yourself! . . ." Razumikhin whispered hotly, just over her shoulder, squeezing her hand hard.

"I'll be back right away!" he cried, turning to Pulcheria Alexandrovna, who had gone numb, and he ran out of the room.

Raskolnikov was waiting for him at the end of the corridor.

"I knew you'd come running," he said. "Go back to them and be with them . . . Be with them tomorrow, too . . . and always. I'll come . . . maybe . . . if I can. Good-bye!"

And without offering his hand, he began walking away.

"But where are you going? Why? What's wrong with you? You can't do this!" Razumikhin kept murmuring, utterly at a loss.

Raskolnikov stopped again.

"Once and for all, never ask me about anything. I have no answers for you . . . Don't come to me. Maybe I'll come here. Leave me . . . but *don't leave them.* Do you understand me?"

It was dark in the corridor; they were standing near a light. For a minute they looked silently at each other. Razumikhin remembered that minute all his life. Raskolnikov's burning and fixed look seemed to grow more intense every moment, penetrating his soul, his consciousness. All at once Razumikhin gave a start. Something strange seemed to pass between them . . . as if the hint of some idea, something horrible, hideous, flitted by and was suddenly understood on both sides . . . Razumikhin turned pale as a corpse.

"You understand now?" Raskolnikov said suddenly, with a painfully contorted face. "Go back, go to them," he added suddenly, and, turning quickly, he walked out of the house . . .

I will not describe here what went on that evening at Pulcheria Alexandrovna's, how Razumikhin went back to them, how he tried to calm them, how he swore that Rodya needed to be allowed some rest in his illness, swore that Rodya would come without fail, would visit them every day, that he was very, very upset, that he should not be irritated; that he, Razumikhin, would keep an eye on him, would find him a doctor, a good doctor, the best, a whole consultation . . . In short, from that evening on Razumikhin became their son and brother.

IV

AND RASKOLNIKOV went straight to the house on the canal where Sonya lived. It was a three-storied, old, and green-colored house. He sought out the caretaker and got vague directions from him as to where Kapernaumov the tailor lived. Having located the entrance to a narrow and dark stairway in the corner of the yard, he went up, finally, to the second floor and came out onto a gallery running around it on the courtyard side. While he was wandering in the darkness and in perplexity with regard to the possible whereabouts of Kapernaumov's entrance, a door opened suddenly, three steps away from him; he took hold of it mechanically.

"Who's there?" a woman's voice asked in alarm.

"It's me . . . to see you," Raskolnikov replied, and stepped into the tiny entryway. There, on a chair with a broken seat, stood a candle in a bent copper candlestick.

"It's you! Lord!" Sonya cried weakly, and stood rooted to the spot.

"Where do I go? In here?"

And, trying not to look at her, Raskolnikov went quickly into the room.

A moment later Sonya came in with the candle, put the candlestick down, and stood before him, completely at a loss, all in some inexpressible agitation, and obviously frightened by his unexpected visit. Color suddenly rushed to her pale face, and tears even came to her eyes . . . She had a feeling of nausea, and shame, and sweetness . . . Raskolnikov quickly turned away and sat down on a chair by the table. He managed to glance around the room as he did so.

It was a big but extremely low-ceilinged room, the only one let by the Kapernaumovs, the locked door to whose apartment was in the wall to the left. Opposite, in the right-hand wall, there was another door, always tightly shut. This led to another, adjoining apartment, with a different number. Sonya's room had something barnlike about it; it was of a very irregular rectangular shape, which gave it an ugly appearance. A wall with three windows looking onto the canal cut somehow obliquely across the room, making one corner, formed of a terribly acute angle, run somewhere into the depths where, in the weak light, it could not even be seen very well; the other corner was too grotesquely obtuse. The whole big room had almost no furniture in it. There was a bed in the corner to the right; a chair next to it, nearer the door. Along the same wall as the bed, just by the door to the other apartment, stood a simple wooden table covered with a dark blue cloth and, at the table, two rush-bottom chairs. Then, against the opposite wall, near the acute corner, there was a small chest of drawers, made of plain wood, standing as if lost in the emptiness. That was all there was in the room. The yellowish, frayed, and shabby wallpaper was blackened in all the corners; it must have been damp and fumy in winter. The poverty was evident; there were not even any curtains over the bed.

Sonya looked silently at her visitor, who was examining her room so attentively and unceremoniously, and at last even began to tremble with fear, as though she were standing before the judge and ruler of her destiny.

"It's late . . . already eleven?" he asked, still without raising his eyes to her.

"Yes," Sonya murmured. "Ah, yes, it is!" she suddenly hurried on, as if the whole way out for her lay there. "The landlord's clock just struck . . . I heard it myself . . . It is!"

"I've come to you for the last time," Raskolnikov went on sullenly, though it was in fact the first time. "I may never see you again . . ."

"You're . . . going away?"

"I don't know . . . tomorrow, everything . . ."

"So you won't be at Katerina Ivanovna's tomorrow?" Sonya's voice faltered.

"I don't know. Tomorrow morning, everything . . . That's not the point; I came to say one word to you . . ."

He raised his pensive eyes to her and suddenly noticed that he was sitting and she was still standing before him.

"Why are you standing? Sit down," he said suddenly, in a changed, quiet and tender voice.

She sat down. He looked at her for about a minute, kindly and almost compassionately.

"How thin you are! Look at your hand! Quite transparent. Fingers like a dead person's."

He took her hand. Sonya smiled weakly.

"I've always been like that," she said.

"Even when you were living at home?"

"Yes."

"Ah, but of course!" he uttered abruptly, and the expression of his face and the sound of his voice suddenly changed again. He looked once more around the room.

"You rent from Kapernaumov?"

"Yes, sir . . ."

"That's their door there?"

"Yes . . . They have a room the same as this one."

"All in one room?"

"Yes, in one room, sir."

"I'd be scared in your room at night," he remarked sullenly.

"The landlords are very nice, very affectionate," Sonya replied, as if she had still not come to her senses or collected her thoughts, "and all the furniture and everything . . . everything is theirs. And they're very kind, and the children often come to see me, too."

"They're the ones who are tongue-tied?"

"Yes, sir . . . He stammers, and he's lame as well. And his wife, too . . . Not that she really stammers, but it's as if she doesn't quite get the words out. She's kind, very. And he's a former household serf. And there are seven children . . . and only the oldest one stammers; the rest are just sick . . . but they don't stammer . . . But how do you know about them?" she added with some surprise.

"Your father told me everything that time. He told me everything about you . . . How you went out at six o'clock, and came back after eight, and how Katerina Ivanovna knelt by your bed."

Sonya was embarrassed.

"I thought I saw him today," she whispered hesitantly.

"Whom?"

"My father. I was walking along the street, nearby, at the corner, around ten o'clock, and he seemed to be walking ahead of me. It looked just like him. I was even going to go to Katerina Ivanovna . . ."

"You were out walking?"

"Yes," Sonya whispered abruptly, embarrassed again and looking down.

"But Katerina Ivanovna all but beat you when you lived at your father's?"

"Ah, no, what are you saying, no!" Sonya looked at him even with some sort of fright.

"So you love her?"

"Love her? But, of co-o-ourse!" Sonya drew the word out plaintively, suddenly clasping her hands together with suffering. "Ah! You don't . . . If only you knew her! She's just like a child. It's as if she's lost her mind . . . from grief. And she used to be so intelligent . . . so generous . . . so kind! You know nothing, nothing . . . ah!"

Sonya spoke as if in despair, worrying and suffering and wringing her hands. Her pale cheeks became flushed again; her eyes had a tormented look. One could see that terribly much had been touched in her, that she wanted terribly to express something, to speak out, to intercede. Some sort of *insatiable* compassion, if one may put it so, showed suddenly in all the features of her face.

"Beat me? How can you! Beat me—Lord! And even if she did beat me, what of it! Well, what of it! You know nothing, nothing . . . She's so unhappy; ah, how unhappy she is! And sick . . . She wants justice . . . She's pure. She believes so much that there should be justice in everything, and she demands it . . . Even if you tortured her, she wouldn't act unjustly. She herself doesn't notice how impossible it all is that there should be justice in people, and it vexes her . . . Like a child, like a child! She's a just woman!"

"And what will become of you?"

Sonya looked at him questioningly.

"They're all on your hands. True, it was all on you before as well, and it was to you that your late father came to beg for the hair of the dog. Well, what will become of you now?"

"I don't know," Sonya said sadly.

"Will they stay there?"

"I don't know, they owe rent for the apartment; only I heard today that the landlady said she wants to turn them out, and Katerina Ivanovna says herself that she won't stay a moment longer."

"How is she so brave? She's counting on you?"

"Ah, no, don't talk like that! . . . We're all one, we live as one." Sonya again became all excited and even vexed, just like a canary or some other little bird getting angry. "And what is she to do? What, what is she to do?" she repeated, hotly and excitedly. "And how she cried, how she cried today! She's losing her mind, did you notice? She is; she keeps worrying like a little girl that everything should be done properly tomorrow, the meal and everything . . . then she wrings her hands, coughs up blood, cries, and suddenly starts beating her head against the wall as if in despair. And then she gets comforted again; she keeps hoping in you; she says you'll be her helper now, and that she'll borrow a little money somewhere, and go back with me to her town, and start an institution for noble girls, and she'll make me a supervisor, and a completely new, beautiful life will begin for us, and she kisses me, embraces me, comforts me, and she really believes it! She really believes in her fantasies! Well, how can one contradict her? And she

spent the whole day today washing, cleaning, mending; she brought
the tub into the room by herself, with her weak strength, out of breath,
and just collapsed on the bed; and she and I also went to the market
in the morning to buy shoes for Polechka and Lenya, because theirs
fell to pieces, only we didn't have enough money, it was much more
than we could spend, and she had picked out such lovely shoes, because
she has taste, you don't know . . . She just cried right there in the shop,
in front of the shopkeepers, because there wasn't enough . . . Ah, it was
such a pity to see!"

"Well, after that one can understand why you . . . live as you do,"
Raskolnikov said, with a bitter smirk.

"And don't you pity her? Don't you?" Sonya heaved herself up
again. "You, I know, you gave her all you had, and you hadn't even
seen anything. And if you'd seen everything, oh, Lord! And so many
times, so many times I've brought her to tears! Just last week! Ah, me!
Only a week before his death. I acted cruelly! And I've done it so many
times, so many times. Ah, it's been so painful to remember it all day
long today!"

Sonya even wrung her hands as she spoke, so painful was it to
remember.

"You, cruel?"

"Yes, me, me! I came then," she continued, weeping, "and my father
said, 'Read to me, Sonya,' he said, 'there's an ache in my head, read
to me . . . here's a book'—he had some book, he got it from Andrei
Semyonovich, he lives here, Lebezyatnikov, he was always getting
such funny books. And I said, 'It's time I was going,' I just didn't want
to read, because I stopped by mainly to show Katerina Ivanovna the
collars; Lizaveta, the dealer, had brought me some cheap collars and
cuffs, pretty, new ones, with a pattern. And Katerina Ivanovna liked
them very much, she put them on and looked at herself in the mirror,
and she liked them very, very much. 'Sonya, please,' she said, 'give
them to me.' She said *please,* and she wanted them so much. But where
would she go in them? She was just remembering her former happy
days! She looked in the mirror, admired herself, and she's had no
dresses, no dresses at all, no things, for so many years now! And she
never asks anything from anybody; she's proud, she'd sooner give
away all she has, but this time she asked—she liked them so much! And

I was sorry to think of giving them away; I said, 'But what for, Katerina Ivanovna?' I said that: 'what for?' I should never have said that to her. She just looked at me, and she took it so hard, so hard, that I refused, and it was such a pity to see . . . And it wasn't because of the collars, but because I refused, I could see that. Ah, if only I could take it all back now, do it over again, all those past words . . . Oh, I . . . but why am I talking about it! . . . it's all the same to you!"

"So you knew Lizaveta, the dealer?"

"Yes . . . Why, did you?" Sonya asked in return, with some surprise.

"Katerina Ivanovna has consumption, a bad case; she'll die soon," Raskolnikov said after a pause, and without answering the question.

"Oh, no, no, no!" And with an unconscious gesture, Sonya seized both his hands, as if pleading that it be no.

"But it's better if she dies."

"No, it's not better, not better, not better at all!" she repeated, fearfully and unwittingly.

"And the children? Where will they go, if you don't take them?"

"Oh, I really don't know!" Sonya cried out, almost in despair, and clutched her head. One could see that the thought had already flashed in her many, many times, and that he had only scared it up again.

"Well, and what if you get ill now, while Katerina Ivanovna is still with you, and you're taken to the hospital—what then?" he insisted mercilessly.

"Ah, don't, don't! That simply can't be!" And Sonya's face became distorted with terrible fright.

"Why can't it?" Raskolnikov went on, with a cruel grin. "You're not insured against it, are you? What will happen to them then? They'll wind up in the street, the lot of them; she'll cough and beg and beat her head against the wall, like today, and the children will cry . . . Then she'll collapse, then the police station, the hospital, she'll die, and the children . . ."

"Oh, no! God won't let it happen!" burst at last from Sonya's straining breast. She listened, looking at him in supplication, her hands clasped in mute entreaty, as if it were on him that everything depended.

Raskolnikov got up and began pacing the room. About a minute passed. Sonya stood with arms and head hanging, in terrible anguish.

"But can't you save? Put something aside for a rainy day?" he asked suddenly, stopping in front of her.

"No," whispered Sonya.

"No, naturally! And have you tried?" he added, all but in mockery.

"I have."

"But it didn't work! Naturally! Why even ask!"

And he began pacing again. Another minute or so passed.

"You don't get money every day?"

Sonya became more embarrassed than before, and color rushed to her face again.

"No," she whispered, with painful effort.

"It's bound to be the same with Polechka," he said suddenly.

"No, no! It can't be! No!" Sonya cried loudly, desperately, as if she had suddenly been stabbed with a knife. "God, God won't allow such horror! . . ."

"He allows it with others."

"No, no! God will protect her! God! . . ." she repeated, beside herself.

"But maybe there isn't any God," Raskolnikov replied, even almost gloatingly, and he looked at her and laughed.

Sonya's face suddenly changed terribly: spasms ran over it. She looked at him with inexpressible reproach, was about to say something, but could not utter a word and simply began sobbing all at once very bitterly, covering her face with her hands.

"You say Katerina Ivanovna is losing her mind, but you're losing your mind yourself," he said, after a pause.

About five minutes passed. He kept pacing up and down, silently and without glancing at her. Finally he went up to her; his eyes were flashing. He took her by the shoulders with both hands and looked straight into her weeping face. His eyes were dry, inflamed, sharp, his lips were twitching . . . With a sudden, quick movement he bent all the way down, leaned towards the floor, and kissed her foot. Sonya recoiled from him in horror, as from a madman. And, indeed, he looked quite mad.

"What is it, what are you doing? Before me!" she murmured, turning pale, and her heart suddenly contracted very painfully.

He rose at once.

"I was not bowing to you, I was bowing to all human suffering," he uttered somehow wildly, and walked to the window. "Listen," he added, returning to her after a minute, "I told one offender today that he wasn't worth your little finger . . . and that I did my sister an honor by sitting her next to you."

"Ah, how could you say that to them! And she was there?" Sonya cried fearfully. "To sit with me! An honor! But I'm . . . dishonorable . . . I'm a great, great sinner! Ah, how could you say that!"

"I said it of you not for your dishonor and sin, but for your great suffering. But that you are a great sinner is true," he added, almost ecstatically, "and most of all you are a sinner because you destroyed yourself and betrayed yourself *in vain.* Isn't that a horror! Isn't it a horror that you live in this filth which you hate so much, and at the same time know yourself (you need only open your eyes) that you're not helping anyone by it, and not saving anyone from anything! But tell me, finally," he spoke almost in a frenzy, "how such shame and baseness can be combined in you beside other opposite and holy feelings? It would be more just, a thousand times more just and reasonable, to jump headfirst into the water and end it at once!"

"And what would become of them?" Sonya asked weakly, glancing at him with suffering, but at the same time as if she were not at all surprised at his question. Raskolnikov looked at her strangely.

He read everything in that one glance of hers. So she really had already thought of it herself. Perhaps many times, in despair, she had seriously considered how to end it all at once, so seriously, indeed, that now she was almost not surprised at his suggestion. She had not even noticed the cruelty of his words (nor had she noticed, of course, the meaning of his reproaches, or his special view of her shame—that was obvious to him). But he fully understood the monstrous pain she suffered, and had long been suffering, at the thought of her dishonorable and shameful position. What, he wondered, what could so far have kept her from deciding to end it all at once? And only here did he understand fully what these poor little orphaned children meant to her, and this pitiful, half-crazed Katerina Ivanovna, with her consumption, and her beating her head against the wall.

But then, too, it was clear to him that Sonya, with her character, and the education which, after all, she did have, could in no way remain as she was. It still stood as a question for him: how had she been able to remain for so much too long a time in such a position and not lose her mind, if it was beyond her strength to drown herself? Of course, he understood that Sonya's position was an accidental social phenomenon, though unfortunately a far from isolated and exceptional one. But it would seem that this very accident, this smattering of education, and the whole of her preceding life, should have killed her at once, with her first step onto that loathsome path. What sustained her? Surely not depravity? All this shame obviously touched her only mechanically; no true depravity, not even a drop of it, had yet penetrated her heart—he could see that; she stood before him in reality . . .

"Three ways are open to her," he thought, "to throw herself into the canal, to go to the madhouse, or . . . or, finally, to throw herself into a depravity that stupefies reason and petrifies the heart." This last thought was the most loathsome of all to him; but he was already a skeptic; he was young, abstract, and consequently cruel; and therefore he could not but believe that the last outcome—that is, depravity—was the most likely.

"But can it be true?" he exclaimed to himself. "Can it be that this being, who has still kept her purity of spirit, in the end will be consciously pulled into this vile, stinking hole? Can it be that the pulling has already begun, and that she has been able to endure so far only because vice no longer seems so loathsome to her? No, no, it can't be!" he kept exclaiming, like Sonya earlier. "No, what has so far kept her from the canal is the thought of sin, and of *them, those ones* . . . And if she hasn't lost her mind so far . . . But who says she hasn't lost her mind? Is she in her right mind? Is it possible to talk as she does? Is it possible for someone in her right mind to reason as she does? Is it possible to sit like that over perdition, right over the stinking hole that's already dragging her in, and wave her hands and stop her ears when she's being told of the danger? What does she expect, a miracle? No doubt. And isn't this all a sign of madness?"

He stubbornly stayed at this thought. He liked this solution more than any other. He began studying her with greater attention.

"So you pray very much to God, Sonya?" he asked her.

Sonya was silent; he stood beside her, waiting for an answer.

"And what would I be without God?" she whispered quickly, energetically, glancing at him fleetingly with suddenly flashing eyes, and she pressed his hand firmly with her own.

"So that's it!" he thought.

"And what does God do for you in return?" he asked, testing her further.

Sonya was silent for a long time, as if she were unable to answer. Her frail chest was all heaving with agitation . . .

"Be still! Don't ask! You're not worthy! . . ." she cried suddenly, looking at him sternly and wrathfully.

"That's it! That's it!" he repeated insistently to himself.

"He does everything!" she whispered quickly, looking down again.

"Here's the solution! Here's the explanation of the solution!" he decided to himself, studying her with greedy curiosity.

With a new, strange, almost painful feeling, he peered at that pale, thin, irregular, and angular little face, those meek blue eyes, capable of flashing with such fire, such severe, energetic feeling, that small body still trembling with indignation and wrath, and it all seemed more and more strange to him, almost impossible. "A holy fool! A holy fool!" he kept saying within himself.[12]

There was a book lying on the chest of drawers. He had noticed it each time he paced the room; now he picked it up and looked. It was the New Testament, in Russian translation.[13] The book was old, used, bound in leather.

"Where did this come from?" he called to her across the room. She was still standing in the same place, three steps from the table.

"It was brought to me," she answered, as if reluctantly, and without glancing at him.

"Who brought it?"

"Lizaveta. I asked her to."

"Lizaveta! How strange!" he thought. Everything about Sonya was becoming more strange and wondrous for him with each passing minute. He took the book over to the candle and began leafing through it.

"Where is the part about Lazarus?" he asked suddenly.

Sonya went on stubbornly looking down, and did not answer.

"Where is it about the raising of Lazarus? Find it for me, Sonya."

She gave him a sidelong glance.

"You're looking in the wrong place . . . it's in the fourth Gospel . . ."
she whispered sternly, without moving towards him.

"Find it and read it to me," he said. He sat down, leaned his elbow
on the table, propped his head in his hand, and looked away sullenly,
preparing to listen.

"About three weeks, and welcome to Bedlam! I'll probably be there
myself, if nothing worse happens," he muttered to himself.

Sonya stepped hesitantly to the table, mistrusting Raskolnikov's
strange wish. Nevertheless, she picked up the book.

"You've never read it?" she asked, glancing at him loweringly across
the table. Her voice was becoming more and more severe.

"Long ago . . . in school. Read it!"

"You never heard it in church?"

"I . . . haven't gone. Do you go often?"

"N-no," whispered Sonya.

Raskolnikov grinned.

"I see . . . Then you won't go tomorrow to bury your father either?"

"Yes, I will. And I went last week . . . for a memorial service."

"For whom?"

"Lizaveta. She was killed with an axe."

His nerves were becoming more and more irritated. His head was
beginning to spin.

"Were you friends with Lizaveta?"

"Yes . . . She was a just woman . . . She came . . . rarely . . . she
couldn't. She and I used to read and . . . talk. She will see God."[14]

How strange these bookish words sounded to him; and here was
another new thing: some sort of mysterious get-togethers with
Lizaveta—two holy fools.

"One might well become a holy fool oneself here! It's catching!" he
thought. "Read!" he suddenly exclaimed insistently and irritably.

Sonya still hesitated. Her heart was pounding. She somehow did not
dare read to him. He looked almost with pain at the "unfortunate
madwoman."

"What is it to you? You don't believe, do you? . . ." she whispered
softly, somehow short of breath.

"Read! I want you to!" he insisted. "You read to Lizaveta!"

Sonya opened the book and found the place. Her hands were trembling; she did not have voice enough. She tried twice to begin, but kept failing to get the first syllable out.

" 'Now a certain man was sick, named Lazarus, of Bethany . . .' "[15] she uttered at last, with effort, but suddenly, at the third word, her voice rose and broke like an overtightened string. Her breath failed, and her chest contracted.

Raskolnikov partly understood why Sonya was hesitant to read to him, and the more he understood it, the more rudely and irritably he insisted on her reading. He understood only too well how hard it was for her now to betray and expose all that was *hers*. He understood that these feelings might indeed constitute her *secret*, as it were, real and long-standing, going back perhaps to her adolescence, when she was still in the family, with her unfortunate father and her grief-maddened stepmother, among the hungry children, the ugly shouts and reproaches. But at the same time he now knew, and knew for certain, that even though she was anguished and terribly afraid of something as she was starting out to read, she also had a tormenting desire to read, in spite of all her anguish and apprehension, and precisely *for him*, so that he would hear it, and precisely *now*—"whatever might come of it afterwards!" . . . He read it in her eyes, understood it from her rapturous excitement . . . She mastered herself, suppressed the spasm in her throat that had made her voice break at the beginning of the verse, and continued her reading of the eleventh chapter of John's Gospel. Thus she read on to the nineteenth verse:

" 'And many of the Jews came to Martha and Mary, to comfort them concerning their brother. Then Martha, as soon as she heard that Jesus was coming, went and met him: but Mary sat still in the house. Then said Martha unto Jesus, Lord, if thou hadst been here, my brother had not died. But I know, that even now, whatsoever thou wilt ask of God, God will give it thee.' "

Here she stopped again, anticipating with shame that her voice was again about to tremble and break . . .

" 'Jesus saith unto her, Thy brother shall rise again. Martha saith unto him, I know that he shall rise again in the resurrection at the last day. Jesus said unto her, *I am the resurrection, and the life:* he that believeth in me, though he were dead, yet shall he live: and whosoever liveth and believeth in me shall never die. Believest thou this? She saith unto him . . .' "

(and catching her breath as if in pain, Sonya read strongly and distinctly, exactly as if she herself were confessing it for all to hear:)

" 'Yea, Lord: I believe that thou art the Christ, the Son of God, which should come into the world.' "

She stopped, quickly raised her eyes to *him,* but mastered herself at once and began to read further. Raskolnikov sat listening motionlessly, without turning, his elbow resting on the table, his eyes looking away.

They read to the thirty-second verse.

" 'Then when Mary was come where Jesus was, and saw him, she fell down at his feet, saying unto him, Lord, if thou hadst been here, my brother had not died. When Jesus therefore saw her weeping, and the Jews also weeping which came with her, he groaned in the spirit, and was troubled, and said, Where have ye laid him? They said unto him, Lord, come and see. Jesus wept. Then said the Jews, Behold how he loved him! And some of them said, Could not this man, which opened the eyes of the blind, have caused that even this man should not have died?' "

Raskolnikov turned and looked at her anxiously: yes, that was it! She was already trembling in a real, true fever. He had expected that. She was approaching the word about the greatest, the unheard-of miracle, and a feeling of great triumph took hold of her. There was an iron ring to her voice; joy and triumph sounded in it and strengthened it. The lines became confused on the page before her, because her sight was dimmed, but she knew by heart what she was reading. At the last verse: "Could not this man, which opened the eyes of the blind . . ." she had lowered her voice, conveying ardently and passionately the doubt, reproach, and reviling of the blind, un-believing Jews, who in another moment, as if thunderstruck, would fall down, weep, and believe . . . "And *he, he* who is also blinded and unbelieving, he, too, will now hear, he, too, will believe—yes, yes! right now, this minute," she dreamed, and she was trembling with joyful expectation.

" 'Jesus therefore again groaning in himself cometh to the grave. It was a cave, and a stone lay upon it. Jesus said, Take ye away the stone.

Martha, the sister of him that was dead, saith unto him, Lord, by this time he stinketh: for he hath been dead *four* days.' "

She strongly emphasized the word *four*.

" 'Jesus saith unto her, Said I not unto thee, that, if thou wouldest believe, thou shouldest see the glory of God? Then they took away the stone from the place where the dead was laid. And Jesus lifted up his eyes, and said, Father, I thank thee that thou hast heard me. And I knew that thou hearest me always: but because of the people which stand by I said it, that they may believe that thou hast sent me. And when he thus had spoken, he cried with a loud voice, Lazarus, come forth. *And he that was dead came forth . . .* ' "

(she read loudly and rapturously, trembling and growing cold, as if she were seeing it with her own eyes:)

" '. . . bound hand and foot with graveclothes: and his face was bound about with a napkin. Jesus saith unto them, Loose him, and let him go.

" '*Then many of the Jews which came to Mary, and had seen the things which Jesus did, believed on him.*' "

Beyond that she did not and could not read; she closed the book and got up quickly from her chair.

"That's all about the raising of Lazarus," she whispered abruptly and sternly, and stood motionless, turned away, not daring and as if ashamed to raise her eyes to him. Her feverish trembling continued. The candle-end had long been burning out in the bent candlestick, casting a dim light in this destitute room upon the murderer and the harlot strangely come together over the reading of the eternal book. Five minutes or more passed.

"I came to talk about business," Raskolnikov suddenly spoke loudly, and, frowning, he rose and went to Sonya. She looked up at him silently. His face was especially stern, and some wild resolution was expressed in it.

"I left my family today," he said, "my mother and sister. I won't go to them now. I've broken with everything there."

"Why?" Sonya asked, as if stunned. Her meeting earlier with his mother and sister had left an extraordinary impression on her, though one not yet clear to herself. She heard the news of the break almost with horror.

"I have only you now," he added. "Let's go together . . . I've come to you. We're cursed together, so let's go together!"

His eyes were flashing. "He's crazy," Sonya thought in her turn.

"Go where?" she asked in fear, and involuntarily stepped back.

"How do I know? I only know that it's on the same path, I know it for certain—that's all. One goal!"

She went on looking at him, understanding nothing. She understood only that he was terribly, infinitely unhappy.

"None of them will understand anything, if you start talking with them," he continued, "but I understand. I need you, and so I've come to you."

"I don't understand . . ." Sonya whispered.

"You'll understand later . . . Haven't you done the same thing? You, too, have stepped over . . . were able to step over. You laid hands on yourself, you destroyed a life . . . *your own* (it's all the same!). You might have lived by the spirit and reason, but you'll end up on the Haymarket . . . But you can't endure it, and if you remain *alone*, you'll lose your mind, like me. You're nearly crazy already; so we must go together, on the same path! Let's go!"

"Why? Why do you say that?" Sonya said, strangely and rebelliously stirred by his words.

"Why? Because it's impossible to remain like this—that's why! It's necessary finally to reason seriously and directly, and not weep and cry like a child that God will not allow it! What if you are indeed taken to the hospital tomorrow? That woman is out of her mind and consumptive, she'll die soon, and the children? Won't Polechka be destroyed? Haven't you seen children here on the street corners, sent out by their mothers to beg? I've learned where these mothers live, and in what circumstances. Children cannot remain children there. There a seven-year-old is depraved and a thief. But children are the image of Christ: 'Theirs is the Kingdom of Heaven.'[16] He taught us to honor and love them, they are the future mankind . . ."

"But what, what can be done, then?" Sonya repeated, weeping hysterically and wringing her hands.

"What can be done? Smash what needs to be smashed, once and for all, and that's it—and take the suffering upon ourselves! What? You don't understand? You'll understand later . . . Freedom and power, but above all, power! Over all trembling creatures, over the whole ant-heap! . . . That is the goal! Remember it! This is my parting word to you! I may be talking to you for the last time. If I don't come tomorrow, you'll hear about everything yourself, and then remember these present words. And sometime later, years later, as life goes on, maybe you'll understand what they meant. But if I come tomorrow, I'll tell you who killed Lizaveta. Good-bye!"

Sonya shuddered all over with fear.

"You mean you know who killed her?" she asked, frozen in horror and looking at him wildly.

"I know and I'll tell . . . you, you alone! I've chosen you. I won't come asking forgiveness, I'll simply tell you. I chose you long ago to tell it to, back when your father was talking about you and Lizaveta was still alive, I thought of it then. Good-bye. Don't give me your hand. Tomorrow!"

He went out. Sonya looked at him as at a madman; but she herself was as if insane, and she felt it. Her head was spinning. "Lord! How does he know who killed Lizaveta? What did those words mean? It's frightening!" But at the same time *the thought* would not enter her mind. No, no, it would not! . . . "Oh, he must be terribly unhappy! . . . He's left his mother and sister. Why? What happened? And what are his intentions? What was it he had said to her? He had kissed her foot and said . . . said (yes, he had said it clearly) that he now could not live without her . . . Oh, Lord!"

Sonya spent the whole night in fever and delirium. She jumped up every now and then, wept, wrung her hands, then dropped into feverish sleep again, and dreamed of Polechka, of Katerina Ivanovna, of Lizaveta, of reading the Gospel, and of him . . . him, with his pale face, his burning eyes . . . He was kissing her feet, weeping . . . Oh, Lord!

Beyond the door to the right, the door that separated Sonya's apartment from the apartment of Gertrude Karlovna Resslich, there was an intervening room, long empty, which belonged to Mrs. Resslich's apartment and was up for rent, as signs on the gates and notices pasted to the windows facing the canal announced. Sonya had long been used to considering this room uninhabited. And meanwhile, all that time, Mr. Svidrigailov had been standing by the door in the empty room and stealthily listening. When Raskolnikov left, he stood for a while, thought, then went on tiptoe into his room, adjacent to the empty room, took a chair, and inaudibly brought it close to the door leading to Sonya's room. He had found the conversation amusing and bemusing, and he had liked it very, very much—so much that he even brought a chair, in order not to be subjected again in the future, tomorrow, for instance, to the unpleasantness of standing on his feet for a whole hour, but to settle himself more comfortably and thus treat himself to a pleasure that was full in all respects.

V

WHEN, at exactly eleven o'clock the next morning, Raskolnikov entered the building that housed the ——y police station, went to the department of the commissioner of investigations, and asked to be announced to Porfiry Petrovich, he was even surprised at how long they kept him waiting: at least ten minutes went by before he was summoned. Whereas, according to his calculations, it seemed they ought to have pounced on him at once. Meanwhile he stood in the waiting room, and people came and went who apparently were not interested in him at all. In the next room, which looked like an office, several scriveners sat writing, and it was obvious that none of them had any idea who or what Raskolnikov was. With an uneasy and mistrustful look he glanced around, trying to see if there were not at least some guard, some mysterious eyes, appointed to watch that he not go away. But there was nothing of the kind: all he saw were some pettily occupied office faces, then some other people, and none of them had any need of him: he could have gone four ways at once. A thought was becoming more and more firmly established in him: if that mysterious man yesterday, that ghost who had come from under the ground, indeed knew everything and had seen everything—would they let him, Raskolnikov, stand here like this and wait quietly? And would they have waited for him here until eleven o'clock, until he himself saw fit to come? It followed that the man either had not denounced him yet, or . . . or simply did not know anything, had not seen anything himself, with his own eyes (and how could he have?), and, consequently, the whole thing that he, Raskolnikov, had gone through yesterday was again a phantom, exaggerated by his troubled and sick imagination. This surmise had begun to strengthen in him even yesterday, during the most intense anxiety and despair. As he thought it all over now and made ready for a new battle, he suddenly felt himself trembling—and indignation even boiled up in him at the thought that he was trembling with fear before the hateful Porfiry Petrovich. It was most terrible for him to meet this man again; he hated him beyond measure, infinitely, and was even afraid of somehow giving himself away by his hatred. And so strong was this indignation that it immediately stopped his trembling; he made ready to go in with a cold and insolent air, and vowed to be silent as much as possible, to look and listen attentively, and, if only this once at least, to overcome his morbidly irritated nature, cost what it might. Just then he was called in to see Porfiry Petrovich.

It turned out that Porfiry Petrovich was alone in his office at the moment. His office was a room neither large nor small; in it stood a big writing desk in front of a sofa upholstered in oilcloth, a bureau, a cabinet in the corner, and a few chairs—all institutional furniture, of yellow polished wood. In the corner of the back wall—or, better, partition—was a closed door; beyond it, behind the partition, there must consequently have been other rooms. When Raskolnikov came in, Porfiry Petrovich immediately closed the door through which he had come, and they remained alone. He met his visitor with an apparently quite cheerful and affable air, and only several minutes later did Raskolnikov notice in him the signs of something like embarrassment—as if he had suddenly been put out, or caught doing something very solitary and secretive.

"Ah, my esteemed sir! Here you are . . . in our parts . . ." Porfiry began, reaching out both hands to him. "Well, do sit down, my dear! Or perhaps you don't like being called esteemed and . . . dear—so, *tout court?*[17] Please don't regard it as familiarity . . . Over here, sir, on the sofa."

Raskolnikov sat down without taking his eyes off him.

"In our parts," the apology for being familiar, the French phrase *"tout court,"* and so on—these were all typical signs. "He reached out both hands to me, and yet he didn't give me either, he drew them back in time," flashed in him suspiciously. Each of them was watching the other, but as soon as their eyes met, quick as lightning they would look away.

"I've brought you this little paper . . . about the watch . . . here, sir. Is that all right, or shall I copy it over?"

"What? A little paper? Right, right . . . don't worry, it's quite all right, sir," Porfiry Petrovich said, as if he were hurrying somewhere, and after saying it, he took the paper and looked it over. "Quite all right, sir. Nothing more is needed," he confirmed in the same patter, and put the paper on the desk. Then, a minute later, already speaking of something else, he took it up again and put it on the bureau.

"You seemed to be saying yesterday that you wished to ask me . . . formally . . . about my acquaintance with this . . . murdered woman?" Raskolnikov tried to begin again. "Why did I put in that *seemed?*" flashed in him like lightning. "And why am I so worried about having put in that *seemed?*" a second thought immediately flashed in him like lightning.

And he suddenly felt that his insecurity, from the mere contact with Porfiry, from two words only, from two glances only, had bushed out to monstrous proportions in a moment . . . and that it was terribly dangerous—frayed nerves, mounting agitation. "It's bad! It's bad! . . . I'll betray myself again."

"Yes, yes, yes! Don't worry! It will keep, it will keep, sir," Porfiry Petrovich muttered, moving back and forth by the desk, but somehow aimlessly, as if darting now to the window, now to the bureau, then back to the desk, first avoiding Raskolnikov's suspicious eyes, then suddenly stopping dead and staring point-blank at him. His plump, round little figure gave it all an extremely strange effect, like a ball rolling in different directions and bouncing off all the walls and corners.

"We'll have time, sir, we'll have time! . . . Do you smoke, by chance? Have you got your own? Here, sir, take a cigarette . . ." he continued, offering his visitor a cigarette. "You know, I'm receiving you here, but my apartment is right there, behind the partition . . . government quarters, sir, but just now I'm renting another for a while. They've been doing a bit of renovating here. It's almost ready now . . . a government apartment is a fine thing, eh? What do you think?"

"Yes, a fine thing," Raskolnikov answered, looking at him almost mockingly.

"A fine thing, a fine thing . . ." Porfiry Petrovich kept repeating, as if he had suddenly begun thinking of something quite different; "yes, a fine thing!" he all but shouted in the end, suddenly fixing his eyes on Raskolnikov and stopping two steps away from him. This silly, multiple repetition that a government apartment is a fine thing was too contradictory, in its triteness, to the serious, reflective, and enigmatic look that he now directed at his visitor.

But this only made Raskolnikov's anger boil the more, and he was no longer able to refrain from making a mocking and rather imprudent challenge.

"You know what," he suddenly asked, looking at him almost insolently, and as if enjoying his own insolence, "it seems there exists a certain legal rule, a certain legal technique—for all possible investigators—to begin from afar at first, with little trifles, or even with something serious but quite unrelated, in order to encourage, so to speak, or, better, to divert the person being interrogated, to lull his prudence, and then suddenly, in the most unexpected way, to stun him right on the head with the most fatal and dangerous question—is it so? I suppose it's mentioned religiously to this day in all the rule books and manuals?"

"Well, well . . . so you think I've been using this government apartment to get you to . . . eh?" And having said this, Porfiry Petrovich squinted, winked; something merry and sly ran across his face, the little wrinkles on his forehead smoothed out, his little eyes narrowed, his features stretched out, and he suddenly dissolved into prolonged, nervous laughter, heaving and swaying with his whole body, and looking straight into Raskolnikov's eyes. The latter began to laugh himself, somewhat forcedly; but when Porfiry, seeing that he was also laughing, went off into such gales of laughter that he almost turned purple, Raskolnikov's loathing suddenly went beyond all prudence; he stopped laughing, frowned, and stared at Porfiry long and hatefully, not taking his eyes off him during this whole long and as if deliberately unceasing fit of laughter. The imprudence, however, was obvious on both sides: it appeared that Porfiry Petrovich was laughing in the face of his visitor, who was meeting his laughter with hatred, and that he was hardly embarrassed by this circumstance. Raskolnikov found the last fact very portentous: he realized that Porfiry Petrovich had certainly also not been at all embarrassed earlier, but on the contrary, that he himself, Raskolnikov, had perhaps stepped into a trap; that evidently there was something here that he was unaware of, some goal; that everything was perhaps prepared already, and now, this minute, would be revealed and come crashing down . . .

He went straight to the point at once, rose from his place, and took his cap.

"Porfiry Petrovich," he began resolutely, but with rather strong irritation, "yesterday you expressed a wish that I come for some sort of interrogations" (he put special emphasis on the word *interrogations*). "I have come. If there is anything you need to ask, ask it; if not, allow me to withdraw. I have no time, I have things to do . . . I have to be at the funeral of that official who was run over, about whom . . . you also know . . ." he added, and at once became angry for having added it, and therefore at once became more irritated. "I am quite sick of it all, sir, do you hear? And have been for a long time . . . that is partly what made me ill . . . In short," he almost shouted, feeling that the phrase about his illness was even more inappropriate, "in short, kindly either ask your questions or let me go, right now . . . and if you ask, do so not otherwise than according to form, sir! I will not allow it otherwise; and so, good-bye for now, since there's nothing for the two of us to do here."

"Lord! What is it? What is there to ask?" Porfiry Petrovich suddenly began clucking, immediately changing his tone and aspect, and instantly ceasing to laugh. "Don't worry, please," he fussed, again rushing in all directions, then suddenly trying to sit Raskolnikov down, "it will keep, it will keep, sir, and it's all just trifles, sir! I am, on the contrary, so glad that you have finally come to us . . . I am receiving you as a guest. And excuse me, dear Rodion Romanovich, for this cursed laughter. Rodion Romanovich—is that right? . . . I'm a nervous man, sir, and you made me laugh by the wittiness of your remark; sometimes, really, I start shaking like a piece of gum rubber and can't stop for half an hour . . . I laugh easily, sir. With my constitution I'm even afraid of a stroke. But do sit down, won't you? . . . Please, my dear, or I'll think you're angry . . ."

Raskolnikov kept silent, listened, and watched, still frowning wrathfully. He sat down nonetheless, but without letting the cap out of his hands.

"I'll tell you one thing about myself, dear Rodion Romanovich, in explanation of my personal characteristics, so to speak," Porfiry Petrovich went on, fussing about the room, and, as before, seeming to avoid meeting his visitor's eyes. "I am, you know, a bachelor, an unworldly and unknowing man, and, moreover, a finished man, a frozen man, sir, gone to seed, and . . . and . . . and have you noticed, Rodion Romanovich, that among us—that is, in our Russia, sir, and most of all in our Petersburg circles—if two intelligent men get together, not very well acquainted yet, but, so to speak, mutually respecting each other, just like you and me now, sir, it will take them a whole half hour to find a topic of conversation—they freeze before each other, they sit feeling mutually embarrassed. Everybody has topics for discussion—ladies, for instance . . . worldly men, for instance, of a higher tone, always have a topic for discussion, *c'est de rigueur*[18]—but people of the neuter kind, like us, are all easily embarrassed and have trouble talking . . . the thinking ones, I mean. Why do you suppose that is, my dear? Do we have no social interests, or is it that we're too honest and don't want to deceive each other, I don't know. Eh? What do you think? And do put your cap aside, sir, it's as if you were just about to leave, really, it's awkward looking at you . . . On the contrary, I'm so glad, sir . . ."

Raskolnikov put down the cap, but remained silent and went on listening seriously and frowningly to Porfiry's empty and inconsistent babble. "What is he trying to do, divert my attention with his silly babble, or what?"

"I won't offer you coffee, sir, this is no place for it; but why shouldn't one sit down for five little minutes with a friend, as a diversion," Porfiry continued in a steady stream, "and you know, sir, all these official duties . . . you won't be offended, my dear, that I keep pacing back and forth like this; excuse me, my dear, I'm so afraid of offending you, but it's simply necessary for me to move, sir. I sit all the time, and I'm so glad to be able to walk around for five minutes or so . . . hemorrhoids, sir . . . I keep thinking of trying gymnastics as a treatment; they say there are state councillors, senior state councillors, even privy councillors, happily skipping rope, sir; that's how it is, this science, in our age, sir . . . yes, sir . . . But concerning these duties here, interrogations, and all these formalities . . . now you, my dear, were just so good as to mention interrogations yourself . . . and you know, really, my dear Rodion Romanovich, these interrogations frequently throw off the interrogator himself more than the one who is being interrogated . . . As you, my dear, so justly and wittily remarked a moment ago." (Raskolnikov had made no such remark.) "One gets mixed up, sir! Really mixed up! And it's all the same thing, all the same thing, like a drum! Now that the reform is coming, they'll at least change our title, heh, heh, heh![19] And concerning our legal techniques—as you were pleased to put it so wittily—there I agree with you completely, sir. Tell me, really, who among all the accused, even the most cloddish peasant, doesn't know, for instance, that they will first lull him with unrelated questions (to use your happy expression) and then suddenly stun him right on the head, with an axe, sir—heh, heh, heh!—right on the head, to use your happy comparison, heh, heh! So you really thought I was talking about this apartment to make you . . . heh, heh! Aren't you an ironical man. Very well, I'll stop! Ah, yes, incidentally, one word calls up another, one thought evokes another— now, you were just pleased to mention form, with regard to a bit of interrogating, that is . . . But what is it about form? You know, sir, in many cases form is nonsense. Oftentimes one may just have a friendly talk, and it's far more advantageous. Form won't run away, allow me to reassure you on that score, sir; but, I ask you, what is form essentially? One cannot bind the investigator with form at every step. The investigator's business is, so to speak, a free art, in its own way, or something like that . . . heh, heh, heh!"

Porfiry Petrovich paused for a moment to catch his breath. The talk was simply pouring out of him, now in senselessly empty phrases, then suddenly letting in some enigmatic little words, and immediately going off into senselessness again. He was almost running back and forth now, moving his fat little legs quicker and quicker, looking down all the time, with his right hand behind his back and his left hand constantly waving and performing various gestures, each time remarkably unsuited to his words. Raskolnikov suddenly noticed that as he was running back and forth he twice seemed almost to pause for a moment by the door, as if he were listening . . . "Is he waiting for something, or what?"

"And you really are entirely right, sir," Porfiry picked up again, looking at Raskolnikov merrily and with remarkable simple-hearted-ness (which startled him and put him on his guard at once), "really, you're right, sir, in choosing to laugh so wittily at our legal forms, heh, heh! Because these profoundly psychological techniques of ours (some of them, naturally) are extremely funny, and perhaps even useless, sir, when they're too bound up with form. Yes, sir . . . I'm talking about form again: well, if I were to regard, or, better, to suspect this, that, or the other person of being a criminal, sir, in some little case entrusted to me . . . You're preparing to be a lawyer, are you not, Rodion Romanovich?"

"Yes, I was . . ."

"Well, then, here you have a little example, so to speak, for the future—I mean, don't think I'd be so bold as to teach you, you who publish such articles on crime! No, sir, but I'll be so bold as to offer you a little example, simply as a fact—so, if I were to regard, for example, this, that, or the other person as a criminal, why, I ask you, should I trouble him before the time comes, even if I have evidence against him, sir? There may be a man, for example, whom it is my duty to arrest quickly, but another man may have a different character, really, sir; and why shouldn't I let him walk around town, heh, heh, sir! No, I can see you don't quite understand, so let me present it to you more clearly, sir: if I were to lock him up too soon, for example, I might thereby be lending him, so to speak, moral support, heh, heh! You laugh?" (Raskolnikov had not even thought of laughing; he was sitting with compressed lips, not taking his feverish gaze from the eyes of Porfiry Petrovich.) "And yet it really is so, sir, particularly with some specimens, because people are multifarious, sir, and there is one practice over all. Now, you were just pleased to mention evidence; well, suppose there is evidence, sir, but evidence, my dear, is mostly double-ended, and I am an investigator and therefore, I confess, a weak man: I would like to present my investigation with, so to speak, mathe-matical clarity; I would like to get hold of a piece of evidence that's something like two times two is four! Something like direct and indis-putable proof! But if I were to lock him up at the wrong time—even

though I'm sure it was *him*—I might well deprive myself of the means
for his further incrimination. Why? Because I would be giving him,
so to speak, a definite position; I would be, so to speak, defining him
and reassuring him psychologically, so that he would be able to hide
from me in his shell: he would understand finally that he is under
arrest. They say that in Sebastopol, right after Alma, intelligent people
were oh so afraid that the enemy might attack any moment in full force
and take Sebastopol at once; but when they saw that the enemy preferred a regular siege and was digging the first parallel, the intelligent
people were ever so glad and reassured, sir: it meant the thing would
drag on for at least two months, because who knew when they'd
manage to take it by regular siege![20] Again you laugh? Again you don't
believe me? And right you are, of course. You are, sir, yes, you are!
These are all particular cases, I agree; the case in point is indeed a
particular one, sir! But at the same time, my good Rodion Romanovich, it must be observed that the general case, the one to which all
legal forms and rules are suited, and on the basis of which they are all
worked out and written down in the books, simply does not exist, for
the very reason that every case, let's say, for instance, every crime, as
soon as it actually occurs, turns at once into a completely particular
case, sir; and sometimes, just think, really completely unlike all the
previous ones, sir. The most comical occurrences sometimes occur this
way, sir. But if I were to leave some gentleman quite alone, not bring
him in or bother him, but so that he knows every hour and every
minute, or at least suspects, that I know everything, all his innermost
secrets, and am watching him day and night, following him vigilantly,
if I were to keep him consciously under eternal suspicion and fear,
then, by God, he might really get into a whirl, sir, he might come
himself and do something that would be like two times two, so to
speak, something with a mathematical look to it—which is quite agreeable, sir. It can happen even with a lumpish peasant, and all the more
so with our sort, the contemporarily intelligent man, and developed in
a certain direction to boot! Because, my dear, it's quite an important
thing to understand in which direction a man is developed. And
nerves, sir, nerves—you've forgotten about them, sir! Because all of
that is so sick, and bad, and irritated nowadays! . . . And there's so much
bile, so much bile in them all! I'll tell you, it's a sort of gold mine on

occasion, sir! And why should I worry that he's walking around town unfettered! Let him, let him walk around meanwhile, let him; I know all the same that he's my dear little victim and that he won't run away from me! Where is he going to run to, heh, heh! Abroad? A Pole would run abroad, but not *him,* especially since I'm watching and have taken measures. Is he going to flee to the depths of the country? But only peasants live there—real, cloddish, Russian peasants; now, a contemporarily developed man would sooner go to prison than live with such foreigners as our good peasants, heh, heh! But that's all nonsense, all external. What is it, to run away! A mere formality; that's not the main thing; no, he won't run away from me, not just because he has nowhere to run to: *psychologically* he won't run away on me, heh, heh! A nice little phrase! He won't run away on me by a law of nature, even if he has somewhere to run to. Have you ever seen a moth near a candle? Well, so he'll keep circling around me, circling around me, as around a candle; freedom will no longer be dear to him, he'll fall to thinking, get entangled, he'll tangle himself all up as in a net, he'll worry himself to death! . . . What's more, he himself will prepare some sort of mathematical trick for me, something like two times two—if I merely allow him a slightly longer intermission . . . And he'll keep on, he'll keep on making circles around me, narrowing the radius more and more, and—whop! He'll fly right into my mouth, and I'll swallow him, sir, and that will be most agreeable, heh, heh, heh! You don't believe me?"

Raskolnikov did not reply; he was sitting pale and motionless, peering with the same strained attention into Porfiry's face.

"A good lesson!" he thought, turning cold. "This isn't even like cat and mouse anymore, as it was yesterday. And it's not for something so useless as to make a show of his strength and . . . let me know it: he's more intelligent than that! There's some other goal here, but what? Eh, it's nonsense, brother, this dodging and trying to scare me! You have no proofs, and that man yesterday doesn't exist! You simply want to throw me off, to irritate me beforehand, and when I'm irritated, whop me—only it's all lies, you won't pull it off, you won't! But why, why let me know so much? . . . Are we counting on bad nerves, or what? . . . No, brother, it's all lies, you won't pull it off, whatever it is you've got prepared . . . Well, we shall see what you've got prepared."

And he braced himself with all his strength, preparing for the terrible and unknown catastrophe. At times he wanted to hurl himself at Porfiry and strangle him on the spot. He had been afraid of this anger from the moment he entered. He was aware that his lips were dry, his heart was pounding, there was foam caked on his lips. But he was still determined to be silent and not say a word until the time came. He realized that this was the best tactic in his position, because he not only would not give anything away, but, on the contrary, would exasperate the enemy with his silence, and perhaps make him give something away himself. At least he hoped for that.

"No, I see you don't believe me, sir; you keep thinking I'm just coming out with harmless jokes," Porfiry picked up, getting merrier and merrier, ceaselessly chuckling with pleasure, and beginning to circle the room again, "and of course you're right, sir; even my figure has been so arranged by God Himself that it evokes only comic thoughts in others; a buffoon, sir; but what I shall tell you, and repeat again, sir, is that you, my dear Rodion Romanovich—you'll excuse an old man—you are still young, sir, in your first youth, so to speak, and therefore you place the most value on human intelligence, following the example of all young men. A playful sharpness of wit and the abstract arguments of reason are what seduce you, sir. Which is exactly like the former Austrian *Hofkriegsrat,* for example, insofar, that is, as I am able to judge of military events: on paper they had Napoleon crushed and taken prisoner, it was all worked out and arranged in the cleverest manner in their study, and then, lo and behold, General Mack surrenders with his entire army, heh, heh, heh![21] I see, I see, Rodion Romanovich, my dear, you're laughing that such a civilian as I should keep picking little examples from military history. A weakness, I can't help it, I love the military profession, and I do so love reading all these military accounts . . . I've decidedly missed my career. I should be serving in the military, really, sir. I might not have become a Napoleon, perhaps, but I'd be a major at least, heh, heh, heh! Well, my dearest, now I'll tell you the whole detailed truth—about that *particular case,* I mean: reality and human nature, sir, are very important things, and oh how they sometimes bring down the most perspicacious calculations! Eh, listen to an old man, I say it seriously, Rodion Romanovich" (as he spoke, the barely thirty-five-year-old Porfiry Petrovich indeed seemed to grow old all at once; his voice even changed, and he became all hunched over); "besides, I'm a sincere man, sir . . . Am I a sincere man, or am I not? What do you think? I'd say I'm completely sincere: I'm telling you all this gratis, and ask no reward for it, heh, heh! Well, sir, to go on: wit, in my opinion, is a splendid thing, sir; it is, so to speak, an adornment of nature and a consolation of life; and what tricks it can perform, it seems, so that some poor little investigator is hard put to figure them out, it seems, since he also gets carried away by his own fantasy, as always happens, because he, too, is a man, sir! But it's human nature that helps the poor investigator out, sir, that's the trouble! And that is what doesn't occur to the young people, carried away by their own wit, 'stepping over all obstacles' (as you were pleased to put it in a most witty and cunning way). Suppose he lies—our man, I mean, *this particular case*, sir, this incognito—and lies splendidly, in the most cunning way; here, it seems, is a triumph; go and enjoy the fruits of your wit; but then—whop! he faints, in the most interesting, the most scandalous place. Suppose he's ill, and the room also happens to be stuffy, but even so, sir! Even so, it makes one think! He lied incomparably, but he failed to reckon on his nature. There's the perfidy, sir! Another time, carried away by the playfulness of his wit, he starts making a fool of a man who suspects him, and turns pale as if on purpose, as if in play, but he turns pale *too naturally*, it's too much like the truth, so again it makes one think! He might hoodwink him to begin with, but overnight the man will reconsider, if he's nobody's fool. And so it is at every step, sir! And that's not all: he himself starts running ahead, poking his nose where no one has asked him, starting conversations about things of which he ought, on the contrary, to keep silent, slipping in various allegories, heh, heh! He'll come himself and start asking why he wasn't arrested long ago, heh, heh, heh! And it can happen with the wittiest man, a psychologist and a writer, sir! Human nature is a mirror, sir, the clearest mirror! Look and admire—there you have it, sir! But why are you so pale, Rodion Romanovich? Is there not enough air? Shall I open the window?"

"Oh, don't bother, please," Raskolnikov cried, and suddenly burst out laughing, "please don't bother!"

Porfiry stood in front of him, waited, and suddenly burst out laughing himself. Raskolnikov rose from the sofa, suddenly putting an abrupt stop to his completely hysterical laughter.

"Porfiry Petrovich!" he said loudly and distinctly, though he could barely stand on his trembling legs, "at last I see clearly that you do definitely suspect me of murdering that old woman and her sister Lizaveta. For my own part I declare to you that I have long been sick of it all. If you believe you have the right to prosecute me legally, then prosecute me; or to arrest me, then arrest me. But to torment me and laugh in my face, that I will not allow!"

His lips trembled all at once, his eyes lit up with fury, and his hitherto restrained voice rang out:

"I will not allow it, sir!" he suddenly shouted, banging his fist on the table with all his might. "Do you hear, Porfiry Petrovich? I will not allow it!"

"Ah, Lord, what's this now!" Porfiry Petrovich exclaimed, looking thoroughly frightened. "My good Rodion Romanovich! My heart and soul! My dearest! What's the matter!"

"I will not allow it!" Raskolnikov shouted once more.

"Not so loud, my dear! People will hear you, they'll come running! And what shall we tell them? Only think!" Porfiry Petrovich whispered in horror, bringing his face very close to Raskolnikov's face.

"I will not allow it, I will not allow it!" Raskolnikov repeated mechanically, but suddenly also in a complete whisper.

Porfiry quickly turned and ran to open the window.

"To let in some air, some fresh air! And do drink some water, my dear; this is a fit, sir!" And he rushed to the door to send for water, but there turned out to be a carafe of water right there in the corner.

"Drink, my dear," he whispered, rushing to him with the carafe, "maybe it will help . . ." Porfiry Petrovich's alarm and his sympathy itself were so natural that Raskolnikov fell silent and began to stare at him with wild curiosity. He did not accept the water, however.

"Rodion Romanovich, my dear! but you'll drive yourself out of your mind this way, I assure you, a-ah! Do drink! A little sip, at least!"

He succeeded after all in making him take the glass of water in his hands. Raskolnikov mechanically brought it to his lips, but then, recollecting himself, set it on the table with loathing.

"Yes, sir, a fit, that's what we've just had, sir! Go on this way, my dear, and you'll have your former illness back," Porfiry Petrovich began clucking in friendly sympathy, though he still looked somewhat at a loss. "Lord! How is it you take no care of yourself at all? Then, too, Dmitri Prokofych came to see me yesterday—I agree, I agree, I have a caustic nature, a nasty one, but look what he deduced from it! . . . Lord! He came yesterday, after you, we were having dinner, he talked and talked, I just threw up my hands; well, I thought . . . ah, my Lord! Don't tell me you sent him! But sit down, my dear, do sit down, for Christ's sake!"

"No, I didn't send him. But I knew he went to you and why he went," Raskolnikov replied sharply.

"You knew?"

"Yes. What of it?"

"Here's what, my dear Rodion Romanovich—that this is not all I know about your exploits; I've been informed of everything, sir! I know about how you went *to rent the apartment,* just at nightfall, when it was getting dark, and began ringing the bell and asking about blood, which left the workmen and caretakers perplexed. I quite understand what state you were in at the time . . . but even so, you'll simply drive yourself out of your mind this way, by God! You'll get yourself into a whirl! You're boiling too much with indignation, sir, with noble indignation, sir, at being wronged first by fate and then by the police, and so you rush here and there, trying, so to speak, to make everyone talk the sooner and thus put an end to it all at once, because you're sick of these stupidities and all these suspicions. Isn't that so? I've guessed your mood, haven't I? . . . Only this way it's not just yourself but also Razumikhin that you'll get into a whirl on me; because he's too *kind* a man for this, you know it yourself. You are ill, but he is a virtuous man, and so the illness is catching for him . . . I'll explain, my dear, when you're calmer . . . but do sit down, for Christ's sake! Please rest, you look awful; do sit down."

Raskolnikov sat down; his trembling was going away and he was beginning to feel hot all over. In deep amazement, tensely, he listened to the alarmed and amiably solicitous Porfiry Petrovich. But he did not believe a word he said, though he felt some strange inclination to believe. Porfiry's unexpected words about the apartment thoroughly struck him. "So he knows about the apartment, but how?" suddenly crossed his mind. "And he tells it to me himself!"

"Yes, sir, we had a case almost exactly like that in our legal practice, a psychological case, a morbid one, sir," Porfiry went on pattering. "There was a man who also slapped a murder on himself, sir, and how he did it! He came out with a whole hallucination, presented facts, described circumstances, confused and bewildered us one and all—and why? Quite unintentionally, he himself had been partly the cause of the murder, but only partly, and when he learned that he had given a pretext to the murderers, he became anguished, stupefied, began imagining things, went quite off his head, and convinced himself that he was the murderer! But the governing Senate finally examined the case and the unfortunate man was acquitted and put under proper care. Thanks to the governing Senate! Ah, well, tsk, tsk, tsk! So, what then, my dear? This way you may get yourself into a delirium, if you have such urges to irritate your nerves, going around at night ringing doorbells and asking about blood! I've studied all this psychology in practice, sir. Sometimes it can drive a man to jump out the window or off a bell-tower, and it's such a tempting sensation, sir. The same with doorbells, sir . . . An illness, Rodion Romanovich, an illness! You've been neglecting your illness too much, sir. You ought to get the advice of an experienced physician—what use is this fat fellow of yours! . . . You're delirious! You're doing all this simply and solely in delirium! . . ."

For a moment everything started whirling around Raskolnikov.

"Can it be, can it be," flashed in him, "that he's lying even now? Impossible, impossible!" He pushed the thought away from him, sensing beforehand to what degree of rage and fury it might lead him, sensing that he might lose his mind from rage.

"It was not in delirium, it was in reality!" he cried out, straining all the powers of his reason to penetrate Porfiry's game. "In reality, in reality! Do you hear?"

"Yes, I understand, and I hear, sir! Yesterday, too, you said it was not in delirium, you even especially stressed that it was not in delirium!

Everything you can say, I understand, sir! Ahh! . . . But Rodion Romanovich, my good man, at least listen to the following circumstances. If you were indeed a criminal in reality, or somehow mixed up in this cursed case, well, for heaven's sake, would you yourself stress that you were doing it all not in delirium but, on the contrary, in full consciousness? And stress it especially, stress it with such special obstinacy—now, could that be, could it be, for heaven's sake? Quite the opposite, I should think. Because if there really was anything to it, you would be bound precisely to stress that it was certainly done in delirium! Right? Am I right?"

Something sly could be heard in the question. Raskolnikov drew all the way back on the sofa, away from Porfiry, who was leaning towards him, and stared at him silently, point-blank, in bewilderment.

"Or else, to do with Mr. Razumikhin—to do, that is, with whether he came to talk yesterday on his own or at your instigation—you ought precisely to have said that he came on his own, and to have concealed that it was at your instigation! But you're not concealing it! You precisely stress that it was at your instigation!"

Raskolnikov had done no such thing. A chill ran down his spine.

"You keep lying," he said slowly and weakly, his lips twisted into a pained smile. "You want to show me again that you know my whole game, that you know all my answers beforehand," he said, himself almost aware that he was no longer weighing his words as he should. "You want to bully me . . . or else you're simply laughing at me. . . ."

He continued to stare at him point-blank as he said this, and suddenly a boundless anger again flashed in his eyes.

"You keep lying!" he cried out. "You know perfectly well that the criminal's best dodge is to conceal as little as possible of what need not be concealed. I don't believe you!"

"You're quite a dodger yourself!" Porfiry tittered. "There's just no getting along with you, my dear; you've got some monomania sitting in you. So you don't believe me? But I shall tell you that you do in fact believe me, you've already believed me for a foot, and I'm going to get you to believe me for a whole yard, because I'm genuinely fond of you and sincerely wish you well."

Raskolnikov's lips trembled.

"Yes, I do, sir, and I'll tell you one last thing, sir," he went on, taking Raskolnikov lightly and amiably by the arm, a little above the elbow, "I'll tell you one last thing, sir: watch out for your illness. Besides, your family has now come to you; give a thought to them. You ought to soothe them and pamper them, and all you do is frighten them . . ."

"What's that to you? How do you know it? Why are you so interested? It means you're spying on me and want me to see it?"

"But, my dear, I learned it all from you, from you yourself! You don't even notice that in your excitement you're the first one to tell everything, both to me and to others. I also learned many interesting details yesterday from Mr. Razumikhin, Dmitri Prokofych. No, sir, you interrupted me just now, but I shall tell you that, for all your wit, your insecurity has made you lose a sober view of things. Here's an example, on that same theme, to do with the doorbells: I let you have such a precious thing, such a fact (it is a complete fact, sir!), just like that, lock, stock, and barrel—I, an investigator! And you see nothing in it? But, if I had even the slightest suspicion of you, is that how I ought to have acted? On the contrary, I ought first to have lulled your suspicions, giving no sign that I was already informed of this fact; to have thus diverted you in the opposite direction; and then suddenly to have stunned you on the head as with an axe (to use your own expression): 'And what, sir, were you pleased to be doing in the murdered woman's apartment at ten o'clock in the evening, or even almost eleven? And why were you ringing the bell? And why did you ask about the blood? And why did you bewilder the caretakers and incite them to go to the police station, to the lieutenant of the precinct?' That's how I ought to have acted, if I had even the slightest suspicion of you. I ought to have taken your evidence in accordance with all the forms, made a search, and perhaps have arrested you as well . . . Since I have acted otherwise, it follows that I have no suspicions of you! But you've lost a sober view and don't see anything, I repeat, sir!"

Raskolnikov shuddered all over, so that Porfiry Petrovich noticed it only too clearly.

"You're lying still!" he cried. "I don't know what your purposes are, but you keep lying . . . You talked in a different sense a moment ago, and I'm surely not mistaken . . . You're lying!"

"Lying, am I?" Porfiry picked up, obviously excited, but preserving

a most merry and mocking look, and seeming not in the least concerned with Mr. Raskolnikov's opinion of him. "Lying, am I? . . . Well,
and how did I act with you just now (I, an investigator), prompting
you and letting you in on all the means of defense, and coming out
with all this psychology for you myself: 'Illness, delirium, you felt all
offended; melancholy, policemen,' and all the rest of it? Eh? Heh, heh,
heh! Though, by the way—incidentally speaking—all these psychological means of defense, these excuses and dodges, are quite untenable,
and double-ended besides: 'Illness, delirium, dreams,' they say, 'I imagined it, I don't remember'—maybe so, but why is it, my dear, that in
one's illness and delirium one imagines precisely these dreams, and not
others? One might have had others, sir? Right? Heh, heh, heh, heh!"

Raskolnikov looked at him proudly and disdainfully.

"In short," he said, loudly and insistently, getting up and pushing
Porfiry a little aside, "in short, I want to know: do you acknowledge
me to be finally free of suspicion, or *not?* Speak, Porfiry Petrovich,
speak positively and finally, and right now, quickly!"

"What an assignment! Ah, you're a real assignment!" Porfiry exclaimed, with a perfectly merry, sly, and not in the least worried look.
"But why do you want to know, why do you want to know so much,
when we haven't even begun to bother you in the least! You're like
a child: just let me touch the fire! And why do you worry so much?
Why do you thrust yourself upon us, for what reason? Eh? Heh, heh,
heh!"

"I repeat," Raskolnikov cried furiously, "that I can no longer
endure . . ."

"What, sir? The uncertainty?" Porfiry interrupted.

"Don't taunt me! I won't have it! . . . I tell you, I won't have
it! . . . I cannot and I will not have it! . . . Do you hear! Do you hear!"
he cried, banging his fist on the table again.

"Quiet, quiet! They'll hear you! I warn you seriously: look out for
yourself. I'm not joking, sir!" Porfiry said in a whisper, but in his face
this time there was nothing of that earlier womanish, good-natured,
and alarmed expression; on the contrary, now he was *ordering* outright, sternly, frowning, and as if suddenly breaking through all secrets
and ambiguities. But only for a moment. Puzzled at first, Raskolnikov
suddenly flew into a real frenzy; but, strangely, he again obeyed the

order to speak more softly, though he was in the most violent paroxysm of rage.

"I will not allow you to torture me!" he began whispering, as before, realizing immediately, with pain and hatred, that he was unable to disobey the order, and getting into even more of a rage at the thought of it. "Arrest me, search me, but be so good as to act according to form and not to toy with me, sir! Do not dare . . ."

"Now, don't go worrying about form," Porfiry interrupted, with his usual sly smile, and as if even delightedly admiring Raskolnikov. "I invited you here unofficially, my dear, only as a friend!"

"I don't want your friendship, and I spit on it! Do you hear? Now look: I'm taking my cap and leaving. What are you going to say to that, if you were intending to arrest me?"

He seized his cap and walked to the door.

"But don't you want to see my little surprise?" Porfiry tittered, seizing his arm again just above the elbow, and stopping him at the door. He was obviously becoming more and more merry and playful, which was finally driving Raskolnikov into a fury.

"What little surprise? What is it?" he asked, suddenly stopping and looking at Porfiry in fear.

"A little surprise, sir, sitting there behind my door, heh, heh, heh!" (He pointed his finger at the closed door in the partition, which led to his government apartment.) "I even locked it in so that it wouldn't run away."

"What is it? Where? What? . . ." Raskolnikov went over to the door and tried to open it, but it was locked.

"It's locked, sir, and here is the key!"

And indeed he showed him the key, having taken it from his pocket.

"You're still lying!" Raskolnikov screamed, no longer restraining himself. "You're lying, you damned punchinello!" And he rushed at Porfiry, who retreated towards the door, but was not at all afraid.

"I understand everything, everything!" he leaped close to him. "You're lying and taunting me so that I'll give myself away . . ."

"But one could hardly give oneself away any more, my dear Rodion Romanovich. You're beside yourself. Don't shout, I really will call people, sir!"

"Lies! You've got nothing! Call your people! You knew I was sick and wanted to annoy me to the point of rage, to get me to give myself away, that was your purpose! No, show me your facts! I understand everything! You have no facts, all you have are just miserable, worthless guesses, Zamyotovian guesses! . . . You knew my character, you wanted to drive me into a frenzy and then suddenly stun me with priests and deputies . . . Is it them you're waiting for? Eh? What are you waiting for? Where? Let's have it!"

"But what deputies could there be, my dear! You have quite an imagination! This way one can't even go by form, as you say; you don't know the procedure, my friend . . . But form won't run away, sir, as you'll see for yourself! . . ." Porfiry muttered, with an ear towards the door.

Indeed, at that moment there seemed to be some noise just behind the door to the other room.

"Ah, they're coming!" cried Raskolnikov. "You sent for them! . . . You've been waiting for them! You calculated . . . Well, let's have them all here—deputies, witnesses, whatever you like . . . go on! I'm ready! Ready! . . ."

But here a strange incident occurred, something so unexpected, in the ordinary course of things, that certainly neither Raskolnikov nor Porfiry Petrovich could have reckoned on such a denouement.

VI

AFTERWARDS, remembering this moment, Raskolnikov pictured it all in the following way.

The noise from behind the door quickly increased all at once, and the door opened a little.

"What is it?" Porfiry Petrovich exclaimed in annoyance. "Didn't I warn you . . ."

No answer came for a moment, but one could see that several people were outside the door, and that someone was apparently being pushed aside.

"What is it in there?" Porfiry Petrovich repeated worriedly.

"We've brought the prisoner Nikolai," someone's voice was heard.

"No! Away! Not now! . . . How did he get here? What is this disorder?" Porfiry cried, rushing to the door.

"But he . . ." the same voice tried to begin again and suddenly stopped short.

For two seconds, not more, a real struggle took place; then it was as if someone suddenly pushed someone violently aside, after which a certain very pale man stepped straight into Porfiry Petrovich's office.

The man's appearance, at first sight, was very strange. He was staring straight ahead of him, but as if seeing no one. Determination flashed in his eyes, but at the same time there was a deathly pallor on his face, as though he were being led out to execution. His completely white lips quivered slightly.

He was still very young, dressed as a commoner, of average height, lean, with his hair cut like a bowl, and with gaunt, dry-looking features. The man he had unexpectedly pushed aside was the first to dash into the room after him, and managed to seize him by the shoulder: it was one of the guards; but Nikolai jerked his arm and tore himself free again.

A crowd of several curious onlookers formed in the doorway. Some of them made attempts to enter. Everything described here took place in no more than a moment.

"Away! It's too soon! Wait till you're called! . . . Why did you bring him ahead of time?" Porfiry Petrovich muttered, extremely annoyed and as if thrown off. But all at once Nikolai went down on his knees.

"What's this now?" Porfiry cried in amazement.

"I'm guilty. The sin is mine! I am the murderer!" Nikolai suddenly pronounced, somewhat breathlessly, but in a rather loud voice.

The silence lasted for about ten seconds, as though everyone were simply stunned; even the guard recoiled and no longer tried to approach Nikolai, but retreated mechanically towards the door and stood there without moving.

"What is this?" cried Porfiry Petrovich, coming out of his momentary stupor.

"I am . . . the murderer . . ." Nikolai repeated, after a short silence.

"What . . . you . . . what . . . who did you kill?" Porfiry Petrovich was obviously at a loss.

Again Nikolai was silent for a moment.

"Alyona Ivanovna and her sister, Lizaveta Ivanovna—I . . . killed them . . . with an axe. My mind was darkened . . ." he added suddenly, and again fell silent. He was still on his knees.

For a few moments Porfiry Petrovich stood as if pondering, then he roused himself up again and waved away the uninvited witnesses. They vanished instantly, and the door was closed. Then he looked at Raskolnikov, who was standing in the corner gazing wildly at Nikolai, made a move towards him, but suddenly stopped, looked at him, immediately shifted his eyes to Nikolai, then back to Raskolnikov, then back to Nikolai, and suddenly, as if carried away, he fell upon Nikolai again.

"Why are you rushing ahead with your darkening?" he shouted at him almost spitefully. "I haven't asked you yet whether your mind was darkened or not . . . Tell me, you killed them?"

"I am the murderer . . . I'm giving testimony . . ." Nikolai said.

"Ehh! What did you kill them with?"

"An axe. I had it ready."

"Eh, he's rushing! Alone?"

Nikolai did not understand the question.

"Did you do it alone?"

"Alone. And Mitka's not guilty, and he's not privy to any of it."

"Don't rush with Mitka! Ehh! . . . And how was it, how was it that you went running down the stairs then? The caretakers met both of you, didn't they?"

"That was to throw you off . . . that's why I ran then . . . with Mitka," Nikolai replied hurriedly, as if he had prepared the answer beforehand.

"So, there it is!" Porfiry cried out spitefully. "He's not using his own words!" he muttered, as if to himself, and suddenly he noticed Raskolnikov again.

He had evidently been so carried away with Nikolai that for a moment he even forgot all about Raskolnikov. Now he suddenly recollected himself, was even embarrassed . . .

"Rodion Romanovich, my dear! Excuse me, sir," he dashed to him, "this simply won't do; if you please, sir . . . there's nothing for you to . . . I myself . . . see what surprises! . . . if you please, sir! . . ."

And taking him by the arm, he showed him to the door.

"It seems you didn't expect this?" said Raskolnikov, who of course understood nothing clearly yet but had already managed to cheer up considerably.

"You didn't expect it either, my dear. Look how your hand is shaking! Heh, heh!"

"You're shaking, too, Porfiry Petrovich."

"Indeed I am, sir; I didn't expect this! . . ."

They were standing in the doorway. Porfiry was waiting impatiently for Raskolnikov to go out.

"So you're not going to show me your little surprise?" Raskolnikov said suddenly.

"He says it, and his teeth are still chattering in his mouth, heh, heh! What an ironical man you are! Well, sir, come again."

"It's *good-bye,* I should think."

"As God wills, sir, as God wills!" Porfiry muttered, his smile becoming somehow twisted.

As he passed through the office, Raskolnikov noticed that many people were looking at him intently. Among the crowd in the waiting room he managed to make out the two caretakers from *that* house, the ones he had incited to go to the police that night. They were standing and waiting for something. But as soon as he walked out to the stairs, he suddenly heard the voice of Porfiry Petrovich behind him. Turning around, he saw that he was hurrying after him, all out of breath.

"One little word, Rodion Romanovich, sir; concerning everything else, it's as God wills, but all the same we'll have to ask you a thing or two formally, sir . . . so we'll be seeing each other right enough, sir."

And Porfiry stood in front of him, smiling.

"Right enough, sir," he added once more.

It might be supposed that he wanted to say something more, but it somehow would not get itself said.

"And you must forgive me, Porfiry Petrovich, about these things just now . . . I lost my temper," Raskolnikov began, now thoroughly cheered up, so much so that he could not resist the desire to show off.

"Never mind, sir, never mind . . ." Porfiry picked up almost joyfully. "And I myself, sir . . . I have a venomous character, I confess, I confess! So we'll be seeing each other, sir. God willing, we shall indeed, sir!"

"And finally get to know each other?" Raskolnikov picked up.

"And finally get to know each other," Porfiry Petrovich agreed, narrowing his eyes and looking at him rather seriously. "So, now you're off to the name-day party, sir?"

"To the funeral, sir!"

"Ah, yes, the funeral, that is! Your health, do look after your health, sir . . ."

"And I really don't know what to wish you in return!" replied Raskolnikov, who was already starting down the stairs but suddenly turned back to Porfiry. "I would wish you greater success, but, you see, your job is so comical!"

"How is it comical, sir?" Porfiry, who had also turned to go, instantly pricked up his ears.

"Well, just take this poor Mikolka, whom you must have tortured and tormented psychologically, the way you do, until he confessed; you must have been proving it to him day and night: 'You are the murderer, you are the murderer . . .'—well, and now that he's confessed, you're going to pick him apart bone by bone: 'You're lying, you're not the murderer! You couldn't have been! You're not using your own words!' How can it not be a comical job after that?"

"Heh, heh, heh! So you noticed I just told Nikolai that he wasn't 'using his own words'?"

"How could I not?"

"Heh, heh! Sharp-witted, you're sharp-witted, sir. You notice everything! Truly a playful mind, sir! And you do touch the most comical string . . . heh, heh! They say it's Gogol, among writers, who had this trait in the highest degree?"[22]

"Yes, Gogol."

"Yes, Gogol, sir . . . Till we have the pleasure again, sir."

"Till we have the pleasure again . . ."

Raskolnikov went straight home. He was so puzzled and confused that, having come home and thrown himself on the sofa, he sat there for a quarter of an hour simply resting and trying at least somehow to collect his thoughts. He did not even venture to reason about Nikolai: he felt that he was defeated, that in Nikolai's confession there was something inexplicable, astonishing, which at the moment he was totally unable to understand. But Nikolai's confession was an actual fact. The consequences of this fact became clear to him at once: the lie could not but be revealed, and then they would set to work on him again. But at least he was free until then, and he absolutely had to do something for himself, because the danger was unavoidable.

To what extent, however? The situation was beginning to clarify itself. Recalling his whole recent scene with Porfiry, *roughly*, in its general outlines, he could not help shuddering with horror again. Of course, he did not know all of Porfiry's purposes yet, he could not grasp all his calculations. But part of the game had been revealed, and certainly no one knew better than he how terrible this "move" in Porfiry's game was for him. A little more and he *might* have given himself away completely, and factually now. Knowing the morbidity of his character, having correctly grasped and penetrated it at first sight, Porfiry had acted almost unerringly, albeit too resolutely. There was no question that Raskolnikov had managed to compromise himself far too much today, but still it had not gone as far as *facts*; it was all still relative. But was it right, was it right, the way he understood it now? Was he not mistaken? What precisely had Porfiry been driving at today? Did he really have anything prepared today? And what precisely? Was he really expecting something, or not? How precisely would they have parted today, had it not been for the arrival of an unexpected catastrophe through Nikolai?

Porfiry had shown almost the whole of his game; he was taking a risk, of course, but he had shown it, and (Raskolnikov kept thinking) if Porfiry really had something more, he would have shown that, too. What was this "surprise"? A mockery, perhaps? Did it mean anything, or not? Could it have concealed anything resembling a fact, a positive accusation? That man yesterday? Where had he dropped to? Where was he today? Because if Porfiry had anything positive, it must certainly be connected with that man yesterday . . .

He was sitting on the sofa, his head hanging down, his elbows resting on his knees, and his face buried in his hands. A nervous trembling still shook his whole body. Finally he got up, took his cap, thought, and made for the door.

He somehow had a presentiment that for today, at least, he could almost certainly consider himself safe. Suddenly his heart felt almost joyful: he wanted to hasten to Katerina Ivanovna's. To be sure, he was late for the funeral, but he would still be in time for the memorial meal, and there, now, he would see Sonya.

He stopped, thought, and a sickly smile forced itself to his lips.

"Today! Today!" he repeated to himself. "Yes, today! It must be . . ."

He was just about to open the door, when it suddenly began to open by itself. He trembled and jumped back. The door was opening slowly and quietly, and suddenly a figure appeared—of yesterday's man *from under the ground.*

The man stopped on the threshold, looked silently at Raskolnikov, and took a step into the room. He was exactly the same as yesterday, the same figure, the same clothes, but in his face and eyes a great change had taken place: he now looked somehow rueful, and, having stood for a little, he sighed deeply. He need only have put his palm to his cheek and leaned his head to one side, to complete his resemblance to a peasant woman.

"What do you want?" Raskolnikov asked, going dead.

The man paused and then suddenly bowed deeply to him, almost to the ground. At least he touched the ground with one finger of his right hand.

"What is this?" Raskolnikov cried out.

"I am guilty," the man said softly.

"Of what?"

"Of wicked thoughts."

The two stood looking at each other.

"I felt bad. When you came that time, maybe under the influence, and told the caretakers to go to the precinct, and asked about blood, I felt bad because it all came to nothing, and you were taken for drunk. And I felt so bad that I lost my sleep. And, remembering the address, we came here yesterday and asked . . ."

"Who came?" Raskolnikov interrupted, instantly beginning to recall.

"I came, that is. I did you a bad turn."

"You're from that house, then?"

"But I was standing with them in the gateway that time, don't you remember? We have our handcraft there, from old times. We're furriers, tradespeople, we work at home . . . but most of all I felt bad . . ."

And all at once Raskolnikov clearly recalled the whole scene in the gateway two days ago; he realized that besides the caretakers several other people had been standing there, and women as well. He recalled one voice suggesting that he be taken straight to the police. He could not recall the speaker's face, and even now he did not recognize him, but he remembered that he had even made him some reply then, and turned to him . . .

So this was the solution to yesterday's horror. Most horrible was the thought that he had really almost perished, almost destroyed himself, because of such a *worthless* circumstance. So except for the renting of the apartment and the talk about blood, this man had nothing to tell. So Porfiry also had nothing, nothing except this *delirium,* no facts except for *psychology,* which is *double-ended,* nothing positive. So if no more facts emerged (and they must not emerge, they must not, they must not!), then . . . then what could they possibly do to him? How could they expose him finally, even if they should arrest him? And so Porfiry had learned about the apartment only now, only that day, and knew nothing before.

"Was it you who told Porfiry today . . . that I went there?" he cried, struck by the sudden idea.

"What Porfiry?"

"The chief investigator."

"Yes, me. The caretakers wouldn't go that time, so I went."

"Today?"

"I was there just a minute before you. And I heard everything, everything, the way he was tormenting you."

"Where? What? When?"

"But, right there, behind the partition, I was sitting there the whole time."

"What? So the surprise was you? But how could it have happened? For pity's sake!"

"Seeing as the caretakers didn't want to go on my words," the tradesman began, "because they said it was late by then and he might even be angry that they came at the wrong time, I felt bad, and lost my sleep, and began finding things out. And having found out yesterday, I went today. The first time I came, he wasn't there. I tarried an hour longer, and then he couldn't see me. The third time I came, they let me in. I began reporting to him everything as it was, and he began rushing around the room and beat himself on the chest with his fist: 'What are you doing to me, you robbers?' he said. 'If I'd known anything of the sort, I'd have gone and brought him in under guard!' Then he ran out, called someone, and began talking to him in the corner, and then he came back to me, and began questioning and chiding me. And he reproached me very much; and I informed him of everything, and said that you didn't dare answer anything to my words yesterday, and that you didn't recognize me. And here he began running around again, and kept beating himself on the chest, and he was angry, and running around, and when you were announced— 'Well,' he said, 'get behind the partition, sit there for now, don't move, no matter what you hear,' and he himself brought me a chair there and locked me in; 'I may ask for you,' he said. And when they brought Nikolai, he took me out, just after you: 'I'll want you again,' he said, 'I'll question you again' . . ."

"And did he ask Nikolai any questions while you were there?"

"As soon as he took you out, he immediately took me out as well, and began questioning Nikolai."

The tradesman stopped and suddenly bowed again, touching the floor with his finger.

"For my slander and my wickedness, forgive me."

"God will forgive," Raskolnikov replied, and as soon as he uttered it, the tradesman bowed to him, not to the ground this time but from the waist, turned slowly, and walked out of the room. "Everything's double-ended, now everything's double-ended," Raskolnikov kept repeating, and he walked out of the room more cheerful than ever.

"The struggle's not over yet," he said with a spiteful grin, on his way down the stairs. The spite was directed at himself: with scorn and shame he looked back on his "faintheartedness."

Part Five

I

THE MORNING that followed his fatal talk with Dunechka and Pulcheria Alexandrovna had its sobering effect on Pyotr Petrovich as well. To his greatest displeasure, he was forced little by little to accept as a fact, accomplished and irreversible, that which even yesterday had seemed to him an almost fantastic event, which, though real, was still somehow impossible. The black serpent of stung vanity had sucked all night at his heart. Having gotten out of bed, Pyotr Petrovich at once looked in the mirror. He feared the bile might have risen in him during the night. So far, however, all was well in that regard, and, having considered his white and noble aspect, grown slightly fat of late, Pyotr Petrovich even took comfort for a moment, feeling quite sure of finding a bride for himself somewhere in another place, and perhaps even a cut above this one; but he came to his senses at once and spat aside vigorously, thereby evoking a silent but sarcastic smile in his young friend and cohabitant, Andrei Semyonovich Lebezyatnikov. Pyotr Petrovich noticed this smile, and inwardly set it down at once against his young friend's account. Of late he had managed to set a lot against his account. He grew doubly spiteful at the sudden realization that he ought not to have informed Andrei Semyonovich yesterday about yesterday's results. That was his second mistake yesterday, made in the heat of the moment, from overexpansiveness, in irritation . . . Then, throughout the morning, as if by design, nuisance followed nuisance. Some trouble even awaited him in the Senate, in connection with a case he was pleading there. But he was especially irritated with the owner of the apartment he had rented with a view to his impending marriage and decorated at his own expense: the owner, some German craftsman grown rich, would in no way agree to break the just concluded contract, and demanded the full forfeit mentioned in it, notwithstanding that Pyotr Petrovich would be turning the apartment back to him almost entirely done over. In the same way, the furniture store refused to return even a single rouble of the deposit for furniture bought but not yet delivered to the apartment. "I'm not going to get married just for the sake of the furniture!" Pyotr Petrovich snarled to himself, and at the same moment a desperate hope flashed in him once more: "But can it all be so irrevocably lost and finished? Can't I try one more time?" Again the thought of Dunechka needled his heart seductively. He endured this moment with pain, and certainly, had it been possible right then to kill Raskolnikov merely by wishing, Pyotr Petrovich would immediately have voiced this wish.

"Moreover, it was also a mistake not to give them any money at all," he was thinking, as he sadly made his way back to Lebezyatnikov's closet. "Devil take it, why did I turn into such a Jew? There wasn't even any calculation in it! I thought I'd keep them on a short tether for a bit, and get them to see me as their Providence, and now look! . . . Pah! . . . No, if I'd handed them, say, fifteen hundred meanwhile, for the trousseau, and for presents, for all sorts of little boxes, toilet cases, trinkets, fabrics, and all that trash from Knop's, and from the English store,[1] things would be better now . . . and firmer! They wouldn't have refused me so easily! They're of such mold that they'd be sure to regard it as their duty, in case of refusal, to return the gifts and the money; and to return them would be a bit difficult, and a pity! And conscience would prick them: how can you suddenly chase a man out like this, when all along he's been so generous and rather delicate? . . . Hm! I missed that one!" And snarling once more, Pyotr Petrovich told himself then and there—but only himself, naturally—that he was a fool.

Having come to this conclusion, he returned home twice as angry and irritated as when he had left. The preparations for the memorial meal in Katerina Ivanovna's room partly drew his curiosity. He had already heard something about this memorial meal yesterday; he even had some memory of having been invited himself; but, busy with his own troubles, he had passed over all these other things without notice. Hastening to inquire of Mrs. Lippewechsel, who in Katerina Ivanovna's absence (she was at the cemetery) was bustling about the table that was being laid, he learned that the memorial meal was to be a grand affair, that nearly all the tenants had been invited, among them even those unknown to the deceased, that even Andrei Semyonovich Lebezyatnikov had been invited, in spite of his past quarrel with

Katerina Ivanovna, and finally that he himself, Pyotr Petrovich, not only was invited but was even expected with great impatience, since he was perhaps the most important guest among all the tenants. Amalia Ivanovna herself had been invited with great honors, in spite of all past unpleasantnesses, and was therefore now hustling and bustling about, almost taking a delight in it; moreover, she was quite dressed up, in mourning but all of it new, silk, frills and fancies, and she was proud of it. All these facts and details gave Pyotr Petrovich a certain idea, and he went to his room—that is, to Andrei Semyonovich Lebezyatnikov's room—somewhat thoughtful. The thing was that, as he had learned, Raskolnikov was also among the invited guests.

Andrei Semyonovich, for some reason, had stayed at home that whole morning. Between this gentleman and Pyotr Petrovich a certain strange, though somewhat natural, relationship had come about: Pyotr Petrovich despised and hated him, even beyond measure, and had done so almost from the very day he came to stay with him; yet at the same time he was as if a bit wary of him. He was staying with him during his visit to Petersburg not just from miserly economy alone; though this was almost the main reason, there was also another reason here. While still in the provinces, he had heard of Andrei Semyonovich, his former ward, as one of the foremost young progressivists, who was even playing an important role in certain curious and fabled circles. Pyotr Petrovich was struck by this. These powerful, all-knowing, all-despising, and all-exposing circles had long frightened Pyotr Petrovich, with some peculiar, though perfectly undefined, fear. Of course, on his own, and living in the provinces besides, he was unable to form, even approximately, an exact notion of anything *of that sort.* He had heard, as everyone had, that there existed, especially in Petersburg, certain progressivists, nihilists, exposers, and so on and so forth, but, like many others, he exaggerated and distorted the meaning and significance of these names to the point of absurdity. What he had feared most of all, for several years now, was *exposure,* and this was the chief ground for his permanent, exaggerated uneasiness, especially when he dreamed of transferring his activities to Petersburg. In this respect he was *scared,* as they say, the way little children are sometimes *scared.* Some years ago, in the provinces, when he was just embarking on his career, he had met with two cases in which rather important personages of the province, whom he had latched on to and who until then had been his patrons, were cruelly exposed. One case ended somehow especially scandalously for the exposed personage, and the other even all but ended in real trouble. This was why Pyotr Petrovich decided, upon arriving in Petersburg, to find out at once how matters stood, and, if need be, to head things off just in case and curry favor with "our young generations." To this end he put his hopes in Andrei Semyonovich, and in any case, as during his visit to Raskolnikov, for example, he already knew how to round off certain phrases he had borrowed somewhere . . .

Of course, he soon managed to discern in Andrei Semyonovich an extremely trite and simple little man. But this did not in the least reassure or encourage Pyotr Petrovich. Even if he were convinced that all progressivists were the same sort of little fools, it would still not have allayed his uneasiness. Properly speaking, these teachings, ideas, systems (with which Andrei Semyonovich simply pounced upon him), were none of his affair. He had his own object. He needed only to find out at once and quickly what went on *here,* and how. Did *these people* have any power, or did they not have any power? Was there anything for him to fear personally, or was there not? Would they expose him if he undertook this or that, or would they not expose him? And if they would expose him, then what for, and what exactly was it that one got exposed for nowadays? Furthermore, could he not somehow get in good with them and at the same time hoodwink them a bit, if they were indeed so powerful? Was it the thing to do, or not? Could he not, for instance, bolster his career a bit precisely by means of them? In short, he was faced with hundreds of questions.

This Andrei Semyonovich was a thin-blooded and scrofulous little man, small of stature, who worked as an official somewhere, was strangely towheaded, and had side-whiskers shaped like mutton-chops, which were his great pride. What's more, his eyes were almost constantly ailing. His heart was rather soft, but his speech was quite self-confident and on occasion extremely presumptuous—which, compared with his little figure, almost always came out funny. Amalia Ivanovna, however, counted him among her most honored tenants, meaning that he did not drink and that he paid his rent regularly. In spite of all these qualities, Andrei Semyonovich was indeed a bit stupid.

He subscribed himself to progress and "our young generations" out of passion. He was one of that numerous and diverse legion of vulgarians, feeble miscreates, half-taught petty tyrants who make a point of instantly latching on to the most fashionable current idea, only to vulgarize it at once, to make an instant caricature of everything they themselves serve, sometimes quite sincerely.

However, though he was a very kind little man, Lebezyatnikov was also beginning to find his cohabitant and former guardian, Pyotr Petrovich, partly unbearable. It came about somehow mutually and inadvertently on both sides. Simple as Andrei Semyonovich was, he nevertheless began gradually to realize that Pyotr Petrovich was hoodwinking him and secretly despised him, and that "he was not the right sort of man at all." He had tried expounding Fourier's system and Darwin's theory to him, but Pyotr Petrovich, especially of late, had begun listening somehow too sarcastically, and most recently had even become abusive. The thing was that he had begun to perceive, by instinct, that Lebezyatnikov was not only a trite and silly little man, but perhaps also a bit of a liar; that he had no connections of any importance even in his own circle, but had only heard things third hand; moreover, he perhaps did not even know his own *propaganda* business properly, because he got too confused; and so it was not for the likes of him to be an exposer! Incidentally, let us note in passing that Pyotr Petrovich, during this week and a half, had willingly accepted (especially at the beginning) some rather peculiar praise from Andrei Semyonovich; that is, he did not object, for example, but remained silent, when Andrei Semyonovich ascribed to him a readiness to contribute to the future and imminent establishing of a new "commune" somewhere in Meshchanskaya Street, or not to hinder Dunechka, for example, if in the very first month of marriage she should decide to take a lover, or not to have his future children baptized, and so on and so forth—all in the same vein.[2] Pyotr Petrovich, as was his custom, did not object to such qualities being ascribed to him, and allowed himself to be praised even in such a way—so pleasant did he find every sort of praise.

Pyotr Petrovich, who for some reason had cashed several five percent bank notes that morning, sat at the table and counted through the bundles of bills and series. Andrei Semyonovich, who almost never had any money, was pacing the room, pretending to himself that he looked upon all those bundles with indifference, and even with contempt. Pyotr Petrovich would in no way have believed, for example, that Andrei Semyonovich could indeed look upon so much money with indifference; and Andrei Semyonovich, in his turn, reflected bitterly that Pyotr Petrovich was indeed capable of having such thoughts about him, and, furthermore, was perhaps glad of the chance to prod and tease his young friend with the laid-out bundles of bills, reminding him of his nonentity and all the difference supposedly existing between the two of them.

He found him, this time, unprecedentedly irritable and inattentive, even though he, Andrei Semyonovich, had begun to develop for him his favorite theme about the establishment of a new, special "commune." The brief objections and remarks that escaped Pyotr Petrovich in the intervals between the clicking of beads on the abacus, breathed the most obvious and deliberately impolite mockery. But the "humane" Andrei Semyonovich ascribed Pyotr Petrovich's state of mind to the impression of yesterday's break with Dunechka, and was burning with the desire to take up the subject at once: he had something progressive and propagandizing to say on that account, which would comfort his honorable friend and "undoubtedly" be useful in his further development.

"What is this memorial meal that this . . . widow is arranging?" Pyotr Petrovich asked suddenly, interrupting Andrei Semyonovich at the most interesting point.

"As if you didn't know; I spoke with you on the subject just yesterday, and developed my thought about all these rites . . . But she invited you, too, I heard it. You spoke with her yourself yesterday . . ."

"I never expected the destitute fool would dump on this one meal all the money she got from that other fool . . . Raskolnikov. I was even amazed as I passed by just now; the preparations, the wines! . . . A number of people have been invited—devil knows what's going on!" Pyotr Petrovich continued, inquiring and driving at the conversation as if with some purpose. "What? You say I was invited, too?" he suddenly added, raising his head. "When was that? I don't remember it, sir. I won't go, however. Why should I? I just talked with her yesterday, in passing, about the possibility of her receiving a year's salary in a lump sum, as the destitute widow of an official. Maybe that's why she invited me? Heh, heh!"

"I don't intend to go either," said Lebezyatnikov.

"Surely not! You gave her a thrashing with your own hands. Naturally, you're ashamed, heh, heh, heh!"

"Who gave a thrashing? To whom?" Lebezyatnikov became all flustered, and even blushed.

"Why, you did; you thrashed Katerina Ivanovna, about a month ago, didn't you? I heard it yesterday, sir . . . So much for your convictions! . . . And it leaves the woman question a bit lame. Heh, heh, heh!"

And, as if feeling better, Pyotr Petrovich began clicking his abacus again.

"That is all nonsense and slander!" Lebezyatnikov flared up, always fearful of being reminded of this story. "It wasn't like that at all! It was different . . . You heard it wrong; it's gossip! I merely defended myself then. She attacked me first with her claws . . . She plucked out one whole side of my whiskers . . . Every human being, I hope, is allowed to defend his own person. Besides, I will not allow anyone to use violence against me . . . On principle. Because it amounts to despotism. What was I to do: just stand there? I only pushed her away."

"Heh, heh, heh!" Luzhin went on chuckling maliciously.

"You're picking at me because you're angry and irritated yourself . . . But it's nonsense, and has nothing to do with the woman question at all, not at all! You don't understand it rightly; I even thought that if it's so well accepted that woman is the equal of man in everything, even in strength (as has already been affirmed), then there ought to be equality here as well. Of course, I reasoned later that essentially there should be no such question, because there also should be no fighting, and that instances of fighting are unthinkable in the future society . . . and it's strange, of course, to look for equality in fighting. I'm not that stupid . . . although fighting, by the way, is . . . that is, later there won't be any, but now there's still . . . pah! the devil! You throw a man off! I won't go to the memorial meal, but it's not on account of that trouble; I won't go on principle, so as not to participate in the vile prejudice of such a meal, that's why! However, it would even be possible to go, just like that, to laugh . . . A pity there won't be any priests. Otherwise, I'd certainly go."

"You mean, to sit at someone else's table and immediately spit upon it, as well as upon those who invited you. Is that it?"

"Not at all to spit, but to protest. With a useful purpose. I might contribute indirectly to development and propaganda. It's the duty of every man to develop and propagandize, and the sharper the better, perhaps. I might sow an idea, a seed . . . From this seed a fact will grow. How am I offending them? They'll be offended at first, but then they'll see for themselves that I've been useful. Didn't they accuse Terebyeva at first (the one who is now in a commune) because, when she walked out on her family and . . . gave herself, she wrote to her mother and father that she did not want to live among prejudices and was entering into a civil marriage, and it was supposedly all too rude—towards fathers, that is—and she could have spared them and written more gently? That's all nonsense, in my opinion, and it shouldn't have been any gentler; on the contrary, on the contrary, it's here that one needs to protest. Take Varents, now; she lived for seven years with her husband, abandoned her two children, snapped out at once in a letter to the husband: 'I realized that I could not be happy with you. I will never forgive you for deceiving me, by concealing from me the existence of a different social order, by means of communes. I recently learned all about it from a magnanimous man to whom I have given myself, and together we are setting up a commune. I say it directly, because I consider it dishonest to deceive you. Remain as you choose. Do not hope to bring me back, you are too late. I wish you happiness.' That's how such letters are written!"

"And is this the same Terebyeva you told me about, the one who is now in her third civil marriage?"

"Only the second, if you're really counting! But even if it were the fourth, or the fifteenth, it's all nonsense! And if ever I've regretted that my father and mother are dead, it's certainly now. I've even dreamed several times of how I'd smack them with a protest, if only they were alive! I'd set it all up on purpose . . . A 'severed member' and all that—pah! who cares! I'd show them! They'd get a surprise! Really, it's too bad I haven't got anybody!"

"To surprise, you mean? Heh, heh! Well, be that as you like," Pyotr Petrovich interrupted, "but tell me something: you do know this dead man's daughter, the frail one? Is it completely true what they say about her, eh?"

"What if it is? In my opinion—I mean, according to my personal conviction—that is the most normal condition for a woman. And why not? I mean, *distinguons.*[3] In today's society it is, of course, not quite normal, because it's forced, but in the future it will be perfectly normal, because free. But now, too, she had the right: she was suffering, and this was her reserve, her capital, so to speak, which she had every right to dispose of. Naturally, there will be no need of reserves in the future society; but her role will be designated by a different significance, it will be conditioned harmoniously and rationally. As far as Sofya Semyonovna personally is concerned, at present I look upon her actions as an energetic and embodied protest against the social order, and I deeply respect her for it. I even rejoice to look at her!"

"Yet I was told that it was you who drove her out of this house!"

Lebezyatnikov even became furious.

"That is more gossip!" he shouted. "It was not like that at all, not at all! It really was not like that! That's all Katerina Ivanovna's lies, because she understood nothing! I was not making up to Sofya Semyonovna at all! I was simply developing her, quite disinterestedly, trying to arouse a protest in her . . . The protest was all I was after, and anyway, Sofya Semyonovna couldn't have gone on staying in the house as she was!"

"Were you inviting her to a commune?"

"You keep laughing, and very inappropriately, if I may say so. You don't understand anything! There are no such roles in a commune. Communes are set up precisely so that there will be no such roles. In a commune, the present essence of this role will be entirely changed, and what is stupid here will become intelligent there, what is unnatural here, under the present circumstances, will there become perfectly natural. Everything depends on what circumstances and what environment man lives in. Environment is everything, and man himself is nothing. And even now I'm on good terms with Sofya Semyonovna, which may serve you as proof that she never regarded me as her enemy and offender. Yes! I'm now enticing her into a commune, only on a totally, totally different basis! What's so funny? We want to set up our own commune, a special one, only on a much broader basis than the previous ones. We've gone further in our convictions. We negate more! If Dobrolyubov rose from the grave, I'd argue with him. As for Belinsky, I'd pack him away![4] And meanwhile I'm continuing to develop Sofya Semyonovna. She has a beautiful, beautiful nature!"

"So you're finding a use for this beautiful nature, eh? Heh, heh!"

"No, no! Oh, no! Quite the contrary!"

"Come now, quite the contrary! Heh, heh, heh! What a phrase!"

"No, believe me! What reasons do I have for concealing it from you, pray tell? On the contrary, I even find it strange myself: with me she's somehow especially, somehow fearfully chaste and modest!"

"And, of course, you're developing her . . . heh, heh! . . . by proving to her that all these modesties are nonsense? . . ."

"Not at all! Not at all! Oh, how crudely, even stupidly—forgive me—you understand the word development! You really understand n-nothing! Oh, God, you're still so . . . unready! We seek woman's freedom, and you have only one thing on your mind . . . Setting aside entirely the question of chastity and womanly modesty as in themselves useless and even prejudicial, I fully, fully allow for her chastity with me, because—it's entirely her will, entirely her right. Naturally, if she herself said to me: 'I want to have you,' I would regard myself as highly fortunate, because I like the girl very much; but for now, for now at least, certainly no one has ever treated her more politely and courteously than I, or with more respect for her dignity . . . I wait and hope—that's all!"

"Well, you'd better give her some present. I bet you haven't thought of that."

"You understand n-nothing, I tell you! She's in that sort of position, of course, but the question here is different! Quite different! You simply despise her. Seeing a fact which you mistakenly consider worth despising, you deny her any humane regard as a person. You still don't know her nature! Only it's a great pity that lately she has somehow ceased reading altogether and no longer takes any books from me. And she used to. It's a pity, too, that with all her energy and determination to protest—which she has already proved once—she still seems to have too little self-sufficiency, or independence, so to speak, too little nega- tion, to be able to break away completely from certain prejudices and

. . . stupidities. In spite of that, she has an excellent understanding of certain questions. She understood splendidly the question of kissing hands, for instance—that is, that a man insults a woman with inequality if he kisses her hand.[5] The question was debated among us, and I immediately told her. She also listened attentively about the workers' associations in France. Now I'm explaining to her the question of freedom of entry into rooms in the future society."

"What on earth does that mean?"

"The question was being debated recently, whether a member of a commune has the right to enter another member's room, either a man's or a woman's, at any time . . . well, and it was decided that he does . . ."

"Well, and what if he or she is occupied at the moment with vital necessities, heh, heh!"

Andrei Semyonovich even became angry.

"And you just keep at it, at these cursed 'necessities'!" he cried out with hatred. "Pah, I'm so angry and annoyed with myself for mentioning these cursed necessities prematurely, when I was explaining the system to you that time! Devil take it! It's a stumbling block for all your kind, and worst of all—they start tossing it around even before they know what it's about! And just as if they were right! Just as if they were proud of something! Pah! I've insisted several times that this whole question cannot be explained to novices except at the very end, once he's already convinced of the system, once the person has already been developed and directed. And what, pray tell, do you find so shameful and contemptible even in cesspits? I, first, I'm ready to clean out any cesspits you like! There isn't even any self-sacrifice in it! It's simply work, a noble activity, useful for society, as worthy as any other, and certainly much higher, for example, than the activity of some Raphael or Pushkin, because it's more useful!"[6]

"And more noble, more noble, heh, heh, heh!"

"What do you mean by 'noble'? I don't understand such expressions as ways of defining human activity. 'More noble,' 'more magnanimous'—it's all nonsense, absurdities, old prejudicial words, which I negate! What is noble is whatever is *useful* for mankind! I understand only the one word: *useful!* Snigger all you like, but it's true!"

Pyotr Petrovich was laughing very much. He had already finished counting his money and tucked it away. However, part of it for some reason remained on the table. This "cesspit question," in spite of all its triviality, had served several times before as a pretext for quarrels and disagreements between Pyotr Petrovich and his young friend. The whole stupidity lay in the fact that Andrei Semyonovich really got angry, while Luzhin was just letting off steam, and at the present moment wanted especially to anger Lebezyatnikov.

"It's because of your failure yesterday that you're so angry and carping," Lebezyatnikov burst out at last. Generally speaking, in spite of all his "independence" and all his "protests," he somehow did not dare to oppose Pyotr Petrovich and generally maintained a certain respectfulness towards him, habitual from years past.

"You'd better tell me one thing," Pyotr Petrovich interrupted haughtily and with vexation. "Can you, sir . . . or, better, are you really on sufficiently close terms with the aforementioned young lady that you could ask her right now to come here, to this room, for a minute? I think they've all returned from the cemetery by now . . . I hear people walking around . . . I would like to see her—this person, I mean, sir."

"But what for?" Lebezyatnikov asked in surprise.

"I just want to, sir. I'll be moving out of here today or tomorrow, and therefore I wished to tell her . . . However, please stay here during our talk. That will be even better. Otherwise you might think God knows what."

"I'd think precisely nothing . . . I merely asked, and if you have some business, nothing could be easier than to call her away. I'll go now. And rest assured that I shall not interfere with you."

Indeed, about five minutes later Lebezyatnikov returned with Sonechka. She came in greatly surprised and, as usual, timidly. She was always timid on such occasions, and was very afraid of new faces and new acquaintances, had been afraid even before, in her childhood, and was now all the more so . . . Pyotr Petrovich greeted her "courteously and affectionately," though with a certain shade of some cheery familiarity, befitting, however, in Pyotr Petrovich's opinion, to such a respectable and solid man as himself with regard to such a young and, in a certain sense, *interesting* being. He hastened to "encourage" her and sat her down across the table from himself. Sonya sat down, looked around—at Lebezyatnikov, at the money lying on the table, and suddenly at Pyotr Petrovich again, and then could no longer tear her eyes away, as if they were riveted to him. Lebezyatnikov made a move towards the door. Pyotr Petrovich stood up, gestured to Sonya to remain seated, and stopped Lebezyatnikov at the door.

"This Raskolnikov—is he there? Has he come?" he asked him in a whisper.

"Raskolnikov? Yes. But why? Yes, he's there . . . He just came in, I saw him . . . But why?"

"Well, then I especially ask you to stay here with us, and not to leave me alone with this . . . girl. It's a trifling matter, but people will draw God knows what conclusions. I don't want Raskolnikov to tell *them* . . . You see what I mean?"

"Oh, I do, I do!" Lebezyatnikov suddenly understood. "Yes, you have the right . . . To be sure, in my personal opinion you're carrying your apprehensions too far, but . . . all the same, you have the right. I'll stay, if you like. I'll stand here at the window and not interfere with you . . . I think you have the right . . ."

Pyotr Petrovich went back to his sofa, sat down facing Sonya, looked at her attentively, and suddenly assumed an extremely imposing, even somewhat stern, expression, as if to say: "Don't you think anything of the sort, miss." Sonya became utterly embarrassed.

"First, please make my excuses, Sofya Semyonovna, to your much respected mother . . . Am I right? I mean, Katerina Ivanovna is like a mother for you?" Pyotr Petrovich began quite imposingly, albeit rather affectionately. One could see that he had the most friendly intentions.

"Exactly right, sir, right, like a mother, sir," Sonya replied hastily and fearfully.

"Well, so make my excuses to her, that owing to unrelated circumstances I am forced to stay away and will not be coming to your pancakes . . . I mean, memorial meal, in spite of your mother's charming invitation."

"Right, sir, I'll tell her, at once, sir," and Sonechka hastily jumped up from the chair.

"I haven't *finished* yet," Pyotr Petrovich stopped her, smiling at her simplicity and ignorance of propriety, "and you little know me, my good Sofya Semyonovna, if you thought that for this unimportant reason, of concern to me alone, I would trouble someone such as yourself, and ask you to come and see me personally. I have a different object, miss."

Sonya hastily sat down. The gray and iridescent bills which had not been removed from the table again began flashing in her eyes, but she quickly turned her face away and raised it towards Pyotr Petrovich: it suddenly seemed terribly indecent, especially for *her,* to stare at someone else's money. She tried to fix her eyes on Pyotr Petrovich's gold lorgnette, which he held in place with his left hand, and at the same time on the massive, heavy, extremely beautiful ring, with its yellow stone, on the middle finger of that hand—but suddenly she looked away from that as well, and, not knowing what else to do, ended by again staring straight into Pyotr Petrovich's eyes. After another pause, even more imposing than the previous one, the man went on:

"I happened yesterday, in passing, to exchange a few words with the unfortunate Katerina Ivanovna. Those few words were enough for me to see that she is—if I may put it so—in an unnatural condition . . ."

"Yes, sir . . . unnatural, sir," Sonya kept hurriedly yessing him.

"Or, to put it more simply and clearly—she is sick."

"Yes, sir, more simply and clear . . . yes, sick, sir."

"So, miss. And thus, from a feeling of humaneness and . . . and . . . and commiseration, so to speak, I should like to be of some use, foreseeing her inevitably unfortunate lot. It seems that this entire, most destitute family now depends just on you alone."

"Allow me to ask," Sonya suddenly stood up, "what was it that you told her yesterday about the possibility of a pension? Because she told me yesterday that you were taking it upon yourself to obtain a pension for her. Is it true, sir?"

"By no means, miss, and in some sense it's even an absurdity. I merely alluded to temporary assistance for the widow of an official who has died in service—provided one has connections—but it appears that your deceased parent not only did not serve out his term, but had not served at all recently. In short, though there might be hope, it is quite ephemeral, because essentially there are no rights to assistance in this case, and even quite the opposite . . . And she's already thinking about a pension, heh, heh, heh! A perky lady!"

"Yes, sir, about a pension . . . Because she's trusting and kind, and her kindness makes her believe everything, and . . . and . . . and . . . that's how her mind is . . . Yes, sir . . . excuse me, sir," Sonya said, and again got up to leave.

"If you please, you haven't heard me out yet, miss."

"Right, sir, I haven't heard you out," Sonya muttered.

"Sit down, then, miss."

Sonya became terribly abashed and sat down again, for the third time.

"Seeing what situation she is in, with the unfortunate little ones, I should like—as I have already said—insofar as I can, to be of some use—I mean, insofar as I can, as they say, and no further. One could, for example, organize a benefit subscription for her, or a lottery, so to speak . . . or something of the sort—as is always done in such cases by relatives, or even by outsiders who wish generally to help. That is what I intended to tell you about. It can be done, miss."

"Yes, sir, very good, sir . . . For that, sir, God will . . ." Sonya babbled, looking fixedly at Pyotr Petrovich.

"It can be done, miss, but . . . that's for later, miss . . . I mean, we could even begin today. We'll see each other in the evening, talk it over, and, so to speak, lay the foundations. Come to see me here at, say, seven o'clock. Andrei Semyonovich, I hope, will also take part . . . But . . . there is one circumstance here which ought to be mentioned beforehand and carefully. It was for this, Sofya Semyonovna, that I troubled you to come here. Namely, miss, that in my opinion to give money into the hands of Katerina Ivanovna herself is dangerous and ought not to be done; and the proof of it is—this very memorial meal today. Not having, so to speak, even a crust of daily food for tomorrow, nor . . . well, nor shoes, nor anything, today she buys Jamaica rum, and, I think, even Madeira, and . . . and . . . and coffee. I saw it as I passed by. Tomorrow it will all fall on you again, to the last piece of bread; now, this is absurd, miss. And therefore the subscription, in my personal opinion, ought to be done in such a way that the unfortunate widow, so to speak, does not even know about the money, and only you, for instance, know about it. Am I right in saying so?"

"I don't know, sir. It's only today that she's been like this . . . once in her life . . . she wanted so much to commemorate, to honor, to remember . . . otherwise she's very intelligent, sir. However, as you wish, sir, and I'll be very, very, very . . . and they'll all be . . . and God will . . . and the orphans, sir . . ."

Sonya did not finish, and began crying.

"So, miss. Well, do keep it in mind; and now be good enough to accept, in the interests of your relative, on this first occasion, a sum feasible for me personally. I am quite, quite anxious that my name not be mentioned in this connection. Here, miss, having my own cares, so to speak, this is all I am able to . . ."

And Pyotr Petrovich handed Sonya a ten-rouble bill, after carefully unfolding it. Sonya took it, blushed, jumped up, murmured something, and hastily began bowing her way out. Pyotr Petrovich solemnly accompanied her to the door. She sprang out of the room at last, all agitated and exhausted, and returned in great embarrassment to Katerina Ivanovna.

During the course of this whole scene, Andrei Semyonovich either stood by the window or paced the room, not wishing to interrupt the conversation; but when Sonya left, he suddenly went up to Pyotr Petrovich and solemnly offered him his hand.

"I heard everything, and *saw* everything," he said, with special emphasis on the word *saw*. "What a noble thing—that is, I meant to say, humane! You wished to avoid gratitude, I could see! And though I confess to you that, on principle, I cannot sympathize with private philanthropy, because it not only does not eradicate evil at the root, but even nourishes it still more, nevertheless I cannot help confessing that I looked upon your action with pleasure—yes, yes, I like it."

"Eh, what nonsense!" Pyotr Petrovich muttered, a bit disturbed, and looking somehow closely at Lebezyatnikov.

"No, it's not nonsense! A man insulted and irritated as you are by yesterday's incident, and at the same time capable of thinking of the misfortune of others—such a man, sir . . . though by his actions he may be making a social mistake—nevertheless . . . is worthy of respect! I did not even expect it of you, Pyotr Petrovich, the less so since according to your ideas—oh! how your ideas still hinder you! How troubled you are, for instance, by yesterday's failure," the good little Andrei Semyonovich went on exclaiming, once more feeling fervently inclined towards Pyotr Petrovich, "but why, why the absolute need for this marriage, this *legal* marriage, my most noble and most amiable Pyotr Petrovich? Why this absolute need for *legality* in marriage? Well, beat me if you like, but I'm glad, glad that it fell through, that you are free, that you are not yet altogether lost to mankind, glad . . . You see, I've spoken my mind."

"Because I don't want to wear horns and breed up other men's children—that's why I need a legal marriage," Luzhin said, just to make a reply. He was especially pensive and preoccupied with something.

"Children? You've touched upon children?" Andrei Semyonovich gave a start, like a war horse hearing the sound of trumpets. "Children are a social question, and the question is of the first importance, I agree; but the question of children will be resolved differently. There are even some who negate children altogether, as they do every suggestion of the family. We'll talk about children later, but now let us turn our attention to horns! I confess, this is my weak spot. This nasty, Pushkinian, hussar's expression is even unthinkable in the future lexicon.[7] Besides, what are horns? Oh, delusion! What horns? Why horns? What nonsense! On the contrary, in civil marriage there won't be any horns! Horns are simply the natural consequence of every legal marriage, its correction, so to speak, a protest, so that in this sense they are not humiliating in the least . . . And—absurd as it is to think of it—if ever I wind up in a legal marriage, I will even be glad of your thrice-cursed horns; in that case I'll say to my wife: 'My friend, before now I have only loved you, but now I respect you, because you've been able to protest!'[8] You laugh? That's because you're not strong enough to tear yourself free of prejudices! Devil take it, don't I know precisely what makes it so unpleasant when you're deceived in the legal sort? But that is merely the base consequence of a base fact, in which both parties are humiliated. But when the horns are given openly, as in a civil marriage, then they no longer exist, they are unthinkable, and lose even the name of horns. On the contrary, your wife will merely be proving how much she respects you, by considering you incapable of opposing her happiness and developed enough not to take revenge on her for her new husband. Devil take it, I sometimes dream that if I were given in marriage—pah!—if I were to marry (civilly or legally, it makes no difference), I think I'd bring my wife a lover myself, if she was too slow in taking one. 'My friend,' I'd say, 'I love you, but beyond that I wish you to respect me—here!' Is it right, is it right what I'm saying? . . ."

Pyotr Petrovich was chuckling as he listened, but with no particular enthusiasm. Indeed, he was scarcely even listening. He was actually thinking over something else, and even Lebezyatnikov finally noticed it. Pyotr Petrovich was even excited; he rubbed his hands and kept lapsing into thought. All this Andrei Semyonovich realized and recalled afterwards . . .

II

I T WOULD BE difficult to point to exactly what caused the idea of this witless memorial meal to be born in Katerina Ivanovna's unsettled head. Indeed, nearly ten roubles had been thrown away on it, out of the more than twenty she had received from Raskolnikov for Marmeladov's actual funeral. Perhaps Katerina Ivanovna considered it her duty towards the dead man to honor his memory "properly," so that all the tenants would know, Amalia Ivanovna especially, that he was "not only in no way worse than they, but maybe even much better," and that none of them had the right to "turn up his nose" at him. Perhaps what had greatest influence here was that special *poor man's pride*, which brings it about that in some of the social rituals obligatory for one and all in our daily life, many poor people turn themselves inside out and spend every last kopeck of their savings, only so as to be "no worse than others" and "not to be condemned" somehow by these others. It is quite probable that Katerina Ivanovna wished, precisely on that occasion, precisely at that moment when it seemed she had been abandoned by everyone in the world, to show all these "worthless and nasty tenants" not only that she "knew how to live and how to entertain," but that she had even been brought up for an altogether different lot, that she had been brought up "in a noble, one might even say aristocratic, colonel's house," and was not at all prepared for sweeping the floor herself and washing the children's rags at night. Such paroxysms of pride and vanity sometimes visit the poorest and most downtrodden people, and at times turn into an irksome and irrepressible need in them. Katerina Ivanovna, moreover, was not the downtrodden sort at all; she could be utterly crushed by circumstances, but to make her morally *downtrodden*—that is, to intimidate her and break her will—was impossible. Moreover, Sonechka had quite good grounds for saying of her that her mind was becoming deranged. True, one could not say it positively and finally as yet, but indeed, recently, during the whole past year, her poor head had been too tormented not to have become at least partially damaged. An acute development of consumption, physicians say, also leads to a deranging of the mental faculties.

Wines in plural and in great variety there were not, nor was there any *Madeira;* all this had been exaggerated; but there was wine. There were vodka, rum, and Lisbon, all of the worst quality, but all in sufficient quantity. Of food, besides *kutya,*[9] there were three or four dishes (pancakes among them), all from Amalia Ivanovna's kitchen, and in addition two samovars were being prepared for tea and punch, which were supposed to follow the meal. The purchasing had been seen to by Katerina Ivanovna herself, with the help of one tenant, a pathetic little Pole, who for God knows what reason was living at Mrs. Lippewechsel's, and who immediately attached himself to Katerina Ivanovna as an errand boy, and had spent the whole day yesterday and all that morning running around with his tongue hanging out, seeming especially anxious that this last circumstance be noticed. He came running to Katerina Ivanovna for every trifle, even ran to look for her in the Gostiny Arcade, kept calling her *"pani chorunżina,"*[10] until at last she got thoroughly fed up with him, though at first she had said that without this "obliging and magnanimous" man she would utterly have perished. It was a property of Katerina Ivanovna's character hastily to dress up any first-comer in the best and brightest colors, to shower him with praises, which made some even feel ashamed, to invent various nonexistent circumstances for praising him, and to believe with perfect sincerity and candor in their reality, and then suddenly, all at once, to become disillusioned, to cut short, berate, and drive out the person whom, only a few hours earlier, she had literally worshipped. She was naturally of an easily amused, cheerful, and peaceable character, but continual misfortunes and failures had made her wish and demand so *fiercely* that everyone live in peace and joy, and *not dare* to live otherwise, that the slightest dissonance in life, the least failure, would at once send her almost into a frenzy, and in the space of an instant, after the brightest hopes and fantasies, she would begin cursing her fate, tearing and throwing whatever she got hold of, and beating her head against the wall. Suddenly, for some reason, Amalia Ivanovna also acquired an extraordinary significance and extraordinary respect from Katerina Ivanovna, perhaps solely because this memorial meal got started and Amalia Ivanovna decided wholeheartedly to participate in all the chores: she undertook to lay the table, to provide linen, dishes, and so on, and to prepare the food in her kitchen. Katerina Ivanovna left her in charge when she went to the cemetery, and gave her full authority. Indeed, everything was done up famously: the tablecloth was even quite clean; the dishes, forks, knives, wineglasses, goblets, cups—all miscellaneous, of course, in all sorts of shapes and sizes, borrowed from various tenants—were in place at the right time; and Amalia Ivanovna, feeling that she had done a superb job, met the people coming back even with a certain pride, all decked out in a bonnet with new mourning ribbons and a black dress. This pride, though merited, for some reason displeased Katerina Ivanovna: "Really, as if they couldn't even have set the table without Amalia Ivanovna!" The bonnet with its new ribbons also displeased her: "Is this stupid German woman proud, by any chance, of being the landlady and agreeing out of charity to help her poor tenants? Out of charity! I ask you! In the house of Katerina Ivanovna's papa, who was a colonel and all but a governor, the table was sometimes laid for forty persons, and this same Amalia Ivanovna, or, more properly, Ludwigovna, wouldn't even have been allowed into the kitchen . . ." However, Katerina Ivanovna resolved not to air her feelings for the time being, though she decided in her heart that Amalia Ivanovna absolutely had to be brought up short that very day and reminded of her proper place, or else she would start fancying God knows what about herself, but for the time being she was simply cool to her. Yet another unpleasantness contributed to Katerina Ivanovna's irritation: almost none of the tenants who had been invited actually came to the funeral, except for the little Pole, who did manage to run over to the cemetery; yet for the memorial meal—for the food, that is—all the poorest and most insignificant of them appeared, many not even looking like themselves, just some sort of trash. And those who were a bit older and a bit more solid, as if on purpose, by conspiracy, all stayed away. Pyotr Petrovich Luzhin, for example, the most solid, one might say, of all the tenants, did not appear, and yet the evening before, Katerina Ivanovna had managed to tell the whole world—that is, Amalia Ivanovna, Polechka, Sonya, and the little Pole—that he was a most noble and magnanimous man, with the most vast connections and wealth, her first husband's old friend, received in her father's house, and that he had promised to use every means to obtain a considerable pension for her. Let us note here that when Katerina Ivanovna did boast of someone's connections and wealth, it was without any thought for herself, without any personal calculation, quite disinterestedly, so to speak, from a fullness of heart, only for the pleasure of praising, and so as to give even more worth to what she praised. Along with Luzhin, and no doubt "following his example," that "nasty scoundrel Lebezyatnikov" also failed to appear. "Who does he think he is? He was invited only out of charity, and then only because he's sharing a room with Pyotr Petrovich and is his acquaintance, so that it would have been awkward not to invite him." Absent as well were a certain genteel lady and her "overripe maiden" daughter, who, though they had been living in Amalia Ivanovna's rooms for only about two weeks, had already complained several times of noise and shouting from the Marmeladovs' room, especially when the deceased would return home drunk, of which Katerina Ivanovna had, of course, already been informed by Amalia Ivanovna herself when, squabbling with Katerina Ivanovna and threatening to turn out the whole family, she had shouted at the top of her voice that they were disturbing "noble tenants whose foot they were not worth." Katerina Ivanovna now made a point of inviting this lady and her daughter whose "foot she supposedly was not worth," the more so as prior to this, in chance meetings, the woman always turned haughtily away—now they would know that there were "people who had nobler thoughts and feelings, and invited guests without holding any grudges," and they would see that Katerina Ivanovna was accustomed to quite a different lot in life. This was to be explained to them without fail at the table, as was the governorship of her late papa, and along with that an indirect remark would be made about there being no point in turning away from meetings, as it was an extremely stupid thing to do. There was a fat lieutenant-colonel (actually a retired captain) who also did not come, but it turned out that he had been "out cold" since the previous evening. In short, the only ones who came were: the little Pole; then a miserable runt of a clerk, mute, covered with blackheads, in a greasy frock coat, and with a disgusting smell; and then a deaf and almost completely blind old man, who had once worked in some post office, and whom someone from time immemorial and for unknown reasons had been keeping at Amalia Ivanovna's. There was also a drunken retired lieutenant, actually a supply officer, who had a most indecent and loud laugh, and, "just imagine," was not wearing a waistcoat! One of them sat right down at the table without so much as a bow to Katerina Ivanovna, and finally one personage, for lack of clothes, appeared in his dressing gown, but this was already an impossible degree of indecency, and, through the efforts of Amalia Ivanovna and the little Pole, he was successfully removed. The little Pole, however, brought along two other little Poles, who had never even lived at Amalia Ivanovna's, and whom no one had seen in the house before. Katerina Ivanovna found all this quite unpleasantly annoying. "Whom were all these preparations made for, then?" To gain space, the children were not even put at the table, which took up the whole room anyway, but had to eat in the back corner on a trunk, the two little ones sitting on a bench, while Polechka, being a big girl, looked after them, fed them, and wiped their little noses "as is proper for noble children." In short, Katerina Ivanovna had, against her will, to meet everyone with heightened dignity and even condescension. To some she gave an especially stern look, haughtily inviting them to sit down at the table. Considering Amalia Ivanovna for some reason answerable for all those who failed to come, she suddenly began treating her with great negligence, which Amalia Ivanovna noticed at once and greatly resented. Such a beginning promised no good end. Finally they all sat down.

Raskolnikov came in at almost the same moment as they returned from the cemetery. Katerina Ivanovna was terribly glad to see him, first because he was the only "educated man" among all the guests and "as everyone knew, was preparing to occupy a professor's chair at the local university in two years' time," and second because he immediately and respectfully apologized to her for having been unable to attend the funeral, in spite of his wishes. She simply fell upon him, seated him at the table directly to her left (Amalia Ivanovna was sitting to her right), and in spite of her constant fussing and concern that the serving be correct and that there be enough for everyone, in spite of the tormenting cough that interrupted and choked her every moment and that seemed to have settled in her especially over the past two days, she constantly turned to Raskolnikov and hastened to pour out to him in a half whisper all her pent-up feelings and all her righteous indignation at the failed memorial meal—this indignation frequently giving way to the most gay and irrepressible laughter at the assembled guests, and predominantly at the landlady herself.

"It's all this cuckoo-bird's fault. You know who I'm talking about—her, her!" and Katerina Ivanovna nodded towards the landlady. "Look at her eyes popping out! She feels we're talking about her, but she can't catch anything, so she's gawking at us. Pah, what an owl! Ha, ha, ha! . . . Hem, hem, hem! And what is she trying to show with that bonnet of hers! Hem, hem, hem! Have you noticed, she keeps wanting everyone to think she's patronizing me and doing me a great honor by her presence! I asked her, as a decent woman, to invite the better sort of people—namely, my late husband's acquaintances—and look who she's brought! Clowns! Sluts! Look at that one with the pimply face: some sort of snot on two legs! And those little Poles . . . ha, ha, ha! Hem, hem, hem! Nobody, nobody has ever seen them here; I've never seen them myself; so why did they come, I ask you? Sitting side by side so decorously. Hey, *panie!*"[11] she called out suddenly to one of them, "did you have any pancakes? Have some more! Drink some beer, some beer! Don't you want some vodka? Look, he jumped up, he's bowing, look, look! The poor fellows must be quite hungry! Never mind, let them eat. At least they're not making any noise, only . . . only, really, I'm afraid for the landlady's silver spoons! . . . Amalia Ivanovna!" she suddenly addressed her, almost aloud, "if by any chance they steal your spoons, I won't answer for them, I warn you beforehand! Ha, ha, ha!" She simply dissolved, turning to Raskolnikov again, and again nodding towards the landlady, delighted with her little escapade. "She didn't get it, again she didn't get it! She sits there gawking, look—an owl, a real owl, a barn owl in new ribbons, ha, ha, ha!"

Here her laughter again turned into an unbearable coughing, which lasted for about five minutes. There was blood left on her handkerchief; drops of sweat stood out on her forehead. She silently showed the blood to Raskolnikov and, having only just caught her breath, at once began whispering to him again in great animation and with flushed spots on her cheeks:

"You see, I gave her a most subtle errand, one might say—to invite that lady and her daughter, you know the ones I'm talking about? It was necessary to behave in the most delicate manner here, to act most skillfully, but she managed it so that this visiting fool, this presumptuous creature, this worthless provincial, simply because she's some sort of major's widow and has come to ask for a pension, and is wearing out her skirt-hems in all the offices, because at the age of fifty-five she blackens her eyebrows, powders her face, and wears rouge (as everyone knows) . . . and such a creature not only did not deem it necessary to come, but did not even send an apology for being unable to come, as common courtesy demands in such cases! But I cannot understand why Pyotr Petrovich hasn't come. And where is Sonya? Where did she go? Ah, here she is at last! Why, Sonya, where have you been? It's strange of you to be so unpunctual even at your own father's funeral. Rodion Romanych, let her sit next to you. Here's a place for you, Sonechka . . . take what you'd like. Have some fish in aspic, that's the best. They'll bring more pancakes soon. Did the children have any? Polechka, do you have everything there? Hem, hem, hem! All right, then. Be a good girl, Lenya; and you, Kolya, stop swinging your feet; sit like a noble child. What's that you're saying, Sonechka?"

Sonya hastened to convey at once Pyotr Petrovich's apology to her, trying to speak loudly enough for everyone to hear, and choosing the most respectful expressions, which she even invented and embellished a bit on Pyotr Petrovich's behalf. She added that Pyotr Petrovich had asked her to say especially that as soon as he could, he would come at once to talk over certain *matters* privately, and to discuss what could be done and undertaken in the future, and so on and so forth.

Sonya knew that this would calm and appease Katerina Ivanovna, that it would flatter her, and, above all—would satisfy her pride. She sat down next to Raskolnikov, having hastily bowed to him and looked curiously at him in passing. For the rest of the time, however, she somehow avoided looking at him or speaking to him. She even seemed absentminded, though she kept peering into Katerina Ivanovna's face in order to please her. Neither she nor Katerina Ivanovna was wearing mourning, for lack of dresses. Sonya had on something brown, of a darkish shade; Katerina Ivanovna was wearing her only dress, a dark cotton one with stripes. The news about Pyotr Petrovich went over swimmingly. Having listened to Sonya with an air of importance, Katerina Ivanovna, with the same importance, inquired after Pyotr Petrovich's health. Then, immediately and almost aloud, she *whispered* to Raskolnikov that it would indeed be strange for such a respected and solid man as Pyotr Petrovich to find himself in such "extraordinary company," in spite of all his devotion to her family and his old friendship with her papa.

"That is why I am so especially grateful to you, Rodion Romanych, for not scorning my bread and salt, even in such circumstances," she added, almost aloud.[12] "However, I'm sure that only your special friendship with my poor late husband prompted you to keep your word."

Then once again, with pride and dignity, she surveyed her guests, and suddenly, with special solicitude, inquired loudly of the old man across the table: "Wouldn't he care for some more stew, and had he tried the Lisbon wine?" The old man did not reply and for a long time could not understand what he was being asked, though his neighbors even began nudging him for the fun of it. He only looked around open-mouthed, which fueled the general merriment even more.

"What a dolt! Look, look! Why did they bring him? As for Pyotr Petrovich, I've always been confident of him," Katerina Ivanovna continued to Raskolnikov, "and he certainly bears no resemblance ..." (she addressed Amalia Ivanovna sharply and loudly, and with an extremely stern look, under which even Amalia Ivanovna quailed) "no resemblance to those frippery skirt-swishers of yours, whom my papa wouldn't even have taken as cooks into his kitchen, and as for my late husband, he, of course, would have been doing them an honor by receiving them, and then only out of his inexhaustible kindness."

"Yes, ma'am, he liked his drink; he liked it, that he did, ma'am!" the retired supply officer suddenly exclaimed, emptying his twelfth glass of vodka.

"My late husband indeed had that weakness, and everyone knows it," Katerina Ivanovna simply fastened on him all at once, "but he was a kind and noble man, who loved and respected his family; the only bad thing was that in his kindness he trusted too much in all sorts of depraved people, and God alone knows who he didn't drink with, even people who weren't worth his shoe sole! Imagine, Rodion Romanovich, they found a gingerbread rooster in his pocket: he was walking around dead drunk, yet he remembered the children."

"A roo-ooster? Did you say a roo-ooster?" cried the supply gentleman.

Katerina Ivanovna did not deign to answer him. She lapsed into thought about something and sighed.

"You no doubt think, as everyone else does, that I was too strict with him," she went on, addressing Raskolnikov. "But it wasn't so! He respected me, he respected me very, very much! He was a man of good soul! And I oftentimes felt so sorry for him! He used to sit and look at me from the corner, and I'd feel such pity for him, I'd have liked to be nice to him, but then I'd think to myself: 'I'll be nice to him, and he'll just get drunk again.' It was only by strictness that it was possible to restrain him at all."

"Yes, ma'am, it did go on, the hair-pulling, that it did, more than once, ma'am," the supply man bellowed again, and poured another glass of vodka into himself.

"Not just hair-pulling but even the broom would be a useful treatment for some fools. I'm not talking about my late husband now," Katerina Ivanovna snapped at the supply man.

The flushed spots on her cheeks glowed brighter and brighter; her chest was heaving. Another minute and she would be ready to start a scene. Many were chuckling; evidently many found it enjoyable. They began nudging the supply man and whispering something to him. Obviously they wanted to set them at each other.

"And ma-a-ay I ask on what account, ma'am," the supply man began, "that is, on whose noble account . . . you have just been so good as to . . . but, no! Nonsense! A widow! A widow-woman! I forgive . . . I pass!" and he knocked back some more vodka.

Raskolnikov sat and listened silently and with loathing. And he ate only out of politeness, barely touching the food that Katerina Ivanovna was constantly putting on his plate, and then only to avoid offending her. He kept a close eye on Sonya. But Sonya was becoming more and more anxious and preoccupied; she, too, anticipated that the memorial meal was not going to end peaceably, and watched with fear Katerina Ivanovna's mounting irritation. She knew, incidentally, that she herself, Sonya, was the main reason that the two visiting ladies had treated Katerina Ivanovna's invitation so contemptuously. She had heard from Amalia Ivanovna herself that the mother was even offended at the invitation and had posed the question: "How could she possibly place her daughter next to *that girl?*" Sonya had a feeling that this had somehow already become known to Katerina Ivanovna; and an offense to her, Sonya, meant more to Katerina Ivanovna than an offense to herself personally, or to her children, or to her papa; in short, it was a mortal offense, and Sonya knew that now Katerina Ivanovna would not rest "until she had proved to those skirt-swishers that they were both . . ." and so on and so forth. As if on purpose, someone sent Sonya a plate from the other end of the table with two hearts on it pierced by an arrow, molded in black bread. Katerina Ivanovna flared up and at once loudly remarked across the table that whoever had sent it was, of course, "a drunken ass." Amalia Ivanovna, who also anticipated something bad, and furthermore was insulted to the bottom of her soul by Katerina Ivanovna's haughtiness, in order to divert the unpleasant mood of the company, and at the same time raise herself in the general esteem, suddenly, out of the blue, began telling of how an acquaintance of hers, "Karl from the pharmacy," had taken a cab one night, and the driver "vanted to kill him, and Karl he pegged him fery, fery much not to kill him, and he vept and clasped his hands, and he vas shcared, and from fear vas pierced his heart." Katerina Ivanovna, though she smiled, immediately observed that Amalia Ivanovna ought not to tell anecdotes in Russian. The woman became even more offended, and replied that her "fater aus Berlin vas a fery, fery important mann and vent mit his hands into the pockets." The easily amused Katerina Ivanovna could not help herself and burst into a terrible fit of laughter, so that Amalia Ivanovna began to lose all patience and could barely contain herself.

"What a barn owl!" Katerina Ivanovna whispered again to Raskolnikov, almost cheerfully. "She meant to say he kept his hands in his pockets, but it came out that he picked people's pockets, hem, hem!

And have you noticed, Rodion Romanovich, once and for all, that all these Petersburg foreigners—that is, Germans mainly, wherever they come from—are all stupider than we are! You must agree, one simply cannot talk about how 'Karl from the pharmacy from fear vas pierced his heart,' and how he (the young snot!) 'clasped his hands, and vept, and pegged fery much' instead of just tying the driver up! Ah, the dunderhead! And yet she thinks it's very touching and doesn't suspect how stupid she is! In my opinion, this drunken supply man is a good deal smarter; at least one can see he's a boozer and has drunk up the last of his wits; but these people are all so well-behaved, so serious . . . Look at her sitting there with her eyes popping out. She's angry! She's angry! Ha, ha, ha! Hem, hem, hem!"

Having cheered up, Katerina Ivanovna immediately got carried away with various details, and suddenly began to talk of how, with the aid of the obtained pension, she would certainly start an institute for noble girls in her native town of T——. This was something Katerina Ivanovna herself had not yet spoken of with Raskolnikov, and she was immediately carried away with the most tempting details. All at once, no one knew how, she was holding in her hands that same "certificate of merit" which Raskolnikov had heard about from the late Marmeladov, when he was explaining to him in the tavern that Katerina Ivanovna, his spouse, on her graduation from the institute, had danced with a shawl "before the governor and other personages." This certificate of merit was now obviously meant to serve as evidence of Katerina Ivanovna's right to start an institute of her own; but above all it had been kept ready with the purpose of finally confounding "those two frippery skirt-swishers" in case they should come to the memorial meal, and proving clearly to them that Katerina Ivanovna was from a most noble, "one might even say aristocratic, house, a colonel's daughter, and certainly better than the sort of adventuresses who have been multiplying in such quantity lately." The certificate of merit was immediately handed around among the drunken guests, which Katerina Ivanovna did not prevent, because it did indeed mention *en toutes lettres*[13] that she was the daughter of a court councillor and chevalier of an order, and therefore indeed almost a colonel's daughter. Burning with excitement, Katerina Ivanovna immediately expanded on all the details of this wonderful and peaceful future life in T——, the school-masters she would invite to give lessons in her institute, the venerable old Frenchman, Mangot, who had taught French to Katerina Ivanovna herself at the institute, and was now living out his old age in T——, and who would certainly come to her on quite suitable terms. Finally, it came to Sonya as well, "who would go to T—— together with Katerina Ivanovna and help her there in everything." Here someone suddenly snorted at the other end of the table. Though Katerina Ivanovna at once made a pretense of scornfully ignoring the laughter that arose at the end of the table, she deliberately raised her voice at once and began talking animatedly about Sofya Semyonovna's undoubted abilities to serve as her assistant, about "her meekness, patience, self-denial, nobility, and education," and she patted Sonya on the cheek and, rising a little, warmly kissed her twice. Sonya flushed, and Katerina Ivanovna suddenly burst into tears, immediately observing of herself that "she was a nervous fool, and much too upset, and that it was time to end, and since the meal was over, why not serve tea." At the same moment, Amalia Ivanovna, now utterly offended because she had not taken the least part in the entire conversation and no one would even listen to her, suddenly risked a last attempt and, with concealed anguish, ventured to offer Katerina Ivanovna an extremely sensible and profound observation about the necessity, in the future institute, of paying special attention to the girls' clean linen *(die Wäsche)* and "of making sure dere iss vun such good lady" *(die Dame)* "who should look vell after the linen," and second, "that all the young girls mussn't sneak any novel by night to read." Katerina Ivanovna, who was really upset and very tired, and was already thoroughly sick of the memorial meal, immediately "snapped" at Amalia Ivanovna that she was "pouring out drivel" and understood nothing; that it was for the head matron to worry about *die Wäsche,* not the directress of a noble institute; and as far as reading novels was concerned, that was all simply indecencies and she begged her to keep quiet. Amalia Ivanovna flushed and, getting angry, remarked that she was only "vishing vell" and that she "fery much vished vell," but that "for a long time she vasn't the geld paid for the apartment." Katerina Ivanovna "put her down" at once, declaring that she was lying when she said she "vished her vell," because just yesterday, while the dead man was still laid out on the table,[14] she had been tormenting her about the apartment. To this Amalia Ivanovna responded, quite consistently, that she had "infited those ladies, but the ladies didn't come, because those been noble ladies, and to a not noble lady they cannot come." Katerina Ivanovna immediately "underscored" for her that since she was a slut, she was no judge of true nobility. This was too much for Amalia Ivanovna, and she declared at once that her "fater aus Berlin vas fery, fery important mann and vent mitt both hands into the pockets and alvays made like that: poof! poof!" and for a more lifelike portrayal of her fater, Amalia Ivanovna jumped up from her chair, thrust both hands into her pockets, puffed out her cheeks, and began producing some sounds vaguely resembling "poof, poof" with her mouth, to the accompaniment of loud guffaws from all the tenants, who, anticipating a skirmish, deliberately encouraged Amalia Ivanovna with their approval. Now this Katerina Ivanovna could not tolerate, and she immediately "rapped out" for all to hear that Amalia Ivanovna perhaps never even had a fater; that Amalia Ivanovna was simply a drunken Petersburg Finn and must have lived somewhere formerly as a kitchen maid, if not something worse. Amalia Ivanovna turned red as a lobster and started shrieking that it was maybe Katerina Ivanovna who "hat no fater at all, but that she hat a fater aus Berlin, and he vore a frock coat this long and made poof, poof, poof all the time!" Katerina Ivanovna observed contemptuously that her origins were known to all, and that it was stated in print on that same certificate of merit that her father was a colonel, and that Amalia Ivanovna's father (if she had any father) must have been some Petersburg Finn who sold milk; but most likely there was no father at all, because to this day it was unknown whether Amalia Ivanovna's patronymic was Ivanovna or Ludwigovna. At this, Amalia Ivanovna became utterly enraged and, banging her fist on the table, began shrieking that she was Amal-Ivan, not Ludwigovna, that her fater's name "vas Johann, and he vas Burgomeister," and that Katerina Ivanovna's fater "vas never vonce Burgomeister." Katerina Ivanovna rose from her chair and sternly, in an ostensibly calm voice (though she was all pale and her chest was heaving deeply), remarked to her that if she ever dared "to place her wretched little fater on the same level with her dear papa, she, Katerina Ivanovna, would tear her bonnet off and trample it under her feet." Having heard this, Amalia Ivanovna started running around the room, shouting with all her might that she was the landlady and that Katerina Ivanovna must "in vun minute facate the apartment"; then for some reason she rushed to gather up the silver spoons from the table. A row and an uproar ensued; the children started to cry. Sonya rushed and tried to hold Katerina Ivanovna back; but when Amalia Ivanovna suddenly shouted something about a yellow pass, Katerina Ivanovna pushed Sonya away and made for Amalia Ivanovna in order to carry out at once her threat concerning the bonnet. At that moment the door opened, and Pyotr Petrovich Luzhin appeared on the threshold of the room. He stood and with stern, attentive eyes surveyed the whole company. Katerina Ivanovna rushed to him.

III

"PYOTR PETROVICH!" she exclaimed, "you protect us at least! Bring home to this stupid creature that she dare not treat a noble lady in misfortune this way, that there are courts for such things . . . I'll go to the governor-general himself . . . She'll answer . . . Remember my father's bread and salt; protect the orphans."

"Excuse me, madam . . . Excuse me, excuse me, madam," Pyotr Petrovich brushed her aside. "As you are aware, I did not have the honor of knowing your father . . . excuse me, madam!" (Someone guffawed loudly.) "And I have no intention of participating in your ceaseless strife with Amalia Ivanovna . . . I have come for my own purposes . . . and wish to speak at once with your stepdaughter, Sofya . . . Ivanovna . . . I believe? Allow me to pass, ma'am."

And edging past Katerina Ivanovna, Pyotr Petrovich made his way to the opposite corner, where Sonya was.

Katerina Ivanovna simply stood there as if thunderstruck. She could not understand how Pyotr Petrovich could disavow her dear papa's bread and salt. Having once invented this bread and salt, she now believed in it religiously. She was also struck by Pyotr Petrovich's tone—businesslike, dry, even full of some contemptuous threat. And everyone else somehow gradually became hushed at his appearance. Besides the fact that this "businesslike and serious" man was so sharply out of harmony with the whole company, besides that, one could see that he had come for something important, that probably only some extraordinary reason could have drawn him into such company, and that, therefore, something was about to happen, there was going to be something. Raskolnikov, who was standing next to Sonya, stepped aside to let him pass; Pyotr Petrovich seemed to take no notice of him. A minute later, Lebezyatnikov also appeared on the threshold; he did not come into the room, but stood there with some special curiosity, almost astonishment; he listened carefully, but it seemed that for a long time there was something he could not understand.

"Excuse me for possibly interrupting you, but the matter is rather important," Pyotr Petrovich remarked somehow generally, not addressing anyone in particular. "I'm even glad to have the public here. Amalia Ivanovna, I humbly ask you, in your quality as landlady, to pay attention to my forthcoming conversation with Sofya Ivanovna. Sofya Ivanovna," he continued, turning directly to Sonya, who was extremely surprised and already frightened beforehand, "a state bank note belonging to me, in the amount of one hundred roubles, disappeared from my table in the room of my friend, Andrei Semyonovich Lebezyatnikov, immediately following your visit. If, in one way or another, you know and can point out to us its present whereabouts, I assure you on my word of honor, and I call all of you as witnesses, that the matter will end right here. Otherwise, I shall be forced to take quite serious measures, in which case . . . you will have only yourself to blame, miss!"

Complete silence fell over the room. Even the crying children became quiet. Sonya stood deathly pale, looking at Luzhin, unable to make any reply. It was as if she still did not understand. Several seconds passed.

"Well, miss, what is it to be?" Luzhin asked, looking at her fixedly.

"I don't know . . . I don't know anything . . ." Sonya finally said in a weak voice.

"No? You don't know?" Luzhin asked again, and paused for another few seconds. "Think, mademoiselle," he began sternly, but still as if admonishing her, "consider well; I am willing to give you more time for reflection. Kindly realize, mademoiselle, that if I were not so sure, then naturally, with my experience, I would not risk accusing you so directly; for I myself, in a certain sense, am answerable for such a direct and public accusation, if it is false, or even merely mistaken. I am aware of that. This morning, for my own purposes, I cashed several five percent notes for the nominal value of three thousand roubles. I have a record of the transaction in my wallet. On returning home—Andrei Semyonovich is my witness here—I began counting the money and, having counted out two thousand three hundred roubles, I put them away in my wallet, and put the wallet into the side pocket of my frock coat. There were about five hundred left on the table, in bank notes, among them three notes for a hundred roubles each. At that moment you arrived (summoned by me)—and all the while you were with me, you were extremely embarrassed, so that you even got up and for some reason hastened to leave three times in the middle of the conversation, though our conversation was not yet finished. Andrei Semyonovich can witness to all that. Probably, mademoiselle, you yourself will not refuse to state and corroborate that I summoned you, through Andrei Semyonovich, for the sole purpose of discussing with you the orphaned and helpless situation of your relative, Katerina Ivanovna (whom I have been unable to join for the memorial meal), and how useful it would be to organize something like a subscription, a lottery, or what have you, for her benefit. You thanked me and even shed a few tears (I am telling everything as it happened, first, to remind you of it, and second, to show you that not the slightest detail has erased itself from my memory). Then I took from the table a ten-rouble bank note and handed it to you, in my own name, for the sake of your relative's interests and in view of a first contribution. Andrei Semyonovich saw all this. Then I accompanied you to the door—still with the same embarrassment on your part—after which, remaining alone with Andrei Semyonovich and talking with him for about ten minutes, Andrei Semyonovich left, and I turned again to the table with the money lying on it, intending to count it and set it aside, as I had meant to do earlier. To my surprise, from among the other hundred-rouble bills, one was missing. Now, kindly consider: I really can in no way suspect Andrei Semyonovich, miss; I'm even ashamed of the suggestion. That I made a mistake in counting is also not possible, because I had finished all my accounts a moment before you came, and found the result correct. You can only agree that, recalling your embarrassment, your haste to leave, and the fact that you kept your hands on the table for some time; considering, finally, your social position and its attendant habits, I was *forced,* with horror, so to speak, and even against my will, to arrive at a suspicion—a cruel one, of course, but—a justified one, miss! I will also add and repeat that, in spite of all my *obvious* certainty, I am aware that there is still some risk present for me in this accusation of mine. But, as you see, I did not take it idly; I rose up, and let me tell you why: solely, miss, solely on account of your blackest ingratitude! What? I invite you in the interests of your most destitute relative, I offer you a feasible donation of ten roubles, and right then and there you repay all that with such an act! No, miss, that is not nice! You must be taught a lesson, miss. Consider, then; moreover, I beg you as a true friend (for you could have no better friend at this moment) to come to your senses! Otherwise, I shall be implacable! Well then, miss?"

"I took nothing from you," Sonya whispered in terror. "You gave me ten roubles—here, take it." Sonya pulled a handkerchief from her pocket, found the knot, untied it, took out the ten-rouble bill, and held her hand out to Luzhin.

"And the other hundred roubles you simply do not admit?" he said reproachfully and insistently, without taking the bill.

Sonya looked around. They were all staring at her with such terrible, stern, mocking, hateful faces. She glanced at Raskolnikov . . . he was standing by the wall, arms folded, looking at her with fiery eyes.

"Oh, Lord!" escaped from Sonya.

"Amalia Ivanovna, we shall have to inform the police, and therefore I humbly ask you to send meanwhile for the caretaker," Luzhin said softly and even tenderly.

"*Gott der Barmherzige!*[15] I just known she vas shtealing!" Amalia Ivanovna clasped her hands.

"You just knew?" Luzhin picked up. "Then you had at least some grounds for such conclusions before this. I beg you, most respected Amalia Ivanovna, to remember your words, which in any case have been spoken in front of witnesses."

Loud talk suddenly arose on all sides. Everyone stirred.

"Wha-a-at!" Katerina Ivanovna suddenly cried, having come to her senses, and, as if tearing herself loose, she rushed at Luzhin. "What! You accuse her of stealing? Sonya? Ah, scoundrels, scoundrels!" And rushing to Sonya, she embraced her with her withered arms, as in a vise.

"Sonya! How dared you take ten roubles from him! Oh, foolish girl! Give it to me! Give me the ten roubles at once—there!"

And snatching the bill from Sonya, Katerina Ivanovna crumpled it in her hand, drew back, and hurled it violently straight into Luzhin's face. The ball of paper hit him in the eye and bounced onto the floor. Amalia Ivanovna rushed to pick up the money. Pyotr Petrovich became angry.

"Restrain this madwoman!" he shouted.

At that moment several more faces appeared in the doorway beside Lebezyatnikov; the two visiting ladies were among those peeking in.

"What! Mad? Mad, am I? Fool!" shrieked Katerina Ivanovna. "You, you're a fool, a pettifogger, a base man! Sonya, Sonya take his money? Sonya a thief? Why, she'd sooner give you money, fool!" And Katerina Ivanovna laughed hysterically. "Have you ever seen such a fool?" she was rushing in all directions, pointing out Luzhin to them all. "What! And you, too?" she noticed the landlady. "You're in it, too, you sausage-maker! You, too, claim that she 'vas shtealing,' you vile Prussian chicken-leg in a crinoline! Ah, you! . . . you! But she hasn't even left the room; as soon as she came from seeing you, you scoundrel, she sat down at once just beside Rodion Romanovich! . . . Search her! Since she hasn't gone anywhere, it means the money must still be on her! Search, then, go ahead and search! Only if you don't find anything, then, excuse me, my dear, but you'll answer for it! To the sovereign, the sovereign, I'll run to the merciful tsar himself, I'll throw myself at his feet, now, today! I'm an orphan! They'll let me in! You think they won't let me in? Lies! I'll get there! I will! Was it her meekness you were counting on? Were you hoping for that? But I'm perky enough myself, brother! You won't pull it off! Search, then! Search, search, go ahead and search!"

And Katerina Ivanovna, in a frenzy, tugged at Luzhin, pulling him towards Sonya.

"I'm prepared to, and I'll answer for it . . . but calm yourself, madam, calm yourself! I see only too well how perky you are! . . . But it . . . it . . . you see, ma'am," Luzhin muttered, "the police ought to be present . . . though, anyway, there are more than enough witnesses as it is . . . I'm prepared to . . . But in any case it's embarrassing for a man . . . by reason of his sex . . . If Amalia Ivanovna were to help . . . though, anyway, it's not how things are done . . . You see, ma'am?"

"Anyone you like! Let anyone you like search her!" cried Katerina Ivanovna. "Sonya, turn your pockets out for them! There, there! Look, monster, this one's empty, the handkerchief was in it, the pocket's empty, see? Here, here's the other one! See, see?"

And Katerina Ivanovna did not so much turn as yank the pockets inside out, one after the other. But from the second, the right-hand pocket, a piece of paper suddenly flew out and, describing a parabola in the air, fell at Luzhin's feet. Everyone saw it; many cried out. Pyotr Petrovich bent down, picked up the paper from the floor with two fingers, held it aloft for everyone to see, and unfolded it. It was a hundred-rouble bill, folded in eight. Pyotr Petrovich made a circle with his hand, showing the bill all around.

"Thief! Out from the apartment! Politz! Politz!" screamed Amalia Ivanovna. "They should to Tsiberia be chased! Out!"

Exclamations came flying from all sides. Raskolnikov was silent, not taking his eyes off Sonya, but from time to time shifting them quickly to Luzhin. Sonya stood where she was, as if unconscious; she was almost not even surprised. Color suddenly rushed to her cheeks; she uttered a short cry and covered her face with her hands.

"No, it wasn't me! I didn't take it! I don't know anything!" she cried in a heart-rending wail, and rushed to Katerina Ivanovna, who seized her and pressed her hard to herself, as if wishing to shield her from everyone with her own breast.

"Sonya! Sonya! I don't believe them! You see I don't believe them!" Katerina Ivanovna cried (in spite of all the obviousness), rocking her in her arms like a child, giving her countless kisses, catching her hands and simply devouring them with kisses. "As if you could take anything! What stupid people they all are! Oh, Lord! You're stupid, stupid," she cried, addressing them all, "you still don't know what a heart she has, what a girl she is! As if she would take anything! Why, she'd strip off her last dress and sell it, and go barefoot, and give everything to you if you needed it—that's how she is! She got a yellow pass because my children were perishing from hunger, she sold herself for us! . . . Ah, husband, husband! Ah, my poor, dead husband! Do you see? Do you see? Here's your memorial meal! Lord! But defend her! Why are you all standing there! Rodion Romanovich! Why don't you take her part? Do you believe it, too? None of you is worth her little finger, none of you, none, none, none! Lord, defend us finally!"

The cries of the poor, consumptive, bereaved Katerina Ivanovna seemed to produce a strong effect on the public. There was so much pathos, so much suffering in her withered, consumptive face, contorted by pain, in her withered lips flecked with blood, in her hoarsely crying voice, in her sobbing, so much like a child's, in her trusting, childlike, and at the same time desperate plea for defense, that they all seemed moved to pity the unfortunate woman. Pyotr Petrovich, at least, was immediately *moved to pity.*

"Madam! Madam!" he exclaimed in an imposing voice. "This fact does not concern you! No one would dare accuse you of any intent or complicity, the less so since you discovered it yourself by turning her pockets out: consequently you suspected nothing. I'm quite, quite prepared to show pity if poverty, so to speak, was also what drove Sofya Semyonovna to it, but why is it, mademoiselle, that you did not want to confess? Fear of disgrace? The first step? Or perhaps you felt at a loss? It's understandable; it's quite understandable . . . But, in any case, how could you get yourself into such qualities! Gentlemen!" he addressed everyone present, "gentlemen! Pitying and, so to speak, commiserating, I am perhaps ready to forgive, even now, in spite of the personal insults I have received. May this present shame serve you, mademoiselle, as a lesson for the future," he turned to Sonya, "the rest I shall let pass, and so be it, I have done. Enough!"

Pyotr Petrovich gave Raskolnikov a sidelong look. Their glances met. Raskolnikov's burning eyes were ready to reduce him to ashes. Katerina Ivanovna, meanwhile, seemed not even to be listening anymore; she was madly embracing and kissing Sonya. The children also took hold of Sonya from all sides with their little arms, and Polechka—though without quite understanding what was the matter—seemed all drowned in tears, choking back her sobs and hiding her pretty little face, swollen with weeping, on Sonya's shoulder.

"How vile!" a loud voice suddenly came from the doorway.

Pyotr Petrovich quickly turned around.

"What vileness!" Lebezyatnikov repeated, staring him straight in the eye.

Pyotr Petrovich even seemed to give a start. Everyone noticed it. (They remembered it afterwards.) Lebezyatnikov took a step into the room.

"And you dare hold me up as a witness?" he said, approaching Pyotr Petrovich.

"What do you mean, Andrei Semyonovich? What are you talking about?" Luzhin muttered.

"I mean that you are . . . a slanderer, that is what my words mean!" Lebezyatnikov said hotly, giving him a stern look with his weak-sighted eyes. He was terribly angry. Raskolnikov simply fastened his eyes on him, as though catching and weighing every word. Again there was another silence. Pyotr Petrovich was even almost at a loss, especially for the first moment.

"If it's me you are . . ." he began, stammering, "but what's the matter with you? Have you lost your mind?"

"I haven't lost my mind, and you are . . . a swindler! Ah, how vile of you! I kept listening, I kept listening on purpose, so as to understand it all, because, I must admit, even now it doesn't seem quite logical . . . But what you did it for, I cannot understand."

"But what have I done? Will you stop talking in these nonsensical riddles? Or maybe you've been drinking?"

"Maybe you drink, you vile man, but not me! I never even touch vodka, because it's against my convictions! Imagine, he, he himself, with his own hands, gave that hundred-rouble bill to Sofya Semyonovna—I saw it, I am a witness, I'll swear an oath to it! He, he did it!" Lebezyatnikov repeated, addressing one and all.

"Are you cracked or what, you milksop!" Luzhin shrieked. "She herself, in person, right in front of you—she herself, here and now, in front of everyone, confirmed that she received nothing but ten roubles from me. How, in that case, could I have given it to her?"

"I saw it, I saw it!" Lebezyatnikov exclaimed and insisted. "And though it's against my convictions, I'm ready to go this very minute and swear whatever oath you like in court, because I saw you slip it to her on the sly! Only, like a fool, I thought you were slipping it to her out of philanthropy! At the door, as you were saying good-bye to her, when she turned away and you were shaking her hand, with your other hand, your left hand, you put a piece of paper into her pocket on the sly. I saw it! I did!"

Luzhin went pale.

"What lies!" he exclaimed boldly. "And besides, how could you make out a piece of paper, when you were standing by the window? You imagined it . . . with your weak-sighted eyes. You're raving!"

"No, I didn't imagine it! I saw everything, everything, even though I was standing far away; and though it is indeed difficult to make out a piece of paper from the window—you're right about that—in this particular case I knew for certain that it was precisely a hundred-rouble note, because when you went to give Sofya Semyonovna the ten-rouble bill—I saw this myself—you took a hundred-rouble note from the table at the same time (I saw it because I was standing up close then, and since a certain idea immediately occurred to me, I didn't forget that you had the note in your hand). You folded it and kept it clutched in your hand all the time. Then I forgot about it for a while, but when you were getting up, you passed it from your right hand to your left and nearly dropped it; then I remembered again, because then the same idea came to me—namely, that you wanted to be philanthropic to her in secret from me. You can imagine how I began watching—and so I saw how you managed to slip it into her pocket. I saw it, I did, I'll swear an oath to it!"

Lebezyatnikov was almost breathless. Various exclamations began coming from all sides, mostly indicating surprise, but some of the exclamations also took on a menacing tone. Everyone pressed towards Pyotr Petrovich. Katerina Ivanovna rushed to Lebezyatnikov.

"Andrei Semyonovich! I was mistaken about you! Defend her! You alone are on her side! She's an orphan; God has sent you! Andrei Semyonovich, you dear, sweet man!"

And Katerina Ivanovna, almost unconscious of what she was doing, threw herself on her knees before him.

"Hogwash!" screamed Luzhin, enraged to the point of fury. "You're pouring out hogwash, sir! 'I forgot, I remembered, I forgot'—what is all that! You mean I slipped it to her on purpose? Why? With what aim? What do I have in common with this . . ."

"Why? That I myself don't understand, but it's certain that I'm telling a true fact! I'm so far from being mistaken—you loathsome, criminal man—that I remember precisely how a question occurred to me at once in this connection, precisely as I was thanking you and shaking your hand. Precisely why did you put it into her pocket on the sly? That is, precisely why on the sly? Could it be simply because you wanted to conceal it from me, knowing that I hold opposite convictions and negate private philanthropy, which cures nothing radically? And so I decided that you were indeed ashamed to give away such a chunk in front of me, and besides, I thought, maybe he wants to give her a surprise, to astonish her when she finds a full hundred roubles in her pocket. (Because some philanthropists like very much to smear their philanthropies around like that, I know.) Then I also thought you might want to test her—that is, to see if she'd come and thank you when she found it. Then, that you wanted to avoid her gratitude, and that—how does it go?—that the right hand, or whatever, shouldn't know . . . something like that, in short[16] . . . Well, and so many other thoughts came to my mind then that I decided to think it all over later, but still considered it indelicate to reveal to you that I knew the secret. Again, however, still another question immediately came to my mind: that Sofya Semyonovna, for all I knew, might lose the money before she noticed it, which is why I decided to come here, to call her aside, and inform her that a hundred roubles had been put in her pocket. But on the way I stopped first to see the Kobylyatnikov ladies and give them *The General Conclusion of the Positive Method*, and especially to recommend an article by Piederit (and, incidentally, one by Wagner as well);[17] then I came here and found a whole scene going on! How, then, how could I have all these thoughts and arguments if I hadn't actually seen you put the hundred roubles in her pocket?"

When Andrei Semyonovich finished his verbose argument, with such a logical conclusion at the close of the speech, he was terribly tired and sweat was even running down his face. Alas, he did not know how to explain himself properly even in Russian (though he knew no other language), so that he somehow immediately became all exhausted, and even seemed to have grown thinner after his forensic exploit. Nevertheless, his speech produced an extraordinary effect. He had spoken with such ardor, with such conviction, that everyone seemed to believe him. Pyotr Petrovich felt things were going badly.

"What do I care if some foolish questions came into your head?" he cried out. "That is no proof, sir! You may have raved it all up in a dream, that's all! And I tell you that you are lying, sir! Lying and slandering because of some grudge against me, and, namely, because you're angry at my disagreeing with your freethinking and godless social proposals, that's what, sir!"

But this dodge proved useless to Pyotr Petrovich. On the contrary, murmuring was heard on all sides.

"Ah, so you're off on that track now!" cried Lebezyatnikov. "Lies! Call the police, and I'll swear an oath to it! The one thing I can't understand is why he risked such a base act! Oh, you vile, pathetic man!"

"I can explain why he risked such an act, and if need be I'll swear an oath to it myself!" Raskolnikov spoke finally in a firm voice, stepping forward.

He appeared firm and calm. It somehow became clear to everyone at a glance that he really knew what it was all about and that the denouement had arrived.

"It's all perfectly clear to me now," Raskolnikov went on, addressing Lebezyatnikov directly. "From the very beginning of this scene, I suspected there was some nasty hoax in it; I began suspecting it on account of certain particular circumstances, known only to myself, which I will presently explain to everyone: they are the crux of the matter! And you, Andrei Semyonovich, with your invaluable evidence, have finally made it all clear to me. I ask all of you, all of you, to listen carefully: this gentleman" (he pointed to Luzhin) "recently became engaged to a certain girl—namely, to my sister, Avdotya Romanovna Raskolnikov. But, having come to Petersburg, at our first meeting, the day before yesterday, he quarreled with me, and I threw him out of my place, for which there are witnesses. The man is very angry . . . I was not aware the day before yesterday that he was staying in your room, Andrei Semyonovich, and that consequently, on the same day that we quarreled—the day before yesterday, that is—he was a witness to my giving some money, as a friend of the late Mr. Marmeladov, to his wife, Katerina Ivanovna, for the funeral. He immediately wrote a note to my mother and informed her that I had given all my money not to Katerina Ivanovna, but to Sofya Semyonovna, and along with that made references in the meanest terms about . . . about Sofya Semyonovna's character—that is, he hinted at the character of my relations with Sofya Semyonovna. All this, you understand, with the aim of making me quarrel with my mother and sister, by suggesting to them that I was squandering their last money, which they had sent to help me, for ignoble purposes. Yesterday evening, before my mother and sister, and in his presence, I re-established the truth, proving that I had given the money to Katerina Ivanovna for the funeral, and not to Sofya Semyonovna, and that the day before yesterday I was not yet even acquainted with Sofya Semyonovna and had never set eyes on her. I also added that he, Pyotr Petrovich Luzhin, for all his virtues, was not worth the little finger of Sofya Semyonovna, of whom he spoke so badly. And to his question, whether I would sit Sofya Semyonovna next to my sister, I answered that I had already done so that same day. Angry that my mother and sister did not want to quarrel with me over his calumny, he became more unpardonably rude to them with every word. A final break ensued, and he was thrown out of the house. All this took place yesterday evening. Here I ask you to pay particular attention: suppose he now managed to prove that Sofya Semyonovna was a thief; then, first of all, he would prove to my sister and mother that he was almost right in his suspicions; that he was justly angry with me for putting my sister and Sofya Semyonovna on the same level; that in attacking me he was thereby also defending and protecting the honor of my sister, and his bride. In short, by means of all this he might even make me quarrel with my family again, and could certainly hope to win back their favor. I say nothing of his revenge on me personally, since he has reasons to suppose that Sofya Semyonovna's honor and happiness are very dear to me. That was the whole of his calculation! That is how I understand this business! That is the reason for it, and there can be no other!"

Thus, or almost thus, Raskolnikov ended his speech, interrupted frequently by exclamations from the public, who listened, however, very attentively. But in spite of all the interruptions, he spoke sharply, calmly, precisely, clearly, firmly. His sharp voice, his convinced tone and stern face produced an extraordinary effect on everyone.

"Right, right, that's right!" Lebezyatnikov confirmed delightedly.

"It must be right, because he precisely asked me, as soon as Sofya Semyonovna came to our room, whether you were here, whether I had seen you among Katerina Ivanovna's guests. He called me over to the window for that, and asked me quietly. That means he wanted to be sure you were here! It's right, it's all right!"

Luzhin was silent and only smiled contemptuously. He was very pale, however. He seemed to be pondering how he might wriggle out of it. He would perhaps have been glad to drop it all and leave, but at the present moment that was almost impossible; it would have amounted to a direct admission that the accusations being hurled at him were true and that he had indeed slandered Sofya Semyonovna. Besides, the public, who were a bit drunk to begin with, were much too excited. The supply man, though he had not understood it all, shouted more than anyone, and suggested certain measures quite unpleasant for Luzhin. But there were some who were not drunk; people came and gathered from all the rooms. The three little Poles were all terribly angry, and ceaselessly shouted *"Panie łajdak!"*[18] at him, muttering some other Polish threats in addition. Sonya had listened with strained attention, but also as if not understanding it all, as if coming out of a swoon. She simply would not take her eyes from Raskolnikov, feeling that he was her whole defense. Katerina Ivanovna was breathing hoarsely and with difficulty, and seemed terribly exhausted. Amalia Ivanovna stood there most stupidly of all, her mouth hanging open, grasping nothing whatsoever. She saw only that Pyotr Petrovich had somehow been caught. Raskolnikov asked to speak again, but this time he was not given a chance to finish: everyone was shouting and crowding around Luzhin with threats and curses. Yet Pyotr Petrovich did not turn coward. Seeing that the case of Sonya's accusation was utterly lost, he resorted to outright insolence.

"Excuse me, gentlemen, excuse me; don't crowd, let me pass!" he said, making his way through the throng. "And kindly stop your threatening; I assure you nothing will come of it, you won't do anything, I'm not to be intimidated, quite the opposite, gentlemen, it is you who will have to answer for using force to cover up a criminal case. The thief has been more than exposed, and I shall pursue it, sirs. The courts are not so blind . . . or drunk; they will not believe two notorious atheists, agitators, and freethinkers, accusing me out of personal vengeance, which they, in their foolishness, admit themselves . . . So, sirs, excuse me!"

"Be so good as to move out, and don't leave a trace of yourself behind in my room! It's all over between us! When I think how I turned myself inside out explaining things to him . . . for two whole weeks! . . ."

"But I told you myself that I was vacating today, Andrei Semyonovich, and it was you who were trying to keep me here; now I shall only add that you are a fool, sir. I hope you may find a cure for your wits, and your weak-sighted eyes. Excuse me, gentlemen!"

He pushed his way through; but the supply man did not want to let him off so easily, just with abuse: he snatched a glass from the table, hauled off, and hurled it at Pyotr Petrovich; but the glass flew straight at Amalia Ivanovna. She shrieked, and the supply man, who had lost his balance as he swung, went crashing to the floor under the table. Pyotr Petrovich returned to his room, and half an hour later was no longer in the house. Sonya, timid by nature, had known even before that it was easier to ruin her than anyone else, and that whoever wanted to could offend her almost with impunity. But even so, until that very moment she had always thought it somehow possible to avoid disaster—by prudence, meekness, submissiveness to one and all. The disillusionment was too much for her. She was capable, of course, of enduring everything, even this, with patience and almost without a murmur. But for the first moment it was too much for her. In spite of her triumph and vindication—when the initial fear and the initial stupor had passed, when she had grasped and understood everything clearly—the feeling of helplessness and offense painfully wrung her heart. She became hysterical. Finally, unable to bear it, she rushed out of the room and ran home. This was almost immediately after Luzhin left. Amalia Ivanovna, when she was hit by the glass, amid the loud laughter of all those present, also could no longer bear this hangover from someone else's spree. With a shriek, she flung herself wildly at Katerina Ivanovna, whom she blamed for everything.

"Facate the apartment! At vonce! March!" And with these words she began seizing anything of Katerina Ivanovna's she could lay her hands on and throwing it to the floor. Nearly dead to begin with, all but in a faint, breathless, pale, Katerina Ivanovna jumped up from the bed (on which she had fallen in exhaustion) and rushed at Amalia Ivanovna. But the struggle was too unequal; she was pushed away like a feather.

"What! As if that godless slander weren't enough—this creature is at me, too! What! I'm driven from my apartment on the day of my husband's funeral, after my bread and salt, thrown out into the street, with the orphans! But where can I go?" the poor woman screamed, sobbing and gasping. "Lord!" she suddenly cried, her eyes flashing, "is there really no justice? Who else are you going to protect if not us orphans? Ah, no, we shall see! There is justice and truth in the world, there is, I'll find it! Just wait, you godless creature! Polechka, stay with the children; I'll be right back! Wait for me, even in the street! We'll see whether there's truth in the world!"

And throwing over her head the same green flannel shawl that the late Marmeladov had mentioned in his story, Katerina Ivanovna pushed her way through the disorderly and drunken crowd of tenants who still crowded the room, and ran shouting and weeping out into the street—with the vague purpose of finding justice somewhere, at once, immediately, and whatever the cost. Terrified, Polechka hid with the children in the corner, on the trunk, where, embracing the two little ones and trembling all over, she began waiting for her mother's return. Amalia Ivanovna rushed about the room, shrieked, wailed, flung everything she came upon to the floor, in a great rage. The tenants were all bawling without rhyme or reason—some finished saying whatever they could about the just-occurred incident; others quarreled and swore; still others began singing songs . . .

"And now it's also time for me to go!" thought Raskolnikov. "Well, Sofya Semyonovna, we'll see what you have to say now!"

And he set out for Sonya's place.

IV

RASKOLNIKOV had been an energetic and spirited advocate of Sonya against Luzhin, even though he was burdened with so much horror and suffering in his own soul. But having suffered so much that morning, he was as if glad of the chance to change his impressions, which were becoming unbearable—to say nothing of all that was personal and heartfelt in his desire to defend Sonya. Besides, the meeting he now faced with Sonya had been on his mind, and troubled him terribly, especially at moments: he *had* to tell her who killed Lizaveta, and foresaw a terrible torment for himself, which he tried, as it were, to wave away. And therefore, when he exclaimed, as he was leaving Katerina Ivanovna's: "Well, what are you going to say now, Sofya Semyonovna?" he was evidently still in some externally aroused state of high spirits and defiance from his recent triumph over Luzhin. But a strange thing happened to him. When he reached Kapernaumov's apartment, he felt suddenly powerless and afraid. Thoughtful, he stood outside the door with a strange question: "Need I tell her who killed Lizaveta?" The question was strange because he suddenly felt at the same time that it was impossible not only not to tell her, but even to put the moment off, however briefly. He did not yet know why it was impossible; he only *felt* it, and the tormenting awareness of his powerlessness before necessity almost crushed him. In order not to reason and suffer any longer, he quickly opened the door and looked at Sonya from the threshold. She was sitting with her elbows resting on the table, her face buried in her hands, but when she saw Raskolnikov, she hurriedly rose and went to meet him, as if she had been waiting for him.

"What would have happened to me without you!" she said quickly, coming up to him in the middle of the room. Obviously it was just this that she was in a hurry to say to him. This was why she had been waiting for him.

Raskolnikov walked over to the table and sat down on the chair from which she had just risen. She stood in front of him, two steps away, exactly as the day before.

"Well, Sonya?" he said, and suddenly felt that his voice was trembling. "So the whole matter indeed rested on your 'social position and its accompanying habits.' Did you understand that just now?"

Suffering showed on her face.

"Only don't talk to me like you did yesterday," she interrupted him. "Please, don't start. There's enough pain as it is . . ."

She smiled hurriedly, for fear he might not like her reproach.

"It was stupid of me to leave. What's going on there now? I was about to go back, but kept thinking . . . you might come."

He told her that Amalia Ivanovna was throwing them out of the apartment, and that Katerina Ivanovna had run off somewhere "in search of truth."

"Ah, my God!" Sonya heaved herself up. "Let's go quickly . . ." And she seized her cape.

"It's the same thing eternally!" Raskolnikov cried out in vexation. "All you ever think about is them! Stay with me a little."

"But . . . Katerina Ivanovna?"

"Katerina Ivanovna certainly won't do without you; she'll come here herself, since she ran away from the house," he added peevishly. "If she doesn't find you here, you'll be blamed for it . . ."

In painful indecision, Sonya sat down on a chair. Raskolnikov was silent, looking at the ground and thinking something over.

"Suppose Luzhin didn't want to do it this time," he began, without glancing at Sonya. "Well, but if he had wanted to, or if it had somehow entered into his calculations, he'd have locked you up in prison, if Lebezyatnikov and I hadn't happened to be there. Eh?"

"Yes," she said in a weak voice. "Yes!" she repeated, distracted and alarmed.

"And I really might have happened not to be there! And as for Lebezyatnikov, he turned up quite accidentally."

Sonya was silent.

"Well, and what if it had been prison? What then? Remember what I said yesterday?"

Again she did not reply. He waited.

"And I thought you'd cry out again: 'Ah, stop, don't say it!'" Raskolnikov laughed, but somehow with a strain. "What now, still silent?" he asked after a moment. "We've got to talk about something! I, namely, would be interested in finding out how you would now resolve a certain 'question,' as Lebezyatnikov says." (It seemed he was beginning to get confused.) "No, really, I'm serious. Imagine to yourself, Sonya, that you knew all of Luzhin's intentions beforehand, knew (I mean, for certain) that as a result of them Katerina Ivanovna would perish altogether, and the children as well, and with you thrown in (just so, *thrown in,* since you consider yourself nothing). Polechka, too . . . because she'll go the same way. Well, so, if all this was suddenly given to you to decide: is it for him or for them to go on living; that is, should Luzhin live and commit abominations, or should Katerina Ivanovna die? How would you decide which of them was to die? That's what I'm asking."

Sonya looked at him worriedly: she could detect something peculiar in this uncertain speech, approaching its object from afar.

"I had a feeling you were going to ask something like that," she said, looking at him searchingly.

"Well, so you did; all the same, how is one to decide?"

"Why do you ask about what cannot be?" Sonya said with loathing.

"So it's better for Luzhin to live and commit abominations! You don't dare to decide even in this?"

"But I cannot know divine Providence . . . And why do you ask what cannot be asked? Why such empty questions? How could it come about that it should depend on my decision? And who put me here to judge who is to live and who is not to live?"

"Once divine Providence gets mixed up in it, there's nothing to be done," Raskolnikov growled sullenly.

"You'd better say straight out what you want!" Sonya cried with suffering. "You're leading up to something again . . . Can it be that you came only to torment me?"

She could not help herself and suddenly began weeping bitterly. He looked at her in gloomy anguish. About five minutes passed.

"Yes, you're right, Sonya," he said at last, softly. He had changed suddenly; his affectedly insolent and powerlessly challenging tone had disappeared. Even his voice became suddenly weaker. "I told you yesterday that I would not come to ask forgiveness, and now I've begun by almost asking forgiveness . . . I was speaking about Luzhin and Providence for my own sake . . . I was seeking forgiveness, Sonya . . ."

He tried to smile, but this pale smile told of something powerless and incomplete. He bent his head and covered his face with his hands.

And suddenly a strange, unexpected feeling of corrosive hatred for Sonya came over his heart. As if surprised and frightened by this feeling, he suddenly raised his head and looked at her intently, but he met her anxious and painfully caring eyes fixed upon him; here was love; his hatred vanished like a phantom. That was not it; he had mistaken one feeling for another. All it meant was that *the moment* had come.

Again he covered his face with his hands and bent his head. Suddenly he turned pale, got up from the chair, looked at Sonya, and, without saying anything, went mechanically and sat on her bed.

This moment, as it felt to him, was terribly like the one when he had stood behind the old woman, having already freed the axe from its loop, and realized that "there was not another moment to lose."

"What's the matter?" Sonya asked, becoming terribly timid.

He could not utter a word. This was not the way, this was not at all the way he had intended to *announce* it, and he himself did not understand what was happening with him now. She quietly went over, sat down on the bed beside him, and waited, without taking her eyes from him. Her heart was pounding and sinking. It became unbearable: he turned his deathly pale face to her; he twisted his lips powerlessly in an effort to utter something. Horror swept over Sonya's heart.

"What's the matter with you?" she repeated, moving slightly away from him.

"Nothing, Sonya. Don't be afraid . . . Nonsense! Really, if you stop and think, it's—nonsense," he muttered, with the look of a man lost in delirium. "Only why did I come to torment you?" he suddenly added, looking at her. "Really, why? That's what I keep asking myself, Sonya . . ."

Perhaps he had asked himself this question a quarter of an hour before, but now he spoke quite powerlessly, hardly aware of himself, and feeling a ceaseless trembling all over.

"Oh, how tormented you are!" she said with suffering, peering at him.

"It's all nonsense! . . . Listen, Sonya" (suddenly, for some reason, he gave a pale and powerless smile, which lasted about two seconds), "do you remember what I wanted to tell you yesterday?"

Sonya waited uneasily.

"I said, as I was leaving, that I was perhaps saying good-bye to you forever, but that if I came today, I'd tell you . . . who killed Lizaveta."

She suddenly began trembling all over.

"So, you see, I've come to tell you."

"Then, yesterday, you really . . ." she whispered with difficulty. "But how do you know?" she added quickly, as if suddenly coming to her senses.

Sonya began breathing with difficulty. Her face was becoming paler and paler.

"I know."

She was silent for a minute or so.

"What, has *he* been found?" she asked timidly.

"No, he hasn't."

"Then how do you know about *it?*" she asked again, barely audibly, and again after almost a minute's silence.

He turned to her and looked at her very, very intently.

"Guess," he said, with his former twisted and powerless smile.

It was as if a shudder ran through her whole body.

"But you . . . I . . . why do you . . . frighten me so?" she said, smiling like a child.

"I must be a great friend of *his* . . . since I know," Raskolnikov went on, still looking relentlessly in her face, as if he were no longer able to take his eyes away. "This Lizaveta . . . he didn't want to kill her . . . He killed her . . . accidentally . . . He wanted to kill the old woman . . . when she was alone . . . and he went there . . . And then Lizaveta came in . . . Then he . . . killed her, too."

Another terrible minute passed. They both went on looking at each other.

"So you can't guess?" he suddenly asked, feeling as if he were throwing himself from a bell-tower.

"N-no," Sonya whispered, barely audibly.

"Take a good look."

Again, as soon as he said this, a former, familiar sensation suddenly turned his soul to ice: he looked at her, and suddenly in her face he seemed to see the face of Lizaveta. He vividly recalled the expression of Lizaveta's face as he was approaching her with the axe and she was backing away from him towards the wall, her hand held out, with a completely childlike fright on her face, exactly as when little children suddenly begin to be frightened of something, stare fixedly and uneasily at what frightens them, back away, and, holding out a little hand, are preparing to cry. Almost the same thing now happened with Sonya as well: just as powerlessly, with the same fright, she looked at him for a time; then suddenly, holding out her left hand, she rested her fingers barely, lightly, on his chest, and slowly began to get up from the bed, backing farther and farther away from him, while looking at him more and more fixedly. Her terror suddenly communicated itself to him: exactly the same fright showed on his face as well; he began looking at her in exactly the same way, and even with almost the same *childlike* smile.

"You've guessed?" he whispered at last.

"Lord!" a terrible cry tore itself from her breast. Powerlessly she fell onto the bed, face down on the pillows. But after a moment she quickly got up again, quickly moved closer to him, seized both his hands, and, squeezing them tightly with her thin fingers, as in a vise, again began looking fixedly in his face, as though her eyes were glued to him. With this last, desperate look she wanted to seek out and catch hold of at least some last hope for herself. But there was no hope; no doubt remained; it was all *so!* Even later, afterwards, when she remembered this moment, she found it both strange and wondrous: precisely why had she seen *at once* that there was no longer any doubt? She could not really say, for instance, that she had anticipated anything of the sort. And yet now, as soon as he told her, it suddenly seemed to her that she really had anticipated *this* very thing.

"Come, Sonya, enough! Don't torment me!" he begged with suffering.

This was not the way, this was not at all the way he had intended to reveal it to her, but *thus* it came out.

As if forgetting herself, she jumped up and, wringing her hands, walked halfway across the room; but she came back quickly and sat down again beside him, almost touching him, shoulder to shoulder. All at once, as if pierced, she gave a start, cried out, and, not knowing why, threw herself on her knees before him.

"What, what have you done to yourself!" she said desperately, and, jumping up from her knees, threw herself on his neck, embraced him, and pressed him very, very tightly in her arms.

Raskolnikov recoiled and looked at her with a sad smile.

"You're so strange, Sonya—you embrace me and kiss me, when I've just told you *about that.* You're forgetting yourself."

"No one, no one in the whole world, is unhappier than you are now!" she exclaimed, as if in a frenzy, not hearing his remark, and suddenly burst into sobs, as if in hysterics.

A feeling long unfamiliar to him flooded his soul and softened it all at once. He did not resist: two tears rolled from his eyes and hung on his lashes.

"So you won't leave me, Sonya?" he said, looking at her almost with hope.

"No, no, never, not anywhere!" Sonya cried out. "I'll follow you, I'll go wherever you go! Oh, Lord! . . . Ah, wretched me! . . . Why, why didn't I know you before! Why didn't you come before? Oh, Lord!"

"Well, so I've come."

"Now you've come! Oh, what's to be done now! . . . Together, together!" she kept repeating, as if oblivious, and again she embraced him. "I'll go to hard labor with you!" He suddenly seemed to flinch; the former hateful and almost arrogant smile forced itself to his lips.

"But maybe I don't want to go to hard labor, Sonya," he said.

Sonya glanced at him quickly.

After her first passionate and tormenting sympathy for the unhappy man, the horrible idea of the murder struck her again. In the changed tone of his words she suddenly could hear the murderer. She looked at him in amazement. As yet she knew nothing of why, or how, or for what it had been. Now all these questions flared up at once in her consciousness. And again she did not believe it: "He, he a murderer? Is it really possible?"

"What is this! Where am I!" she said, deeply perplexed, as if she had still not come to her senses. "But you, you, you're so . . . how could you make yourself do it? . . . What is this!"

"To rob her, of course. Stop it, Sonya!" he replied somehow wearily, and as if with vexation.

Sonya stood as if stunned, but suddenly exclaimed:

"You were hungry! You . . . it was to help your mother? Yes?"

"No, Sonya, no," he murmured, turning away and hanging his

head. "I wasn't so hungry . . . I did want to help my mother, but . . . that's not quite right either . . . don't torment me, Sonya!"

Sonya clasped her hands.

"But can it be, can it be that it's all actually true? Lord, what sort of truth is this! Who can believe it? . . . And how is it, how is it that you could give away your last penny, and yet kill in order to rob! Ahh! . . ." she suddenly cried out, "that money you gave to Katerina Ivanovna . . . that money . . . Lord, was that the same money . . ."

"No, Sonya," he interrupted hastily, "don't worry, it wasn't the same money! That was money my mother sent to me, through a merchant; it came when I was sick, and I gave it away the same day . . . Razumikhin saw . . . it was he who received it for me . . . it was my money, my own, really mine."

Sonya listened to him in perplexity and tried as hard as she could to understand something.

"And *that* money . . . though I don't even know if there was any money," he added softly and as if pensively. "I took a purse from around her neck then, a suede purse . . . a fat one, stuffed full . . . but I didn't look inside, I must not have had time . . . And the things—there were just some cuff-links and little chains—I buried all the things along with the purse under a stone in some unknown courtyard on V——y Prospect, the very next morning . . . It's all still there . . ."

Sonya was listening as hard as she could.

"Well, then why . . . how can you say it was for the sake of robbery, if you didn't take anything?" she said quickly, grasping at a straw.

"I don't know . . . I haven't decided yet—whether to take the money or not," he spoke pensively, and all at once, as if recollecting himself, he grinned quickly and briefly. "Ah, what a stupid thing to come out with, eh?"

The thought flashed through Sonya: "Can he be mad?" But she abandoned it at once: no, there was something else here. She understood nothing here, nothing at all.

"You know, Sonya," he said suddenly, with a sort of inspiration, "you know, I can tell you this much: if I'd killed them only because I was hungry," he went on, stressing each word, and looking at her mysteriously but sincerely, "I would now be . . . *happy!* You should know that!

"And what is it to you, what is it to you," he cried out after a moment, even with some sort of despair, "what is it to you if I've now confessed that I did a bad thing? This stupid triumph over me—what is it to you? Ah, Sonya, was it for this that I came to you today!"

Sonya again wanted to say something, but kept silent.

"That is why I called you to go with me yesterday, because you are the only one I have left."

"Called me where?" Sonya asked timidly.

"Not to steal, not to kill, don't worry, not for that," he grinned caustically. "We're different . . . And you know, Sonya, it's only now, only now that I understand *where* I was calling you yesterday. And yesterday, when I was calling you, I didn't know where myself. I called you for one thing, I came to you for one thing: that you not leave me. You won't leave me, Sonya?"

She pressed his hand.

"And why, why did I tell her, why did I reveal it to her!" he exclaimed in despair after a moment, looking at her with infinite pain. "Now you're waiting for explanations from me, Sonya, you're sitting and waiting, I can see that; and what am I going to tell you? Because you won't understand any of it; you'll only wear yourself out with suffering . . . because of me! So, now you're crying and embracing me again—so, why are you embracing me? Because I couldn't endure it myself, and have come to shift the burden onto another: 'You suffer, too; it will be so much the easier for me!' Can you really love such a scoundrel?"

"But aren't you suffering as well?" cried Sonya.

The same feeling flooded his soul again, and softened it again for a moment.

"I have a wicked heart, Sonya; take note of that, it can explain a lot. That's why I came, because I'm wicked. There are those who wouldn't have come. But I am a coward and . . . a scoundrel! Well . . . and what if I am! All this is not it . . . I have to speak now, and I don't even know how to begin . . ."

He stopped and fell to thinking.

"Ahh, we're so different!" he cried out again. "We're not a match. And why, why did I come! I'll never forgive myself for it!"

"No, no, it's good that you came!" Sonya exclaimed. "It's better that I know! Much better!"

He looked at her with pain.

"Why not, after all!" he said, as if reconsidering, "since that is how it was! You see, I wanted to become a Napoleon, that's why I killed . . . Well, is it clear now?"

"N-no," Sonya whispered, naively and timidly, "but go on, just go on! I'll understand, I'll understand everything *within myself!*" she kept entreating him.

"You will? All right, we'll see!"

He fell silent, and thought it over for a long time.

"The thing is that I once asked myself this question: how would it have been if Napoleon, for example, had happened to be in my place, and didn't have Toulon, or Egypt, or the crossing of Mont Blanc to start his career, but, instead of all these beautiful and monumental things, had quite simply some ridiculous old crone, a leginstrar's widow, whom on top of that he had to kill in order to filch money from her trunk (for his career, you understand)—well, so, could he have made himself do it if there was no other way out? Wouldn't he have shrunk from it because it was so unmonumental and . . . and sinful? Well, I tell you, I suffered a terribly long time over this 'question,' so that I was terribly ashamed when I finally realized (somehow all at once) not only that he would not shrink, but that it wouldn't even occur to him that it was unmonumental . . . and he wouldn't understand at all what there was to shrink from. And if there was indeed no other path for him, he'd up and throttle her before she could make a peep, without a moment's thoughtfulness! . . . So I, too . . . came out of my thoughtfulness . . . I throttled her . . . following the example of my authority . . . And that's exactly how it was! You think it's funny? Yes, Sonya, the funniest thing is that maybe that's precisely how it was . . ."

Sonya did not think it was funny at all.

"You'd better tell me straight out . . . without examples," she asked, still more timidly, and barely audibly.

He turned to her, looked at her sadly, and took her hands.

"You're right again, Sonya. It's all nonsense, almost sheer babble!

You see, my mother, as you know, has almost nothing. My sister received an education only by chance, and is doomed to drag herself about as a governess. All their hopes were in me alone. I was studying, but I couldn't support myself at the university and had to take a leave for a while. Even if things had managed to go on that way, then in about ten or twelve years (if circumstances turned out well) I could still only hope to become some sort of teacher or official with a thousand-rouble salary . . ." (He was speaking as if by rote.) "And by then my mother would have withered away with cares and grief, and I still wouldn't be able to set her at ease, and my sister . . . well, something even worse might have happened with my sister! . . . And who wants to spend his whole life passing everything by, turning away from everything; to forget his mother, and politely endure, for example, his sister's offense? Why? So that, having buried them, he can acquire new ones—a wife and children—and then leave them, too, without a kopeck or a crust of bread? Well . . . well, so I decided to take possession of the old woman's money and use it for my first years, without tormenting my mother, to support myself at the university, and for the first steps after the university, and to do it all sweepingly, radically, so as to set up a whole new career entirely and start out on a new, independent path . . . Well . . . well, that's all . . . Well, that I killed the old woman—of course, it was a bad thing to do . . . well, but enough of that!"

In some sort of powerlessness he dragged himself to the end of his story and hung his head.

"Oh, that's not it, not it," Sonya exclaimed in anguish, "how can it be so . . . no, that's not it, not it!"

"You can see for yourself that's not it! . . . yet it's the truth, I told it sincerely!"

"What kind of truth is it! Oh, Lord!"

"I only killed a louse, Sonya, a useless, nasty, pernicious louse."

"A human being—a louse!"

"Not a louse, I know it myself," he replied, looking at her strangely. "Anyway, I'm lying, Sonya," he added, "I've been lying for a long time . . . All that is not it; you're right in saying so. There are quite different reasons here, quite, quite different! . . . I haven't talked with anyone for a long time, Sonya . . . I have a bad headache now."

His eyes were burning with a feverish fire. He was almost beginning to rave; a troubled smile wandered over his lips. A terrible powerlessness showed through his agitated state of mind. Sonya realized how he was suffering. Her head, too, was beginning to spin. And he spoke so strangely: one seemed to understand something, but . . . "but what is it! What is it! Oh, Lord!" And she wrung her hands in despair.

"No, Sonya, that's not it!" he began again, suddenly raising his head, as if an unexpected turn of thought had struck him and aroused him anew. "That's not it! Better . . . suppose (yes! it's really better this way), suppose that I'm vain, jealous, spiteful, loathsome, vengeful, well . . . and perhaps also inclined to madness. (Let's have it all at once! There's been talk of madness already, I've noticed!) I just told you I couldn't support myself at the university. But, you know, maybe I could have. Mother would have sent me whatever was needed for the fees; and I could have earned enough for boots, clothes, and bread myself; that's certain! There were lessons; I was being offered fifty kopecks. Razumikhin works! But I turned spiteful and didn't want to. Precisely, I *turned spiteful* (it's a good phrase!). Then I hid in my corner like a spider. You were in my kennel, you saw it . . . And do you know, Sonya, low ceilings and cramped rooms cramp the soul and mind! Oh, how I hated that kennel! And yet I didn't want to leave it. I purposely didn't want to! For days on end I wouldn't go out, and didn't want to work, and didn't even want to eat, and went on lying there. If Nastasya brought something, I'd eat; if not, the day would go by; I purposely didn't ask, out of spite. At night there was no light; I used to lie in the dark, rather than earn money for candles. I was supposed to be studying, but I sold my books; and on my table, on my papers and notebooks, there's a finger-thick layer of dust even now. I liked to lie and think. And I kept on thinking . . . And I kept on having such dreams, all sorts of strange dreams, there's no point in telling what they were about! Only at the same time I also began imagining . . . No, that's not right! Again I'm not telling it right! You see, I kept asking myself then: am I so stupid that, if others are stupid and I know for certain they're stupid, I myself don't want to be smarter? Then I learned, Sonya, that if one waits for everyone to become smarter, it will take too long . . . And then I also learned that it will never happen, that people will never change, and no one can remake them, and it's not worth the effort! Yes, it's true! It's their law . . . A law, Sonya! It's true! . . . And I know now, Sonya, that he who is firm and strong in mind and spirit will rule over them! He who dares much will be right in their eyes. He who can spit on what is greatest will be their lawgiver, and he who dares the most will be the rightest of all! Thus it has been until now, and thus it will always be. Only a blind man can fail to see it!"

Though Raskolnikov was looking at Sonya as he said this, he was no longer concerned with whether she understood or not. The fever had him wholly in its grip. He was in some sort of gloomy ecstasy. (Indeed, he had not talked with anyone for a very long time!) Sonya understood that this gloomy catechism had become his faith and law.

"Then I realized, Sonya," he went on ecstatically, "that power is given only to the one who dares to reach down and take it. Here there is one thing, one thing only: one has only to dare! And then a thought took shape in me, for the first time in my life, one that nobody had ever thought before me! Nobody! It suddenly came to me as bright as the sun: how is it that no man before now has dared or dares yet, while passing by all this absurdity, quite simply to take the whole thing by the tail and whisk it off to the devil! I . . . I wanted *to dare*, and I killed . . . I just wanted to dare, Sonya, that's the whole reason!"

"Oh, be still, be still!" cried Sonya, clasping her hands. "You deserted God, and God has stricken you, and given you over to the devil! . . ."

"By the way, Sonya, when I was lying in the dark and imagining it all, was it the devil confounding me, eh?"

"Be still! Don't laugh, blasphemer, you understand nothing, simply nothing! Oh, Lord! Nothing, he understands nothing!"

"Be still, Sonya, I'm not laughing at all, I know myself that a devil was dragging me. Be still, Sonya, be still!" he repeated gloomily and insistently. "I know everything. I thought it all out and whispered it all out when I was lying there in the dark . . . I argued it all out with myself, to the last little trace, and I know everything, everything! And I was so sick, so sick of all this babble then! I wanted to forget everything and start anew, Sonya, and to stop babbling. Do you really think I went into it headlong, like a fool? No, I went into it like a bright boy, and that's what ruined me! And do you really think I didn't at least know, for example, that since I'd begun questioning and querying myself: do I have the right to have power?—it meant that I do not have the right to have power? Or that if I pose the question: is man a louse?—it means that *for me* man is not a louse, but that he is a louse for the one to whom it never occurs, who goes straight ahead without any questions . . . Because, if I tormented myself for so many days: would Napoleon have gone ahead or not?—it means I must already have felt clearly that I was not Napoleon . . . I endured all, all the torment of all this babble, Sonya, and I longed to shake it all off my back: I wanted to kill without casuistry, Sonya, to kill for myself, for myself alone! I didn't want to lie about it even to myself! It was not to help my mother that I killed—nonsense! I did not kill so that, having obtained means and power, I could become a benefactor of mankind. Nonsense! I simply killed—killed for myself, for myself alone—and whether I would later become anyone's benefactor, or would spend my life like a spider, catching everyone in my web and sucking the life-sap out of everyone, should at that moment have made no difference to me! . . . And it was not money above all that I wanted when I killed, Sonya; not money so much as something else . . . I know all this now . . . Understand me: perhaps, continuing on that same path, I would never again repeat the murder. There was something else I wanted to know; something else was nudging my arm. I wanted to find out then, and find out quickly, whether I was a louse like all the rest, or a man? Would I be able to step over, or not! Would I dare to reach down and take, or not? Am I a trembling creature, or do I have the *right* . . ."

"To kill? The right to kill?" Sonya clasped her hands.

"Ahh, Sonya!" he cried irritably, and was about to make some objection to her, but remained scornfully silent. "Don't interrupt me, Sonya! I wanted to prove only one thing to you: that the devil did drag me there then, but afterwards he explained to me that I had no right to go there, because I'm exactly the same louse as all the rest! He made a mockery of me, and so I've come to you now! Welcome your guest! If I weren't a louse, would I have come to you? Listen: when I went to the old woman that time, I went only *to try* . . . You should know that!"

"And you killed! Killed!"

"But how did I kill, really? Is that any way to kill? Is that how one goes about killing, the way I went about it then? Some day I'll tell you how I went about it . . . Was it the old crone I killed? I killed myself, not the old crone! Whopped myself right then and there, forever! . . . And it was the devil killed the old crone, not me . . . Enough, enough, Sonya, enough! Let me be," he suddenly cried out in convulsive anguish, "let me be!"

He leaned his elbows on his knees and pressed his head with his palms as with a pincers.

"Such suffering!" burst in a painful wail from Sonya.

"Well, what to do now, tell me!" he said, suddenly raising his head and looking at her, his face hideously distorted by despair.

"What to do!" she exclaimed, suddenly jumping up from her place, and her eyes, still full of tears, suddenly flashed. "Stand up!" (She seized him by the shoulder; he rose, looking at her almost in amazement.) "Go now, this minute, stand in the crossroads, bow down, and first kiss the earth you've defiled, then bow to the whole world, on all four sides, and say aloud to everyone: 'I have killed!' Then God will send you life again. Will you go? Will you go?" she kept asking him, all trembling as if in a fit, seizing both his hands, squeezing them tightly in her own, and looking at him with fiery eyes.

He was amazed and even struck by her sudden ecstasy.

"So it's hard labor, is it, Sonya? I must go and denounce myself?" he asked gloomily.

"Accept suffering and redeem yourself by it, that's what you must do."

"No! I won't go to them, Sonya."

"And live, how will you live? What will you live with?" Sonya exclaimed. "Is it possible now? How will you talk to your mother? (Oh, and them, what will become of them now!) But what am I saying! You've already abandoned your mother and sister. You have, you've already abandoned them. Oh, Lord!" she cried, "he already knows it all himself! But how, how can one live with no human being! What will become of you now!"

"Don't be a child, Sonya," he said softly. "How am I guilty before them? Why should I go? What should I tell them? It's all just a phantom . . . They expend people by the million themselves, and what's more they consider it a virtue. They're cheats and scoundrels, Sonya! . . . I won't go. And what should I say: that I killed but didn't dare take the money, that I hid it under a stone?" he added, with a caustic grin. "They'll just laugh at me; they'll say I was a fool not to take it. A coward and a fool! They won't understand a thing, Sonya, not a thing—and they're not worthy to understand. Why should I go? I won't go. Don't be a child, Sonya . . ."

"You'll suffer too much, too much," she repeated, stretching out her hands to him in desperate supplication.

"*Still,* maybe I've slapped myself with it," he remarked gloomily, as if deep in thought, "maybe I'm *still* a man and not a louse, and was being too quick to condemn myself . . . I'll *still* fight."

A haughty smile was forcing itself to his lips.

"To bear such suffering! And for your whole life, your whole life! . . ."

"I'll get used to it . . ." he said, grimly and pensively. "Listen," he began after a moment, "enough tears; it's time for business: I came to tell you that they're after me now, trying to catch me . . ."

"Ah!" Sonya cried fearfully.

"So you cry out! You yourself want me to go to hard labor, and now you're afraid? Only here's what: I'm not going to let them get me. I'll still fight them; they won't be able to do anything. They don't have any real evidence. I was in great danger yesterday, I thought I was already ruined, but things got better today. All their evidence is double-ended; I mean, I can turn their accusations in my own favor, understand? And I will, because now I know how it's done . . . But they'll certainly put me in jail. If it weren't for one incident, they might have put me in today; certainly, they may *still* even do it today . . . Only it's nothing, Sonya: I'll sit there, and then they'll let me go . . . because they don't have one real proof, and they never will, I promise you. And they can't keep anyone behind bars with what they have. Well, enough . . . I just wanted you to know . . . I'll try to manage things with my mother and sister somehow so as to reassure them and not frighten them . . . My sister now seems provided for . . . so my mother is, too . . . Well, that's all. Be careful, though. Will you come and visit me when I'm in jail?"

"Oh, I will! I will!"

The two were sitting side by side, sad and crushed, as if they had been washed up alone on a deserted shore after a storm. He looked at Sonya and felt how much of her love was on him, and, strangely, he suddenly felt it heavy and painful to be loved like that. Yes, it was a strange and terrible feeling! On his way to see Sonya, he had felt she was his only hope and his only way out; he had thought he would be able to unload at least part of his torment; but now, suddenly, when her whole heart turned to him, he suddenly felt and realized that he was incomparably more unhappy than he had been before.

"Sonya," he said, "you'd better not visit me when I'm in jail."

Sonya did not reply; she was weeping. Several minutes passed.

"Do you have a cross on you?" she suddenly asked unexpectedly, as if suddenly remembering.

At first he did not understand the question.

"You don't, do you? Here, take this cypress one. I have another, a brass one, Lizaveta's. Lizaveta and I exchanged crosses; she gave me her cross, and I gave her my little icon. I'll wear Lizaveta's now, and you can have this one. Take it . . . it's mine! It's mine!" she insisted. "We'll go to suffer together, and we'll bear the cross together! . . ."

"Give it to me!" said Raskolnikov. He did not want to upset her. But he immediately drew back the hand he had held out to take the cross.

"Not now, Sonya. Better later," he added, to reassure her.

"Yes, yes, that will be better, better," she picked up enthusiastically. "When you go to your suffering, then you'll put it on. You'll come to me, I'll put it on you, we'll pray and go."

At that moment someone knocked three times at the door.

"Sofya Semyonovna, may I come in?" someone's very familiar and polite voice was heard.

Sonya rushed to the door in fear. The blond physiognomy of Mr. Lebezyatnikov peeked into the room.

V

LEBEZYATNIKOV looked alarmed.

"I must see you, Sofya Semyonovna. Excuse me . . . I thought I'd find you here," he turned suddenly to Raskolnikov, "that is, I thought nothing . . . of the sort . . . but I precisely thought . . . Katerina Ivanovna has gone out of her mind there at our place," he suddenly said abruptly to Sonya, abandoning Raskolnikov.

Sonya gave a cry.

"That is, it seems so anyway. However . . . We don't know what to do, that's the thing! She came back . . . it seems she was thrown out of somewhere, maybe beaten as well . . . it seems so at least . . . She ran to see Semyon Zakharych's superior but didn't find him at home; he was out having dinner at some other general's . . . Imagine, she flew over to where this dinner was . . . to this other general's, and imagine—she really insisted, she called Semyon Zakharych's superior out and, it seems, away from the table at that. You can imagine what came of it. Naturally, she was chased away; and, according to her, she swore and threw something at him. Which is quite likely . . . How it happened that she wasn't arrested is beyond me! Now she's telling everyone about it, including Amalia Ivanovna, only it's hard to understand her, she's shouting and thrashing about . . . Ah, yes: she's saying and shouting that since everyone has abandoned her now, she'll take the children and go into the street with a barrel-organ, and the children will sing and dance, and so will she, and collect money, and stand every day under the general's window . . . 'Let them see,' she says, 'how the noble children of a civil servant are going about begging in the streets!' She beats all the children, and they cry. She's teaching Lenya to sing 'The Little Farm,' and the boy to dance, and Polina Mikhailovna as well; she's tearing up all the clothes, making them some sort of little hats like actors; and she herself is going to carry a basin and bang on it for music . . . She won't listen to anything . . . Imagine, you see? It's simply impossible."

Lebezyatnikov would have gone on longer, but Sonya, who had been listening to him almost without breathing, suddenly snatched her cape and hat and ran out of the room, putting them on as she ran. Raskolnikov went out after her, and Lebezyatnikov after him.

"She's certainly gone mad!" he said to Raskolnikov, as they came out to the street. "I just didn't want to frighten Sofya Semyonovna, so I said 'it seems,' but there isn't any doubt. It's those little knobs they say come out on the brain in consumption; too bad I don't know any medicine. By the way, I tried to convince her, but she won't listen to anything."

"You told her about the little knobs?"

"I mean, not exactly about the little knobs. Besides, she wouldn't have understood anything. But what I say is this: if one convinces a person logically that he essentially has nothing to cry about, he'll stop crying. That's clear. Or are you convinced that he won't?"

"Life would be too easy that way," Raskolnikov replied.

"I beg your pardon, I beg your pardon, of course it's quite hard for Katerina Ivanovna to understand, but do you know that in Paris serious experiments have already been performed with regard to the possibility of curing mad people by working through logical conviction alone? A professor there, who died recently, a serious scientist, fancied that such treatment should be possible. His basic idea is that there's no specific disorder in a mad person's organism, but that madness is, so to speak, a logical error, an error of judgment, a mistaken view of things. He would gradually prove his patient wrong, and imagine, they say he achieved results! But since he used showers at the same time, the results of the treatment are, of course, subject to doubt . . . Or so it seems."

Raskolnikov had long since stopped listening. Having reached his house, he nodded to Lebezyatnikov and turned in at the gateway. Lebezyatnikov came to his senses, looked around, and ran on.

Raskolnikov walked into his closet and stood in the middle of it. Why had he come back here? He looked around at the shabby, yellowish wallpaper, the dust, his sofa . . . Some sharp, incessant rapping was coming from the courtyard, as if something, some nail, was being hammered in somewhere . . . He went to the window, stood on tiptoe, and for a long time, with an extremely attentive look, peered down into the courtyard. But the courtyard was empty; whoever was doing the rapping could not be seen. In the wing to the left, open windows could be seen here and there; pots with scrawny geraniums. Laundry was hanging outside the windows . . . He knew it all by heart. He turned away and sat down on the sofa.

Never, never before had he felt himself so terribly lonely!

Yes, he felt once again that he might indeed come to hate Sonya, and precisely now, when he had made her more miserable. Why had he gone to her to beg for her tears? Why was it so necessary for him to eat up her life? Oh, meanness!

"I'll stay alone!" he suddenly said resolutely. "And she won't come to the jail!"

After about five minutes, he raised his head and smiled strangely. The thought was a strange one: "Perhaps hard labor would indeed be better," it had suddenly occurred to him.

He did not remember how long he had been sitting in his room with vague thoughts crowding in his head. Suddenly the door opened and Avdotya Romanovna came in. She stopped first and looked at him from the threshold, as he had done earlier at Sonya's; then she went and sat down on a chair facing him, in the same place as yesterday. He looked at her silently and somehow unthinkingly.

"Don't be angry, brother, I've come only for a moment," said Dunya. The expression of her face was thoughtful but not stern. Her eyes were clear and gentle. He could see that this one, too, had come to him with love.

"Brother, I know everything now, *everything*. Dmitri Prokofych has explained and told me everything. You are being persecuted and tormented because of a stupid and odious suspicion . . . Dmitri Prokofych told me that there isn't any danger and that you needn't take it with such horror. I disagree. I *fully understand* all the resentment you must feel, and that this indignation may leave its mark forever. That is what I am afraid of. I do not judge and have no right to judge you for abandoning us, and forgive me if I reproached you before. I feel in myself that if I had such a great grief, I, too, would leave everyone. I won't tell mother *about this*, but I'll talk about you constantly, and I'll tell her, on your behalf, that you will come very soon. Don't suffer over her; *I* will set her at ease; but don't make her suffer either—come at least once; remember she's your mother! I've come now only to say" (Dunya began to get up) "that in case you should need me for something, or should need . . . my whole life, or . . . call me, and I'll come. Good-bye!"

She turned sharply and walked to the door.

"Dunya!" Raskolnikov stopped her, got up, and went to her. "This Razumikhin, Dmitri Prokofych, is a very good man."

Dunya blushed a little.

"Well?" she asked, after waiting a moment.

"He is a practical man, hard-working, honest, and capable of deep love . . . Good-bye, Dunya."

Dunya flushed all over, and then suddenly became alarmed.

"What is it, brother, are we really parting forever, since you're making me . . . such bequests?"

"Never mind . . . good-bye . . ."

He turned and walked away from her to the window. She stood, looked at him uneasily, and left in alarm.

No, he was not cold towards her. There had been a moment (the very last) when he had wanted terribly to embrace her tightly, to make it a real *farewell*, and even *to tell her*, but he had not even dared to give her his hand.

"She might shudder later when she remembered that I embraced her now; she might say I stole her kiss!

"And will *this one* endure, or will she not?" he added to himself, after a few minutes. "No, she will not; *her kind* cannot endure! Her kind can never endure . . ."

And he thought of Sonya.

There came a breath of fresh air from the window. The light outside was no longer shining so brightly. He suddenly took his cap and went out.

Of course, he could not and did not want to concern himself with his ill condition. But all this ceaseless anxiety and all this horror of the soul could not go without consequences. And if he was not yet lying in real delirium, it was perhaps precisely because this ceaseless inner anxiety still kept him on his feet and conscious, but somehow artificially, for a time.

He wandered aimlessly. The sun was going down. Some particular anguish had begun telling in him lately. There was nothing particularly acute or burning in it; but there came from it a breath of something permanent, eternal, a presentiment of unending years of this cold, deadening anguish, a presentiment of some eternity on "a square foot of space." This feeling usually began to torment him even more strongly in the evening hours.

"Try keeping yourself from doing something stupid, with these stupid, purely physical ailments that depend only on some sunset! One could wind up going not just to Sonya, but to Dunya!" he muttered hatefully.

Someone called out to him. He turned around. Lebezyatnikov rushed up to him.

"Imagine, I was just at your place, I've been looking for you. Imagine, she carried out her intention and took the children away! Sofya Semyonovna and I had a hard time finding them. She's banging on a frying pan, making the children sing and dance. The children are crying. They stand at intersections and outside of shops. Foolish people are running after them. Come on!"

"And Sonya? . . ." Raskolnikov asked in alarm, hurrying after Lebezyatnikov.

"Simply in a frenzy. That is, Sofya Semyonovna's not in a frenzy, but Katerina Ivanovna is; however, Sofya Semyonovna's in a frenzy, too. And Katerina Ivanovna is in a complete frenzy. She's gone finally crazy, I tell you. They'll be taken to the police. You can imagine what effect that will have . . . They're at the canal now, near the ——sky Bridge, not far from Sofya Semyonovna's. Nearby."

At the canal, not very far from the bridge, two houses away from where Sonya lived, a small crowd of people had gathered. Boys and girls especially came running. The hoarse, strained voice of Katerina Ivanovna could already be heard from the bridge. And indeed it was a strange spectacle, capable of attracting the interest of the street public. Katerina Ivanovna, in her old dress, the flannel shawl, and a battered straw hat shoved to one side in an ugly lump, was indeed in a real frenzy. She was tired and short of breath. Her worn-out, consumptive face showed more suffering than ever (besides, a consumptive always looks more sick and disfigured outside, in the sun, than at home), but her agitated state would not leave her, and she was becoming more irritated every moment. She kept rushing to the children, yelling at them, coaxing them, teaching them right there, in front of people, how to dance and what to sing; she would start explaining to them why it was necessary, despair over their slow-wittedness, beat them . . . Then, before she had finished, she would rush to the public; if she noticed an even slightly well-dressed person stopping to look, she would immediately start explaining to him that this was what the children "of a noble, one might even say aristocratic, house" had been driven to. If she heard laughter or some taunting little remark from the crowd, she would immediately fall upon the impudent ones and start squabbling with them. Some, indeed, were laughing; others were shaking their heads; in general, everyone was curious to see the crazy woman with her frightened children. The frying pan Lebezyatnikov had spoken of was not there; at least Raskolnikov did not see it; but instead of banging on a frying pan, Katerina Ivanovna would begin clapping out the rhythm with her dry palms, making Polechka sing and Lenya and Kolya dance, even beginning to sing along herself, but breaking off each time at the second note with a racking cough, at which she would again fall into despair, curse her cough, and even weep. Most of all it was the frightened tears of Kolya and Lenya that drove her to distraction. There had indeed been an attempt to dress the children up in street-singers' costumes. The boy was wearing a turban of some red and white material, to represent a Turk. No costume could be found for Lenya; all she had was a red knitted worsted hat (or rather nightcap) from the late Semyon Zakharych, with a broken ostrich feather stuck in it that once belonged to Katerina Ivanovna's grandmother and had been kept until now in the trunk as a family curio. Polechka was wearing her usual little dress. Timid and lost, she watched her mother, would not leave her side, hiding her tears, guessing at her mother's madness, and looking around uneasily. The street and the crowd frightened her terribly. Sonya doggedly followed Katerina Ivanovna, weeping and begging her all the while to go back home. But Katerina Ivanovna was implacable.

"Stop, Sonya, stop!" she shouted in a hurried patter, choking and coughing. "You don't know what you're asking, you're like a child! I've already told you I won't go back to that drunken German woman. Let them all, let all of Petersburg see how a gentleman's children go begging, though their father served faithfully and honestly all his life and, one might say, died in service." (Katerina Ivanovna had already managed to create this fantasy and believe in it blindly.) "Let him see, let that worthless runt of a general see. And how stupid you are, Sonya: what are we going to eat now, tell me? We've preyed upon you enough, I don't want any more of it! Ah, Rodion Romanych, it's you!" she exclaimed, noticing Raskolnikov and rushing to him. "Please explain to this little fool that this is the smartest thing we could do! Even organ-grinders make a living, and we'll be picked out at once, people will see that we're a poor, noble family of orphans, driven into abject poverty, and that runt of a general—he'll lose his position, you'll see! We'll stand under his windows every day, and when the sovereign drives by I'll kneel, push them all forward, and point to them: 'Protect us, father!' He's the father of all orphans, he's merciful, he'll protect us, you'll see, and that runt of a general, he'll . . . Lenya! *Tenez-vous droite!*[19] You, Kolya, are going to dance again now. Why are you whimpering? He's whimpering again! What, what are you afraid of now, you little fool! Lord! What am I to do with them, Rodion Romanych! If you knew how muddleheaded they are! What can one do with the likes of them! . . ."

And, almost weeping herself (which did not hinder her constant, incessant pattering), she pointed to the whimpering children. Raskolnikov tried to persuade her to go back, and even said, hoping to touch her vanity, that it was not proper for her to walk the streets as organgrinders do, since she was preparing to be the directress of an institute for noble girls . . .

"An institute, ha, ha, ha! Castles in Spain!" cried Katerina Ivanovna, her laughter followed immediately by a fit of coughing. "No, Rodion Romanych, the dream is over! Everyone's abandoned us! And that runt of a general . . . You know, Rodion Romanych, I flung an inkpot at him—it just happened to be standing there, in the anteroom, on the table next to the visitors' book, so I signed my name, flung it at him, and ran away. Oh, vile, vile men! But spit on them; I'll feed mine myself now, I won't bow to anybody! We've tormented her enough." (She pointed to Sonya.) "Polechka, how much have we collected, show me! What? Just two kopecks? Oh, the villains! They don't give anything, they just run after us with their tongues hanging out! Now, what's that blockhead laughing at?" (She pointed to a man in the crowd.) "It's all because Kolka here is so slow-witted; he's a nuisance! What do you want, Polechka? Speak French to me, *parlez-moi français.* I've been teaching you, you know several phrases! . . . Otherwise how can they tell you're educated children, from a noble family, and not at all like the rest of the organ-grinders; we're not putting on some 'Petrushka' in the street,[20] we'll sing them a proper romance . . . Ah, yes! What are we going to sing? You keep interrupting me, and we . . . you see, Rodion Romanych, we stopped here to choose what to sing—something Kolya can also dance to . . . because, can you imagine, we haven't prepared anything; we must decide and rehearse it all perfectly, then we'll go to the Nevsky Prospect, where there are many more people of high society, and we'll be noticed at once: Lenya knows 'The Little Farm' . . . Only it's always 'The Little Farm,' the same 'Little Farm,' everybody sings it! We ought to sing something much more noble . . . Well, what have you come up with, Polya, you could at least help your mother! Memory, my memory's gone, or I'd have remembered something! We can't sing 'A Hussar Leaning on His Sabre,' really! Ah, let's sing *'Cinq sous'* in French. I taught it to you, I know I did. And the main thing is that it's in French, so people will see at once that you're a nobleman's children, and it will be much more moving . . . Or why not even *'Malborough s'en va-t-en guerre,'*[21] because it's a perfect children's song and they use it as a lullaby in aristocratic houses.

> *'Malborough s'en va-t-en guerre,*
> *Ne sait quand reviendra . . .'* "

she began singing . . . "But no, better *'Cinq sous'!* Now, Kolya, put your hands on your hips, quickly, and you, Lenya, turn around, too, the opposite way, and Polechka and I will sing and clap along!

> *'Cinq sous, cinq sous,*
> *Pour monter notre ménage . . .'*[22]

Hem, hem, hem!" (And she went off into a fit of coughing.) "Straighten your dress, Polechka, the shoulders are slipping down," she remarked through her coughing, gasping for breath. "You must behave especially properly and on a fine footing now, so that everyone can see you're noble children. I said then that the bodice ought to be cut longer and made from two lengths. It's all you and your advice, Sonya: 'Shorter, shorter'—and as a result the child's completely disfigured . . . Ah, what's all this crying, stupid children! Well, Kolya, start, quickly, quickly, quickly—oh, what an unbearable child! . . .

> *'Cinq sous, cinq sous . . .'*

Another soldier! Well, what do you want?"

Indeed, a policeman was forcing his way through the crowd. But at the same time a gentleman in a uniform and greatcoat, an imposing official of about fifty with an order around his neck (this last fact rather pleased Katerina Ivanovna, and was not without effect on the policeman), approached and silently gave Katerina Ivanovna a green three-rouble bill. His face expressed genuine compassion. Katerina Ivanovna accepted and bowed to him politely, even ceremoniously.

"I thank you, my dear sir," she began haughtily. "The reasons that have prompted us . . . take the money, Polechka. You see, there do exist noble and magnanimous people, who are ready at once to help a poor gentlewoman in misfortune. You see before you, my dear sir, the orphans of a noble family, with, one might even say, the most aristocratic connections . . . And that runt of a general was sitting there eating grouse . . . he stamped his foot at me for bothering him . . . 'Your Excellency,' I said, 'protect the orphans, seeing that you knew the late Semyon Zakharych so well,' I said, 'and his own daughter was slandered on the day of his death by the worst of all scoundrels . . .' That soldier again! Protect me!" she cried to the official. "Why won't that soldier leave me alone! We already ran away from one on Meshchanskaya . . . what business is it of yours, fool!"

"Because it's prohibited in the streets. Kindly stop this outrage."

"You're the outrageous one! It's the same as going around with a barrel-organ. What business is it of yours?"

"Concerning a barrel-organ, a permit is required for that; and with yourself and your behavior, you're stirring people up, madam. Kindly tell me where you live."

"What! A permit!" Katerina Ivanovna yelled. "I buried my husband today, what's this about a permit!"

"Madam, madam, calm yourself," the official tried to begin, "come, I'll take you . . . It's improper here, in the crowd, you are not well . . ."

"My dear sir, my dear sir, you know nothing!" Katerina Ivanovna shouted. "We'll go to the Nevsky Prospect—Sonya, Sonya! Where is she? She's crying, too! What's the matter with you all! . . . Kolya, Lenya, where are you going?" she suddenly cried out in fear. "Oh, stupid children! Kolya, Lenya, but where are they going! . . ."

It so happened that Kolya and Lenya, utterly frightened by the street crowd and the antics of their mad mother, and seeing, finally, a policeman who wanted to take them and lead them off somewhere, suddenly, as if by agreement, seized each other by the hand and broke into a run. Shouting and weeping, poor Katerina Ivanovna rushed after them. It was grotesque and pitiful to see her running, weeping, choking. Sonya and Polechka rushed after her.

"Bring them back, bring them back, Sonya! Oh, stupid, ungrateful children! . . . Polya! Catch them . . . It's for your sake that I . . ."

She stumbled in mid-run and fell.

"She's hurt! She's bleeding! Oh, Lord!" Sonya cried out, bending over her.

Everyone came running, everyone crowded around. Raskolnikov and Lebezyatnikov were among the first to reach her; the official also came quickly, and after him came the policeman as well, having groaned, "Oh, no!" and waved his hand, anticipating that the matter was going to take a troublesome turn.

"Move on! Move on!" he drove away the people who were crowding around.

"She's dying!" someone cried.

"She's lost her mind!" said another.

"God forbid!" one woman said, crossing herself. "Did they catch the lad and the girl? Here they are, the older girl caught them . . . Little loonies!"

But when they looked closely at Katerina Ivanovna, they saw that she had not injured herself against the stone at all, as Sonya thought, but that the blood staining the pavement was flowing through her mouth from her chest.

"This I know, I've seen it before," the official murmured to Raskolnikov and Lebezyatnikov. "It's consumption, sir; the blood flows out like that and chokes them. I witnessed it just recently with a relation of mine; about a glass and a half . . . all at once, sir . . . Anyway, what can we do; she's dying."

"Here, here, to my place!" Sonya begged. "I live right here! . . . This house, the second one down . . . To my place, quickly, quickly! . . ." She was rushing from one person to another. "Send for a doctor . . . Oh, Lord!"

Through the efforts of the official the matter was settled; the policeman even helped to transport Katerina Ivanovna. She was brought to

Sonya's room in an almost dead faint and laid on the bed. The bleeding continued, but she seemed to begin to come to her senses. Along with Sonya, Raskolnikov, and Lebezyatnikov, the official and the policeman also entered the room, the latter after dispersing the crowd, some of whom had accompanied them right to the door. Polechka brought Kolya and Lenya in, holding them by their hands; they were trembling and crying. The Kapernaumovs also came from their room: the man himself, lame and one-eyed, of odd appearance, his bristling hair and side-whiskers standing on end; his wife, who somehow looked forever frightened; and several children, with faces frozen in permanent surprise and open mouths. Amidst all this public, Svidrigailov also suddenly appeared. Raskolnikov looked at him in surprise, not understanding where he had come from and not remembering having seen him in the crowd.

There was talk of a doctor and a priest. The official, though he whispered to Raskolnikov that a doctor now seemed superfluous, still ordered one to be sent for. Kapernaumov ran himself.

Meanwhile Katerina Ivanovna recovered her breath, and the bleeding stopped for a while. She looked with pained but intent and penetrating eyes at the pale and trembling Sonya, who was wiping the drops of sweat from her forehead with a handkerchief; finally, she asked to sit up. With help, she sat up on the bed, supported on both sides.

"Where are the children?" she asked, in a weak voice. "Did you bring them, Polya? Oh, you stupid ones! . . . Why did you run away . . . ahh!"

Her withered lips were still all bloody. She moved her eyes, looking around.

"So this is how you live, Sonya! I've never even been here . . . now is my chance . . ."

She looked at her with suffering.

"We've sucked you dry, Sonya . . . Polya, Lenya, Kolya, come here . . . Well, Sonya, here they all are, take them . . . I'm handing them over to you . . . I've had enough! . . . The ball is over! Gh-a! . . . Lay me back; at least let me die in peace . . ."

They laid her back again on the pillow.

"What? A priest? . . . No need . . . Where's your spare rouble? . . . There are no sins on me! . . . God should forgive me anyway . . . He knows how I've suffered! . . . And if He doesn't, He doesn't! . . ."

A restless delirium was taking hold of her more and more. From time to time she gave a start, moved her eyes around, recognized everyone for a moment, but her consciousness would immediately give way to delirium again. Her breathing was hoarse and labored, and it was as if something were gurgling in her throat.

"I said to him, 'Your Excellency! . . .'" she exclaimed, drawing a breath after each word, " 'this Amalia Ludwigovna' . . . ah! Lenya, Kolya! Hands on your hips, quickly, quickly, *glissez, glissez, pas de Basque!*[23] Tap your feet . . . Be a graceful child.

'Du hast Diamanten und Perlen' . . .

How does it go? I wish we could sing . . .

*'Du hast die schönsten Augen,
Mädchen, was willst du mehr?'*[24]

Well, really, I must say! *Was willst du mehr*—what's he thinking of, the blockhead! . . . Ah, yes, here's another:

'In the noonday heat, in a vale of Daghestan' . . .[25]

Ah, how I loved . . . I loved that song to the point of adoration, Polechka! . . . You know, your father . . . used to sing it when he was still my fiancé . . . Oh, those days! . . . If only, if only we could sing it! How, how does it go now . . . I've forgotten . . . remind me how it goes!" She was extremely agitated and was making an effort to raise herself. Finally, in a terrible, hoarse, straining voice, she began to sing, crying out and choking at every word, with a look of some mounting fear:

" 'In the noonday heat! . . . in a vale! . . . of Daghestan! . . .
With a bullet in my breast!' . . .

Your Excellency!" she suddenly screamed in a rending scream, dissolving in tears. "Protect the orphans! Having known the bread and salt of the late Semyon Zakharych! . . . One might even say, aristocratic! . . . Gh-a!" She gave a sudden start, came to herself, and looked around in some sort of horror, but immediately recognized Sonya. "Sonya, Sonya!" she said meekly and tenderly, as if surprised to see her there in front of her. "Sonya, dear, you're here, too?"

They raised her up again.

"Enough! . . . It's time! . . . Farewell, hapless girl! . . . The nag's been overdriven! . . . Too much stra-a-ain!" she cried desperately and hatefully, and her head fell back on the pillow.

She became oblivious again, but this last oblivion did not continue long. Her pale yellow, withered face turned up, her mouth opened, her legs straightened convulsively. She drew a very deep breath and died.

Sonya fell on her corpse, put her arms around her, and lay motionless, her head resting on the deceased woman's withered breast. Polechka fell down at her mother's feet and kissed them, sobbing. Kolya and Lenya, not yet understanding what had happened, but sensing something very awful, seized each other's shoulders and, staring into each other's eyes, suddenly, together, at the same time, opened their mouths and began howling. They were both still in their costumes: he in the turban, she in the nightcap with an ostrich feather.

And how had that "certificate of merit" suddenly turned up on the bed, near Katerina Ivanovna? It was lying right there by the pillow; Raskolnikov saw it.

He walked over to the window. Lebezyatnikov ran up to him.

"She's dead!" Lebezyatnikov said.

"Rodion Romanovich, I have a couple of necessary words for you," Svidrigailov approached. Lebezyatnikov yielded his place at once and delicately effaced himself. Svidrigailov drew the surprised Raskolnikov still further into the corner.

"All this bother—that is, the funeral and the rest of it—I will take upon myself. It's a matter of money, you know, and, as I told you, I have some to spare. I'll place these two younglings and Polechka in some orphanage, of the better sort, and settle fifteen hundred roubles on each of them, for their coming of age, so that Sofya Semyonovna can be completely at ease. And I'll get her out of the quagmire, because she's a nice girl, isn't she? So, sir, you can tell Avdotya Romanovna that that is how I used her ten thousand."

"What's the purpose of all this philanthropizing?" asked Raskolnikov.

"Ehh! Such a mistrustful man!" laughed Svidrigailov. "I did tell you I had this money to spare. Well, and simply, humanly speaking, can you not allow it? She wasn't some sort of 'louse,' was she" (he jabbed his finger towards the corner where the deceased woman lay), "like some little old money-lender? Well, you'll agree, well, 'is it, indeed, for Luzhin to live and commit abominations, or for her to die?' And if it weren't for my help, then 'Polechka, for example, will go there, too, the same way . . .' "

He said this with the look of some *winking*, merry slyness, not taking his eyes off Raskolnikov. Raskolnikov turned pale and cold, hearing the very phrases he had spoken to Sonya. He quickly recoiled and looked wildly at Svidrigailov.

"How d-do you . . . know?" he whispered, scarcely breathing.

"But I'm staying here, just the other side of the wall, at Madame Resslich's. Kapernaumov is here, and there—Madame Resslich, an ancient and most faithful friend. I'm a neighbor, sir."

"You?"

"Me," Svidrigailov went on, heaving with laughter. "And I assure you on my honor, dearest Rodion Romanovich, that you have got me extremely interested. I told you we'd become close, I predicted it— well, and so we have. You'll see what a congenial man I am. You'll see that one can get along with me after all . . ."

Part Six

I

A STRANGE TIME came for Raskolnikov: it was as if fog suddenly fell around him and confined him in a hopeless and heavy solitude. Recalling this time later, long afterwards, he suspected that his consciousness had sometimes grown dim, as it were, and that this had continued, with some intervals, until the final catastrophe. He was positively convinced that he had been mistaken about many things then; for example, the times and periods of certain events. At least, remembering afterwards, and trying to figure out what he remembered, he learned much about himself, going by information he received from others. He would, for example, confuse one event with another; he would consider something to be the consequence of an event that existed only in his imagination. At times he was overcome by a morbidly painful anxiety, which would even turn into panic fear. But he also remembered that he would have moments, hours, and perhaps even days, full of apathy, which came over him as if in opposition to his former fear—an apathy resembling the morbidly indifferent state of some dying people. Generally, during those last days, he even tried, as it were, to flee from a clear and full understanding of his situation; some essential facts, which called for an immediate explanation, especially burdened him; but how glad he would have been to free himself, to flee from certain cares, to forget which, however, would in his situation have threatened complete and inevitable ruin.

He was especially anxious about Svidrigailov; one might even say he had become stuck, as it were, on Svidrigailov. Since the time of Svidrigailov's words, spoken all too clearly and all too threateningly for him, in Sonya's apartment, at the moment of Katerina Ivanovna's death, the usual flow of his thoughts seemed disrupted. But even though this new fact troubled him greatly, Raskolnikov was somehow in no hurry to clarify the matter. At times, suddenly finding himself somewhere in a remote and solitary part of the city, in some wretched tavern, alone at a table, pondering, and scarcely recalling how he had ended up there, he would suddenly remember about Svidrigailov: the all too clear and alarming awareness would suddenly come to him that he also had to make arrangements with this man as soon as he could, and, if possible, come to a final resolution. Once, having gone somewhere beyond the city gates, he even fancied that he was waiting for Svidrigailov and that they had agreed to meet there. Another time he woke before dawn, on the ground somewhere, in the bushes, and almost without understanding how he had strayed there. However, in the first two or three days after Katerina Ivanovna's death, he had already met Svidrigailov a couple of times, almost always at Sonya's apartment, where he would come by somehow aimlessly, but almost always just for a minute. They always exchanged a few brief phrases and never once spoke of the capital point, as if it had somehow arranged itself between them that they would be silent about it for the time being. Katerina Ivanovna's body was still lying in the coffin. Svidrigailov had taken charge of the funeral and was bustling about. Sonya was also very busy. At their last meeting, Svidrigailov explained to Raskolnikov that he had somehow finished with Katerina Ivanovna's children, and had done so successfully; that, thanks to one connection or another, he had managed to find the right persons, with whose help it had been possible to place all three orphans, immediately, in institutions quite proper for them; that the money set aside for them had also helped considerably, because it was much easier to place orphans with capital than poor ones. He also said something about Sonya, promised to stop by at Raskolnikov's one of those days, and mentioned that he "wished to ask his advice; that he'd like very much to talk things over; that there were certain matters . . ." This conversation took place in the corridor, near the stairs. Svidrigailov looked intently into Raskolnikov's eyes and suddenly, after a pause, lowered his voice and asked:

"But what is it, Rodion Romanych? You're not yourself at all! Really! You listen and look, but it's as if you don't understand. You must cheer up. Let's do have a talk; only it's a pity there are so many things to be done, other people's and my own . . . Ehh, Rodion Romanych," he suddenly added, "what every man of us needs is air, air, air, sir . . . That first of all!"

He suddenly stepped aside to allow a priest and a reader, who were coming up the stairs, to pass. They were going to hold a memorial service.[1] On Svidrigailov's orders, these were held punctually twice a day. Svidrigailov went on his way. Raskolnikov stood, thought, and then followed the priest into Sonya's apartment.

He stopped in the doorway. The service began, quietly, ceremoniously, sadly. Ever since childhood, there had always been something heavy and mystically terrible for him in the awareness of death and the feeling of the presence of death; besides, it was long since he had heard a memorial service. Besides, there was also something else here, too terrible and disquieting. He looked at the children: they were all kneeling by the coffin, and Polechka was crying. Behind them, weeping softly and as if timidly, Sonya was praying. "And in these days she hasn't once glanced at me, hasn't said a word to me," suddenly came to Raskolnikov's mind. The room was brightly lit by the sun; the smoke from the incense was rising in clouds; the priest was reading "Give rest, O Lord . . ."[2] Raskolnikov stood there through the whole service. The priest, as he gave the blessing and took his leave, looked around somehow strangely. After the service, Raskolnikov went up to Sonya. She suddenly took both his hands and leaned her head on his shoulder. This brief gesture even struck Raskolnikov as puzzling; it was even strange: what, not the least loathing for him, not the least revulsion, not the least tremor in her hand? Here was some sort of boundlessness of one's own humiliation. So he understood it, at least. Sonya said nothing. Raskolnikov pressed her hand and walked out. He felt terribly heavy. Had it been possible to go somewhere that minute and remain utterly alone, even for the whole of his life, he would have counted himself happy. But the thing was that, though he had been almost always alone recently, he could never feel that he was alone. It had happened that he would leave town, go out to the high road, once he even went as far as a little wood; but the more solitary the place was, the stronger was his awareness as of someone's near and disquieting presence, not frightening so much as somehow extremely vexing, so that he would hurriedly return to the city, mingle with the crowd, go into eating-houses, taverns, to the flea market, the Haymarket. Here it seemed easier, and even more solitary. In one chop-house, towards evening, people were singing songs: he sat for a whole hour listening, and remembered that he had even enjoyed it. But towards the end he suddenly became uneasy again, as if he had suddenly begun to be tormented by remorse: "So I'm sitting here listening to songs, but is this what I ought to be doing?" he somehow thought. However, he realized immediately that this was not the only thing troubling him; there was something that called for immediate resolution, but which it was impossible to grasp or convey in words. It was all wound up into a sort of ball. "No, better some kind of fight! Better Porfiry again . . . or Svidrigailov . . . The sooner to meet someone's challenge, someone's attack . . . Yes, yes!" he thought. He left the chop-house and almost broke into a run. The thought of Dunya and his mother for some reason suddenly seemed to fill him with panic fear. This was the night when he woke up, before morning, in the bushes, on Krestovsky Island, all chilled, in a fever; he went home, arriving early in the morning. The fever left him after a few hours of sleep, but it was late when he woke up: already two o'clock in the afternoon.

He remembered that Katerina Ivanovna's funeral had been appointed for that day, and was glad not to be present at it. Nastasya brought him something to eat; he ate and drank with great appetite, all but greedily. His head was fresher, and he himself was calmer, than during those last three days. He even marveled, fleetingly, at his earlier influxes of panic fear. The door opened and Razumikhin came in.

"Aha! he's eating! That means he's not sick!" Razumikhin said, and, taking a chair, he sat down at the table across from Raskolnikov. He was troubled and did not try to conceal it. He spoke with obvious vexation, but without hurrying and without raising his voice especially. One might have thought there was some special and even exceptional intention lodged in him. "Listen," he began resolutely, "devil take you all, as far as I'm concerned, but from what I see now, I see clearly that I can't understand anything; please don't think I've come to question you—I spit on it! I don't want it myself! Reveal everything now, all your secrets, and maybe I won't even listen, I'll just spit and walk away. I've come only to find out personally and finally: first of all, is it true that you're mad? You see, a belief exists (well, somewhere or other) that you may be mad, or very much inclined that way. I'll confess to you, I myself was strongly inclined to support that opinion, judging, first, by your stupid and partly vile actions (unexplainable by anything), and, second, by your recent behavior with your mother and sister. Only a monster and a scoundrel, if not a madman, would act with them as you did; consequently, you're a madman . . ."

"How long ago did you see them?"

"Just now. And you haven't seen them since then? Where have you been hanging around, may I ask; I've come by here three times already. Your mother has been seriously ill since yesterday. She wanted to come here; Avdotya Romanovna tried to hold her back, but she wouldn't listen to anything: 'If he's sick,' she said, 'if he's going mad, who will help him if not his mother?' We all came here, because we couldn't let her come alone. We kept telling her to calm down all the way to your very door. We came in; you weren't home; here's where she sat. She sat for ten minutes, silently, with us standing over her. She got up and said: 'If he can go out, and is therefore well and has simply forgotten his mother, then it's indecent and shameful for a mother to stand on his doorstep and beg for affection as for a handout.' She went home and came down sick; now she has a fever: 'I see,' she says, 'he has time enough for *that one of his.*' She thinks *that one* is Sofya Semyonovna, your fiancée or your mistress, I really don't know. I went to Sofya Semyonovna's at once, because I wanted to find out everything, brother—I came and saw a coffin standing there, children crying. Sofya Semyonovna was trying their mourning clothes on them. You weren't there. I looked in, apologized, and left, and reported to Avdotya Romanovna. So it's all nonsense, and there isn't any *that one* involved; so it must be madness. But here you sit gobbling boiled beef as if you hadn't eaten for three days. Granted madmen also eat, but you, though you haven't said a word to me . . . are not mad! I'll swear to it. Whatever else you are, you're not mad. And so, devil take you all, because there's some mystery here, some secret, and I have no intention of breaking my head over your secrets. I've just come to swear at you," he concluded, getting up, "to vent my feelings, and now I know what to do!"

"What are you going to do now?"

"What do you care what I'm going to do now?"

"Look out, you'll go on a binge!"

"How . . . how did you know?"

"What else?"

Razumikhin paused for a minute.

"You've always been a very reasonable man, and you've never, ever been mad," he suddenly observed with ardor. "It's true—I'll go on a binge! Good-bye!" And he made a move to leave.

"I was talking about you, Razumikhin, two days ago, I think, with my sister."

"About me! But . . . where could you have seen her two days ago?" Razumikhin stopped, and even paled a little. One could guess that his heart had begun pounding slowly and tensely in his chest.

"She came here, alone, sat down and talked to me."

"She did!"

"Yes, she did."

"What did you tell her . . . about me, I mean?"

"I told her that you're a very good, honest, and hard-working man. I didn't tell her that you loved her, because she knows it herself."

"Knows it herself?"

"What else! Wherever I may go, whatever happens to me—you will remain their Providence. I'm handing them over to you, so to speak, Razumikhin. I say this because I know perfectly well how much you love her and am convinced of the purity of your heart. I also know that she can love you as well, and perhaps even already does. Now decide for yourself, as best you can, whether you want to go on a binge or not."

"Rodka . . . you see . . . well . . . Ah, the devil! And where do you plan on going? You see, if it's all a secret, let it stay that way! But I . . . I'll find out the secret . . . And I'm certain that it's some sort of nonsense and terribly trifling, and that it's all your own doing. But, anyway, you're a most excellent man! A most excellent man! . . ."

"And I was precisely about to add, when you interrupted me, that you had quite a good thought just now about not finding out these mysteries and secrets. Let it be for now, and don't worry. You'll learn everything in due time, precisely when you should. Yesterday a certain person told me that man needs air, air, air! I want to go to him now and find out what he meant by that."

Razumikhin stood pensive and agitated, figuring something out.

"He's a political conspirator! For sure! And he's about to take some decisive step—for sure! It can't be otherwise, and . . . and Dunya knows . . ." he suddenly thought to himself.

"So Avdotya Romanovna comes to see you," he said, stressing each word, "and you yourself want to see a man who says we need air, more air, and . . . and, therefore, this letter, too . . . is something of the same sort," he concluded, as if to himself.

"What letter?"

"She received a certain letter today; it troubled her very much. Very. Even too much. I began talking about you—she asked me to be quiet. Then . . . then she said we might be parting very soon, and began thanking me ardently for something; then she went to her room and locked herself in."

"She received a letter?" Raskolnikov pensively repeated the question.

"Yes, a letter; and you didn't know? Hm."

They were both silent for a short time.

"Good-bye, Rodion. I . . . there was a time, brother . . . anyway, good-bye. You see, there was a time . . . Well, good-bye! I must go, too. And I won't drink. There's no need now . . . Forget it!"

He hurried out, but having left and almost closed the door behind him, he suddenly opened it again and said, looking somewhere aside:

"By the way! Remember that murder, you know, Porfiry's case—the old woman? Well, you ought to know that the murderer has been found, he confessed and presented all the proofs himself. It was one of those workmen, those painters, just think of it; remember me defending them here? Would you believe that that whole scene of laughing and fighting on the stairs with his friend, when the others were going up, the caretaker and the two witnesses, was set up by him on purpose, precisely as a blind? What cunning, what presence of mind, in such a young pup! It's hard to believe; but he explained it all, he confessed it all himself! And what a sucker I was! Well, I suppose it's simply the genius of shamming and resourcefulness, the genius of the legal blind—and so there's nothing to be especially surprised at! Such people do exist, don't they? And that his character broke down and he confessed, makes me believe him all the more. It's more plausible . . . But how, how could I have been such a sucker! I was crawling the walls for them!"

"Tell me, please, where did you learn this, and why does it interest you so much?" Raskolnikov asked, with visible excitement.

"Come, now! Why does it interest me! What a question! . . . I learned it from Porfiry, among others. But mainly from Porfiry."

"From Porfiry?"

"From Porfiry."

"And what . . . what does he say?" Raskolnikov asked fearfully.

"He explained it to me perfectly. Psychologically, in his own way."

"Explained it? He explained it to you himself?"

"Himself, himself. Good-bye! I'll tell you a bit more later, but right now I have something to do. There . . . there was a time when I thought . . . But what of it; later! . . . Why should I get drunk now. You've got me drunk without wine. Because I am drunk, Rodka! I'm drunk without wine now. Well, good-bye; I'll come again, very soon."

He walked out.

"He's a political conspirator, he is, for sure, for sure!" Razumikhin decided to himself finally, as he slowly went down the stairs. "And he's drawn his sister into it; that's very, very likely, given Avdotya Romanovna's character. They've started meeting together . . . And she, too, dropped me a hint. It all comes out precisely that way, from many of her words . . . and phrases . . . and hints! And how else can all this tangle be explained? Hm! And I almost thought . . . Oh, Lord, how could I dream of it! Yes, sir, that was an eclipse, and I am guilty before him! It was he who brought this eclipse on me then, by the light, in the corridor. Pah! What a nasty, crude, mean thought on my part! Good boy, Mikolka, for confessing . . . And all the earlier things are explained now! That illness of his then, all that strange behavior, even before, before, still at the university, he was always so gloomy, sullen . . . But then, what does this letter mean? There might be something there as well. Who is the letter from? I suspect . . . Hm. No, I'm going to find it all out."

He remembered and put together everything about Dunechka, and his heart sank. He tore from his place and ran.

Raskolnikov, as soon as Razumikhin left, got up, turned towards the window, bumped into one corner, then into another, as if forgetting how small his kennel was, and . . . sat down again on the sofa. He was altogether renewed, as it were; again the fight—it meant a way out had been found!

"Yes, it means a way out has been found! For everything had

become too stifling and confined, too painfully oppressive, overcome by some sort of druggedness. Since that very scene with Mikolka at Porfiry's, he had been suffocating in a cramped space, with no way out. After Mikolka, on the same day, there had been the scene at Sonya's; he had handled it and ended it not at all, not at all as he might have imagined to himself beforehand . . . which meant he had become weak, instantly and radically! All at once! And he had agreed with Sonya then, he had agreed, agreed in his heart, that he would not be able to live like that, alone, with such a thing on his soul! And Svidrigailov? Svidrigailov's a riddle . . . Svidrigailov troubles him, it's true, but somehow not from that side. Maybe he'll have to face a struggle with Svidrigailov as well. Svidrigailov may also be a whole way out; but Porfiry's a different matter.

"So it was Porfiry himself who explained it to Razumikhin, explained it *psychologically!* He's bringing in his cursed psychology again! Porfiry, indeed! As if Porfiry could believe even for a moment in Mikolka's guilt, after what had passed between them then, after that face-to-face scene just before Mikolka, of which there could be no correct interpretation except *one!*" (Several times during those days scraps of that whole scene with Porfiry had flashed and recalled themselves to Raskolnikov; he could not have borne the recollection as a whole.) "Such words had been spoken between them then, such movements and gestures had been made, such looks had been exchanged, certain things had been said in such a tone, it had reached such limits, that thereafter it was not for Mikolka (whom Porfiry had figured out by heart from the first word and gesture), it was not for Mikolka to shake the very foundations of his convictions.

"And now look! Even Razumikhin has begun to suspect! So that scene in the corridor, by the light, did not go in vain. He went rushing to Porfiry . . . But why did the man start hoodwinking him like that? What is he aiming at in using Mikolka as a blind with Razumikhin? He certainly must have something in mind; there's an intention here, but what? True, much time has passed since that morning—much too much, and not a word or a breath from Porfiry. Well, that, of course, was worse than . . ." Raskolnikov took his cap and, pensive, started out of the room. For the first day in all that time he felt himself, at least, of sound mind. "I must finish with Svidrigailov," he thought, "at all costs, as soon as possible: he, too, seems to be waiting for me to come to him." And at that moment such hatred rose up from his weary heart that he might have killed either one of them: Svidrigailov or Porfiry. At least he felt that if not now, then later he would be able to do so. "We'll see, we'll see," he repeated silently.

But no sooner had he opened the door to the entryway than he suddenly ran into Porfiry himself. He was coming in. Raskolnikov was dumbfounded for a moment. Strangely, he was not very surprised to see Porfiry and was almost not afraid of him. He was merely startled, but he quickly, instantly, readied himself. "The denouement, perhaps! But how is it that he came up so softly, like a cat, and I heard nothing? Can he have been eavesdropping?"

"You weren't expecting a visitor, Rodion Romanovich," Porfiry Petrovich exclaimed, laughing. "I've been meaning to drop in for a long time; then I was passing by and thought—why not stop for five minutes and see how he is? Are you on your way somewhere? I won't keep you. Just one little cigarette, if I may."

"Sit down, Porfiry Petrovich, do sit down." Raskolnikov invited his visitor to take a seat, ostensibly in so pleased and friendly a manner that he would indeed have marveled could he have seen himself. The dregs, the leavings, were being scraped out! Thus a man will sometimes suffer half an hour of mortal fear with a robber, but once the knife is finally at his throat, even fear vanishes. He sat down facing Porfiry and looked at him without blinking. Porfiry narrowed his eyes and began lighting a cigarette.

"Well, speak, speak" seemed about to leap from Raskolnikov's heart. "Well, why, why, why don't you speak?"

II

"THESE CIGARETTES, really!" Porfiry finally began to speak, having lighted up and caught his breath. "Harm, nothing but harm, yet I can't give them up! I cough, sir, there's a tickling in the throat and a shortness of breath. I'm a coward, you know, so the other day I went to B——n; he examines every patient for a minimum of half an hour; he even burst out laughing when he looked at me: he tapped and listened—by the way, he said, tobacco's not good for you, your lungs are distended. Well, and how am I going to quit? What'll I replace it with? I don't drink, sir, that's the whole trouble, heh, heh, heh—that I don't drink, that's the trouble! Everything's relative, Rodion Romanych, everything's relative!"

"What is this? Is he starting with the same old officialism again, or what!" Raskolnikov thought with loathing. The whole scene of their last meeting suddenly came back to him, and a wave of the same feeling as then flooded his heart.

"I already came to see you two days ago, in the evening—didn't you know?" Porfiry Petrovich continued, looking around the room. "I came in, into this same room. Like today, I was passing by and thought—why not repay his little visit? I came up, the door was wide open; I looked around, waited, and didn't even tell the maid—just went away. You don't lock your place?"

Raskolnikov's face was growing darker and darker. Porfiry seemed to guess his thoughts.

"I've come to explain myself, my good Rodion Romanych, to explain myself, sir! I'm obliged, and I owe you an explanation, sir," he went on with a little smile, and even slapped Raskolnikov lightly on the knee with his palm, but at almost the same moment his face suddenly assumed a serious and preoccupied air; it even became as if veiled with sadness, to Raskolnikov's surprise. He had never yet seen or suspected him of having such a face. "A strange scene took place between us last time, Rodion Romanych. One might say that in our first meeting, too, a strange scene also took place between us; but then . . . Well, so one thing leads to another! You see, sir, I have perhaps come out very guilty before you; I feel it, sir. For you must remember how we parted: your nerves were humming and your knees trembling, and my nerves were humming and my knees trembling. And, you know, it came out somehow improperly between us then, not in gentlemanly fashion. And we are gentlemen, after all; that is, in any case, we are gentlemen first—that has to be understood, sir. You must remember what it was coming to . . . even altogether indecent, sir."

"What's with him? Who does he think I am?" Raskolnikov asked himself in amazement, raising his head and staring at Porfiry.

"In my judgment, it would be better now if we were to proceed with frankness," Porfiry Petrovich continued, throwing his head back slightly and lowering his eyes, as if wishing no longer to embarrass his former victim with his look, and as if scorning his former ways and tricks. "Yes, sir, such suspicions and such scenes cannot go on for long. Mikolka resolved it for us then, otherwise I don't know what it would have come to between us. That cursed little tradesman was sitting behind my partition then—can you imagine? Of course, you know that already, and I am informed that he went to see you afterwards; but what you supposed then was not true: I hadn't sent for anyone, and I hadn't made any arrangements yet. You ask why I hadn't made any arrangements? What can I say: I was as if bowled over by it all then. I'd barely even managed to send for the caretakers. (I'll bet you noticed the caretakers as you passed by.) A thought raced through me then, a certain thought, quick as lightning; I was firmly convinced then, you see, Rodion Romanych. After all, I thought, though I may let one slip for a time, I'll catch another by the tail—but what's mine, what's mine, at least, I won't let slip. You are all too irritable, Rodion Romanych, by nature, sir; even too much so, sir, what with all the other basic qualities of your character and heart, which I flatter myself with the hope of having partly comprehended, sir. Well, of course, even then I, too, could consider that it doesn't always happen for a man just to stand up and blurt out all his innermost secrets. Though it does happen, especially when the man has been driven out of all patience, but, in any case, rarely. That I, too, could consider for myself. No, I thought, if only I had at least some little trace! At least the tiniest little trace, just one, but one you could get your hands on, some real thing, not just this psychology. Because, I thought, if a man is guilty, then, of course, it's possible anyway to expect something substantial from him; it's even permissible to count on the most unexpected results. I was counting on your character, Rodion Romanych, on your character most of all! I had much hope in you then."

"But you . . . but why do you go on talking this way now?" Raskolnikov muttered at last, without making much sense of his own question. "What's he talking about?" he felt utterly at a loss. "Can he really take me for innocent?"

"Why am I talking this way? But I've come to explain myself, sir; I regard it, so to speak, as my sacred duty. I want to tell you everything to the last drop, as it all was, the whole history of all that darkening, so to speak. I made you suffer through a great deal, Rodion Romanych. I am not a monster, sir. I, too, can well understand how it must be for a man to drag all this with him when he's aggrieved but at the same time proud, domineering, and impatient—above all, impatient! In any case, sir, I regard you as a most noble man, and even as having the rudiments of magnanimity, though I do not agree with you in all your convictions, which I consider it my duty to announce beforehand, directly, and with complete frankness, for above all I have no wish to deceive. Having come to know you, I feel an attachment to you. Perhaps you will burst out laughing at such words from me? You have the right, sir. I know that you disliked me even at first sight, because essentially there is nothing to like me for, sir. Regard it as you will, but I now wish, for my part, to use every means to straighten out the impression produced, and to prove that I am a man of heart and conscience. I say it sincerely, sir."

Porfiry Petrovich paused with dignity. Raskolnikov felt the influx of some new fear. The thought that Porfiry regarded him as innocent suddenly began to frighten him.

"To tell everything in order, as it suddenly began then, is hardly necessary," Porfiry Petrovich continued. "I think it's even superfluous. And it's unlikely I'd be able to, sir. Because how could I explain it thoroughly? First there were rumors. To say what these rumors were, from whom they came, and when . . . and on what occasion, strictly speaking, the matter got as far as you—is, I think, also superfluous. And for me personally, it began by accident, a quite accidental accident, something which in the highest degree might or might not have happened—and what was it? Hm, I think there's no need to say. All these rumors and accidents converged in me then into a single thought. I confess frankly—for if one is going to confess, it should be everything—I was the first to hit on you then. Take, for instance, all those labels the old woman wrote on the things, and so on and so forth—it's all nonsense, sir. One can count off a hundred such things. I also accidentally learned in detail then about the scene in the police office—also by accident, sir—and not just in passing, but from a special narrator, a capital one, who, without realizing it, handled the scene remarkably. One thing leads to another, one thing leads to another, my dear Rodion Romanych! So, how could I not turn in a certain direction? A hundred rabbits will never make a horse, a hundred suspicions will never make a proof, as a certain English proverb says, and that's only reasonable; but the passions, sir, try overcoming the passions—for an investigator is also a man, sir. Then I also remembered your little article in that little magazine; you remember, we spoke of it in detail during your first visit. I scoffed then, but that was only to provoke you to further things. I repeat, you're impatient, and very ill, Rodion Romanych. That you are daring, presumptuous, serious, and . . . have felt, have already felt a great deal—all this I have known for a long time, sir. All these feelings are familiar to me, and I read your little article as a familiar one. It was worked out on sleepless nights and in a frenzy, with a heaving and pounding heart, with suppressed enthusiasm. And it's a dangerous thing in young people, this suppressed, proud enthusiasm! I scoffed a bit then, but now I shall tell you that in general—that is, as an amateur—I'm terribly fond of these first, youthful, ardent tests of the pen. Smoke, mist, a string twanging in the mist.[3] Your article is absurd and fantastic, but there are flashes of such sincerity in it, there is pride in it, youthful and incorruptible, there is the courage of despair; it's a gloomy article, sir, but that's a good thing. I read your little article, and laid it aside, and . . . as I laid it aside, I thought: 'Well, for this man it won't end there!' Well, tell me now, with such a foregoing, how could I not be carried away by the subsequent! Ah, Lord! But am I really saying anything? Am I affirming anything now? I simply noted it at the time. 'What's in it?' I thought. There's nothing here—I mean, exactly nothing, and perhaps the final degree of nothing. And for me, an investigator, to be carried away like that is even altogether unfitting: here I've got Mikolka on my hands, and with facts now—whatever you say, they're facts! And he, too, comes with his psychology; I must give some attention to him, too; because it's a matter of life and death. Why am I explaining it all to you now? So that you may know and, what with your mind and heart, not accuse me of behaving maliciously that time. It wasn't malicious, sir, I say it sincerely, heh, heh! Are you wondering why I didn't come here for a search then? But I did, sir, I did, heh, heh, I came, sir, while you were lying here sick in your little bed. Not officially, and not in person, but I came, sir. Everything was examined here, in your apartment, down to the last hair, while the tracks were still fresh; but—

umsonst![4] I thought: now the man will come, will come of himself, and very soon; if he's guilty, he'll certainly come. Another man wouldn't come, but this one will. And do you remember how Mr. Razumikhin began letting it slip to you? It was we who arranged that in order to get you stirred up; we spread the rumor on purpose, so that Mr. Razumikhin would let it slip to you, because he's the kind of man who cannot contain his indignation. What struck Mr. Zamyotov most of all was your wrath and your open daring, suddenly to blurt out in the tavern: 'I killed her!' Too daring, sir, too bold; and I thought, if he's guilty, then he's a fierce fighter! That's what I thought then, sir. So I waited! I waited as hard as I could, and as for Zamyotov, you simply crushed him then, and . . . that's the whole catch, that this cursed psychology is double-ended! And so I waited for you, and look, what a godsend—you came! My heart fairly skipped a beat! Eh! Now, what made you come just then? And that laughter, that laughter of yours as you walked in then, remember? I saw through it all at once, like a pane of glass, but if I hadn't been waiting for you in such a special way, I wouldn't have noticed anything in your laughter. That's what it means to be in the right frame of mind. And Mr. Razumikhin then— ah! and the stone, the stone, remember the stone, the one the things are hidden under? I can just see it there, somewhere in a kitchen garden—didn't you mention a kitchen garden to Zamyotov, and then again at my place? And when we began going through your article, when you were explaining it—one just takes your every word in a double sense, as if there were another sitting under it! And so, Rodion Romanych, in this way I reached the outermost pillars, and bumped my head, and then I came to my senses. No, I said, what's the matter with me! For if you like, I said, all this down to the last trace can be explained in the opposite sense, and it will come out even more naturally. What a torment, sir! 'No,' I thought, 'better some little trace! . . .' And then, when I heard about those little bells, I even stopped dead, I even began shivering. 'Now,' I thought, 'here's that little trace! This is it!' And I wasn't reasoning then, I simply didn't want to. I'd have given a thousand roubles from my own pocket just to have seen you *with my own eyes:* how you walked a hundred steps beside the little tradesman that time, after he said 'murderer' to your face, and you didn't dare ask him anything for the whole hundred steps! . . . Well, and that chill in the spine? Those little bells, in your illness, in half-delirium? And so, Rodion Romanych, why should you be surprised, after all that, if I was playing such tricks with you then? And why did you yourself come just at that moment? It's as if someone was prompting you, too, by God, and if Mikolka hadn't separated us . . . and do you remember Mikolka then? Do you remember him well? A bolt, that's what it was like, sir! Wasn't it like a bolt from the clouds? A thunderbolt! Well, and how did I meet it? I didn't believe the thunderbolt, not a whit, you could see that! And later, after you left, when he began answering some points quite, quite neatly, so that I was surprised myself, even then I didn't believe a pennyworth of it! That's what it means to be strong as adamant. No, I thought, not by a long shot! There's no Mikolka here!"

"Razumikhin was just telling me that you're still accusing Nikolai, and were assuring Razumikhin of it yourself . . ."

His breath failed him, and he did not finish. He had listened in inexpressible excitement to the way this man who had seen through him to the very bottom disavowed himself. He was afraid to believe it, and he did not believe it. In the still ambiguous words he greedily sought and hoped to catch something more precise and final.

"That Mr. Razumikhin!" Porfiry exclaimed, as if rejoicing at the question from Raskolnikov, who up to then had been silent. "Heh, heh, heh! But Mr. Razumikhin simply had to be gotten out of the way: two's company, three's a crowd. Mr. Razumikhin is something else, sir; he's an outsider; he came running, all pale in the face . . . Well, God bless him, why get him mixed up in it! As for Mikolka, would you like to hear about that subject—I mean, as I understand it? First of all, he's still immature, a child, and not so much a coward as something like a sort of artist. Really, sir, don't laugh that I interpret him this way. He's innocent and susceptible to everything. He has heart; he's fanciful. He sings, he dances, and they say he can tell stories so that people come from all over to hear him. And he goes to school, and he laughs his head off if somebody just shows him a finger, and he gets dead drunk, not really from depravity, but in spells, when he's given drink, again like a child. He stole that time, for instance, and he doesn't realize it—he 'just picked it up from the ground; what kind of stealing is that?' And do you know he's a schismatic? Or not really a schismatic, but a sectarian; there were Runners in his family, and he himself recently spent two whole years in a village, under the spiritual direction of a certain elder.⁵ I learned all this from Mikolka and from his Zaraisk friends. What's more, all he wanted was to flee to the desert! He was zealous, prayed to God at night, and read, just couldn't stop reading—the old books, the 'true' ones. Petersburg had a strong effect on him, especially the female sex, yes, and wine, too. He's susceptible, sir, he forgot the elder and all the rest. It's known to me that a certain artist took a liking to him, used to go and see him, and then this incident came along! So, what with all this intimidation—hang yourself! Run away! What can we do about the ideas people have of our juridics! There are some who are terrified of 'having the law on them.' Whose fault is that? Maybe something will come from the new courts. Oh, God grant it! And so, sir, once in prison, he evidently remembered his honorable elder; the Bible also appeared again. Do you know, Rodion Romanych, what 'suffering' means for some of them? Not for the sake of someone, but simply 'the need for suffering'; to embrace suffering, that is, and if it comes from the authorities—so much the better. In my time there was a most humble convict in prison; for a year he sat on the stove at night reading the Bible; so he kept reading it and read himself up so much that, you know, out of the blue, he grabbed a brick and threw it at the warden, without any wrong on the warden's part. And how did he throw it? He aimed it on purpose to miss by a yard, so as not to cause any harm!⁶ Well, everyone knows what's in store for a convict who throws himself armed at the authorities: so he 'embraced suffering.' And now I suspect that Mikolka also wants to 'embrace suffering' or something of the sort. I know it for certain, and even with facts, sir. Only he doesn't know that I know. What, won't you allow that such a nation as ours produces fantastic people? All over the place! The elder has started acting up in him now; he recalled him especially after the noose. However, he'll come and tell me everything himself. You think he'll hold out? Wait, he'll deny it yet. I'm expecting him to come any time now and deny his evidence. I've grown fond of this Mikolka and am studying him thoroughly. And what do you think! Heh, heh! He answered some points quite neatly—evidently picked up the necessary information, prepared himself cleverly—but on other points he's all at sea, doesn't know a blessed thing, and doesn't even suspect that he doesn't know! No, my good Rodion Romanych, there's no Mikolka here! Here we have a fantastic, gloomy case, a modern case, a situation of our times, when the human heart is clouded, when one hears cited the phrase that blood 'refreshes,' when people preach a whole life of comfort. There are bookish dreams here, sir, there is a heart chafed by theories; we see here a resolve to take the first step, but a resolve of a certain kind—he resolved on it, but as if he were falling off a mountain or plunging down from a bell-tower, and then arrived at the crime as if he weren't using his own legs. He forgot to lock the door behind him, but killed, killed two people, according to a theory. He killed, but wasn't able to take the money, and what he did manage to grab, he went and hid under a stone. It wasn't enough for him to endure the torment of standing behind the door while the door was being forced and the bell was ringing—no, later he goes back to the empty apartment, in half-delirium, to remind himself of that little bell, feeling a need to experience again that spinal chill . . . Well, let's say he was sick then, but here's another thing: he killed, and yet he considers himself an honest man, despises people, walks around like a pale angel—no, forget Mikolka, my dear Rodion Romanych, there's no Mikolka here!"

These last words, after everything that had been said before and that had seemed so much like a disavowal, were too unexpected. Raskolnikov began trembling all over as if he had been pierced through.

"Then . . . who did . . . kill them? . . ." he asked, unable to restrain himself, in a suffocating voice. Porfiry Petrovich even recoiled against the back of his chair, as if he, too, were quite unexpectedly amazed at the question.

"What? Who killed them? . . ." he repeated, as if not believing his ears. "But *you* did, Rodion Romanych! You killed them, sir . . ." he added, almost in a whisper, in a completely convinced voice.

Raskolnikov jumped up from the sofa, stood for a few seconds, and sat down again without saying a word. Brief spasms suddenly passed over his face.

"Your poor lip is twitching again, like the other day," Porfiry Petrovich muttered, even as if sympathetically. "It seems, Rodion Romanych, that you did not understand me rightly," he added after a short pause. "That's why you're so amazed, sir. I precisely came with the intention of saying everything this time, and of bringing it all out in the open."

"It wasn't me," Raskolnikov whispered, just as frightened little children do when they are caught red-handed.

"No, it was you, Rodion Romanych, it was you, sir, there's no one else," Porfiry whispered sternly and with conviction.

They both fell silent, and the silence even lasted strangely long, for about ten minutes. Raskolnikov leaned his elbows on the table and silently ran his fingers through his hair. Porfiry Petrovich sat quietly and waited. Suddenly Raskolnikov looked contemptuously at Porfiry.

"You're up to your old tricks again, Porfiry Petrovich! You just cling to the same methods: aren't you sick of it, really?"

"Eh, come on, what do I care about methods now! It would be different if there were witnesses here; but we're alone, whispering to each other. You can see I didn't come to hunt you down and catch you like a hare. Whether you confess or not—it's all the same to me right now. I'm convinced in myself, even without you."

"In that case, why did you come?" Raskolnikov asked irritably. "I'll ask you my former question: if you consider me guilty, why don't you put me in jail?"

"Well, what a question! Let me answer you point by point: first, it's not to my advantage simply to lock you up straight away."

"How not to your advantage! If you're convinced, then you ought . . ."

"Eh, what if I am convinced? So far it's all just my dreams, sir. And what's the point of putting you there *for a rest?* You know it would be, since you're begging for it yourself. I'll bring in that little trades-man, for example, to give evidence against you, and you'll say to him: 'Are you drunk, or what? Who saw me with you? I simply took you for a drunk, and in fact you were drunk,' and what am I to say to that, especially since your story is more plausible than his, because his is just psychology—which, with a mug like his, is even indecent—and you'll have gone straight to the mark, because he does drink, the scoundrel, heavily, and is all too well known for it. And I myself have frankly admitted to you several times already that this psychology is double-ended, and that the other end is bigger, and much more plausible, and that so far I have nothing else against you. And though I'm going to lock you up all the same, and have even come myself (which is not at all how it's done) to announce everything to you beforehand, all the same I'm telling you directly (which is also not how it's done) that it will not be to my advantage. Now, secondly, sir, I've come to you because . . ."

"Ah, yes, secondly . . ." (Raskolnikov was still suffocating.)

"Because, as I announced earlier, I think I owe you an explanation. I don't want you to consider me a monster, especially since I am sincerely disposed towards you, believe it or not. As a result of which, thirdly, I've come to you with an open and direct offer—that you yourself come and confess your guilt. That will be infinitely more advantageous for you, and more advantageous for me as well—since it will be taken off my back. Now, tell me, is that sincere on my part, or not?"

Raskolnikov thought for about a minute.

"Listen, Porfiry Petrovich, you said yourself it was just psychology, and meanwhile you've gone off into mathematics. But what if you're actually mistaken now?"

"No, Rodion Romanych, I'm not mistaken. I've got that little trace. I did find that little trace then, sir—a godsend!"

"What little trace?"

"I won't tell you, Rodion Romanych. And in any case I have no right to put it off any longer; I shall lock you up, sir. So consider for yourself: it's all the same to me *now,* and consequently it's just for your sake alone. By God, it will be better, Rodion Romanych."

Raskolnikov grinned spitefully.

"That's not only ridiculous, it's even shameless. Now, even if I were guilty (which I'm not saying at all), why on earth should I come and confess my guilt, when you yourself say I'll be put in there *for a rest?*"

"Eh, Rodion Romanych, don't believe entirely in words; maybe it won't be entirely *for a rest!* That's just a theory, and my theory besides, sir, and what sort of authority am I for you? I might be concealing something from you even now, sir. Why should I up and pour out everything for you, heh, heh! Another thing: what do you mean, what advantage? Do you know what a reduction of sentence you'd get for that? Because when is it that you'd be coming, at what moment? Just consider that! When another man has already taken the crime on himself and confused the whole case! And I swear to you by God Himself that I'll set it up and arrange things 'there' so that your confession will come out as quite unexpected. We'll do away entirely with all this psychology, and I'll turn all the suspicions of you to nothing, so that your crime will appear as some sort of darkening—because, in all conscience, it was a darkening. I'm an honest man, Rodion Romanych, I'll keep my word."

Raskolnikov lapsed into a sad silence and his head drooped; he thought for a long time and finally grinned again, but this time his smile was meek and sad.

"Eh, don't!" he said, as if he were now entirely done dissembling with Porfiry. "It's not worth it! I don't want your reduction at all!"

"Now, that's what I was afraid of!" Porfiry exclaimed hotly and as if involuntarily. "That's what I was afraid of, that you don't want our reduction."

Raskolnikov gave him a sad and imposing look.

"Ah, don't disdain life!" Porfiry went on. "You still have a lot of it ahead of you. How can you not want a reduction, how can you say that? What an impatient man you are!"

"A lot of what ahead of me?"

"Of life! What, are you a prophet? How much do you know? Seek and ye shall find. Maybe it's just here that God has been waiting for you. And the fetters, well, they're not forever . . ."

"They'll reduce the sentence . . ." Raskolnikov laughed.

"Or maybe you're afraid of the bourgeois shame of it, or something? It's possible you're afraid without knowing it yourself—you being so young! But, even so, you're not one to be afraid or ashamed of confessing your guilt."

"Ehh, I spit on it!" Raskolnikov whispered scornfully and with loathing, as though he did not even wish to speak. He again made a move to get up, as if he wanted to go somewhere, but again sat down in visible despair.

"You spit on it, really! You've lost your faith and you think I'm crudely flattering you; but how much have you lived so far? How much do you understand? He came up with a theory, and now he's ashamed because it didn't work, because it came out too unoriginally! True, it did come out meanly, but even so you're not such a hopeless scoundrel. Not such a scoundrel at all! At least you didn't addle your brain for long, you went all at once to the outermost pillars. Do you know how I regard you? I regard you as one of those men who could have their guts cut out, and would stand and look at his torturers with a smile—provided he's found faith, or God. Well, go and find it, and you will live. First of all, you've needed a change of air for a long time. And suffering is also a good thing, after all. Suffer, then. Mikolka may be right in wanting to suffer. I know belief doesn't come easily—but don't be too clever about it, just give yourself directly to life, without reasoning; don't worry—it will carry you straight to shore and set you on your feet. What shore? How do I know? I only believe that you have much life ahead of you. I know you're taking what I say now as a prepared oration, but maybe you'll remember it later and find it useful; that's why I'm saying it to you. It's good that you only killed a little old woman. If you'd come up with a different theory, you might have done something a hundred million times more hideous! Maybe you should still thank God; how do you know, maybe God is saving you for something. Be of great heart, and fear less. Have you turned coward before the great fulfillment you now face? No, it's a shameful thing to turn coward here. Since you've taken such a step, stand firm now. It's a matter of justice. So, go and do what justice demands. I know you don't believe it, but, by God, life will carry you. And then you'll get to like it. All you need is air now—air, air!"

Raskolnikov even gave a start.

"And you, who are you?" he cried out. "What sort of prophet are you? From the heights of what majestic calm are you uttering these most wise prophecies?"

"Who am I? I'm a finished man, that's all. A man who can, perhaps, sympathize and empathize, who does, perhaps, even know something—but completely finished. But you are quite a different matter: God has prepared a life for you (though, who knows, maybe it will also pass like smoke and nothing will happen). What matter that you'll be passing into a different category of people? You're not going to miss your comforts, are you, with a heart like yours? What matter if no one will see you for a long time? The point lies in you, not in time. Become a sun and everyone will see you. The sun must be the sun first of all. Why are you smiling again—because I'm such a Schiller? I bet you think I'm trying to cajole you! And, who knows, maybe that's just what I'm doing, heh, heh, heh! Perhaps, Rodion Romanych, you shouldn't take me at my word, perhaps you even should never believe me completely—for such is my bent, I agree. Only I would like to add this: you yourself seem able to judge how far I am a base man and how far I am honest!"

"And when do you plan to arrest me?"

"Oh, I can give you a day and a half, or two, to walk around. Think, my dear, pray to God. It's to your advantage, by God, it's to your advantage."

"And what if I run away?" Raskolnikov asked, grinning somehow strangely.

"You won't. A peasant would run away, a fashionable sectarian would run away—the lackey of another man's thought—because it's enough to show him the tip of a finger and, like Midshipman Dyrka, he'll believe anything for the rest of his life.[7] But you no longer believe your own theory—what would you run away on? And what would you do as a fugitive? It's nasty and hard to be a fugitive, and first of all you need a life and a definite position, the proper air; and would that be any air for you? You'd run away, and come back on your own. *It's impossible for you to do without us.* And if I lock you up in jail, you'll sit there for a month, or maybe two, or maybe three, and then suddenly and—mark my words—on your own, you'll come, perhaps even quite unexpectedly for yourself. You won't know an hour beforehand that you're going to come and confess your guilt. And I'm even sure you'll 'decide to embrace suffering'; you won't take my word for it now, but you'll come round to it yourself. Because suffering, Rodion Romanych, is a great thing; don't look at me, fat as I am, that's no matter, but I do know—don't laugh at this—that there is an idea in suffering. Mikolka is right. No, you won't run away, Rodion Romanych."

Raskolnikov got up from his place and took his cap. Porfiry Petrovich also got up.

"Going for a stroll? It should be a fine evening, if only we don't have a thunderstorm. Though that might be good; it would freshen the air . . ."

He also reached for his cap.

"Porfiry Petrovich," Raskolnikov said with stern insistence, "please don't take it into your head that I've confessed to you today. You're a strange person, and I've been listening to you only out of curiosity. But I did not confess anything . . . Remember that."

"I know, yes, I'll remember—well, really, he's even trembling! Don't worry, my dear; be it as you will. Walk around a little; only you can't walk around for too long. And, just in case, I have a little request to make of you," he added, lowering his voice. "It's a bit ticklish, but important: if—I mean, just in case (which, by the way, I don't believe; I consider you quite incapable of it), if, I say—just so, in any such case—you should have the wish, during these forty or fifty hours, to end this matter somehow differently, in some fantastic way—such as by raising your hand against yourself (an absurd suggestion, but perhaps you'll forgive me for it)—then leave a brief but explicit note. A couple of lines, just two little lines, and mention the stone; it will be more noble, sir. Well, sir, good-bye . . . I wish you kind thoughts and good undertakings!"

Porfiry went out, somehow stooping, and as if avoiding Raskolnikov's eyes. Raskolnikov went to the window and waited with irritable impatience until he calculated Porfiry had had enough time to reach the street and move some distance away. Then he, too, hurriedly left the room.

III

HE WAS HURRYING to Svidrigailov. What he could hope for from him, he himself did not know. But the man had some hidden power over him. Once he realized it, he could no longer rest, and, besides, the time had now come.

One question especially tormented him on the way: had Svidrigailov gone to Porfiry?

No, as far as he was able to judge, he had not—he would have sworn to it! He thought it over again and again, recalled Porfiry's entire visit, and realized: no, he had not; of course he had not!

But if he had not gone yet, would he or would he not go to Porfiry? For the time being it seemed to him that he would not go. Why? He could not have explained that either, but even if he could have explained it, he would not have racked his brains much over it just now.

All this tormented him, yet at the same time he somehow could not be bothered with it. Strangely, though no one might have believed it, his present, immediate fate somehow concerned him only faintly, absentmindedly. Something else, much more important and urgent—to do with himself and himself alone, but something else, some main thing—was tormenting him now. Besides, he felt a boundless moral fatigue, though his mind had worked better that morning than in all those recent days.

And was it worthwhile now, after everything that had happened, to try to overcome all these measly new difficulties? Was it worthwhile, for example, trying to intrigue so that Svidrigailov would not go to Porfiry; to investigate, to make inquiries, to lose time on some Svidrigailov!

Oh, how sick he was of it all!

And yet here he was hurrying to Svidrigailov; could it be that he expected something *new* from him—directions, a way out? People do grasp at straws! Could it be fate, or some instinct, bringing them together? Perhaps it was only weariness, despair; perhaps it was not Svidrigailov but someone else he needed, and Svidrigailov just happened to be there. Sonya? But why should he go to Sonya now? To ask for her tears again? Besides, Sonya was terrible for him now. Sonya represented an implacable sentence, a decision not to be changed. It was either her way or his. Especially at that moment he was in no condition to see her. No, would it not be better to try Svidrigailov, to see what was there? And he could not help admitting to himself that for a long time he had really seemed to need the man for something.

Well, but what could there be in common between them? Even their evildoing could not be the same. Moreover, the man was very unpleasant, obviously extremely depraved, undoubtedly cunning and deceitful, perhaps quite wicked. There were such stories going around about him. True, he had taken some trouble over Katerina Ivanovna's children; but who knew what for or what it meant? The man eternally had his projects and intentions.

Still another thought had kept flashing in Raskolnikov all those days, and troubled him terribly, though he had even tried to drive it away from him, so difficult did he find it! He sometimes thought: Svidrigailov kept hovering around him, and was doing so even now;

Svidrigailov had found out his secret; Svidrigailov had once had designs on Dunya. And did he have them still? One could almost certainly say *yes*. And what if now, having found out his secret and thus gained power over him, he should want to use it as a weapon against Dunya?

This thought had tormented him at times, even in his sleep, but the first time it had appeared to him with such conscious clarity was now, as he was going to Svidrigailov. The thought alone drove him into a black rage. First of all, everything would be changed then, even in his own position: he would immediately have to reveal his secret to Dunechka. He would perhaps have to betray himself in order to divert Dunechka from some rash step. The letter? Dunya had received some letter that morning! Who in Petersburg could be sending her letters? (Luzhin, perhaps?) True, Razumikhin was on guard there; but Razumikhin did not know anything. Perhaps he would have to confide in Razumikhin as well? Raskolnikov loathed the thought of it.

"In any case, I must see Svidrigailov as soon as possible," he decided finally to himself. "Thank God, it's not details that are needed here so much as the essence of the matter; but if, if he's really capable, if Svidrigailov is plotting something against Dunya—then . . ."

Raskolnikov had become so tired in all that time, over that whole month, that he could no longer resolve such questions otherwise than with one resolution: "Then I will kill him," he thought, in cold despair. A heavy feeling weighed on his heart; he stopped in the middle of the street and began looking around: what way had he taken, and where had he come to? He was on ——sky Prospect, thirty or forty steps from the Haymarket, which he had passed through. The entire second floor of the building to his left was occupied by a tavern. The windows were all wide open; the tavern, judging by the figures moving in the windows, was packed full. In the main room, singers were pouring themselves out, a clarinet and fiddle were playing, a Turkish drum was beating. Women's squeals could be heard. He was about to go back, wondering why he had turned onto ——sky Prospect, when suddenly, in one of the last open windows of the tavern, he saw Svidrigailov, sitting at a tea table just by the window, a pipe in his teeth. This struck him terribly, to the point of horror. Svidrigailov was observing him, gazing at him silently, and, what also struck Raskolnikov at once, seemed about to get up in order to slip away quietly before he was noticed. Raskolnikov immediately pretended he had not noticed him and looked away pensively, while continuing to observe him out of the corner of his eye. His heart was beating anxiously. He was right: Svidrigailov obviously did not want to be seen. He took the pipe from his mouth and was already trying to hide; but, having stood up and pushed his chair back, he must suddenly have noticed that Raskolnikov had seen and was watching him. Between them there occurred something resembling the scene of their first meeting at Raskolnikov's, when he had been asleep. A mischievous smile appeared on Svidrigailov's face and widened more and more. They both knew that each of them had seen and was watching the other. Finally, Svidrigailov burst into loud laughter.

"Well, well! Come in, then, if you like; I'm here!" he called from the window.

Raskolnikov went up to the tavern.

He found him in a very small back room, with one window, adjacent to the main room where shopkeepers, clerks, and a great many people of all sorts were drinking tea at twenty little tables, to the shouting of a desperate chorus of singers. From somewhere came the click of billiard balls. On the table in front of Svidrigailov stood an open bottle of champagne and a half-filled glass. Also in the room were a boy organ-grinder with a small barrel-organ, and a healthy, ruddy-cheeked girl in a tucked-up striped skirt and a Tyrolean hat with ribbons, a singer, about eighteen years old, who, in spite of the chorus in the next room, was singing some lackey song in a rather husky contralto to the organ-grinder's accompaniment . . .

"That'll do now!" Svidrigailov interrupted her as Raskolnikov came in.

The girl broke off at once and stood waiting respectfully. She had also been singing her rhymed lackey stuff with a serious and respectful look on her face.

"Hey, Filipp, a glass!" cried Svidrigailov.

"I won't drink any wine," said Raskolnikov.

"As you wish; it wasn't for you. Drink, Katya! No more for today—off you go!" He poured her a full glass of wine and laid out a yellow bank note. Katya drank the wine down as women do—that is, without a pause, in twenty sips—took the money, kissed Svidrigailov's hand, which he quite seriously allowed to be kissed, and walked out of the room. The boy with the barrel-organ trailed after her. They had both been brought in from the street. Svidrigailov had not spent even a week in Petersburg, but everything around him was already on some sort of patriarchal footing. The tavern lackey, Filipp, was also by now a "familiar" and quite obsequious. The door to the main room could be locked; Svidrigailov seemed at home in this room and spent, perhaps, whole days in it. The tavern was dirty, wretched, not even of a middling sort.

"I was on my way to your place, I was looking for you," Raskolnikov began, "but why did I suddenly turn down ——sky Prospect just now from the Haymarket! I never turn or come this way. I turn right from the Haymarket. And this isn't the way to your place. I just turned and here you are! It's strange!"

"Why don't you say straight out: it's a miracle!"

"Because it may only be chance."

"Just look how they all have this twist in them!" Svidrigailov guffawed. "Even if they secretly believe in miracles, they won't admit it! And now you say it 'may' only be chance. They're all such little cowards here when it comes to their own opinion, you can't imagine, Rodion Romanych! I'm not talking about you. You have your own opinion and were not afraid to have it. It was that in you that drew my curiosity."

"And nothing else?"

"But surely that's enough."

Svidrigailov was obviously in an excited state, but only a little; he had drunk only half a glass of wine.

"I believe you came to see me before you found out that I was capable of having what you refer to as my own opinion," Raskolnikov observed.

"Well, it was a different matter then. Each of us takes his own steps. And as for the miracle, let me say that you seem to have slept through these past two or three days. I myself suggested this tavern to you, and there was no miracle in your coming straight here; I gave you all the directions myself, described the place where it stands, and told you the hours when I could be found here. Remember?"

"I forgot," Raskolnikov answered in surprise.

"I believe it. I told you twice. The address got stamped automatically in your memory. So you turned here automatically, strictly following my directions without knowing it yourself. I had no hope that you understood me as I was telling it to you then. You give yourself away too much, Rodion Romanych. And another thing: I'm convinced that many people in Petersburg talk to themselves as they walk. This is a city of half-crazy people. If we had any science, then physicians, lawyers, and philosophers could do the most valuable research on Petersburg, each in his own field. One seldom finds a place where there are so many gloomy, sharp, and strange influences on the soul of man as in Petersburg. The climatic influences alone are already worth something! And at the same time this is the administrative center of the whole of Russia, and its character must be reflected in everything. But that's not the point now; the point is that I've already observed you several times from the side. You walk out of the house with your head still high. After twenty steps you lower it and put your hands behind your back. You look but apparently no longer see anything either in front of you or to the sides. Finally you begin moving your lips and talking to yourself, sometimes freeing one hand and declaiming, and finally you stop in the middle of the street for a long time. It's really not good, sir. Someone besides me may notice you, and that is not at all to your advantage. It makes no difference to me, in fact, and I'm not going to cure you, but, of course, you understand me."

"And do you know that I'm being followed?" Raskolnikov asked, glancing at him searchingly.

"No, I know nothing about that," Svidrigailov answered, as if in surprise.

"Well, then let's leave me alone," Raskolnikov muttered, frowning.

"All right, let's leave you alone."

"Better tell me, if you come here to drink and twice told me to come to you here, why did you hide and try to leave just now, when I looked in the window from the street? I noticed it very well."

"Heh, heh! And why, when I was standing in your doorway that time, did you lie on your sofa with your eyes shut, pretending you were asleep, when you weren't asleep at all? I noticed it very well."

"I may have had . . . reasons . . . you know that yourself."

"And I may have had my reasons, though you are not going to know them."

Raskolnikov lowered his right elbow to the table, propped his chin from underneath with the fingers of his right hand, and fixed his eyes on Svidrigailov. For a minute or so he studied his face, which had always struck him before as well. It was somehow a strange face, more like a mask: white, ruddy, with ruddy, scarlet lips, a light blond beard, and still quite thick blond hair. The eyes were somehow too blue, and their look was somehow too heavy and immobile. There was something terribly unpleasant in this handsome and, considering the man's age, extremely youthful face. Svidrigailov's clothes were stylish, summery, light; especially stylish was his linen. On his finger there was an enormous ring with an expensive stone.

"But do I really have to bother with you as well?" Raskolnikov said suddenly, coming out into the open with convulsive impatience. "Though you're perhaps a most dangerous man, if you should decide to do me harm, I don't want to go against myself anymore. I'll show you now that I don't care as much about myself as you probably think. Know, then, that I've come to tell you straight out: if you still harbor your former intentions towards my sister, and if you think of using some recent discovery for that end, I will kill you before you can put me in jail. My word is good: you know I'm capable of keeping it. Second, if you want to announce something to me—because it has seemed to me all along as if you had something to tell me—do so quickly, because time is precious, and very soon it may be too late."

"Where are you off to in such a hurry?" Svidrigailov asked, studying him curiously.

"Each of us takes his own steps," Raskolnikov said glumly and impatiently.

"You yourself just invited me to be sincere, and now you refuse to answer the very first question," Svidrigailov observed with a smile. "You keep thinking I have some purposes, and so you look at me suspiciously. Well, that's quite understandable in your position. But however much I may wish to become closer to you, I still won't go to the trouble of reassuring you to the contrary. By God, the game isn't worth the candle; besides, I wasn't intending to talk with you about anything very special."

"Then why did you need me so much? You've been wooing around me, haven't you?"

"Simply as a curious subject for observation. I liked you for your fantastic situation—that's why! Besides, you're the brother of a person in whom I was very much interested; and, finally, there was a time when I heard terribly much and terribly often about you from that person, from which I concluded that you have a great influence over her; isn't that enough? Heh, heh, heh! However, I confess that your question is too complicated for me, and I find it difficult to answer. Let's say, for example, that you've come to me now not just on business, but for a little something new—right? Am I right?" Svidrigailov insisted, with a mischievous smile. "Now, just imagine that I, while still on my way here, on the train, was also counting on you, that you would also tell me a *little something new,* that I'd manage to come by something from you! See what rich men we are!"

"What could you come by?"

"Who can say? How should I know what? You see the sort of wretched tavern I spend all my time sitting in; and I relish it—that is, not that I relish it, but just that one needs a place to sit down. Well, take even this poor Katya—did you see her? . . . If I were at least a glutton, for example, a club gourmand—but look what I'm able to eat!" (He jabbed his finger towards the corner, where the leftovers of a terrible beefsteak with potatoes stood on a little table, on a tin plate.) "Have you had dinner, by the way? I had a bite, and don't want any more. Wine, for example, I don't drink at all. None, except for champagne, and even then only one glass in a whole evening, and even then I get a headache. I asked for it to be served now as a bracer, because I'm on my way somewhere, so you're seeing me in an unusual state of mind. That's why I hid myself like a schoolboy, because I thought you'd get in my way; but I think" (he took out his watch) "I can spend an hour with you; it's half past four now. Believe me, if only I were at least something—a landowner, say, or a father, an uhlan, a photographer, a journalist . . . n-nothing, no profession! Sometimes I'm even bored. Really, I thought you'd tell me something new."

"But who are you, and why did you come here?"

"Who am I? Oh, you know: a nobleman, served two years in the cavalry, then hung around here in Petersburg, then married Marfa Petrovna and lived on the estate. That's my biography!"

"You're a gambler, I believe?"

"No, hardly. A sharper is not a gambler."

"And you were a sharper?"

"Yes, I was a sharper."

"Did you ever get thrashed?"

"It happened. What of it?"

"Well, so you could also have been challenged to a duel . . . and that generally makes things lively."

"I won't contradict you, and, besides, I'm no expert at philosophizing. I confess to you that I hurried here rather more in connection with women."

"As soon as you'd buried Marfa Petrovna?"

"Why, yes." Svidrigailov smiled with winning frankness. "And what of it? You seem to find something bad in my talking that way about women?"

"You mean, do I find anything bad in depravity?"

"Depravity! Well, listen to that! However, for the sake of order, I'll answer you first about women in general; you know, I'm inclined to be talkative. Tell me, why should I restrain myself? Why should I give up women, if I'm so fond of them? At least it's an occupation."

"So all you're hoping for here is depravity?"

"Well, call it depravity if you wish! You and your depravity! At least it's a direct question; I like that. In this depravity there's at least something permanent, even based on nature, and not subject to fantasy, something that abides in the blood like a perpetually burning coal, eternally inflaming, which for a long time, even with age, one may not be able to extinguish so easily. Wouldn't you agree that it's an occupation of sorts?"

"What is there to be so glad about? It's a disease, and a dangerous one."

"Ah, listen to that! I admit it's a disease, like everything that goes beyond measure—and here one is bound to go beyond measure—but, first of all, that means one thing for one man and another for another, and, second, one must of course maintain a certain measure and calculation in everything, even if it's vile; but what can one do? Without that, really, one might perhaps have to shoot oneself. I agree that a decent man is obliged to be bored, but even so . . ."

"And could you shoot yourself?"

"Come, now!" Svidrigailov parried with loathing. "Do me a favor, don't speak of it," he added hurriedly, and even without any of the fanfaronade that had showed in his previous words. Even his face seemed to change. "I'll confess it's an unfortunate weakness, but what can I do: I'm afraid of death and don't like hearing it talked about. You know, I'm something of a mystic."

"Ah! Marfa Petrovna's ghosts! What, do they keep coming?"

"Away! Don't mention them! No, not in Petersburg yet; and anyway, devil take them!" he cried, with a sort of irritated look. "No, better let's talk about . . . although . . . Hm! Eh, there's no time, I can't stay with you long, more's the pity! I'd have found something to tell you."

"What is it, a woman?"

"Yes, a woman, just some chance occasion . . . no, it's not that."

"Well, and the vileness of the whole situation no longer affects you? You've already lost the power to stop?"

"So you're also appealing to power? Heh, heh, heh! You surprised me just now, Rodion Romanych, though I knew beforehand that it would be like this. And you talk to me of depravity and aesthetics! You—a Schiller! You—an idealist! Of course, it all had to be just like this, and it would be surprising if it were otherwise, but all the same it's strange when it really happens . . . Ah, what a pity there's no time, because you yourself are a most curious subject! By the way, are you fond of Schiller? I'm terribly fond of him."

"What a fanfaron you are, really!" Raskolnikov said with some loathing.

"Not so, by God!" Svidrigailov replied, guffawing. "Though I won't argue, let it be fanfaron; and why not a bit of fanfaronade, since it's quite harmless? I lived for seven years on Marfa Petrovna's estate, and so now, having fallen upon an intelligent man like you—intelligent and curious in the highest degree—I'm simply glad of a little chat, and, besides, I've drunk this half glass of wine and it's already gone to my head a bit. And, above all, there is one circumstance that has braced me very much, but which I . . . shall pass over in silence. Where are you going?" Svidrigailov suddenly asked in alarm.

Raskolnikov was getting up. He felt both wretched and stifled, and somehow awkward that he had come there. He was convinced that Svidrigailov was the emptiest and most paltry villain in the world.

"Ehh! Sit down, stay," Svidrigailov begged, "at least order some tea. Do stay, I won't talk nonsense—about myself, I mean. I'll tell you something. Shall I tell you how a woman, to put it in your style, was 'saving' me? This will even be an answer to your first question, because the person is your sister. May I tell you? It'll kill some time."

"Tell me, then, but I hope you . . ."

"Oh, don't worry! Besides, even in such a bad and empty man as I am, Avdotya Romanovna can inspire nothing but the deepest respect."

IV

"YOU PERHAPS KNOW (and, incidentally, I told you myself)," Svidrigailov began, "that I was being held in debtors' prison here, for an enormous sum, and without the least prospect of paying it. There's no point in detailing how Marfa Petrovna bought me off then; do you know to what degree of stupefaction love can sometimes lead a woman? She was an honest woman, very far from stupid (though completely uneducated). Imagine, then, that this same jealous and honest woman made up her mind, after many terrible frenzies and reproaches, to stoop to a certain sort of contract with me, which she indeed fulfilled throughout our marriage. The thing was that she was considerably older than I and, besides, constantly kept some sort of clove in her mouth. I had enough swinishness in my soul, and honesty of a sort, to announce to her straight off that I could not be completely faithful to her. This admission drove her into a frenzy, but I think she in some way liked my crude frankness: 'If he announces it beforehand like this, it means he doesn't want to deceive me'—well, and for a jealous woman that is the primary thing. After many tears, an oral contract was concluded between us along the following lines: first, I would never leave Marfa Petrovna and would always remain her husband; second, I would never go away anywhere without her permission; third, I would never keep a permanent mistress; fourth, in return for this, Marfa Petrovna would allow me to cast an eye occasionally on the serving girls, but not otherwise than with her secret knowledge; fifth, God forbid I should love a woman of our own rank; sixth, if, God forbid, I should perchance be visited by some great and serious passion, I would have to confide it to Marfa Petrovna. With regard to this last point, however, Marfa Petrovna felt rather at ease all the while; she was an intelligent woman and consequently could not look upon me as anything other than a profligate and a skirt-chaser who was incapable of serious love. But an intelligent woman and a jealous woman are two different things, and that's just the trouble. To make an impartial judgment of some people, one has *a priori* to renounce certain preconceived opinions and one's habitual attitude to the people and things that ordinarily surround one. I have the right to trust your judgment more than anyone else's. Perhaps you've already heard a great deal that was ridiculous and absurd about Marfa Petrovna. Indeed, some of her habits were quite ridiculous; but I'll tell you straight out that I sincerely regret the countless griefs of which I was the cause. Well, and that's enough, I think, to make a fairly decent *oraison funèbre*[8] for the most tender wife of a most tender husband. On the occasions when we quarreled, I was silent for the most part and did not become irritated, and this gentlemanliness almost always achieved its purpose; it affected her, and even pleased her; there were occasions when she was even proud of me. But all the same your dear sister was too much for her. And how did it ever happen that she risked taking such a beauty into her house as a governess! I explain it by Marfa Petrovna's being herself a fiery and susceptible woman, and quite simply falling in love herself—literally falling in love—with your dear sister. And Avdotya Romanovna is a good one, too! I understood very well, at first glance, that things were bad here, and—what do you think?—I decided not even to raise my eyes to her. But Avdotya Romanovna herself took the first step—will you believe that? And will you believe that Marfa Petrovna at first even went so far as to be angry with me for my constant silence about your sister, for being so indifferent to her ceaseless and enamored reports about Avdotya Romanovna? I don't understand what she wanted! Well, and of course Marfa Petrovna told

Avdotya Romanovna all her innermost secrets about me. She had the unfortunate trait of telling decidedly everyone all our family secrets, and of constantly complaining to everyone about me; how could she pass over such a new and wonderful friend? I suppose they even talked about nothing else but me, and no doubt all those dark, mysterious tales that are ascribed to me became known to Avdotya Romanovna . . . I'll bet you've already heard something of the sort as well?"

"I have. Luzhin even accused you of causing a child's death. Is it true?"

"Do me a favor, leave all those trivialities alone," Svidrigailov brushed the question aside, gruffly and with loathing. "If it's so necessary for you to learn about all that nonsense, I'll tell you specially some time, but now . . ."

"There was also talk of some servant on the estate, and that you seemed to have been the cause of something."

"Do me a favor—enough!" Svidrigailov interrupted again with obvious impatience.

"Was that the same servant who came to fill your pipe after his death . . . the one you told me about yourself?" Raskolnikov was becoming more and more irritated.

Svidrigailov looked intently at Raskolnikov, who thought he saw a spiteful grin flash momentarily, like lightning, in his eyes, but Svidrigailov restrained himself and answered quite politely:

"The very same. I see that you, too, find all this extremely interesting, and will regard it as my duty, when the first occasion offers, to satisfy your curiosity on all points. Devil take it! I see I may actually strike people as a romantic figure. Judge, then, how grateful I must be to the late Marfa Petrovna for having told so many curious and mysterious things about me to your dear sister. I dare not judge the impression, but in any case it was to my advantage. With all the natural loathing Avdotya Romanovna felt for me, and in spite of my ever gloomy and repellent look—in the end she felt pity for me, pity for the lost man. And when a girl's heart is moved to *pity*, that is, of course, most dangerous for her. She's sure to want to 'save' him then, to bring him to reason, to resurrect him, to call him to nobler aims, to regenerate him into a new life and new activity—well, everyone knows what can be dreamt up in that vein. I saw at once that the bird was flying into my net on its own, and prepared myself in my turn. You seem to be frowning, Rodion Romanych? Never mind, sir, it all came down to trifles. (Devil take it, I'm drinking too much wine!) You know, from the very beginning I've always felt sorry that fate did not grant your sister to be born in the second or third century of our era, as the daughter of some princeling or some other sort of ruler, or a proconsul in Asia Minor. She would undoubtedly have been among those who suffered martyrdom, and would have smiled, of course, while her breast was burned with red-hot iron tongs. She would have chosen it on purpose, and in the fourth or fifth century she would have gone to the Egyptian desert and lived there for thirty years, feeding on roots, ecstasies, and visions.[9] She's thirsting for just that, and demands to endure some torment for someone without delay, and if she doesn't get this torment, she may perhaps jump out the window. I've heard something about a certain Mr. Razumikhin. He's said to be a reasonable man (and his name also shows it; he must be a seminarian)[10]—well, then let him take care of your sister. In short, I think I understood her, and count it to my credit. But at the time—that is, at the beginning of our acquaintance—you know yourself that one is always somehow more light-minded and foolish, one's view is mistaken, one sees the wrong things. Devil take it, why is she so good-looking? It's not my fault! In short, it began with the most irrepressible sensual impulse in me. Avdotya Romanovna is terribly chaste, to an unseen, unheard-of degree. (Note that; I'm telling it to you as a fact about your sister. She is chaste, possibly, to the point of illness, in spite of all her broad intelligence, and it will do her harm.) There happened to be a certain girl there named Parasha, dark-eyed Parasha, who had just been brought from another village, a serving-girl, whom I had never seen before—very pretty, but incredibly stupid: burst into tears, raised the rooftops with her howling, and the result was a scandal. Once, after dinner, Avdotya Romanovna came specially looking for me alone on a path in the garden, and with flashing eyes *demanded* that I leave poor Parasha alone. It was almost our first conversation tête-à-tête. I naturally considered it an honor to satisfy her wish, tried to pretend I was struck, embarrassed—well, in short, played my role none too badly. Communications began, secret conversations, sermons, lectures, entreaties, supplications, even tears—would you believe it, even tears!

That's how strong the passion for propaganda is in some girls! I, of course, blamed it all on my fate, pretended to be hungering and thirsting for light, and, finally, employed the greatest and surest means of conquering a woman's heart, a means which has never yet failed anyone, which works decidedly on one and all, without exception—the well-known means of flattery. There's nothing in the world more difficult than candor, and nothing easier than flattery. If there is only the hundredth part of a false note in candor, there is immediately a dissonance, and then—scandal. But with flattery, even if everything is false down to the last little note, it is still agreeable and is listened to not without pleasure; crude though the pleasure may be, it is still a pleasure. And however crude the flattery may be, at least half of it is sure to seem true. And that is so for all levels of development and strata of society. Even a vestal virgin can be seduced by flattery. Not to mention ordinary people. I can't help laughing when I remember how I once seduced a certain lady who was devoted to her husband, her children, and her own virtues. It was so much fun, and so little work! And the lady was indeed virtuous, in her own way at least. My whole tactic consisted in being simply crushed and prostrate before her chastity at every moment. I flattered her infernally, and as soon as I obtained so much as the squeezing of her hand, or even just a look from her, I would reproach myself for having wrested it from her, because she had resisted, had resisted so much that I would never have gotten so far had I not been so depraved myself; because she, in her innocence, did not foresee any perfidy and succumbed inadvertently, without knowing, without thinking, and so on and so forth. In short, I obtained everything, and my lady remained convinced in the highest degree that she was innocent and chaste and had fulfilled all her duties and obligations, and had been ruined quite accidentally. And how angry she was with me when I declared to her finally that according to my sincere conviction she was seeking pleasure as much as I was. Poor Marfa Petrovna was also terribly susceptible to flattery, and if ever I had wanted, I could, of course, have transferred her entire estate to my name while she was still alive. (However, I'm drinking a terrible amount of wine and babbling away.) I hope you won't be angry if I now mention that the same effect began to show itself with Avdotya Romanovna. But I was stupid and impatient and spoiled the whole thing myself. Several times even before (and once somehow especially) Avdotya Romanovna had been terribly displeased by the look in my eyes—can you believe it? In short, a certain fire kept flaring up in them more and more strongly and imprudently, which frightened her and in the end became hateful to her. There's no point in going over the details, but we parted. Here again I was stupid. I began jeering in the crudest way regarding all these propagandas and conversions; Parasha appeared on the scene again, and not only her—in short, Sodom began. Ah, Rodion Romanych, if you'd seen at least once in your life how your dear sister's eyes can flash at times! It doesn't matter that I'm drunk now and have already finished a whole glass of wine, I'm telling the truth; I assure you that I used to see those eyes in my dreams; the rustling of her dress finally became unbearable to me. Really, I thought I'd get the falling sickness; I never imagined I could reach such a frenzy. In short, it was necessary to make peace—but it was no longer possible. And can you imagine what I did then? Oh, the degree of stupefaction to which rage can lead a man! Never undertake anything in a rage, Rodion Romanych! Considering that Avdotya Romanovna was essentially a beggar (ah, excuse me, that's not what I wanted . . . but isn't it all the same, if the concept is the same?), in short, that she was living by the work of her own hands, that she was supporting both her mother and you (ah, the devil, you're scowling again . . .), I decided to offer her all my money (I could have realized as much as thirty thousand even then) on condition that she elope with me, say, here to Petersburg. Naturally, I would swear eternal love, bliss, and so on and so forth. Believe me, I was so smitten that if she'd told me: Stick a knife into Marfa Petrovna, or poison her, and marry me—the thing would have been done at once! But it all ended in the catastrophe you already know about, and you can judge for yourself what a rage I was driven to when I discovered that Marfa Petrovna had procured that meanest of little clerks, Luzhin, and had almost put together a marriage—which would be essentially the same as what I was offering. Right? Right? Am I right? I notice you've begun listening rather attentively . . . an interesting young man . . ."

Svidrigailov impatiently pounded his fist on the table. He was flushed. Raskolnikov saw clearly that the glass or glass and a half of champagne he had drunk, sipping at it imperceptibly, was having a morbid effect on him, and decided to make use of his chance. He found Svidrigailov very suspicious.

"Well, after that, I'm fully convinced that you had my sister in mind when you came here," he said to Svidrigailov, directly and without reticence, in order to provoke him even more.

"Eh, come on," Svidrigailov suddenly seemed to catch himself, "didn't I tell you . . . and besides, your sister can't stand me."

"That she can't stand you I'm also convinced of, but that's not the point now."

"Are you so convinced of it?" (Svidrigailov narrowed his eyes and smiled mockingly.) "You're right, she doesn't love me; but never swear yourself to what has gone on between husband and wife, or between two lovers. There's always a little corner here that's always unknown to the whole world and is known only to the two of them. Will you swear that Avdotya Romanovna looked upon me with loathing?"

"I notice from certain words and phrases in your account that you still have your plans and the most immediate intentions on Dunya— vile ones, naturally."

"What! Did such words and phrases escape me?" Svidrigailov became most naively frightened all at once, paying not the slightest attention to the epithet applied to his intentions.

"Yes, and they're still escaping you. What, for instance, are you so afraid of? Why are you suddenly so frightened?"

"Me? Afraid and frightened? Frightened of you? It's rather you who should be afraid of me, *cher ami*. But what drivel . . . However, I see that I'm drunk; I nearly let things slip again. Devil take wine! Ho, there! Water!"

He grabbed the bottle and hurled it unceremoniously out the window. Filipp brought water.

"That's all nonsense," said Svidrigailov, wetting a towel and putting it to his head, "and I can haul you up short and reduce your suspicions to dust with a single word. Do you know, for instance, that I am getting married?"

"You told me that before."

"Did I? I forgot. But I couldn't have spoken positively then, because I hadn't seen the bride yet; it was just an intention. Well, but now I have a bride, and the matter is settled, and if it weren't for some

pressing matters, I'd certainly take you to see them—because I want
to ask your advice. Eh, the devil! I only have ten minutes left. See, look
at the time; however, I'll tell you, because it's an interesting little thing
in its own way; my marriage, I mean—where are you going? Leaving
again?"

"No, I wouldn't leave now."

"Wouldn't leave at all? We'll see. I'll take you there, truly, to show
you the bride, only not now; now it will soon be time for you to go.
You to the right, and I to the left. Do you know this Resslich? This
same Resslich who rents me the room—eh? You hear? No, what are
you thinking, the same one they say, about the girl, in the water, in
winter—well, do you hear? Do you? Well, so she's the one who cooked
it all up for me; you're bored like this, she said, amuse yourself a little.
And I really am a gloomy, boring man. You think I'm cheerful? No,
I'm gloomy: I don't do any harm, I just sit in the corner; sometimes
no one can get a word out of me for three days. And Resslich, that
rogue, I'll tell you, here's what she has in mind: I'll get bored, abandon
my wife, and leave; then she'll get the wife and put her into circula-
tion—among our own set, that is, or a little higher up. There's this
paralyzed father, she says, a retired official, sits in a chair and hasn't
moved his legs for three years. There's also a mother, she says, a
reasonable lady, the mother is. The son serves somewhere in the provinces, doesn't help them. One daughter is married and doesn't visit;
there are two little nephews on their hands (as if their own weren't
enough), and their last daughter's a schoolgirl, they took her out of
school without letting her finish, in a month she'll be just sixteen,
which means in a month she can be married. To me, that is. We went
there; it was very funny. I introduced myself: a landowner, a widower,
from a notable family, with such-and-such connections, with money—
so what if I'm fifty and she's not sixteen yet? Who's looking at that?
But isn't it tempting, eh? It's tempting, ha, ha! You should have seen
me talking with the papa and mama! People would have paid just to
see me then. She comes out, curtsies—can you imagine, she's still in
a short dress; an unopened bud—she blushes, turns pink as the dawn
(they had told her, of course). I don't know how you feel about
women's faces, but to my mind those sixteen years, those still childish
eyes, that timidity, those bashful little tears—to my mind they're better

than beauty, and on top of that she's just like a picture. Fair hair fluffed up in little curls like a lamb's, plump little crimson lips, little feet—lovely! . . . So we got acquainted, I announced that I was in a hurry owing to family circumstances, and the very next day—that is, two days ago—they gave us their blessing. Since then, the moment I come in I take her on my knees and don't let her get down . . . Well, she blushes like the dawn, and I kiss her all the time; and the mama naturally impresses upon her that this, you see, is your husband, and it ought to be this way—in short, clover! And this present position, as a fiancé, may in fact be better than that of a husband. It's what's called *la nature et la vérité!*[11] Ha, ha! I've talked with her a couple of times—the girl is far from stupid; once in a while she gives me a glance on the sly—it burns right through. And you know, she has the face of a Raphael Madonna. Because the Sistine Madonna has a fantastic face, the face of a mournful holy fool, has that ever struck you? Well, hers is the same sort. As soon as they blessed us, the next day, I came with fifteen hundred roubles' worth: a set of diamonds, another of pearls, and a lady's silver toilet case—this big—with all kinds of things in it, so that even her Madonna's face began to glow. I took her on my knees yesterday, but I must have done it too unceremoniously—she became all flushed, tears started, but though she didn't want to show it, she was all aflame herself. Everyone left for a moment, there were just the two of us, she suddenly threw herself on my neck (the first time on her own), embraced me with her little arms, kissed me, and vowed that she would be an obedient, faithful, and good wife to me, that she would make me happy, that she would spend her whole life on it, every minute of her life, would sacrifice everything, everything, and in re-turn for all that she wished to have *only my respect,* and she said, 'I need nothing else, nothing, nothing, no presents!' You must agree that to hear such a confession, in private, from such a dear sixteen-year-old angel, in a lace dress, with fluffed-up little curls, with a blush of maidenly modesty and tears of enthusiasm in her eyes, you must agree it's rather tempting. It is tempting, isn't it? It's worth something, eh? Well, isn't it? Well . . . so, listen . . . let's go and see my fiancée . . . only not now!"

"In short, it's this monstrous difference in age and development that arouses your sensuality! Can you really get married like that?"

"And why not? Of course. Every man looks out for himself, and he has the happiest life who manages to hoodwink himself best of all. Ha, ha! But who are you to go running full tilt into virtue? Spare me, my dear, I'm a sinful man. Heh, heh, heh!"

"Nevertheless, you provided for Katerina Ivanovna's children. However . . . however, you had your own reasons for that . . . I understand it all now."

"I like children generally; like them very much," Svidrigailov guffawed. "In this connection I can even tell you about a most curious episode, which is still going on. On the very day of my arrival, I went to look at all these various cesspools—well, after seven years I really leaped at them! You've probably noticed that I've been in no rush to get together with my bunch, I mean my former friends and acquaintances. And I'll do without them for as long as possible. You know, on Marfa Petrovna's estate I was tormented to death by the memory of all these mysterious places, these little corners where, if you know, you can find quite a lot. Devil take it! The people are drinking, the educated youth are burning themselves up in idleness, in unrealizable dreams and fancies, crippling themselves with theories; Yids come flocking from somewhere, hiding the money away, and the rest of it falls into depravity. This city breathed its familiar breath on me from the first hours. I wound up at a so-called dance hall—a terrible cesspool (but I like my cesspools precisely with a bit of filth)—well, there was a cancan, the like of which is not and never was in my time. Yes, sir, there's progress there. Suddenly I see a girl of about thirteen, in a lovely dress, dancing with a virtuoso, and with another one *vis-à-vis*. And her mother is sitting on a chair by the wall. Well, you can imagine what the cancan is! The girl gets embarrassed, blushes, finally feels offended and begins to cry. The virtuoso picks her up and begins twirling her around and performing in front of her; everyone is roaring with laughter and—I love our public, even a cancan public, at such moments—they laugh and shout: 'That's the way, serves them right! Shouldn't bring children here!' Well, I spit on it, it's none of my business whether they console themselves logically or not! I immediately picked out my place, sat down next to the mother, and started telling her that I, too, was a visitor, and, oh, what boors they all were here, that they couldn't recognize true virtue or feel any rightly deserved respect; made it known to her that I had a lot of money; offered to take them home in my carriage; brought them home, became acquainted (they'd just arrived, were subletting some closet from tenants). It was announced to me that she and her daughter could not regard my acquaintance as anything but an honor; I discovered that they had neither stick nor stone, and had come to petition for something in some office; I offered help, money; I discovered that they had gone to the dance hall by mistake, thinking it was a place where they actually taught dancing; I, for my part, offered to contribute to the young lady's education—French language and dancing lessons. They accepted with delight, considered it an honor, and I've kept up the acquaintance . . . If you like, we can go there—only not now."

"Stop, stop your mean, vile anecdotes, you depraved, mean, sensual man!"

"Look at our Schiller, what a Schiller, just look at him! *Où va-t-elle la vertu se nicher?*[12] And you know, I'll go on telling you such things on purpose, just to hear your little outcries. Delightful!"

"Isn't it! And do you think I don't seem ludicrous to myself right now?" Raskolnikov muttered spitefully.

Svidrigailov was roaring with laughter; finally he called for Filipp, paid, and began getting up. "Oh, am I drunk! *Assez causé!*"[13] he said. "Delightful!"

"What else but delightful," Raskolnikov exclaimed, also getting up. "Of course it's delightful for a played-out profligate to tell about such adventures—with some monstrous intention of the same sort in mind—and under such circumstances besides, and to such a man as me . . . Quite arousing."

"Well, in that case," Svidrigailov replied, even with some surprise, scrutinizing Raskolnikov, "in that case, you're rather a cynic yourself. Anyway, you've got enormous material in you. You can understand a lot, quite a lot . . . well, and you can also do a lot. Well, but enough. I sincerely regret having talked so little with you, but you won't get away from me . . . Just wait . . ."

Svidrigailov left the tavern. Raskolnikov walked out after him. Svidrigailov was not very drunk, however; it had gone to his head only momentarily, and the drunkenness was passing off every minute. He was very preoccupied with something, something very important, and was frowning. Some prospect obviously worried and troubled him. In the past few minutes he had also somehow suddenly changed towards Raskolnikov, had become more rude and mocking. Raskolnikov noticed all this and was also alarmed. Svidrigailov became very suspicious to him; he decided to follow him.

They went down to the sidewalk.

"You go right, and I'll go left, or perhaps vice versa, only—*adieu, mon plaisir*,[14] see you—gladly—soon!"

And he turned right, towards the Haymarket.

V

RASKOLNIKOV walked behind him.

"What's the meaning of this!" Svidrigailov exclaimed, turning around. "I believe I said . . ."

"It means that I'm not going to leave you alone right now."

"Wha-a-at?"

The two men stopped and looked at each other for a minute or so, as if sizing each other up.

"From all your half-drunken stories," Raskolnikov snapped sharply, "I've *positively* concluded that you not only have not abandoned your most vile designs on my sister, but are even more occupied with them than ever. It is known to me that my sister received some sort of letter this morning. You were unable to sit still all this while . . . Suppose you did dig yourself up some wife along the way; it means nothing. I wish personally to make sure . . ."

Raskolnikov himself could hardly have said precisely what he wanted now, or precisely what he wished personally to make sure of.

"Is that so! And would you like me to call the police right now?"

"Go ahead!"

Again they stood facing each other for a minute. Finally, Svidrigailov's expression changed. Having assured himself that Raskolnikov was not afraid of the threat, he suddenly assumed a most cheerful and friendly look.

"Aren't you the one! I purposely did not start talking with you about your affair, though naturally I'm eaten up with curiosity. It's a fantastic affair. I tried to put it off until next time, but, really, you could

even rouse a dead man . . . Well, come along, only I'll tell you beforehand that I'm only going home for a moment, to pick up some money;
then I'll lock the apartment, take a carriage, and go off to the Islands
for the whole evening. Well, do you think you're going to follow me?"

"To the apartment, for the moment; not yours but Sofya Semyonovna's, to apologize for not being at the funeral."

"Do as you please, but Sofya Semyonovna isn't home. She took all
the children to a certain lady, an aristocratic old lady, a former acquaintance of mine from the old days, who is the patroness of some
orphanages. I charmed the lady by paying the fees for all three of
Katerina Ivanovna's younglings and donating money to the institutions as well; finally, I told her Sofya Semyonovna's story, with full
honors, not concealing anything. The effect was indescribable. That's
why Sofya Semyonovna had an appointment to go straight to the
——y Hotel, where this lady is temporarily present, after her summer
house."

"No matter, I'll still come."

"As you wish, only I'm no part of it; it's nothing to me! Here's the
house. Tell me, am I right that you look at me suspiciously because I
myself have been so delicate all along and haven't bothered you with
any questions . . . you understand? It seems a remarkable thing to you,
I'll bet on it! Well, so much for being delicate!"

"And eavesdropping at doors!"

"Ah, so it's that now!" Svidrigailov laughed. "Yes, I'd be surprised
if you let that go unnoticed, after all that's happened. Ha, ha! I did
catch something about your antics that time . . . there . . . which you
were telling to Sofya Semyonovna, but still, what does it mean? Perhaps I'm a thoroughly backward man and unable to understand anything. Explain, my dear, for God's sake! Enlighten me with the latest
principles."

"You couldn't have heard anything; it's all lies!"

"I don't mean that, not that (though I did hear a thing or two all
the same), no, what I mean is that you keep moaning and groaning all
the time! Schiller is constantly being embarrassed in you. And now I'm
told that one can't eavesdrop at doors. In that case, go and tell the
authorities; say thus and so, I've had this mishap: there was a little
mistake in my theory. But if you're convinced that one cannot eaves-

drop at doors, but can go around whacking old crones with whatever comes to hand, to your heart's content, then leave quickly for America somewhere! Flee, young man! Maybe there's still time. I say it sincerely. Are you out of money or something? I'll give you enough for the trip."

"That's not at all what I'm thinking about," Raskolnikov interrupted with loathing.

"I understand (don't trouble yourself, by the way: you needn't say much if you don't want to); I understand what sort of questions are in vogue with you: moral ones, right? Questions of the citizen and the human being? Forget them; what do you need them for now? Heh, heh! Is it because you're still a citizen and a human being? But in that case you shouldn't have butted into this; there's no point in tackling business that isn't yours. So, shoot yourself; or what, you don't want to?"

"You seem to be taunting me on purpose so that I'll leave you alone now . . ."

"What an odd man! But we're already here, welcome to the stairs. See, there's Sofya Semyonovna's door; look, no one's home! You don't believe me? Ask Kapernaumov; she leaves them the key. Here's Madame de Kapernaumov herself, eh? What? (She's a bit deaf.) Gone out? Where? Well, did you hear now? She's not in, and may not be back until late in the evening. Well, let's go to my place now. Didn't you want to go there, too? So, here we are, at my place. Madame Resslich isn't home. The woman is eternally bustling about, but she's a good woman, I assure you . . . she might be of use to you, if you were a little more reasonable. Well, now observe if you please: I take this five percent note from the bureau (see how many I've got left!), but this one's going to the money-changer's today. Well, did you see? No point in losing more time. The bureau is being locked, the apartment is being locked, and we're on the stairs again. Well, do you want us to hire a carriage? Because I'm off to the Islands. Would you like to go for a ride? Look, I'm taking this carriage to Yelagin Island. What? You refuse? Can't keep it up? Never mind, let's go for a ride. Looks like it may rain; never mind, we'll raise the top . . ."

Svidrigailov was already sitting in the carriage. Raskolnikov judged that his suspicions, at least this time, were unwarranted. Without a word of reply, he turned and went back in the direction of the Haymarket. If he had looked behind him at least once on his way, he would have had time to see how Svidrigailov, after driving no more than a hundred paces, paid for the carriage and ended up on the sidewalk himself. But he could no longer see anything, and had already turned the corner. A profound loathing drew him away from Svidrigailov. "How could I, even for a moment, expect something from this crude villain, this sensual profligate and scoundrel!" he exclaimed involuntarily. True, Raskolnikov pronounced his judgment too hastily and light-mindedly. There was something in all that had to do with Svidrigailov which endowed him with at least a certain originality, if not mysteriousness. And as far as his sister was concerned in all this, here Raskolnikov remained convinced quite assuredly that Svidrigailov would not leave her alone. But it was becoming too difficult and unbearable to go on thinking and rethinking it all!

As usual, once he was alone, after going about twenty steps, he fell into deep thoughtfulness. Having walked out onto the bridge, he stopped by the railing and began looking at the water. And meanwhile Avdotya Romanovna was standing close by him.

He had met her as he started across the bridge but had passed by without noticing her. Dunechka had never before met him like this in the street, and was struck to the point of fear. She stopped and did not know whether to call out to him or not. Suddenly she noticed Svidrigailov coming hurriedly from the direction of the Haymarket.

He seemed to be approaching secretively and cautiously. He did not walk out on the bridge, but stopped to one side on the sidewalk, trying as well as he could not to be seen by Raskolnikov. He had noticed Dunya long since and began making signs to her. It appeared to her from his signs that he was begging her not to call her brother, but to leave him alone and come to him.

And Dunya did so. She quietly passed around her brother and went up to Svidrigailov.

"Come along, quickly," Svidrigailov whispered to her. "I do not wish Rodion Romanovich to know of our meeting. I must warn you that I've just been sitting with him, not far from here, in a tavern, where he came looking for me himself, and I had trouble getting rid of him. He somehow knows about my letter to you and suspects something. Of course, it was not you who revealed it? But if not, then who was it?"

"Here, we've already turned the corner," Dunya interrupted, "my brother won't see us now. I declare to you that I will not go farther with you. Tell me everything here; it can all be said in the street."

"First, it can by no means be said in the street; second, you must also hear Sofya Semyonovna; third, I have some documents to show you . . . Well, and finally, if you won't agree to come to my place, I'll give up all explanations and leave at once. At the same time I beg you not to forget that a rather curious secret of your beloved brother's is entirely in my hands."

Dunya stood hesitantly, and looked at Svidrigailov with piercing eyes.

"What are you afraid of?" the latter remarked calmly. "The city is not the country. And in the country you caused me more harm than I did you, but here . . ."

"Has Sofya Semyonovna been warned?"

"No, I didn't say a word to her, and am not even sure that she's at home now. However, she probably is. She buried her relation today: on such a day one doesn't go around visiting. For the time being I don't want to tell anyone about it, and even partly regret having told you. At this point the slightest imprudence is the same as a denunciation. I live just here, here in this house, the one we're coming to. Here's our caretaker; the caretaker knows me very well; look, he's bowing; he sees me coming with a lady, and of course has already managed to notice your face—that will prove useful to you, if you're very afraid and suspicious of me. Excuse me for speaking so crudely. I'm subletting from tenants. Sofya Semyonovna lives on the other side of my wall; she also sublets from tenants. The whole floor is full of tenants. Why are you afraid, then, like a child? Or am I really so frightening?"

Svidrigailov's face twisted into a condescending smile, but he could no longer bother about smiling. His heart was pounding, and his breath was taken away. He deliberately raised his voice to conceal his growing excitement, but Dunya failed to notice this special excitement; she was too irritated by his remark that she was afraid of him like a child and found him so frightening.

"Though I know that you are a man . . . without honor, I am not in the least afraid of you. Go ahead," she said with apparent calm, but her face was very pale.

Svidrigailov stopped at Sonya's apartment.

"Allow me to inquire whether she is at home. No. Worse luck! But I know she can come any minute. If she's stepped out, it must be to see a certain lady, about the orphans. Their mother has died. I also mixed into it and made arrangements. If Sofya Semyonovna doesn't come back in ten minutes, I'll send her to you, this very day if you like; now here's my apartment. Here are my two rooms. My landlady, Mrs. Resslich, lives behind that door. Now look here, I'll show you my main documents: this door leads from my bedroom to two completely vacant rooms, which are for rent. Here they are . . . you should take a somewhat more attentive look at this . . ."

Svidrigailov occupied two rather spacious furnished rooms. Dunya was looking around mistrustfully, but did not notice anything special either in the decor or in the layout of the rooms, though there were things to be noticed—for instance, that Svidrigailov's apartment was somehow placed between two almost uninhabited apartments. His entrance was not direct from the corridor, but through the landlady's two rooms, which were nearly empty. And, having opened the locked door from the bedroom, Svidrigailov showed Dunya the other apartment, also empty, which was for rent. Dunya stood on the threshold, not understanding why she was being invited to look, but Svidrigailov hastened to explain.

"Now, look here, in this second large room. Notice this door; it's locked. By the door there's a chair, the only chair in either room. I brought it from my apartment, to listen more comfortably. Just the other side of the door stands Sofya Semyonovna's table; she was sitting there, talking with Rodion Romanych. And I was here eavesdropping, sitting on the chair, two evenings in a row, each time for two hours or so—and, of course, I'd be able to find something out, don't you think?"

"You were eavesdropping?"

"Yes, I was eavesdropping; now come back to my place; there's nowhere even to sit down here."

He led Avdotya Romanovna back to his first room, which served him as a living room, and offered her a chair. He himself sat at the other end of the table, at least seven feet away from her, but probably his eyes were already shining with the same flame that had once so frightened Dunechka. She gave a start and again looked around mistrustfully. It was an involuntary gesture; she clearly did not want to show her mistrust. But the isolated situation of Svidrigailov's apartment finally struck her. She would have liked to ask at least if the landlady was at home, but she did not ask . . . out of pride. Besides, there was in her heart another, immeasurably greater suffering than fear for herself. She was unbearably tormented.

"Here is your letter," she began, placing it on the table. "How can what you write be possible? You allude to a crime supposedly committed by my brother. You allude to it all too clearly, you cannot talk your way out of it now. Know, then, that I heard that stupid tale even before this, and I do not believe a single word of it. It is a vile and ridiculous suspicion. I know the story, and how and why it was invented. You cannot possibly have any proof. You promised to prove it: speak, then! But know beforehand that I don't believe you! I don't! . . ."

Dunechka spoke in a rapid patter, and for a moment color rushed to her face.

"If you don't believe me, how did it happen that you risked coming alone to see me? Why did you come, then? Only out of curiosity?"

"Don't torment me—speak, speak!"

"You're a brave girl, needless to say. By God, I thought you'd ask Mr. Razumikhin to accompany you here. But he was not with you, or anywhere in the vicinity—I did check. That is courageous; it means you wanted to spare Rodion Romanych. But then, everything in you is divine . . . As for your brother, what can I tell you? You just saw him yourself. A nice sight?"

"But you're not just basing it on that?"

"No, not on that, but on his own words. For two evenings in a row he came here to see Sofya Semyonovna. I showed you where they were sitting. He told her his full confession. He is a murderer. He killed the old woman, the money-lender, the official's widow, to whom he had also pawned things; he killed her sister as well, a small-time dealer named Lizaveta, who chanced to walk in during her sister's murder. He killed them both with an axe, which he had brought with him. He killed them in order to rob them, and he did rob them; he took money and some things . . . He himself told it all word for word to Sofya Semyonovna; she's the only one who knows the secret, but she did not participate in the murder either by word or by deed, but, on the contrary, was as horrified as you are now. Don't worry, she won't betray him."

"It cannot be!" Dunya murmured with pale, deadened lips; she was breathless. "It cannot be, there's no reason, not the slightest, no motive . . . It's a lie! A lie!"

"He robbed her, that's the whole reason. He took money and some things. True, according to his own confession, he did not put either the money or the things to any use, but went and hid them somewhere under a stone, where they're lying still. But that was because he didn't dare use them."

"But is it conceivable that he could steal, rob, that he could even think of it?" Dunya cried out, jumping up from her chair. "You know him, you've seen him! Could he be a thief?"

It was as if she were imploring Svidrigailov; she forgot all her fear.

"There are thousands and millions of combinations and gradations here, Avdotya Romanovna. A thief steals, but then he knows in himself that he's a scoundrel; but I've heard of one gentleman who broke into the mail, and who can tell about him, maybe he really thought he was doing a decent thing! Naturally, I would not have believed it, just as you don't, if I'd been told it by some third person. But I did believe my own ears. He also explained all his reasons to Sofya Semyonovna; and at first she did not even believe her ears, but in the end she believed her eyes, her own eyes. Because he himself was telling it to her personally."

"And what are . . . the reasons!"

"That's a long story, Avdotya Romanovna. What we have here is—how shall I express it for you—a theory of sorts; it's the same as if I should find, for example, that an isolated evildoing is permissible if the main purpose is good. A single evil and a hundred good deeds! Of course, it's also offensive for a young man of merit and measureless vanity to know that if he had, for example, a mere three thousand or so, his whole career, the whole future in terms of his life's purpose, would shape itself differently—and yet the three thousand aren't there. Add to that the vexations of hunger, cramped quarters, rags, and a lively sense of the beauty of his social position, as well as that of his sister and mother. But above all vanity, pride and vanity—though, God knows, perhaps even with good inclinations . . . I'm not blaming him, please don't think that; it's none of my business. There was also a certain little theory of his—a so-so theory—according to which people are divided, you see, into raw material and special people, meaning people for whom, owing to their high position, the law does not exist, people, on the contrary, who themselves devise laws for the rest, for the raw material—that is, for the trash. Not bad, a so-so little theory; *une théorie comme une autre.* [15] He got terribly carried away with Napoleon—that is, essentially what carried him away was that a great many men of genius disregarded isolated evil and stepped over it without hesitation. He seems to have imagined that he, too, was a man of genius—that is, he was sure of it for a time. He suffered greatly, and suffers still, from the thought that though he knew how to devise the theory, he was unable to step over without hesitation and therefore is not a man of genius. Now that, for a vain young man, is truly humiliating, especially in our age . . ."

"And remorse of conscience? You mean you deny him all moral feeling? Is that what he's like?"

"Ah, Avdotya Romanovna, things have all become clouded now—though, by the way, they never were in any particular order. Russian people are generally broad people, Avdotya Romanovna, broad as their land, and greatly inclined to the fantastic, the disorderly; but it's disastrous to be broad without special genius. And do you remember how much you and I used to talk in the same way, and about the same subject, sitting by ourselves on the terrace, every evening after supper? You used to reproach me precisely with this broadness. Who knows, maybe at the same time as we were talking, he was lying here and thinking his thoughts. In our educated society, Avdotya Romanovna, we have no especially sacred traditions; except for what someone somehow pieces together from old books . . . or something drawn from the old chronicles. But they are mostly scholars and, you know, they're all dunces in their way, so that for a man of the world it's even indecent. However, you generally know my opinion; I'm certainly not accusing anyone. I myself am an idler and I keep to that. But we've already talked about it more than once. I even had the happiness of interesting you with my judgments . . . You are very pale, Avdotya Romanovna!"

"I know this theory of his. I read his article in a magazine, about people to whom everything is permitted . . . Razumikhin brought it to me . . ."

"Mr. Razumikhin? Your brother's article? In a magazine? Is there such an article? I didn't know. Now that is most certainly curious! But where are you going, Avdotya Romanovna?"

"I want to see Sofya Semyonovna," Dunechka said in a weak voice. "How can I get to her? Maybe she's come back; I absolutely must see her now. Let her . . ."

Avdotya Romanovna could not finish; her breath literally failed her.

"Sofya Semyonovna will not come back before nightfall. So I suppose. She ought to have come very soon, but if not, it will be very late . . ."

"Ah, so you're lying! I see . . . you've been lying . . . it was all a lie! I don't believe you! I don't! I don't!" Dunechka cried out in a real frenzy, completely losing her head.[16]

Almost in a faint, she fell onto the chair that Svidrigailov hastened to move towards her.

"Avdotya Romanovna, what's wrong? Come to your senses! Here's some water. Take a sip . . ."

He sprinkled her with water. Dunechka started and came to her senses.

"It's affected her strongly!" Svidrigailov muttered to himself, frowning. "Avdotya Romanovna, calm yourself! I assure you, he has friends. We will save him, rescue him. Do you want me to take him abroad? I have money; I can get a ticket in three days. And as for the murder, he'll still have time to do many good deeds, so it will all be made up for; calm yourself. He still may be a great man. How are you now? How do you feel?"

"Wicked man! He's still jeering! Let me . . ."

"Where are you going? Where?"

"To him. Where is he? Do you know? Why is this door locked? We came in this door, and now it's locked. When did you manage to lock it?"

"We couldn't really shout for the whole house to hear what we were just talking about. I'm not jeering at all; I'm simply tired of speaking this language. Now, where are you going to go in such a state? Or do you want to betray him? You'll drive him into a rage, and he'll betray himself. I want you to know that he's being watched, they're already on his trail. You'll only give him away. Wait. I saw him and spoke with him just now; he can still be saved. Wait, sit down, let's think it over together. That's why I sent for you, to talk about it alone with you and think it over carefully. Do sit down!"

"How can you save him? Can he be saved?"

Dunya sat down. Svidrigailov sat beside her.

"It all depends on you, on you, on you alone," he began, with flashing eyes, almost in a whisper, becoming confused, and even failing to articulate some words in his excitement.

Dunya drew further back from him in fear. He, too, was trembling all over.

"You . . . one word from you, and he is saved! I . . . I will save him. I have money, and friends. I'll send him away at once, and I'll get a passport, two passports. One for him, the other for me. I have friends; I have practical people . . . Do you want me to? I'll also get a passport for you . . . your mother . . . what do you need Razumikhin for? I, too, love you . . . I love you infinitely. Let me kiss the hem of your dress—let me, let me! I can't bear its rustling! Tell me: 'Do this,' and I'll do it! I'll do anything. I'll do the impossible. What you believe, I will believe. I'll do anything, anything! No, don't look at me like that! You know you're killing me . . . ."

He was even beginning to rave. Something happened to him suddenly, as if it all suddenly went to his head. Dunya jumped up and rushed to the door.

"Open! Open!" she cried through the door, calling to someone and shaking the door with her hands. "Open, please! Is anyone there?"

Svidrigailov stood up and recovered himself. A spiteful and mocking smile was slowly forcing itself to his still trembling lips.

"No one is there," he said softly and evenly, "the landlady has gone out, and shouting like that is a wasted effort; you're only upsetting yourself for nothing."

"Where is the key? Open the door at once, at once, you vile man!"[17]

"I've lost the key; I can't find it."

"Ah! So it's force!" Dunya cried out, turned pale as death, and rushed to the corner, where she quickly shielded herself with a little table that happened to be there. She did not scream; but she fastened her eyes on her tormentor and closely followed his every movement. Svidrigailov did not move from where he was, and stood facing her at the other end of the room. He even regained his composure, at least externally. But his face was as pale as before, and the mocking smile had not left it.

"You just mentioned 'force,' Avdotya Romanovna. If it's to be force, you can judge for yourself that I've taken measures. Sofya Semyonovna is not at home; the Kapernaumovs are very far, five locked doors away. Finally, I am at least twice as strong as you are, and, besides, I have nothing to fear, because you cannot complain afterwards either: you really won't want to betray your brother, will you? Besides, no one will believe you: why on earth should a girl go alone to a single man's apartment? So that even if you sacrifice your brother, you still won't prove anything: force is very difficult to prove, Avdotya Romanovna."

"Scoundrel!" Dunya whispered indignantly.

"As you please, but note that I was speaking only by way of suggestion. According to my own personal conviction, you are entirely right: force is an abomination. What I was getting at was that there would be exactly nothing on your conscience even if . . . even if you wished to save your brother voluntarily, in the way I have offered. It would mean you were simply submitting to circumstances—well, to force, finally, if it's impossible to do without the word. Think about it; the fates of your brother and your mother are in your hands. And I shall be your slave . . . all my life . . . I'll wait here . . ."

Svidrigailov sat down on the sofa, about eight steps away from Dunya. For her there was no longer the slightest doubt of his unshakeable determination. Besides, she knew him . . .

Suddenly she took a revolver from her pocket, cocked it, and lowered the hand holding the revolver to the little table. Svidrigailov jumped up from his seat.

"Aha! So that's how it is!" he cried out in surprise, but with a spiteful grin. "Well, that completely changes the course of things! You're making it much easier for me, Avdotya Romanovna! And where did you get the revolver? Can it be Mr. Razumikhin? Hah, but that's my revolver! An old acquaintance! And how I was hunting for it then! . . . So those shooting lessons I had the honor of giving you in the country weren't wasted after all."

"It's not your revolver, it's Marfa Petrovna's, whom you killed, villain![18] Nothing in her house was yours. I took it as soon as I began to suspect what you were capable of. If you dare take just one step, I swear I'll kill you!"

Dunya was in a frenzy. She held the revolver ready.

"Well, and your brother? I ask out of curiosity," Svidrigailov said, still standing in the same place.

"Denounce him if you like! Don't move! Not a step! I'll shoot! You poisoned your wife, I know it; you're a murderer yourself! . . ."

"And are you firmly convinced that I poisoned Marfa Petrovna?"

"You did! You hinted it to me yourself; you spoke to me about poison . . . I know you went to get it . . . you had it ready . . . It was certainly you . . . scoundrel!"

"Even if that were true, it was because of you . . . you would still be the cause of it."

"You're lying! I hated you always, always . . ."

"Aha, Avdotya Romanovna! You've obviously forgotten how in the heat of propaganda you were already inclining and melting . . . I saw it in your dear eyes; remember, in the evening, in the moonlight, and with a nightingale singing?"

"You're lying!" (Rage shone in Dunya's eyes.) "You're lying, slanderer!"

"Lying, am I? Well, maybe I am. So I lied. Women oughtn't to be reminded of these little things." (He grinned.) "I know you'll shoot, you pretty little beast. Go on, shoot!"

Dunya raised the revolver and, deathly pale, her white lower lip trembling, her large black eyes flashing like fire, looked at him, having made up her mind, calculating, and waiting for the first movement from his side. He had never yet seen her so beautiful. The fire that flashed from her eyes as she raised the revolver seemed to burn him, and his heart was wrung with pain. He took a step, and a shot rang out. The bullet grazed his hair and struck the wall behind him. He stopped and laughed softly:

"The wasp has stung! She aims straight at the head . . . What's this? Blood?" He took out a handkerchief to wipe away the blood that was flowing in a thin trickle from his right temple; the bullet must have slightly touched his scalp. Dunya lowered the revolver and looked at Svidrigailov not really in fear but in some wild perplexity. It was as if she herself did not understand what she had done or what was happening.

"Well, so you missed! Shoot again, I'm waiting," Svidrigailov said softly, still grinning, but somehow gloomily. "This way I'll have time to seize you before you cock it!"

Dunechka gave a start, quickly cocked the revolver, and raised it again.

"Let me be!" she said in despair. "I swear, I'll shoot again . . . I'll . . . kill you! . . ."

"Well, so . . . from three paces you could hardly fail to kill me. Well, but if you don't . . . then . . ." His eyes flashed, and he took two more steps.

Dunechka pulled the trigger—a misfire!

"You didn't load it properly. Never mind! You've got another cap left. Put it right; I'll wait."[19]

He stood in front of her, two steps away, waiting and looking at her with wild determination, his grim eyes inflamed with passion. Dunya realized that he would rather die than let her go. "And . . . and of course she would kill him now, from two paces! . . ."

Suddenly she threw the revolver aside.

"She threw it down!" Svidrigailov said in surprise, and drew a deep breath. It was as if something had all at once been lifted from his heart, and perhaps not just the burden of mortal fear—which, besides, he had hardly felt in that minute. It was a deliverance from another, more sorrowful and gloomy feeling, the full force of which he himself would have been unable to define.

He went up to Dunya and gently put his arm around her waist. She did not resist but, all trembling like a leaf, looked at him with imploring eyes. He wanted to say something, his lips twisted, but he was unable to speak.

"Let me go!" Dunya said imploringly.[20]

Svidrigailov started; this *let me* was spoken somehow differently from the previous one.

"So you don't love me?" he asked softly.

Dunya moved her head negatively.

"And . . . you can't . . . ever?" he whispered in despair.

"Never!" whispered Dunya.

A moment of terrible, mute struggle passed in Svidrigailov's soul. He looked at her with an inexpressible look. Suddenly he withdrew his arm, turned away, walked quickly to the window, and stood in front of it.

Another moment passed.

"Here's the key!" (He took it from the left pocket of his coat and placed it on the table behind him, without looking and without turning to Dunya.) "Take it; go quickly! . . ."

He went on staring out the window.

Dunya approached the table to take the key.

"Quickly! Quickly!" Svidrigailov repeated, still without moving and without turning around. But in this "quickly" some terrible note must have sounded.

Dunya understood it, seized the key, rushed to the door, quickly unlocked it, and burst out of the room. A moment later, beside herself, she rushed madly to the canal and ran in the direction of the ——y Bridge.

Svidrigailov stood by the window for about three minutes; at last, he quietly turned, looked around, and slowly passed his hand over his forehead. A strange smile twisted his face, a pitiful, sad, weak smile, a smile of despair. Blood, already drying, stained his palm; he looked at the blood spitefully; then he wet a towel and washed his temple. The revolver Dunya had thrown aside, which had landed near the door, suddenly caught his eye. He picked it up and examined it. It was a small pocket revolver with a three-shot cylinder, of old-fashioned construction; there were two loads and one cap left. It could be fired one more time. He thought a moment, put the revolver into his pocket, took his hat, and went out.

VI

ALL THAT EVENING until ten o'clock he spent in various taverns and cesspools, passing from one to the other. Somewhere he came across Katya, who sang another lackey song about some "scoundrel and tyrant" who

> "Began kissing Katya."

Svidrigailov bought drinks for Katya, and the organ-grinder, and the singers, and the lackeys, and two wretched little scriveners. He took up with these scriveners, in fact, because they both had crooked noses: one was crooked to the right, the other to the left. This struck Svidrigailov. They drew him finally to some pleasure garden, where he paid for them and for the entrance. In this garden were one spindly, three-year-old fir tree and three little bushes. Besides that, a "Vauxhall" had also been built, actually a bar, but one could also get tea there; and a few green tables and chairs were standing around.[21] A chorus of bad singers and some drunken German from Munich, like a clown with a red nose, but for some reason extremely downcast, were entertaining the public. The little scriveners quarreled with some other little scriveners and started a fight. They chose Svidrigailov as their arbiter. He arbitrated between them for a quarter of an hour, but they shouted so much that there was not the slightest possibility of making anything out. In all likelihood one of them had stolen something and even managed to sell it at once to some Jew who happened to be there; but, having sold it, he did not want to share the proceeds with his friend. In the end the stolen object turned out to be a teaspoon belonging to the vauxhall. It was found missing from the vauxhall, and the affair began to take on troublesome dimensions. Svidrigailov paid for the spoon, got up, and walked out of the garden. It was around ten o'clock. He himself had not drunk a drop of wine the whole time, but had only ordered some tea in the vauxhall, and even that more for propriety's sake. Meanwhile the evening was close and lowering. By ten o'clock terrible clouds had approached from all sides; thunder rolled, and rain poured down like a waterfall. It did not come in drops, but lashed the ground in steady streams. Lightning flashed every moment, and one could count to five in the course of each flash. Drenched to the skin, he arrived home, locked himself in, opened his bureau, took out all his money, and tore up two or three papers. Then, having thrust the money into his pocket, he thought of changing his clothes, but looking out the window and hearing the thunder and rain, he waved his hand, took his hat, and walked out without locking his apartment. He went straight to Sonya. She was at home.

She was not alone; with her were Kapernaumov's four little children. Sofya Semyonovna was giving them tea. She met Svidrigailov silently and respectfully, looked with surprise at his wet clothes, but did not say a word. The children all ran away at once in indescribable terror.

Svidrigailov sat at the table and asked Sonya to sit near him. She timidly prepared to listen.

"Sofya Semyonovna," Svidrigailov said, "I shall perhaps be leaving for America, and as we are probably seeing each other for the last time, I have come to make certain arrangements. So, you saw that lady today? I know what she said to you; you needn't repeat it." (Sonya stirred and blushed.) "Those people have their ways. As far as your sisters and brother are concerned, they are indeed provided for, and the money due them I have placed where it ought to be, in sure hands, with a receipt for each of them. But you had better take the receipts, just in case. Here, take them! Well, now that's done. Here are three five-percent notes, for three thousand altogether. Take them for yourself, for yourself personally, and let it be between us, so that no one knows, no matter what you may hear. And you'll need them, because, Sofya Semyonovna, to live like this, as you have been, is bad, and it's no longer necessary."

"You have been such a benefactor to me, sir, and the orphans, and the dead woman," Sonya rushed on, "that if I have so far thanked you so little, you mustn't take it . . ."

"Eh, enough, enough."

"And this money, Arkady Ivanovich, I'm very grateful to you, but I have no need of it now. I can always earn enough for myself; you mustn't take it as ingratitude: if you're so charitable, sir, this money . . ."

"It's for you, for you, Sofya Semyonovna, and, please, with no special words on the subject, because I really haven't time. And you will need it. There are two ways open for Rodion Romanovich: a bullet in the head, or Siberia." (Sonya looked wildly at him and trembled.) "Don't worry, I know everything, from him, and I'm not a babbler, I won't tell anyone. You did well to advise him that he should go and denounce himself. It would be much more advantageous for him. Now, what if it's Siberia—he'll go, and you'll follow him, is that so? Is it so? Well, and if it's so, then you'll need money. You'll need it for him, understand? In giving it to you, it's as if I were giving it to him. Besides, you did promise Amalia Ivanovna that you would pay her the debt; I heard you. Why do you so rashly take such contracts and obligations upon yourself, Sofya Semyonovna? It was Katerina Ivanovna who was left owing to the German woman, not you; so just spit on the German woman. You can't survive in the world that way. Now, if anyone ever asks you—tomorrow, say, or the day after tomorrow—about me, or anything concerning me (and they will ask you), don't mention that I came to you, and by no means show them the money or tell anyone that I gave it to you. Well, now good-bye." (He got up from his chair.) "Bow to Rodion Romanych for me. By the way, for the time being why don't you keep the money with, say, Mr. Razumikhin? Do you know Mr. Razumikhin? Of course you do. A so-so fellow. Take it to him tomorrow, or . . . when the time comes. And until then hide it well away."

Sonya had also jumped up from her chair and was looking at him in fear. She wanted very much to say something, to ask something, but in those first moments she did not dare or know how to begin.

"But how can you . . . how can you go now, sir, in such rain?"

"What? To go off to America and be afraid of rain? Heh, heh! Farewell, my good Sofya Semyonovna! Live, and live long, you'll be needed by others. Incidentally . . . tell Mr. Razumikhin that I bow to him. Tell him just that: Arkady Ivanovich Svidrigailov bows to you. Do it without fail."

He went out, leaving Sonya in amazement, in fear, and in some vague and somber apprehension.

It later turned out that on that same evening, after eleven o'clock, he paid yet another quite eccentric and unexpected visit. It had still not stopped raining. Soaking wet, at twenty minutes past eleven, he walked into the small apartment of his fiancée's parents on Vasilievsky Island, at the corner of the Third Line and Maly Prospect. He had difficulty getting them to open, and at first produced a great commotion; but Arkady Ivanovich, when he chose, could be a man of quite beguiling manners, so that the original (and, incidentally, quite shrewd) surmise of the fiancée's sensible parents—that Arkady Ivanovich was most likely so cockeyed drunk that he no longer knew what he was doing—immediately collapsed of itself. The paralyzed parent was rolled out in his chair to meet Arkady Ivanovich by the fiancée's tenderhearted and sensible mother, who, as was her custom, began at once with certain roundabout questions. (This woman never asked direct questions, but always resorted first to smiles and the rubbing of hands, and then, if she wanted to find out something certainly and accurately, such as when Arkady Ivanovich would be pleased to have the wedding take place, she would begin with the most curious and even greedy questions about Paris and court life there, and only later come around in due course to the Third Line on Vasilievsky Island.) At some other time all this would, of course, have inspired great respect, but on this occasion Arkady Ivanovich turned out to be somehow especially impatient and flatly demanded to see his fiancée, though he had been informed at the very beginning that the fiancée had already gone to bed. Naturally, the fiancée appeared. Arkady Ivanovich told her directly that because of a certain rather important circumstance he was obliged to leave Petersburg for some time, and therefore he had brought her various bank notes worth fifteen thousand roubles in silver, which he asked her to accept from him as a gift, since he had been intending for a long time to give her this trifle before the wedding. Of course, these explanations by no means revealed any logical connection between the gift and his urgent departure, or the unavoidable necessity of coming for that purpose at midnight, in the rain, but the thing nevertheless came off quite neatly. Even the requisite ohs and ahs, questions and exclamations, suddenly became somehow remarkably moderate and restrained; to make up for which, the most ardent gratitude was shown, and was even reinforced by tears from the most sensible mother. Arkady Ivanovich stood up, laughed, kissed the fiancée, patted her on the cheek, repeated that he would be coming back soon, and, noticing in her eyes not only a child's curiosity but also some mute and very serious question, he thought for a moment, kissed her a second time, and sincerely regretted in his soul that the gift would immediately be taken and locked up by the most sensible of mothers. He walked out, leaving everyone in an extremely excited state. But the tenderhearted mama at once, in a half-whispered patter, resolved some of the more important perplexities, saying that Arkady Ivanovich was a big man, a man with affairs and connections, and a very rich one—God knew what was in his head, he chose to go away and so he went, he chose to give money and so he gave it, and therefore there was nothing to marvel at. Of course, it was strange that he was all wet, but Englishmen, for example, are even more eccentric, and such high-toned people never pay attention to what is said about them, and never stand on ceremony. Maybe he went around like that on purpose to show that he was not afraid of anybody. And the main thing was not to say a word about it to anyone, because God knew what might still come of it, and the money should be locked up quickly, and most certainly the best thing in all this was that Fedosya had stayed in the kitchen the whole time, and the main thing was that they should by no means, by no means, by no means ever say anything to that cunning old fox Resslich, and so on and so forth. They sat and whispered until two o'clock. The fiancée, however, went to bed much earlier, surprised and a little sad.

And meanwhile, at midnight precisely, Svidrigailov was crossing the ——kov Bridge in the direction of the Petersburg side. The rain had stopped, but the wind was blowing. He was beginning to shiver, and for a moment he looked down at the black water of the Little Neva with some special curiosity, and even questioningly. But soon he felt it was much too cold for him to be standing there over the water; he turned away and went on to the ——y Prospect. He had been walking down the endless ——y Prospect for a long time, almost half an hour, more than once stumbling on the wooden pavement in the dark, but without ceasing to look curiously for something on the right side of the prospect. Driving by recently, he had noticed somewhere there, towards the end of the prospect, a hotel, wooden but spacious, and its name, as far as he could remember, was something like "The Adrianople." He was not mistaken in his reckoning: in such a backwater, the hotel was such a conspicuous point that one could not possibly fail to find it, even in the dark. It was a long, blackened, wooden building, in which, despite the late hour, lights were still burning and a certain animation could be noticed. He went in and asked the ragamuffin he met in the corridor for a room. The ragamuffin, looking Svidrigailov over, roused himself and at once led him to a remote room, stuffy and small, somewhere at the very end of the corridor, in a corner, under the stairs. But it was the only room; all the others were occupied. The ragamuffin had a questioning look.

"Is there tea?" Svidrigailov asked.

"It's possible, sir."

"What else is there?"

"Veal, sir, vodka, hors d'oeuvres."

"Bring some veal and tea."

"And you won't require anything else?" the ragamuffin asked, even in some perplexity.

"Nothing, nothing."

The ragamuffin withdrew, thoroughly disappointed.

"Must be a nice place," Svidrigailov thought, "why didn't I know about it? I, too, probably look like someone coming back from a *café-chantant*, and who already got into something on the way. Curious, however; who would stay and spend the night here?"

He lighted the candle and looked the room over in more detail. It was a closet, such a small one that Svidrigailov could barely fit into it, with a single window; a very dirty bed, a simple painted table, and a chair took up almost all the space. The walls looked as though they had been knocked together from boards, and the shabby wallpaper was so dusty and tattered that, while it was still possible to guess its color (yellow), the pattern was no longer discernible. A portion of the wall and ceiling was cut away at an angle, as is usual in garrets, but here there was a stairway above it. Svidrigailov put down the candle, sat on the bed, and lapsed into thought. But a strange, incessant whispering in the next closet, which sometimes rose almost to a shout, suddenly drew his attention. This whispering had not ceased from the moment he entered. He began to listen: someone was scolding and almost tearfully reproaching someone else, but only one voice could be heard. Svidrigailov stood up, shaded the candle with his hand, and at once a crack flashed in the wall; he went up and began to look through it.

There were two guests, in a room somewhat larger than his own. One of them, coatless, with extremely curly hair and a red, inflamed face, was standing in the pose of an orator, legs apart to keep his balance, and, beating his breast with his fist, in a voice full of pathos, was reproaching the other with being a beggar and even having no rank, claiming that he had dragged him from the mud and could throw him out whenever he wanted, and that only the finger of God sees it all. The reproached friend sat on a chair looking like someone who has a great desire to sneeze but cannot manage to do it. From time to time he glanced at the orator with dull and bovine eyes, but evidently had no idea what it was all about, and most likely had not even heard any of it. On the table, where a candle was burning down, stood an almost empty carafe of vodka, wineglasses, bread, tumblers, pickles, and the dishes from a long-since-finished tea. Having examined this picture attentively, Svidrigailov left the crack with indifference and again sat down on the bed.

The ragamuffin, who came back with the tea and veal, could not refrain from asking once more: "Will anything else be required?" and having again heard a negative reply, withdrew for good. Svidrigailov fell upon the tea to warm himself, and drank a whole glassful, but could not eat even a single bite for total loss of appetite. He was apparently beginning to have a fever. He took off his coat and jacket, wrapped himself in a blanket, and lay on the bed. This was annoying: "It would be better to be well at such a moment," he thought, and grinned. The room was stuffy, the candlelight was dim, the noise of the wind came from outside, a mouse was scratching somewhere in a corner, and the whole room seemed to smell of mice and something leathery. He lay as if dreaming: one thought gave way to another. It seemed he would have liked very much to catch hold of at least something particular in his imagination. "It's outside the window, must be some garden," he thought, "trees rustling; how I dislike the rustling of trees at night, in a storm, in the darkness—a nasty feeling!" And he remembered that as he was passing by the Petrovsky Park earlier he had even thought of it with loathing. Here he incidentally remembered the ——kov Bridge as well, and the Little Neva, and again he seemed to feel cold, as he had then when he was standing over the water. "Never in my life have I liked water, not even in landscapes," he thought again, and again suddenly grinned at a certain strange thought: "Well, it seems it ought to be all the same now, with regard to all this aesthetics and comfort, but it's precisely now that I've become particular, the way an animal makes sure to choose a place for itself . . . on a similar occasion. I ought precisely to have turned in at the Petrovsky Park earlier! It must have seemed dark and cold, heh, heh! One all but requires pleasant sensations! . . . By the way, why don't I put out the candle?" (He blew it out.) "The neighbors have gone to bed," he thought, seeing no light from the crack. "Well, Marfa Petrovna, why don't you come now, if you like? It's dark, and the place is suitable, and the moment is an original one. But it's precisely now that you won't come . . ."

Suddenly, for some reason, he remembered how earlier, an hour before carrying out his designs on Dunechka, he had recommended that Raskolnikov entrust her to Razumikhin's protection. "In fact, perhaps I said it more to egg myself on, as Raskolnikov guessed. What a rogue this Raskolnikov is, however! He's taken a lot on himself. Might become a big rogue in time, when the nonsense gets out of him, but now he wants *too much* to live! On that point these people are scoundrels. Well, devil take him, he can do what he likes, it's nothing to me."

He still could not fall asleep. Little by little today's image of Dunechka began to emerge before him, and a sudden trembling ran down his body. "No, that has to be dropped now," he thought, coming to himself, "I have to think of something else. How strange and funny: I've never had a great hatred for anyone, never even wished especially to revenge myself on anyone—it's a bad sign, a bad sign! I didn't like arguing either, and never got into a temper—also a bad sign! And look at all I promised her today—pah, the devil! And she might really have ground me up somehow . . ." He again fell silent and clenched his teeth: again Dunechka's image appeared before him exactly as she had been when, after firing the first time, terribly frightened, she lowered the revolver and looked at him numbly, so that he could have seized her twice over, and she would not have raised a hand to defend herself if he had not reminded her. He remembered it was just as if he had felt sorry for her at that moment, as if his heart had been wrung . . . "Eh, devil take it! These thoughts again! It all has to be dropped, dropped! . . ."

He was beginning to doze off; the feverish trembling was going away; suddenly something seemed to run over his arm and leg under the blanket. He jumped: "Pah, the devil, a mouse no less!" he thought. "It's the veal I left on the table . . ." He was terribly reluctant to uncover himself, get out of bed, freeze; but suddenly something again scurried unpleasantly over his leg; he tore the blanket off and lighted the candle. Trembling with feverish chill, he bent down to examine the bed—there was nothing; he shook the blanket and suddenly a mouse jumped out on the sheet. He rushed to catch it; but the mouse, refusing to get off the bed, flashed zigzagging in all directions, slipped from under his fingers, ran across his hand, and suddenly darted under the pillow; he threw the pillow aside, but instantly felt something jump onto his chest, scurry over his body, and down his back under his shirt. He shuddered nervously, and woke up. The room was dark, he was lying in bed wrapped up in the blanket as before, the wind was howling outside the window. "What nastiness!" he thought vexedly.

He got up and sat on the edge of the bed, his back to the window. "Better not to sleep at all," he decided. From the window, however, there came a cold, damp draft; without getting up, he pulled the blanket over him and wrapped himself in it. He did not light the candle. He was not thinking of anything, and did not want to think; but reveries rose one after another, fragments of thoughts with no beginning, no end, no connection. As if he were falling into a half slumber. Perhaps it was the cold, or the darkness, or the dampness, or the wind howling outside the window and swaying the trees, that called up in him some stubborn, fantastic inclination and desire—but he began to picture flowers. He imagined a lovely landscape; a bright, warm, almost hot day, a feast-day, the day of the Trinity.[22] A rich, luxurious country cottage in the English style, all sunk in fragrant flowerbeds, with rows surrounding the entire house; the porch, entwined with climbing plants, filled with banks of roses; a bright, cool stairway, laid with sumptuous carpet, adorned with rare flowers in Chinese jars. He noticed especially the bouquets of white and tender narcissus, in jars of water on the windowsills, bending on long, bright green, fleshy stems, with their heavy, sweet scent. He was even reluctant to leave them; but he went up the stairs and entered a large, high-ceilinged room, and here again, at the windows, by the doors opening to the terrace, on the terrace itself, everywhere there were flowers. The floors were strewn with freshly cut, fragrant grass, the windows were open, fresh, light, cool air penetrated the room, birds chirped outside the windows, and in the middle of the room, on tables covered with white satin cloths, stood a coffin. The coffin was lined with white gros de Naples silk and abundantly trimmed with white ruche. Garlands of flowers twined it on all sides. All in flowers, a girl was lying in it, in a white lace dress, her hands, as if carved from marble, folded and pressed to her breast. But her loose hair, hair of a light blond color, was wet; it was twined with a wreath of roses. The stern and already stiff profile of her face also seemed carved from marble, but the smile on her pale lips was full of some unchildlike, boundless grief and great complaint. Svidrigailov knew the girl: no icons, no lighted candles stood by the coffin, no prayers were heard. The girl was a suicide—by drowning.[23] She was only fourteen, but hers was already a broken heart, and it destroyed itself, insulted by an offense that had horrified and astonished this young child's consciousness, that had covered her angelically pure soul with undeserved shame, and torn from her a last cry of despair, not heeded but insolently defiled in the black night, in the darkness, in the cold, in the damp thaw, while the wind was howling . . .

Svidrigailov came to his senses, got up from the bed, and stepped to the window. He fumbled for the latch and opened it. Wind swept furiously into his small closet and coated as if with hoarfrost his face and chest, covered only by a shirt. There must indeed have been something like a garden outside the window, and it, too, seemed to be a pleasure garden; probably singers would be singing there in the daytime, and tea would be served at the tables. But now drops came flying in the window from the trees and bushes, and it was dark as a cellar, so that one could just barely distinguish certain darker spots, signifying objects. Bending down and leaning his elbows on the windowsill, for all of five minutes Svidrigailov stared into the darkness without tearing himself away. From the blackness and the night a cannon shot resounded, then another.

"Ah, the signal! The water's rising," he thought.[24] "Towards morning it will flood all the lower places, the streets; it will pour into the basements and cellars, the cellar rats will float up, and amid rain and wind people, cursing and drenched, will begin transferring their stuff to the upper floors . . . I wonder what time it is now?" And as soon as he thought of it, somewhere nearby, ticking and as if hurrying as fast as it could, a wall clock struck three. "Aha! It will be daybreak in an hour! What's the use of waiting? I'll leave now, go straight to the Petrovsky: somewhere there I'll choose a big bush doused all over with rain, so that if you barely touch it with your shoulder, millions of drops will shower down on your head . . ." He withdrew from the window, locked it, lighted the candle, pulled on his waistcoat and overcoat, put his hat on, and went out to the corridor with his candle to hunt up the ragamuffin, asleep somewhere in a closet amid some junk and candle-ends, pay him for the room, and leave the hotel. "The best moment; one even couldn't pick a better one!"

He spent much time walking through the long, narrow corridor without finding anyone, and was just about to call out when suddenly, in a dark corner, between an old wardrobe and a door, he made out some strange object, something as if alive. He bent down with the candle and saw a child—a girl of about five, not more, in a wretched little dress soaked through like a dishrag, who was shivering and crying. She seemed not to be afraid of Svidrigailov, but looked at him in dull astonishment with her big, black eyes, sobbing now and then, as children do who have been crying for a long time, but have now stopped and are even comforted, and yet every once in a while suddenly sob. The girl's little face was pale and exhausted; she was stiff with cold, but "how did she get here? She must have hidden herself here and not slept all night." He began questioning her. The girl suddenly came to life and began prattling something to him very, very quickly in her child's language. There was something in it about "mommy" and that "mommy was gonna beat her," about some cup she had "bwoken." The girl talked nonstop. It was possible to make out haphazardly from all she said that she was an unloved child, beaten down and terrorized by her mother, some eternally drunken cook, probably from this same hotel; that the girl had broken her mama's cup, and was so afraid that she ran away earlier in the evening; she must have hidden for a long time somewhere in the yard, in the rain, and finally crept in here, hidden behind the wardrobe, and stayed in this corner all night, crying, shivering from the damp, the darkness, and the fear that for all this she would now be beaten badly. He picked her up in his arms, went to his room, sat her on his bed, and began to undress her. The torn little shoes on her bare feet were as wet as if they had lain all night in a puddle. After undressing her, he placed her on the bed, covered her, and wrapped her up completely, head and all, in the blanket. She fell asleep at once. Having done all this, he again lapsed into sullen thought.

"The idea of getting involved!" he suddenly decided, with a heavy and spiteful feeling. "What nonsense!" Annoyed, he picked up the candle, so as to go and find the ragamuffin at all costs and quickly leave the place. "Eh, this girl!" he thought with a curse, already opening the door, but he went back once more to see if she was asleep and how she was sleeping. He carefully lifted the blanket. The little girl was soundly and blissfully asleep. She had warmed up under the blanket, and color had already spread over her pale cheeks. But, strangely, this color appeared brighter and deeper than a child's red cheeks would ordinarily be. "It's the flush of fever," Svidrigailov thought; it was just like the flush from wine, as if she had been given a whole glass to drink. Her scarlet lips were as if burning, aflame—but what is this? It suddenly seems to him as if her long black eyelashes are fluttering and blinking, as if they are opening, and a coy, sharp eye, winking somehow in an unchildlike way, is peeping out from under them, as if the girl is not asleep but pretending. Yes, so it is: her lips are expanding into a smile, the corners of her mouth are quivering, as if she were still restraining herself. But now she has lost all restraint; now it is laughter, obvious laughter; something insolent, defiant, shines in this completely unchildlike face; it is depravity, it is the face of a scarlet woman, the insolent face of a woman for sale, of the French sort. Now, without hiding it at all, both eyes open: they look him over with a fiery and shameless glance, they beckon to him, they laugh . . . There is something infinitely hideous and insulting in this laughter, in these eyes, in all this vileness in the face of a child. "What! A five-year-old!" Svidrigailov whispered in genuine horror. "This . . . what is this?" But by now she has fully turned her whole burning face to him, she reaches her arms out . . . "Ah, cursed one!" Svidrigailov cried out in horror, raising his hand over her . . . But at that moment he woke up.

He was still in bed, wrapped in the blanket as before; the candle had not been lighted; the windowpanes were pale with the full light of day.

"Nightmares all night long!" He raised himself angrily, feeling all broken; his bones ached. There was a completely dense fog outside, and nothing could be distinguished. It was nearly five o'clock; he had overslept! He got up and put on his still damp jacket and overcoat. Having felt for the revolver in his pocket, he took it out and adjusted the cap; then he sat down, took a notebook from his pocket, and wrote a few lines in large script on the front and most conspicuous page. After reading them over, he lapsed into thought, resting his elbow on the table. The revolver and the notebook lay just by his elbow. Flies woke up and swarmed all over the untouched portion of veal that lay there on the table. He watched them for a long time and finally with his free right hand began trying to catch one. He exhausted himself with the long effort, but still could not catch it. Finally, catching himself in this interesting occupation, he came to his senses, gave a start, got up, and resolutely walked out of the room. A moment later he was in the street.

Thick, milky fog lay over the city. Svidrigailov walked along the slippery, dirty, wooden pavement in the direction of the Little Neva. In imagination he could see the water of the Little Neva as it had risen high overnight, Petrovsky Island, wet paths, wet grass, wet trees and bushes, and finally that very bush . . . Annoyed, he began staring at the houses in order to think about something else. There was not a passer-by, not a coachman to be met on the prospect. The bright yellow wooden houses with their closed shutters looked cheerless and dirty. The cold and damp chilled his whole body through, and he began to shiver. From time to time he came across shop or greengrocer's signs, and he read each one carefully. Then the wooden pavement came to an end. He was in front of a big stone building. A dirty, shivering little mutt, tail between its legs, ran across his path. Someone was lying, dead drunk, in an overcoat, face down on the sidewalk. He glanced at him and went on. To the left a tall watchtower caught his eye. "Hah!" he thought, "here's the place; why go to Petrovsky? At least in front of an official witness . . ." He almost grinned at this new thought, and turned down ——sky Street. It was there that the big building with the watchtower stood. By the big locked gates of the building, leaning with his shoulder against them, stood a little man wrapped in a gray soldier's greatcoat and wearing a brass Achilles helmet.[25] With drowsy eyes, coldly, he glanced sidelong at the approaching Svidrigailov. His face bore that expression of eternal, grumbling sorrow that is so sourly imprinted upon all faces of the Jewish tribe without exception. The two of them, Svidrigailov and Achilles, studied each other silently for a while. Achilles finally thought it out of order for a man who was not drunk to be standing there in front of him, three steps away, staring at him point-blank and saying nothing.

"Zo vat do you vant here?" he said, still without moving or changing his position.

"Nothing, brother. Good morning!" Svidrigailov replied.

"It's de wrong place."

"I'm off to foreign lands, brother."

"To foreign lands?"

"To America."

"America?"

Svidrigailov took out the revolver and cocked it. Achilles raised his eyebrows.

"Zo vat's dis, a choke? It's de wrong place!"

"But why is it the wrong place?"

"Because it's de wrong place!"

"Well, never mind, brother. It's a good place. If they start asking you, just tell them he went to America."

He put the revolver to his right temple.

"Oi, dat's not allowed, it's de wrong place!" Achilles roused himself, his pupils widening more and more.

Svidrigailov pulled the trigger.

VII

T HAT SAME DAY, but in the evening, past six o'clock, Raskolnikov was approaching the apartment of his mother and sister—the apartment in Bakaleev's house where Razumikhin had placed them. The entrance to the stairway was from the street. Raskolnikov was still slowing his steps and as if hesitating whether to go in or not. But he would not have turned back for anything in the world; his decision had

been taken. "Besides, it doesn't matter, they still don't know anything," he was thinking, "and they're already used to considering me
an odd man . . ." His clothes were terrible: everything was dirty, torn,
tattered, after a whole night out in the rain. His face was almost
disfigured by weariness, bad weather, physical exhaustion, and the
nearly twenty-four-hour struggle with himself. He had spent the
whole night alone, God knows where. But at least he had made up his
mind.

He knocked at the door; his mother opened. Dunechka was not
there. Even the serving-girl happened not to be there. Pulcheria Alexandrovna was speechless at first from joyful amazement; then she
seized him by the hand and pulled him into the room.

"So here you are!" she began, faltering with joy. "Don't be angry
with me, Rodya, for greeting you so foolishly, with tears: I'm laughing,
not crying. You think I'm crying? No, I'm rejoicing, but I have this
foolish habit: tears pour out of me. I've had it ever since your father's
death; I cry at everything. Sit down, darling, you must be tired, I can
see. Ah, how dirty you've gotten."

"I was out in the rain yesterday, mama . . ." Raskolnikov tried to
begin.

"Don't, oh, don't!" Pulcheria Alexandrovna burst out, interrupting
him. "You thought I'd just up and start questioning you, from my
former woman's habit, but don't worry. I do understand, I understand
everything now, I now know how things are done here, and really, I
can see for myself that it's more intelligent here. I've judged once and
for all: is it for me to understand your considerations and demand
reports from you? God knows what affairs and plans you may have in
your head, or what ideas may be born there; so why should I nudge
your arm and ask what you're thinking about? And now I'm . . . Ah,
Lord! But why am I rushing up and down like a lunatic? . . . Now I'm
reading your article in the magazine, Rodya; Dmitri Prokofych
brought it. I just gasped when I saw it: fool that I am, I thought to
myself, this is what he's busy with, this is the solution to it all! Perhaps
he has new ideas in his head right now; he's thinking them over, and
I'm tormenting and confusing him. Well, I'm reading it, my dear, and
of course there are many things I don't understand; however, that's as
it must be: how could I?"

"Show it to me, mother!"

Raskolnikov took the little journal and glanced briefly at his article. Contradictory as it was to his situation and condition, he still felt that strange and mordantly sweet sensation an author experiences on seeing himself in print for the first time; besides, his twenty-three years showed themselves. This lasted only a moment. Having read a few lines, he frowned and a terrible anguish wrung his heart. The whole of his soul's struggle over the past months came back to him all at once. In disgust and vexation, he flung the article down on the table.

"But, foolish as I am, Rodya, I'm able to judge all the same that you will soon be one of the foremost men, if not the very foremost, in our learned world. And they dared to think you were mad. Ha, ha, ha! You don't know, but they did think that! Ah, base worms, how can they understand what intelligence is! And Dunechka nearly believed it, too—fancy that! Your late father twice sent things to magazines— poems first (I still have the notebook, I'll show it to you someday), and then a whole long story (I begged to be the one to copy it out), and how we both prayed it would be accepted—but it wasn't! It grieved me so, six or seven days ago, Rodya, to look at your clothes, the way you live, what you eat, how you dress. But now I see that I was being foolish again, because if you wanted, you could get everything for yourself at once, with your mind and talent. It means that for the time being you don't want to, and are occupied with far more important matters . . ."

"Dunya's not home, mother?"

"No, Rodya. I quite often don't see her at home; she leaves me by myself. Dmitri Prokofych, bless him, comes to sit with me, and keeps talking about you. He loves and respects you, my dear. I'm not saying that your sister is so very inconsiderate of me. I'm not complaining. She has her character, I have mine; she's got some sort of secrets now; well, I don't have any secrets from either of you. Of course, I'm firmly convinced that Dunya is far too intelligent and, besides, she loves both you and me . . . but I really don't know where it will all end. You've made me happy by coming, Rodya, but she has missed seeing you; she'll come and I'll say: your brother stopped by while you were out, and where, may I ask, have you been spending your time? Don't spoil me too much, Rodya: stop by if you can, and if you can't—there's no help for it, I'll just wait. I'll know that you love me even so, and that's enough for me. I'll read your writings, I'll hear about you from everyone, and once in a while you'll stop by to see me yourself—what could be better? For you did come now to comfort your mother, I see that . . ."

Here Pulcheria Alexandrovna suddenly started to cry.

"Me again! Don't look at your foolish mother! Ah, Lord, but why am I sitting here like this," she exclaimed, jumping up from her place. "There's coffee, and I haven't offered you any! That's what it means to be a selfish old woman. Just a moment, just a moment!"

"Forget it, mama, I'm going now. I didn't come for that. Please listen to me."

Pulcheria Alexandrovna timidly went up to him.

"Mama, whatever happens, whatever you hear about me, whatever they tell you about me, will you still love me as you do now?" he asked suddenly, from the fullness of his heart, as if not thinking about his words or weighing them.

"Rodya, Rodya, what's the matter with you? How can you ask me that! And who is going to tell me anything about you? No, I won't believe anyone at all, and whoever comes to me I'll simply chase away."

"I've come to assure you that I have always loved you, and I'm glad we're alone now, I'm even glad that Dunechka isn't here," he went on with the same impulsiveness. "I've come to tell you straight out that, although you will be unhappy, you must know all the same that your son loves you right now more than himself, and whatever you may have thought about me being cruel and not loving you, it's all untrue. I'll never cease to love you . . . Well, and enough; I thought I had to do this, to begin with this . . ."

Pulcheria Alexandrovna was silently embracing him, pressing him to her, and weeping softly.

"What's the matter with you, Rodya, I don't know," she said at last. "I thought all this time that we were simply bothering you, but now I see every sign that there is a great grief ahead of you, and that's why you are in anguish. I've foreseen it for a long time, Rodya. Forgive me for beginning to speak of it; I think about it all the time and don't sleep nights. Your sister, too, spent the whole of last night in delirium, and kept mentioning you. I heard something but understood none of it. I went around all morning as if I were facing execution, waiting for something, anticipating—and here it is! Rodya, Rodya, what is it? Are you going away somewhere, or what?"

"I'm going away."

"That's what I thought! But I can come with you, too, if you want. And Dunya; she loves you, she loves you very much, and Sofya Semyonovna, maybe she can come with us if you want; you see, I'll willingly take her like a daughter. Dmitri Prokofych will help us all get ready . . . but . . . where are you . . . going?"

"Good-bye, mama."

"What! This very day!" she cried out, as if she were losing him forever.

"I can't, I have to go, I must . . ."

"And I can't go with you?"

"No, but kneel and pray to God for me. Maybe your prayer will be heard."

"Let me cross you, let me bless you! So, so. Oh, God, what are we doing?"

Yes, he was glad, he was very glad that no one was there, that he and his mother were alone. It was as if his heart softened all at once, to make up for all that terrible time. He fell down before her, he kissed her feet, and they both wept, embracing each other. And this time she was not surprised and did not ask any questions. She had long understood that something terrible was happening with her son, and now some awful moment had come round for him.

"Rodya, my dear, my first-born," she said, sobbing, "you're the same now as when you were little and used to come to me in the same way and embrace me and kiss me in the same way; when your father was still alive and times were hard, you gave us comfort simply by being with us; and when I buried your father—how often we used to weep over his grave, embracing each other as we're doing now. And if I've been weeping for so long, it's because my mother's heart foreboded calamity. As soon as I saw you that first time, in the evening—remember, when we'd only just arrived?—I understood everything from your eyes alone, and my heart shook within me, and today, as I opened the door to you, I looked and thought, well, the fatal hour must be here. Rodya, Rodya, you're not going now?"

"No."

"You'll come again?"

"Yes . . . I'll come."

"Rodya, don't be angry, I daren't even ask any questions, I know I daren't, but all the same tell me just two words, are you going somewhere far away?"

"Very far."

"What is there, some job, a career for you, or what?"

"Whatever God sends . . . only pray for me . . ."

Raskolnikov went to the door, but she clutched at him and looked desperately in his eyes. Her face became distorted with terror.

"Enough, mama," Raskolnikov said, deeply regretting his decision to come.

"Not forever? It's not forever yet? You will come, will you come tomorrow?"

"I'll come, I'll come, good-bye."

He finally tore himself away.

The evening was fresh, warm, and bright; the weather had cleared that morning. Raskolnikov was going to his apartment; he was hurrying. He wished to be done with everything before sundown. And until then he had no wish to meet anyone. Going up to his apartment, he noticed that Nastasya tore herself away from the samovar and watched him intently, following him with her eyes. "I hope nobody's there," he thought. With loathing, he imagined Porfiry. But when he reached his room and opened the door, he saw Dunechka. She was sitting there all by herself, deep in thought, and seemed to have been waiting for him a long time. He stopped on the threshold. She rose from the sofa in alarm and stood up straight before him. The look she fixed upon him showed horror and unappeasable grief. And from that look alone he understood immediately that she knew everything.

"Well, shall I come in or go away?" he asked mistrustfully.

"I've been sitting the whole day with Sofya Semyonovna; we were both waiting for you. We thought you would surely come there."

Raskolnikov went into the room and sat down on a chair in exhaustion.

"I'm somehow weak, Dunya; very tired, really; and I wished to be in full possession of myself at least at this moment."

He quickly raised his mistrustful eyes to her.

"But where were you all night?"

"I don't remember very well; you see, sister, I wanted to make my mind up finally, and walked many times by the Neva; that I remember. I wanted to end it there, but . . . I couldn't make up my mind . . ." he whispered, again glancing mistrustfully at Dunya.

"Thank God! We were so afraid of just that, Sofya Semyonovna and I! So you still believe in life—thank God, thank God!"

Raskolnikov grinned bitterly.

"I didn't believe, but just now, with mother, I wept as we embraced each other; I don't believe, but I asked her to pray for me. God knows how these things work, Dunechka, I don't understand any of it."

"You went to see mother? And you told her?" Dunya exclaimed in horror. "Could you possibly dare to tell her?"

"No, I didn't tell her . . . in words; but she understood a great deal. She heard you raving last night. I'm sure she already understands half of it. Maybe it was a bad thing that I went. I don't even know why I did it. I'm a vile man, Dunya."

"A vile man, yet you're ready to go and suffer! You are going, aren't you?"

"I am. Right now. Yes, it was to avoid this shame that I wanted to drown myself, Dunya, but I thought, as I was already standing over the water, that if I've considered myself a strong man all along, then let me not be afraid of shame now," he said, getting ahead of himself. "Is that pride, Dunya?"

"Yes, it's pride, Rodya."

It was as if fire flashed in his extinguished eyes, as if he were pleased to think there was still pride in him.

"And you don't think, sister, that I simply got scared of the water?" he asked, with a hideous smirk, peeking into her face.

"Oh, Rodya, enough!" Dunya exclaimed bitterly.

The silence lasted for about two minutes. He sat downcast, staring

at the ground; Dunechka stood at the other end of the table and looked
at him with suffering. Suddenly he stood up.

"It's late, it's time. I'm now going to give myself up. But why I'm
going to give myself up, I don't know."

Big tears were rolling down her cheeks.

"You're crying, sister, but can you give me your hand?"

"Did you doubt it?"

She embraced him tightly.

"By going to suffer, haven't you already washed away half your
crime?" she cried out, pressing him in her arms and kissing him.

"Crime? What crime?" he suddenly cried out in some unexpected
rage. "I killed a vile, pernicious louse, a little old money-lending crone
who was of no use to anyone, to kill whom is worth forty sins forgiven,
who sucked the life-sap from the poor—is that a crime? I'm not thinking of it, nor am I thinking of washing it away. And why is everyone
jabbing at me from all sides: 'Crime! Crime!' Only now do I see clearly
all the absurdity of my faintheartedness, now that I've already decided
to go to this needless shame! I decided on it simply from my own
vileness and giftlessness, and perhaps also for my own advantage, as
was suggested by this . . . Porfiry!"

"Brother, brother, what are you saying! You shed blood!" Dunya
cried out in despair.

"Which everyone sheds," he picked up, almost in a frenzy, "which
is and always has been shed in torrents in this world, which men spill
like champagne, and for which they're crowned on the Capitoline and
afterwards called benefactors of mankind.²⁶ But just look closer and try
to see! I wished people well and would have done hundreds, thousands
of good deeds, instead of this one stupidity—or not even stupidity, but
simply clumsiness, because the whole idea was by no means as stupid
as it seems now that it failed (everything that fails seems stupid!). By
this stupidity, I merely wanted to put myself in an independent position, to take the first step, to acquire means, and later everything would
be made up for by the—comparatively—immeasurable usefulness . . .
But I, I could not endure even the first step, because I'm a scoundrel!
That's the whole point! But even so I won't look at it with your eyes:
if I'd succeeded, I'd have been crowned, but now I'm walking into the
trap!"

"But that's not it, that's not it at all! Brother, what are you saying!"

"Ah, the wrong form, not so good aesthetically! Well, I decidedly do not understand why hurling bombs at people, according to all the rules of siege warfare, is a more respectable form. Fear of aesthetics is the first sign of powerlessness! . . . Never, never have I been more clearly aware of it than now, and now more than ever I fail to understand my crime! Never, never have I been stronger or more certain than now! . . ."

Color even came to his pale, worn-out face. But as he was uttering this last exclamation, his eyes suddenly met Dunya's, and so great, so great was the anguish for him in those eyes that he came involuntarily to his senses. He felt that after all he had made these two poor women unhappy. After all, it was he who had caused . . .

"Dunya, dear! If I am guilty, forgive me (though if I'm guilty, I cannot be forgiven). Good-bye! Let's not argue! It's time, it really is. Don't follow me, I beg you, I still have to stop at . . . But go now, at once, and stay with mother. I beg you to do that. It is my last, my greatest request of you. Don't leave her for a moment; I left her in such anxiety that she'll hardly survive it: she'll either die or lose her mind. So be with her! Razumikhin will stay by you; I talked with him . . . Don't weep over me: I'll try to be both courageous and honest all my life, even though I'm a murderer. Perhaps you'll hear my name someday. I won't disgrace you, you'll see; I'll still prove . . . well, good-bye for now," he hastened to finish, again noticing some strange expression in Dunya's eyes at his last words and promises. "Why are you crying so? Don't cry, don't; we're not parting forever! . . . Ah, yes! Wait, I forgot! . . ."

He went to the table, took a thick, dusty book, opened it, and took from between the pages a small watercolor portrait on ivory. It was a portrait of his landlady's daughter, his former fiancée, who had died of a fever, the same strange girl who had wanted to go into a convent. He gazed at that expressive and sickly little face for a moment, kissed the portrait, and handed it to Dunechka.

"With her I used to talk a lot—about *that*, too—with her alone," he said, reflecting. "I confided much to her heart of what later came true so hideously. Don't worry," he turned to Dunya, "she didn't agree with it, as you don't, and I'm glad she's no longer here. The main thing, the main thing is that now everything will go a new way, it will break in two," he cried out suddenly, returning again to his anguish, "everything, everything, and am I ready for that? Do I myself want it? They say the ordeal is necessary for me! Why, why all these senseless ordeals? Why, am I going to have a better understanding then, when I'm crushed by suffering and idiocy, in senile powerlessness after twenty years of hard labor, than I have now? And why, then, should I live? And why do I agree to such a life now? Oh, I knew I was a scoundrel as I was standing over the Neva at dawn today!"

They both finally left. It was hard for Dunya, but she loved him! She began to walk away, but having gone about fifty steps, she turned once more to look at him. He was still in sight. When he reached the corner, he, too, turned around; their eyes met for a last time; but noticing that she was looking at him, he impatiently and even irritably waved his hand at her to go on, and himself sharply turned the corner.

"I'm wicked, I see that," he thought to himself, feeling ashamed a moment later of his irritated gesture to Dunya. "But why do they love me so, when I'm unworthy of it! Oh, if only I were alone and no one loved me, and I myself had never loved anyone! *None of this would be!* Curious, is it possible that in these next fifteen or twenty years my soul will become so humbled that I'll reverently snivel in front of people, calling myself a robber with every word? Yes, precisely, precisely! That's why they're going to exile me now, that's what they want . . . Look at them all scuttling up and down the street, and each one of them is a scoundrel and a robber by his very nature; worse than that—an idiot! But let exile pass me by, and they'll all go wild with noble indignation! Oh, how I hate them all!"

He fell to pondering deeply "by what process it might come about that he would finally humble himself before them all without reasoning, humble himself from conviction? But, after all, why not? Of course, that is how it should be. Won't twenty years of unremitting oppression finish him off completely? Water wears away stone. But why, why live in that case? Why am I going now, if I know myself that it will all be precisely so, as if by the book, and not otherwise!"

It was perhaps the hundredth time he had asked himself that question since the previous evening, and yet he was going.

VIII

WHEN HE CAME to Sonya's, dusk was already falling. Sonya had been waiting for him all day in terrible anxiety. She had waited together with Dunya, who, remembering Svidrigailov's words of the day before that Sonya "knew about it," had come to her that morning. We shall not relate the details of the conversation and the tears of the two women, or how close they became to each other. From this meeting Dunya drew at least one consolation, that her brother would not be alone: he had gone first to her, to Sonya, with his confession; in her he had sought a human being when he needed a human being; and she would go with him wherever fate sent him. She had not asked, but she knew it would be so. She looked at Sonya even with a certain reverence, and at first almost embarrassed her by the reverent feeling with which she treated her. Sonya was all but on the verge of tears: she considered herself, on the contrary, unworthy even to glance at Dunya. The beautiful image of Dunya as she had bowed to her with such attention and respect at the time of their first meeting at Raskolnikov's, had since remained forever in her soul as one of the most beautiful and unattainable visions of her life.

Dunechka finally could not stand it and left Sonya to go and wait for her brother in his apartment; she kept thinking he might come there first. Left alone, Sonya immediately began to be tormented by fear at the thought that he might indeed commit suicide. Dunya was afraid of the same thing. But they had competed all day long in reassuring each other by every possible argument that it could not be so, and had felt calmer while they were together. Once they parted, however, they both began thinking only of that. Sonya kept recalling how Svidrigailov had told her the day before that there were two ways open for Raskolnikov—Siberia, or . . . She knew, besides, his vanity, his presumption, his self-conceit, and his unbelief. "Can it be that he has only faintheartedness and the fear of death to make him live?" she thought at last, in despair. Meanwhile the sun was going down. She stood sadly by the window, gazing out—but from the window only the blank, unpainted wall of the neighboring house could be seen. At last, when she had become completely convinced that the unfortunate man was dead—he walked into her room.

A joyful cry burst from her breast. But, looking closely at his face, she suddenly grew pale.

"Well, so!" Raskolnikov said, grinning, "I've come for your crosses, Sonya. You're the one who was sending me to the crossroads; why turn coward now that it's come to business?"

Sonya looked at him in amazement. His tone seemed strange to her; a cold shiver ran through her body; but a moment later she realized that all of it—both the tone and the words—was put on. He even stared somehow into the corner as he talked to her, as if trying to avoid looking her straight in the face.

"You see, Sonya, I figure that it may be more advantageous this way. There's a certain circumstance . . . Well, but it's a long tale to tell, and there's no point. Only, you know what makes me mad? It irks me that all those stupid, beastly mugs will immediately surround me, gaping at me with their eyeballs hanging out, asking me their stupid questions, which I will have to answer—pointing their fingers at me . . . Pah! You know, I'm not going to go to Porfiry; I'm sick of him. Better if I go to my friend Gunpowder—now that will be a surprise, that will make an effect of sorts! And I'd better be more cool-headed; I've gotten too bilious lately. Would you believe it, I all but shook my fist at my sister just now, simply because she turned to look at me a last time. Swinishness, that's the name for it! Eh, see what I've come to! Well, so where are the crosses?"

It was as if he were not himself. He was unable to stay still even for a minute, unable to focus his attention on any one subject; his thoughts leaped over each other; his speech wandered; his hands were trembling slightly.

Sonya silently took two crosses from a drawer, one of cypress, the other of brass; she crossed herself, crossed him, and hung the cypress cross around his neck.

"So this is a symbol of my taking a cross upon myself, heh, heh! That's right, I haven't suffered enough yet! Cypress, for simple folk; the brass one, Lizaveta's, you're keeping for yourself—can I see it? So she was wearing it . . . at that moment? I also know of two similar crosses, a silver one and a little icon. I let them drop on the old crone's chest that time. It would really be more to the point if I put those on now . . . It's all nonsense, however; I'm forgetting the real business; I'm somehow distracted! . . . You see, Sonya, as a matter of fact I came to forewarn you, so that you'd know . . . Well, that's all . . . That's the only reason I came. (Hm. I thought I'd have more to say, though.) Anyway, you yourself wanted me to go; well, so I'll be locked up in jail and your wish will be fulfilled; so, why are you crying? You, too? Stop; enough! Oh, how hard this all is for me!"

Feeling came to life in him, however; his heart was wrung as he looked at her. "But this one, why this one?" he thought to himself. "What am I to her? Why is she crying, why is she getting me ready, like mother or Dunya? She'll be my nursemaid!"

"Cross yourself, pray once at least," Sonya asked in a trembling, timid voice.

"Oh, that, yes, as much as you like! And in all sincerity, Sonya, in all sincerity . . ."

He wanted, however, to say something else.

He crossed himself several times. Sonya seized her shawl and threw it over her head. It was a green flannel shawl, probably the same one Marmeladov had mentioned, the "family shawl." Raskolnikov thought fleetingly of it, but he did not ask. Indeed, he now began to feel himself that he was terribly distracted and somehow hideously alarmed. That frightened him. It also suddenly struck him that Sonya wanted to go with him.

"What's this! Where are you going? Stay, stay! I'll go alone," he cried out in fainthearted vexation, and almost angrily walked to the door. "No need for a whole retinue!" he muttered on his way out.

Sonya was left standing in the middle of the room. He had not even said good-bye to her; he had already forgotten her; a corrosive and rebellious doubt was seething in his soul.

"But is it right, is it all so right?" he thought again, going down the stairs. "Can it be that it's impossible to stop now and revise it all . . . and not go?"

But still he was going. He sensed all at once that there was finally no point in asking himself questions. Coming out to the street, he remembered that he had not said good-bye to Sonya, that she had stayed in the middle of the room in her green shawl, not daring to stir after his shout, and he stopped for an instant. At that same moment a thought suddenly dawned on him brightly—as though it had been waiting to strike him at the last.

"Then why did I go to her now? What for? I told her it was for business; and what was this business? There wasn't any business at all! To announce that I was *going?* But what of it? What was the need! Is it that I love her? I don't, do I? Didn't I just chase her away like a dog? Was it really crosses I wanted from her? Oh, how low I've fallen! No—I wanted her tears, I wanted to see her frightened, to look at her heartache and torment! I wanted to cling at least to something, to linger, to look at a human being! And I dared have such hopes for myself, such dreams, abject as I am, worthless—a scoundrel, a scoundrel!"

He was walking along the canal bank and had not much farther to go. But on reaching the bridge he stopped for a moment and suddenly turned aside, crossed it, and went to the Haymarket.

He looked greedily to right and left, peered intently at every object, but could not focus his attention on anything; everything slipped away. "In a week, say, or a month, I'll be taken somewhere in one of those prison vans over this bridge, and how will I look at the canal then? I must try to remember it," flashed through his head. "This sign, say—how will I read these same letters then? Here they've written 'Compiny,' so I must remember this *i*, this letter *i*, and look at it in a month, at this same *i;* how will I look at it then? What will I be feeling and thinking then? . . . God, how base it all must be, all these present . . . cares of mine! Of course, it must all be rather curious . . . in its own way . . . (ha, ha, ha! what a thought!). I'm becoming a child, swaggering to myself; why am I shaming myself? Pah, they shove so! This fat one—must be a German—who just shoved me: does he know whom he was shoving? Here's a woman with a child, begging for alms; curious that she should consider me more fortunate than herself. Maybe I'll give her something just for the oddity of it. Hah, a five-kopeck piece managed to survive in my pocket, I wonder how! Yes, yes . . . take it, mother!"

"God keep you!" came the weepy voice of the beggar-woman.

He walked into the Haymarket. It was unpleasant, very unpleasant, for him to encounter people, yet he was going precisely where he could see the most people. He would have given anything in the world to be left alone, yet he felt himself that he could not have remained alone for a minute. A drunk man was acting up in the crowd; he was trying to dance, but kept losing his balance. People were standing around him. Raskolnikov squeezed through the crowd, watched the drunk man for a few minutes, and suddenly guffawed shortly and abruptly. A moment later he had already forgotten about him and did not even see him, though he went on looking at him. Finally he walked away, not even remembering where he was; but when he came to the middle of the square, a certain movement suddenly occurred with him, a certain sensation seized him all at once, took hold of him entirely— body and mind.

He suddenly remembered Sonya's words: "Go to the crossroads, bow down to people, kiss the earth, because you have sinned before it as well, and say aloud to the whole world: 'I am a murderer!' " He trembled all over as he remembered it. And so crushed was he by the hopeless anguish and anxiety of this whole time, and especially of the last few hours, that he simply threw himself into the possibility of this wholesome, new, full sensation. It came to him suddenly in a sort of fit, caught fire in his soul from a single spark, and suddenly, like a flame, engulfed him. Everything softened in him all at once, and the tears flowed. He simply fell to the earth where he stood . . .

He knelt in the middle of the square, bowed to the earth, and kissed that filthy earth with delight and happiness. He stood up and then bowed once more.

"This one's plastered all right!" a fellow near him observed.

There was laughter.

"It's that he's going to Jerusalem, brothers, and he's saying good-bye to his children and his motherland and bowing to the whole world, giving a kiss to the metropolitan city of Saint Petersburg and its soil," some drunken little tradesman added.

"Still a young lad!" a third one put in.

"From gentlefolk!" someone observed in an imposing voice.

"You can't tell nowadays who's gentlefolk and who isn't."

All this talk and commentary held Raskolnikov back, and the words "I killed," which were perhaps on the tip of his tongue, froze in him. However, he calmly endured all these exclamations, and without looking back went straight down the side street in the direction of the police station. On the way an apparition flashed before him, but he was not surprised by it; he had already anticipated that it must be so. As he bowed down the second time in the Haymarket, turning to the left, he had seen Sonya standing about fifty steps away. She was hiding from him behind one of the wooden stalls in the square, which meant that she had accompanied him throughout his sorrowful procession! Raskolnikov felt and understood in that moment, once and for all, that Sonya was now with him forever and would follow him even to the ends of the earth, wherever his fate took him. His whole heart turned over inside him . . . but—here he was at the fatal place . . .

He walked quite briskly into the courtyard. He had to go up to the third floor. "So far so good," he thought. Generally, it seemed to him that the fatal moment was still far off, that there was still much time left, that he could still think many things over.

Again the same trash, the same eggshells on the winding stairs, again the wide-open doors to the apartments, again the same kitchens emitting fumes and stench. Raskolnikov had not been back here since that time. His legs were going numb and giving way under him, but went on walking. He stopped for a moment to catch his breath and straighten himself up, so as to enter *like a human being*. "But why? What for?" he suddenly thought, having caught his own movement. "If I am indeed to drink this cup, what difference does it make? The fouler the better." At that moment the picture of Ilya Petrovich Gunpowder flashed in his imagination. "Must I really go to him? Why not to someone else? Why not to Nikodim Fomich? Turn around and go to the police chief himself, to his place? At least things could be arranged in a homelike fashion . . . No, no! To Gunpowder, to Gunpowder! If I'm to drink, I'll drink it all at once . . ."

Turning cold and barely conscious of himself, he opened the door to the office. This time very few people were there, some caretaker and some other simple fellow. The guard did not even peek out from behind his partition. Raskolnikov went into the next room. "Maybe it's still possible not to tell them," flashed in him. Here some person from among the scribes, dressed in a civilian jacket, was settling down to write something at a desk. In the corner another scrivener was about to take his seat. Zamyotov was not there. Nikodim Fomich was, of course, not there either.

"No one's here?" Raskolnikov asked, addressing the person at the desk.

"Who do you want?"

"Aha-a-a! Fee, fi, fo, fum, I smell the smell of a Russian man . . . or how does the tale go . . . I forget! Gr-r-reetings!" a familiar voice cried out suddenly.

Raskolnikov shook. There stood Gunpowder; he walked out suddenly from the third room. "This is fate itself," Raskolnikov thought. "Why is he here?"

"Come to see us? What's the occasion? . . ." Ilya Petrovich exclaimed. (He was apparently in a most excellent and even somewhat excited state of mind.) "If it's on business, you've come too early. I myself just happen to be . . . However, anything I can do. I must confess . . . what's your, your . . . Excuse me . . ."

"Raskolnikov."

"There you are—Raskolnikov! You don't suppose I really forgot! No, please, you mustn't regard me as such a . . . Rodion Ro . . . Ro . . . Rodionych, isn't it?"

"Rodion Romanych."

"Yes, yes, of course! Rodion Romanych, Rodion Romanych! Just what I was getting at. I even made a number of inquiries. I—shall I confess to you?—I have been genuinely grieved that you and I were so . . . it was later explained to me, I learned that the young writer—scholar, even . . . the first steps, so to speak . . . Oh, Lord! And who among writers and scholars did not make some original steps to begin with! My wife and I, we both respect literature—my wife even to the point of passion! . . . Literature and artistry! One need only be a gentleman, and the rest can all be acquired by talent, knowledge, reason, genius! A hat—now what, for instance, is a hat? A hat is a pancake, I can buy one at Zimmerman's; but that which is kept under the hat, and is covered by the hat, that I cannot buy, sir! . . . I'll confess I even wanted to go and explain myself to you, but I thought perhaps you . . . However, I haven't even asked: do you in fact need anything? I hear your family has come?"

"Yes, my mother and sister."

"I've even had the honor and happiness of meeting your sister—an educated and charming person. I'll confess I regretted that you and I got so worked up that time. A mishap! And that I gave you a certain kind of look then, on the occasion of your fainting—that was explained afterwards in a most brilliant manner! Overzealousness and fanaticism! I understand your indignation. Perhaps you're changing apartments on the occasion of your family's arrival?"

"N-no, I just . . . I came to ask . . . I thought I'd find Zamyotov here."

"Ah, yes! You became friends; I heard, sir. Well, Zamyotov is no longer with us—you've missed him. Yes, sir, we've lost Alexander Grigorievich! He's been unavailable since yesterday; he's moved on . . . and as he was moving on he quarreled with everybody . . . even quite discourteously . . . A flighty youngster, nothing more; he might even give one hopes; but what can be done with them, these brilliant young men of ours! He wants to take some examination or other, but with us that's all just talk and swagger, and so much for the examination. It's quite another matter with you, for example, or let's say your friend, Mr. Razumikhin! Your career is a scholarly one, and you won't be put off by any setbacks! For you, all these beauties of life, one might say, *nihil est*[27]—ascetic, monk, hermit that you are! . . . For you, it's a book, a pen behind the ear, scholarly research—there's where your spirit soars! I myself am somewhat . . . have you read Livingstone's diaries,[28] may I ask?"

"No."

"But I have. Nowadays, by the way, there are a great many nihilists spreading around; well, it's quite understandable; what sort of times are these, I ask you! But I'm being too . . . by the way, you're surely not a nihilist![29] Tell me frankly, frankly!"

"N-no."

"No, you see, you can be frank with me, don't be embarrassed, just as if you were alone with yourself! Duty is one thing, and . . . what is another? . . . You thought I was going to say *pleasure*—no, sir, you've guessed wrong! Not pleasure, but the feeling of a citizen and a human being, the feeling of humaneness and love for the Almighty. I may be an official person and acting in the line of duty, but I must always feel the citizen and human being in myself, and be accountable for it . . . Now, you were so good as to bring up Zamyotov. Zamyotov! He'd go and cause a French-style scandal in some disreputable establishment, over a glass of champagne or Don wine—that's what your Zamyotov is! While I, perhaps, so to speak, am consumed with devotion and lofty feelings, and furthermore I have significance, rank, I occupy a position! I'm a married man, I have children. I fulfill the duties of a citizen and a human being, and who is he, may I ask? I advert to you as a man ennobled by education. And there are also these midwives spreading around in extraordinary numbers."

Raskolnikov raised his eyebrows questioningly. The words of Ilya Petrovich, who had obviously just gotten up from the table, came clattering and spilling out at him for the most part as empty sounds. But even so he somehow understood part of them; he looked on questioningly, not knowing where it would end.

"I'm talking about these crop-haired wenches," the garrulous Ilya Petrovich went on. "I've nicknamed them midwives, and personally I find the nickname completely satisfactory. Heh, heh! They force their way into the Academy, study anatomy; now tell me, if I get sick, am I going to call a girl to treat me? Heh, heh!"[30]

Ilya Petrovich guffawed, thoroughly pleased with his witticisms.

"Well, let's say it's an immoderate thirst for enlightenment; but once enlightened, it's enough. Why abuse it? Why insult noble persons the way that scoundrel Zamyotov does? Why did he insult me, I ask you? And then, too, there are so many suicides spreading around—you can't even imagine. They spend their last money and then kill themselves. Girls, boys, old folk . . . Only this morning there was a report about some recently arrived gentleman. Nil Pavlych, hey, Nil Pavlych! What's the name of that gentleman, the one we just had the report about, who shot himself on the Petersburg side?"

"Svidrigailov," someone responded huskily and indifferently from the other room.

Raskolnikov gave a start.

"Svidrigailov! Svidrigailov shot himself!" he cried out.

"What, you know Svidrigailov?"

"Yes . . . I do . . . he came recently . . ."

"Right, he came recently, lost his wife, a man of wanton behavior, and all of a sudden he shot himself, and so scandalously, you can't even imagine . . . left a few words in his notebook, that he was dying in his right mind and asked that no one be blamed for his death. The man had money, they say. And how do you happen to know him?"

"I . . . was acquainted . . . my sister lived with them as a governess . . ."

"Aha, aha, aha . . . But you can tell us about him, then. You didn't even suspect?"

"I saw him yesterday . . . he . . . was drinking wine . . . I knew nothing."

Raskolnikov felt as if something had fallen on him and crushed him.

"You seem to have turned pale again. This is a stuffy place . . ."

"Yes, it's time I was going, sir," Raskolnikov muttered. "Excuse me for having troubled . . ."

"Oh, heavens, as much as you like! It's my pleasure, and I'm glad to say . . ."

Ilya Petrovich even offered him his hand.

"I just wanted . . . to see Zamyotov . . ."

"I understand, I understand, and it's been my pleasure."

"I'm . . . very glad . . . good-bye, sir . . ." Raskolnikov smiled.

He walked out; he was reeling. His head was spinning. He could not feel his legs under him. He started down the stairs, propping himself against the wall with his right arm. It seemed to him that some caretaker with a book in his hands pushed him as he climbed past on his way up to the office, that some little mutt was barking its head off somewhere on a lower floor, and that some woman threw a rolling pin at it and shouted. He went on down the stairs and came out into the courtyard. There in the courtyard, not far from the entrance, stood Sonya, pale, numb all over, and she gave him a wild, wild look. He stopped before her. Something pained and tormented, something desperate, showed in her face. She clasped her hands. A hideous, lost smile forced itself to his lips. He stood a while, grinned, and turned back upstairs to the office.

Ilya Petrovich was sitting down, rummaging through some papers. Before him stood the same peasant who had just pushed Raskolnikov on his way up the stairs.

"A-a-ah? You again! Did you leave something behind? . . . But what's the matter?"

Raskolnikov, his lips pale, a fixed look in his eyes, went straight up to the desk, leaned on it with his hand, tried to say something, but could not; only incoherent sounds came out.

"You're not well! A chair! Here, sit down on the chair, sit down! Water!"

Raskolnikov sank down on the chair, but would not take his eyes from the quite unpleasantly surprised face of Ilya Petrovich. For a minute or so they went on looking at each other and waiting. Water was brought.

"It was I . . ." Raskolnikov tried to begin.

"Drink some water."

Raskolnikov pushed the water aside with his hand and said softly, with some pauses, but distinctly:

"It was I who killed the official's old widow and her sister Lizaveta with an axe and robbed them."

Ilya Petrovich opened his mouth. People came running from all sides.

Raskolnikov repeated his statement . . . .

. . . .

Epilogue

I

SIBERIA. On the bank of a wide, desolate river stands a town, one of the administrative centers of Russia; in the town there is a fortress; in the fortress, a prison.[1] In the prison, already confined for nine months, is exiled convict of the second class Rodion Raskolnikov. Almost a year and a half has passed since the day of his crime.

The court proceedings in his case went without great difficulties. The criminal firmly, precisely, and clearly supported his statement, without confusing the circumstances, without softening them in his favor, without distorting the facts, without forgetting the slightest detail. He recounted the whole process of the murder to the last trace: explained the mystery of the *pledge* (the piece of wood with the metal strip), which had been found in the murdered woman's hand; told in detail how he had taken the keys from the old woman, described the keys, described the trunk and what it was filled with, even enumerated some of the particular objects that were in it; explained the riddle of Lizaveta's murder; told how Koch had come and knocked, and the student after him, and repeated everything they had said between themselves; told how he, the criminal, had then run down the stairs and heard the shrieks of Mikolka and Mitka; how he had hidden in the empty apartment, then gone home; and in conclusion he pointed them to the stone in the courtyard on Voznesensky Prospect, near the gateway, under which the articles and purse were found. In short, it turned out to be a clear case. The investigators and judges were very surprised, incidentally, that he had hidden the purse and articles under the stone without making any use of them, and most of all that he not only did not remember in detail all the things he had actually carried off, but was even mistaken as to their number. Indeed, the circumstance that he had not once opened the purse and did not even know exactly how much money was in it appeared incredible (there turned out to be three hundred and seventeen silver roubles and three twenty-kopeck pieces in the purse; from lying so long under the stone, some of the topmost bills, the largest, had become quite damaged). For a long time they strove to discover why the accused would lie precisely about this one circumstance, when he had confessed voluntarily and truthfully to everything else. Finally, some of them (especially from among the psychologists) even admitted the possibility that he had indeed not looked into the purse and therefore did not know what was in it, and thus, without knowing, had gone and put it under the stone, but from this they concluded at once that the crime itself could not have occurred otherwise than in some sort of temporary insanity, including, so to speak, a morbid monomania of murder and robbery, with no further aim or calculation of profit. This fell in opportunely with the latest fashionable theory of temporary insanity, which in our time they so often try to apply to certain criminals. Furthermore, Raskolnikov's long-standing hypochondriac state of mind was attested to with precision by many witnesses, by Dr. Zossimov, former friends, the landlady, the maid. All this contributed greatly to the conclusion that Raskolnikov was not quite like the ordinary murderer, outlaw, and robber, but that something else was involved. To the great annoyance of those who defended this opinion, the criminal did almost nothing to defend himself; to the ultimate questions of precisely what had inclined him to homicide and what had prompted him to commit robbery, he answered quite clearly, with the crudest exactitude, that the cause of it all lay in his bad situation, his poverty and helplessness, his wish to fortify the first steps of his life's career with the help of the three thousand roubles, at least, that he counted on finding at the murdered woman's. He had resolved on the murder as a result of his frivolous and fainthearted nature, further exasperated by hardship and failure. And to the question of what precisely had prompted him to come and confess his guilt, he answered directly that it was sincere repentance. There was something almost crude about it all . . .

The sentence nevertheless turned out to be more merciful than might have been expected, given the crime committed, perhaps precisely because the criminal not only did not try to justify himself, but even seemed to show a desire to inculpate himself still more. All the strange and particular circumstances of the case were taken into consideration. The criminal's illness and distress prior to committing the crime were not subject to the least doubt. That he had not made use of what he had stolen was attributed partly to the influence of awakened repentance, partly to the not quite sound state of his mental capacities at the time the murder was committed. The circumstance of the accidental killing of Lizaveta even served as an example in support of the latter suggestion: the man commits two murders, and at the same time forgets that the door is standing open! Finally, the confession of his guilt, at the very time when the case had become extraordinarily tangled as a result of the false self-accusation of a dispirited fanatic (Nikolai), and when, moreover, there was not only no clear evidence against the real criminal, but hardly even any suspicion (Porfiry Petrovich had fully kept his word)—all this contributed in the end to mitigating the accused man's sentence.

Besides which, other circumstances quite unexpectedly came out that greatly favored the accused. The former student Razumikhin dug up information somewhere and presented proofs that the criminal Raskolnikov, while at the university, had used his last resources to help a poor and consumptive fellow student, and had practically supported him for half a year. And when the student died, he had looked after his surviving old and paralytic father (whom his dead friend had fed and supported by his own efforts almost since the age of thirteen), finally placed the old man in a hospital, and when he died as well, buried him. All this information had a certain favorable influence on the deciding of Raskolnikov's fate. His former landlady, the mother of Raskolnikov's late fiancée, the widow Zarnitsyn, also testified that while they were still living in the other house, at Five Corners, Raskolnikov, during a fire one night, had carried two small children out of an apartment already in flames and had been burned in the process. This fact was carefully investigated and quite well attested to by many witnesses. In short, the outcome was that the criminal was sentenced to penal servitude of the second class for a term of only eight years, in consideration of his having come to confess his guilt and other mitigating circumstances.

At the very beginning of the proceedings, Raskolnikov's mother became ill. Dunya and Razumikhin found it possible to take her away from Petersburg for the whole time of the trial. Razumikhin chose a town on a railway line, and only a short distance from Petersburg, so that he could follow regularly all the circumstances of the proceedings and at the same time see Avdotya Romanovna as often as possible. Pulcheria Alexandrovna's illness was of some strange, nervous sort, and was accompanied by something like madness, at least partial, if not complete. Dunya, on coming home from her last meeting with her brother, had found her mother already quite ill, in fever and delirium. That same evening she arranged with Razumikhin how precisely to answer her mother's questions about her brother, and they even invented a whole story for her mother about Raskolnikov going somewhere far away, to the Russian border, on some private mission that would finally bring him both money and fame. But they were struck that Pulcheria Alexandrovna never asked them anything about any of it, either then or later. On the contrary, she turned out to have a whole story of her own about her son's sudden departure; she would tell with tears of how he had come to say good-bye to her; she would let it be known by hints that she alone was informed of many quite important and mysterious circumstances, and that Rodya had many quite powerful enemies, so that he had even been forced to go into hiding. As for his future career, to her it also seemed unquestionable and brilliant, once certain hostile circumstances passed; she assured Razumikhin that in time her son would even be a statesman, as was proved by his article and by his brilliant literary talent. She read this article incessantly, sometimes even aloud; she all but slept with it; yet she hardly ever asked precisely where Rodya was at present, in spite of the fact that people obviously avoided talking to her about it—which in itself might have aroused her suspicions. Finally, they began to be frightened by Pulcheria Alexandrovna's strange silence on certain issues. She did not even complain, for instance, that there were no letters from him, whereas before, when she was living in her little town, she had lived only in the hope and expectation of soon receiving a letter from her beloved Rodya. This last circumstance was all too inexplicable, and greatly troubled Dunya; the thought kept occurring to her that her mother had perhaps sensed something terrible in her son's fate and was afraid to ask questions lest she find out something still more terrible. In any event, Dunya saw clearly that Pulcheria Alexandrovna was not in her right mind.

A couple of times, however, it happened that she herself led the conversation in such a way that it was impossible in answering her not to mention precisely where Rodya was then; and when, willy-nilly, the answers came out unsatisfactory and suspicious, she would all at once turn extremely sad, gloomy, and silent, and would remain so for quite a long time. Dunya saw at last that it was hard to go on lying and inventing, and came to a final conclusion that it was better to be completely silent on certain issues; but it was becoming more and more clear, to the point of obviousness, that the poor mother suspected something terrible. Dunya incidentally remembered her brother saying that their mother had listened to her raving on the eve of that last, fatal day, after her scene with Svidrigailov: had she managed to hear something then? Often, sometimes after several days or even weeks of gloomy, sullen silence and wordless tears, the sick woman would become somehow hysterically animated and begin suddenly to talk aloud, almost without stop, about her son, about her hopes, about the future . . . Her fantasies were sometimes very strange. They humored her, yessed her (she herself perhaps saw clearly that they yessed her only to humor her), but she still went on talking . . .

The sentence came five months after the criminal went and confessed. Razumikhin saw him in prison whenever he possibly could. So did Sonya. Finally it came time to part. Dunya swore to her brother that the parting was not forever; so did Razumikhin. A project had firmly shaped itself in Razumikhin's young and ardent head, to lay, as far as possible, over the next three or four years, at least the foundations of a future fortune, to save at least some money, and move to Siberia, where the soil was rich in all respects, and workers, people, and capital were scarce; to settle there in the same town where Rodya was, and . . . begin a new life together. On saying farewell, they all wept. Raskolnikov had been very pensive during those last days, inquired often about his mother, was constantly worried about her. He even suffered too much over her, which alarmed Dunya. Having learned in detail of his mother's ailing spirits, he became very gloomy. With Sonya he was for some reason especially taciturn the whole time. Sonya had long since made her preparations, with the help of the money left her by Svidrigailov, and was ready to follow the party of convicts with which he would be sent. No word had been spoken of it between her and Raskolnikov, but they both knew it would be so. During the last farewell, he kept smiling strangely at the fervent assurances of his sister and Razumikhin about their happy future when he would be done with hard labor, and foretold that his mother's ailing condition would soon end in grief. He and Sonya finally set off.

Two months later Dunechka married Razumikhin. The wedding was sad and quiet. Among those invited, by the way, were Porfiry Petrovich and Zossimov. All the time recently, Razumikhin had had the look of a man who has firmly made up his mind. Dunya believed blindly that he would carry out all his intentions, and could not but believe it: an iron will could be seen in the man. Incidentally, he began attending university lectures again, to complete his studies. They were both constantly making plans for the future; both firmly counted on moving to Siberia without fail in five years' time. Until then they relied on Sonya being there . . .

Pulcheria Alexandrovna gladly blessed her daughter's marriage to Razumikhin; but after the marriage she seemed to become still more sad and preoccupied. To give her a moment's pleasure, Razumikhin incidentally told her the fact about the student and his decrepit father, and how Rodya had been burned and was even laid up after saving two little children from death the year before. This news sent Pulcheria Alexandrovna, whose mind was unsettled to begin with, almost into a state of ecstasy. She talked of it incessantly, even got into conversations in the street (though Dunya always accompanied her). In public carriages, in shops, having caught hold of at least some listener, she would bring the conversation around to her son, his article, how he had helped the student, had been burned in the fire, and so on. Dunechka simply did not know how to restrain her. Besides the danger of such an ecstatic, morbid state of mind, there could also have been trouble if someone had remembered Raskolnikov's name in connection with the recent trial and happened to mention it. Pulcheria Alexandrovna even found out the address of the mother of the two children saved from the fire and was absolutely set on going to see her. In the end her anxiety grew beyond limits. She sometimes suddenly started to cry, often fell ill and raved feverishly. One morning she announced outright that by her calculations Rodya was soon to arrive, that she remembered how he himself had mentioned, as he was saying good-bye to her, that they should expect him in exactly nine months. She began tidying up everything in the apartment and preparing to meet him, began decorating the room where he was to live (her own), cleaned the furniture, washed and hung up new curtains, and so on. Dunya was worried but said nothing, and even helped her arrange the room for her brother's reception. After a troubled day spent in ceaseless fantasies, in joyful dreams and tears, she fell ill during the night, and by morning was in a fever and raving. She became delirious. Two weeks later she died. In her raving certain words escaped her from which it could be concluded that she had a far greater suspicion of her son's terrible fate than had even been supposed.

Raskolnikov did not learn of his mother's death for a long time, though a correspondence with Petersburg had been established from the very beginning of his installation in Siberia. It was arranged through Sonya, who wrote regularly every month to the name of Razumikhin in Petersburg, and from Petersburg regularly received an answer every month. To Dunya and Razumikhin, Sonya's letters at first seemed somehow dry and unsatisfactory; but in the end they both found that they even could not have been written better, because as a result these letters gave a most complete and precise idea of their unfortunate brother's lot. Sonya's letters were filled with the most ordinary actuality, the most simple and clear description of all the circumstances of Raskolnikov's life at hard labor. They contained no account of her own hopes, no guessing about the future, no descriptions of her own feelings. In place of attempts to explain the state of his soul, or the whole of his inner life generally, there stood only facts—that is, his own words, detailed reports of the condition of his health, of what he had wanted at their meeting on such-and-such a day, what he had asked her, what he had told her to do, and so on. All this news was given in great detail. In the end the image of their unfortunate brother stood forth of itself, clearly and precisely drawn; no mistake was possible here, because these were all true facts.

But Dunya and her husband could derive little joy from this news, especially at the beginning. Sonya ceaselessly reported that he was constantly sullen, taciturn, and even almost uninterested in the news she brought him each time from the letters she received; that he sometimes asked about his mother; and that when, seeing he had begun to guess the truth, she finally told him of her death, to her surprise even the news of his mother's death seemed not to affect him too greatly, or so at least it appeared to her from the outside. She told them, among other things, that although he seemed so immersed in himself, as if he had closed himself off from everyone, his attitude towards his new life was very direct and simple; that he understood his position clearly, expected nothing better in the near future, had no frivolous hopes (so natural in his position), and was surprised at almost nothing amid his new surroundings, so little resembling anything previous. She reported that his health was satisfactory. He went to work, neither volunteering nor trying to avoid it. Was almost indifferent to food, but the food was so bad, except on Sundays and feast days, that in the end he had eagerly accepted a little money from her, Sonya, so that he could have tea every day; as for all the rest, he asked her not to worry, insisting that all this concern for him only annoyed him. Sonya wrote further that he had been placed together with all the others in prison; that she had not seen the inside of the barracks, but assumed it was crowded, ugly, and unhealthy; that he slept on a plank bed with a piece of felt under him and did not want to make any other arrangements for himself. But that he lived so poorly and crudely not at all from some preconceived plan or purpose, but simply from inattention and outward indifference to his lot. Sonya wrote directly that, especially at the beginning, he not only was not interested in her visits, but was even almost vexed with her, spoke reluctantly, and was even rude to her, but that in the end their meetings became a habit for him and even almost a necessity, so that he even grieved very much when she was sick for a few days and unable to visit him. And that she saw him on feast days by the prison gates or in the guardroom, where he would be summoned to see her for a few minutes; and on weekdays at work, where she came to see him either in the workshops, at the brick factory, or in the sheds on the banks of the Irtysh. About herself Sonya reported that she had managed to acquire some acquaintances and patrons in town; that she did sewing, and since there were almost no dressmakers in town, she had even become indispensable in many homes; only she did not mention that through her Raskolnikov had also come under the patronage of the authorities, that his work had been lightened, and so on. Finally came the news (Dunya had even noticed some special anxiety and alarm in her latest letters) that he shunned everyone, that the convicts in the prison did not like him; that he kept silent for whole days at a time and was becoming very pale. Suddenly, in her latest letter, Sonya wrote that he was quite seriously ill, and was in the hospital, in the convict ward . . .

II

HE HAD BEEN SICK for some time; but it was not the horrors of convict life, or the work, or the food, or the shaved head, or the patchwork clothes that broke him: oh, what did he care about all these pains and torments! On the contrary, he was even glad of the work: by wearing himself out physically at work, he at least earned himself several hours of peaceful sleep. And what did the food—that watery cabbage soup with cockroaches—matter to him? In his former life as a student, he often had not had even that. His clothes were warm and adapted to his way of life. He did not even feel the chains on him. Was he to be ashamed of his shaved head and two-colored jacket? But before whom? Sonya? Sonya was afraid of him, and should he be ashamed before her?

But what, then? He was indeed ashamed even before Sonya, whom he tormented because of it with his contemptuous and rude treatment. But he was ashamed not of a shaved head and chains: his pride was badly wounded; and it was from wounded pride that he fell ill. Oh, how happy he would have been if he could have condemned himself! He could have endured everything then, even shame and disgrace. But he judged himself severely, and his hardened conscience did not find any especially terrible guilt in his past, except perhaps a simple *blunder* that could have happened to anyone. He was ashamed precisely because he, Raskolnikov, had perished so blindly, hopelessly, vainly, and stupidly, by some sort of decree of blind fate, and had to reconcile himself and submit to the "meaninglessness" of such a decree if he wanted to find at least some peace for himself.

Pointless and purposeless anxiety in the present, and in the future one endless sacrifice by which nothing would be gained—that was what he had to look forward to in this world. And what matter that in eight years he would be only thirty-two and could still begin to live again! Why should he live? With what in mind? Striving for what? To live in order to exist? But even before, he had been ready to give his existence a thousand times over for an idea, a hope, even a fantasy. Existence alone had never been enough for him; he had always wanted more. Perhaps it was only from the force of his desires that he had regarded himself as a man to whom more was permitted than to others.

If only fate had sent him repentance—burning repentance, that breaks the heart, that drives sleep away, such repentance as torments one into dreaming of the noose or the watery deeps! Oh, he would have been glad of it! Torments and tears—that, too, was life. But he did not repent of his crime.

He might at least have raged at his own stupidity, as he had once raged at the hideous and utterly stupid actions that had brought him to prison. But now that he was in prison, and *at liberty,* he reconsidered and reflected upon all his former actions and did not find them at all as stupid and hideous as they had seemed to him once, at that fatal time.

"How," he pondered, "how was my thought any stupider than all the other thoughts and theories that have been swarming and colliding in the world, ever since the world began? It's enough simply to take a broad, completely independent view of the matter, free of all common influences, and then my thought will surely not seem so . . . strange. Oh, nay-sayers and penny philosophers, why do you stop halfway!

"Now, what do they find so hideous in my action?" he kept saying to himself. "That it was an evildoing? What does the word 'evildoing' mean? My conscience is clear. Of course, a criminal act was committed; of course, the letter of the law was broken and blood was shed; well, then, have my head for the letter of the law . . . and enough! Of course, in that case even many benefactors of mankind, who did not inherit power but seized it for themselves, ought to have been executed at their very first steps. But those men endured their steps, and therefore *they were right,* while I did not endure, and so I had no right to permit myself that step."

This alone he recognized as his crime: that he had not endured it, but had gone and confessed.

And he suffered from another thought: why had he not killed himself then? Why, when he was standing over the river then, had he preferred to go and confess? Was there really such force in this desire to live, and was it so difficult to overcome it? Had not Svidrigailov, who was afraid of death, overcome it?

In torment he asked himself this question, and could not understand that even then, when he was standing over the river, he may have sensed a profound lie in himself and in his convictions. He did not understand that this sense might herald a future break in his life, his future resurrection, his future new vision of life.

Instead he allowed only for the dull burden of instinct here, which it was not for him to break through, and which (again owing to weakness and worthlessness) he had been unable to step over. He looked at his fellow convicts and was amazed: how they, too, all loved life, how they valued it! It precisely seemed to him that in prison they loved and valued it even more, cherished it even more than in freedom. What terrible pains and torments had some of them not endured—the tramps, for instance! Could some one ray of sunlight mean so much to them, a deep forest, a cool spring somewhere in the untrodden wilderness, noticed two years before, to meet which the tramp dreams as he dreams of meeting his mistress, sees it in his sleep, green grass growing around it, a bird singing in a bush? Looking further, he found examples still more inexplicable.

In prison, in his surroundings, he did not notice much, of course, and really did not want to notice. He lived somehow with lowered eyes: it was repulsive and unbearable to look. But in the end many things began to surprise him, and he somehow involuntarily began to notice what he had not even suspected before. But, generally, he came to be surprised most of all by the terrible and impassable abyss that lay between him and all these people. It was as if he and they belonged to different nations. He and they looked at each other with mistrust and hostility. He knew and understood the general reasons for such disunion; but he had never before assumed that these reasons were in fact so deep and strong. There were also exiled Poles there, political prisoners. They simply regarded all these people as ignorant slaves and haughtily disdained them; but Raskolnikov could not take such a view: he saw clearly that these ignorant men were in many respects much smarter than the Poles themselves. There were also Russians who all too readily despised these people—a former officer and two seminarians; Raskolnikov clearly saw their mistake as well.

As for him, he was disliked and avoided by everyone. In the end they even began to hate him—why, he did not know. Men far more criminal than he despised him, laughed at him, laughed at his crime.

"You're a gentleman!" they said to him. "What did you take up an axe for; it's no business for a gentleman."

During the second week of the Great Lent, it was his turn to fast and go to services together with his barracks.[2] He went to church and prayed together with the others. For some reason unknown to him, a quarrel broke out one day; they all fell on him at once with ferocity.

"You're godless! You don't believe in God!" they shouted. "You ought to be killed!"

He had never talked with them about God or belief, but they wanted to kill him for being godless; he kept silent and did not argue with them. One convict flew at him in a perfect frenzy; Raskolnikov waited for him calmly and silently: his eyebrows did not move, not a feature of his face trembled. A guard managed to step between him and the murderer just in time—otherwise blood would have been shed.

Still another question remained insoluble for him: why had they all come to love Sonya so much? She had not tried to win them over; they met her only rarely, at work now and then, when she would come for a moment to see him. And yet they all knew her, knew also that she had followed *after him,* knew how she lived and where she lived. She had never given them money or done them any special favors. Only once, at Christmas, she brought alms for the whole prison: pies and kalatchi.[3] But, little by little, certain closer relations sprang up between them and Sonya. She wrote letters for them to their families, and posted them. When their male or female relations came to town, they would instruct them to leave things and even money for them in Sonya's hands. Their wives and mistresses knew her and visited her. And when she came to see Raskolnikov at work, or met a party of convicts on the way to work, they would all take their hats off, they would all bow to her: "Little mother, Sofya Semyonovna, our tender, fond little mother!"—so the coarse, branded convicts would say to this small and frail being. She would smile and bow in return, and they all liked it when she smiled to them. They even liked the way she walked; they would turn and follow her with their eyes to see how she walked, and praise her; they even praised her for being so small; they were even at a loss what not to praise her for. They even came to her with their ailments.

He lay in the hospital all through the end of Lent and Holy Week. As he began to recover, he remembered his dreams from when he was still lying in feverish delirium. In his illness he had dreamed that the whole world was doomed to fall victim to some terrible, as yet unknown and unseen pestilence spreading to Europe from the depths of Asia. Everyone was to perish, except for certain, very few, chosen ones. Some new trichinae had appeared, microscopic creatures that lodged themselves in men's bodies. But these creatures were spirits, endowed with reason and will. Those who received them into themselves immediately became possessed and mad. But never, never had people considered themselves so intelligent and unshakeable in the truth as did these infected ones. Never had they thought their judgments, their scientific conclusions, their moral convictions and beliefs more unshakeable. Entire settlements, entire cities and nations would be infected and go mad. Everyone became anxious, and no one understood anyone else; each thought the truth was contained in himself alone, and suffered looking at others, beat his breast, wept, and wrung his hands. They did not know whom or how to judge, could not agree on what to regard as evil, what as good. They did not know whom to accuse, whom to vindicate. People killed each other in some sort of meaningless spite. They gathered into whole armies against each other, but, already on the march, the armies would suddenly begin destroying themselves, the ranks would break up, the soldiers would fall upon one another, stabbing and cutting, biting and eating one another. In the cities the bells rang all day long: everyone was being summoned, but no one knew who was summoning them or why, and everyone felt anxious. The most ordinary trades ceased, because everyone offered his own ideas, his own corrections, and no one could agree. Agriculture ceased. Here and there people would band together, agree among themselves to do something, swear never to part—but immediately begin something completely different from what they themselves had just suggested, begin accusing one another, fighting, stabbing. Fires broke out; famine broke out. Everyone and everything was perishing. The pestilence grew and spread further and further. Only a few people in the whole world could be saved; they were pure and chosen, destined to begin a new generation of people and a new life, to renew and purify the earth; but no one had seen these people anywhere, no one had heard their words or voices.

It pained Raskolnikov that this senseless delirium echoed so sadly and tormentingly in his memory, that the impression of these feverish dreams refused to go away for so long. It was already the second week after Holy Week; warm, clear spring days had set in; the windows in the convict ward were opened (barred windows, with a sentry pacing beneath them). Sonya had been able to visit him in the ward only twice during the whole period of his illness; each time she had to ask for permission, and that was difficult. But she had often come to the hospital courtyard, under the windows, especially towards evening, or sometimes just to stand in the yard for a short while and look at least from afar at the windows of the ward. Once, towards evening, Raskolnikov, then almost fully recovered, fell asleep; waking again, he chanced to go to the window and suddenly saw Sonya far away, by the hospital gate. She stood as if she were waiting for something. At that moment, something seemed to pierce his heart; he started and quickly stepped away from the window. The next day Sonya did not come, nor the day after; he noticed that he was waiting worriedly for her. At last he was discharged. When he came to the prison, he learned from the convicts that Sofya Semyonovna was sick in bed at home and not going out anywhere.

He was very worried and sent to inquire after her. Soon he learned that her illness was not dangerous. Having learned in her turn that he missed her and was so concerned about her, Sonya sent him a penciled note informing him that she was feeling much better, that she had a slight, insignificant cold, and that soon, very soon, she would come to see him at work. His heart was beating heavily and painfully as he read this note.

Again it was a clear, warm day. Early in the morning, at about six o'clock, he went to work in a shed on the riverbank, where gypsum was baked in a kiln and afterwards ground. Only three workers went there. One of them took a guard and went back to the fortress to get some tool; the second began splitting firewood and putting it into the kiln. Raskolnikov walked out of the shed and right to the bank, sat down on some logs piled near the shed, and began looking at the wide, desolate river. From the high bank a wide view of the surrounding countryside opened out. A barely audible song came from the far bank opposite. There, on the boundless, sun-bathed steppe, nomadic yurts could be seen, like barely visible black specks. There was freedom, there a different people lived, quite unlike those here, there time itself seemed to stop, as if the centuries of Abraham and his flocks had not passed. Raskolnikov sat and stared fixedly, not tearing his eyes away; his thought turned to reverie, to contemplation; he was not thinking of anything, but some anguish troubled and tormented him.

Suddenly Sonya was beside him. She came up almost inaudibly and sat down next to him. It was still very early; the morning chill had not softened yet. She was wearing her poor old wrap and the green shawl. Her face still bore signs of illness; it had become thinner, paler, more pinched. She smiled to him amiably and joyfully, but gave him her hand as timidly as ever.

She always gave him her hand timidly; sometimes she even did not give it at all, as if fearing he might push it away. He always took her hand as if with loathing, always met her as if with vexation, was sometimes obstinately silent during the whole time of her visit. There were occasions when she trembled before him and went away in deep grief. But this time their hands did not separate; he glanced at her quickly and fleetingly, said nothing, and lowered his eyes to the ground. They were alone; no one saw them. The guard had his back turned at the moment.

How it happened he himself did not know, but suddenly it was as if something lifted him and flung him down at her feet. He wept and embraced her knees. For the first moment she was terribly frightened, and her whole face went numb. She jumped up and looked at him, trembling. But all at once, in that same moment, she understood everything. Infinite happiness lit up in her eyes; she understood, and for her there was no longer any doubt that he loved her, loved her infinitely, and that at last the moment had come . . .

They wanted to speak but could not. Tears stood in their eyes. They were both pale and thin, but in those pale, sick faces there already shone the dawn of a renewed future, of a complete resurrection into a new life. They were resurrected by love; the heart of each held infinite sources of life for the heart of the other.

They resolved to wait and endure. They still had seven years more, and until then so much unbearable suffering and so much infinite happiness! But he was risen and he knew it, he felt it fully with the whole of his renewed being, and she—she lived just by his life alone!

In the evening of the same day, when the barracks were locked, Raskolnikov lay on his plank bed and thought of her. It had even seemed to him that day as if all the convicts, his former enemies, already looked at him differently. He had even addressed them himself and been answered amiably. He recalled it all now, but that was how it had to be: did not everything have to change now?

He was thinking of her. He remembered how he had constantly tormented her and torn her heart; remembered her poor, thin little face; but he was almost not even tormented by these memories: he knew by what infinite love he would now redeem all her sufferings.

And what were they, all, *all* those torments of the past! Everything, even his crime, even his sentence and exile, seemed to him now, in the first impulse, to be some strange, external fact, as if it had not even happened to him. However, that evening he could not think long or continuously of anything, could not concentrate his mind on any-thing; besides, he would have been unable to resolve anything con-sciously just then; he could only feel. Instead of dialectics, there was life, and something completely different had to work itself out in his consciousness.

Under his pillow lay the Gospels. He took the book out mechani-cally. It belonged to her, it was the same one from which she had read to him about the raising of Lazarus. At the beginning of his hard labor he had thought she would hound him with religion, would be forever talking about the Gospels and forcing books on him. But to his greatest amazement, she never once spoke of it, never once even offered him the Gospels. He had asked her for it himself not long before his illness, and she had silently brought him the book. He had not even opened it yet.

Nor did he open it now, but a thought flashed in him: "Can her convictions not be my convictions now? Her feelings, her aspirations, at least . . ."

She, too, had been greatly excited all that day, and during the night even fell ill again. But she was so happy that she almost became frightened of her happiness. Seven years, *only* seven years! At the beginning of their happiness there were moments when they were both ready to look at those seven years as if they were seven days. He did not even know that a new life would not be given him for nothing, that it still had to be dearly bought, to be paid for with a great future deed . . .

But here begins a new account, the account of a man's gradual renewal, the account of his gradual regeneration, his gradual transition from one world to another, his acquaintance with a new, hitherto completely unknown reality. It might make the subject of a new story—but our present story is ended.

Notes

Biblical references in the text and notes are given in the King James Version. *Crime and Punishment* is abbreviated here as *C&P*. Our notes are indebted to the extensive commentaries provided in the Soviet Academy of Sciences edition published in 1973.

PART ONE

1. Zimmerman was a famous hatter with a shop on Nevsky Prospect in Petersburg. Dostoevsky owned a Zimmerman hat.

2. There were nine grades of councillors in the Russian civil service; titular councillor was the ninth, or lowest.

3. It was customary for Russians to identify themselves formally by giving their social "rank" as well as their name. "Student"—and thus "former student"—was such a rank. The reader will find mention of ranks throughout *C&P*. The lowest was "simple person" or peasant; "tradesman" was a bit higher; and so on.

4. The hay barges on the Neva were well known in Petersburg during the 1860s as a place where beggars and bums spent the night.

5. The "yellow pass" was an official certificate issued to prostitutes.

6. See Matthew 10:26: "there is nothing covered, that shall not be revealed; and hid, that shall not be known."

7. Pontius Pilate's words about Christ; see John 19:5.

8. Dancing with a shawl was an honor granted to the most successful students of girls' boarding schools at graduation.

9. It was possible to "live in a corner," that is, to rent only part of a room, though Marmeladov turns out to be renting a whole room from Mrs. Lippewechsel.

10. Cyrus the Great (600?–529 B.C.), king of Persia from 550–529, founder of the Persian empire.

11. A Russian translation of *The Physiology of Everyday Life*, by the English philosopher and critic George Henry Lewes (1817–78), was published in Moscow in 1861. Dostoevsky owned a copy of the second edition. The book, influenced by the thought of the French positivist Auguste Comte (1798–1857), suited the practical-minded tastes of the time and was especially popular among progressive young women.

12. State councillor was the fifth grade of councillors in the civil service; a fairly high position.

13. See Psalm 68:2: "as wax melteth before the fire, so let the wicked perish at the presence of God."

14. "The Little Farm" was a popular Russian song of the mid-nineteenth century, with words by A. V. Koltsov (1809–42), a poet of humble origin.

15. See Luke 7:47.

16. See Revelation 13:15–16.

17. The second petition of the Lord's Prayer; see Matthew 6:10, Luke 11:2.

18. Petersburg, owing to its northern latitude (60°N), has "white nights" during the summer. In July the sun sets at around 8:30 P.M., with twilight lasting almost until midnight; sunrise is at approximately 4:00 A.M., preceded by a long, pale dawn.

19. Like civil servants, students in Russia wore uniforms, including a visored cap and a greatcoat.

20. The first half of a saying; the second half (obviously) is: "because you may have to drink from it."

21. It was a custom of local people in small towns or villages to smear with tar the gates of someone against whom they wanted to express their moral indignation.

22. Court councillor was the seventh grade of councillors in the civil service.

23. The Russian Senate in Petersburg functioned as the highest court of law as well as a managerial and administrative body; it remained answerable to the tsar.

24. The feast of the Dormition of the Mother of God (the Assumption, in Roman Catholicism), celebrated on August 15. According to the canons of the Orthodox Church, weddings may not be celebrated during periods of fasting. The fast preceding the feast of the Dormition is from August 1 to August 14.

25. The Kazan Mother of God (generally showing just the head and shoulders of the Virgin, with a frontal half-figure of the infant Christ giving a blessing) is perhaps the most widespread icon of the Mother of God in Russia. Its prototype was discovered in Kazan in 1579.

26. Golgotha ("the place of a skull" in Aramaic; latinized as "Calvary") is the name of the place just outside Jerusalem where Christ was crucified. See Matthew 27:33, Mark 15:22, John 19:17.

27. A broad reference to the works and ideas of the German poet and playwright Friedrich Schiller (1759–1805), who stood, in Dostoevsky's keyboard of references, for notions of the ideal, the "great and beautiful," and a simplified struggle for freedom, all with a Romantic glow. Having loved Schiller's poetry as a young man, Dostoevsky indulged in a good deal of indirect mockery of him in his later works. Further references to Schiller in *C&P* are all in the same tone.

28. The Order of St. Anne (the mother of the Virgin; "Anna" in Russian) was a military and civil distinction, awarded by the tsar. It had two degrees, the higher being worn on the breast, the lower around the neck.

29. Schleswig-Holstein, in the north of Germany, bordering on Jutland, was fought over by Denmark and Prussia in the mid-1860s, before being annexed by Prussia in 1866. The struggle was much discussed in the Russian press of the time, by Dostoevsky among others.

30. The situation of Latvians under Russian rule was so bad that even poor Germans of the region considered them as slaves—another issue taken up by the Russian press in the 1860s.

31. The Jesuits (members of the Society of Jesus, a religious order founded by St. Ignatius Loyola in 1534) were popularly considered masters of casuistry.

32. Though Raskolnikov has just heard about Svidrigailov in his mother's letter, for Dostoevsky and his contemporaries the name was not unknown. In several issues of the newspaper *Iskra*, in 1861, the doings of a wealthy provincial landowner and his minion Svidrigailov had been discussed. The name came to suggest a type of shady dealer and intriguer, and might have been used as Raskolnikov uses it here.

33. Following the publication, in 1865, of a Russian translation of *Man and the Development of His Abilities: An Experiment in Social Physics,* by the Belgian mathematician and statistician Adolphe Quételet (1796–1874), there was discussion in the press about the percentages of victims destined by nature to crime and prostitution. Quételet's followers tried to establish the statistical regularity of human actions in society. Quételet and his German disciple Adolf Wagner (1835–1917) were hailed as pillars of the science of moral statistics.

34. A series of islands (Petrovsky, Krestovsky, Yelagin) in the delta of the Neva west of Petersburg where wealthier people had summer houses.

35. Alexander Pushkin (1799–1837), the greatest of Russian poets; Ivan Turgenev (1818–83), novelist, Dostoevsky's contemporary and acquaintance. Dostoevsky had the highest admiration for Pushkin, whose short story "The Queen of Spades" may be considered one of the "sources" of *C&P*. His relations with Turgenev were often strained, and artistically the two were opposites.

36. The dream that follows contains autobiographical elements; in his notes for the novel, Dostoevsky mentions a broken-winded horse he had seen as a child.

37. Kutya (koot*yah*) is a special dish offered to people at the end of a memorial service and, in some places, on Christmas Eve, made from rice (or barley, or wheat) and raisins, sweetened with honey.

38. A kichka (*kee*chka) is a headdress with two peaks or "horns" on the sides, worn only by married women.

39. In his poem "Before Evening" from the cycle *About the Weather* (1859), Nikolai Nekrasov (1821–77) describes a scene of a horse being beaten "on its meek eyes." Dostoevsky seems to have been deeply moved by the poem; it is referred to at some length in *The Brothers Karamazov.*

40. Collegiate registrar was the fourteenth, or lowest, grade in the Russian civil service.

PART TWO

1. "Thank you" (German). Louisa Ivanovna's speech further on, like Mrs. Lippewechsel's later in the novel, is full of German words and Germanisms; these will not be glossed in our notes.

2. The Russian word *tsugunder*, used in the phrase "to send [someone] to *tsugunder*," is a borrowing from German of much-disputed etymology. The phrase means generally "to arrest" or "to deal with." Ilya Petrovich obviously uses it for its Germanic ring, and we have altered the spelling accordingly.

3. A *molieben* (molyehben) is an Orthodox prayer service for a special occasion, commemoration, or thanksgiving. Koch is evidently of German origin, therefore most likely not Orthodox, which is why Nikodim Fomich is so struck.

4. In her memoirs, Dostoevsky's wife, Anna Grigorievna, mentions that in the first weeks of their married life Dostoevsky took her to a certain yard during a walk and showed her the stone under which his Raskolnikov hid the stolen objects. When she asked what he himself had been doing in that deserted yard, Dostoevsky replied, "The same thing as other passers-by."

5. The *Confessions* of Jean-Jacques Rousseau (1712–78) was translated into Russian in the 1860s. His younger Russian contemporary, Alexander Radishchev (1749–1802), author of *A Journey from Petersburg to Moscow*, was exiled to Siberia by the empress Catherine the Great because of his outspoken attacks on social abuses.

6. This title is an ironic reference to the controversy surrounding the "woman question" that began in the 1860s.

7. The streets on Vasilievsky Island, called "Lines," were laid out in a grid like the streets of Manhattan, and have numbers in place of names.

8. The Winter Palace, residence of the tsars.

9. The cathedral is St. Isaac's. Designed in a mixed style suggesting a neoclassical interpretation of St. Peter's in Rome, it is heavily ornamented with sculptures, including (as Soviet guides say) "four life-size angels." There was a small chapel of St. Nicholas built on to the Nikolaevsky Bridge; both were made of wood and burned down in 1916.

10. Apparently his real name is Vrazumikhin, derived from the Russian verb meaning "to bring to reason," but is habitually simplified to Razumikhin, from the verb "to reason." Or else he is simply joking.

11. A low-class or poor people's way of sipping tea through a lump of sugar held in the teeth. The aim was to save sugar, it being considered a luxury to dissolve sugar in one's tea.

12. Five Corners, still so called, is an intersection in Petersburg where five streets meet.

13. I. G. Charmeur was a well-known Petersburg tailor; Dostoevsky had his own suits made by Charmeur.

14. The Palais de Cristal (later referred to in *C&P* as the Crystal Palace) was a hotel/restaurant, opened in Petersburg in 1862, but not in the area where Dostoevsky locates the establishment described here. His deliberate use of the name was most likely intended to remind his readers of earlier mentions of "the Crystal Palace" in *Notes from Underground* (1864) and elsewhere, referring to the great glass hall built in London for the International Exposition of 1851. In polemics with his ideological opponent the radical writer N. G. Chernyshevsky (1828–89), who saw this Crystal Palace as an image

of the ideal living space for the future communal society (in his 1862 novel *What Is to Be Done?*), Dostoevsky's man from underground likens it to a chicken coop.

15. Peski ("the Sands") and Kolomna were neighborhoods on the outskirts of Petersburg.

16. Xavier Jouvain, of Grenoble, brought about a revolution in glove-making with his invention, in 1834, of a special mold for shaping gloves.

17. The actual proverb is much terser in Russian; Luzhin bungles it, as if he were making a "literal" translation, something like, "If you throw one stone at two birds, you may not kill either of them."

18. Luzhin's words here echo ideas of the English economist and philosopher Jeremy Bentham (1748–1832), which were the subject of great polemics in Russia at the time. They also contain suggestions of Chernyshevsky's theory of "rational egoism."

19. A "band" of forgers, including a university lecturer, was indeed uncovered in Moscow in 1865. At his trial, the lecturer gave explanations similar to those quoted by Razumikhin further on. The murder of the embassy secretary is also an allusion to an actual trial, mentioned in Dostoevsky's notebooks, involving a retired army lieutenant who made an attempt on the life of a Russian embassy secretary in Paris.

20. Raskolnikov read about this "narrow ledge" in Book II, chapter 2, of Victor Hugo's *Notre Dame de Paris* (1831), first published in Russian translation in Dostoevsky's short-lived magazine *Time* in 1862.

21. Ivan Ivanovich Izler was the owner of a man-made suburban spa in Petersburg called "Mineral Waters," very popular in the 1860s. The Petersburg newspapers of 1865 were full of news about the arrival in the city of a young midget couple, Massimo and Bartola, said to be descendants of the ancient Aztecs. The unusual number of fires in Petersburg and then throughout Russia in 1862 were sometimes blamed on revolutionary students. Dostoevsky tried to oppose these rumors in his magazine, *Time,* but the articles were not passed by the censors.

22. This account of the nervous accomplice comes from an actual event reported in a Moscow newspaper in 1865.

23. "Enough talk!" (French). According to his wife's memoirs, this was one of Dostoevsky's own favorite phrases. He borrowed it from Vautrin, a character in the novels of Honoré de Balzac (1799–1850). Dostoevsky was a great admirer of Balzac, whose Rastignac is a fictional precursor of Raskolnikov.

24. The civil equivalent of the military rank of colonel.

25. A provincial marshal of nobility was, prior to the reforms of the 1860s, the highest elected officer in a province.

26. The names in Katerina Ivanovna's account are allegorical but plausible: Bezzemelny means "landless," and Shchegolskoy means "foppish." This lends an air of fantasy to her memories. "Kammerjunker," borrowed by Russian from the German, was an honorary court title.

27. Consecrated bread and wine of the Eucharist, reserved by the priest for such occasions.

28. Dostoevsky himself underwent such a sentencing and pardon in 1849, after being arrested for subversive activities. He often uses the experience metaphorically.

PART THREE

1. Anton Rubinstein (1829–94), Russian composer and world-famous pianist. He founded the Petersburg Conservatory in 1859.

2. The upper chamber of the Prussian legislature of the time.

3. Marie Antoinette de Lorraine (1755–93), archduchess of Austria, married to Louis XVI of France, was imprisoned during the French Revolution and then guillotined. Dostoevsky mentions her name in his notes for *C&P*.

4. "Drop dead, dogs, if you don't like it!" (French).

5. The Mitrofanievsky Cemetery, established in 1831 during a cholera epidemic, was considered a cemetery for the poor. A meal, called a "memorial meal" (*pominki* in Russian), is traditionally served following a funeral.

6. Refers to the beggar Lazarus in the Gospel parable (see Luke 16:19–31), who eats crumbs from the rich man's table. Metaphorically, the common Russian saying "to sing Lazarus" means to complain of one's fate. A song about the poor man Lazarus was often sung by blind beggars asking for alms.

7. The term "phalanstery" was coined by the French utopian socialist thinker Charles Fourier (1772–1837) to designate the physical and productive arrangements for living in the future communal society. Dostoevsky's interest in "Fourierism" as a young man led to his arrest by the tsar's agents in 1849.

8. "Ivan the Great" is a bell-tower in the Moscow Kremlin.

9. Lycurgus, semilegendary lawgiver of ancient Sparta, is said to have lived in the ninth century B.C. Solon (630?–560? B.C.), lawgiver and reformer of the Athenian state, was one of the "seven sages of Greece." Muhammad and Napoleon, among other things, also codified the laws of their nations.

10. The French phrase means "long live the eternal war." The New Jerusalem appears at the end of Revelation (21:1–3) in St. John's vision of "the holy city . . . coming down from God out of heaven." However, the Saint-Simonians, followers of the utopian socialist Claude-Henri de Saint-Simon (1760–1825), interpreted this vision as foretelling a future paradise on earth and a new golden age. Saint-Simon's thought, a sort of neo-Christianity, was popular in Russia during the 1840s.

11. See John 11:1–45. This is not the beggar Lazarus, but Lazarus the brother of Martha and Mary, whom Jesus raises from the dead. The theme of the raising of Lazarus, central to the novel, is here introduced from an unexpected quarter, and meets an unexpected response.

12. A temperature of 30° on the Réaumur scale is the equivalent of 100°F or 38°C.

13. Raskolnikov mentally lists the steps in Napoleon's career. Napoleon (1769–1821) first distinguished himself as an artillery captain in the battle of Toulon in the south of France (1793). In 1795 he used his artillery to suppress a royalist uprising in Paris. After an unfortunate campaign in the Middle East, in August 1799 he abandoned his

army in Egypt and hastily returned alone to Paris to seize power (the remnants of the army were finally repatriated only two years later). In his disastrous Russian campaign of 1812, he lost all but a few thousand of his 500,000-man army, and most of his artillery. The "pun in Vilno" refers to Napoleon's remark after leaving Russia: *"Du sublime au ridicule, il n'y a qu'un pas"* ("From the sublime to the ridiculous is only one step"), quoted by Victor Hugo in the preface to his historical drama *Cromwell* (1827).

14. The phrase, almost a quotation, appears in the writings of Victor Considérant (1808–93), a French utopian socialist thinker, follower of Fourier.

15. The expression "trembling creature," from the Koran, also appears in Pushkin's cycle of poems *Imitations of the Koran* (1824), where Dostoevsky may have found it.

PART FOUR

1. A misquotation of a famous line from the Roman playwright Terence (190–159 B.C.): *homo sum, humani nihil a me alienum puto* ("I am a man, nothing human is alien to me"). Svidrigailov's error is a common one (repeated by the devil in *The Brothers Karamazov*).

2. "It's honest warfare" (French).

3. "Freedom of expression" in Svidrigailov's ironic phrase is *glasnost* in the original. The whipping of the German woman, an event that took place in 1860, was widely commented on in the newspapers. The "Outrageous Act of *The Age*" refers to the title of a polemical article published in the *St. Petersburg Gazette* (3 March 1861) protesting against an attack on the movement for women's emancipation in the weekly magazine *The Age*. The article in *The Age* had denounced an event at which a woman gave a public reading from Pushkin's *Egyptian Nights:* the reading of Cleopatra's challenge to men (to spend a night with her in exchange for their lives) was considered an immoral act revealing the true aims of the proponents of women's emancipation. "Those dark eyes" refers to the description of the lady as she was reading.

4. After the emancipation of the serfs in 1861, peasants were allotted arable land, which was taken from the landowners; forests and water meadows were not included in such allotments.

5. Dussot owned a famous restaurant in Petersburg frequented by high society. *Pointes* (French for points or spits of land) here refers to a pleasure garden on Yelagin Island.

6. "Wine doesn't agree with me" (French).

7. Berg was the owner of amusement attractions in Petersburg. Known as "the famous Petersburg aeronaut," he was often mentioned in newspapers during the mid-1860s.

8. "So as to please you" (French).

9. "Give rest with thy saints, O Christ, to the soul of thy servant . . ." is the first phrase of a hymn *(kontakion)* from the Orthodox funeral service. "The food" refers to the traditional memorial meal following a funeral.

10. Prince Svirbey and Madame Prilukov are not known. Vyazemsky's house was a Petersburg flophouse where the dregs of society spent their nights.

11. Razumikhin has earlier played on the sound of his name (see Part Two, note 10). Here Luzhin is misled by its meaning. "Rassudkin" comes from *rassudok:* reason, intellect, common sense.

12. A "holy fool" (*yurodivyi* in Russian) can be a saintly person or ascetic whose saintliness is expressed as "folly." Holy fools of this sort were known early in Christian tradition, but in later common usage "holy fool" also came to mean a crazy person or simpleton.

13. The language of the Russian Orthodox Church is Old Slavonic, not Russian. The Bible was first translated into Russian in the early nineteenth century.

14. See Matthew 5:8: "Blessed are the pure in heart: for they shall see God."

15. Here and further on Sonya reads from John 11:1-45.

16. An imprecise quotation of Matthew 19:14.

17. "Simply" or "without adornments" (French).

18. "It's obligatory" (French).

19. The judicial reforms of 1864 introduced, among many more important changes, a new nomenclature for police and court personnel.

20. During the Crimean War (1853–56), after defeating the Russian army at the Alma River (September 8, 1854), the allied forces (England, France, Turkey, the Piedmont) laid siege to Sebastopol, finally taking the city eleven months later.

21. The *Hofkriegsrat* was the supreme military council of Austria. Field Marshal Karl Mack (1752–1828) was surrounded by the French army at Ulm in 1805 and surrendered his 30,000 men to Napoleon without a fight. Mack's arrival at Russian headquarters after this defeat is described in Tolstoy's *War and Peace,* in a chapter published in *The Russian Herald* (1866, No. 2), between the publication in the same magazine of the first and the remaining parts of *C&P.*

22. Nikolai Gogol (1809–52), prose writer and dramatist, was the greatest of Dostoevsky's predecessors. Dostoevsky was deeply indebted to him as an artist, particularly in his notion of "fantastic realism"; his works are full of references, hidden parodies, and polemical responses to the writings of the great satirist.

PART FIVE

1. Knop was the owner of a toiletry shop on Nevsky Prospect in Petersburg. The English Shop also sold imported toiletries, among other things.

2. This passage humorously summarizes some of the issues of concern to radicals of the early 1860s. Communes had begun to appear in Petersburg under the influence of Fourier and of Chernyshevsky's novel *What Is to Be Done?* (there was in fact a commune on Meshchanskaya Street).

3. "Let's distinguish" (French).

4. Nikolai A. Dobrolyubov (1836–61) was a radical literary critic and associate of Chernyshevsky. His career was cut short by consumption. Vissarion Belinsky (1811–

48), a liberal critic of the previous and more idealistic generation, achieved great prominence in his time. He was among the earliest to recognize Gogol's genius, and championed Dostoevsky's first novel, *Poor Folk* (1846).

5. Lebezyatnikov is alluding to Vera Pavlovna's argument in Chernyshevsky's *What Is to Be Done?* The question of "freedom of entry into rooms" is also discussed in the same novel.

6. An allusion to arguments about art and usefulness propounded by certain radical critics of the day, particularly D. I. Pisarev (1840–68), a great disparager of Pushkin, who is said to have wept when he read *C&P*, before hastening to write a critical review of the novel.

7. Pushkin mentions "horns" in at least three poems, "horns" and "hussars" in one of them ("Couplets," 1816).

8. A parody of ideas about love and jealousy in Chernyshevsky's novel *What Is to Be Done?*

9. See Part One, note 37.

10. "Lady cornet's wife" (Polish); an absurd compliment.

11. *Panie* (*pah*nyeh) is the respectful term of direct address for a gentleman in Polish, as *pani* is for a lady.

12. Bread and salt, literal or metaphorical, is a symbol of hospitality in Russia.

13. "In black and white" (French).

14. It was customary in Russia for a corpse to be laid out on a table until it was put in the coffin.

15. "Oh, merciful God!" (German).

16. See Matthew 6:3: "But when thou doest alms, let not thy left hand know what thy right hand doeth . . ."

17. *The General Conclusion of the Positive Method* was a collection of articles on various scientific subjects, mainly physiology and psychology, translated from German into Russian and published in 1866. Piederit was a German medical writer; Adolf Wagner, a follower of Quételet, was a proponent of "moral statistics" (see Part One, note 33).

18. "Sir, you are a scoundrel!" (Polish).

19. "Stand up straight!" (French).

20. Petrushka is a Russian clown; shows involving his antics were put on at fairs and in the streets.

21. "A Hussar Leaning on His Sabre" is a well-known song, with words by the poet Konstantin Batyushkov (1787–1855). "*Cinq sous*" ("Five pennies") is a French popular song. "*Malborough s'en va-t-en guerre*" ("Malborough's going to war") is a widely known French song about John Churchill, Duke of Marlborough (1650–1722), who led the English forces in the War of the Spanish Succession in the Low Countries. The Duke's name is variously misspelled in French transcriptions as "Malbrough," "Malbrouk," or "Malborough," as Dostoevsky has it here.

22. "Malborough's going to war / Doesn't know when he'll come back . . ." "Five pennies, five pennies / To set up our household . . ."

23. French dance terms: "slide, slide, the Basque step."

24. Lines from the poem "Back in My Native Land" from the *Book of Songs,* by the German poet Heinrich Heine (1797–1856), set to music by Franz Schubert: "You have diamonds and pearls . . . / You have the most beautiful eyes, / Maiden, what more do you want?"

25. A setting of the poem "The Dream" by Mikhail Lermontov (1814–41).

PART SIX

1. A reader reads the responses and assists the priest in the memorial service (*panikhida* in Russian).

2. Part of a prayer for the dead: "Give rest, O Lord, to the soul of thy departed servant."

3. An inexact quotation from "Diary of a Madman" by Nikolai Gogol.

4. "In vain!" (German).

5. The word "schismatic" (*raskolnik* in Russian) rings oddly in the original because of its closeness to the protagonist's name. It refers to the Old Believers, who split off from the Russian Orthodox Church in disagreement over the reforms of the patriarch Nikon in the mid-seventeenth century. "Runners" refers to a sect of the Old Believers that emerged in the eighteenth century; believing that the Orthodox Church and all civil authorities were under the sway of the Antichrist, they fled from every form of obedience to social institutions and "sojourned" in forests and desert places; hence they were first called "sojourners" and later "runners." The institution of elders is a venerable one in Orthodox tradition (there is a short treatise on elders in Book One of *The Brothers Karamazov*). An elder, generally speaking, is a spiritual director, to whom the one seeking direction owes the strictest obedience.

6. Dostoevsky describes this convict in *Notes from the Dead House* (1860), a semifictional account of his own prison experiences.

7. Midshipman Dyrka (*dyrka* means "hole" in Russian) is mentioned in Gogol's comedy *The Wedding,* but Porfiry Petrovich has apparently confused him with another character in the play, the easily amused Midshipman Petukhov (*petukh* means "rooster").

8. "Funeral oration" (French).

9. Svidrigailov has in mind the early persecutions of Christians, and then the life of St. Mary of Egypt, a fifth-century saint greatly venerated in the Orthodox Church, a former prostitute who converted to Christianity and withdrew to the Egyptian desert where she spent more than forty years in solitude.

10. Not necessarily a theological student, but generally a poor scholar, probably from a clerical family. Such families often had names (like Razumikhin) derived from words designating Christian virtues.

11. "Nature and truth" (French). Dostoevsky uses this phrase (compare *l'homme de la nature et de la vérité,* in *Notes from Underground*) in ironic reference to the thought of Jean-Jacques Rousseau (see Part Two, note 5).

12. "Where is virtue going to build her nest?" (French). The playwright Molière (1622–73) is said to have asked this of a beggar who thought he had made a mistake in giving him a gold piece.

13. "Enough talk!" (French). See Part Two, note 23.

14. "Good-bye, my pleasure" (French).

15. "As good a theory as any" (French).

16. Here Dunya suddenly addresses Svidrigailov in the familiar second person singular, which Russians generally use only with family and intimate friends. The shift has a strong effect for the Russian reader, suggesting more to their relationship than has appeared so far.

17. Here again Dunya uses the second person singular.

18. Dunya speaks in the second person singular through "You're lying, slanderer!" Svidrigailov twice responds in kind.

19. The revolver is of the old cap-and-ball variety, midway between a firelock and the later cartridge pistol. The chambers were hand-loaded and fired by a separate percussion cap. In the "misfire" the cap apparently went off but did not fire the charge.

20. Here they both begin to speak in the second person singular, through "ever?"

21. The original Vauxhall was a seventeenth-century pleasure garden in London. Here the term refers to an outdoor space for concerts and entertainment, with a tea-house, tables, and so on. Russian borrowed the word from English; evidently vauxhalls were a new thing in the 1860s.

22. In the Orthodox Church, the Sunday of Pentecost, fifty days after Easter.

23. The Church does not grant suicides Christian burial or offer prayers for them.

24. Cannon shots fired from the Petropavlovsky Fortress in Petersburg served as a flood warning; they also signaled such events as the spring thaw, military victories, fires, or the birth of a son to the imperial household.

25. The brass helmets worn by Russian (and not only Russian) firemen in the nineteenth century were descendants of the crested helmets supposed to have been worn by such Greek heroes as Achilles.

26. Julius Caesar was crowned high priest and military tribune in the temple of Jupiter on the Capitoline Hill in Rome, at the start of his rise to power.

27. *Nihil est:* "it is nothing" or "nothing is" (Latin).

28. David Livingstone (1813–73), famous Scottish explorer of central and southern Africa, published a book on his travels along the Zambezi River in 1865; it was soon translated into Russian.

29. "Nihilism" was a new movement among the radical Russian youth, emerging just around the time that Dostoevsky was writing *C&P*, the mentality and consequences of which he partly explores in the novel. The aims of the nihilists, as the name suggests, were essentially negative—the destruction of the existing social order, without stipulating what should replace it. In this they "stepped beyond" the earlier utopian socialists; they "negated more," as Lebezyatnikov puts it. Their ideology was anti-idealist, concerned with immediate action and practical results.

30. Ilya Petrovich's words reflect common attacks on women who sought higher

education. In the 1860s women were allowed education only as teachers or midwives. The Academy he refers to is the medical school.

EPILOGUE

1. The setting and conditions of Raskolnikov's hard labor are drawn from Dosto-evsky's own experiences as a convict. The four years he spent in prison at Omsk, on the Irtysh River, are described in *Notes from the Dead House.*

2. Special services are held on weekdays during the Great Lent (in the Orthodox Church, the forty-day fast preceding Holy Week, which in turn precedes Easter Sunday). The prisoners probably took turns attending these services because the church was too small to accommodate all of them at once.

3. Kalatchi: plural of kalatch, a very fine white bread shaped like a purse with a looped handle.

A Note on the Type

This book was set in Janson. The hot-metal version of Janson was a recutting made direct from type cast from matrices long thought to have been made by the Dutchman Anton Janson, who was a practicing type founder in Leipzig during the years 1668–87. However, it has been conclusively demonstrated that these types are actually the work of Nicholas Kis (1650–1702), a Hungarian, who most probably learned his trade from the master Dutch type founder Dirk Voskens. The type is an excellent example of the influential and sturdy Dutch types that prevailed in England up to the time William Caslon (1692–1766) developed his own incomparable designs from them.

Composed, printed, and bound by
The Haddon Craftsmen, Inc., Scranton, Pennsylvania

Designed by Peter A. Andersen